Longings

Susan Lewis is the bestselling author of twenty-three novels. She is also the author of *Just One More Day*, a moving memoir of her childhood in Bristol. She lives in Gloucestershire. Her website address is www.susanlewis.com

Acclaim for Susan Lewis

'One of the best around' *Independent on Sunday*

'Spellbinding! ... you just keep turning the pages, with the atmosphere growing more and more intense as the story leads to its dramatic climax' *Daily Mail*

'Mystery and romance *par excellence*' *Sun*

'The tale of conspiracy and steamy passion will keep you intrigued until the final page' *Bella*

'A multi-faceted tearjerker' *heat*

'Erotic and exciting' *Sunday Times*

'We use the phrase honest truth too lightly: it should be reserved for books – deeply moving books – like this' Alan Coren

'Susan Lewis strikes gold again ... gripping' *Options*

Also by Susan Lewis

A Class Apart
Dance While You Can
Stolen Beginnings
Obsession
Vengeance
Summer Madness
Last Resort
Wildfire
Chasing Dreams
Taking Chances
Cruel Venus
Strange Allure
Silent Truths
Wicked Beauty
Intimate Strangers
The Hornbeam Tree
The Mill House
A French Affair
Missing
Out of the Shadows
Lost Innocence
The Choice

Just One More Day, A Memoir

SUSAN LEWIS

Darkest Longings

arrow books

Published by Arrow Books 2007

11

Copyright © Susan Lewis 1992

Susan Lewis has asserted her right under the Copyright, Designs
and Patents Act 1988 to be identified as the author of this work

First published in Great Britain in 1992 by William Heinemann
First published by Arrow Books in 1998
Arrow Books
Random House, 20 Vauxhall Bridge Road,
London SW1V 2SA

www.penguin.co.uk

Addresses for companies within The Random House Group Limited can be
found at: www.randomhouse.co.uk/offices.htm

The Random House Group Limited Reg. No. 954009

A CIP catalogue record for this book
is available from the British Library

ISBN 9780099514671

Penguin Random House is committed to a sustainable future for
our business, our readers and our planet. This book is made from
Forest Stewardship Council® certified paper.

Printed and bound in Great Britain by Clays Ltd, Elcograf S.p.A.

This book is dedicated to my father . . .

Acknowledgements

I should like to express my gratitude to Madame La Comtesse du Petit-Thovârs for the help she gave in the preparation of this book. For inviting me into her home and allowing me to base the story around the ancestral home of the Petit-Thouars – though I must stress that no characters in the book are based on her family. My thanks also to Richard Hazlewood for the help and advice he gave, not to mention the many introductions. Also to Monsieur et Madame Rutault and Madame Amos.

Most especially of all I should like to thank Pamela Brunet and her husband Amedé for the research and translations they carried out on my behalf.

And lastly my love and thanks to my family and friends for their unwavering support following the death of my father.

'Are you feeling nervous, *chérie*?'

Claudine's gaze moved slowly from the passing French countryside to rest upon her father. It was over an hour since they had boarded the train in Paris, but this was the first time either of them had spoken. As their eyes met, Claudine's full mouth curved into a secretive, almost self-mocking smile, and Beavis smiled too as he watched his extraordinary daughter sweep a hand through the tumbling raven hair that bounced unfashionably around her shoulders, and stretch out her long legs to settle them on the seat beside him.

She didn't answer his question, but leaned her head back against the cushion and returned her attention to the passing fields.

Yes, she was nervous. Who wouldn't be, in her shoes? But apart from the occasional tug she gave to the feather which curled over the brim of the hat lying in her lap, there was nothing in her manner to indicate either the unease or the excitement that randomly coasted between her heart and her stomach. She looked up ahead and saw the front of the train as it rounded a curve in the track, steam billowing from the funnel in a chain of ephemeral white clouds. Again she smiled, then looking back to her father, who was still watching her, she started to laugh.

'Are you surprised that we've come this far?' she asked.

'If I am, I shouldn't be.'

'Meaning?'

He arched his brows comically and pulled at his moustache. 'You know perfectly well what I mean.'

'That nothing is more irresistible to your hare-brained daughter than territory where angels – perhaps even fools – fear to tread?'

'Precisely.'

'But, Papa, it was your idea,' she reminded him.

'So it was. I'd almost forgotten,' he chuckled. Then, more seriously, he added, 'But we don't have to be here, *chérie*.' He often used the French term of endearment, even when they were speaking English – it was a habit he had fallen into during twenty-seven years of marriage to a Frenchwoman. 'It's not too late,' he continued, 'we can turn back to England, you have only to say the word.' For all sorts of reasons, that would now be extremely difficult, but he felt obliged to say it all the same.

'Oh, Papa! To have come all this way and then not actually see him! I should die of curiosity.'

Satisfied with her answer, Beavis returned to his newspaper. But it took only a few minutes for him to realize that he was reading the same paragraph over and over again. His mind was full of his daughter and the meeting that would take place two days from now at the Château de Lorvoire.

He took out a cigarette and lit it, filling their first-class compartment with the bitter-sweet smell of Turkish tobacco. As Claudine inhaled the aroma she closed her eyes, reminding him of her mother, and for the first time since her death Beavis was grateful that Antoinette wasn't there to express her thoughts on what he was doing. Not that he harboured any doubts about bringing Claudine to France – on the contrary, he firmly believed that his plans for his daughter were in her own best interest – but he couldn't help feeling that Antoinette might have handled things with a little more subtlety.

But what was he supposed to do? As a man, he had no experience in handling these matters; all he knew was that, at twenty-two, it was high time Claudine was married.

Everyone told him so, particularly his sister-in-law, Céline. During Claudine's debutante year in London Céline had, of course, done her best to introduce Claudine to as many eligible young men as possible – and no doubt several ineligible ones too, if he knew Céline, but at the time Claudine had had other ideas, and she and Dissy, her best friend, had taken themselves off to New York to stay with a girl they had shared a room with at finishing school, Melissa von Merity. Beavis knew the von Merity family, so he had agreed to the plan. He hadn't been prepared for Claudine to spend almost three years in New York, and he most certainly hadn't been prepared for the fierce independence she had acquired during her stay there – which, together with her inherent sense of humour and her undeniable beauty, had turned her into a force even he found difficult to reckon with.

She had returned to London six months ago, in time to see in the New Year – 1937. In that time Dissy had married Lord Poppleton, and Claudine, as Céline had told him in no uncertain terms, had been left to run wild. He knew that Claudine had received several proposals of marriage, both in New York and in London, but for reasons known only to herself she had refused them all. So, not unnaturally, he had been more than surprised when she seemed to welcome the suggestion first put to him by his old friends the Comte and Comtesse de Rassey de Lorvoire, that their two families should unite.

Céline's response, on the other hand, had come as no surprise at all. She had never, she told him, in her worst nightmares, imagined he would be capable of even considering marrying his precious daughter to a man like François de Lorvoire. Beavis, who was well aware of Parisian society's views on the Lorvoires' eldest son, had listened patiently to everything Céline had to say and then told her, quite calmly, that his mind was made up. After which he had extracted her promise that, should Claudine raise no objection to the marriage, she, Céline, would do nothing to dissuade her.

Yet now, with the hurdle of Claudine's agreement so easily surmounted, he couldn't help wondering why his daughter had shown such readiness to accept the proposal. She knew nothing about François de Lorvoire, yet she appeared almost eager to marry him. He was intrigued to know why. She had a will of iron, and he wouldn't have relished the prospect of fighting her if she had set her mind against the idea. He wondered, too, about the shattering of her illusions yet to come . . . But Claudine would handle it; he was quite resolved that François was the right husband for her, he admired the man – no matter what Céline might say. Though how Antoinette would have felt about the match did, in truth, unsettle him somewhat.

Able to read her father's face only too well, Claudine put aside her hat and leaned forward to take his hand. Her blue eyes were dancing, but her voice was gentle as she said, 'Papa, I know you're thinking about *Maman* and what she would say if she knew what we were about. But try to remember, darling, that I am a grown woman now, I can – and do – make decisions for myself. You know I wouldn't be here if I didn't want to be.'

Beavis' face clouded for a moment. Then, with a touch of irony, he said, 'That is precisely what baffles me, *chérie*. Why, when you've had so many offers from men who are eminently suitable, are you so willing to give yourself to a man you've never even met?'

'Because it is what *you* want, Papa,' she answered, her eyes gravely wide.

His answering look told her that he didn't believe a word of it, and laughing, she threw back her head, curled her feet under her, and resting an elbow on the window ledge, was once again intent upon the passing landscape.

She was amused by her father's bewilderment, knowing that he had been fully prepared to assert his parental authority on this matter had it proved necessary. Of course, had she not wanted the marriage herself, she'd have fought, and won . . . She knew he was surprised by her compliance, but thankfully he hadn't questioned her too closely, so she had not found herself compelled to lie. And lie she would have done, rather than tell him why she was willing to marry François de Lorvoire – a man whom, as Beavis had quite rightly pointed out, she had never met.

Of course, she had heard a great deal about the de Rassey de Lorvoire family as she grew up. Her father and the old Comte had been firm friends ever since they served together in the Great War, and Antoinette Rafferty and Solange de Lorvoire, François' mother, had corresponded for many years and had frequently spent time together in Paris. But Claudine had never met the de Lorvoires; she had been at school, or too busy with her horses at Rafferty Lodge to accompany her mother on her shopping sprees. And, curiously, she didn't recollect any mention ever being made of François, who was fourteen years older than she was, and would surely have been cutting a figure in society long before her mother died. That fact rather amused her now, for what little she had managed to learn about François during the last few weeks suggested that whatever there was to say about him had probably been considered too shocking for her young ears.

In fact, his reputation was proving to be thoroughly intriguing. Just this past week she had discovered that one had only to mention his name in polite Parisian circles to set the conversation alight with any kind of unsavoury rumour. Take the other night, at the home of Constance and Charles Delaforge. She had gone alone, since Beavis had business to attend to, and had casually mentioned that she was looking forward to meeting the Lorvoire family at the weekend, their eldest son François in particular, because she had heard so much about him. From the look on the faces around her, she might just have let forth a stream of profanities. Constance had glared, Charles had started muttering under his breath, then suddenly the old duchess sitting beside her had drawn herself up, and cried in a voice pinched with distress, 'I forgive you, Claudine, but only because you cannot know what anguish it causes me to hear that man's name spoken. If you knew what he has done . . . *Mon Dieu!*' And she had covered her face with her hands.

Constance had flown to her side to comfort her, but the duchess had continued to quake. 'Why poor Solange should be cursed with such a son is beyond me,' she had sobbed. 'I'm sure it's why she never comes to Paris now. How could she hold her head up after after what happened . . . Oh, Constance! Not a day passes but I think of dear Hortense. Poor, poor, Hortense, how we all still miss her.' And with that, she had swept from the room.

The duchess's performance had thoroughly amused Claudine, but she had tactfully hidden her smiles, as she had her curiosity regarding 'poor, poor, Hortense' until just the night before, when she had met her friend Henriette at the Hungarian Embassy ball. At first it had proved impossible to get Henriette to speak of anything other than her recent engagement to Claude, the dashing young vicomte she'd arrived with. Claudine had listened with mounting impatience, waiting her chance, until Henriette babbled excitedly 'And now we've to find *you* a husband, Claudine. Oh, you must marry a Frenchman, please, please. Don't throw yourself away on one of those stuffy old English, I couldn't bear it. I want you to live here, in Paris, so I can see you all the time.'

Claudine's lovely slanting eyes sparkled with humour. 'I don't think that should present too much of a problem, *chérie*. Now, tell me, what has François de Lorvoire been up to?'

'François de Lorvoire?' Henriette repeated, clearly surprised by such an abrupt change of subject.

'Henriette, you must have heard. Something to do with . . .'

'Oh!' Henriette gasped, covering her mouth with her hand. 'You mean you've heard about Aimée de Garenaux?' Claudine hadn't, but was not about to interrupt. 'Well, I can't say I'm surprised,' Henriette rushed on. 'I should think the whole world knows by now. Such a silly creature she is. Really, Claudine, this time I think one can hardly say it was François' fault. Except that he might have behaved with a little more chivalry. But then everyone knows that François . . .'

'Henriette!' Claudine cried. 'What happened?'

Henriette's pretty green eyes widened with surprise at the impatience in Claudine's voice. 'Why this sudden interest in François de Lorvoire?' she asked, eyeing her friend suspiciously. 'I wasn't aware you even knew him.'

'I'll tell you later. Now, what happened with Aimée?'

Henriette shrugged, and fluffing out the taffeta folds of her ball gown, she sank into the sumptuous leather sofa behind her. 'Well,' she said, 'the stupid girl took it into her head not only to fall in love with him, but to follow him to Lyon. You know, Claudine, why everyone makes such a fuss about him is quite beyond me, it gives me the shivers just to look at him. Have you ever seen him? It's like coming face to face with the devil . . . Anyway, as I said, Aimée followed him to Lyon. Everyone is trying to say now that François abducted her, but it's not true. I'm not saying he's not capable of such an outrage, but in this instance Aimée confessed to me before she went that she intended to make him marry her. I warned her what he was like, but she wouldn't listen. Maybe I should have told her mother, but she'd sworn me to secrecy, and how was I to know it would end the way it did?'

'How did it end?' Claudine asked, enjoying the story immensely.

'She went to his hotel late at night, and told the people on the desk that she was his wife, so they let her into his room. When he came back, she was there, waiting for him. She then informed him that if he didn't agree to marry her she would tell the whole world he had forced himself upon her – raped her! At least, that's what she told me she was going to do. I can only assume she went ahead with her plan, but what François said – or did – in response I have no idea, Aimée refuses to talk about it now. All I know is that he left her there, alone, in the middle of the night, and returned to Paris. Whether he actually ravished her before he left, none of us knows, but I imagine he did. Anyway, he went straight to her home, got her father out of bed to inform him of his daughter's whereabouts, and told him that if the girl was no longer a virgin he had no doubt the blame would be laid at his door, but that Monsieur de Garenaux was to understand he had no intention of marrying her. And now poor Aimée, stupid Aimée, has been shipped off to Morocco to stay with her grandparents. You may well laugh, Claudine,' Henriette said, her own lips beginning to twitch, 'but what if poor Aimée is pregnant?'

'Somehow I rather doubt it,' Claudine answered. 'Don't you?'

'If it were anyone but him, I would. But, *oh là*, she was so stupid. If only she had listened to me. The man is not only a philanderer but a confirmed bachelor, everyone knows so. As he told my papa once, there is not a woman alive who could change his mind on that point. Though if you ask me, he flatters himself to think that anyone would want to. The only reason why women throw themselves at him the way they do – and usually they're given a hefty push by their mothers – is because he is so rich and will inherit the de Lorvoire title when his father dies. It certainly has nothing to do with looks or charm. But now you are to tell me, why are you asking about him?'

A light gleamed in Claudine's eyes, and in a rustle of skirts she sat down beside Henriette. 'Because,' she said, taking Henriette's fragile white hands between her own, 'I'm going to marry him.'

She watched Henriette's angelic face as her friend blinked several times before her mouth actually fell open. Until that moment Claudine had not intended to tell Henriette, or indeed anyone, about her arranged marriage, but as she listened to Henriette an idea had crystallized in her mind – though whether it was a good one or not, it was now too late to decide, for the words were already spoken. There would be repercussions, naturally. Her father might be angry that she had revealed her secret, Tante Céline most certainly would be; and how François and his family might view the indiscretion she had no idea. But one thing she was sure of: telling Henriette about the proposed marriage was tantamount to telling all of Paris, and once Parisian society expected the match, no one in her family would now try to dissuade her from it.

At last Henriette recovered the power of speech. 'Claudine, you are teasing me,' she breathed. 'You aren't serious, I know you're not. But what a strange joke.'

'It isn't a joke, Henriette. I shall meet him for the first time on Sunday, and soon after that we shall be married.'

Henriette's face puckered with confusion as she searched her friend's beautiful blue eyes. 'I don't want to believe you, Claudine,' she said finally. 'Common sense tells me this can't be true, but I have a horrible feeling that for once you aren't teasing.'

Claudine was trying not to laugh. 'No, Henriette,' she said softly, 'I'm not teasing. I am going to marry François de Lorvoire.'

Henriette started to shake her head. 'No, Claudine,' she

said, 'no. I can't let you do this. I should have stopped Aimée and I feel dreadful that I didn't, but she's hardly my responsibility. With you it's different. With you I am going to put my foot down. You are not to go near that man, do you hear? You are to promise me that you will never have anything to do with him.'

'I'm afraid it's too late,' Claudine grinned.

'Too late! But no, if you've not met him yet it can't be too late. And if you insist on going to the rendezvous, Claudine, I shall inform your father. But how has this come about? If you don't know him, how can you have an assignation with him on Sunday? Oh Claudine, no,' she cried, tightening her grip on her friend's hands, 'you can't do this. You don't know him, he's a monster. He's wicked, he's evil. He won't marry you, he'll use you, just like all the . . .'

'He *will* marry me, Henriette.'

'No! No! Claudine, you're not listening to me. If it were anyone else I know you would succeed. You're so beautiful, what man wouldn't want to marry you? But you'll never succeed with François de Lorvoire. He'll never marry you, Claudine, *never!*'

Henriette was near to tears by now, and her hands were gripping Claudine's so fiercely that Claudine almost winced with the pain. But as she began to explain the arrangement her father had made with the Comte de Rassey de Lorvoire and his son, the hands around hers slowly relaxed their hold.

'But he swore he would never marry,' Henriette breathed, hardly able to take it all in. 'What has happened to change his mind?'

Claudine shrugged, unable to enlighten her friend – except to say that she believed the Comte, who had saved her father's life during the Battle of Verdun, probably wanted to ensure that the name of de Rassey de Lorvoire would continue. Henriette immediately pointed out that

François had a younger brother, Lucien – and this was something that rather confused Claudine too, since the de Lorvoire line could obviously be continued by Lucien, and Lucien's children. But as she had no explanation to offer on that score, Claudine simply hugged her friend and said, 'What does it matter why he has changed his mind? He has, and so we will be married. As I said, it is all arranged.'

Henriette suddenly drew her hands away, and the expression that came over her face saddened Claudine. 'I don't know you any more, Claudine,' she said. 'I don't understand you. You have the pick of men in London and Paris, New York too, yet you are allowing yourself to be given away in marriage to a man who . . . Oh no, I can't bear to think of it. Do you need me to tell you that marriage is not an adventure? It isn't one of your games, Claudine. You and the Lorvoires are Catholics: once you are married to François not all the money in the world, not even your father, will be able to rescue you.'

'You are assuming that I will want to be "rescued",' Claudine replied with a smile.

'I'm not assuming, I know. For heaven's sake, Claudine, I told you, the man is . . . You must have heard about Hortense de Bourchain. How can you even contemplate this marriage, knowing what he did to her?'

'Ah, yes, Hortense,' Claudine said – but at that moment, to her unutterable frustration, Claude de la Chevasse arrived to whisk his fiancée into the next waltz.

And now, here she was on a train taking her through the Loire Valley to a new life that was beginning to conjure up such fantastic images in her mind, she was beginning to question her own sanity. Even so, she knew that nothing, simply nothing, was going to stop her from meeting François de Lorvoire now. And knowing Henriette as she did, the news of her arranged marriage would be all over Paris by now, so that not even Tante Céline would try to talk her out of it – the scandal if the marriage didn't go ahead would be too much for her to bear. And as for the sudden bouts of nervousness she was experiencing? Well, that was because François was, indisputably, an experienced lover, whereas she . . . But she would talk to Tante Céline about that, at the earliest possible opportunity.

Élise Pascale's blouse was hanging from her shoulders, the top of her silk camisole was hooked beneath her breasts. She looked down at the big dark hands as they caressed her abundant milky white flesh, then sucked in her breath as his fingers closed around her painfully aroused nipples. Her head fell back against the wall and his lips crushed hers, parting them to make way for his tongue.

They were standing on the landing outside her apartment; the key was in her right hand, and with her left she was stroking him through his trousers. For a moment he stood back to look at her, then, as a door slammed somewhere downstairs, he slowly lowered his mouth to her breasts, holding her about the waist as he sucked. Her hand tightened around him, and as he bit harder she started to moan. Then his hands were lifting her skirt, pushing it up to her waist, and she heard him chuckle quietly as he saw she was wearing no knickers. There was both tenderness and savagery in his touch, and an almost sadistic pleasure in the way he was teasing her. She had never in her life experienced anything to match the eroticism of François de Lorvoire's love-making.

As he stood straight, she looked up into his face and saw that he was laughing. He could sense her mounting frustration, he knew only too well how he affected her, but she simply let him look at her, knowing that he would take her when he was ready.

Five minutes later they were lying naked on her bed. For a long time he lay still as she kissed and caressed him, then finally he pushed her onto her back and stood up. As she watched him, every pulse in her body throbbing, he walked to the foot of the bed, took her ankles in his hands and dragged her to the edge. Then he hooked her feet around the two posts, caught her hips between his hands and lifted her to meet him. She could feel the tip of his penis brushing against her, and almost choking on the intensity of her longing, she looked down as slowly he eased himself into her.

Within minutes she was writhing, gasping, sobbing as he pounded his body against hers; his fingers dug into her buttocks, then caught her breasts and pulled hard on her nipples. He watched her face, waiting until she had lost all sense of everything beyond what he was doing to her. Then, knowing his own control was about to break, he quickly pulled her up and pressed his lips brutally over hcrs.

Her legs gripped his waist, her nails clawed his shoulders, then she was crying out his name, and he was shooting his semen into her with rapid, excruciating strokes.

When it was over he lay down on the bed beside her, and she snuggled against him, resting her head on his chest and curling a leg over his. He didn't speak for a long time, and she knew that his thoughts had long since moved from the confines of that room. If she was lucky, though, they would make love again before he left.

And probably they would have, had she not made the grave mistake of telling him something she had overheard when she had dropped in at the Hungarian Embassy ball in the early hours of that morning.

An ominous silence followed her words. Then he asked her to repeat them.

'It would appear,' she said, smiling to cover her unease, 'that *l'Anglaise* has seen fit to reveal the secret of your forthcoming nuptials. All of Paris is talking about it.'

Still he didn't move, but as she reached up to pull his face round to hers, he swung his legs to the floor. She started to protest, to ask where he was going, but one glimpse of his expression was enough to tell her that she would be wise to keep silent.

– 2 –

Céline du Verdon stretched her long legs across the window seat, allowing her pastel cotton dress to fall open almost to mid-thigh. Her dark blonde hair was loose, falling in natural waves around her shoulders, and her delicately lined face was for once free of make-up. The tall windows beside her were open, and she inhaled deeply the rich, earthy aroma that seeped up from the rain-spattered lawns. Now the sun was shining again, scorching the gardens with an intensity unusual in early June. At the end of the wide, sloping lawns the doves were poking their faces warily out of the dovecote, and somewhere out of sight she could hear the gardeners beginning work again.

She was sitting in the spacious airy drawing-room she had favoured since her arrival at the Château de Montvisse. With its faded oriental rugs, matching pair of japanned sofas, three giltwood armchairs and *secretaire-cabinet* behind the door, it was a pleasant change from the over-furnished salons and parlours of Paris. Of course, she was a Parisienne at heart, and nothing would ever change that, but though it hurt her to admit it, the strain of being one of the city's great society hostesses was becoming a little too much – Céline du Verdon was getting older. With the exception of her brother-in-law, Beavis Rafferty, there wasn't a soul in the world who now knew her true age. Even she became confused on the rare occasions when she put herself to the task of remembering, something she did only when Beavis was around, for he took much delight in reminding her that she was exactly the same age as he was, to the day: fifty-one. Younger sisters were such mischief-makers, Céline thought. It really had been too tiresome of Antoinette to inform her husband of this inconsequential fact. Dear Antoinette, how she missed her – how they all missed her. But there was always darling Claudine, who was so like her mother that seeing her gave almost as much pain as it did pleasure.

Glancing at the ormolu clock, the sole occupant of the mantleshelf, Céline gave a gentle sigh, slipped off her shoes and curled her feet under her like a schoolgirl. It was approaching four in the afternoon. The humidity outside was unendurable but, protected by the old stone walls of the château, the rooms inside were wonderfully cool and still . . . And then there was a curt knock on the door, before it swung open.

'Yes, Brigitte?' Céline sighed, closing her eyes. She and her maid had been together for so many years that she could sense Brigitte's presence as accurately as she could her moods.

'*Madame*,' Brigitte said stiffly, 'your guests will arrive very soon now.'

'Yes?' Céline answered, drawing out the word and knowing full well what was on Brigitte's mind.

'I implore you, *madame*, to make yourself presentable.'

'What do you mean, Brigitte?'

Brigitte's small frame pumped up with outrage. 'It is not fitting for a lady such as yourself to be without stockings, *madame*. And that dress, *pah*! You look like a lady who sells pegs on the side of the streets.'

'Brigitte, I adore you. And I adore you most of all when you are angry with me.'

'*Madame*, I am very angry. You are mocking me, and now all the servants are laughing at me because I cannot dress you correctly. Why do you have to hurt me like this?'

Céline felt a flutter of sympathy, and was just beginning to resign herself to going upstairs to change into the smart afternoon suit dear Coco had created for her when the sound of a car on the gravel drive told her it was too late. Beavis and Claudine had arrived. She had to struggle to hold back the laughter as she saw the stricken expression on Brigitte's face.

'Come here, Brigitte,' she said, as she unwound her legs and pulled herself gracefully to her feet.

Obediently Brigitte crossed the room, her rubber soles squeaking, her starched uniform rustling, and allowed Céline to fold her into an embrace. The overwhelming love she felt for her mistress swamped her pride and brought tears into her eyes.

'Now,' Céline said, releasing her, 'come with me to greet Claudine. You know how you have been longing to see her. So let's forget my appearance, because it really isn't important.'

'Oh, *madame*, how can you say such a thing?' Brigitte gasped, but Céline was already sweeping out of the room.

Outside, in the small octagonal entrance hall, Pierre, who had been waiting all afternoon for the arrival of Monsieur and Mademoiselle Rafferty, leapt up from the conversation seat where he had been dozing and threw the front doors wide.

'Tante Céline!' Claudine cried, stepping from the car as her aunt's tall figure emerged from the darkness of the doorway.

'*Ma chérie*,' Céline laughed, as her niece embraced her. 'How are you? Let me look at you. Oh, but you're so beautiful you are dazzling my eyes. And that hat. Where did you get it *chérie*, it is simply divine. And your hair, so much hair, so wild and such a colour. How can I have forgotten such a colour?' She sighed wistfully as she tousled the coppery black curls. 'Oh Claudine, it has been too long since I have seen you. But you are here now.' And she hugged her again.

'Do I get one of those?' Beavis' deep voice demanded.

Céline looked up, and as her eyes softened into a smile meant only for him, she passed her niece into Brigitte's more formal embrace and turned to her brother-in-law.

'What a pleasure,' she purred. 'How happy I am to see you both.' Her body trembled with the memory of the last time Beavis had held her in his arms. Sensing that he too was remembering, she allowed her hips to brush gently against his before slipping out of his arms. It was a pity that there would be no love-making on this visit, but they had discussed it during his most recent trip to Paris and had come to the conclusion that neither of them wanted to run the risk of Claudine finding out. She might not understand, might even think they had been conducting a liaison while her mother was still alive – though Beavis had loved Antoinette far too much ever to be unfaithful, and Céline, while not quite so circumspect where other lovers were concerned, would never have done anything to hurt her sister.

'You are breathtaking, Céline,' Beavis told her, his grey eyes twinkling mischievously as he held her at arms' length and looked at her. 'I don't think I have ever seen you quite so . . . quite so . . . No, I am lost for words, but the countryside evidently agrees with you. You look like a teenager when you must be . . .'

'I'll have Jean bring us some champagne,' Céline cut in quickly. 'I do so love champagne at this time of day, don't you, *chérie?*' she said, slipping an arm around Claudine's shoulders.

'I love champagne at any time of the day, Tante Céline,' Claudine informed her, 'and so do you. Oh Papa!' she cried, suddenly, 'we've left Tante Céline's gifts in the car,' and she tripped lightly back down the steps to where Pierre was trying to balance the brightly-coloured packages one on top of the other.

'Gifts? For me?' Céline sighed, wondering how her niece managed to look so cool in such heat. 'Ah, how like her mother she is. Everyone must have a gift for every occasion. Beavis, you must be impoverished by now with such extravagance in your family.'

But for once Beavis' attention was not on his daughter. 'If you insist on looking so desirable, Céline,' he said, 'this pact of ours is not going to be easy to keep.' He spoke in English, so that Brigitte and the other servants who had collected in the hall to welcome them wouldn't understand.

'Maybe it wasn't such a good idea anyway,' Céline murmured, aware of the warmth that was spreading through her body. 'But for now we shall content ourselves with a glass of champagne, before I show you around this funny little château I've taken for the summer. I have put you in the west tower, *mon cher*, where I thought you might be less tempted to bumble about in the night trying to find me.'

'How very thoughtful of you. But the kind of temptation you exercise, Céline, makes light work of the darkest corridors and stairways. And by the way, I resent the suggestion that I might bumble.'

They passed an extremely pleasant hour sipping Roederer and extolling the virtues of Chinon, the medieval town which lay along the banks of the River Vienne, five kilometers from Montvisse. Their chauffeur, Claudine told Céline, had given her and Beavis a guided tour along the quai and through the narrow cobbled streets, where the houses built for the servants of Charles VII at the beginning of the fifteenth century were not only still standing, but still lived in.

'And the château!' Claudine cried. 'How can the French have allowed such a tragedy? It sits there at the top of the hill, right above the town – a ruin! Even so, it's enchanting,

Tante Céline – we must visit it before you return to Paris. Do you think we'll be allowed inside? They say Joan of Arc was there once . . .'

Céline watched her niece move round the room and listened to her rich, honeyed voice. She had been to London only twice since Claudine's return from New York, but on both occasions had found herself marvelling at the way her niece had changed. It wasn't only that the child had become a woman; the woman had, over and above her extraordinary beauty, something so compelling about her that it almost took your breath away. She had a confidence, a sophistication Céline had believed it impossible to attain in a city like New York – and yet at the same time there was an impish naiveté about her, a freshness to her sophistication, that made Céline feel both old and young at the same time. And the happiness, together with the self-mocking humour that shone from those extraordinary wide and slanting eyes, was so infectious that it wasn't any wonder Claudine drew a crowd around her wherever she went.

But the thing about Claudine that had most disturbed and delighted Céline when she was last in London was her incredible body. If ever there was a body made for love, it was Claudine's. Those magnificent full breasts, the curvaceous hips, the endlessly long legs, were almost a miracle. And her skin, so soft, so honey-pale, and so inviting . . . Plenty of men Céline knew, had been crazy for Claudine. And on the occasions when she had seen her niece naked, she had invariably found herself wondering about the man who would bring that body to life, the man who would kiss and caress those achingly ripe breasts, who would introduce Claudine to the unsurpassable pleasures her own body could give.

Now, Céline closed her eyes, trying to block out the image of François de Rassey de Lorvoire and concentrate on what her niece was saying. But the image was persistent, it was as if de Lorvoire were there in the room, mocking her, taunting her with that dark, mysterious power that seemed to spill from his black eyes. What would a man like de Lorvoire do with such innocence as Claudine's? It was an innocence not many would detect, but Céline was in no doubt that he would recognize it at a glance. He would destroy it. He would crush Claudine as ruthlessly as the presses of the Lorvoire vineyards crushed the cabernet grapes. Oh, that such a man should be the one to take the virginity that Claudine had protected so lovingly, the virginity she had always sworn would never be given before the night of her wedding. To think that she had saved herself for a man like François de Lorvoire! Céline thought it might almost break her heart.

She tried to pull herself together, to tell herself she was over-reacting. And certainly, when she came to speak of him to Claudine later, she must try hard not to let her prejudice show. The fact that de Lorvoire had remained so resolutely impervious to her own charms – resolutely impervious! an understatement worthy of the driest Englishman! – must not be allowed to have any bearing on the way she behaved now. Of course, she wasn't the only one he had spurned, nor was she the only one to have suffered such humiliation in rejection. Even now she was unsure why she had tried to seduce him – except that once the rumour started that he was homosexual, she had been determined to find out if it was true. He had merely laughed in her face; she had hurled the accusation at him, screaming it at the top of her voice as she clutched the sheets about her body in a vain attempt to preserve the remaining shreds of her dignity.

How that loss of dignity had hurt! But it was her own fault. Where was the dignity in receiving a man lying naked on your bed and offering yourself to him in any way he might care to choose? In having him pick up your clothes, drop them into your lap and tell you he took great exception to being called to your home for tea and being offered something markedly less appetizing than cake . . . That was when she had thrown the accusation at him – but she should have known better. François de Lorvoire cared nothing for what society thought of him. The malice of those he had scorned could vent itself as it chose – it would not affect him. He was a man without emotion – a man without morals.

And he was a man, Céline now knew, with a mistress. A mistress who not only adored him, but satisfied him in a way only a great courtesan could – completely and unconditionally. She was Élise Pascale, arguably the most beautiful woman in all France; a woman who had come from nowhere and succeeded with de Lorvoire where all others had failed. For de Lorvoire she had thrown off every other lover and, if the rumours circulating in Paris were to be believed, he in turn had devoted himself to Élise. If that was true, where did it leave her precious Claudine? How could she even begin to compete with a woman so experienced in the art of lovemaking? A woman who knew exactly what it took to satisfy the sophisticated tastes of a man like François de Lorvoire.

Céline's only hope now was that Claudine's dream would be shattered the instant she set eyes on him. This thought cheered her a little, for de Lorvoire could not, by any stretch of the imagination, be described as handsome, and she sensed that Claudine had an image of him that was as romantic as it was false. No, Céline told herself now, she refused to worry any more, she would leave it to Claudine. Claudine might be headstrong and impulsive, but she most certainly wasn't stupid: she would understand soon enough that all that was required of her was to become a Lorvoire brood mare – and if she knew anything at all about her niece's spirit, that would be the end of the whole business.

'I don't think Tante Céline is with us, Papa.' Claudine's

voice cut into her thoughts, and Céline opened her eyes to find Beavis standing over her ready to pour the last of the champagne into her glass, and Claudine laughing softly at her aunt's apparent lack of attention.

'I am sorry, *chérie*,' she said, 'it is the heat. What were you saying?'

'Only that Magaly will be arriving from Paris tomorrow with my new wardrobe,' Claudine answered. 'Nothing important.'

'Magaly?'

'My maid, Tante Céline,' Claudine smiled.

'Of course, Magaly.' Then, seeming to collect her wits, Céline rose, stood on tip-toe and kissed Beavis on either cheek, saying, 'Claudine and I are going to take a walk in the garden, dearest, so you may go off to the study and use the telephone. No, don't look at me like that, I know you always have business to attend to – and Claudine and I want to have a nice woman-to-woman talk, is that not right, *chérie?*'

Knowing only too well what her aunt wished to discuss with her, the corner of Claudine's mouth dropped in a wry smile, and sitting forward on the sofa, she treated her father to an extremely bawdy wink. Beavis choked on the last of his champagne, but the merriment in his eyes showed the delight he took in his daughter.

'Come along, *chérie*,' Céline chuckled, as she held out her hand to Claudine. 'We'll stroll through the trees down to the river, it shouldn't be too hot if we keep in the shade, and there's something I want to show you.'

They parted company with Beavis outside the library, then wandered arm in arm out of the front door, round the lake in the courtyard and through the stable blocks to the avenue of limes at the rear of the house, which led down to the banks of the River Vienne.

'So tell me how you are feeling, now you are here,' Céline said, as they ambled through the dappled shadows.

Letting her head fall back, Claudine gazed up at the sparkling archway of branches above them and let out a soft groan. 'I don't know, Tante Céline, truly I don't. Perhaps I'm insane even to be contemplating this, but I know I'm going to go through with it.'

'Meeting him or marrying him?'

'Both. That is, of course, if he wants to marry me. Maybe when he meets me he'll change his mind.'

Céline gave her beautiful niece a long, considering glance. 'He won't change his mind, *chérie*.' She paused. 'But what about love, Claudine?' she said softly. 'Have you given that no thought at all?'

Claudine chuckled. 'I think about it all the time.'

'And?'

'Again, I don't know. Maybe we will fall in love, who knows?'

It was on the tip of Céline's tongue to tell her that that would never happen, but she stopped herself. Which of them could predict the future? Who could say that de Lorvoire wouldn't fall in love with her? God knew, Claudine had turned into as captivating a woman as she'd ever seen, so maybe she would win his heart – if indeed he had one. But then she remembered Élise Pascale, and it was as if the ground beneath her was tilting, plummeting her into despair.

For a moment she toyed with the idea of telling Claudine about La Pascale, but again she kept silent. Claudine might be an innocent, but she knew enough about the French way of life to know that most French husbands had mistresses. And, of course, if Claudine were to marry de Lorvoire there was nothing to stop her taking a lover, too – after she had given birth to the heir, naturally. But Céline judged it better not to say any of that to Claudine just now – and besides, there was still the hope that Claudine would see how foolish she was being before things got as far as marriage. Though how successful she would be in defying her father, Céline wasn't at all sure.

Suddenly Claudine laughed. 'I know you're longing to talk me out of this, Tante Céline.'

'You're right, I am,' Céline said. 'Maybe I should tell you why.'

'There's no need. I've heard enough about François de Lorvoire in these past weeks to know that he's the most unsavoury character you could wish to meet.'

'But you don't believe what you hear?'

Claudine shrugged.

Céline looked at her. 'So, would you like me to tell you about him?'

'Do you know, I don't think I would,' Claudine answered, after a moment or two. 'What I'd like now is to meet him for myself.' Then, after another pause: 'However, there is one thing you could tell me.'

'Yes?' Céline prompted when Claudine didn't continue.

Claudine's eyes were wandering dreamily about her, taking in the glorious spectacle of nature left to tend itself – the trees that rose on either side of them, the carpets of green and yellow that spread as far as the eye could see. Then her lips curved in a secret smile as she decided that, no, she wouldn't ask about Hortense after all. She would save that question for François. Instead she turned to her aunt, gave her a brief kiss on the cheek, and as they approached the steps in the tall grass which led down to the river, she skipped on ahead, lifting her dress to stop it catching on the thistles and revealing the dark bands at the top of her stockings as she tripped down to the water's edge.

Watching her go, so unselfconscious, so natural, Céline felt a jolt of painful love shoot through her heart. Claudine reached the roughened sandy beach, kicked off her shoes, rolled down her stockings and splashed into the river. 'This is heavenly, Tante Céline,' she cried, throwing out her arms and spinning round and round. 'It's so beautiful here. Just look at the sunlight on the water, look at the poppies, look at the trees and the sky. I love it here, Tante Céline, I love it so much I want to hold it in my arms.'

And how, Céline thought, could François de Lorvoire, were he here to see her, not want to do the same to her? Surely even he could not remain impervious to such charm, such guileless joy, such unsullied beauty. And again that brief flicker of hope ignited in her breast. Perhaps he would love her; perhaps beneath that implacable exterior there was a heart.

'Is there a rowing boat here?' Claudine called. 'It would be wonderful to row across to that forest over there, don't you think? To sail about under the branches hanging over the water.'

She had stopped spinning, and her head was on one side as she contemplated the opposite bank where the trees crowded one upon the other, the river lapping at their roots and the sun scorching their topmost leaves where they rose high, high into the sky. There was something mystical about that forest, she felt; she wanted to go closer, to find out what it was.

'That is what I wanted to show you,' Céline answered. 'It's the de Lorvoire forest. It spreads all over the hillside, much further than you can see, and the château is in amongst it, hidden from view.'

'The Lorvoire château is surrounded by those trees?'

'Yes. But there's a steep meadow in front of the château, and lawns on either side – like a kind of oasis in the middle of the forest.'

Claudine gazed in wonder. Then she turned to face her aunt, who had come to stand at the edge of the river. 'I'm going to be happy here, Tante Céline,' she said softly.

Céline smiled, and wondered if Claudine had ever known what it was to be anything other than happy. But of course –

her mother had died when she was sixteen years old, and Céline knew that still, even now, Claudine missed her terribly. And that was another thing she admired so much in her niece, her indomitable courage, her understanding and selflessness that had helped to hold Beavis together when Antoinette fell to her death on that fateful Italian holiday. Her own grief Claudine had nursed privately, confiding in no one but Céline.

Claudine was looking down at the grey-brown water lapping about her ankles. Then, lifting her head, she said in a voice of quiet but unmistakable passion, 'I am going to marry him, Tante Céline.'

'But why?' Céline asked gently. 'Why, when . . .'

'Because I have to.'

'No, *chérie*, you don't have to. I will speak with your father . . .'

'I have to,' Claudine repeated.

Céline's confusion showed, and smiling, Claudine waded out of the water to put an arm around her aunt. 'I have to,' she said, 'because all of Paris knows that I'm here, and why.'

The colour started to drain from Céline's face and her pale eyes widened in horror as she took in the full meaning of what Claudine had said. 'What!' she gasped.

'I'm afraid so,' Claudine answered, with mock gravity. 'You see, I told Henriette, and you know how hopeless she is at keeping a secret, especially one like this.'

For a moment Céline was lost for words. 'Oh no!' she moaned at last, covering her face with her hands. 'Don't you realize, Claudine, that if you decide to refuse him now, all of Paris will assume that *he* has refused *you*. You will be yet another in the long line of François de Lorvoire's rejected women!' Her voice rose in anguish as she contemplated the derision that not only Claudine, but she too, would have to suffer as a result of her niece's thoughtlessness.

'But if I marry him,' Claudine said, very softly, 'there won't be any scandal, now will there, Tante Céline?'

Once again Céline found herself bereft of speech. She stared straight into Claudine's piercing blue eyes as the realization hit her. 'You did it on purpose, didn't you?' she said. 'You made sure that the marriage arrangement would be common knowledge, so that fear of scandal would force me to withdraw my opposition to it.' Suddenly her anger gave way to distress. 'But why are you so set on this marriage, Claudine? Tell me why, I beg you.'

'It isn't only I who want it, Tante Céline,' Claudine said mildly. 'When the proposal was put to François, he didn't object, he's told his family, and Papa, that he will marry me. And just as he has promised Papa to marry *me*, I promise you I'll marry *him*.'

'But *why?*'

'Because I am twenty-two years old and in danger of becoming an old maid?'

'Claudine, you are mocking me. I know you; there's something behind all this that you're not telling me or your Papa.'

'If there is,' Claudine countered, 'then maybe it's a secret I want to keep.'

Céline fell silent. After what Claudine had done, the marriage was now almost a *fait accompli* – and yet how could she stand by and watch her niece ruin her life? 'I promised your father I would do nothing to interfere,' she said slowly, 'but I am going to break that promise. I am going to stop this marriage, Claudine. I am going to stop it for your own sake, and one day you will thank me for it.'

'No!' Claudine's eyes held a dangerous gleam, and her aunt stepped back, almost as if she had been struck. 'This is my life, Tante Céline, and I will do with it as *I* see fit. I have made the decision to marry François de Lorvoire, and if you do anything to jeopardize that, then so help me, Tante Céline, I'll . . . I'll . . .'

'Claudine!' her aunt gasped. 'Are you threatening me?'

Suddenly Claudine's eyes were alive with laughter. 'Do you know,' she grinned, 'I rather think I am. But I am serious, Tante Céline. I am no longer a child. My life, my destiny, are in my hands now. And the reasons I have for going through with this marriage are mine, and mine alone.'

Céline closed her eyes as her anger deflated. 'Oh, this is all such a mess,' she sighed, gazing out across the river to the Lorvoire forest. 'How has it happened? I know your Papa loves you . . .' Her eyes moved back to Claudine's and she gave her a weak smile as she said, 'I can't give up, Claudine. I will go and speak to your Papa again now. All is not lost yet.' And turning, she began to walk slowly back to the château.

With the brown water of the River Vienne lapping her toes, Claudine stood and watched her aunt disappear along the avenue of limes. How hard Tante Céline had tried to make her divulge the reason behind her determination to marry François! But how could she tell her when the truth was so ridiculous? Heaven knows, she would laugh herself if she was told such a story, but when something like that happened to you, when it touched your own life, it was a different matter altogether. Somehow, you couldn't shrug it off, no matter how hard you tried. And when life was unfolding in precisely the manner the old woman had described . . .

She picked up her shoes and wandered over to the long grass where she sat down, resting her elbows on her knees, propping her chin on her hands, and staring sightlessly at the river as it flowed past.

That was why she was here, that was why she was going to marry François de Lorvoire. Because of an old gypsy, who had sent the village children to tell her she must come and see her. She hadn't sought the gypsy out herself; she had just returned to her Hertfordshire home from New York, and hadn't even known the fair was nearby until the children told her. But the gypsy woman had known about her; so she had gone, not out of vanity, not even out of curiosity, but out of a desire to please the children.

Afterwards, she had all but forgotten what the gypsy said, until six weeks ago her father returned from Rome, having stopped en route for a brief stay at the Château de Lorvoire. Then it had all come flooding back.

'There is a man,' the gypsy had said, 'a very handsome man, much older than you. I think perhaps he is your father. He will come to you and tell you something you will find strange at first, but you must listen to him, because your future is in his words. Your future lies across the sea, in a foreign land, but I see it is not such a foreign land to you.' The old woman had looked up from Claudine's palm and searched her eyes. 'Your father is English, I think,' she said. 'Your mother not.'

When Claudine nodded, the odd, foreign-looking face smiled, before it was lost in shadow again as the gypsy bent her head. 'Tell me no more,' she murmured. Then there was a long silence, and Claudine could hear the shouts and laughter outside and the sound of the fairground organ as it piped and whistled a medley of cheerful tunes only a few yards from the tiny domed tent in which she sat.

At last the old woman spoke again. 'You will do what your father tells you, even though there will be many who warn you against it.'

'But what is it?' Claudine asked.

'It is marriage. There is a man, again older than you.' The woman stopped. 'But wait!' she said. 'There are two men. Yes, I see two men. The man who will be your husband, and the other ... There is a great love.' She looked up, and there was an odd light in her eyes that made Claudine want to shiver. 'And there is a greater danger,' she rasped. 'I cannot tell which of them ...'

'Danger?' Claudine repeated, when the old woman did not go on.

She shook her head. 'It is more than danger. There are many influences . . . influences that will be beyond your control. And always there are these two men. What is your name?'

'Claudine.'

The gypsy smiled, revealing the gaps between her stained teeth. 'I cannot say which of these men will bring you happiness, Claudine, all I can say is that there is a long road to travel before you find it, many mistakes to be made and lessons to be learned along the way. My advice is to listen to your heart, because it is a truer friend to you even than those who believe they know what is right for you. Your marriage will cause much trouble, but it will happen soon, sooner than you think, and it will change your life.'

Claudine found herself smiling as the gnarled old fingers closed protectively around hers. 'It is not right that I should tell you more,' she said. 'The lines in your hand fork many times, you will decide which route to take as you approach them. But perhaps you can avoid the pain, perhaps you can overcome the fear and the danger if I tell you that there is love there for you, a love so great that few people find it in this life – but you will find it, and you will find it where you least expect it . . . But never forget, child, that things are not always as they seem.'

'Not always as they seem . . .' The words echoed through Claudine's mind as she sat there on the banks of the Vienne, while the early evening breeze drifted through the trees of the Lorvoire forest.

So, absurd as it was, that was why she was here, on the brink of a new life, a life she could hardly begin to imagine – because an old woman had told her to trust her instincts. And since the day her father had first put the suggestion of this marriage to her, Claudine's instinct had told her that it was right. Just as her instinct was telling her now that the ambiguity of the gypsy's final words concerned François de Lorvoire.

But the other man, the second man, who was he? And was he the danger, or was *he* the great love? Again, as she had many times these past six weeks, Claudine searched her mind for the elusive words the gypsy had spoken. She had said something more, something about the other man that was important. But Claudine simply couldn't remember what it was.

– 3 –

Breakfast on Sunday morning was served on the garden roof of the château's east wing, overlooking the orchard of dwarf-like fruit trees and the maize fields beyond. The breeze was no more than a whisper of warm air carrying the mingled scents of roses, cut grass and freshly ground coffee. The only sounds were the billing and cooing of the doves and the distant clatter of dishes in the kitchens below.

The previous day, Magaly had arrived from Paris bearing the dresses, suits, hats, shoes and lingerie Claudine had been fitted for during her stay. Even Céline, whose shopping sprees were legendary, had been amazed at how much Claudine had managed to purchase in such a short time, but she was even more impressed once the garments had been removed from their protective coverings.

Claudine's knowledge of what suited her had always been exceptional, but on this occasion she had managed to excel herself. With amusement, Céline noted that virtually every designer in Paris was represented in the garments that spilled from the endless number of tissue-strewn boxes scattered around her niece's bedchamber, from Schiaparelli's startling pinks and circus prints, to Piguet's sumptuously risqué evening gowns, to Mainbocher's sophisticated day-time elegance.

Now, with so many things to choose from and with such

an important day ahead, the conversation over breakfast was quite naturally about what Claudine should wear. Beavis, with his head buried in the newspaper and a plate of untouched kedgeree in front of him, paid scant attention to Céline's deliberations on what would be correct for an afternoon party in the country. Though the news from Germany and Japan came as no surprise to him, it was nonetheless disturbing, and he was beginning to wonder just how long he would be able to stay in Touraine. Long enough, he hoped, to see his daughter's wedding.

Finally, heaving a weary sigh, he put the newspaper down just as Céline, looking utterly charming in her peach satin peignoir, signalled to Jean for more coffee. 'I have quite run out of suggestions, *chérie*,' she declared to Claudine, 'but I have a suspicion that you have already made up your mind.'

'Do you know, Tante Céline,' Claudine responded in a conspiratorial tone, 'I do believe I have.'

'Beavis!' Céline cried. 'She is impossible. Quite, quite impossible. Thank you, Jean,' she added, as he refilled her cup.

Chuckling, Beavis picked up his fork. 'What time are they expecting us?' he asked.

'Around three. After lunch – which, knowing you two, you will be able to eat. As for me, I am simply too nervous even for breakfast. Claudine, are you really going to eat all that?' she said, as Claudine returned from the hot-plate with another helping of kedgeree.

Claudine looked down at her plate. And it was then, quite unexpectedly, that the first pang of apprehension wrenched at her stomach, completely obliterating her appetite. 'I *was* going to,' she said uncertainly. She sat down, and started to look anxiously around the table.

'They're under the newspaper,' Beavis said, and watched Céline's bewildered expression as Claudine located the cigarette packet and took one out.

'You have an uncanny knack of doing that,' Céline remarked, smiling despite herself at the way Beavis had read his daughter's mind. 'Perhaps, as an encore, you can enlighten me as to what she is intending to wear today.'

'Now that,' Beavis answered, 'is beyond even me.'

Claudine, still clad in black jodhpurs, riding boots and a white silk shirt after her early morning canter across the fields, got up from the table, wandered to the edge of the terrace and leaned against the ornate railings. Her sudden attack of nerves had disturbed her deeply; part of her was so happy that she wanted to throw out her arms and embrace the world, and part of her longed to flee back to London. It was the first time since she'd arrived in France that she had experienced anything approaching fear, and now that it had begun, she was finding it difficult to overcome.

She drew on her cigarette and turned to gaze out at the shimmering horizon. Then, tossing her hair back over her shoulders, she perched one leg on the railing, and ran through in her mind the recent imaginary conversations she'd had with François. How silly they seemed now! She wondered if he had thought about her at all. But of course, he must have done; no matter what everyone said, he couldn't be *completely* lacking in sensibility. She rather doubted that he was suffering from sudden attacks of nerves, though. How naive of her not to have foreseen that she would.

Throughout the remainder of the morning she roamed the towers and stairways of the château. She went to the library and sat at the *bureau de dame*, trying to write a letter to Dissy in London, but got no further than 'Dearest Dissy'. Thinking she would prefer it, Beavis and Céline left her alone, but there were moments when Claudine longed to speak to them about the way she was feeling. As she bathed, then dressed herself for the afternoon ahead, she was torn by a bewildering paradox of emotions –anticipation and apprehension, excitement and dread. And to make matters worse, the instincts she had relied upon to guide her through seemed to be completely lost in the confusion.

Well, there's only one thing for it, she told herself, as at three o'clock precisely Céline's chauffeur turned the car from the forest road into the steep, winding drive which approached the west wing of the Lorvoire château; that is, to remember that when I had my wits about me, I had no doubts at all. Just because I feel now as though I'm journeying beyond the borders of reality doesn't mean I'm not doing the right thing. And with that decided, she settled herself back against the leather upholstery of Céline's Armstrong Siddeley to await the first glimpse of her future home.

When it came, it was as though someone had caught hold of her heart and stopped it beating for a moment. Her eyes dilated and her lips parted as she sat forward in her seat. Never could she have envisaged such mesmerizing splendour: the fairy-tale magic of the soaring towers, the massive creamy-white façade, the magnificent Renaissance windows. And then there were the gardens, which fanned gently out from the château towards the surrounding forest, whose impenetrable green foliage was like a bastion, protecting the Château de Lorvoire from everything but the elements.

'Well, *chérie*,' her father said, as the car pulled slowly to a stop in front of the château, 'a charming little place, wouldn't you say?'

But as Claudine turned to look at him, Beavis felt himself almost choked with a welter of emotion. He couldn't remember ever having seen her so lovely. Her bright blue eyes were blazing with such passion it almost dazzled him, and his heart melted as a breeze from the car's open window caught the fiery black curls, and blew them across her lips.

'I know what I say,' Céline said. 'I say that if François de

Lorvoire can bring the same light to Claudine's eyes as his home has, then I will bless this marriage with all my heart.'

Claudine stared at her aunt as a sudden bolt of nervousness soared inside her. This was *his* home. This was where she would live *with François de Lorvoire*. How strange it suddenly seemed. She looked around, and for one perplexing moment felt detached from herself, as though her thoughts had scattered like the pearls of a broken necklace.

Then, seeing the puzzled faces of her aunt and her father, an impish light flared in her eyes and she began to get out of the car, saying, 'Come along, you two, this lamb has waited long enough to be led to the slaughter,' and she was still smiling as she led them up the steps, and the liveried butler ushered them through the hall and into a magnificent walnut-panelled drawing-room.

Claudine had not been sure quite what to expect when she first arrived at the Lorvoire château, but one thing she had certainly not anticipated was that she would find herself confronted by a room so filled with people. The noise was deafening, the air heavy with a mixture of scent and cigarette smoke. Several people turned as the door opened, and for one horrifying moment, as Claudine stood on the threshold in the clinging black woollen dress by Charles Creed, with the red, navy and white striped piqué that matched the crown of her little black straw hat, it occurred to her that they might all be de Rassey de Lorvoire relatives. Seeing her stricken face, and reading the situation perfectly, Beavis leaned towards her and whispered, 'The Comtesse thought it might be easier if there were people here, friends and acquaintances, so that you could be introduced to François as naturally as possible.'

Claudine's relief was evident, but then Beavis ruined everything by adding: 'Of course, now that you've let the cat out of the bag and informed the whole world why you are in

Touraine . . .' He broke off, wincing, as Claudine's heel found his toe.

Assuming her most radiant smile, Claudine held out her hands towards Solange de Lorvoire, a tall, rangy woman with startlingly wide amber eyes and oddly cropped grey hair, who had that moment finished beating a path through the crowd and was clearly intent upon taking Claudine in her arms.

'*Ma chérie!*' she cried, kissing Claudine on both cheeks. 'Ah, *ma chérie!* Let me look at you. Oh, but you are so like your mother it almost breaks my heart. How is it that we have never met when I have heard so much about you? And you are even more beautiful than they say. But look at me, I am going to cry, I am so happy. Ah, Louis,' she said, as the distinguished-looking man beside her passed her his handkerchief, 'do you see Antoinette's daughter? Is she not the loveliest creature? Beavis, why have you been hiding her from us? Why have you never brought her to Lorvoire before?'

'Solange,' Beavis answered, the twinkle in his grey eyes belying the formal tone of his voice, 'may I present my daughter, Claudine. Claudine, the Comtesse de Rassey de Lorvoire and her long-suffering husband, Louis.'

'Oh, but it is I who do the suffering, Claudine,' the Comtesse assured her. 'It is always we women who do the suffering, don't you agree?'

Laughing as she looked from one to the other, Claudine said: 'I am so pleased to meet you at last, *madame.*'

'Oh no, I won't hear of "*madame*", you must call me Solange. Ah, Céline!' she cried. 'I didn't see you standing there, *chérie*. But you look so divine. Is that Molyneux you are wearing? He has done you proud, my dear. I wish I could wear a hat like that, but . . . You know, I think I shall! If you don't mind what people say, then why should I? Louis, do you hear me, I'm going to buy a hat like Céline's. Now tell me, Céline, how do you manage to keep yourself looking so young when I know for certain that you must be at least fifty?'

Claudine, both amused and bewildered, suddenly found herself looking into the aristocratic face of the Comte. He gave her the smallest of winks, then, removing the round spectacles perched on the end of his large Roman nose, held out his arms to welcome her. There was such warmth in his tired, shadowy eyes that for a moment she was almost overwhelmed – then found herself spluttering with laughter as he whispered in English, 'Never mind Solange, she's batty. Harmless, but batty.' Then, letting her go, he turned to Beavis. 'Now, my friend, there is someone over here I've been wanting you to meet . . .' and Claudine blinked several times as she recognized the name of the French Prime Minister.

'Is that really Léon Blum?' she whispered to Céline.

'Of course, *chérie*.'

'But what on earth is he doing here? He's a communist.'

'Odd isn't it?' Céline responded, casting her eyes about the room to see whom she recognized. 'Now,' she said, 'who shall we introduce you to first?'

For the next half-hour a sea of faces passed before Claudine's eyes, most of them unknown to her. She was aware that her presence was exciting a great deal of comment amongst the guests, who seemed to include politicians, aristocrats, soldiers, writers, musicians and even a couple of actors. But there was only one person who could hold any interest for Claudine, though, as thoroughly as she searched the room with her eyes, she couldn't see anyone who might conceivably be him.

At last she managed to get a moment alone with Céline. 'For heaven's sake,' she whispered, 'which one is he?'

'Now, *chérie*, you're not to be angry,' Céline whispered back, 'but he hasn't come.'

Claudine's face paled as the excitement that had charged her veins ever since she first walked into the room, evaporated so abruptly it was as though someone had landed a blow to her stomach. Then seeing the gleam of *I told you so* in Céline's eyes, she turned sharply away.

So he hadn't come. She didn't know why she should feel so crushed; after all, with everything she had heard about him she should have expected something like this. And yet, could he really be so ungallant as to humiliate her in front of all these people? It was true that if she had learned anything at all about François de Lorvoire, it was that he cared nothing for social graces. Yet she had hoped, believed, that with her he would be different . . . Now his absence made more than a mockery of that, it showed her how utterly naive and foolish she was.

The next ten minutes were some of the longest she had ever known, as she flirted and joked with guests while all the time anger welled inside her. It was directed at herself as well as at François, for didn't she have only herself to blame that many of the de Lorvoire guests would know the reason for her presence here? She was certain she could already see the delight on their faces as they witnessed François' humiliation of her – and suddenly she hated him with an overpowering intensity that threatened to drive her out of this room, out of the château, out of the de Lorvoires' lives for ever.

'Steady,' her father murmured beside her, his hand on her arm. 'Be patient.'

'Be patient!' she hissed. 'Do you think I've come here to be humiliated like this?'

Beavis smiled. 'Would it calm you if I told you that he's arrived?'

Her answer was snatched by the sickening lurch of her heart, and unable to stop herself, she looked desperately round the room.

Beavis shook his head. 'He's upstairs, changing. He was delayed in Paris, he . . .'

'There you are, Claudine!'

They turned to find Solange holding the hand of a remarkably striking young woman dressed and coiffured in the height of Paris fashion. She was, Claudine surmised, about her own age, but it was difficult to judge when her face bore an expression of such blatant hostility. This, Solange told them proudly, was her daughter, Monique.

Again, Claudine met the hostile gaze, and wondered what on earth she could have done to provoke it. '*Enchantée*,' she said, holding out her hand and smiling.

'*Enchantée*,' Monique repeated, but though she returned the smile, her eyes remained cold.

'You two are going to be *such* good friends,' Solange enthused.

The situation was temporarily saved by Beavis, who stepped forward to embrace Monique in the French way. To Claudine's surprise, Monique responded with genuine warmth, and for a few moments she felt as though she were looking at a different person. Then those suspicious amber eyes, with their cumbersome black brows, were upon her again as Monique embarked upon a formal recital of welcome.

Claudine remained silent throughout, smiling politely until Monique had finished. Then, to her amazement, as she was about to reply Monique turned on her heel and walked back into the body of the party.

'Well!' Claudine gasped, turning to her father, and to Solange's delight they burst out laughing.

'You see!' Solange cried. 'I told you you would love her!'

'Oh, I do,' Claudine answered. 'Really I . . .'

She stopped, and the smile vanished from her face as her eyes were suddenly arrested by the massive figure standing just inside the door. He was talking to Léon Blum and a man her father had introduced earlier as Colonel Rivet, and though Claudine had never seen him before in her life she knew beyond all doubt that she was looking at François de Lorvoire.

For the moment shock paralysed her senses so that all she could do was stare. Not in her wildest dreams had she imagined him to look like that. He was tall, taller even than Beavis, and his unfashionably long hair, which was combed straight back from his forehead and curled over his collar, was as black as night. His head was bowed and he appeared intent upon what his companions were saying, then he turned slightly, and Claudine started as she saw the pronounced hook of his nose beneath the heavy, hawk-like eyes. His mouth was set in a firm line of concentration, but she could see the cruelty in it as clearly as she could see the hideous scar that curved jaggedly round his cheek bone to his jaw. He was the ugliest, most sinister-looking man she had ever seen.

Her mind started a slow spin, adding a strange light-headedness to her stupor. She was both appalled and mesmerized; she couldn't tear her eyes away as she felt herself responding to the bewildering force of his presence. It seemed to fill the room, to push aside the guests, opening a path between them and pull her towards him. But he wasn't even looking at her, he didn't know she was there. Her lips parted, but still she made no sound, and her eyes remained unblinking as a remote tightening sensation spread throughout her body, engulfing her in feelings she couldn't begin to recognize.

Beside her, her father, though he was making a pretence of talking to Solange, was quite aware of his daughter's confusion. Then suddenly Louis was there too, taking his wife by the arm and leading her away, almost as if he knew that Beavis and Claudine needed this moment to themselves. Claudine looked at her father, still too shaken to find her voice.

'I know what you're thinking,' he said.

'But why? Why did you. . . ?'

'Claudine,' he interrupted, 'I have, from the start, made it clear to you that the decision is yours. You have, of course, put yourself in an extremely difficult position by letting everyone know why you are here. However, should you . . .'

'But he's so . . . Oh, dear God, Papa.'

Beavis looked across the room with a grim smile. Then turning back to her, he said, 'You will, *of course*, meet him.'

It was the closest to an order she had ever heard him give. It made her feel dizzy, and it brought, too, a suffocating sense of betrayal. But worse was the feeling that she was suddenly a stranger to herself; new sensations were confusing her, frightening her almost. Then, as though they had a will of their own, she found her eyes moving back to François. He was talking now to Anton Veronne, a man Claudine had always considered handsome. Yet strangely, beside François Anton seemed almost insignificant. Then she realized that so too did all the men around him.

Again she looked at François, and this time her mouth dried with shock. He was looking at her, and his expression made her want to step behind her father, to have him protect her from such malevolence. But sensing her intention, Beavis moved away into the crowd, leaving her still bound by that invidious gaze.

Claudine blinked. It was inconceivable that someone could have such an effect on her – but then she had never before met anyone who emanated such power. She was afraid, though she didn't know why, and yet she was unable to wrest her eyes from his. In the end, François was the first to turn away, but as he released her eyes, instead of being relieved she felt as though she had been cast adrift, left to drown in her own internal confusion, and without realizing what she was doing she found her arms starting to move from her sides as if they were seeking something to save her.

'It's all right, *chérie*, I'm here.'

Claudine spun round to find Céline standing beside her with a glass of brandy. 'Drink it,' she insisted. 'You've had a shock, you need something.'

'A shock?'

'Don't pretend, Claudine, I saw your face.'

Unthinkingly Claudine took the brandy and sipped it. 'Did you see the way he looked at me, Tante Céline?' she whispered. 'It was as if he hated me.'

Céline smiled. 'No, *chérie*, he doesn't hate you. It is simply the way he looks. Which, I take it, is nothing like what you imagined.'

Already beginning to realize how ridiculous she had made herself, and acutely aware of the curious glances being thrown in her direction, Claudine forced herself to smile. To her surprise, this actually made her feel better – and suddenly her indomitable sense of humour broke free of the lingering pinions of shock, so that she actually laughed aloud at her melodramatic reaction to her first sight of the man she had vowed to marry. 'Never mind,' she said, giving Céline an impulsive hug. 'Anyway, now I shall go and meet him.'

But to her consternation, he seemed to have disappeared.

'What an infuriating man,' she muttered. And then her heart gave a monstrous lurch as a voice behind her said, 'Would you be looking for me, by any chance?'

With every pulse hammering in her body, Claudine turned around, and steeling herself, lifted her head to meet the black eyes that gazed down at her from beneath their hooded lids. For one fleeting second she thought she detected a glint of humour in them, but then his shadowed face was once again as severe as the tone of his deep, strangely alluring voice, as he said to Céline, 'If you can bring yourself to do it, I should appreciate an introduction, Céline.'

Céline's response was delivered through gritted teeth. 'Claudine, may I present François de Rassey de Lorvoire. François, my niece, Claudine Rafferty.'

'Thank you,' he answered. 'Now, as Mademoiselle Rafferty has seen fit to inform half of Paris as to the purpose of her visit here today, I'm sure there are a number of people in this room requiring details of her first introduction to me. Perhaps you would care to oblige, Céline.'

Céline's gasp of outrage took his eyes, which had not yet moved from Claudine's, to hers. 'How dare you!' she hissed. 'I am not a servant to be dismissed . . .'

'Céline, please go.'

Claudine watched as her aunt drew herself to her full height and stalked off. Then turning back to François, she said, 'Was it necessary to be so rude?'

'Shall we just say I try not to disappoint expectation,' he answered smoothly. 'Now, unless you want to stand here being ogled by the entire gathering, I suggest we take a walk in the garden.'

There was an unmistakable lull in the general conversation as François held open the door for her to walk out ahead of him. She followed him through the dimly lit hall, past the wide mahogany staircase and into a small, untidy sitting-room. Curtains fluttered at the tall, open windows, and François stepped over the sill onto the gravelled courtyard outside, then turned back to give her his hand.

For a moment Claudine was confounded by the extreme tightness of her skirt, and looking up, saw his eyes narrow with impatience at her hesitation. By the time she had hitched her dress up over her thighs, however, he had already started down the wide stone steps that led down to the water garden. He neither stopped nor turned round when she started to follow – and pride prevented her from hurrying after him.

When at last she caught up with him, he was standing

with one foot on the low wall surrounding a small, circular fountain where three cherubs with arms and wings entwined in stone spouted water from their pouting lips. He had rested his arms on his knee and was gazing thoughtfully down at the goldfish darting about in the pool.

Joining him, Claudine perched on the wall, and crossing her legs demurely at the ankles began trailing a hand through the cool water. After a while the silence became uncomfortable. She was hunting about in her mind for a way to begin, yet at the same time was stubbornly determined not to. After all, he was the host, it was the correct thing for him to address her first. But the awkwardness became so insufferable that, unable to disguise her irritation, she said at last, 'Do you intend to speak at all?'

To her amazement and outrage, he merely threw her a quick glance, then returned to his study of the fish.

She stood up, and as she walked round him he pulled at his bow tie, loosening the knot until it was free of his collar. Then he resumed his stance. The most infuriating thing was that he gave every appearance of being completely oblivious to her discomfort.

'What were you thinking when you looked at me earlier?' she demanded.

Casting her a look from the corner of his eye, he said, 'I wasn't aware of thinking anything.'

Claudine decided to swallow her temper and try a different approach. 'Papa tells me you were delayed in Paris,' she ventured.

There was a brief pause before he spoke, but still he didn't look up. 'My apologies for keeping you waiting.' His tone was so thick with sarcasm that she felt the colour rush to her cheeks.

'If the apology were meant I'd accept it,' she snapped. 'As it is . . .'

He made no response to her unfinished sentence though

she stared furiously at him for several minutes. Then, before she could give herself time to think, she had kicked his foot from the wall so that he was suddenly ankle-deep in the fountain. To hell with him, she thought, as she marched angrily along the cobbled path. Then, hearing the slosh of water as he drew his foot from the fountain, she started to grin. She felt even better when she heard his footsteps behind her, but she didn't stop until she reached a nearby lily pound, by which time her shoulders were shaking with suppressed laughter.

'I take it,' he said, as he came to stand beside her, 'that it is your childish behaviour that so amuses you.'

'Actually, no,' she replied. 'It's your pomposity that so amuses me. And after just these few minutes of knowing you, I can already understand why Tante Céline dislikes you so intensely.'

When she looked up into his face she could see that her words had not succeeded in ruffling him at all, but when he looked back at her she felt a horrible heat burn across her cheeks, and turned quickly away.

'Tell me,' he said, 'has Céline ever cared to enlarge upon why she dislikes me so intensely?'

'Are you going to tell me?' she countered.

'No.'

They lapsed into silence again, and Claudine, assuming an air of nonchalance, looked about her. They were on the edge of the forest here, and there were several inviting pathways leading into the trees.

'Why are you making this so difficult?' she asked eventually.

His answering laugh was more of a sneer. 'My dear girl,' he said, 'if you are expecting protestations of love and promises of undying devotion, then I am afraid you are going to be disappointed.'

'I was expecting nothing of the kind,' she snapped. But a

small interior voice told her that that wasn't strictly true. Suddenly she had had enough and reaching up to remove the pin from her hat, she shook out her curls, and started off into the forest. Should he take it upon himself to come after her, then maybe she would try again – providing he apologised first, of course – but as it was, she really didn't see why she should put up with his rudeness any longer. And so, hitching her skirt up over her knees and gripping the branches to help her up the steep path, she climbed higher and higher into the woods.

As she reached the brink of the hill the shadows gave way to bright sunlight, and she found herself in a narrow meadow from which there was the most magnificent view over the next valley. Every hillside, for as far as the eye could see, was covered with row upon row, acre upon acre of leafy vines, and at the heart of the valley, where the river shimmered and sparkled in the sunlight, was a cluster of tiny cottages.

The unexpected and awe-inspiring spectacles of nature never failed to move Claudine, and by the time François came up behind her she was too delighted to bother about his earlier unpleasantness, or to feel any satisfaction that he had followed her again.

'It's so beautiful,' she murmured.

'I'm glad you like it,' he said, coming to stand next to her.

'And these are all your vineyards?'

'Yes,' he answered.

Every time he drew near her, she felt a thrill of such excitement, such recklessness . . . She should be repulsed by his ugliness, and yet . . . She could not make sense of what she was feeling. Could it be fear? All she knew for certain was that she found his physical presence deeply disturbing, and she moved away from him, walking on across the hilltop and gazing down at the unyielding symmetry of the vines as the wind swept through her hair.

Far below she saw someone waving. She lifted her hat and waved back. 'Who is it?' she called out to François.

'Armand,' he answered, when he was close enough not to have to shout. 'Armand St Jacques. He's the *Chef de Caves*, and also the *vigneron*. In other words, Armand runs the place – as his father did and his grandfather before him. Theirs is the expertise, ours is the name.'

'Aren't you involved at all in the wine-making?'

He shook his head. 'Only in the selling.'

He was looking past her into the middle-distance, apparently unaware of the way she was searching his face. She watched him closely for several minutes, fascinated by the way his gruesome face was almost transformed when he wasn't scowling. With those macabre features and that hideously disfiguring scar he could never be described as handsome, but when he looked as he did at that moment, his eyes devoid of rancour and his mouth relaxed in something close to a smile, there was an air about him that she found positively intriguing.

'Tell me,' she said softly, 'why did you change your mind about marriage?'

Instantly the frown returned, and as his eyes bored into hers she felt herself grow suddenly weak. 'Change my mind?' he echoed.

Quickly she turned away, stunned by her peculiar reaction, but her voice was perfectly steady as she said, 'I thought, at least everyone else seems to think, that you had vowed never to marry.'

His laugh was bitter. 'For once the gossip-mongers are right, if a little exaggerated.'

'So, why?'

'I think,' he said, starting to turn away, 'that you would prefer not to know the answer to that.'

'I think,' she said, following him, 'that if I am to marry you, I had better know the answer.'

'Then I shall tell you – after I have proposed and you have accepted.'

'Are you so sure that I will accept? And do you very much care, one way or the other?'

At that he stopped and turned to face her. To her dismay, she found herself caught by those black, impenetrable eyes, and again she felt that strange response to him sweeping through her body. 'Claudine,' he said coldly, 'when I feel that the time is right, I shall ask you to marry me. I shall ask you because it is the wish of our fathers to unite our families. Whether you accept my proposal is a decision only you can make, but I can assure you that I have no personal feelings on the matter whatsoever.'

'You rather give me the impression that I would be doing you the greatest favour if I were to refuse,' she said, in a tone that disgusted her by its peevishness.

'The words are yours,' he said, 'not mine.'

She was not a naturally violent person, but in the space of less than half an hour she had not only kicked him, but was now shaking with the urge to slap him. 'I understand now,' she seethed, 'why your reputation is so foul. You are not only rude and insensitive, you are unpardonably offensive. In fact, I would go so far as to say that you are a truly despicable man.'

'So I believe,' he answered lightly.

For one horrifying moment Claudine thought she was going to cry – and since she would rather die than give him the satisfaction of witnessing that, she stormed back into the forest. She had gone no more than a few yards when, to her inexpressible humiliation, she slipped in the undergrowth and bumped several feet down the path on her bottom in the most undignified – not to mention, painful – manner. It was the final straw: the tears streamed from her eyes, and at the same time, as she buried her face in her hands, her body convulsed with sobs of laughter.

She heard him coming down behind her, and when she looked up it was to find him standing over her, holding out her hat. 'Yours, I believe,' he said.

'Thank you,' she said, wiping the back of her hand over her cheeks. Then, as she reached out to take the hat she noticed the damp patch at the bottom of his trousers, and unable to contain herself, was consumed by another paroxysm of laughter.

He waited, with an unmistakable air of boredom, for her to pull herself together, then offered her a hand to help her to her feet.

'Tell me,' she said, as she tried not to notice the way his hand swallowed hers in its grip, 'do you have a sense of humour? The stories they tell about you in Paris suggest you might.'

'There are very few things that concern me, Claudine,' he said, letting go of her and starting to walk on. 'And society gossip is not one of them.'

'Then, may I venture to ask what does concern you?'

'No.'

When they had reached the water-garden again, Claudine stopped at the fountain and sat down. For one alarming moment she thought François was going to walk on, but he halted a few paces away, keeping his back to her.

'May I ask how you received the scar on your face?' she said.

'No.'

'Am I allowed to ask anything at all?'

He turned slowly, but made no move towards her as he said, 'Inquisitiveness is not a quality I find attractive.'

'Do you intend ever to be anything but rude to me?'

'That depends very much on you.'

Not knowing quite how to answer that, she sat quietly, hoping he might say more. At last, to break the silence she asked, 'Do you know my father well?'

'Yes.'

'Do you like him?'

'I have a great admiration for him.'

'Well, couldn't you at least be civil to his daughter, then? Especially if she is going to marry you.'

'If there is to be a marriage between us, Claudine, then it will be one of convenience only. Beavis is fully aware of that.'

'Must it preclude friendship?'

He looked away, but she could tell that her question had annoyed him. 'Why does it have to be you who marries, then,' she went on angrily, 'if you hate the idea so much? You have a brother, couldn't he have rescued you from this obviously repugnant state of affairs?'

At that he gave a shout of mirthless laughter, and his eyes gleamed balefully as he turned to look at her. 'From the moment you meet my brother,' he said, 'it will be one of the greatest regrets of your life that he won the toss of the coin.'

She frowned. 'The toss of the coin?'

He merely smiled, but this time there was something so pernicious in the smile that though he was standing several feet away, she felt herself shrink back.

'Earlier,' she said, 'I thought you hated me. But I was wrong. You despise me, don't you?'

'Does it matter what my feelings are for you?'

'If I'm to marry you, then of course it does!' she cried.

His eyes were suddenly harder than ever as the thick brows pulled together and the wide nostrils of his beaked nose flared. 'If you care about such trivialities, perhaps you should return to England before your disappointment becomes an embarrassment to us both,' he said, and sliding his hands into his pockets, he turned and walked back to the house.

Claudine was still sitting at the fountain when Céline came

to find her half an hour later. In that time she had managed to overcome the worst of her fury, but her sense of outrage was still so strong that she had not yet dared to go back into the house. She was stunned by the effect he had on her – was still having. It was almost as if he had molested her, as if his monstrous presence had actually invaded her – though their only physical contact had been when he touched her hand. She was confused and hurt, she wanted to repay him for the way he had insulted her. But she wanted more than that; much more.

She started as her aunt's shadow fell across the water; for one dreadful moment she thought he had returned. But when she saw Céline's anxious face looking down at her, she got to her feet, smiling brightly and holding out her hands.

'Sitting here all alone, *chérie?*' Céline asked uncertainly as she took her hands. 'Where is François?'

'Didn't he rejoin the party?'

Céline shook her head, and Claudine smiled as she remembered that of course he would have had to change his clothes.

'How was your. . . ? How did. . . ? Céline laughed, 'I don't know how to put it,' she said.

'How was our first meeting?' Claudine suggested, helpfully. 'It was . . . eventful.'

'But what do you think of him?'

'I imagine, the same as he thinks of me.'

Céline's face brightened as she let go of Claudine's hands and embraced her. 'Oh, thank heavens, *chérie.* So you will put all this nonsense behind you now and return to London?'

'Oh, Tante Céline,' Claudine laughed, 'to think that you have such little faith in my charms!' She pushed her aunt away, but keeping her hands on her shoulders, she said, 'You are presuming, are you not, that he found me . . . how shall I put it? Not to his taste?'

Céline's eyes rounded. 'You mean, I am wrong? You mean that he has. . . ?' She blinked. 'Has he asked you to marry him?'

'Not yet, but he will.'

'And you are going to accept?'

'Of course.'

Céline took a step back from her niece, and stared at her. 'Claudine,' she said, 'what has happened to you? You are not yourself. Your eyes, they are so cold. What has he done to you? Oh to think that I could have allowed this to happen, what would your poor mother say if she could see you now?'

'Please don't distress yourself,' Claudine smiled. 'François has done nothing to me, except perhaps to open my eyes to the reality of what our marriage will be like. And maybe it would help you to know that I want this marriage now with all my heart.'

'Your heart? *Mon Dieu*! You have fallen in love with him!'

Laughing, Claudine slipped an arm around her aunt's shoulders and started to lead her back to the house. 'You are jumping to conclusions, Tante Céline,' she said. 'I mentioned nothing about love.'

And after that she refused to discuss him any further, for in truth she had no idea why she was still so determined to marry François when she found him so utterly abhorrent, and when every shred of common sense she possessed was screaming at her to leave Touraine and never return.

– 4 –

In the days that followed her first encounter with François, Claudine became aware that the boundaries of her world were beginning to draw in. It was as though anywhere beyond Lorvoire and Montvisse had become so far distant as no longer to matter: the focus of her life was here, these few acres of French countryside – and the man she was unshakably determined to marry.

It surprised her a little to find that she harboured no desire to return to the glamorous, carefree life she had pursued in London, and there were moments, as she roamed about the gardens of Montvisse, or gazed at herself in the mirror while Magaly fought with her wilful hair, when she found herself as intimidated and perplexed by her determination to marry him as she was by François himself. The emotion she experienced every time she thought of him was always enough to restore the unparalleled sense of purpose he had left her with – and yet, whenever she thought seriously about her future she felt as though she was being sucked into an ever-changing mirage, in which that saturnine, almost sinister presence dominated and eclipsed her. But despite the confusion, she was determined to see the marriage through, and there was nothing in her outward manner to indicate either the resentment she bore François, or the self-loathing she felt whenever she recalled her behaviour that day in the water-garden. On the contrary, she gave every appearance of being happier than Céline could remember, which, given Claudine's intrinsic joy in life, was quite something to witness.

In the middle of the week Claudine's Lagonda arrived from England. To see her niece hover round Pierre for a full two hours while he checked the car over, to see her take a cloth herself to make sure every inch of the chrome glistened like new, Céline found fatiguing enough, but when, with a whoop of delight, Claudine dragged her into the car and zoomed off down the drive, her hair flying in the wind and a cloud of dust billowing behind them, she was so agitated by fear that she thought she might never recover.

It was the first and last time Céline ever graced the Lagonda with her presence, but fortunately Magaly, who had not a faint-hearted bone in her body, enjoyed nothing more than an afternoon spin in the country with her mistress – especially when that country was her own beloved France – so Claudine was not deprived of company during the frequent excursions she took to distract herself from contemplating her future with François de Lorvoire.

Solange and Monique visited the Château de Montvisse on several occasions. Monique's hostility remained as obdurate as ever, and the fact that Claudine was so obviously entertained by the way Monique disagreed with everything she said, only succeeded in making matters worse. The Comtesse chose not to notice her daughter's attitude; her way of dealing with anything unpleasant, as Claudine had come to realize, was simply to pretend it didn't exist. Already Claudine had become inordinately fond of Solange, delighting in her dotty little ways and outrageous comments –which were mostly directed at Céline.

During these visits François was never mentioned; it was as if all concerned – with the exception of Claudine – were embarrassed by his abrupt return to Paris. Claudine knew he was there because her father had told her so during one of the frequent telephone calls he had made since his own departure for the capital. From François himself there had been no communication at all, a fact that both annoyed and pleased her. On balance, she thought she was probably more pleased than annoyed, for she had a great many decisions to make before she saw him again. For one thing, she had no intention of being thrown like the last time – or of allowing him the final word. Next time they met, she would be the one to take control of the situation, and she would make certain he understood that under no circumstances would she tolerate his appalling manners once they were married.

The other problem Claudine felt she must sort out before

much longer was Monique's dislike. She knew now that Monique was two years older than her, that she was devoted to her two brothers, and that she had had a very poor time of it romantically. When Céline told her this last fact, Claudine was surprised, for Monique's wealth and position obviously made her an excellent match, and she was also remarkably attractive. Still, if Monique's character was as like her elder brother's as Claudine suspected, it was hardly surprising she was still unmarried. Nevertheless, she was determined to win Monique's friendship, though it wasn't going to be easy, she mused now, eyeing Monique as she sat beside her mother on one of the Japanese sofas in Céline's favourite drawing-room. Monique was balancing a cup and saucer in her hands, and looking haughtier than ever in a pastel-rose flannel suit, silk stockings and short-veiled hat.

'I'm so delighted that you have fallen in love with our countryside, *chérie*,' Solange was saying. 'I must say, I don't think there's a place on earth to beat it. Have you been for many walks?'

Claudine turned her eyes from Monique to smile affectionately at the Comtesse. 'Yes, lots,' she answered, 'but I have to confess I try to avoid the long grass as I have a mortal dread of snakes.'

'Oh, but I *love* snakes,' Monique cried theatrically. 'They are such graceful creatures, so beautiful.'

'Perhaps, then,' Claudine said smoothly, 'you would care to come for a walk with me, Monique, help me to conquer my fear.'

Monique's small nostrils flared. 'But I am so busy at the château,' she answered, tossing her head in a way that made her sleek black hair bob gently on her shoulders. 'I really don't have time for walks. However, I'm sure *Maman* would be only too happy to oblige.'

'What?' Solange cried, turning her head rapidly between

Claudine and Monique. 'Oblige? Of course, anything, *chérie*. Absolutely anything.'

'Then that is settled,' Claudine said, with an impish grin. 'And perhaps,' she added, avoiding Céline's eyes, 'while we are walking Solange, you might care to tell me about your son Lucien. He's the only member of your family I haven't yet met.'

Céline sighed inwardly. Wasn't that just like Claudine? She obviously hadn't missed the silence that had so far surrounded Lucien's name.

'Ah, Lucien!' Solange trilled. 'My boy. My baby. He is coming home tomorrow.'

'*Maman*, he came home yesterday,' Monique reminded her gently.

'And where has he been?' asked Claudine.

Monique's lips puckered with annoyance. 'He's been in Spain, fighting with the International Brigade. Lucien is a born soldier, he has no time for frivolities.'

That was on odd thing to say, Claudine thought. 'What kind of frivolities do you mean, Monique?' she asked mildly.

'I mean romance,' Monique responded, not in the least fazed.

Claudine smiled. 'Then he is like his brother.'

'Exactly.'

'And does he look like his brother?'

There was an awkward pause. 'Lucien,' Céline answered at last, 'is an exceptionally handsome young man, Claudine.'

Claudine turned back to Monique, and not even attempting to suppress the laughter in her voice, said, 'A handsome young man, and wedded to the army. What a tragedy for French womanhood!'

Again there was a long, uncomfortable silence. It was Solange who broke it, announcing suddenly: 'Hitler's coming!'

Céline's cup hit her saucer with a clatter, and swallowing

hard to stop herself from choking, she said, 'He is?' Her eyes were dancing. 'When, *chérie?*'

'I'm not certain, but I heard François telling Louis just the other day. I can't quite decide which room to put him in.'

'*Maman,*' Monique said patiently, 'I don't think François meant that he was coming to stay – at least not at Lorvoire.'

'What a relief!' Solange cried. 'I find it so difficult to refuse anyone hospitality, but I've heard such dreadful things about the man, haven't you, Céline? What he did to all those poor people in Gibraltar a few weeks ago! It's quite beyond me why the British put up with that, you know.'

'You mean Guernica, *Maman,*' Monique told her. 'And Guernica is in Spain, it has nothing to do with the British.'

'Oh. Well, the point is, the man is German, which doesn't do much to commend him to anyone, does it?'

'I think François is mistaken about him coming here,' said Céline. 'Paris is full of scaremongers, but I'm surprised at François. He doesn't normally go in for that sort of gossip.'

'Well, all I know is that François and his charming friend Charles told Louis that Hitler was coming. I know, because I was listening outside the door.'

'Solange!' Céline laughed. 'You are the only person alive who could describe Colonel Charles de Gaulle as charming! But I can assure you, *chérie*, France is perfectly safe now that we have the Maginot Line. There can't be any question of Hitler coming.'

'Unless of course François *has* invited him to Lorvoire,' Claudine remarked to no one in particular.

'I consider that remark in very poor taste,' Monique said acidly. 'To suggest that François even knows Adolf Hitler –'

'But François knows everyone!' Solange declared. 'He meets them when he is taking our wine for them to taste.

Why, he's even met the King of England, that lovely Edward.'

'Edward is no longer the King of England, *Maman*. He abdicated at the end of last year.'

'So he did. Tell me, did you ever meet the Simpson woman, Claudine?'

'Only once,' Claudine answered. 'We were introduced at a charity ball. She was rather pleasant, I thought, but it'll be a long time before the English forgive her for stealing their king.'

'In my opinion,' said Solange, 'the English should count themselves lucky that they have one at all. France has never been the same since the Revolution.'

As Céline and Claudine struggled to choke back their laughter, Monique rose from the sofa. 'I think,' she said stiffly, 'that it is time *Maman* and I were leaving.'

'Must we, *chérie*?' Solange protested.

'Yes, *Maman*, we must.'

'And we were having such fun,' Solange grumbled as she pulled her reedy frame up from the sofa.

'If you like,' Claudine said, 'I could drive you back to the château in my car, Monique, and your mother could stay a little longer.'

'Your car, Claudine!' Solange interrupted. 'Oh, I'd just love to have a ride in your car!'

'Oh no,' Céline muttered under her breath.

'And I'd love to take you,' Claudine said, giving up on Monique. 'Shall we race them Solange? See who gets to the château first? – Monique and your chauffeur, or you and me in the Lagonda?'

'How splendid!' And Solange, flushed with excitement, made for the door, Claudine following after her.

For several moments after they had gone, Monique stood still in the middle of the room, her face pinched with resentment. Céline walked over to her and slipped an arm round her shoulders. 'What is the matter, *chérie*?' she said kindly. 'You are not normally unfriendly, but you have hardly uttered a civil word to Claudine since she arrived. Why don't you tell me what's on your mind?'

Suddenly it was as though something inside Monique had snapped. 'If you must know, then I don't want her to charm my family or to make friends with people in the area,' she cried. 'I don't want her to like them or them to like her. If they do, she'll never leave. And she can't stay, she *can't*!' She tried to pull away from Céline, but Céline, gently lifting her chin, forced Monique's tear-filled eyes to meet her own.

'It's Lucien, isn't it?' she said.

Monique's lovely face was suddenly tortured by anguish. 'Come along, *chérie*,' Céline said, 'come and sit down.'

'But *Maman*. Is she safe with Claudine in that car?'

'I can assure you that they will arrive at the château in one piece.' Céline led Monique to the sofa, then sat down beside her. 'Claudine may be a little wild at times, but she is not completely lacking in sense.'

'Unlike *Maman*,' Monique said ruefully.

Céline chuckled. 'And neither is your mother as dizzy as she would have us all believe.'

'I know,' Monique sighed. 'It's just her only way of coping with it all.'

Céline bowed her head, then reaching out for Monique's hands, she took them between her own and said, 'You're afraid, *chérie*, aren't you? You are afraid that Claudine will fall in love with Lucien.'

Again Monique's eyes were swamped by tears as she tried to turn away.

'It's all right, I understand,' Céline soothed. 'I know how much you love François, how much you love both your brothers. But you must try to forget what happened with Hortense, *chérie*. It was an accident.'

'Of course it was an accident! How could it have been

anything else? Oh, I know what everyone was saying at the time, but Lucien couldn't help it, Céline, he didn't mean things to turn out the way they did. He loves François as much as I do. They are close, as close as brothers can be.'

'That is true,' Céline acknowledged. It was perhaps the one thing she admired about François, his devotion to his family. 'But now you are afraid that the same thing is going to happen again?'

'Aren't you?'

'No,' Céline lied. 'And neither is Beavis. He and François have spoken about what happened to Hortense, and he has no reservations about François marrying Claudine.'

'Then he is a fool! François will never love her, they will never have the kind of marriage you want for her. Do you know what François said to me after their meeting last week? Claudine was frivolous beyond endurance, and that if he hadn't given his word to Beavis he would call the whole thing off. Don't you see she'll marry him, and he won't love her, and then she'll, she'll – '

'Fall in love with Lucien?'

'She's bound to, Céline! Everyone does.' Monique buried her face in her hands. 'I don't understand why she hasn't returned to London. Why is she still here, Céline? What is she trying to prove by marrying François?'

'I've no idea, *chérie*. That's a question only Claudine can answer. But he hasn't asked her yet. Maybe she will refuse him.'

Monique took a deep breath. 'Do you think so? Do you think she might?' She sighed. 'Oh, if only she weren't so beautiful . . .'

'Are you going to tell her about Hortense?' Céline said, after a pause.

'No. François has forbidden it.'

Again there was silence. 'Lucien will be there at the château when she arrives with *Maman*,' Monique said miserably.

'Then better they meet now, while Claudine is still free to make her choice,' Céline replied. 'And there is one fundamental difference between Hortense and Claudine, Monique, which is that François is not in love with Claudine. So if she should fall in love with Lucien now, there will be no harm done.'

Monique didn't bother to answer. There were a thousand thoughts spinning around her head, and every one of them was yet another reason why Claudine should not be allowed to stay in Lorvoire. But she would never tell them to Céline, she would never tell anyone. She was too ashamed even to voice them to herself.

When Monique had left, Céline sat quietly thinking over their conversation. She had a feeling that Monique had only skimmed the surface of her resentment of Claudine, but what really lay at the root of it she couldn't be sure. Perhaps, as she said, she was just deeply concerned to protect her brothers from another catastrophe like the one with Hortense. Claudine knew nothing about Hortense, of course, and Beavis had forbidden Céline to tell her. And she herself, Céline reflected, did not know exactly what had happened on that fateful night. Only François and Lucien knew; and perhaps their father. And Hortense, she thought, with a shiver.

Well, she shrugged, getting up from the sofa, there was really no point in worrying any further. It seemed as if Claudine was determined to marry François, and nothing would dissuade her – probably not even his brother Lucien.

As the shiny red Lagonda skidded to a halt on the gravel outside the Château de Lorvoire, Claudine was laughing so hard she almost lost control of the car. Solange had been singing heartily the whole way; then, on entering the drive she had torn off her hat, hauled herself to her feet, and was now giving a splendid rendition of an old and extremely bawdy music-hall song, clutching the windscreen and jerking her head from side to side as the wind stood her greying tufts of hair on end. Claudine was hooting on the horn to keep her company, and so intent were they upon the climax of their performance that neither of them noticed the young man come out of the château and circle round behind the car, looking it over with marked appreciation and smiling at the din coming from within. It wasn't until he came to stand beside Solange, hands on hips and head tilted humorously to one side, that they both saw him – whereupon Solange abandoned her song to a screech of joy and threw herself into his arms.

'Lucien!' she cried, and laughing, her younger son scooped her out of the car and set her down in front of him. Then, to Claudine's delight, Solange hooked him round the waist and started to quick-step him round the forecourt. As she watched them enjoying themselves so naturally, Claudine's heart was full. How hard it was to believe that François belonged to the same family!

At last Lucien twirled his mother to a halt, and slipping an arm around her shoulders, turned back to the car. As they came towards her Claudine's heart gave an involuntary leap, and for a fleeting moment she felt as though she were in a dream where faces change beyond belief, reality turns into fantasy. It was as though François was approaching her, mocking her, letting her see how handsome he could be if only his eyes were blue and his smile was as ready and sincere as his brother's.

She blinked, trying to clear her vision, then found herself placing her hand in Lucien's as he said, 'Captain Lucien de Lorvoire at your service, *mademoiselle*.'

The twinkle in his eyes was so infectious that Claudine felt the laughter spring to her own as she made a curtsey to his bow. 'Delighted to make your acquaintance, *Monsieur le Capitaine*.'

They both turned to Solange, who was bobbing excitedly up and down beside them. 'Do you know who this is, Lucien?' she cried. 'Can you guess?'

Lucien frowned thoughtfully, then casting a sidelong glance at Claudine, he said, 'I imagine, unless I am greatly mistaken, that this is none other than Mademoiselle Rafferty.'

'Yes!' Solange clapped her hands together delightedly. 'And isn't she beautiful? And she drives like a maniac, Lucien, just like you. Oh, it was such fun, and if Papa will allow it I think I shall go again.'

'If it makes you happy, *Maman*, then I am sure Papa will allow it. But don't you think that perhaps you've had enough for today?'

As Solange's face fell, Claudine had to fight the impulse to hug her. 'You could be right,' Solange sighed. 'All right, I shall leave you two to get to know one another. Such a shame you're not in uniform, Lucien. He looks so dashing in his uniform, you know.' Then, leaning towards Lucien, she whispered, 'If you're feeling exceptionally brave, *chéri*, you should ask Claudine to take you for a spin, but I warn you, she's a better driver than you.' And before he could answer she tripped lightly up the steps and disappeared inside the château.

Laughing, Lucien turned back to Claudine. 'She's incorrigible,' he said.

'I think she's adorable,' Claudine smiled, as she met his clear blue eyes. They looked at each other for several moments, openly assessing one another and both amused by the frankness they were displaying, until, rubbing his hands together in a businesslike manner, Lucien turned to the car.

'So, how about that spin?'

Claudine inclined her head, and waving her hand towards the passenger seat, pulled open the driver's door. 'I warn you, this is not for the faint-hearted.'

'Then do your worst, *mademoiselle*,' he said, jumping in.

'Are you ready?' she called, as she revved the engine and slid it into gear.

'Go!' he shouted in English.

And with a spin of the wheel and a screech of tyres, she swung the car round and sped off down the drive, leaving a cloud of dust billowing in their wake.

'Where would you like to go?' she yelled, as they squealed out of the drive onto the forest road.

'Surprise me.'

Claudine tossed him a look, then pressed her foot hard to the floor and headed full speed through the trees towards the village of Lorvoire.

'You're crazy,' he shouted, as they all but took off going over a humpback bridge.

'Had enough?'

'Never!'

Laughing, she turned her eyes back to the road – and just in the nick of time, for they had suddenly swallowed the distance between the bridge and a lumbering tractor. Claudine steered the car up the bank, round the tractor, across the road again and into a ditch, where they came to an unceremonious halt.

'And *Maman* thinks you're a better driver than me!' Lucien declared, rubbing his forehead where it had bumped the windscreen.

Claudine was laughing so hard that for a moment she couldn't speak. 'But I am,' she finally spluttered. 'If you'd been driving I'll bet you'd have braked.'

'Damn right I would,' he said, getting out of the car to inspect it for damage. He slapped his hand on the bonnet as if to give it the all-clear, then turned to wave down the old man who was chugging up in his tractor. Claudine, who was just beginning to get out of the car, took one look at the farmer's outraged face and decided that it would be wise to leave the explaining to Lucien.

'Oh no you don't!' Lucien said, pulling her out from behind him. But just as she was assuming her most winsome smile and bracing herself for the wrath to come, the old man suddenly seemed to surrender.

'*Monsieur le Capitaine*,' he muttered, clutching the beret from his balding head. 'I didn't realize it was you in the car. Pardon me for saying so, *monsieur*, but you could have been killed, driving like that.'

'My sentiments exactly, Thomas,' Lucien told him heartily. 'It would appear that *mademoiselle*'s tutor has not adequately schooled her in the art of braking, don't you agree? But you may rest assured, Thomas, I shall see to it personally that she does no further damage to our ditches.'

Thomas leaned conspiratorially towards him. 'I don't think they should ever have let women behind the wheel myself, *monsieur*. They don't have what it takes to control a machine like that. No wits.'

'None at all,' Lucien agreed solemnly.

Unable to stop herself, Claudine gave a snort of indignation, which brought such an imperious arch to old Thomas's brows that Lucien had to turn away before the old man realized he was laughing.

'Incidently, Thomas,' he went on, once he had himself back under control, 'before you do the decent thing and get us out of this mess, I think I'd better do you the honour of a formal introduction. Thomas Crouy, meet Mademoiselle Claudine Rafferty, possibly the future Comtesse de Lorvoire.'

He was looking at Claudine, waiting for her confirmation, but Claudine was watching Thomas, whose confusion was so apparent that she rushed forward to clasp his hand between hers, apologizing for being such a hazard on the roads, lamenting the shame of having so few wits, and promising to take more care in the future . . .

'That was a rotten thing to do,' she told Lucien, as ten

minutes later they waved Thomas goodbye and drove off at a respectable pace.

'I know,' he confessed, 'but he can be such a pompous old cake at times. And better he finds out now who you are than later. Imagine how he would feel then?'

She threw him a quick glance, then flattened the accelerator and sent the car shooting off down the road into the open countryside.

A few minutes later, halfway up a hill, he yelled for her to stop, and with a screeching of brakes she pulled into the roadside. 'Over the brink of that hill are the de Lorvoire vineyards,' Lucien said, 'and below them, at the heart of the valley, is the Vienne and the village. It's a view you shouldn't miss, so we'll walk from here.'

'As you like,' she murmured, but instead of getting out of the car she closed her eyes, stretched her arms above her head and inhaled the fresh country air. Then, allowing her head to fall back against the seat, she sat quietly watching the tiny patches of white cloud as they drifted across the sky.

'What are you thinking?' Lucien asked, watching her with amusement and not a little fascination.

As she turned to smile at him she was pleasantly struck by how relaxed she felt in his company, as if she had known him for ten years rather than ten minutes. 'I'm not sure I'm thinking anything,' she said softly.

He nodded. 'Mm, as Thomas said, no wits.' And he started to walk on up the hill, his hands buried in the pockets of his corduroy trousers and the silk back of his waistcoat billowing in the breeze.

Claudine smiled. Effortless charm, dark good looks and ready humour – Lucien really was very attractive! It might be quite hard to resist him, if it wasn't for the fact that . . . She stopped smiling, and got out of the car.

'So,' he said, falling into step with her as she joined him, 'how are you finding it all?'

'If by that you mean Lorvoire, would it be too sentimental to say I'm in grave danger of losing my heart?'

'But you haven't seen it yet. At least, not the village.'

'I've seen it from the top of the hill over there.' She pointed to where she and François had stood a week ago.

'One of the best views,' he admitted. 'Who told you about it?'

She smiled as she remembered how she had come to be there. 'As a matter of fact, I found it for myself. I was in a mind to escape your brother at the time.'

He grinned. 'And did you succeed?'

Claudine thought about that for a moment, then said, 'No, but I'd be lying if I said he came after me with passion beating in his heart.'

Lucien gave a shout of laughter. 'So how *did* you find my brother?' he said.

'Rather sore that he lost the toss of the coin,' she answered, gazing nonchalantly about her.

Lucien came to an abrupt halt. 'He *told* you about that?'

'Not in so many words,' she answered, turning back to look at him. 'But that is what happened, isn't it? Two confirmed bachelors tossed a coin to decide which of them must make the ultimate sacrifice?'

As they stared at one another, the corner of Lucien's mouth curved in a sheepish grin. 'I can see there's no point in lying,' he said.

'None whatsoever,' she agreed happily.

They started to walk on, keeping in single file as Thomas rolled past in his tractor. 'Has François asked you to marry him yet?' Lucien asked bluntly, as he caught her up.

'No. Did you think he would on our first meeting?'

'As a matter of fact, I did. Whenever François has something unpleasant to do, he usually gets it over with as quickly as possible. And I could have phrased that a little more tactfully, couldn't I?'

Claudine laughed. 'Never mind. Besides, it suggests he might have found the prospect a little less unpleasant than you imagined!'

Knowing precisely what François' first impression of her had been, Lucien passed no comment. Instead he asked, 'What about you? Have you decided what your answer will be when he does get around to asking?'

'Oh yes. I will marry him. And he'll ask me the very next time he is at Lorvoire.'

'He will?' Lucien said, highly entertained by this answer. 'And when will that be?'

'I'm afraid I don't have the faintest idea. François has not seen fit to communicate with me since he left for Paris last Monday.'

'Very remiss of him. Also very like him. But maybe it will put your mind at rest to know that he is returning to Lorvoire this evening.'

Claudine's eyes closed as her stomach lurched sickeningly. 'This evening?' she repeated, in a small voice. It was one thing to have brave resolutions when he was so far away, it was quite another when she was faced with carrying them out so soon. 'Your mother didn't mention it,' she said, trying to sound indifferent.

'That's because she didn't know. He telephoned early this afternoon, while she and Monique were over at Montvisse with you. I'd like to be able to tell you that he is rushing back to be at your side, but I believe his unscheduled return has a little more to do with my own presence at the château.'

'You are so gallant, Lucien,' she said breezily.

'The truth, Claudine,' he said seriously, 'always the truth between us. What do you say?'

'I'd like that very much,' she answered with surprise, but equal sincerity; and they smiled.

When they reached the top of the hill they stopped, and

Lucien draped an arm loosely about her shoulders as he pointed out the tiny houses below, the *mairie* and the café. She was glad of not having to speak. As they stood there, two lone figures at the top of the hill, ruffled gently by the breeze and embraced by the sun's warmth, and she listened to Lucien telling her how he and François used to hide from their nanny in the forest, then row along the Vienne to the village where Sebastien St Jacques would scoop them up onto his horse and take them back to the château, she was aware of a deep feeling building inside her that was beyond words.

'Over there.' Lucien's voice seemed suddenly louder, and for a moment she was startled, and a little sad, to realize that it wasn't François standing there with her – François, who hadn't seen fit to share anything of his past with her. Then in her mind's eye she caught a glimpse of that cold, brutal face, and realized she was in danger of confusing the François of her imagination with the François of grim reality – and her hands tightened in resentment. Quickly she pulled herself together and looked to where Lucien was pointing, at a large house partly hidden by the church. 'That's where Armand St Jacques lives,' he told her, 'old Sebastien's son. Armand is probably the closest friend François and I have.'

'Then I'd like to meet him,' Claudine said.

'I doubt he'll be there at this time of day,' Lucien answered, letting her go and starting to stroll on down the hill. 'He'll be out checking the vines. He lives alone with his mother, Liliane. Armand's wife died giving birth to their son, almost two years ago now, then his son died too. He took their deaths very hard. He does nothing but work in the wine caves and vineyards, or drink alone at the café. Even Monique has trouble persuading him into the château these days, and there was a time when he couldn't refuse my sister anything. Speaking of Monique,' he said, making an obvious effort to lighten the conversation, '*Maman* informs me you've become the best of friends.'

'Ah, well,' Claudine said, 'I wouldn't have put it quite like that myself. However, we shall be. One day. Now, come along, I'm going to race you to the bottom of the hill.' And snatching the shoes off her feet, she sprinted on ahead of him.

Knowing he could outdistance her with the minimum of effort, Lucien held back, watching as her long legs flew through the grass, her red and grey checked skirt flapping about her knees, her scarlet silk blouse ballooning out behind her, her incredible hair rising on the wind.

He had hidden his surprise well when he first set eyes on her, for nothing François had told him on the telephone had prepared him for such incredible beauty – or such vivacity. But most intriguing of all was the effect she was having on him now. He had known her for barely more than half an hour, hardly a serious word had passed between them, yet for some reason he felt an overpowering protectiveness towards her. But that was crazy. What did he want to protect her from? His own brother?

Lucien frowned as he remembered François' words. 'She is not only vain, she is unspeakably trivial. She entertains such disgusting notions of romance that I can hardly bear to look at her. Far better that you had won the toss, Lucien, for you would know what to do with her. However, a pact is a pact, so you need have no fears about me fulfilling my duty. Unless, of course, I can persuade her to refuse me.'

François had never had much patience with women, particularly those who fell in love with him. And looking at Claudine through his brother's eyes, Lucien could see that beside the worldly sophistication of Élise Pascale, Claudine might appear embarrassingly gauche. But there was more to her than François gave her credit for – or would allow himself to see. There was something that set her apart from other women, and it wasn't just her extraordinary beauty. Everything about her seemed so natural, so lacking in artifice – admittedly qualities that François might not choose to find attractive – yet there was no denying she had a quick, intelligent mind and a ready wit, and she emanated such spirit, such tenacity, that Lucien was amazed that even François could remain immune. And even La Pascale couldn't compete with the still youthful loveliness of that face or the tender smoothness of that honey skin . . . He felt suddenly saddened by the pain François would cause her, the heartache and the loneliness she would have to suffer, being married to a man like his brother. And because of the kind of woman she was, he could already see the hopeless struggle she would put up to make her marriage work. He hoped she had the courage, the stamina, to survive.

'Don't think I don't realize you're letting me win!' she called back to him over her shoulder.

'Of course I am!' he shouted back.

As they were nearing the bottom of the hill, Claudine stopped and flopped down on the grass, trying to catch her breath. 'You're incorrigible, Lucien de Lorvoire,' she gasped as he sat down beside her, his breathing as steady as if he had walked down the hill.

And you, he thought, looking at her with a sudden blinding realization, are a virgin. Why that thought had struck him now, he had no idea, but unprompted though it was, he knew it to be true. He gazed into her eyes – and suddenly he longed to be the one to take her, the one to introduce that unbearably sensuous body to the pleasures of love. To leave her to the indifference of François seemed a crime . . . yet wasn't it an even greater crime that he should harbour such a thought after what had happened in the past? When they were both of them, François most of all, still paying the price for what had happened to Hortense?

'Oh no, I've torn my stockings,' Claudine complained, running a finger over the ladder that was snaking along her calf. 'And again there! What a wreck I am! Oh, well, there's nothing else for it, I'll simply have to take them off.'

Lucien's eyes lit up, and leaning back on one elbow, he snapped off a blade of grass and put it between his teeth, ready to watch.

Claudine eyed him dangerously, and laughing, he rolled onto his stomach while she unhooked her suspenders.

'Is your father with you at Montvisse?' he asked, gazing through the columns of vines which spread across the hillside in front of him.

'Not at the moment, he's in Paris. He's coming back sometime this week, though. Do you know him?'

'Of course. I knew your mother too. You're very like her.'

She gathered up her stockings and pushed them into her skirt pocket. Then, sitting cross-legged facing him, she said, 'What about François? Did he know my mother?'

'Yes. He was very fond of her as I remember.'

'It's strange, isn't it?' she mused. 'I mean, how fond François is of my parents when he seems to despise me.'

Lucien turned onto his back to look at her, and studied her remarkable face for some time before, fighting back a sudden surge of anger, he said, 'It's not you that François despises. It's . . .'

'Yes?' she prompted.

He sat up, and throwing away the blade of grass, he said, 'There's a lot you don't know about François, Claudine. I only wish you could have met him before . . .'

'Before what?'

He looked at her as if in some way assessing her. 'Obviously your father hasn't told you,' he said, and this time she detected the anger in his voice. 'But maybe Beavis doesn't know. I thought François had told him, had explained, but . . .'

'Explained what? Lucien, you're talking in riddles.' Then she cried out as he suddenly grasped her shoulders, and his frown was so like François' that she found herself cowering away.

'Why are you marrying him, Claudine?' he growled. 'Why?'

'Lucien, you're hurting me!'

'Why?' he repeated, tightening his grip. 'What is it that's driving you into this marriage? Surely it's not your father, he wouldn't force you to do something you found repellent. And you do find him repellent, don't you?'

'No! Yes! I don't know! Lucien, please – '

'The truth!'

'Then the truth is that, yes, at first I did.'

'And now?'

'I don't know. All I know is that I'm going to marry him.'

'He'll hurt you, Claudine.'

'I can look after myself.'

'Don't be naive. François isn't like other men, you must have seen that already. You won't be able to manipulate him, you . . .'

'I don't want to manipulate him, I want to marry him. I can't explain it, I don't even understand it myself, but I want to be his wife and I want to have his children. That's what he wants of me, isn't it? To have his children?'

'Thats all he wants of you, Claudine.' He leaned forward, staring into her face. 'Don't do this to yourself, Claudine. Go back to England and forget you ever met him. Go now, before it's too late.'

'I can't!' she cried. 'I can't leave. I already love him.'

Lucien stared at her. She stared back, so shocked by what she had said that the whole world seemed to have suddenly careered to a halt. All she was aware of was the strange buzzing in her ears and the pressure of Lucien's fingers on her arms.

Finally he let her go, but his eyes were still on hers as he said quietly, 'Is that true?'

She lowered her head, and eventually she shook it.

'But you said it.'

'I know.'

Long minutes passed. 'Lucien,' Claudine said at last. 'If François wasn't always the way he is now, did the change have anything to with a woman? Was it by any chance someone called Hortense?'

It was some time before Lucien spoke, and to her relief the humour was once again beginning to flicker in his eyes. 'You are incredible, Claudine. How do you know about Hortense? Or should I say, what do you know about Hortense?'

'Nothing. Except that she was described to me at a dinner party as "poor, poor, Hortense".'

Lucien looked at her, his eyes resting on her full, shapely lips. It was with a relief bordering on disloyalty that he realized Beavis must have believed François' account of what happened that night with Hortense – or he would never have agreed to the marriage. It wasn't that he had ever seriously doubted his brother, but – contrary to what everyone thought – he had not actually been there that night, and there had always been that nagging suspicion . . . For he, like the rest of the de Lorvoire family, knew there was a dark side to François that rendered him capable of almost anything.

'If you're concocting some story to fob me off with, Lucien,' Claudine remarked, 'then may I remind you that it was your idea that we should *always* tell each other the truth.'

Lucien shot her a look from the corner of his eye. 'It's because I have no wish to lie to you that I can tell you nothing about Hortense,' he said. 'Besides, I haven't actually admitted that it was Hortense who was responsible for changing François.'

Claudine leapt to her feet. 'What a thoroughy infuriating person you are!' she declared. 'But I shall find out, I promise you.'

'And I can promise you that you will only find out the truth when François himself decides to tell you,' Lucien replied, pulling himself to his feet. 'Now, what do you say to leaving our exploration of the village until another day? We've been gone for some time now, and *Maman* will start to fret.'

'I could always,' Claudine said, as they rounded the top of the hill and started the descent to the car, 'ask Tante Céline about Hortense. Or any other hostess in Paris, come to that.'

'Yes, you could,' he acknowledged, 'but I think you know as well as I do that you won't discover the truth from them.'

Claudine was silent then, and by the time they rounded the bend in the drive leading to the château – rather more sedately than they had driven down it, since Lucien was now behind the wheel – she was so deep in thought that she didn't notice the large black Citröen parked outside the door until Lucien pulled alongside it and casually remarked that François had returned.

Her immediate impulse was to leap into the driving seat and speed off into the sunset, but she somehow managed to control herself, and walked round the car with studied calm.

'Aren't you coming inside?' Lucien said.

'I don't think so,' she answered casually, getting into the driving seat and slamming the door. 'Tante Céline will be wondering what's happened to me.'

'You can always telephone.'

Realizing he was teasing her, she poked out her tongue. Then, leaning forward to restart the engine, her hand suddenly froze. She knew, even before she lifted her head, that he was there. She looked up, aware of the pulsating heat in her chest. He was standing on the steps of the château, watching her. He seemed immense in the long, dark coat that hung from his shoulders, and even at a distance the scar on his face appeared livid and menacing. The smile faded from her lips, and she was profoundly glad she was sitting down, for every muscle in her body seemed to have turned to jelly. Then, to her relief, Lucien was bounding up the steps to greet his brother, slapping him on the back and calling him all manner of insulting names.

By the time François turned back to her, Claudine was fully in control of herself, and stepping as majestically as she could from the car, she walked towards the brothers and held out her hand to François.

Taking it, he said, 'It is a pleasure to see you again.'

Biting hard on the sarcasm that was longing to spring from her lips, she smiled and said, 'Thank you. I trust your stay in Paris was a pleasant one?'

'Moderately so.'

His apparent indifference to the silence that followed, coupled with his pointed failure to invite her inside, inflamed her temper so that her cheeks started to burn with it. 'As I am clearly no longer welcome, perhaps I had better go,' she said – and immediately regretted the peevish resentment in her voice.

'Perhaps Lucien would like to see you back to your car.' François nodded to his brother, then turned on his heel and started back up the steps to the château.

'François!' As he turned, she thought she caught a flicker of amusement pass between the brothers, but she was too angry to care. 'I would like *you* to see me to my car, if it's not too much trouble,' she snapped.

Sensing that his presence was no longer required, Lucien disappeared inside the château while, stuffing his hands into his trouser pockets, François strolled lazily back down the steps. He stood in front of her, gazing down into her eyes. 'You have every right to expect an apology for my lack of communication this week,' he said, surprising her so much that she actually jumped. 'And naturally, I do apologize. It is my intention to call on you first thing tomorrow, so that perhaps we may get to know one another a little better. As for my manners, I hope you will find them a little less offensive than when we last met. For that I apologize also.'

'And for the way you snubbed me a moment ago?'

His austere face became even more unsightly as he drew his heavy brows together. 'Again, I must ask your forgiveness. But you seemed so relaxed in my brother's company, and so appalled when you saw me, that I have to confess I was jealous. Childish of me, I know, but there it is.'

'You are a liar!' she declared. 'You couldn't give a damn . . . Where are you taking me?' she demanded, as he slipped a hand under her arm and started to walk her away from the château.

'To your car, of course,' he answered.

'Don't patronize me!' she shouted, wrenching herself from his grip.

'Am I to spend the entire afternoon apologizing, Claudine?'

She wanted to sting him with words, to kick him even, but his use of her name had a sudden, deeply disturbing effect on her, and for a moment she was powerless.

'Let me tell you,' he said, as he opened her car door. 'You are every bit as beautiful with your hair spilling about your face like that, and with no make-up and no stockings on, as you were the first time I met you. So you are wrong to say I couldn't give a damn. I would have to be either insensate or dead to remain impervious to you.'

She was so stunned that she could do nothing more than slide speechlessly into her car.

'I will send the chauffeur to collect you at Montvisse tomorrow. We shall take out the horses. You do ride, I take it?'

'Yes.'

'Would eight o'clock be too early?'

'No.'

'Then I shall look forward to the pleasure of your company.'

Dumbly she started the engine as he walked away.

'François,' she called, as he started to mount the steps.

He turned back, the thick line of his brows raised in mild irritation.

'Thank you for the compliment.'

'It was nothing.'

And it wasn't until she reached the end of the drive that she realized that that was precisely what he meant.

François found Lucien in the dining-room, helping himself to fruit from the generous bowl on the huge mahogany table. The long windows at the far end of the room looked out over the steep meadow at the front of the château, and in the distance, through the trees, he could see Claudine's car as she drove along the forest road towards Chinon. Charolais cows were grazing in the shade of the forest, and two gardeners marched back and forth across the bank, cutting the grass.

The dining-room was a large room, but the wood-panelled walls, frescoed ceiling and worn rococo furniture gave it a feeling of intimacy, as did the paintings depicting scenes from the de Rassey de Lorvoire military past, and the crumbling stone fireplace, which at this time of year was regularly filled with fresh flowers. It was the room where the family took all their meals, including breakfast, and Lucien and François often came here to talk.

'So,' François said, closing the door behind him, 'I am glad to see you looking so well, Lucien.' He sat on one of the high-backed dining chairs and stretched out his long legs to rest his feet on the table. 'What brings you home?' he enquired, as he reached out to pull a grape from the bunch closest to him. 'If my information serves me correctly, the Spanish war is far from over.'

'Your information is correct. The Basque country is having a pretty rough time of it just now.' Lucien shrugged, then bit into an apple. 'The Nationalists will win, of course.'

'Of course.'

'Don't you care?'

'The only thing that concerns me is that my brother might lose his life fighting on the losing side.'

'But it would be all right for me to die if I were on the winning side?'

'Lucien, if you are asking for my permission to die, then I withhold it, unconditionally.'

'Then, to oblige you, *mon frère*, I shall do my best to stay alive. But the fight continues, and I shall remain on the side of those whose cause I judge to be worthy.'

'Very commendable. And if France should need you?'

'Then of course it would be my patriotic duty to return to my regiment.'

'A soldier and a patriot. You put me to shame, Lucien.'

At that Lucien gave a shout of laughter. 'Shame! You don't know the meaning of the word, François. But tell me, do you think France will have need of its army?'

'If you're asking me whether there will be a war in Europe, then how could I possibly know?'

'Because, François, you know everything. And you have been seen only this week at both the Élysée Palace and the Foreign Office.'

'From both of which I obtained some satisfactory orders for our wine.'

Lucien grinned. François always had been a difficult person to hold a straightforward conversation with, but he had always enjoyed their verbal sparring sessions. 'And no doubt a wealth of information the Germans would kill for,' he remarked mildly.

François raised his eyebrows, then popped another grape into his mouth. 'I don't know where you get such notions, Lucien. Who in their right mind is going to give such information to the proprietor of a vineyard? And even if they should, what on earth could I be expected to do with it?'

'Oh, I'm sure you'd find something, François. Now, is there going to be a war?'

'Some say so, yes. But perhaps not for a year or two. Hitler isn't quite ready for us yet.'

'So we are just going to sit and wait for him?'

'Would you prefer that *France* declared war? I can assure you, she would be extremely foolish to do so. Apart from anything else, she is quite unprepared.'

Lucien thought about that for a while, then said, 'Her defence is shaping up.'

François shifted in his chair. 'If you are referring to our new ministry and its plans for the extension of the Maginot Line, I can tell you that Hitler and Goering make jokes at the dinner table about it. And so, might I add, do certain Frenchmen.'

'You being one of them?'

'In the right company, yes. After all, it is quite amusing when you consider that as long ago as '34 it was known that Germany had ninety-three flights of first-line aircraft – fourteen hundred planes. How many do you suppose they have now? More to the point, how many do you suppose *we* have?'

'Do you really hold your own country in such contempt, François?' Lucien said, taking a last bite from his apple before pitching it into the coal-scuttle.

'It is difficult not to when there are so many dunderheads running it.'

'And if France does go to war, will you fight?'

'I shall do everything in my power to avoid it. So I'm afraid, *mon frère*, that preserving the military honour and glory of the family name is up to you.'

'As the continuance of the family name is up to you?' Lucien countered.

François held his eyes for a moment, then looking away, he plucked another grape and rolled it between his fingers. At last he said in a low voice, 'You have brought the information?'

Lucien nodded.

François' eyes were gleaming as he threw the grape into his mouth and heaved himself to his feet. 'You trusted no one else to bring it?'

'It wasn't a matter of trust. In the wrong hands that information could be lethal – I couldn't, *wouldn't* ask anyone else to risk his life for it. Not when I have no idea what you intend to do with it.'

'I don't ask questions, Lucien, and neither should you.'

They both turned as the door in the far corner opened and Fabienne, one of the young kitchen-maids, came in.

'Oh, *messieurs*,' she said, obviously startled to see them there. 'I am sorry, I shall go away.' She started to turn, but then remembering why she had come, said, 'I must set the table for dinner, *messieurs*.'

'We were just leaving,' Lucien smiled, allowing his eyes to linger on the firm breasts straining against the thin cotton of her uniform.

With cold detachment, François watched the agonized lust that burned in Fabienne's eyes as she too allowed her gaze to wander over Lucien's handsome body. François had seen his brother provoke such a reaction in countless women; once it had amused him, now it merely bored him.

'If you're going to put the silly wretch out of her misery,' he told his brother when Fabienne had left them, 'might I suggest you take her to your room this time? Papa tells me

Jean-Paul has still not recovered from last time, when he found you in such a compromising position with whatever-her-name-was.'

'Carlotta. And I can assure you, François, Jean-Paul's embarrassment was nothing compared to mine. After all, what sort of fellow is it that enjoys being found with his trousers about his knees?'

'And what sort of fellow is it, Lucien, that seduces kitchen-maids in the pantry?'

'One who was dragged there in the first place!'

François laughed, and placing a hand on his brother's shoulder, said, 'I'm going to spend an hour with Papa before dinner, and you strike me as though you might benefit from a cold bath.'

'Whereas you, I presume, are immune to such charms.'

'Not always.'

Lucien grinned. 'But there's none to match La Pascale?'

François cocked an eyebrow, and laughing, they parted company.

Lucien walked off along the hall, where he let himself through a low door and started to climb the crooked wooden staircase which spiralled through the tower to his room at the top of the south wing. When he reached it, he found Monique waiting for him on the threshold.

He wasn't altogether surprised to see her. She had tried to talk to him that morning, before she and Solange departed for Montvisse, and though he had managed to avoid her then, he had known that sooner or later she would catch up with him. Treating her to one of his winning smiles, he put an arm around her shoulders and led her into his dressing-room, saying, 'So, *mon petit chou*, you have something on your mind. Something you wish to discuss with me?'

'You know I have, Lucien,' she said, with a smile of exasperation. 'And you know, too what it's about.'

He nodded. 'Henri Stubert?' He was referring to Monique's latest beau, who was also one of his comrades-in-arms.

Monique's lips tightened, and the nostrils of her haughtily-arched de Lorvoire nose flared. 'I'll thank you, Lucien, never to mention that man's name in my hearing again,' she snapped.

'Oh? But I thought you two . . .'

'I received a letter from him a week ago, informing me of his engagement to Sybille Giffard, whoever she may be. Don't tell me you didn't know about it.'

'But I didn't,' he answered truthfully. However, he had been aware that Henri, like many before him, found his sister somewhat over-zealous in her affections.

'Well, it doesn't matter,' Monique declared, lifting her chin defiantly. 'I had begun to tire of him anyway.'

He watched her pick a thread from the sleeve of his uniform which was hanging on the closet door, and saw the slight tremble of her fingers. He knew that Henri's rejection did matter, and he longed to say something that might comfort her, but he knew too that she would rather die than admit to the hurt.

'So,' he said, 'what is it that you wish to talk to me about if it isn't Henri?'

'I want to know why you are here.'

He saw the expression in her wide, amber eyes, and the corner of his mouth dropped in a smile. He knew now what was on her mind. 'Does there have to be a reason?' he teased, taking her hand and leading her to the sofa. 'After all, this is my home. And you are my family,' he added, crossing one leg over the other as he sat down beside her.

'Lucien!' she said meaningfully.

'All right, all right,' he said, holding up his hands. 'Why do you think I'm here?'

She cast a quick glance at the door, then in a low voice she said, 'You have brought something for François, haven't you?'

'Monique!' he cried. 'I thought it was only *Maman* who listened at doors.'

'It is,' she said, laughing despite herself, and he thought how lovely she was when she smiled. 'But that revolting little man, Erich von Pappen, rang here earlier, while you were out and before François arrived. He wanted to know if you had seen François yet.'

'He did, did he?'

'Yes.' She turned to face him. 'Who exactly is Erich von Pappen, Lucien?'

'You'll have to ask François that question, I'm afraid.'

'Perhaps I will,' she said, though they both knew that it was unlikely she would. 'But why did he want to know if *you* had seen François? No, Lucien, please. I know you're going to lie to me, but I won't stand for it. You've brought information here for François, haven't you? Information from von Pappen. Look, I don't want to know what it is. I have a feeling it would be better, safer, for both of you, if I don't. But I need to know that you will never do this again, Lucien. It's a dangerous game that François plays, but he's an expert at it. I don't want you to become involved.'

Lucien gave a shout of laughter, and clasping his hands about her face, he kissed the tip of her nose. 'You are worrying unnecessarily, Monique, I promise you.'

'No!' The colour in her cheeks had deepened. 'We have both known for some time what François is about, and I don't want you getting mixed up in it. There's not another person in the world I would say this to, but you know as well as I do that François . . .' She stopped.

'Go on,' he prompted, the challenge gleaming in his lucid blue eyes.

Monique looked away, lowering her head so that her hair hid her face. 'I can't,' she whispered.

'Then I shall say it for you.' But when it came to it, even he couldn't bring himself to voice the word that he knew was searing the tip of her tongue. So instead he said, 'You believe that François buys information, then sells it – not where it might do the most good, but where it will fetch the best price.'

'Don't you?'

Lucien thought about that for a long time. It was true that François played a dangerous game with the information he gathered, that he was not always ethical in the way he obtained it or the way he sold it. But his brother's business was his own, and Lucien knew better than to interfere. Just as he knew it would be unwise to say anything that might add to Monique's concern. In the end, he said, 'If it will put your mind at rest, I can tell you that in this instance he will be selling it where it does the most good.'

'How do you know?'

'Because I know who he bought it from.'

'Erich von Pappen!' she said angrily. 'A German!'

'Well then, François is hardly going to buy from the Germans to sell to the Germans, is he now?'

Slowly Monique shook her head, but her eyes were still full of doubt. 'There are times, Lucien,' she whispered, 'when I wouldn't put anything past François. He's my brother and I love him, I would never do anything to hurt or betray him, but sometimes I feel as though I don't know him.'

Lucien took her in his arms and rested her head on his shoulder. He felt her start to tremble. 'And he would never do anything to hurt or betray you, you must know that,' he said, stroking her hair.

'That's not what I'm worried about,' she said, her voice muffled by his shoulder.

'I know. But as you said yourself, François knows what he is doing. And if it helps, then I give you my word that I won't get involved again.'

As he tilted her face to his, he was wondering what she would do if he were to tell her what the information was that he had carried from von Pappen. But she had been right when she said it would be safer for them all if she didn't know. The fact that Adolph Hitler had announced to his inner circle his preliminary plans to annex Austria, was more than a dangerous thing to know. But at least, this time, he could be certain that François was selling the information to the French; it was rare, with François, that things were so blessedly simple.

And then, for no logical reason, an image of Claudine came into his mind – Claudine standing on the hilltop overlooking Lorvoire, tall and straight, her magnificent hair with its shades of blueish copper blowing in the wind, her eyes sparkling with laughter. And then, in his mind's eye, he saw her as she later struggled to hide the confusion of her feelings for François . . . But there had been no confusion when she had stood at the foot of the château steps, those splendid almond-shaped eyes blazing with fury as François so crudely dismissed her. Lucien smiled as he remembered how his brother had turned back; it was probably the only time in his adult life that he had witnessed François obeying a woman. But the way François had so casually changed the subject when he referred to Claudine earlier, was enough to tell him that his brother had acted out of indifference – that he considered Claudine nothing more than a small irritant in his life, which would from time to time need his attention.

'What are you thinking about?' Monique whispered.

Lucien's eyes moved back to hers. 'François,' he answered, 'and Claudine.'

Monique's face darkened. Then, to his amazement, she jumped angrily to her feet and ran from the room – but not before Lucien had seen the tears in her eyes.

Marcel, the de Lorvoire chauffeur, arrived at Montvisse a few minutes before eight o'clock the following morning. Claudine was ready and waiting in the small octagonal hall, wearing her blue velvet riding jacket, a high-necked ruffled blouse and a new pair of tailor-made fawn jodhpurs. Her hair had been coiled into a diamond-studded snood by Magaly, and in her gloved hands she carried her hat and crop.

After being endlessly quizzed by Tante Céline the previous evening about the time she had spent with Lucien, she had retired early to bed only to pass an almost sleepless night. She was still shaken, not only by her extraordinary and bewildering confession to Lucien that she was in love with François – which was absurd in the extreme – but by the way François himself had behaved after she lost her temper. Of course, she was under no illusion that his feelings towards her had changed, she knew perfectly well that he had merely been humouring her; but she couldn't deny the pleasure it had given her to hear him admit to being jealous. She had no idea what it had cost him to say it, but she sincerely hoped it was a lot. Though that was unlikely, she realized despondently – as unlikely as that *he* would be losing any sleep over *her*. At that she had closed her eyes and drawn the sheets over her head, but pride made an uncomfortable pillow, and it wasn't until the first light of dawn that she had finally fallen into an uneasy slumber.

Now, as she sat back in her seat behind Marcel on the way to Lorvoire, she was for once oblivious to the poppies springing up at the roadside, the wide open spaces around her filled with maize fields and vineyards, and the way the sunlight danced on the Vienne as they crossed the bridge at

Chinon. She was too engrossed in what she was going to say to François that morning to think of anything else. Her decisions might have been more easily reached were François de Lorvoire not a man of such unpredictable and infuriating response. However, there was one thing she was resolved upon, even though her stomach reacted violently each time she thought of it, and she had as yet no clear idea of how she would approach it. But approach it she would. Why should she be subjected any longer to that abominable man's game of procrastination? He was going to ask her to marry him – and he was going to ask her today.

When the chauffeur pulled up outside the château she remained in the car, waiting for him to open the door, flatly refusing to admit to herself that she was nervous. But there was no denying the sudden rise in her spirits when she saw that it was raining: perhaps there would be no rendezvous with François this morning after all! With a wry grin, she stepped out of the car. That man really does bring out the coward in me! she thought ruefully.

Jean-Paul, the butler, had his umbrella at the ready, and after greeting her with the respectful informality that was typical of the de Lorvoire household, he took her into the hall, then led her through the drawing-room to the library, where François was sitting in a leather armchair reading the newspaper.

The instant she saw him, Claudine felt as though a great cavern had opened up inside her, leaving her bereft of everything but her thudding heart. Quickly she averted her eyes, taking in the shelves of leather-bound books, the ornate writing desk, the grey marble fireplace ... Behind her, Jean-Paul cleared his throat, and finally François looked up.

'Ah, good morning,' he said in English, and putting the paper to one side, he stood up. Then, sweeping an arm towards the window, he continued in French, 'As you can see, it is not the weather for a ride. Perhaps later, if the rain subsides. In the meantime, may I offer you some breakfast?'

'Just coffee, thank you,' Claudine answered, pulling off her gloves and noting with relief that her hands were steady. François looked past her and nodded, then she heard the door close behind Jean-Paul.

The room was so quiet she could hear the clock ticking on the marble mantlepiece. François walked to the window, and lifting one shining black riding boot onto the window-seat, he folded his arms and leaned a shoulder against the wall. His hair was wet, and she wondered if it was from the rain or an early morning shower. Then, to her alarm, her skin started to burn at the thought of him taking a shower; it was extraordinary to think that one day they might share that kind of intimacy – that she would come to know the habits of this man. Looking at him now, she tried to imagine what it would be like to see him smile, to hear him laugh, to have him hold her in his arms and kiss her – make love to her.

'You look rather pale this morning,' he remarked. 'Are you sickening for something?'

'Er, no,' she stumbled. 'No, not at all. I didn't sleep too well, I'm afraid.'

'I trust there is nothing troubling you?' His hooded eyes were regarding her intently, and the unmistakable challenge he had thrown her was enough to restore her equilibrium and bring the fire back to her veins.

'As a matter of fact,' she said, tossing her whip and hat onto a table, and sinking into a chair, 'there is.'

'I have a feeling,' he said, turning and sitting on the window-seat to face her, 'that you're going to tell me what it is.'

'And I have a feeling that you already know.'

His smile was odious in its arrogance, but he said nothing.

'Lucien told me yesterday,' she went on, 'that if you have

something unpleasant to do, then it is your custom to dispense with it as quickly as possible.'

'My brother knows me well.'

'Then I should appreciate it if you were to ask me to marry you now, and have it done with.'

If he was surprised at her bluntness, he didn't show it. 'But surely, asking you to marry me can hardly be described as dispensing with something disagreeable,' he said.

The ambiguity of this remark did not escape her. 'You are suggesting that instead of dispensing with me, you will be tying yourself to me?'

He inclined his head and sat back, blocking the window with his huge shoulders. 'If that is the way you wish to interpret it . . .'

Fortunately, since she was at a loss for what to say next, the door opened then, and Fabienne brought in the coffee which she set out on the table beside Claudine. As she started to pour François rose to his feet and waved her away.

'So,' he said, as he poured the coffee himself, 'the lady is eager for my proposal?'

She almost snatched the cup from him then set it back on the table and sat forward in her chair. 'Why do you have to be so damned difficult about this? We both know why I am here, you have spoken to my father already, so why don't you put us both out of our misery?'

'Misery? You really are eager, Claudine.' His picked up his cup and perched on the edge of the table. After a while he lifted his head to stare out of the window, giving her the distinct impression that his mind was elsewhere.

Her jaw tightened as she clenched her teeth in an effort to hold back her anger. 'Aren't you in the least bit intrigued as to what my answer will be?' she said stiffly.

'I already know what your answer will be,' he answered. 'If you were going to refuse me, you would have left Touraine by now.'

'Perhaps I wanted to give myself the satisfaction of seeing your face when I turned you down,' she said in an icy voice.

'Perhaps,' he admitted. 'But I doubt it.'

Her outrage was swallowing her words at such a rate that her mouth was opening and closing in the most mortifying silent fury, and for one horrible moment, just for the need to make a noise, she came very close to thumping her hand on the table.

Her temper seemed to amuse him, and wandering over to the chair facing hers, he settled into it, resting one foot on the other knee and leaning back with a critical air, as if he were assessing a theatrical performance.

'I have never,' she declared, 'in all my life, met anyone as utterly detestable as you. You make me say and do things I never dreamed of doing before this. I had no idea, until now, that I was even capable of feeling such dislike as I feel for you.'

'It cheers me to hear it. At twenty-two it's about time you grew up.'

'And what is that supposed to mean?'

'It means that you have all the hallmarks of an over-indulged child. It's high time your eyes were opened to the reality of the world and the people in it. You will find, I'm afraid, that not everyone is as *nice*, or as obedient to your whims, as you would like them to be.'

'How dare you say that! How dare you even suggest . . .'

'I dare,' he interrupted. 'Also, I will not be dictated to. If you want a proposal of marriage from me, you will get it when I am ready and not before.'

She leapt to her feet, and gathering up her crop and hat, she stalked out of the library, through the drawing-room and into the hall.

'Claudine,' he said, strolling out behind her, 'it is raining outside and you don't have your car.'

'I don't care,' she snapped. 'I'd rather walk home than

stay another moment in this house with you.' And flinging the door wide, she ran out into the rain.

Any thought she might have had that he would follow her was firmly dispelled when the door closed behind her. For the moment she was too angry to care, and with her head held high she marched off down the drive, furious with herself for having been so spineless as to run away, but too proud to turn back. But by the time she approached the gates she was regretting her hastiness even more; apart from anything else, it was a very long walk back to Montvisse.

Then she heard the gratifying sound of a car crunching along the gravel behind her, and with the smug feeling of having scored a victory, she stuck her nose in the air and quickened her pace, determined that he should beg before she deigned to get in. But as the car pulled alongside, she saw that it wasn't François who was following her, but Marcel.

Without a word, she climbed into the back of the Bentley. However, instead of turning out of the drive onto the forest road, Marcel put the car into reverse and took her back to the château, where François was waiting at the bottom of the steps.

He opened the car door and waited for her to get out, but she stubbornly refused to move. In the end he reached in, took her by the wrist and hauled her out.

She stood facing him, her limpid blue eyes flashing with rage. Neither of them spoke, but the air between them was charged with antagonism. In the end he raised an eyebrow, as if suddenly bored with the whole charade – and before she could stop herself, she had lifted her crop to strike him. In one swift movement he snatched it from her and passed it to Marcel.

'Go inside,' he said.

'Don't tell me what to do!' she seethed.

He took a step towards her, and grabbing her hand, he

twisted it between them. 'Either you walk back into that house of your own volition, or I drag you. The choice is yours.'

'Why?' she cried, willing herself not to struggle no matter how painful his grip. 'Give me one good reason why I should!'

'Because there is something I wish to say to you that I think you would prefer I didn't say here, in front of Marcel and all the other servants who are no doubt watching from the windows.'

Once they were back in the library and he had closed the door behind them, he waited for her to turn and face him.

'Well?' she said, trying not to be thrown by the appalling contempt in his eyes.

He regarded her for some time, then in a chillingly matter-of-fact tone he said, 'I don't want to marry you, Claudine. I don't want you as my wife.'

'Then what the hell am I doing here?' she spat. 'You're the one who made the agreement with my father.'

He walked past her to stand in front of the empty hearth. 'Do you think I imagined for one minute that you would seriously entertain the idea of an arranged marriage?' he said, turning to face her.

'Why shouldn't I?' she shot back. 'It's not so unusual. Hundreds of people marry by arrangement.'

'But you have no need to. Your father was quite adamant about that, even to me. So why don't you go back to England and marry someone there? From what I hear, there are plenty of suitable men who would be only too happy to oblige.'

That brought a smile to her lips and she sauntered towards him, stopping at the table where the coffee was laid out. 'And from what I hear,' she drawled, as she started to pour, 'there are plenty of women in Paris simply longing to hook you. So why me? Why enter into an arrangement with *my* father?'

'You already know the answer to that.'

'Meaning that I was your father's choice, not yours?'

'Isn't that what arranged marriages are all about?'

She nodded slowly. 'But now you are faced with it, you haven't got the guts to go through with it. Is that right?'

'It's not a question of guts.'

'Then what is it a question of?'

When he didn't answer, she took a sip of the lukewarm coffee. Her eyes, over the rim of the cup, were holding his. 'What's the matter, François?' she said, replacing the cup on the table. 'Isn't she suitable?'

'Isn't who suitable?' he said, with a sigh of exasperation.

'The woman who is my rival for your affections, of course.'

He closed his eyes, and turning to lean against the mantleshelf, he rested his head on the heel of his hand. The last thing he wanted now was an argument about Élise Pascale. 'Who are you talking about, Claudine?' he said.

'I believe her name is Hortense,' she answered.

Not a muscle of his body moved, but she was acutely aware that the air in the room had suddenly changed. Then, before she knew what was happening, his hand shot out and he jerked her towards him. The expression on his face was horrifying. His pupils were boring into hers with blinding hatred, the gruesome scar was pulsating with life, and the fire of his breath scalded her face. 'Who told you about Hortense?' he snarled.

'No one,' she answered, doing nothing to break free.

'Then how do you know her name?'

'I heard it at a dinner party.'

'What do you know?' he growled, pulling her even closer. 'What did they tell you?'

'Nothing!' she cried. 'Nothing at all!'

'Then why call her a rival?'

'Well, isn't she?'

His lips curled with loathing and he pushed her away.

She fell across the chair behind her, hitting her head on the winged back. 'You disgust me,' he spat.

'Isn't she?' she repeated, in a virulent whisper.

He didn't answer, but she could see that his control was still very close to breaking.

'Why don't you marry her, François?' she goaded. 'Or won't she have you?'

'Leave it, Claudine,' he warned, 'just leave it.'

'Not until you tell me . . .'

'I said *leave it*!' he roared.

But she couldn't. Something inside her was making her push him, and she could not stop it. 'Who is she, François? Tell me. You loved her, didn't you? You loved her, but she didn't love you.'

He closed his eyes and let his head fall back.

'But there's more to it than that,' she went on. 'There has to be, or . . .' The old duchess's words swept into her mind then. 'Poor Hortense, how we all still miss her.' 'Where is she, François? Where is your beloved Hortense? Did she run away with someone else? Did she. . . ?'

His fist crashed against the mantlepiece as he yelled, 'She's *dead*!'

Claudine sat motionless, her eyes wide with shock as she stared up at him. The word was still there, hanging in the air between them as if it had cast a paralysing spell.

Finally he pushed the hair back from his face and looked up. Then, as he stared at her, his mouth started to twist in a sadistic smile. 'Would you like to know how she died?' he sneered. 'Would you like to know how Hortense de Bourchain lost her life?' Claudine started to shake her head, but he went on. 'I killed her, that's how. *I* killed her. It's how I received the scar on my face – you wanted to know that too, didn't you? Well, Hortense did it! She scarred my face and I killed her for it. I murdered her. So, do you want to marry me now? Do you want to marry a killer?'

Claudine flinched as if he had hit her, then closed her eyes as his face started to swim before her. She was too agitated to speak, too horrified to look at him again, and yet at the same time something deep within her was forcing her to look beneath the terrible words, compelling her to understand why he was doing this. Then, almost without knowing what she was doing, her head snapped up, and looking at him through a blaze of anger she hissed, 'Yes, I'll marry you!'

It was a long time before he tore his eyes from hers. At last he did and walked across the room to his father's desk, where he stood with his back to her. She watched him, waiting for him to speak. In the end he turned to face her, and leaning against the edge of the desk, he said, 'So you're prepared to marry a killer?'

She pulled herself up from the chair and went to stand in front of him. Then raising her chin so that she was looking clear into his eyes, she said, 'No, I'm *going* to marry a liar.'

His laugh was harsh. 'A liar, she says. And what makes you so sure I'm lying?'

'Because you are,' she said. 'You're doing it to stop me wanting to marry you.'

He lowered his head, then looking up again, he sneered, 'Go home, Claudine. Go back to England.' When she merely continued to stare at him with those unnervingly beautiful eyes, he laughed. 'You're nothing but a child! A child in a woman's body.'

Still she didn't answer, but watched as his expression changed to one of savage amusement.

'You would like me to make you a woman?' he said nastily.

She looked down as he lifted a hand and laid it over her breast. Then she looked back to his face.

'*Why* do you want to marry me, Claudine?' he said.

'Does there have to be a reason?'

His eyes narrowed, then it was suddenly as if the fight had

gone out of him, and shaking his head slowly, he said, 'No,' and put his hand back on the table beside him.

It was odd, she thought, that the only sensation she could feel was his hand on her breast, even though he had taken it away. She knew that at any moment the life would return to her body, that she would be able to move again, but as long as his eyes held hers it was as though she was imprisoned by his scrutiny.

As if he knew the effect he was having on her, his mouth curled in disdain. 'You'll live to regret this day, Claudine. You think yourself clever now for the way you wrenched a proposal from me, but in a year from now, ten years from now, you'll look back on this day . . .' He stopped, and as his eyes swept across her lips she felt her breath start to quicken. 'What does it matter?' he said. 'It's your life, not mine. If you want to throw it away . . . Shall we set the date?'

Before she could answer, the door burst open and Solange came bounding across the room in a hair-net and dressing-gown. *'Oh là là*, I knew it was going to happen today!' she cried, gathering Claudine into her arms. 'I had the feeling, in the middle of the night. I woke Louis to tell him. Oh, François, *mon cheri*, she is going to make you such a wonderful wife. I am so happy. We must tell Jean-Paul to bring the champagne. Monique! Where is Monique! She must call Céline and tell her to come right away. Ah, Claudine, you are going to make my Louis such a happy man today.'

As Claudine returned the embrace, her eyes found François', and with the briefest flicker of his brows he acknowledged his defeat.

'I don't suppose,' she said, as Solange went rushing off to find Jean-Paul, 'that I stand any chance of a more romantic proposal?'

'You suppose correctly.'

She leaned her head to one side and studied him for a while. 'Do you really despise me?'

'It is difficult to despise someone for whom one has no feelings at all.'

A smile spread across her lips, then she began to laugh as she retrieved her hat and crop and walked to the door. When she reached it, she glanced back over her shoulder. 'As I said before, I am going to marry a liar,' she declared, and with a triumphant grin she turned to follow Solange from the room.

– 6 –

The engagement was announced, the date for the wedding was set: it was to take place at the Royal Abbey of Fontevraud at the beginning of September, less than three months away. The haste was because Beavis could remain in France only until mid-September, when he was obliged to leave for a spell of duty in Berlin – but Claudine was used to having her calendar dictated by the diplomatic corps, and she felt too that, given the circumstances, à long engagement would be nothing short of a farce. As far as she was concerned, the quicker they were married the better. François expressed no feelings on the matter at all.

He remained at Lorvoire for five days after the announcement of their engagement, then left for Paris. While he was gone he made no contact with Claudine, though she knew he was regularly in touch with his father. She could not decide whether she was glad that his disturbing presence was removed from her, or whether – in some curious way she could not define – she missed him. Once or twice she allowed herself to consider what he had told her about Hortense, but she did not dwell on it, for she was quite convinced he had been lying. She also tried to dismiss from her mind the peculiar emotions he stirred in her – and did her best to spend a calm and cheerful time helping Solange and Tante Céline with the wedding arrangements.

Then, one morning, four days before he'd said he would return, Claudine arrived at Lorvoire to find François' car parked in the courtyard outside the wine caves. At the sight of the large black Citröen her heart somersaulted violently, and as she drew up alongside it, she saw him standing just inside the entrance to one of the caves talking to Armand St Jacques. Slowly she climbed from the car, waiting for him to see her, but when he did eventually look up, he merely turned away again and continued his conversation.

Seething with indignation, and without even thinking what she would say when she got there, she marched towards him. Before she reached the cave Armand came out, and seeing the look on her face, instantly made himself scarce.

Claudine barely noticed him. François had his back to her now, and seemed intent on the bottles lined up on a counter in front of him. Hearing her footsteps, he looked up, and the harsh impatience that flashed across his face inflamed her temper even further.

'What are you doing here?' he snapped, before she could speak.

She stared at him, her anger for the moment blunted by his rudeness.

'Why haven't you returned to England?' he demanded.

'England?' she repeated stupidly.

For several moments he glared at her, then with a shrug he said, 'Do you not have affairs to attend to in England?'

'No,' she answered, anger tightening her beautiful features. 'My father's lawyers and the staff at Rafferty Lodge are dealing with matters there.'

'So you are staying here, in Touraine, until we are married?'

'Unless you have any objection?'

He gave a derisive laugh. Then suddenly his eyes were hard, and leaning his face towards hers, he hissed, 'What do you want from me?'

'*Nothing!*' she seethed, cowering from the venom in his voice.

'Then go! Go away from here. I don't want you!'

She couldn't help flinching at the malice in his voice, but quickly mustering the full might of her fury, she said, 'If you think your atrocious behaviour is going to make me change my mind, then think again, François. The only way you're going to get out of this marriage now is to call it off yourself.'

For a long moment they glared at one another. Then, to her horror, Claudine found that she was remembering the feel of his fingers as they curled about her breast. The shock of the pleasure it gave her slaked through her body as powerfully as the loathing which hammered at her heart. She struggled to break free of those eyes, but she was bound by their magnetism. Her senses were reeling, she felt she would drown in the sheer force of him. Then she saw the sneer on his lips, the contempt that disfigured his face more brutally than the scar, and at last she was able to turn away. She was dazed by what was happening to her: she knew she hated him, yet she felt so drawn to him that at times it was as though she were in danger of losing herself in him.

In the dining-room of the château she found Solange waiting for her, her lively grey hair standing on end and Louis' spectacles perched on the tip of her nose. The table in front of her was in chaos, strewn with cards and envelopes, lists and letters. Today they were to begin the enormous task of sending out invitations. Solange looked so bemused that Claudine felt a great wave of affection for her, and dismissing François from her mind, she sat down to help.

She didn't see him again until midday, when Tante

Céline arrived for lunch and he walked into the dining-room with her. Claudine got up to greet her aunt, studiously ignoring François, but as she was about to sit down again he put a hand on her arm. 'I've brought you something from Paris,' he said.

Claudine stared at him. She watched him reach into his pocket and pull out a small box bearing the insignia of Van Cleef and Arpels. He did not look at her as he put the box into her hand, but simply stepped back, waiting for her to look inside.

When she did, her mouth fell open. Beside her Tante Céline gasped, and Solange clapped her hands in delight. The diamond was flawless and the size of a centime. Claudine looked up at François, but he was staring at the ring, his face devoid of expression. But as she lifted it from the velvet crease to raise it to the light, he took it from her, picked up her left hand and slid the diamond onto the third finger. It was a perfect fit.

'I hope you like it,' he said softly.

Again she looked up at him, dimly aware that her breathing had all but stopped. 'I like it very much,' she answered.

He nodded, and with a flicker of one eyebrow, he turned and walked from the room.

After that, Claudine threw herself into the wedding plans with renewed enthusiasm – while Solange took to rushing about Lorvoire creating one muddle after another. After three days Louis threw up his hands in despair, declaring that he'd given up all hope of ever knowing a moment's peace again, while François complained that he had not been embraced so often since he was an infant.

'Oh *Maman*, not again,' he would groan as she clasped him to her, but there was a gentleness in his eyes as he kissed her that brought a lump to Claudine's throat. For her there was no such display of affection; for all the attention he paid her she might just as well not have been there. But all that would change once they were married, she told herself, and treating him to the same chilly disdain as he showed her, she went about her business.

A week after he'd given her the ring, François went away again, informing her, through Tante Céline, that she should not expect him back before the end of the month. After his departure, at Solange's insistence, Claudine became a daily visitor at Lorvoire in order that she should get to know the household better. It was a happy time for them all: the old gramophone was dragged from a cupboard, and she and Solange whirled about the neglected ballroom while Louis sat quietly in a corner, his round glasses teetering on the end of his nose and his feet tapping to the spritely rhythm.

As that scorchingly hot summer progressed the château saw other visitors too, as noble families from all over the region beat a path to Lorvoire, eager to get a glimpse of the English beauty who was to marry François. The hospitality they received was, by normal standards, unusual: there were games of *cache-cache* in the forest and rowing races on the river, cricket on the sloping bank of the meadow and dancing in the courtyard. But they all seemed to enjoy themselves, and on the rare occasions François was at home, though he never deigned to join in, Claudine occasionally caught him smiling. But never at her. For her there was only the stark hostility she was coming to know so well. But why should she care, she asked herself defiantly, when everyone else welcomed her so warmly?

The wedding was drawing closer, and it was time to leave the château and go to Paris, where Claudine's wedding gown was being created by the House of Worth, and almost every other designer of note had a hand in her trousseau. Claudine and Tante Céline stayed with the de Lorvoires at the house in the Bois de Boulogne, where the afternoon parties, while not quite as unorthodox as those at Lorvoire, were nonetheless lively. In return they were bombarded with invitations to the theatre and the ballet, to private concerts and to dinner with friends, and once, but only once, they went in a party of twelve to the most famous cabaret in Paris, the *Lapin à Gill*. The original plan had been to visit the *Bal Bullier* where, so Claudine had heard, it was difficult to tell the men from the women, and ladies of the night paraded naked through the ballroom – but Louis had drawn the line at that.

That was towards the end of August, and François returned from a three-week trip to North Africa the morning after their exotic night out. He was highly amused to hear that his parents had set foot inside such an establishment, and rather regretted that he could not stay, he said, if this was the kind of entertainment they were going in for – but he must leave again the following day as he had business to attend to in Marseilles, and he wanted to call in at Lorvoire on the way, not only to see Armand but also to check on the work that was being carried out on his apartment in the west wing of the château, to make it ready for Claudine.

Claudine experienced some very strange feelings when she heard that, but she showed none of them when he joined their party at the theatre that night, where he sat beside her, watching as she offered her left hand to those who came into their box to get a glimpse of the by-now famous Van Cleef and Arpels diamond. He accepted their congratulations graciously, but his attitude towards Claudine remained cold and aloof.

After the play they all went on for a late supper before returning to the Bois de Boulogne, and Monique was the only one to see François slip out of the house after everyone had retired to bed. She knew where he was going, for she had made a brief call on Élise Pascale herself that day, and François had telephoned while she was there to tell Élise to expect him.

Monique had no idea at what hour of the morning he returned, but he was there at breakfast when she joined the table, as were Louis and Claudine. Often, when François and Claudine were in the same room, Monique would study them, trying to work out exactly what was going on between them, but as the date of the wedding drew closer their relationship became more and more of a mystery to her. They made a striking couple – François so tall, so powerful and so ugly, Claudine so beautiful, so vibrant and so happy – yet they rarely spoke to one another, and never, simply *never* touched each other. Yet oddly, whenever they looked at one another they seemed suddenly enclosed in a world of their own. But perplexing as their relationship was, Monique felt certain that Claudine didn't love François any more than he loved her.

As for her own relationship with Claudine, as each day passed Monique was growing to hate her more. She was no longer afraid that Claudine would come between Lucien and François; now she only longed to be rid of her so that her own private hell of jealousy would be at an end. Each night, as the wedding drew closer, she lay awake reliving the rejections she had suffered. She wept for her own wedding – the wedding she had always dreamed of, but which now, perhaps, would never be. She smarted with the pain of her loneliness, and ached with the memory of being loved. She did not know what she had done to turn her lovers away, she only knew that if there was to be a wedding at Lorvoire, it should be hers. She deserved it for all the suffering, all the heartache she had known – not Claudine, who had never had a moment's unhappiness in her life.

Had she seen any way to destroy Claudine's happiness, Monique would have taken it. She had even toyed with the idea of telling her about Élise, but Élise herself had warned against it. There was no knowing how François might view their interference, Élise said, and besides, knowing that he had a mistress wasn't in any way guaranteed to make Claudine change her mind. And so Monique nursed her hatred in silence. When she was with Claudine she worked hard to hide her feelings – with such success that even her own parents believed the two of them had struck up a firm friendship. The only person she had not managed to deceive was Claudine herself.

Quite what she was going to do about her future sister-in-law, Claudine didn't yet know. She had worked out for herself what lay at the root of Monique's enmity, and though she had no intention of calling off her wedding she was already wondering what she could do to make it less painful for Monique. It was a shame, she thought, that she couldn't discuss the matter with François – but then he told her something that pushed every other thought from her mind. He had arranged their honeymoon, which was to be in Biarritz. Honeymoon. The word alone was enough to send her nerves galloping into disarray. So too was any thought of intimacy with François, who had not as yet even attempted to kiss her . . .

A week after his departure for Marseilles, she was at the opera, though paying scant attention to what was happening on stage as she was engaged in a rather gratifying fantasy in which François came bursting into their box, grabbed her by the hands and dragged her off to a secret place to tell her how much he loved her. She didn't get as far as to what her response might be to such an unlikely occurrence, as some twenty minutes into the first act she became aware that someone was watching her. She glanced around the darkened opera house, but all eyes seemed to be on the stage. However, the feeling didn't go away, and when the lights came up for the interval she looked again to see who it might be.

'What is it, *chérie?*' Céline asked when she saw the puzzled frown on her niece's face.

'Oh, nothing,' Claudine answered.

'Come, have a glass of champagne. And perhaps tonight we should go straight home after the performance. We've an early start for Touraine tomorrow, and you must be tired after all this gaiety in Paris.'

'Claudine, tired!' Louis exclaimed. 'How I have longed for the day!'

They all laughed, but as Claudine turned in her seat she was again aware of someone watching her, and this time as she scanned the faces in the adjacent boxes, her attention was caught by the downward sweep of a fan. Then, to her amazement, she found herself looking into eyes of the most beautiful woman she had ever seen. Instantly the smile dropped from Claudine's face, for she knew beyond a doubt that this was the person who'd been studying her. She was breathtaking. With her heavy, honey-blonde hair, delicate ivory skin and seductive eyes, she looked like a Greek goddess reclining in the glow of golden light that fell around her.

Finally, with a barely perceptible nod of her head, the woman looked away, and collecting herself, Claudine turned back to her aunt.

'Tante Céline,' she whispered. 'Tell me, do you know that woman over there? She's been staring at me ever since we arrived.'

Céline followed her niece's gaze, and Claudine felt her stiffen. 'Ah no, you're imagining things, *chérie*,' Céline said.

'But do you know her?'

Céline glanced quickly at Louis, who gave a brief nod. 'She's Élise Pascale,' Céline said.

The name meant nothing to Claudine. 'Can we meet her?' she wanted to know.

'I think not, *chérie*.'

'But why?'

'Because she is not quite . . . how can I put it? She is not quite . . .'

'She is what we in polite circles call a courtesan,' Louis supplied.

'Oh,' Claudine said, drawing out the word as her eyes brightened with laughter. She looked back at Élise. 'How absolutely fascinating,' she whispered. 'I'd still like to meet her!'

Of course it was out of the question, and it was to Céline's profound relief that Louis came to the rescue once again by saying, 'I would prefer that you didn't, *chérie*. I wouldn't want her putting ideas into Solange's head.'

They all burst out laughing, and as the curtain rose for the second act of Milhaud's *Le Pauvre Matelot*, the conversation was, to Céline's relief, at an end.

Later, as they were leaving the theatre, Claudine scanned the foyer in the hope of getting a closer look at Élise Pascale. When she saw her her heart gave a sudden vicious lurch as she saw an appallingly familiar figure leaving Élise and coming towards them through the crowd. She'd had no idea François was planning to return to Paris that night – nor, it seemed, had anyone else. He had just arrived from Marseilles, he explained, and had come to meet them in the hope of joining them for dinner. And so, their plans for an early night abandoned, they joined another group of friends and strolled off down the avenue de l'Opéra for a lobster supper at Drouant's.

The following morning François escorted them to the railway station, where he assured his mother that he would be home in time for dinner the next day. Lucien, however, would not be home tomorrow, he told her in response to her urgent enquiry.

'But he is coming to the wedding, isn't he?' Solange cried, as Louis gently pushed her onto the train.

As she asked this question at least once a day, François rolled his eyes and said, 'Yes, *Maman*, Lucien will be coming to the wedding if he can.' And he smiled at her shriek of delight.

'And what about you? Will you be coming to the wedding?'

He turned to find Claudine standing beside him. Her hat cast a light shadow over her eyes, and in her pastel chiffon dress, with the steam billowing around her, she was like an apparition.

'A strange question,' he remarked.

'A strange engagement,' she countered.

He looked at her for a long moment, but she was unable to read his eyes.

'It's the first of September today,' she said. 'You have ten days in which to change your mind.'

'So have you,' he answered, and her cheeks flooded with colour at the way she felt suddenly naked beneath the lascivious smile that curved his thin lips, the eyes that swept the length of her body.

'I have no intention of changing my mind,' she said, through clenched teeth.

'A pity,' he replied, and held the door open for her to board the train.

The day of the wedding dawned. The evening before, Claudine had moved into one of the guest rooms in the west tower of the château de Lorvoire – a circular room with wide, arched windows that overlooked the meadow and gardens at the front and side of the house. The four-poster bed was of carved oak, the hangings, like the window curtains, pale yellow brocade, and the Heriz carpet was a field of sea-green. There were two Louis XV armoires, and a Sormani kingwood and marquetry dressing-table on which Magaly had set out her ivory-backed hairbrushes, silver-topped bottles and two vases of flowers.

Since she had woken at six o'clock Claudine had been

aware of the day's excitement. Through the leaded windows she had watched the caterers arrive, then the florists. Then there had come designers and hairdressers, an army of extra staff hired for the day, and a band of musicians. She had seen Tante Céline's car draw up outside, and heard the clatter of horses' hooves as her father and Lucien returned from an early morning ride.

There had been several knocks on her door, mainly from Dissy, who had arrived with her husband, Lord Poppleton, at the start of the week. But Claudine wasn't ready to see anyone yet today – not even her best friend. She was perched on the edge of the bed, staring into space as she struggled to make sense of her astonishing reaction to what she had discovered last night, when she crept upstairs to take a look at the apartment she would be sharing with François.

The first room she entered had been a pleasant surprise – an elegant but intimate drawing-room, with fringed lampshades over brass lamps, candy-striped sofas and armchairs, and big windows opening onto a terrace that was only feet away from the trees on the hillside behind the château. But it was when she opened the door to her left that the extraordinary reaction started. It was a bedroom, a very beautiful bedroom, with rose-silk-panelled walls, matching bed linen and carpets, rosewood furniture, marble fireplace and high, arched French windows. But a sixth sense was telling her something else about the room. And then her heart started a strange, unsteady rhythm. This was her room, she realized; hers alone.

'What do you think?'

She turned to find Lucien watching her from the sitting-room door, hands in pockets, one shoulder leaning casually against the doorframe.

'I'm not sure,' she answered shortly. 'I haven't seen it all yet.'

He frowned. 'You seem angry.'

'Angry? Why should I be angry?'

He shrugged. 'Shall we take a look around, then?'

She nodded. After all, she was telling herself, it was quite normal for husband and wife to have separate rooms, wasn't it? But why, then, did she feel so disturbed? She took the hand Lucien held out to her, and allowed him to lead her across the sitting-room to a room she hadn't yet entered.

It was, as she had expected, another bedroom. It was plain, uncluttered and unmistakably masculine – just as the other had been unmistakably feminine. From the moment she walked into it Claudine felt she was trespassing, and would go no further than the foot of the vast oak bed, though Lucien explored the bathroom and dressing-room, loudly voicing his approval. She showed him her own suite. At the far end of it was another door which, when she opened it, led out onto a narrow landing. Across the landing, Lucien showed her, was the nursery; and the door at the end of the corridor opened onto a bridge leading from the château into the forest behind. He and François had often used it as an escape route when they were children.

'So,' he declared, as they walked back into the sitting-room, 'my brother has thought of everything, right down to your need to be close to the children – when they come.'

It was that remark, as much as anything, that was causing Claudine so much misgiving now. As she sat on her bed on her wedding morning, the reality of what lay ahead – and of what she felt about it – was at last beginning to come home to her.

She looked down at her hands, at the diamond that glittered in the sunlight, and for a moment her feelings engulfed her. Then suddenly she got up from the bed, dragged the cheval mirror away from the window and stripped off her clothes.

As she gazed at her reflection she tried to see herself

through François' eyes. Tried to imagine his hands on her breasts, his mouth seeking hers, his fingers exploring her most intimate places. His own naked body . . .

She closed her eyes as the heat seared through her veins, and as her fingers closed around her nipples the sensation that shot through her loins snatched the breath from her body. She clutched at the bedpost, biting her lips as she waited for the tide of longing to subside.

How could her body betray her like this? How had this come about when she detested and despised him? Yet, almost from the moment when she discovered that exquisite bedroom in the apartment upstairs, when she realized that even after they were married she was to sleep alone, she had known it was pointless to go on deluding herself. Ugly as he was, cruel and malevolent as she knew he could be, she could no longer deny that she wanted him in a way she had never wanted any other man in her life. She desired him with every fibre of her body, and had done almost from the moment she met him.

She threw back her head and looked up at the ceiling, wanting, but not daring, to scream. Why, dear God, when he so plainly did not want her, did she want him so much?

Suddenly she froze as she heard his voice outside, calling to Lucien. Then hearing him laugh, it was as if all her resolve gathered in a towering surge of defiance; when she looked back at herself in the mirror, her eyes were hard and shining.

'Today,' she whispered to her reflection, 'you are going to marry him. And after that, only you can see to it that he becomes the husband you want him to be. Your desires need not be a weakness, they can be a strength if you learn to use them correctly. And he will want you, one day he will want you every bit as much as you want him.'

She ran her hands down over her hips, then slipped her fingers into the moistness between her legs, and a cry escaped her lips as she discovered the power of her need. How could just the thought of him do this to her?

Quickly she withdrew her fingers, then picking up her négligé, she covered herself and walked to the window. He was there, standing at the centre of the stable yard with Lucien, and as if he sensed her eyes on him, he looked up. But when he saw her, he turned away. She watched him as he strode across the yard, feeling almost faint as she imagined that immense body lying over hers, taking her, violating her. She could almost feel the brutality of his mouth, the ruthlessness of his hands, the . . .

'*Mon Dieu*,' she murmured, and closed her eyes as her fingers were drawn to the ache in her loins.

Suddenly there was a knock on the door. She started, but hearing Dissy's voice she swallowed hard and called for her to come in.

'Ah, ha!' Dissy cried. 'Permission to enter at last!' Then seeing Claudine's naked body through the transparency of her négligé, she laughed. 'A dress rehearsal for the big night?'

'Something like that,' Claudine answered, almost gasping on a sudden onslaught of nerves. 'How are things progressing downstairs?'

'Don't ask! But Jean-Charles and Sophia have arrived with the dress, they'll be wanting to come up soon.'

'I must bathe. Come and talk to me while I do.'

Just then Magaly walked into the room. 'The packing is almost finished,' she said, her round face beaming its habitual smile. 'I shall put your lingerie here on the bed, then go to sort out these people downstairs. Estelle has arrived from the beauty salon with the manicurist. Shall I tell them to come up?'

'Give me half an hour,' Claudine answered. 'Did Jean-Charles remember the shoes?'

'Of course. I telephoned him yesterday to make certain,' and she laughed as Claudine blew her a kiss.

Dissy picked up a nail file and stretched out on the chaise-longue at the side of the bath. 'Did you invite Freddy to stay on at Montvisse after the wedding, or did he invite himself?' she asked. She waited, but there was no answer. From the look on Claudine's face Dissy could see that she hadn't even heard. 'Claudine!' she called. 'Hello!'

Claudine looked up. 'I'm sorry, darling,' she said. 'What were you saying?'

'I was asking about that brother of mine, but it doesn't matter.'

'Oh, Freddy! Hasn't he grown? I would never have recognized him. He tells me he's going to be nineteen at Christmas, and there was me thinking he was still in short trousers.'

'Well, he's at Oxford now, and very definitely in long trousers.'

'He's extremely handsome, Dissy. He has quite a romantic look about him too, don't you think?'

'He cultivates it, darling. He wants to be a poet.'

'Is he any good?'

'I've no idea. Daddy says he's bally awful, but then Daddy would. Mummy, of course, thinks he's better than Byron.'

'And what does Poppy think?' Claudine asked, referring to Dissy's husband, by his nickname.

'Best not repeat it,' Dissy grinned, and laughing, Claudine let her néglige float to the floor and stepped into the bath.

'Clo,' Dissy said thoughtfully, a few minutes later. 'I've been meaning to ask. Is there a reason why you're not having bridesmaids?'

Claudine lay back in the scented water and closed her eyes. 'I suppose,' she said, 'that it just didn't seem appropriate.'

'What? How on earth can bridesmaids not seem appropriate at a wedding?'

With her eyes still closed, Claudine merely raised her eyebrows and said, 'I don't know, but they didn't.'

Dissy stared at her. The absence of bridesmaids wasn't the only thing that struck her as odd about Claudine's wedding. What worried her most was that ever since she'd arrived she had been aware of a change in Claudine herself, which as the week progressed she had no longer been able to dismiss as pre-wedding nerves. And surely it was strange that Claudine had said almost nothing about François – when Dissy had expected her to be talking of nothing else, confiding all the details of the proposal, declaring her undying love. Then there had been the mysterious absence of the bridegroom. Apparently he had been at the château just prior to her arrival, but he had then been called to Paris on urgent business which had kept him there until two days before the wedding.

Oddest of all, perhaps, had been Monique's interrogation. Two days ago, while Claudine was in Chinon meeting François from the train so that they could register their marriage at the town hall, Monique had taken her for a walk in the woods, where she had proceeded to ask all manner of questions about the way Claudine and François felt about each other! If the bridegroom's sister is in the dark about their relationship, Dissy had thought, who *does* know what's going on? Then, she and Monique had talked about Freddy. Dissy had found Monique's interest rather surprising – she must be at least five years older than Freddy, perhaps more.

But it was when she and Monique returned from their walk that Dissy had received the biggest shock of all. The man waiting there on the steps of the château to greet her, Monique proudly informed her, was none other than the future Comte de Rassey de Lorvoire.

Dissy was ashamed now at the way she had stopped dead in her tracks and her mouth had actually fallen open. But he was so ugly, and so . . . Well, so big, standing there beside her lovely Claudine. His hand, when he held it out, had made Dissy shudder, but that was nothing to what she had felt when she looked into his eyes . . . She'd hardly slept a wink that night, and even Poppy had confessed to finding the man a trifle unusual.

However, Claudine had done nothing to invite any comment about her fiancé, nor had she expressed any doubt about what she was doing. 'In which case,' Poppy had said only that morning, 'it would be singularly inappropriate for you to mention your own doubts, Dissy. As we all know, Beavis has done nothing to pressure her into this marriage, so we can only conclude that this is what Claudine wants.'

'But is it what François wants?' Dissy said. 'He doesn't love her, Poppy, I know he doesn't. I can see it in his eyes when he looks at her. If anything, he despises her. And surely she can see it too?'

But if she could, Claudine was saying nothing. And at three o'clock that afternoon Dissy stood amongst the two hundred guests in the Royal Abbey of Fontevraud and watched her best friend, in a dress to make even a royal wedding gown look dowdy, walk down the aisle on the arm of her father, to a man who was as unsightly as his brother – standing beside him in full dress uniform – was handsome.

As they knelt side by side before the priest, Claudine was shaking. She had no idea what she was feeling, she simply listened as the priest's guttural chant echoed solemnly through the abbey and her own heart thudded in her ears. Then François' hand was on her elbow, helping her to her feet, and the priest was whispering to her to remove her veil. She didn't look at François as she did so, but kept her eyes fixed on the priest while François repeated the marriage vows in a warm, gentle voice that belonged to a man she didn't know . . . Then it was time for her to pledge her troth.

A shadow fell over her face, and there was the briefest touch of lips against hers. After that she remembered nothing until the organ suddenly started to play and they were walking back down the aisle.

They returned to the château in Louis' open-topped Bugatti. Marcel drove slowly, so that Claudine could wave to the people who lined the cobbled streets of the villages along the way – Fontevraud, Candés St Martin, St Germain-sur-Vienne – as they called out their good wishes. Beside her, François made no attempt to disguise his loathing of such a display. His discomfort was ridiculous, she thought, and she laughed – but even the sound of her own laughter did nothing to dispel the strange feeling of displacement.

When all the guests had returned, they sat down to the twelve-course wedding feast in the lavishly decorated ballroom of the Château de Lorvoire. Almost every noble family in France was represented, and several members of the English aristocracy were there too. Claudine sipped her champagne and laughed as everyone drank the bride's health, then the bridegroom's, then quite spontaneously, Solange's. Hardly aware of what she was doing, she pushed away the oysters, then the smoked salmon, the turbot, the *grives aux raisins*. When someone called to her, she answered, her eyes dazzling in their beauty and her lips never far from laughter. Beside her François had his back half-turned as he conversed with her father – but Claudine barely noticed.

At seven o'clock the ballroom was cleared and the dancing began. There was much hilarity when Poppy took over the piano and the band picked up the rhythm of the Lambeth Walk, a dance from a London musical, while Dissy taught everyone the steps. Like a child who never tires of the same story, Solange insisted they play it over and over again, until Louis had a quiet word with the band leader, then tangoed his wife off across the floor. Lucien took Claudine, and soon the whole room was a mass of gaily twirling bodies and grandly stamping feet. Claudine danced for what seemed an eternity, moving with the music from a fox-trot to a quick-step, from a rumba to a waltz, changing partners with such frequency that in the end she laughingly pleaded exhaustion, and taking Solange by the hand, started to wander round the room talking to guests.

François remained on the edge of the proceedings, shaking hands where he had to, but mainly engrossed in what Beavis and his father were saying. One subject preoccupied them: the increasing probability of war. François was listening intently; as a British diplomat and a close friend of Neville Chamberlain, Beavis was naturally well-informed, and since the collapse of Léon Blum's government in June and the rise to power of his father's old friend Camille Chautemps, there was much to discuss.

Eventually, aware that Céline was watching him, and knowing that on this occasion he must do what was expected of him, he excused himself and made his way over to Claudine.

She was standing in the middle of a group, laughing at something Lucien was saying, but when they saw him coming the crowd parted to let him through. As everyone around her fell silent, Claudine turned, and when she saw her husband she cocked her head on one side and placed a hand on her hip.

'Would you care to dance?' François said, fixing her with his eyes in a way that seemed to banish the presence of those around her.

'I should be delighted,' she said, and taking the hand he held out to her, she allowed him to lead her to the middle of the floor.

The band, who had been waiting for this moment, smoothly brought the piece they were playing to an end and started an instrumental version of 'The Very Thought Of You'. It was one of Claudine's favourite songs, and as the other dancers cleared the floor and François pulled her into his arms, she wondered if he knew the words. But if he did, he gave no sign, and she wasn't sure whether she was sorry or glad.

'It is unusual, I know, for the bride and groom to have the last dance,' he said, as he led her through her paces, 'but then ours is an unusual alliance, wouldn't you agree?'

'The last dance?' she echoed.

He nodded. 'Unless you're intending to leave in your wedding gown, it is time you went upstairs to change.'

Trying not to mind that he had passed no comment on her dress, with its waterfalls of lace, flowing taffeta skirts and pearl-studded silk bodice, she said, 'How long do I have?'

'As long as you like. But I'd prefer to arrive at Poitiers before midnight.'

'Poitiers?'

'We are spending the night at an hotel there. Did I forget to tell you? My apologies.'

She looked away as she suddenly became aware of his hand in the small of her back. 'Will you be driving us?' she enquired, in a voice that wasn't quite steady.

'Unless you have a notion to do so,' he answered. 'However, if you continue to tremble the way you are now, I wouldn't advise it.'

Her eyes shot to his, but there was no humour in his face; if anything, he seemed bored.

'I'll go upstairs to change,' she said, and turning abruptly, she walked from the dance floor.

An hour later, followed by Céline, Solange, Monique and Dissy, Claudine walked down the grand staircase and into the hall. She was wearing a navy Mainbocher suit with a cerise silk blouse and navy wedged shoes. Magaly had redressed her hair, which was now rolled in a snood under her navy and cerise hat. In the distance she could hear the sounds of the party, which she knew would continue into the small hours of the morning. For one fleeting moment she wished with all her heart that she could stay.

The others were fussing around her, offering her all the advice traditionally given to brides for the first night of their honeymoon. Solange, as usual, was outrageous – but for once Claudine wasn't laughing. She was staring past them to where François stood at the door with Lucien, Beavis and Louis. He too had changed out of his wedding clothes; now he was wearing a dark double-breasted suit and a black trilby hat.

Her eyes closed for a brief moment, then pulling herself together, she walked towards him. 'I'm ready,' she said in a quiet voice.

He turned, but before he could speak Beavis had taken his daughter in his arms. '*Au revoir, chérie*,' he said, and for the first time that day Claudine remembered that her father wouldn't be there when she returned from Biarritz. For a moment she was unable to speak, dreading that her tongue might betray her and announce to everyone present the sudden terror that had seized her. Then, taking a breath, she said goodbye to Beavis and turned to François. Behind her she could hear someone crying – she guessed it was Tante Céline, or perhaps Dissy.

François placed a hand under her arm, and without looking back she walked with him down the steps of the château. It was dark outside, but then the courtyard was flooded with light as Jean-Paul pulled the switch. The black Citröen was there, long and low and startlingly sinister. François opened the door for her to get in. With her eyes fixed straight ahead, she passed him and sat down in the deep leather seat. Then he closed the door behind her, and seconds later he was sitting beside her, starting the engine, easing it into gear. They moved slowly off down the drive. Behind them their families were waving, but neither of them turned back.

Beavis and Céline stood side by side, watching the tail lights until they disappeared from view.

'Like a lamb to the slaughter,' Céline murmured, repeating the words Claudine herself had uttered on these very steps the first time she had come to Lorvoire.

'What was that, *chérie?*' Beavis said, slipping an arm around her.

She looked up into his handsome, smiling face. Then, as her hand moved over his chest, smoothing the brilliant white stiffness of his shirt, she remembered that there was something she had to do, and linking an arm through his, she started to lead him back into the party. 'It's nothing,' she said. 'But I think we need something now to take our minds off our precious girl, don't you?'

Beavis' answering smile was remote; both he and Céline knew that it was unlikely either of them would be able to put Claudine out of their minds for long. But they would have to try, for she was no longer only Beavis' daughter and Céline's niece. First and foremost, now, she was François' wife.

– 7 –

The drive to Poitiers was long and silent. François kept his eyes on the road ahead as in the darkness shadows and light swept through the car. After they had been driving for about an hour, Claudine rested her head against the back of the seat and closed her eyes. She would never have expected to be able to sleep at such a time, but she did for a while, and when she woke she saw they were on the outskirts of a town.

François was smoking a cigarette. 'May I have one?' she said. It was the first word either of them had spoken since leaving Lorvoire.

She smoked in silence, and it was soon after she had

rolled down the window and discarded the last of her cigarette that he turned the car into a dimly lit courtyard, and they came to a halt in front of a rambling old manor house. A coach lamp illuminated the door, and at once a man came out. As they stepped from the car he was smiling a welcome; it was obvious that François was well known to him.

'Monsieur de Lorvoire,' he said, shaking François by the hand. 'And this is your charming wife? I am very pleased to meet you, *madame*. I am Bertrand Raffault, at your service.'

Claudine started at the word '*madame*', then smiled as Bertrand brushed his lips over the back of her hand. She looked at François, and wondered if he was even half as apprehensive as she. He was lighting another cigarette, but otherwise showed not the least sign of nervousness and she determined that she would show none either.

Inside, the manor had retained the look of a very old country house. Glad of the small fire burning in the hearth, and admiring the low, beamed ceiling and the wooden settles, Claudine almost failed to hear it when Bertrand told François in a low voice, 'This message arrived for you about half an hour ago, *monsieur*.'

'Thank you.' François took the folded paper and tucked it into an inside pocket, then picked up a pen to sign the register.

Unable to stop herself, Claudine moved closer to watch what he wrote. *François et Claudine de Rassey de Lorvoire.* Seeing their names together made her feel strangely light-headed, and as she put out her hand to steady herself, François moved his own and their fingers touched. Before she could stop herself she had snatched her hand away – but François didn't seem to notice.

Bertrand ushered them towards the wide, well-trodden staircase. 'I have, as you requested, *monsieur*, prepared the Victory Suite.'

'The Victory Suite?' Claudine said, suppressing a smile. Surely a rather indecorous name for a honeymoon suite?

'They are the rooms,' Bertrand answered, 'so the legend has it, where the English Black Prince celebrated his victory at the Battle of Poitiers in 1356. Myself, I do not believe that the house is so old, but it is a charming thought, don't you agree?'

Claudine refrained from answering. As she mounted the stairs she couldn't help wondering when, and with whom, François had visited this hotel before.

When they reached the first landing, Bertrand walked ahead of them down the corridor to a small black door. Both Claudine and François had to stoop to enter the sparsely furnished sitting-room: low oak beams, a huge fireplace and no windows.

'If you are cold, *madame*,' Bertrand said, 'I can ask Jacques to light a fire for you.'

'That won't be necessary, thank you,' François answered, standing aside as the valet came into the room with their luggage.

Bertrand glanced at Claudine, then opened a door at the back of the room. 'Through here you will find the bedroom, *madame*, and the bathroom is to your right. There is plenty of hot water.'

'Thank you,' she smiled. The room was decidedly Spartan, dominated by the high, wide bed with its faded tapestry covers.

'So now, I will wish you a good night, *monsieur et madame*,' Bertrand said. 'If there is anything you require, then please push the button beside the bed.'

When the door closed behind him, Claudine walked back into the sitting-room, trying to undo the clasp of her bracelet so that she could remove her gloves. She wished her fingers weren't shaking so badly, but as she continued to fumble with the catch François walked towards her, took her hand and calmly undid it.

'Thank you,' she said, half in a whisper.

She pulled off her gloves. Then, as she reached up to take the pin from her hat, she said, 'Aren't you going to read your message?'

'No.'

'But aren't you curious to know who it's from?'

'I know who it's from,' he said, turning to put his hat on the table.

Obviously he had no intention of enlightening her. She decided not to demean herself by asking, and walked back into the bedroom.

'I imagine,' he said, following her in, 'that you would like to use the bathroom for a while.'

She nodded, avoiding his eyes as a warm, prickling sensation crept over her skin.

'In that case,' he said, 'I shall go downstairs to make a telephone call. Perhaps you will be ready for me when I return.'

It was more an instruction than a request, and as he turned to leave the room, Claudine retorted, 'I'll do my best.'

'I expect you will,' he said lightly, and closed the door behind him.

On legs that were trembling as much with indignation as trepidation Claudine went into the bathroom. After the shabby, dark rooms she had seen so far, its white marble tiles and brightly lit mirrors took her by surprise. She pulled a chair up to the mirror, and after studying her face for several minutes, started to unbutton her jacket.

Twenty minutes later, with her glorious hair cascading about her shoulders and the soft, pale silk of her nightgown clinging to her body, she cast one last glance in the mirror, took a deep breath and unlocked the door.

She thought that maybe François had returned without her hearing, but the bedroom and the sitting-room were empty. She stood beside the bed, staring down at it, but found she couldn't bring herself to pull back the covers. After a time she wandered over to the window and stood looking out at the darkened courtyard. Then suddenly she squared her shoulders, walked over to the bed and slipped between the cool cotton sheets.

As she lay there in the silence she thought back to that morning – a lifetime ago now – when her desire for François had reached such a pitch that she had wanted to scream with the force of it. It seemed incredible that she could have felt like that when now she was so dreading him. She wondered again who he had come here with before, whether he had made love to another woman in this bed, and the thought inflamed her with a terrible sense of outrage, made her feel used, and unbearably naive. Then it occurred to her that he might be telephoning that woman even now, and though common sense told her that even François wouldn't do such a thing on his wedding night, she could do nothing to stop the feelings of jealousy that clenched her gut.

He had been gone over an hour by the time she heard the door to the suite creak open. She tensed as she heard him moving about in the next room. Her fury had vanished, and in its place was a choking knot of panic. Then the noises ceased, and she could hear nothing. Long minutes ticked by, and she was just at the point of swallowing her pride and going to find him when the bedroom door opened.

She stared up at him with wide, fearful eyes. She felt almost like a child. But her body was not behaving like a child's, for beneath his sombre black gaze an exquisite ache was opening in her loins and her nipples were beginning to throb as savagely as her heart.

He regarded her for some time, taking in the honey-soft skin of her shoulders, the slender arms that lay on the covers and the tumbling chaos of her hair on the pillow. Then the corner of his mouth dropped, and tugging at his tie, he closed the door.

She knew she should ask him why he had been so long, demand to know who had sent him a message on the night of their honeymoon, but as he walked over to the bed she found that the paralysis of her limbs had now spread to her tongue.

He removed his jacket as he sat down, and she averted her eyes as he started to unbutton his shirt. But then she felt the bed move as he leaned towards the lamp, and she looked back. The last thing she saw before the room plunged into darkness was his hideous profile: the hooked nose, the thin, contemptuous mouth, and the black, greased hair curling at the nape of his neck.

She listened as he removed the rest of his clothes, then the bed dipped as he got in beside her. They lay quietly for a moment, side by side in the darkness, the space between them so narrow that she could feel the warmth of his arm next to hers. She had no idea what he expected of her now, so she closed her eyes, and in an effort to steady her nerves, started to count her heartbeat. Part of her was longing for his arm to go round her, to hear him tell her that it would be all right, but another part of her was shrinking away from him in terror. The confusion of her feelings was terrible, and suddenly there were tears stinging the backs of her eyes.

She allowed one tear to slide unchecked to the pillow, then, as she raised her hand to stop the next, he moved towards her.

Neither of them spoke, but she could feel his breath on her face as his hands sought the hem of her nightgown. She wondered if she should put her arms about his neck, but then he pushed her nightgown up to her waist and threw back the covers, leaving her exposed to the moonlight.

She squeezed her eyes tight shut and fought the urge to cover herself with her hands. Then she tensed even more as his fingers slid between her legs and began easing them apart.

No, not like this! she heard a voice crying inside her. *Please, not like this!*

She felt him move over her as he pulled her legs wider, then he held his weight on one arm as he took his penis and ran the tip of it over her moist flesh to the mouth of her womb. Then his shoulders closed over hers and he placed a hand on either side of her.

'I take it you're a virgin?' he said, in a tone of appalling disinterest. 'Then this might hurt.'

Suddenly, in one almighty surge, the fire returned to her blood, and before he could stop her she had wrenched herself away. 'How dare you treat me like this!' she hissed, twisting out from under him. 'How dare you!' But as she started to scramble from the bed, he grabbed her and threw her back against the pillows.

'You have a duty to perform, Claudine,' he snarled.

'Stop it!' she cried, as his hands dragged her legs apart again. 'Stop! You can't make me . . .'

'Oh, but I can,' he said. 'You are my wife now, remember?' And grabbing her wrists in one hand, he pinned her arms above her head and pushed his legs between hers.

'No!' she cried. 'No! Let me go!'

He pressed his mouth hard against hers, drowning her screams, then using his free hand, he drew her hips towards him and entered her.

The struggle was useless, he was far too strong for her, but nevertheless she managed to wrench her mouth away and sank her teeth into his arm. He only laughed, and squeezing her jaw between his fingers, he turned her face back to his.

'I warned you, Claudine,' he snarled, 'but you wouldn't listen, would you?'

'Get off of me!' she hissed. 'Get your hands off me!'

'All in good time,' he sneered, thrusting himself in and out of her.

'Let go of me now!' she seethed. 'Let go or I'll scream!'

His only response was to tighten his grip on her jaw and slam into her even harder. She writhed and kicked and scratched, but all to no avail, she was trapped beneath him, there was no escape. She lay rigid, eyes closed, lips compressed and fists clenched. Dimly, she was aware that his breathing had quickened, that he was moving even deeper inside her; then she gasped as her whole being seemed suddenly to turn inside out.

It was as though she was alive with him; she could smell him, feel him, taste him, she was submerged in him. She could hear herself sobbing, then she almost screamed as she felt sensation in her start to build to an excruciating pitch. He took her thighs in his hands and pushed them up so that her legs were around his waist, and she clutched at his shoulders, curled her fingers savagely through his hair, feeling that at any moment she was going to explode. His pumping grew harder and harder, then he was touching her so deep inside, filling her so full of himself that she cried out his name. Then suddenly he withdrew.

Her senses reeled with the shock of it, her whole body screamed in protest. She looked up at him, then recoiled as she saw the sadistic smile that curved his lips.

'You're sick!' she cried, wiping the back of her trembling hand across her mouth. 'You're sick, and disgusting!'

'I gave you what you wanted,' he replied, as he rolled off her and sat on the edge of the bed.

'How *dare* you say that . . .'

'I gave you what you wanted,' he repeated, 'and you know it.'

'You *raped* me!' she seethed.

'No,' he said, standing up as he pulled on his undershorts. 'I merely showed you what a ridiculous woman you are.' He was glaring down at her, a vile expression in his eyes. 'I warned you not to marry me, but you had to have your own way, didn't you? And you were prepared to go to any lengths to get it. But have you ever asked yourself why, Claudine? Have you ever stopped to wonder why you were so determined to marry me?'

When she didn't answer, he gave a harsh laugh. 'No, I thought not. Then I'll tell you why. It was because I didn't want you, and you just couldn't face up to that. Your pathetic vanity couldn't accept that there was someone in this world not ready to fall at your feet. That's why you married me. Well, perhaps you can see now what blinkering yourself to get your own way can bring. Marrying me has changed nothing – I still don't want you. All I want is an heir, and as my wife you will make it your business to give me one. And now, since I believe I have cleared your head of any false illusions regarding our union, I shall bid you good-night.'

For a long time after the door had closed behind him, Claudine lay on the bed staring sightlessly at the place where he had stood, too stunned even to think. Eventually she became aware of how cold she was, and as she glanced down at the bare skin of her legs, a tiny flicker of life ignited somewhere very deep inside her.

At first she moved slowly, pulling herself from the bed into the bathroom. Once there, she turned on the taps and began to wash herself, with little energy, but a dim hope that she could cleanse herself of his venom. Once or twice she glanced at herself in the mirror, but she barely recognized the ashen face that looked back at her.

Mechanically she lowered the straps of her nightgown and let it fall to the floor. Her nakedness embarrassed her, and she turned from the mirror. Slowly she began to pull on her clothes. Soon, she told herself, the numbness would leave her mind and she would be able to decide what she should do.

She opened her vanity-case and began packing her toiletries. She had no idea how she was going to get out of the hotel, but there was no question that somehow she must. Then she would take a train to Chinon, and from there a taxi to Montvisse. Her father would still be there, he wasn't leaving for Berlin until the following week. She wouldn't allow herself to think how he would view her sudden return; once he knew the circumstances, surely he would agree that she had done the right thing?

Closing her vanity-case, she picked up her hat and walked back into the bedroom. From the chink of light under the door she guessed that François was still in the sitting-room, but she couldn't run the risk of opening the door to find out. She walked over to the window. It was a struggle to get it open, for it was imperative she make no sound, but eventually the heavy wooden frame responded and she pushed it gently upwards until there was enough room for her to climb through.

First she leaned out to see how she was going to get down, knowing that if it was necessary she would jump. But her painfully thudding heart flooded with relief as she saw the rusty fire-escape only a few feet below the windowledge.

Once she was outside, she eased the window closed, then carefully picked her way down the steps to the moonlit courtyard. Now all she had to do was find the railway station – and again she was in luck, for almost at once she saw a sign in the trees opposite, *Centre Ville*. The station was sure to be somewhere near the centre of the town; not too long a walk, she hoped, because though she doubted that François would go into the bedroom again that night, if he did, there was every chance he would come looking for her.

As she lifted her arm into the light and looked at her watch, she was shivering, and fighting hard against tears. It was one thirty in the morning, just three and a half hours after she had left Lorvoire. With an overpowering sense of sadness, she realized that her wedding party was probably still going on.

Collecting herself, and trying not to be daunted by the looming shadows of the trees, she walked out into the dark, deserted country road.

At about the time Claudine was leaving the hotel in Poitiers, Beavis and Céline were arriving back at Montvisse. All the way home they had sat silently staring in opposite directions, while Céline's chauffeur drove them through the night. Both were acutely aware of the dull red stain of Lorvoire wine on the front of Beavis's shirt. Céline had spilt it just before they left the party, and had been careful to make it look like an accident.

The staff at Montvisse were still up, waiting to attend to Céline's guests as they returned from the wedding. Céline and Beavis were the first to arrive home; they passed through the hall, bidding the servants good-night, then walked up the stairs together, parting company on the landing outside Céline's room.

When Céline went inside she found Brigitte dozing in a chair, but the maid managed to pull herself to her feet as she heard the door open.

'Go to bed, Brigitte,' Céline said, throwing her purse on the dressing-table.

'But I must brush your hair, *madame*, and . . .'

'Go to bed, Brigitte,' Céline repeated.

Had she not been so tired, Brigitte might have been quicker to understand, but as she made to protest again Céline shot her a look, and this time, in no doubt about what was on her mistress's mind, Brigitte bobbed a swift curtesy and did as she was told.

Céline waited, glancing about the room, pleased with the subtle yellow glow from the lamps beside the bed and the position of the cheval mirror in the corner between two occasional chairs. Then she heard footsteps outside the door. Her heart started to pound and her breathing quickened. She spun round as Beavis walked in, without knocking. When she saw the angry look on his face she turned away, lowering her head as if in shame.

He closed the door behind him. 'On countless occasions,' he said harshly, 'I have had to speak to you about your clumsiness.'

Her lips parted and her chest began to heave as he took a step towards her, but she didn't look up.

'My shirt is ruined,' he continued. 'I could have you dismissed for such carelessness, you do realize that?'

'Yes, sir,' she whispered.

'Is that what you want?'

'No, sir.'

'Then you know what must happen?'

'Yes, sir.'

He walked past her, then picking up one of the chairs and placing it in front of the mirror, he said, 'It gives me no pleasure to punish you, but you leave me no alternative. Come over here.'

Keeping her eyes lowered, Céline walked across the room. When she was standing beside him, he sat down on the chair, resting his hands on his knees. 'Pull up your dress,' he said.

Obediently Céline gathered the skirts of her short Molyneux evening dress and pulled them to her waist. Over her white lace suspender-belt she was wearing a pair of pink satin French knickers.

'All right,' he said, watching her reflection in the mirror. 'Have you anything to say for yourself before I begin?'

'Only that I am very sorry, sir. And that I will try not to do it again.'

'Well, we'll just have to see that you don't,' he said, and lifting a hand, he pulled her across his lap. Then arranging her dress so that the hem fell around her shoulders, he slipped his fingers under the elastic of her knickers and pulled them down over her thighs.

By now Céline's breathing was so rapid that she was beginning to shake. As she cast her eyes towards the mirror she could see the reflection of her naked buttocks and the grim determination on Beavis' face. Then, as his hand rose, she closed her eyes, bracing herself for the first blow. When it came, the pain that shot through her body was almost unbearable, but she sank her teeth into her lips to stop from crying out. He lifted his hand again, but this time, as the sharp, stinging slap hit her naked flesh, she could do nothing to stop the moan of pure ecstasy.

He spanked her again and again, until she was bound in a knot of such overpowering arousal she could no longer breathe. But the exquisite torture continued as his long, gentle fingers started to soothe her smarting skin, moving in gentle circles over her buttocks and thighs, caressing and stroking. Then at last, just as she thought she could bear it no longer, his hand came down in one final excruciating slap.

'*Mon Dieu*,' she choked.

He caught her about the waist and pushed her back to her feet. Her dress fell around her knees and her knickers slipped to her ankles. 'Now let that be a lesson to you,' he said.

'Yes, sir,' she murmured, as she stooped to retrieve her knickers.

'Did I give you permission to do that?' he barked.

'No, sir.'

'Then leave them where they are.'

She let her knickers go, and allowed her arms to hang loosely at her sides as she stood before him.

At last he stood up, and putting his hands on his hips he said in a dark voice, 'Unfasten my trousers.'

As she fumbled with his fly, her hands were shaking so badly that in the end he pushed her away. 'Take off your dress,' he said, tugging at his tie.

'But, sir . . .'

'I said take it off!'

Obediently she peeled the ruched bodice from her shoulders and let the dress fall to the floor. Now she was wearing only her white lace brassière, suspender-belt and pale silk stockings.

'Turn round and face the bed,' he told her.

As she did as she was told, he ran two fingers down the crease in her buttocks, then pushing them between her legs, he buried them deep inside her. 'In future,' he said, rotating his fingers as he bent her over, 'you will make it your business never to come into my presence unless you are dressed as you are now.' And withdrawing his fingers, he lowered his trousers and undershorts.

As he entered her, she cried out at the unendurable excitement of it, and clutched the edge of the bed as he tore at the lace holding her breasts. 'Now tell me you spilt the wine purposely,' he growled, as he pulled and squeezed her nipples, while grinding hard against her. 'Tell me that you did it because you knew this would happen.'

'Yes. Oh yes, sir. I wanted you, sir. I wanted you inside me like this, sir.'

'That's it,' he breathed. And as he ran his hands over the insides of her thighs, he lifted her from the floor.

'Oh my God,' she cried, as she felt him push even deeper inside her. Then suddenly she knew she couldn't hold on any longer. 'Please!' she cried. 'Now, please!'

Putting her back to the floor he quickly moved his fingers between her legs, and holding her to him as he expertly stroked and teased her, he slammed into her with long, urgent strokes until he too passed the point of control. As the orgasms shuddered through their bodies, Céline's knees began to give way, but he caught her about the waist and held her up until with one final thrust, the last of his semen leapt from his body.

Both were drenched in sweat, and both were breathing too heavily to speak. He was still inside her, and could feel her muscles clenching him in the dying throes of her climax.

'Ah, Beavis,' she murmured at last, pulling herself upright and leaning back against him. She tilted her head to look up at him, and as he bent to kiss her he wrapped his arms around her, taking her small breasts in his hands.

Eventually he eased himself away, and she moaned softly as he withdrew from her. Then she turned to sit on the bed, and looking at him, she started to laugh.

Bemused, he stared down at himself, then he too began to laugh. His shirt and jacket were open, revealing the hard muscles of his chest and his trousers and undershorts were round his ankles, well below the suspenders that held his socks.

'What do you look like, *chérie*!' she giggled.

'Ludicrous, I should say!' he chuckled. 'But you and your erotic games are enough to make any man forget his dignity.'

'What did you think of the maid?' she murmured, resting her head on his shoulder and trailing her fingers over his thigh.

He looked down at her. 'You have to ask?'

Laughing, she planted a kiss on his cheek, then set about unfastening her suspenders.

When they were both naked, Beavis turned out the lights and they got into bed. For some time they lay quietly in each other's arms until finally Céline whispered, 'What are you thinking?'

In the darkness Beavis frowned. 'Probably the same as you.'

She sighed, and turned in his arms. 'Do you still believe their marriage will work?'

'Why shouldn't I?'

They were quiet again then, and after a few minutes she heard the steady rhythm of his breathing. Assuming that he was asleep, she too closed her eyes.

But Beavis wasn't asleep, it was just that he didn't want to talk. He had hoped that by now the sense of foreboding that had started just before he and Céline left Lorvoire, would have disappeared. But even the delightful episode with Céline hadn't managed to dispel it, and now it was worse than ever.

When he was certain that Céline was asleep, he got up from the bed and lit a cigarette. Even if François had told him the name of the hotel in Poitiers, the idea of telephoning in order to put his mind at rest was, of course, unthinkable. And if he just looked at it rationally for a moment, he would probably see himself for the over-solicitous parent he was. After all, what could possibly have happened to give him such a sense of disaster? If there had been an accident they would have been informed by now. And as for Claudine losing her virginity . . . Well, it had to happen sooner or later, whether he liked it or not.

He ground out his cigarette and walked back to the bed. Knowing he would be unable to sleep, he toyed with the idea of returning to his own room – but Céline would be offended if he did, so he pulled back the sheets and got in beside her.

It was just after five in the morning when Claudine arrived at Montvisse. She hadn't found a train, or a taxi, but a lorry driver who was travelling through the night from Angoulême to Tours had stopped when he saw her walking through the deserted streets of Poitiers in the early hours of the morning. She had hastily explained that she had to return home with the utmost urgency: could he direct her, or even take her, to the nearest railway station?

He laughed. 'There won't be any trains through here until at least seven in the morning,' he said. 'Where are you heading?'

'Chinon. Near Chinon.'

'Get in,' the lorry driver said. 'You'll be far safer in here with me than out there walking the streets. I'm heading for Tours myself, so you won't be much out of my way.'

Ordinarily Claudine would have balked at getting into a vehicle with a stranger, but this wasn't ordinarily ... All through the long drive she sat in the warmth of the small cab while the driver rambled gently on about his wife, his three sons and his seven grandchildren. He knew Claudine wasn't listening, and wondered what lay behind this beautiful young woman's need to get to Chinon with such haste. But he didn't question her, and by the time he dropped her at the gates of Montvisse, he too had fallen silent. Claudine watched him go with an ache in heart, then turned into the avenue of limes and started to walk up the drive.

She found a side door that was open, and let herself into the silent château. Now she was so near her father, the resolve she had gathered in the lorry was beginning to fracture. But she was determined not to break down. No amount of anger or tears would change the situation, she kept telling herself; it could only be handled calmly, with reason and self-control.

She had decided that she must tell her father the whole truth – though now, as she climbed the stairs to Beavis' room at the top of the tower, she was already faltering in her mind over the accusation of rape. But no matter what François thought, she told herself, no matter how her treacherous body had responded, she had *not* wanted him to make love to her ... She hesitated as a burning wave of misery closed around her heart. But she *had* responded, neither she nor François could be in any doubt of it ... The

– 136 –

memory filled her with self-loathing; now, the very thought of those grotesque hands ever touching her body again repelled her.

She tapped gently on her father's door, then let herself in. She was baffled at first by the bright light that flooded the room from the unshuttered windows, then, as she saw the empty bed, an unbearable despondency swept over her. He must have spent the night at Lorvoire; she had no choice but to go downstairs to Tante Céline.

There was no answer when she knocked on her aunt's door, so she pushed it open and peeped in. The shutters were closed, but bright bands of light shone through the slats.

'Tante Céline,' she whispered, as she tip-toed across the room. 'Taunte Céline?'

There was a movement in the bed. Claudine was on the point of speaking again when she froze.

Céline's eyes as they looked up at her were as wide and disbelieving as her own, but Claudine wasn't looking at her aunt. She was looking at her father, who after sleepless hours of worrying about his daughter, had finally fallen into a doze. Suddenly his eyes opened, and he looked straight at Claudine.

There was a moment of dreadful silence, then Claudine turned and ran from the room.

Outside the château, Claudine saw her car. The keys were in it and in a moment she was out of the gates and roaring along the narrow road that ran parallel to the Vienne. She didn't think about where she was going, it didn't matter – she wanted only to drive. And she did drive, furiously, for over half a hour, before she realized she had come dangerously close to running out of petrol and was miles from the nearest pump.

But as she abandoned the Lagonda on the side of the hill

and started to walk up over the brow, she didn't care how she was to get back, or what she was going to do when she did. The drive had succeeded in calming her a little, but she still needed to think; she needed time to sort out in her mind the appalling events of the past twelve hours.

As she walked she took deep, calming breaths, but the shock of finding her father in bed with her aunt was still raw. Every time she thought of it she could see her mother's face . . . How could they have done it? How could they, when Beavis had loved Antoinette so much he would have died for her? But it was Antoinette who had died, and wasn't it just like Cèline to be there with her own special kind of solace? Céline, who had as many lovers as she had dresses, who could have anyone she wanted, had seduced her sister's husband. Perhaps she hadn't even waited for her sister to die.

That thought was so terrible that Claudine buried her face in her hands, and at last, as she sank to her knees in the early morning dew, she allowed the tears to fall. Sobs racked her body, the pain and confusion seemed to tear her heart apart. She wanted her mother now as she had never wanted her before.

It was a long time before she lifted her head again, but when she did, gazing down into the valley of Lorvoire, she found that she felt a little steadier. She was sitting at the top of the hill on the far side of the valley, almost opposite the spot where she had stood with François the first day she met him. What a long time ago that seemed now – and she cringed as she remembered the childish way she had behaved at the fountain. But that was nothing to the way she had acted since.

She recalled the dreadful circumstances of François' proposal, the way she had made herself so ridiculous in her determination to marry him. There was no denying now that she had made the greatest mistake of her life, and it didn't help to know that she had only herself to blame. Everyone had warned her against him, but in her arrogance she had refused to listen, certain that she could be the one to change him. How badly she had needed to grow up! The whole world would know now that Claudine Rafferty had latched herself onto a man who didn't love her, didn't even want her. How they would laugh when they heard what had happened, and how they would pity her.

Engulfed in a wave of desperation, she fell back in the grass, beating her fists against the ground and screaming up at the sky. How could she have done this to herself? How could she have been so stupid and pig-headed?

She thought of the gypsy then, and gave a bitter laugh. Things aren't always what they seem, the old woman had said. And she, like the fool she was, had applied that to François. A great love and a great danger, the gypsy had said. Well, there was no doubt in her mind now that François was the danger. She had only to remember what he had told her about Hortense to know that he was capable of any evil. How she was sickened now by her refusal to believe him! How simple she had been; how unspeakably obtuse . . .

By the time she pulled herself to her feet it was approaching midday, and yet despite her sleepless night she was feeling as though she had at last awoken from a state of stupefying somnambulance. Her mind was finally beginning to clear. One day, she knew, in the not too distant future, the anger and resentment she bore François would cease to exist. But for the moment she must live with it, and she must face him with it – for much as she blamed herself for what had happened, there was no reason on God's earth why he should have treated her the way he had. Now she must face this last hurdle. She must confront him, prove that she could be dignified in defeat, and then she could put the whole thing behind her.

As she wandered back across the hilltop in her crumpled

navy suit, she lifted a hand to her face and pressed gently against the bruises on her jaw. Then, as she glanced at the angry red marks that circled her wrists, she became aware, too, of the dull ache at the top of her thighs.

She tossed her head as again the flame of anger she had struggled to suppress suddenly flared. But she had reached her decision, she was going to give up the fight, and she must not allow herself to think of revenge: who could win against a man like François? An image of his naked body came unbidden to her mind then, and she faltered. But she pushed it away. Nothing, least of all her treacherous bodily desire, was going to weaken her resolve to escape him.

She rounded the crest of the hill and looked down towards her car. Then her breath caught in her throat and she stopped dead. The Lagonda wasn't the only car parked at the side of the road. Beside it was the black Citröen, and standing beside the Citröen, smoking a cigarette and staring right at her, was François. In the early morning sunlight she could see the silver snake of his scar glinting gruesomely. He was wearing the suit he had worn the night before, but now both the jacket and waistcoat were undone, and the collar of his shirt was missing. As she watched he threw away the cigarette and, folding his arms, leaned against the side of his car. His attitude was that of a weary parent waiting for a disobedient child.

A quick temper flashed in her lovely eyes, and she was on the point of turning and walking in the opposite direction when she realized that running away was not the answer. She must face him now, tell him what she had decided, then she could get on with the preparations for her return to England.

Cautiously she started down the hill, but she held her head high and her face set in determination. Nothing in the world would induce her to betray her real feelings – this would be the last time they met, and she would rather die than let him know how badly she still wanted him.

'How did you find me?' she said, when she was close enough for him to hear.

'It wasn't difficult,' he answered. 'It followed that you would run to your father.'

'But he can't have known where I was.'

'No. But he did know you'd gone off in your car.'

'Then why didn't he come after me himself?'

'He would have done, if I hadn't arrived when I did. I pointed out that though I respect the fact that you are his daughter, you are also my wife.'

She flinched, but then she looked him straight in the eye. 'I want our marriage annulled,' she said.

'Do you now?' His tone gave her the distinct impression that that was precisely what he had expected her to say. 'Well, I'm sorry to disappoint you, Claudine, but that isn't possible.'

'What do you mean?'

'To begin with, you need my agreement.'

'And you won't give it?'

'No.'

'But why?' she cried. 'Why, when this marriage is obviously as repugnant to you as it is to me?'

'We shall both learn to tolerate it,' he answered.

She was beginning to panic, and her hands were trembling with the desire to strike his hideous face. 'You raped me!' she hissed. 'Am I supposed to tolerate that?'

He sighed, as if already bored by their exchange. 'It is a legal impossibility for a man to rape his wife,' he said. 'Now, get into the car.'

'I will *not*!' she cried.

He didn't move, but a dangerous glint appeared in his eyes and she felt herself beginning to shrink away. 'I think,' he said, 'that this is as good a moment as any to remind you that less than twenty-four hours ago you swore before God to love, honour and obey me. I do not expect the first, but I unconditionally insist upon the second and the third. Now, get into the car.'

'Why?' she said, casting wildly about in her mind for words she could hit back at him with.

'Because we are going to Biarritz to continue our honeymoon,' he answered.

She froze, and her eyes rounded in horror. 'You're insane,' she breathed. 'You can't seriously believe that I'll continue this farce of a marriage as if nothing had happened?'

'I do. And you will.'

'But people have seen me, they know . . .'

'They know,' he interrupted, 'that we have returned to Lorvoire for Magaly, who incidentally is already packing. Perhaps you would like to thank me for seeing to it that you have company during the long, lonely days beside the sea?'

Her head was beginning to spin. 'What do you mean?' she whispered.

'Only that I shall be unable to spend all my time with you. Of course, I shall return to the hotel each night, when I expect you to perform your wifely duty.'

'I don't believe this is happening,' she said, shaking her head. 'And I don't understand why you want to stay married when you hate the situation as much as I do.'

'You should have thought about what our marriage would be like before you walked down the aisle, Claudine. I gave you no reason to believe that my feelings towards you would change once we were married. If you imagined they would, then I'm sure you know by now that you were deceiving yourself. Now, I won't ask again, so get into the car.'

'Why do you hate me, François?' she said. 'What have I done to make you treat me like this?'

'I don't hate you, Claudine,' he said, opening the car door.

'What about my car?' she asked, so bemused she hardly knew what she was saying.

'Someone will come to fetch it.'

She looked at him, then not knowing what else to do, she got into the car.

'I hate you,' she said quietly as they started back down the hill. 'I despise you. How can you possibly want to make love to someone who feels about you the way I do?'

'But we won't be *making love*, Claudine. We will merely be performing an act in order to conceive children.' His lip curled in a smile. 'And try to remember, while you're reciting the Marseillaise, or whatever it is you women do when you're lying on your backs, that you are not the only one performing a duty.'

Too appalled to speak, she turned to stare out of the window. In the space of a few hours her life had somehow turned into a nightmare from which, it seemed, there was no chance of waking.

– 8 –

The Honourable Frederick Benjamin Prendergast was ambling back through the gardens of Montvisse from the dovecote when he saw the creamy-white Armstrong Siddeley, driven by Céline's chauffeur, pass the black de Lorvoire Bentley under the avenue of limes. The Armstrong Siddeley, he knew, was taking Beavis to the station at Chinon; he had said his farewells to Beavis half an hour before. It had been an awkward meeting, like most of their meetings this past week, since Beavis felt obliged to tell Freddy on each occasion that he would consider it a great favour if Freddy would refrain from mentioning, to anyone, Claudine's impromptu return to the château the morning after her wedding. Freddy repeatedly assured Beavis that he had already forgotten the incident, which brought a grim smile to Beavis' face: he was relieved it was only Freddy who had been up at that hour of the morning, for it would have been an embarrassment, to say the least, to have to ask the other guests to keep silent – and madness to expect them to do so.

However, almost everyone who was staying at the Château de Lorvoire – which included Freddy's sister, Dissy – knew that François and Claudine had made a brief return, and all had found it highly amusing that Claudine was unable to manage for more than a day without her maid. What none of them knew was that she had gone to Montvisse first, and had come in a lorry a good half an hour before François. They did not know, either, that even before François' arrival, Claudine had already sped off again in the Lagonda.

Freddy had seen François go after her, and he had also seen the two of them return, but he had no idea what had gone on behind the closed doors of the library and drawing-room after that. All he knew was that François and Claudine had left the château an hour later, and that when he next saw Céline it was apparent she had been crying.

It wasn't that Freddy had been deliberately spying on the family's comings and goings, it was simply that he had woken that morning with the sunrise, to compose a sonnet for Monique, and had gone to sit at the window of his room, which happened to overlook the avenue of limes ... And Monique had simply adored the sonnet, he thought cheerfully now watching her alight from the Bentley as it came to a stop in front of the château. And thank heavens she spoke English so well, else his sublime efforts might have been in vain.

Seeing him come across the gardens, Monique called out to him, and Freddy's entire body gave a quiver of pure rapture at the way she pronounced his name.

'Monique!' he cried, and running up to her, he caught her hands, kissed them, then held them to his heart.

'*Oh là là*,' she smiled, as she saw the look of adulation in his eyes, and pulling a hand free, she started to tweak at his disorderly thatch of sandy hair. 'What have you been doing, *chéri*?' she said. Then she moved her eyes to his in a way that brought the colour sweeping across his face.

'What do you think?' he said shyly.

'Not another! Oh, Freddy, what am I to do with you?'

He longed to tell her that he was hers to do with as she pleased, but he didn't quite have the courage, so he said, 'Would you like to read it?'

'Where is it?'

'Here, next to my heart,' he said, reaching inside his pullover to take the poem from his shirt pocket.

Monique laughed. 'Then keep it there. I shall read it later, when we . . .'

'When we what?' he prompted.

Her answering smile was so lingeringly provocative that he found himself leaning towards her.

'Freddy,' she murmured. 'You are a naughty boy. I do believe you are thinking to kiss me, right here in front of Montvisse.'

Mortified, Freddy pulled himself together, all his ardour now glowing in his fresh, youthful cheeks, and laughing, Monique turned to Marcel, who promptly leapt from the car and opened the back door for her to get in. 'Come along, *chéri*,' she said, glancing over her shoulder at Freddy.

'Where are we going?'

'Wait and see,' she answered, taking his hand as he got in beside her.

'But aren't you going to call on Céline before you leave?'

'Was she expecting me?'

'Er, no, I don't think so.'

'Then there is no reason for me to do so, is there? You may have me all to yourself this afternoon, Freddy. That is what you want, is it not?'

'I'll say,' he breathed, and she laughed gaily at his boyish enthusiasm as Marcel turned the car round and started back down the drive.

'I am so pleased you have stayed on at Montvisse,' she said, when they were heading along the road towards Chinon.

'It was kind of you to ask Céline if one could,' he responded. 'She's an absolutely spiffing woman, don't you agree?'

'Oh, spiffing,' she said, making him laugh. She adored him most particularly when he smiled.

'You know,' she sighed, 'I had no idea life had become so dreary until you arrived.'

'Oh, but surely life can't be dreary with Claudine around,' he protested. 'Céline tells one she's been on top form ever since she arrived in France.'

Monique smiled, almost to herself. '*Oui, elle a de la presence.*'

Not too sure what that meant, but assuming it was a compliment, Freddy nodded happily.

'She's made quite a change to our lives at Lorvoire,' Monique went on. 'We have all come to love her a great deal, you know. *Maman* is missing her terribly, especially now all the guests have gone. Still I'm sure she's having a simply marvellous time in Biarritz.'

She cast a quick look in Freddy's direction, but so far, pumping him about the morning Claudine and François had returned to Lorvoire had produced no results – he'd made it clear that he wasn't prepared to say anything. For her part, she didn't for one minute believe that nonsense about the maid, but no one else, not even Céline, had confessed to finding the fleeting return unusual, so as yet she had been unable to discover what lay behind it.

'You're very fond of Claudine, aren't you, Freddy?' she said.

'I'll say,' he answered. 'Always have been. Used to hope that one day one might marry her, but of course she's too old for one. I mean, that is to say, she couldn't possibly be interested in someone so young,' he added hastily. 'Not with so many other chaps vying for her attention. That was before she was married, of course. Sure it'll be different now. In love and all that, you know.' It seemed nothing he said was coming out quite right, so he decided to shut up.

'Do you think she is in love with my brother?' Monique said, gazing nonchalantly out of the window as they crossed the bridge at Chinon.

'Oh, absolutely certain of it. Wouldn't have married him otherwise. Would she?'

'Wouldn't she?'

'Grand chap, your brother,' Freddy said, feeling his colour begin to rise again.

'I think so,' she smiled. 'I just hope Claudine does too. And as for François, well, he obviously adores her. I mean, the way he brought her back to Lorvoire the morning after the wedding to collect her maid proves it, doesn't it? But he'll quite ruin her if he insists on indulging her every whim.'

'He's a jolly lucky chap,' Freddy remarked in a dull voice.

Monique sighed, and allowed her head to fall against the back of the seat. 'I do so envy them being so much in love, don't you, *chéri*?'

He took some time to think about that, then with heartfelt solemnity he said, 'Love can be a very painful experience at times.'

'Oh, but it can!' she cried in surprise, but instantly warming to the subject.

He turned to look at her, her lips looked so inviting that he felt his own begin to tremble. For a moment he gazed longingly into her wide amber eyes, but then he turned quickly away, ashamed at the thoughts that were trespassing across his mind. How crude she would think him if she knew the true extent of the passion that beat in his heart, that drummed through his loins and set his blood on fire with ignoble lust. How he longed to hold her, to smother her with kisses and fill her with the rapture she instilled in him! But he had only to look at her to be reminded of what a callow youth he was. A youth whom she had excused the presumption of his adoration, and whose poems she smiled upon in her benevolence.

Swallowing her impatience, Monique looked out of the window. She didn't have much longer to wait, she reminded herself, and one didn't actually expire from a want of kisses, even if just at that moment one felt one might . . .

'Are we going to the village?' Freddy asked a few minutes later as they passed the gates of the Château de Lorvoire.

She nodded. 'I have a message for Liliane St Jacques from *Maman*. Then we shall walk together, and you shall read me your poem, *oui*?'

'*Oui*,' he smiled, and his limpid brown eyes misted with adoration.

They left the car at the edge of the village and tramped over the cobbles, strolling up the steps at the centre of the main street to the old well, where each evening the men heaved up the bucket and splashed themselves with water to rinse away the dust of the fields. Now, in the middle of the afternoon, the village with its grey stone cottages and drab street signs was almost deserted. Monique was a little sorry that there weren't more people to see her with this tall, handsome youth, with his unruly mop of hair, ruddy cheeks and lean, awkward body.

Before his arrival at Montvisse it had never occurred to Monique that she might find a man so much younger than herself attractive, much less fall in love with him, but almost from the moment she had laid eyes on Freddy Prendergast she had felt herself coming to life in a way she hadn't experienced for a long time. She knew, from the poems he wrote her, that he shared her feelings, but she also knew that he was too diffident to presume any further. In a subtle way she had done all she could to encourage him, but so far she had been unable to break through the barrier of his timidity. But she was determined, and after some thought she had decided to bring him to a particular clearing in the forest behind the St Jacques' house.

It was known as the waterfall table, a small oval of flat land with a tiny lake at the centre, filled from a waterfall which flowed through the trees and then down behind the village into the Vienne. Clustered around the lake, protecting it from view, were the roots of the huge forest trees which grew up over the hillside. It was a perfect setting for love, and already Monique's heart was fluttering with the anticipation of what she had resolved to accomplish there.

A few minutes later they rounded the wall of the chapel and climbed the grassy slope to Liliane's house. Freddy waited outside, but Monique was gone only a short time, and soon she and Liliane came out together. The old lady, with her toothless smile, waved to him, then called something after Monique as she came over and took his arm.

'What did she say?' he asked, as they started up through the vineyards towards the forest.

'She was telling me to be sure that Claudine goes to see her the minute she returns.' Then, after a pause, 'It was odd, you know, but she said that Armand saw Claudine's car the morning after the wedding, and that Claudine was driving it. Of course I told her that Armand must have been mistaken, but she absolutely insisted.'

She was watching him out of the corner of her eye, and saw how troubled he looked. Yes, she was almost sure now that, just as she'd suspected, Claudine had returned to Montvisse the morning after her wedding. And the only conclusion to be drawn from that was that Claudine had run away from François. Which meant, of course, that things were already going badly between them. However, instead of the satisfaction that might have given her a week ago, Monique felt only sadness. Now that she was on the brink of finding love herself, she no longer resented it in others. 'Come on,' she said to Freddy. 'What I want now is to listen to your poem.' And she ran on up the hill ahead of him.

Relieved to be let off the hook, as he always had found it hellishly difficult to keep a secret, Freddy started after her, and taking the hand she held out to him, climbed up through the vines with her and into the woods.

'Here,' he said, stopping her as he stooped to pick a flower.

She waited as he tucked it into her hair, then picking one herself, she put it behind his ear and stood back to admire him. '*Tu es très beau*,' she murmured as she gazed into his eyes. Then she stood on tip-toe to brush her lips gently over his before taking his hand and running with him through the trees to the clearing. When they reached it, she stopped and looked up into his face, and with a flutter of joy she saw that his reaction was all she had hoped for.

'Sit here,' she whispered, pulling him down onto the grass beside her. 'Sit here and listen to the waterfall.'

He sat, his eyes transfixed by the beauty of the lake; the way the beams of sunlight streamed through the trees in ephemeral lines of silvery mist that exploded in a glittering mass of light as they touched the water. The way the gnarled, leafy branches drooped to their reflections, and the lily pads floated in the current. After a while Monique pulled him back so that he was lying with his head in her lap. He looked up at her, but she ran her fingers over his eyes, closing them. 'Be still, *chéri*,' she murmured.

They stayed like that for a long time while she stroked his hair, then his face, then his neck. Above them the birds were rustling the trees, while the waterfall trickled and gurgled down through the forest. It was cool, and blissfully calm. In the end Freddy's eyes fluttered open. Monique was resting against the bole of a tree, and pulling himself up on one elbow so that his face was very close to hers, he murmured, ' "Now folds the lily all her sweetness up, And slips into the bosom of the lake: So fold thy self, my dearest, thou, and slip Into my bosom and be lost in me." '

'Oh, Freddy,' she whispered. 'Did you just think of it?'

He smiled. 'Yes, but it was written a long time ago by Tennyson.'

She moved towards him, but as her leg brushed against the treacherous hardness of his body, he turned abruptly away.

'What is it?' she said, putting a hand on his shoulder and turning him back.

As he looked at her, his face was crimson and his eyes flooded with pain. 'It's nothing,' he said, looking down at the ground. 'Nothing at all.'

Monique smiled, and understanding only too well what was troubling him, her heart went out to him in such love and pity that it was all she could do to stop herself taking him in her arms. But she knew it would be wrong to touch him at that moment, so lying back in the grass, she allowed several minutes to tick silently by before she said, 'Have you ever made love to a woman, Freddy?'

He sat up, wrapped his arms about his knees and buried his face.

'Would you like to make love to me?' she said softly.

She watched him, her heart thudding with dread as she waited for the rejection. It was too soon, she had frightened him, and now she would lose him . . . But then his hand reached out for hers and his voice was muffled by his sleeve as he said, 'How can one subject you, the most beautiful woman in the world, to such ignominy? One cannot debase you with the lust one is unable to control.

You are sweet and perfect, and you touch one's soul with your kindness.'

Sitting up, she put an arm about his shoulders and pressed her cheek against his. 'Do I have to tell you, a poet, the beauty of making love?' she said. 'You will not be debasing me, *cheri*, not if you love me.'

'Oh, Monique,' he groaned, and clutching her to him, he pressed his lips brutally to hers.

Gently she pushed him away, then holding his face in her hands she said, 'Let me show you,' and parting her lips, she pulled his mouth back to hers and kissed him with a searing tenderness.

When she let him go, he sobbed and threw himself back in the grass. 'One is so useless!' he cried, flinging an arm across his eyes. 'I want you so much, Monique, but one doesn't know how . . . One has never . . .'

'Ssh,' she said, putting a finger over his lips. Then pushing her hands beneath his pullover, she fanned her fingers across his chest. His eyes were still covered by his arm, but she could feel the rapid beat of his heart. 'Look at me,' she murmured, as she lowered her hands to his waist and began to tug his shirt from his trousers.

He opened his eyes, but she could see that he was too overwhelmed to hold her gaze. Smiling, she took his hand and placed it on her breast. His eyes closed again as he moaned softly. Knowing that he would never have the courage to do it himself, she unbuttoned her blouse, then pulled it free of her skirt and slipped it over her shoulders. 'Look at me,' she said again.

When he saw the sharp points of her nipples pushing against the silk camisole, his breath caught in his throat, but before he could turn away she lifted his hands and kissed them. 'Touch me,' she said. 'Touch me here, Freddy,' and lowering his hands to her breasts, she pressed them against her.

'You are so beautiful,' he murmured. 'Oh, Monique, you are so beautiful.'

She sat quietly as he tentatively lifted her camisole over her breasts and began to fondle her bare skin. Her nipples ached for his lips, but then he took them between his fingers and rolled them gently. She let her head fall back, murmuring and showing him what pleasure he was giving her. Then, when she judged the time right, she lifted a hand and placed it over the front of his trousers.

He froze, then his hands fell to the ground and his head rolled from side to side as he began to groan. Slowly she began to unbutton his fly, watching him and pulling his hand back to her breast.

'When we are married we can do this all the time,' she told him, as she began to ease his trousers over his hips.

'Yes, oh yes,' he moaned, by now too enslaved by the sensation of her fingers as they closed around him to think beyond them.

With one hand she started gently to massage him, while with the other she turned his face to hers. 'Kiss me,' she said, leaning towards him. His lips parted, and as she pushed her tongue between them, she tightened the grip on his penis.

'Oh my God!' he spluttered. 'Oh my God!' The semen was shuddering from his body in urgent, excruciating spurts. 'Oh no!' he cried, pulling himself away from her. 'No, no, no!'

'It doesn't matter,' she said, trying to turn him back. 'Freddy, it doesn't matter.'

But he had covered his face with his hands and raised his leg so that she could no longer see his shame.

'Freddy, I love you!' she cried. 'It doesn't matter. Please, let me hold you.'

'Oh Monique,' he sobbed, as he buried his face in her neck. 'Monique! What a child you must think me.'

'No, you are a man, Freddy. A man who is finding love for the first time.'

'I am so ashamed.'

She smiled, and kissed and stroked his hair until finally he pulled away.

'Can we try again?' he asked. Then, colouring, he added, 'I don't mean today. I mean, can we. . .? Maybe to-morrow. . .'

'Of course, *chéri*. But not tomorrow. I must go with *Maman* to Paris tomorrow. But I shall return next week. You will wait for me?'

'Yes, oh yes!' he gasped.

'Oh, Freddy,' she laughed. 'You are so romantic!'

As they strolled back down the hill, hand in hand, she leaned against him and said, 'I wonder what everyone will say when we tell them?'

'Tell them what?' he said, horrified.

'That we are going to be married, silly,' she laughed. 'When should we tell them? Shall we do it today, when we get back? But no, maybe it's a little too early. I think we should wait until I return from Paris . Oh, Freddy, I'm so happy. I love you so much. I want to hold you in my arms and never let you go. Do you feel the same way, *chéri*? Tell me you love me too. Tell me you've waited all your life for this to happen. But you're only nineteen, how could you have known it would happen so soon? But me, I have been waiting for you. . .

'I knew that one day you would come, that there was a reason for all the rejection I have suffered. But those men, pah! They mean nothing now. They are *épiciers* compared to you – you, who are so sweet and so full of love. How am I going to keep this to myself, Freddy, when I want to shout it from the hilltops? I think, don't you, that we must spend our summers in France, but I can barely wait to see your home, my darling. And soon, very soon, we shall fill it with children . . .'

He let her go on, too stunned to interrupt. All he was thinking was, when, during those few ecstatic moments, had he asked her to marry him? He had no recollection of it, but he must have asked her or she wouldn't be carrying on like this. He felt almost suffocated by his own breath as he tried to speak, tried to assure her that he loved her. Only an hour ago he had hardly been able to stop himself saying it, yet now . . .

Why was it that she suddenly seemed like a stranger when they had just shared such intimate moments? Why was it that he wanted to pull his arm away, to escape her, when earlier the very touch of her fingertips had set him on fire with passion? Why was it that everything she was saying repelled him? The more she went on, the worse it became. Even the sound of her voice, that beautiful throaty voice, now grated on his ears.

By the time her chauffeur had dropped him at Montvisse, and she had promised a thousand times that she would call him that night and then again from Paris the next day, he was beginning to realize that he would never again recapture the feelings he had had beside the lake. He still could not be sure why they had changed, and as he turned from waving Monique off and went into the château, he had no idea what he was going to do about it. He went upstairs to his room, informing the butler that he wouldn't be wanting dinner that evening.

He sat on the edge of his bed, letting the hours slip by. He saw his life's plans, his hopes and dreams float away from him. He longed to talk to someone, but who could he tell? Dissy was no longer in France, and it was unthinkable that he should mention this to Céline. In the end, he realized that there was no way out. If he had asked Monique to marry him during those lust-crazed moments, then it would make him the greatest cad on earth if he were to spurn her after she had all but given herself to him.

At ten o'clock his valet knocked, and with a heavy heart Freddy prepared himself for bed. The joy of being in France had been extinguished, and he longed only to go home.

It was one of those crisp days of early autumn, when the light was so clear that Paris was even more beautiful than in the spring. The leaves on the trees lining the avenue Foch glinted gold in the brilliant sunlight, and the air was bracing. The breeze that wafted in through the open window of Élise Pascale's drawing-room carried not only the sleepy purr and growl of afternoon traffic but also the haunting strains of 'Tout va bien' played on a gramophone in an apartment below.

Élise adored this time of year – but then she adored every time of year, she adored her whole life, and never a day passed when she did not thank the Good Lord for enabling her to use her exceptional beauty to such unforeseen advantage.

It was her striking resemblance to Titian's *Venus of Urbino* that had started her on the road to success, for that was what had first captured the eye of Gustave Gallet, the now forgotten artist who had passed through Toulouse ten years ago, and in return for her favours had taken her to Paris. Before leaving Toulouse her ambition had been merely to marry a man of means and status, and when Gallet first appeared she had already made some headway with the son of the local *préfet*. But the moment Paris was mentioned, she had seen all her dreams start to come true . . . Ever since her daughter was old enough to understand, and right up to the time of her own death, Élise Pascale's mother had read her stories of the great courtesans of France, La Pompadour, Diane de Poitiers, Agnés Sorrel, women whose rise and fall had never ceased to fascinate them both. Élise wanted to be one of them, she wanted her name too to go down in history, and it had angered her that she was living in a France where there were no longer any kings, where she could never be a royal mistress. But then Gustave Gallet had taken her to Paris, and she had known that somehow she was going to make herself the most talked about woman in all France.

Unfortunately, soon after their arrival in the city Gallet had died, and for three years Élise had been an artist's model, moving from one cramped studio to the next. Then she had acquired her own modest apartment on the Quai de la Tournelle, paid for by an ageing film director, Alain Mureau. She had grown fond of Mureau during their eight months together, but when, at a party to celebrate his latest film, she was presented to Gérard, the bohemian son of the Duc de Verlons, she had no compunction whatever in consigning her lover to the past. And with Gérard her career really began to take off, for he took great delight in introducing her to his wealthy and influential friends, and Élise soon discovered that there was little she wouldn't do to get what she wanted, and no one she minded hurting along the way.

And now here she was, luxuriously ensconced on the avenue Foch. She never missed her daily prayer of gratitude – but it was at the shrine of her own voluptuous body that she most frequently worshipped, for it was that wonderful body, that face with its brazenly alluring features, that had got her where she was today. That, and ambition – which had seized her first all those years ago in Toulouse, and even now, despite her success, still burned like a fire in her veins.

And now, as she stood at her drawing-room window looking along the avenue to the Arc de Triomphe, Élise felt so triumphant herself, so happy, that she wanted to laugh. For she was not alone in the room; and her engagements for the rest of the day were even now being cancelled by Gisèle, her maid, who had taken the diary to the telephone in the dining-room so that she should not disturb her mistress and their unexpected visitor.

As yet François had said little, but it was not in his nature to indulge in idle talk, and besides, his presence here, at her apartment, told Élise all she wanted to know. It would be unwise to express her delight, though, even if her heart was singing like a teenager's; François was well aware of the effect he had on her but he hated her to show her feelings. So Élise kept them to herself, and displayed instead the kind of bored sophistication and cat-like indolence he preferred. It was like a game, a game she had come to excel at: always careful to read his moods before she spoke, judging when to disguise her love beneath a mask of indifference; always concealing the deep, secret fear that one day she would lose him. For she loved him as she had never loved any other man.

She took a deep breath, then turned from the window to look across the sumptuously furnished drawing-room. With its muted shades of turquoise and yellow it was a blatantly feminine room, arranged so that every chair and sofa faced the tall arched windows and the white wrought-iron balustrades of the balconies beyond. As she looked at François a teasing light flashed in her narrowed emerald eyes. 'So,' she drawled in her low, husky voice, 'you are married.'

François was sitting in an Aubusson tapestried armchair, his long legs stretched out in front of him, a Gauloise in one hand and a glass of his own wine in the other. For answer, he merely raised an eyebrow, took a final draw on his cigarette and ground it out in the ashtray beside him.

The corners of Élise's soft mouth twitched. Lifting a hand-mirror from the little table beside her, she inspected her delicately rouged lips and patted the waves of her expertly coiffed yellow-gold hair. 'I didn't expect to see you so soon,' she remarked.

When again he didn't answer, she put down her mirror and went to sit near him on the sofa. 'Weren't you supposed to be in Biarritz for *two* weeks?' she asked.

'My wife was eager to leave,' François answered, taking a sip of wine.

'She didn't find Biarritz to her liking?'

He met her eyes, and after a moment or two the corner of his mouth pulled into a smile. 'Shall we just say that my wife prefers to be at Lorvoire?' he said smoothly.

She hated him referring to The Bitch as his wife, but said nothing, understanding that she would be wise to let the matter rest there.

'Have you heard from von Pappen?' he asked, holding out his glass to be refilled.

'I thought he'd left a message for you at Poitiers?'

'He did. Do you know where he is now?'

'In Munich, I believe.'

François was quiet for a moment. Then, as she handed him his wine, he said, 'I am leaving for Berlin in a few days. I want him to meet me there.'

'Berlin?'

'I have a new customer there with a penchant for Lorvoire wine.'

Their eyes met fleetingly, and Élise smiled. Sitting down again, she rested her finely pointed chin on her hand and watched him as he sat once more immersed in the privacy of his thoughts.

It was two years since he had come into her life, and almost as long since she had fallen so desperately in love with him that, when he asked it, she had abandoned every one of her other rich and titled lovers and kept herself for him alone. From that time on, he had become her whole life. Only once had she made the mistake of telling him how she felt about him. In return he had made it plain that he did not love her, and did not now – nor ever would – entertain the slightest intention of marrying a whore from the gutters of Toulouse.

It wasn't the first time he had called her that, but it was the first time she had allowed her fury and pain to get the better of her. The clock she hurled at him had missed, but the bone china pot she threw after it found its mark, and blood began to flow from the barely healed scar on his face as he moved purposefully towards her. Terror kept her fighting, beating her hands against his chest and insulting him with all the foul language she knew, until he threw her across the sofa and began to make love to her. But it was hate, not love, for at the end he had left her begging and screaming for the total satisfaction he sadistically denied her.

'Love me if you must,' he told her when he had had his fill of her, 'but I don't want to hear it. All I want from you is what I have just taken.'

After that she hadn't seen him for a month, during which time she had heard the rumours about Hortense de Bourchain. Immediately she had resolved never to see him again; but when at last he came again, when he stood looking at her with those mesmeric black eyes, she had felt herself drawn to him as a moth to a candle. She had run towards him, ready to embrace him – but he put out a hand and held her at a distance, looking at her. Then, with a smile that twisted through her heart like a knife, he had lifted his hand to her cheek, saying, 'I shall never repeat this, but perhaps you should know that I desire you as I've never desired another woman in my life. I will give you all that I am able to give, and it will be to you, and you alone, that I shall turn for fulfilment. However, your declarations of love revolt me – which is why I spoke as I did. And I warn you, that is the only response you will ever get from me should you be so unwise as to mention your feelings again.'

And then he had pulled her into his arms, and kissed her with a tenderness he had never shown her before. That was when, looking up into those curiously compelling eyes, she first began to recognize the extent of his power.

In the months that followed she had seen him exercise that same anomalous power over politicians and generals, and she began to realize that François was playing some sort of political game. By observing him closely, she soon understood, too, the nature of that game. It was dangerous, more than dangerous, at times it was lethal, but then she had suspected from the beginning that any association with François de Lorvoire would be exceptional . . .

After a time, in quiet ways, she had let him know that she understood what he was doing and that he could trust her. To her surprise he seemed to accept it – though he was always scrupulously careful to conceal from her the precise details of the information he auctioned while they entertained ambassadors, generals and even prime ministers at her apartment; and though she had tried on many occasions, she had never been able to discover the source of his information. What she did know was that he had connections in the corridors of power that went right to the very top, not only in Paris, but in London, Rome and Berlin. In these critical times, such connections could be extremely profitable. She also knew – as their dinner guests did not – that François' patriotism was, to say the least, questionable: his dealings were often complicated, even tortuous, but ultimately the information he had for sale went to the highest bidder. And always before the information was handed over, François would graciously accept a munificent order for the unexceptional though perfectly palatable, Lorvoire wine. For a proprietor of vineyards, selling wine was the most natural cover in the world, and it enabled François to move about Europe without exciting suspicion . . .

Élise looked up. François, emerging from his thoughts, was getting up and walking over to the telephone. She had missed him these past ten days, and now his vast shoulders, arrogant, almost sinister face and powerful hands were arousing her in a way she couldn't ignore. She took a deep breath and swallowed hard, trying to prove to herself that she could – if only this once – conquer her need for him, but as he turned and casually crossed one long leg over the other, resting against the back of a chair, she found herself moving towards him.

A flicker of surprise sparked in his eyes as he saw her standing there, then he smiled as he read what was on her mind. Her heart turned over at the rare expression of tenderness on his face, and already her breath was quickening as he lifted a hand and cupped it around her delicate jaw, drawing her to him. But as his mouth closed over hers, the telephone operator chose that moment to ring back, and he pushed her away.

'Get me Lorvoire four-five-nine,' he said into the receiver.

Élise's carefully schooled features betrayed nothing of what she was feeling, but the fact that he was calling his home angered her. 'I will give you all that I am able to give,' he had said, 'and it will be to you, and you alone, that I shall turn for fulfilment . . .'

There had never been any doubt in her mind that he meant what he had said, and he had never done anything since to suggest that his intentions had changed. In fact he had gone out of his way to tell her of his marriage plans before she could hear them from anyone else, and had even gone on to explain that the Rafferty girl was his father's choice, not his – it was a marriage of convenience. She had been moved by his unprecedented consideration for her feelings, and so convinced of his aversion to the match that she had almost pitied *l'Anglaise*.

That was until she had laid eyes on the bitch.

She had never asked François for a description of his

intended. English women all looked the same as far as she was concerned – buck teeth, rosy cheeks and sturdy thighs. But when La Rafferty had turned out to be at least six years her junior, and so breathtakingly beautiful that all Paris was talking about her, Élise had turned sick with fear and jealousy: Louis de Lorvoire always had known what he was doing, and in the choice of bride for his son he had remained consistent.

By way of comfort, Élise would remind herself of what François had said after his first encounter with The Bitch. 'If it wasn't that Beavis would consider it a great insult, I should ask him to remove his daughter from Lorvoire within the week. As it is, she gives me the distinct impression she has made up her mind to marry me, and seems quite undaunted by the fact that I find her not only superficial but lamentably immature.'

Despite her jealousy, Élise had found his predicament amusing, and had laughed aloud when he'd told her how Claudine had kicked his foot into the fountain. Obviously, Claudine didn't have what it took to handle a man like François: a subtlety and cunning to match his own, and the ability to recognize his changing moods without registering any kind of emotional reaction. Claudine Rafferty was too gauche and too flighty even to begin to understand what was necessary to negotiate the darker side of François' nature. But reality would hit her soon enough, and providing The Bitch wasn't some kind of masochist, it wouldn't be too long, Élise had told herself then, before she went scuttling back to England where she belonged.

But, to Élise's horror, within eight days of meeting the girl François had come to her and demanded that she, Élise, pay a visit to Van Cleef and Arpels to select a ring of betrothal. She had chosen the ring, as she did everything François asked of her, with taste and care, but she had resolved there and then that, if ever it was necessary, she would not hesitate to betray him and let The Bitch know her precious ring had been the choice of her husband's mistress.

When Monique had come to see her, two weeks before the wedding, to suggest that together they might somehow arrange to be rid of Claudine, Élise's initial response had been one of enthusiasm. But then she had remembered François' uncanny knack of finding out the very thing you least wanted him to know – and though he might not want the marriage with Claudine himself, he could not be guaranteed to find interference from other parties – in particular his 'whore from Toulouse' – acceptable.

But as the day of the wedding drew closer, Élise had begun to wonder if she had done the right thing in sending Monique away; their interference might have been welcome after all – for François was now almost beside himself with rage that the girl refused to pull out. 'She behaves as though I am in love with her and refusing to believe it!' he stormed. 'What must I do to prove that I find her the most tedious woman it has ever been my misfortune to meet? God knows, I don't want to be married at all – I don't want a woman meddling in my affairs or wheedling for my attention – but if I must marry, why in hell did my father have to pick someone who is nothing more than a wilful, over-indulged child? I can't understand why my parents are so ridiculously smitten with her. She's a fool. She's even fooled herself into thinking she's in love with me.'

Élise was surprised. 'You've mentioned nothing about this before. Do you really think she's falling in love with you?'

'It isn't what I think, it's what *she* thinks. Well, there's only one way to make her see how ridiculous she is . . .'

That had been two days before the wedding. Then had come Claudine's flight from the honeymoon suite – François had no idea Élise knew about that – followed by an early return from Biarritz. Clearly, François had achieved what he had set out to do and knowing him as she did, Élise shuddered at the thought of the methods he would have employed.

And yet, no matter what had passed between Claudine and François over the past ten days, Élise was still wary. It was a perverse truth that François' unsightliness and his disdain only added to the power of his attraction. Claudine had certainly been strongly attracted before the wedding, even if she wasn't now; who was to say that marriage might not revive the attraction – or even that François might not come to be attracted to Claudine? That was what frightened Élise more than anything else, for if she lost François she lost everything. As his mistress, she, the daughter of a Toulouse *forgeron*, was a member of polite society; she received invitations to the opera and the theatre, she was included on the guest lists for charity balls and excursions to the races at Longchamp. She would never, of course, be invited into the homes of the people she mixed with, but for now at least, it was enough that the men came to her apartment to meet François, and that her skills as a hostess were properly recognized. Often the men came when François was away, but there was never anything furtive or unseemly in their visits, they came simply because they enjoyed her company; the bachelors among them might walk with her in the Tuileries Gardens or take her for coffee to a pavement café in Montmartre. Élise took great pleasure in her popularity, for she had no close friends of her own. Since knowing François she had had no need of them – he gave her everything.

But what really mattered to Élise more than anything else – more than the friends François brought her, the clothes, the jewels, the success – were the hours they spent alone together, when the mere touch of his fingers could inflame her with such desire that she felt without him she might die. No man had ever done to her the things that François de

Lorvoire did, and no man had made such demands of her. She had thought she knew all there was to know about the art of making love, but he had shown her ecstasy and she dreaded above all else to lose it. To lose it to Claudine . . . For if François were ever to make love to Claudine the way he did to her, it would mean only one thing, that he had fallen in love with his wife . . .

Élise, turning these uncomfortable thoughts over in her mind, had wandered from the drawing-room into the bedroom and now stood staring absently down at the bed. She was so deep in thought that she didn't realize François had followed her until she heard the door close behind him.

She turned, and when she saw him standing there, his dark, unshaven face looking meaner than ever, her eyes began to shine with hunger. 'What happened to the telephone call?' she murmured.

'It can wait,' he answered, starting towards her.

'You mean, you aren't eager to speak to your wife?'

He laughed, and reached behind her to pull the clip from her hair. 'As a matter of fact, I was calling my mother. Lucien is leaving Spain and returning to his regiment.'

'Oh?' She turned her head to kiss his hand as his fingers raked gently through her hair. Now wasn't the time to pursue the implications of Lucien's decision, so she only said, 'You've seen Lucien since the wedding?'

'I have,' he confirmed, using his free hand to unfasten his collar. He smiled. 'So you see, there was no need for you to be jealous that I was calling Lorvoire.'

She laughed softly. 'You know me too well.' And putting her arms around his neck, she tilted her face to his.

The touch of his lips was light, but it was enough to send an electrifying thrill through her body. She pressed herself against the hardness of his thighs, but he removed her arms from his neck and went to lie on the bed. It was her cue to undress.

For a while, as she peeled the clothes from the rounded curves of her body, Élise kept her eyes lowered, not wanting him to see her expression ... If François had seen Lucien in the past ten days, it could only mean that he had left Claudine in Biarritz with the maid. And if he was telephoning his mother, it must mean that he had come straight to Paris – to her – leaving Claudine to return to Lorvoire alone.

Élise's sense of triumph was intoxicating. It was highly probable, she thought, that Claudine was afraid of François by now, something which in itself would disgust him. She laughed quietly to herself. There seemed little chance now that this marriage would work – and she, Élise Pascale, was going to do everything in her power to see that it didn't. For no matter how often François told her he would never marry her, she knew that in the end he would. And that would set her apart from all the great courtesans of France. Not for her the humiliation of being cast aside in preference for another: one day she was going to be the Comtesse de Rassey de Lorvoire. And though The Bitch presented an enormous obstacle, Élise Pascale would overcome it – by whatever means she felt compelled to employ.

– 9 –

Still in her dressing-gown and slippers, Claudine was sitting on the sofa in her and François' suite at the Lorvoire château, listening in mounting disbelief to what her sister-in-law was saying. Monique had welcomed her home the night before with astonishing warmth, and then said she would come to her apartment first thing in the morning because she had something of the utmost importance to tell her: but not even in her wildest imaginings had Claudine guessed what it was.

'. . . that's why I've been so longing for you to come home,' Monique gushed, tightening her grip on Claudine's hands. 'I know that's selfish of me when you were on your honeymoon, but you just don't know how wonderful it is to have a sister at last, someone I can confide in. I hope you think of me in the same way. And you know Freddy so well! It'll help him, having you here, a familiar face, and he's so incredibly fond of you. I confess I was a little jealous at first, but now . . . Oh Claudine, I'm so happy. Are you surprised? No, don't deny it, of course you are. Everyone will be when we tell them, but what does the difference in our ages matter when we love each other? There are twelve years between you and François, and no one said a thing about that, did they?'

'Not about that, no,' Claudine murmured. Then forcing a smile, she said, 'Have you set a date for the wedding yet?'

'No, not yet. Perhaps it's a little soon after yours to be thinking about it this year. I've always been rather keen to have a Spring wedding, what do you think? Spring next year?'

'I think it sounds ideal,' Claudine answered, not knowing what else she could say.

'I'll put it to Freddy later, I'm sure he'll agree. He dotes on me, Claudine, it's quite touching to see.'

'And what about you? Do you dote on him?'

Monique gave a squeal of laughter. 'Of course! How can anyone not dote on Freddy? He's so romantic. He writes me poems all the time. If you promise not to tell, I'll show you – they're so passionate I could almost blush when I read them.'

'How much longer is he staying at Montvisse?' Claudine asked. 'I mean, isn't Tante Céline returning to Paris soon?'

'Oh, haven't you heard? But of course you haven't, how could you? Céline has decided to stay on at Montvisse indefinitely, and she's told Freddy he's welcome to stay for as long as he likes. Naturally, I've invited him to Lorvoire, but he says it might be a little *difficult* for him to be under the same roof as me all the time. Isn't he naughty, thinking things like that?'

Claudine couldn't help being glad that at that moment there was a knock on the door and Louis appeared. 'All right to come in?'

'Of course,' Claudine smiled, standing up and holding out her arms. 'How are you? And how's Solange?'

'I couldn't be better,' he said, embracing her. 'And Solange is fine too. Last time I saw her she was doing something drastic to her maid's hair!'

Laughing, Claudine led him to the sofa. 'I'm sorry I was too tired to join you all for dinner last night,' she said.

'Oh, I quite understand, *ma chère*. It was a long journey, and with the weather being so dismal in Biarritz . . . But as you can see, it's no better here. It hasn't stopped raining for three days.'

'Claudine!' a voice suddenly sang out. 'Where are you, *chérie*?' And then Solange bustled in, a scarf tied around her hair, her dressing-gown misbuttoned, and her hands behind her back. As soon as she saw her mother-in-law's intent, childlike face Claudine felt a lump rise in her throat, and she moved quickly to take her in her arms.

'No! Wait!' Solange cried. 'I have something here for you.' And with a flourish she pulled a huge bunch of flowers from behind her back. 'Welcome home!'

'Oh Solange!' Before Claudine could stop them, tears welled up in her eyes. 'Solange,' she said again, as she took the flowers and put an arm about her shoulders. 'I've missed you.'

'Not half as much as she's missed you,' Louis remarked. 'Monique had to take her to Paris at the weekend before she drove me insane.'

'Don't talk about me as if I weren't here,' Solange

retorted haughtily. 'And I won't remind you how many times you telephoned me while I was there, because I lost count. However, suffice it to say you were going insane *without* me.'

Looking at them, Claudine suddenly found herself wondering how two such wonderful people could have fathered a son like François. Quickly, before the tears came, she said, 'I'll take the flowers in to Magaly,' and giving Solange another kiss, she vanished into her bedroom.

Her maid was in the bathroom, rearranging the Lalique bottles on a shelf. 'Can you see to these, Magaly?'

'Of course, *madame*.' Magaly gave her a searching look, but with a small shake of her head Claudine disappeared into her dressing-room. She wouldn't cry any more, and she wouldn't talk about him any more either.

From a dressing-table drawer she took a handkerchief and dabbed at her eyes. Magaly knew everything of course. How could she not when she had spent those ten horrific days in Biarritz with them? But she wouldn't think about that now, she would never think about it again. The tears she had shed every time François left her bed had changed nothing then, and tears would change nothing now. What she needed to do now was to settle down to her new life at the château and the fact that she was his wife, she told herself forcefully, was not to be allowed to affect things *in any way*. What passed between them at night took half an hour or less, and providing she kept out of his way the rest of the time, her life and her emotions were her own to govern.

'Oh, *Maman*, do we have to?' Monique was grumbling as Claudine walked back into the sitting-room.

'Have to what?' Claudine asked brightly.

'*Maman* has arranged for us to visit the de Voisins at Montbazon this afternoon,' Monique answered. 'Couldn't we telephone and explain that Claudine has arrived, so we can't make it today?'

'But they will want to see Claudine too!' Solange cried.

'I should imagine,' Louis interrupted, 'that Claudine is eager to visit her aunt – *alone*,' he added forcefully, seeing his wife's eyes light up at the prospect of a visit to Céline. 'So I think it a very good idea that you take your mother to Montbazon, Monique, then tonight we shall have dinner here and invite Céline and Freddy to join us. How does that sound?'

'Dinner!' Solange shrieked, leaping to her feet. 'We are having dinner here? Then I must go and talk to Arlette.'

'Why doesn't Claudine have a word with the cook?' Louis suggested.

'Claudine! But she's a guest!'

Louis shook his head, and Solange blinked. Then her hands flew to her face and she gave a cry of joyous comprehension. 'And you, *chérie*,' Louis continued, smiling, 'can go and rescue poor Tilde from those new-fangled curlers you've bound her up in.'

'Oh, Tilde! I'd quite forgotten about her!' Solange gasped. She started from the room, then turned back. 'Oh, Claudine,' she said, 'I have a message for you from François. He telephoned last night, after you had gone to bed. He says he will return in time for dinner this evening.' She frowned. 'Or did he say Lucien would be here for dinner? I forget.'

'François is coming this evening,' Louis said, taking off his spectacles and wiping them with his handkerchief. 'Lucien will be here next week.'

Claudine's heart had given a sickening lurch on hearing that François would return so soon, but she was still smiling as she said, 'I've yet to learn what you all like to eat, so I'm not sure I'm the one to talk to Arlette.'

'Nonsense,' Louis answered kindly. 'Arlette knows anyway. And you'll be mistress of Lorvoire one day, so . . .'

'Oh Papa!' Monique exclaimed. 'Claudine has only just

returned from her honeymoon, stop rushing her. *I* will talk to Arlette, and you must take your medication before Doctor Lebrun arrives . . .'

Monique didn't stay long after her father had gone, and to her relief Claudine was left alone for the remainder of the morning. Feigning happiness with her own marriage was one thing, and God knew how difficult that was, but having to pretend to be happy for Monique and Freddy was, just for the moment, beyond her. She was certain, knowing Freddy as she did, that there had been some terrible misunderstanding, but until she spoke to him there was nothing to be done.

Her Lagonda had been brought to Lorvoire while she was in Biarritz, so that afternoon she drove herself over to Montvisse through the pouring rain, the canvas roof firmly in place and the windscreen-wipers creaking frenziedly back and forth. She had done a great deal of thinking while she was in Biarritz, and some of it had been about Tante Céline and her father.

When she had returned to Montvisse on that terrible morning of her flight from Poiters, she had already been in a state of shock, and finding her father and Tante Céline in bed together had been almost more than she could take. Later that day, when she was a little calmer, the three of them had talked; Beavis and Tante Céline left her in no doubt that their relationship had begun long after Antoinette's death, and Claudine had assured them that she understood and forgave them – not that there was really anything to forgive. And she *had* forgiven her father; but somehow it hadn't seemed so easy to forgive Tante Céline, and the last thing that happened before François dragged her off to Biarritz was that she spent a hysterical few minutes calling Tante Céline every bad name she could think of. Her sense of shame at this had contributed to her unhappiness in Biarritz, and what she wanted very much now was to see her aunt and set things right . . . But Tante Céline, Claudine was informed when she arrived at Montvisse, had gone to the beauty salon at Tours and was not expected back until about four o'clock.

Claudine's heart sank. If Tante Céline had gone all the way to Tours on a day when she knew her niece was coming, it surely meant that she was avoiding her – or punishing her. But she cheered up a little when she saw Freddy poke his head out of the library, and with a genuinely warm smile she ran into his arms.

'Oh no, old thing, Céline isn't avoiding you,' Freddy said, when she told him what was on her mind. 'She already had the appointment – she wasn't expecting you back until the end of the week, remember – and one told her to go ahead because one was longing to have you to oneself for a while.'

'Was one indeed?' Claudine said, with a sidelong glance that set his cheeks on fire.

Grinning, she pulled off her gloves, unpinned her hat, then threw them onto the bureau as she flopped into a chair. '*Mon Dieu*, it's cold in here,' she shivered, rubbing her hands as she leaned towards the newly lit fire. 'It's like winter already.'

'How does it feel to be back?' he said. 'Did you like Biarritz?'

'Biarritz was fine,' she answered. 'And how have you found Touraine?'

'Oh, fine.'

The flatness of his voice made her look up, and when she saw the gloomy expression on his face she found it difficult not to smile. 'It's all right, Freddy,' she said, 'Monique's already told me. So come on, out with it, what have you been up to, you rogue? Or shall I call you a Casanova?' she added as she reached for his hand.

'Please, don't!' he said in a pained voice. 'Don't! I have no idea how this has happened, but Clo, one is practically engaged!'

'So I hear,' she chuckled. 'And I take it from your expression that you don't particularly want to be?'

Miserably he shook his head.

'Then you'd better start at the beginning. And don't look so worried, I'm sure we'll find a solution.'

But by the time he had finished his tale of woe, she wasn't quite so sure. Of course, if Freddy were a little more like François he wouldn't have a problem, but being the honourable gentleman he was, he was bound to feel obliged to marry a girl if he so much as kissed her, never mind what he had actually done with Monique. And Monique, of course, had realized that. But instead of being angry with Monique, Claudine was sorry for her. That she should feel so desperate that she had to trick a young boy into marrying her was heart-rending.

'What can one do, Clo?' Freddy said, looking at her with his limpid, puppy-like eyes. 'Do you suppose one will have to go through with it?'

Claudine shook her head. 'I don't know, darling. If I thought it would help I would talk to Monique myself, but . . .'

'Could you!' he cried, squeezing her hands. 'She'll listen to you, I know. She's so terribly, terribly fond of you . . .'

'Is that what she told you?'

'Yes. Oh, yes. *Elle a de la presence*, she said, whatever that means. She thinks you're topping, Clo, and you'll be so much better than one could ever be at letting her down gently.' He stopped, then looking at her sideways, he said, 'Do you think one should just pop back to England, though, before you do it? You know, sort of get out of the way?'

'No, I most certainly do not!' Claudine laughed. 'And neither am *I* going to let her down gently. Don't look at me like that! I'm not saying you have to marry her, but what I am saying is that you have to take responsibility for what you have done. I know she seduced you,' she smiled as Freddy's cheeks started to burn, 'but you have been writing her some rather passionate poetry she tells me . . .'

'But Clo, one didn't mean her to . . .'

'Oh yes one did, Freddy! What you didn't mean her to do was assume you were going to marry her as a result. Now, you are absolutely certain that you didn't actually propose when you were . . . incapable, shall we say?'

'Oh, absolutely! I've thought about it and thought about it, and I just don't see how one could have. I mean, it was the furthest thing from one's mind . . .'

'Hm.' Claudine was silent for a moment. 'Well, what matters now is that we get you out of this mess and back to Oxford before it's too late. The question is, how?'

He gazed up at her pleadingly, and she sat forward to plant a kiss on the end of his nose.

'I know you'll think of something, Clo. I just know you will.'

The telephone started ringing then, and Claudine got up to answer it. 'Well, whatever it is,' she said, 'you have a lesson to learn here, Freddy Prendergast, so you will be the one to let her down gently, not I. Savigny 222,' she said into the receiver. She turned to Freddy, unable to stop the grin spreading across her face. 'Yes, Monique,' she continued into the telephone, 'it is Claudine here. No, I have no idea where Jean or Pierre are, so I answered myself. No, Céline isn't here either, she's in Tours. Yes, yes he is.' She grinned as Freddy started frantically shaking his head. 'I'll put him on.'

Glaring at her, Freddy took the receiver, and Claudine, laughing, went into the drawing-room to save his embarrassment.

Five minutes later, Freddy appeared, his fresh, young face as pink as his tie and his mane of sandy hair in wild disorder. 'Monique asked one to remind you to invite Céline and one to dinner tonight,' he said morosely.

'Of course,' Claudine said. 'Consider yourself invited.' She waited. 'Well,' she pressed, 'what else did she say?'

'Oh, Clo!' he wailed, clasping his head in his hands. 'She wants to announce our engagement. Tonight!'

'Oh, Freddy,' Claudine sighed, trying not to laugh.

He threw himself down on the sofa. 'I'm doomed,' he groaned tragically. 'Doomed!'

'Not necessarily. I'll talk her into postponing it.'

'I don't want a postponement, I want a cancellation!' he cried.

'We don't always get what we want in this life, Freddy,' she said, a little more harshly then she'd intended. He gave her a curious look, and she went on quickly, 'A postponement I can virtually guarantee. Lucien is coming home in a few days time, just for the night *en route* to join his regiment. For that night, assuming François isn't called away, the whole family will be together, and I'll advise Monique to make the announcement then. How does that sound?'

'Better,' he nodded dismally. 'Better, but not perfect.'

'Freddy, you aren't still moping around the place, are you?' Céline was standing at the door, and the instant Claudine saw her, tears stung painfully at her eyes. Hastily she blinked them away – how ridiculous she was to be so moved by the sight of people she loved!

Céline looked back at her niece, then with a smile she lifted her arms and held them out to her. '*Ma chérie,*' she murmured, as Claudine went to her.

'Tante Céline. Oh, Tante Céline, I'm so sorry. I'm so . . .' She stopped as Céline put a finger over her lips.

'There is nothing to be sorry for, *chérie,*' she said. 'We will talk later, but for now I must have some tea.'

Of course they couldn't talk in front of Freddy, but already her aunt had made it clear that she had forgiven the dreadful outburst, and Claudine felt a weight had been lifted from her heart.

Tea was brought, and Claudine heard about what had been happening at Montvisse while she was away, and told them all she wanted them to know about Biarritz. She knew she wasn't deceiving her aunt, even for a minute, but it was vital to her for her own sake to keep up appearances.

It was a little after five when the telephone rang again, and Pierre came to tell Freddy the call was for him. Choking back her laughter at Freddy's anguished face, Claudine waited for him to leave the room before turning to her aunt.

Céline held up her hands. 'I don't want to know,' she said. 'He's got himself into some kind of trouble with Monique de Lorvoire, and as far as I'm concerned he must get himself out of it.'

'My sentiments exactly,' Claudine said. 'But I can't abandon him altogether – after all, he is only nineteen.' She paused and looked Céline straight in the eye. 'Any more than you can bring yourself to abandon me, and I'm twenty-two,' she added meaningfully. 'That is, I take it, why you are staying on at Montvisse?'

Smiling, Céline brushed her fingers over Claudine's face, then helped herself to more tea. 'Am I allowed to ask why you are back from Biarritz so soon?' she said, dropping two lumps of sugar into her cup.

'The weather was atrocious, so François thought it better that we return to Lorvoire,' Claudine answered lightly.

Céline nodded. 'Except that François, so I hear, is in Paris.' Her eyes narrowed as she regarded her niece. 'How are things between you two now?' she said bluntly.

'As good as they'll ever be.'

'Meaning?'

'Meaning that I am over the shock of losing my virginity.'

Céline seemed cross. 'Please don't treat me like an idiot, *chérie*. It would have taken more than that for you to run away on your wedding night, but if you don't want to tell me, then don't.'

Claudine smiled. 'I'm sorry,' she said gently, 'but there's no point in going into why I left him that night, it's history now, and it simply isn't relevant any longer. Things have changed a great deal since. François and I now have a marriage that will suit us both.'

Céline sighed. She didn't like the sound of that at all. 'Why do I get the feeling that you are starting a life sentence?' she said.

'All marriages are life sentences,' Claudine laughed, 'if you want to put it that way. And mine is not so bad. I have Solange and Louis – and Monique and I will be friends eventually. And now that you are staying on in Touraine for a while, I am surrounded by people I love.'

'But . . .'

'*And*,' Claudine interrupted, 'if François and I continue the way we are, it shouldn't be too long before there's a baby at Lorvoire. So then everyone will be happy, including my husband.'

'So you are making love?' Céline said.

'That isn't what François calls it, but yes, I suppose we are.' She looked away. She didn't want to have to go into a detailed account of the nightly struggle between herself and François, particularly since she had now learned that life was a lot easier if she just did as he told her. Though he hadn't liked it much when she started to sing the Marseillaise at the top of her voice . . . She wouldn't do it again . . .

She looked up as the door burst open and Freddy all but fell into the room. 'Clo!' he cried. 'Clo! You know what we were talking about earlier? Well, I've just had the most fortunate phone call, and I think it will solve all my problems!'

By the time Claudine had heard Freddy's plan for extricating himself from Monique, and had said goodbye to Tante Céline, it was early evening. She still wanted to visit Liliane St Jacques, and there was just time, she thought, before she had to get back to the château to change for dinner.

The sky was almost dark as she drove through the village. She could see Armand in the café as she drove past, and for a moment she was tempted to join him, it looked so cosy inside. But it was Liliane, not Armand she had come to see, and there was no cosiness on earth to compare with Liliane St Jacques' kitchen, where garlic and herbs and pots and pans hung all over the unevenly plastered walls, and the ovens always gave out smells so appetizing that Claudine could feel her mouth watering even as she stepped out of the car and made a dash through the rain for the door.

By the time she reached it, it was already open, and Liliane's toothless smile was waiting to greet her. Her black headscarf was tied neatly under her chin, and her shapeless grey dress was covered by a faded, carrot-stained apron. Claudine had met her only a few times before the wedding, but like Solange and Monique she had come to regard her as almost one of the family.

Claudine stooped to embrace her, and Liliane pulled her into the warmth of the kitchen, clucking her delight that she had come to visit so soon. She sat her down at the table, then padded across the flagstones to ladle a cup of hot broth from the pot over the fire. While Claudine drank she continued to clean the vegetables she had set out on the table, all the time recounting in a low, scratchy voice the latest village doings. She knows all there is to know, Claudine thought fondly, but there isn't a malicious bone in her body; she sees good in everyone, even where there's none to see.

After a while Liliane got up and poured them each a tot of Lorvoire wine. Then she turned on the wireless so that Claudine could listen to the last part of the news broadcast, while she added her vegetables to a lamb stew she was cooking for Armand's supper.

The only light in the kitchen came from the fire in the huge stone hearth and the air was warm and steamy. Claudine allowed her eyes to close, only half-listening to the newscaster's dull monotone as he read out the details of a naval agreement Britain had signed with Germany, and the latest information from the Bourse. Her concentration waned altogether then, as she listened to the gentle drum of the rain outside and tried not to think of François. She had almost fallen asleep when suddenly the door opened with a quick burst of cold wind, and Armand came in.

'*Bonsoir*, Armand,' she smiled up at him.

'*Bonsoir, madame.*'

Claudine watched as he stamped the mud from his boots and unbuttoned his jacket. She had met him only once, on the day of her wedding, and she remembered now how much he had surprised her. From what Lucien had told her about the death of his wife and child, she had expected there to be an air of tragedy about him -- but, on the contrary, she had seen humour in his kind, handsome face, and his large blue eyes had shone with laughter as he danced the older women round the ballroom.

'I see you are sampling last year's vintage,' he said, smiling.

'Is it a particularly good one?' she asked, feeling herself responding to his warmth.

He pulled a thoughtful face. 'Not particularly,' he said. 'But it will sell.'

'I'm glad to hear it,' she laughed. 'As a matter of fact, I'm rather glad you're here. There's something I'd like to discuss with you.'

'Oh?' he said, taking off his jacket and hooking it over the back of a chair. He sat down at the head of the table and rested his blond head on his hand, while his mother set a glass before him and started to pour the wine.

'Well, it's more of a suggestion really,' Claudine said. 'François tells me that the grapes are to be harvested soon, and that there always used to be a celebration at the château when they were in. I was wondering if it would be a good idea to revive the tradition. What do you think?'

'Madame de Lorvoire,' Armand said, with irony in his voice, 'you're going to make yourself even more popular than you already are if you continue to come up with suggestions like that.'

'So you'll help?'

'Of course, *madame*.'

'Marvellous. And please stop addressing me as 'madame' when I know full well that you even call the Comte and Comtesse Louis and Solange. Perhaps you can spread the word. About the festival, I mean. See if anyone wants to join us, do anything to help, donate things . . .'

'A Frenchman, donate!' he cried throwing up his hands. 'Don't you know they all have porcupines in their pockets?'

Claudine burst out laughing, and Liliane chuckled too. Armand drained his glass, refilled Claudine's, then rolled back his sleeves and walked over to the enamel sink beneath the window.

'What sort of thing do you have in mind for the celebration?' Liliane asked Claudine.

'I'm not sure yet,' she answered. 'That was why I wanted to talk to you and Armand . . .'

While Claudine and his mother ran through some ideas, Armand turned on the tap and started washing his hands. He had passed Claudine's car on his way in, but it wasn't until he looked at it again now, through the kitchen window – abandoned haphazardly as it was at the bottom of the bank – that he remembered how he had seen her in it the morning after her wedding.

He picked up a towel, and wiping his hands, turned back into the room. Claudine had her back to him, but as he looked at her glorious mane of curls beneath that outrageously frivolous hat, and her delicate white hands lying on the table beside her glass, he experienced a sudden surge of feeling. She was trying hard not to show it, but he had seen it in her eyes: she was lonely and confused and frightened. It made him want to put his arms around her, and tell her he would be there for her if she needed him. But of course that would be an outrageous thing to do. And if he did it, how could he begin to justify it? He could not possibly tell her that the torment in her lovely blue eyes reminded him of the way another woman – another woman who loved François – had looked in the weeks before she died.

Armand knew Claudine had heard of Hortense because Lucien had told him so, but he was certain she didn't know the real truth about what had happened that night in the wine cave. Apart from François, Louis and Doctor Lebrun, Armand guessed that he was probably the only person in the world who did know. He had witnessed it with his own eyes. Even François did not know that; he had never told anyone except his wife, Jacqueline; how, hearing voices, he had come out of the tasting cellar at the back of the cave and stood frozen with horror as he saw François and Hortense struggling with the knife. How he had seen the silver blade, with François' great hand clutched around the handle, plunge into Hortense's chest.

François had been so quick in catching her and running with her to his car that by the time Armand reached the mouth of the cave, he was already speeding down the drive with Hortense's limp body beside him. Then Louis had appeared from nowhere, and from the look on his face it was clear that he too had seen a great deal of what happened.

'He'll be taking her to Doctor Lebrun,' Louis had said in a flat voice.

Armand had simply stared at him, then followed him into the cave. 'How do you know he's taking her to Lebrun?' he asked, his strained voice echoing eerily in the silence.

'I know my son,' Louis answered. 'But if you have any doubts, go after him.' He started to unravel the hose which was hooked on the wall.

'What are you doing?' Armand asked.

'Clearing up the mess.'

For the first time Armand had noticed the blood on the floor, and the sight of it seemed to jolt him back to reality. 'You can't do that!' he cried. 'If François has killed her . . .'

'François didn't kill her!'

'But I saw him! I saw what happened . . .'

'She wasn't dead. When he carried her out, she wasn't dead. Why do you think he's taken her to Lebrun?'

'But Louis, if they don't save her François will be . . .'

'They *will* save her!' Louis had thundered.

But they hadn't. Lebrun had fought for her life all through that night and into the next day, but in the end Hortense died and François was never brought to trial. Armand had no idea what Louis told the de Bourchain family, but they left France soon after, and as far as he knew they had never returned.

It was just over two years now since it happened, and still Armand despised himself for having remained silent. But as Louis pointed out at the time, if the de Bourchain family wanted the matter hushed up, then their wishes had to be respected. And certainly it had been easier that way. It would have been his word against François' and Louis', and though he cared nothing for François, he knew his father would have wanted him to stand by the Comte. If he had spoken out, whether the courts believed him or not he would have had to leave Lorvoire, and that would have broken his mother's heart.

For a long time after that night Armand had been unable

to look at François without remembering what he had seen, without remembering other things, too, that were still, even now, too painful to dwell on. But after a time it had become easier, mainly because François had continued to treat him just as he always had – like a brother. It had been a long struggle, but knowing that his bitterness was hurting no one but himself, Armand had finally learned how to live with it.

Claudine's voice brought him back to the present. 'That's a marvellous idea, Liliane,' she was saying. 'I really think we could hold the entire festival here in your cottage! And it's so kind of Armand to offer to sing for us . . .'

'What?' he barked.

'Ah, so you are still with us,' Claudine grinned, leaning back in her chair. 'We were beginning to wonder.'

'Me sing?' Armand repeated.

'Yes, sing,' she confirmed. 'Any song of your choice. Your mother tells me you have a wonderful voice, and I can play the piano, so I shall expect you for rehearsals up at the château every evening, starting tomorrow, until the grapes are in.'

Armand's eyes moved from her to his mother and back again. 'You're serious!'

'Of course we are,' Claudine said, winking at Liliane. In fact, now that she thought about it the idea was beginning to seem rather a good one. 'That's settled, then,' she said, getting up and picking up her gloves. 'If you know of any more talent in the village, let me know – I think the idea of a cabaret is a splendid one. I shall have to think of something for Solange to do, she's bound to want to join in. I know, perhaps you and she can sing a duet, Armand.'

'Now, hang on a . . .'

'And I shall think of a little play for the children to perform. What do you think, Liliane? We could do *Sleeping Beauty*. Charles Perrault's supposed to have got his inspiration from the château over at Rigny-Ussé, so that keeps it local. Yes, it's getting better all the time. I can hardly wait to tell Solange.' She paused. Armand was staring at her as if she had taken leave of her senses. 'Now,' she said, 'what do you suppose I can give François to do?'

Armand exploded into laughter. 'I'll tell you something,' he said. 'If you can persuade François to do anything at all, then you shall have my unconditional surrender and I will sing with Solange.'

'I accept the challenge,' Claudine said with a grin, holding out her hand. 'And now I really must go.' She was enjoying herself so much that she wished she could stay a little longer, but she must get back to the château for dinner.

'I'll be up at the caves tomorrow,' Armand said, as he opened the door for her. 'If you still want to know something about how we make the wine, then I'll be glad to show you. You asked me about it at the wedding, do you remember?'

'Of course I remember,' she smiled, though he suspected that she didn't. 'I'll look forward to it. What time should I come?'

'Around eleven might be best. The deliveries will be finished by then. Will François be at home tomorrow?'

Armand saw the hunted look come into her eyes. 'Yes,' she said, 'as far as I know.'

'Good. There are a few things I need to go over with him.'

'I'll tell him.' And kissing Liliane on both cheeks, she shook hands with Armand and went out into the damp night air.

Armand stood at the door watching her tail-lights weave back through the village. She's a remarkable woman, he was thinking to himself, quite remarkable. He grinned. And bossy too! When the car lights disappeared from view, he turned back into the cottage and his eyes were alive with laughter as he said to his mother, 'But I can't sing!'

François had already arrived by the time Claudine returned

to the château, though she didn't see him until he came into the drawing-room before dinner. She was sitting in a window-seat discussing the harvest celebration with Solange when the door opened, and without even having to turn round she knew at once that he was there.

As he walked into the room she looked up, but he was engaged in conversation with a man who had introduced himself to her on the stairs earlier as Captain Paul Paillole. He had driven down from Paris with François that afternoon, he had told her, and was looking forward to spending a few days at Lorvoire.

Claudine watched as François spoke quietly to Jean-Paul, the butler, then turned to greet Céline and Freddy. He did not once glance in her direction. She glared at him, longing somehow to humiliate him in return, but she managed to control the urge and continued her conversation with Solange.

Later, over dinner, served in front of a roaring fire in the dining-room, François again conversed mainly with the Captain and his father; Claudine wished she could be as oblivious to his presence as he clearly was to hers. At last she turned her attention to Monique who, she realized with dismay, was talking excitedly about weddings. It hadn't been difficult to persuade her to postpone the announcement of her engagement until the whole family was together, but as she listened to her now, and watched the way her feverish amber eyes continually sought Freddy's, Claudine was overcome with sadness. The way that Freddy planned to free himself from her would cause her real pain; she didn't deserve that kind of rejection, no matter how scheming she had been. Perhaps she should try and have another word with Freddy, Claudine thought, before he talked to Monique . . .

Feeling her aunt's eyes on her, she looked up and smiled, then turned to listen to Captain Paillole.

'Of course,' he was saying, 'the British navy may have a hundred and eighty destroyers, but we in France have fifteen more than the Germans' twenty-two, you know.'

'Nevertheless,' François said, setting down his wine glass, 'if it comes to it – and despite what they say at the Foreign Office, I think we can be fairly certain it will – we shall be relying heavily on the might of the Royal Navy. Statesmen and . . .'

Claudine had spoken almost before she realized. 'But I heard on the news that the Royal Navy have signed an agreement with Germany today, so surely . . .' Her heart-beat suddenly slowed as François moved his thunderous eyes to hers. There was silence round the table, and beneath that inimical gaze she began to feel herself tremble.

Then suddenly Louis laughed, and covering her hand with his, he said, 'Britain and Germany signed that agreement back in July, *ma chère*. What you heard on the news today was the fact that it is running into difficulties already.'

Claudine gazed down at her plate. Her fork was poised over the turbot in its creamy mushroom sauce, but as she dug into it she felt a dryness in her mouth that she knew would prevent her from eating. It had been a simple mistake, that was all, just a simple mistake . . . She stole another look at François and felt herself go tense with fury. But anger wasn't the answer, she had learned that, and reasoning with him was no good either. All she could do was try to ignore him; involve herself in the life of Lorvoire as much as she could, and never, *never* interrupt him when he was speaking . . .

Céline and Freddy didn't stay long after dinner, and to Claudine's relief Monique retired early so she and Solange went upstairs to Claudine's sitting-room for a nightcap. Louis, François and the Captain remained in the library until well past midnight, by which time Claudine was lying in bed, listening to the rain.

Her heart quickened as she heard the door to their apartment open. She could hear François' footsteps as he moved about the sitting-room, and thought how she had lain awake listening for that sound while he was away. Why was it, she wondered angrily, that she felt so empty when he was gone, yet hated him so when he was here?

She reached out to turn off the lamp beside the bed. She didn't want to see his face when he came in, she wanted to pretend that he wasn't really there, that the horrible pounding of his body was happening in a dream. But in her heart she knew that wasn't the real reason why she had turned off the light; she'd done it so that he wouldn't see the pain in her eyes when he got up to go.

When at last the door opened, the light from the sitting-room fell across the bed and she could see his monstrous silhouette as he stood there in the doorway. Though she couldn't see them, she could feel his eyes upon her, and defiantly she stared back. And then, though she could hardly believe her ears, she thought she heard him heave a sigh of resignation at the prospect of having to struggle with her again ... A great surge of anger erupted inside her; she flung back the bedcovers, hoisted her nightdress over her thighs and spat, 'Here you are, this is what you've come for, isn't it?'

His only response was to look at her. Then, loosening his tie and unbuttoning his collar, he walked towards the bed. As he came to a stop beside her, her nails bit into the palms of her hands – but his eyes weren't on her nakedness, they were gazing mockingly into hers. Then, saying nothing, he lifted the blankets and covered her again.

She glared up at him, a buzz of alarm sounding in her head. What foul trick was he about to play her now?

He reached out to turn on the lamp, then slid his hands into his pockets, all the time keeping his eyes fixed calmly on hers. She watched him warily as he sat on the end of the bed, leaning one shoulder against the bedpost and stretching out his legs. She could see the hideous scar that started beneath the corner of his right eye, and the soft light gleaming on the greased smoothness of his hair.

'I have asked the notary to come here tomorrow at three,' he said. 'He will arrange your allowance. If you find the amount unsatisfactory then I will naturally increase it. The money will be yours to do with as you please . . .'

'I have money of my own,' she snapped.

He nodded. 'I am well aware of that. But as I said, the money is yours, to do with as you please. If you choose not to use it . . .' he shrugged '. . . *ça ne fait rien.*'

She eyed him suspiciously; then a thought struck her. 'Guilt money!' she cried. 'Is that what it is? Does it salve your conscience to pay for what you're doing to me? Or is it your sick way of making me feel like a whore?'

His jaw tightened, but he said nothing, his dark face hard and inscrutable. 'I shall be leaving here in a few days,' he continued, just as if she hadn't spoken, 'and shall be away for some weeks. I know you have the highest regard for my mother and father, so I shall trust you not to do anything that could in any way injure or embarrass them.' He threw her a quick look, and she knew that beneath those words lay a warning. 'You will find this difficult to believe, I know,' he went on, 'but I should like you to be happy here at the château, as much for the sake of my family and the children we hope to have, as for your own.'

'You're a liar, François,' she said. 'You care nothing for me, or my happiness. If you did you would let me go. You would end this farce of a marriage and give me the annulment I . . .'

'That subject is closed, Claudine. You are my wife now, for better or for worse, as I am your husband. Try to get used to the idea. It will be easier for you if you do.'

'And what about you? How easy is it for you, having a wife who despises you?'

He smiled, and as he looked at her his eyes seemed to penetrate hers in a way that brought the colour flooding to her cheeks. It was as though he could read everything that was going on inside her mind. 'You will find that I allow you a great deal of freedom in our marriage,' he said, ignoring the question. 'Much more than most wives have, in fact. I require only one thing of you, as you know, and you may be pleased also to know that once you have produced a boy to continue the de Lorvoire line, sexual relations between us will be at an end. Then all I shall require of you is that you are a good mother, and that you are discreet about your lovers.' He stood up. 'Tonight I shall let you sleep in peace. However I shall feel obliged to avail myself of my conjugal rights again before I leave, I will let you know when. In the meantime please be in the library at three tomorrow afternoon to meet the notary.'

He snapped off the light and started back across the room. Claudine's eyes followed him until the door closed behind him, leaving her in darkness. Then suddenly, without giving herself time to think, she leapt out of bed and stormed into the sitting-room.

He was standing at the table, looking at some documents, his hands still in his pockets. When he heard her, he looked up, and a frown of exasperation crossed his face.

'I think you should know,' she fumed, 'that what *you* want, and when *you* choose to do it, just might not be acceptable to *me*.'

To her total confusion, he started to laugh. 'Is this your way,' he said, 'of telling me that you want me in your bed? Now?'

She looked at him in horror. That wasn't what she was saying at all.

'Or have I misunderstood?'

She took a step backwards as he started to amble towards her. 'What are you doing?' she cried, as he turned her round and pushed her back into the bedroom.

She jerked herself away and swung round to face him. The humour had gone from his face, and he seemed bored, waiting for what she was about to say. The frustration was too much for her, and raising her fists she started to hammer them into him. She managed three punches before he caught her hands and twisted them behind her back. The movement brought her body against his, and she felt a bolt of desire strike her with such intensity that it snatched the strength from her legs. But he tightened the grip on her arms, holding her up, and she gasped with the pain of it.

'So,' he said, his mouth very close to hers, 'you have a penchant for violent sex?' He laughed as he saw the expression on her face, but as he looked down at her she felt her lips start to tremble and her eyes flutter closed as she waited for the touch of his mouth. 'However, I'm afraid I am in no mood to oblige you tonight,' he said, 'violently or otherwise.' And he let her go so abruptly that she staggered back against the bed.

She watched the door close behind him, listened as he walked across the sitting-room and into his own room. Her head was spinning, her heart was thudding painfully and her wrists were smarting. She threw herself onto the bed and drew her knees to her chest as if to shut out the insufferable humiliation. What in God's name was happening to her? What had possessed her to go after him like that? For once he had not pressed himself upon her, had been willing to leave her in peace, and she, instead of welcoming it, had . . . When they were in Biarritz, she'd thought she had over-come this insidious longing for him, had managed to control the treachery of her body; but when he had held her against him just now, when she felt his mouth so close to hers, she had wanted him more than ever.

She couldn't understand herself. She was confused, angry, pathetic. Why was she the victim of this consuming desire? Because that was all it was, she told herself; there was no love – there couldn't be when he treated her the way he did. No, she didn't love him, she knew she didn't. And she didn't care that he had rejected her, that he had told her she could take a lover, that he would end what relationship they had once she had done her duty. She didn't care about any of it. She was glad. She hated him, and never wanted him to touch her again . . .

– 10 –

The following morning, the courtyard in front of the wine caves was a hive of activity. Stacks of flattened boxes were being unloaded from one lorry while boxes filled with wine were heaved onto the back of another; Geneviève, the florist from Chinon, and her assistant were lifting the day's supply of flowers for the château out of the back of their Renault van, and Edmond, the butcher's boy, went skidding past on his bicycle *en route* to the kitchen door. Claudine was standing at the window of the small salon, where the family read the newspapers and listened to the wireless after breakfast, watching all that was going on and trying not to smart at how ridiculous she had made herself the night before.

She hadn't slept well, which was hardly surprising, but she was calmer this morning, and now, thinking back to last night, she couldn't help grinning a little at the ease with which François had seen through her, recognizing what she'd wanted even before she knew it herself. No one else could read her the way he did, which was one of the reasons why she detested him so much. It was also, she acknowledged despondently, one of the reasons why she loved him.

She pulled herself up sharply. Of course she didn't love him! It was simply that all these feelings were new to her, and she didn't know how to control them yet. But she would learn, starting today. From now on she would concentrate only on how passionately she hated him, and at the same time she would do everything in her power to show him that she was every bit as capable of resisting him as he was of resisting her.

Again she smiled, pleased to think how quickly she was managing to get her life – and her emotions – back in order. Then, out of the corner of her eye she noticed Armand and François strolling towards the cave furthest from her, and her heart plummeted.

They were engrossed in conversation, and as she watched them she was struck by the contrast between them. Armand, with his startlingly blond hair, was the shorter of the two by at least three inches, but his shoulders were broad and his body was lean and muscular. Armand's eyes too, Claudine thought, remembering their time together the previous evening, were just as compelling as François', though in their own very different way. It was no wonder everyone spoke of him so affectionately when he exuded such kindness and warmth.

The two of them came to a stop behind one of the lorries, and she was about to turn away from the window when she saw Armand raise his hands in the air, as if demonstrating the size of something. She found herself smiling as she watched the ease and humour of his manner, and when François burst out laughing, wished with a sudden pang that she could be there, sharing the joke. She did turn away then, and dropping a quick kiss on Louis' balding head, went off to dress for the busy day ahead of her.

One of the people she planned to see today was Madame Reinberg, who lived in the village, next door to the café. Claudine knew Madame Reinberg by sight, and in her encounters with the village children had been especially attracted by the Reinberg children, little Janette and her younger brother Robert, who was mildly retarded. Liliane had told her yesterday afternoon that Madame Reinberg's husband had deserted her. He had left no note and no money, but he had taken with him a woman from Chinon, and his wife was broken-hearted.

Claudine could do little about the broken heart, but she could ensure that Madame Reinberg's children did not find themselves homeless, and if necessary, she had decided, she would pay the rent herself until a solution was found, out of the money from François' promised allowance — an idea which appealed to her sense of the bizarre, since François was the Reinbergs' landlord. She had, of course, told Solange and Louis what she intended to do, but they had been only too delighted that she was involving herself in the affairs of the village — and now, as she prepared to leave, dressed in a green corduroy skirt, checked wool blouse and thick cardigan, Louis walked with her to her car, telling her to let Gertrude Reinberg know that there was no need for rent this side of Christmas.

'And the other side?' Claudine asked mischievously.

'Oh, I have a feeling you will have come up with a solution by then, *ma chère*.'

'You have such faith in me, Louis!'

'*Bien sûr*,' he chuckled. 'You don't know the meaning of the word failure.'

She wondered for a moment what he meant by that. She was well aware that Louis saw a great deal more than he let on, but he had never said a word to her about her marriage.

'Now,' he said, opening the car door for her, 'don't forget to ask Gustave at the café if he has come across any of those fine Cuban cigars again. I'm willing to pay over the odds, tell him, which is what the old rogue would charge me anyway. And whatever you do, Claudine, don't tell Solange.'

Claudine grinned. Doctor Lebrun allowed Louis three cigars a week and one tot of brandy each night, which was three more cigars and seven more tots than Solange would allow him, which was why Louis had to rely on the rest of his family to smuggle in his luxuries.

As she drove past the wine caves she passed Armand and François. 'See you at eleven,' she called out to Armand.

Armand gave her a salute – and she saw the sardonic lift of François' eyebrows. 'God, he's unbearable,' she muttered through clenched teeth, and pressing her foot hard on the accelerator, she gave a jaunty toss of her head and sped off down the drive.

When she pulled up at the café in Lorvoire, several men were sitting outside playing cards. She knew them all, by now, and had a special greeting for Thomas, the farmer she and Lucien had encountered in his tractor all those months ago. He had taken great pride, she knew, in being the first of the villagers to be introduced to the future Comtesse, and continued to bore his cronies half to death with the story of how he had torn her off a strip for her bad driving.

'Sit down, *madame*,' he croaked in his tobacco-roughened voice. 'Gustave! Bring wine for Madame de Lorvoire.'

Claudine shook her head, laughing. 'It's too early in the day for me, Thomas,' she said. 'And I'll bet your wife is at market and doesn't have the first idea you aren't out in the fields.'

'*Oh là là,*' he chuckled, evidently delighted with his ticking off.

'We hear there's going to be a party up at the château when the grapes are in,' Claude Derlot said, speaking through the cigarette in his teeth and peering up at her with his watery blue eyes.

'I hope so,' she said, 'and I'm looking for volunteers for a cabaret, so you must all think what you could do.' She was turning as she spoke as she'd heard the thunder of tiny feet coming up behind her. 'Now where on earth did you all spring from?' she said, looking down at the group of children who had come to a bashful halt beside her.

'We were playing by the stream,' Richard, one of Thomas's grandchildren, told her, smearing even more mud on his face as he rubbed an eye.

'And don't tell me, you heard my car and thought, *bonbons*!'

The way she said it brought a grin to each of their faces, and she dug into her pockets and handed over the toffees, keeping some aside for Janette and Robert Reinberg.

Gustave, the proprietor of the café, came out then, holding a bottle of Lorvoire wine, and as usual when she saw him Claudine felt her lips begin to twitch. His face, with its florid complexion and bulbous eyes, was almost as fat and round as his belly, and his bushy eyebrows arched so steeply towards his monkish fringe, gave him a look of such extreme surprise, that one felt one's own eyebrows lifting in response. His most arresting feature, though, was a splendid moustache, curled and waxed at the tips, which provided him with the most comical of permanent smiles. Claudine didn't remember ever having seen anyone who looked quite so jolly.

'Ah ha!' he cried. 'You see the sun shines, now that *madame* is back at Lorvoire.'

There were smiles all round. Then, feeling a tug at her pocket, Claudine looked down to discover young Richard trying to steal a toffee.

'*Un voleur*!' she cried, throwing up her hands in horror, and Richard shrieked and scampered off across the square with the other children.

It was a game they often played, but today, instead of going after them Claudine remembered that she had to ask Gustave about the cigars for Louis.

'*Si*, I have been keeping them for him,' he answered.

'Can we have a toffee please, *madame*?' a soft voice asked.

Claudine looked down to find a little girl with an angelic face and an abundance of white-blonde curls staring up at her. She was no more than six years old, and was holding the hand of her even smaller brother. They looked so adorable that Claudine found herself struggling with the urge to gather them up in her arms. 'I'm afraid I'm keeping the toffees that are left for Janette and Robert Reinberg,' she said sadly.

'But *I'm* Janette Reinberg,' the little girl told her, truly believing that Claudine hadn't recognized her.

'No!' Claudine gasped. 'But Janette Reinberg is only a baby and you're such a big girl!'

Janette's face beamed as the toffees were handed over. Robert, with his mouth full, said, 'My Papa has gone away.'

Claudine nodded, and had to swallow a lump in her throat. 'Is *Maman* at home?' she said.

'Yes,' Robert answered, stuffing another toffee in his mouth but never taking his eyes from hers.

Claudine turned back to Gustave. 'I'll collect the cigars later,' she said. Then tucking her purse under her arm and waving goodbye to everyone, she went to knock on Madame Reinberg's door . . .

When she emerged an hour later, the village was deserted. She took a deep breath and closed her eyes. There was a delicious aroma of freshly baked bread coming from the *boulangerie*, and she could hear the rush and gurgle of the river as it flowed behind the cottages on the opposite side of the square. She looked at her watch, wondering if she had time to call on Liliane to ask her where she could buy a secondhand sewing-machine –the possible solution to Madame Reinberg's money problems. Madame Reinberg had been a seamstress in Tours before her marriage, and home sewing and tailoring might restore the poor woman's income, and her pride.

By the time Claudine drove out of the village and headed

back to the château, it was already five past eleven. On the seat beside her were six pots of blackberry jam and a recipe for dry-cured pickled pork, written in code, for Arlette from Liliane, and a box of cigars for Louis from Gustave. She did not think Armand would mind that she was late, and she was feeling in such a good mood that she very much hoped that François had taken himself elsewhere, because she didn't want anything to spoil it.

Smiling, she turned on the wireless, and when she heard the song they were singing she burst out laughing. It was the first time she had heard it in French, but the tune was unmistakable, so she sang along to it in English: 'Who's afraid of the Big Bad Wolf?' It was a pity, she thought, when the song ended, that she couldn't share the joke with François – but of course, if she could there wouldn't be a joke.

Freddy Prendergast was sitting on a wooden bench beside the Montvisse dovecote, watching Monique walk towards him across the lawn. He felt his anxiety deepening with every step she took, and when she came to a stop beside him, he looked up at her and smiled weakly. She looked particularly attractive today, he thought miserably; her dark hair suited her combed back from her face like that, especially when she was smiling so happily. Their eyes met, but he looked away quickly as his misgivings got the better of him, and shuffled awkwardly along the bench to make room for her.

Monique smiled at him fondly. 'Oh, *chéri*,' she said consolingly, 'you are unhappy because we have not been able to spend time alone together for almost a week. It has hurt me too, but I am here now.' She lifted his hand into her lap and gave it a reassuring squeeze. 'I have thought about you all the time, *mon chou*. I read your poems again and again and I tingle all over when I think of how much you love me. I am truly the happiest woman alive.' She took his chin and pulled him round to face her. 'You are not angry, are you, that I wish to wait for Lucien to come home before we announce our engagement?'

Freddy shook his head. 'No, not in the slightest.' His voice sounded high-pitched and nervous. He tried again. 'Not a bit,' he boomed.

'Lucien will be here tomorrow,' she smiled, resting her head on his shoulder, 'and then we shall be able to tell the whole world.' If she was aware of the tension in him she didn't show it, and after a while she looked up at him and whispered, 'Kiss me, Freddy.'

He was suddenly seized with panic, but not knowing what else to do, he planted a quick kiss on her lips, then looked away.

She laughed softly. 'You are afraid that someone is watching us from the window, *oui*?'

He gave a jerky nod and looked desperately towards the sky for Divine intervention.

'I have a surprise for you, *chéri*,' she said. 'Do you want to know what it is?'

No, he most certainly did not, but he found himself saying that he did.

'I have been thinking how we could spend a whole night together,' she told him, 'and now I have the solution. If you come to Lorvoire after dark and climb up into the forest – it is very steep behind the château so you must be sure to take great care – you will find the bridge which leads into the nursery corridor. It is next to Claudine's bedroom, so we will have to be quiet, but if you come after midnight then she will be sure to be sleeping.'

He gaped at her. The woman had clearly taken leave of her senses if she thought for one moment that he would contemplate going into a forest in the dead of night.

'It is perfect, don't you agree?' she said, apparently mistaking his horror for wonder.

A strange noise escaped his lips, and laughing, she leaned forward to kiss them. 'So you will come tonight?' she whispered, treating him to one of her most provocative smiles.

Tonight! She wanted him to go tonight! 'Er, well, er,' he stammered. He cleared his throat. 'Well . . . ' he continued. 'Er, one has a teensy bit of a problem.'

'*Un probléme?*' she repeated, still smiling.

'Yes. Well, it's like this, you see. One has a friend. Well, not a friend exactly; more of a girlfriend.'

He winced as the smile froze on her face, and suddenly the idea of thrashing about in a forest at midnight seemed infinitely preferable to this.

'Go on,' she breathed.

He shrugged, and attempted to smile. 'Well, that's it really. One has a girlfriend.' There *was* more, but he didn't quite have the courage to go through with it now that her face had gone so dreadfully pale.

'But you said, you told me you had never . . . '

'Oh, but we haven't,' he assured her, assuming that she was referring to his virginity and not wanting her to think him a liar. 'Teresa's not *that* sort of girl.'

Even before Monique's hand rang across his cheek, he realized he had made a stupendous blunder.

'I'm sorry,' he gasped. 'One didn't mean to say that. What one meant to say was . . . What one meant, was . . . She's too young. Much, much younger than you.'

He had never seen such a look in his life, and groaning, he dropped his head in his hands. He could feel her trembling, and was just beginning to wish he had never set foot in France, never mind Montvisse, when to his unmitigated horror she started to plead. 'But couldn't we have just one night together?' she begged. 'You could still come to the château . . . It doesn't matter that you . . .'

'I can't!' he wailed. 'It's not that I don't want to, because I do, very much, but you see, Teresa . . . Well, Teresa is coming here, to Montvisse, today.'

She stared at him, her eyes wide and uncomprehending, until finally, to his utter dismay, she seemed to crumple before his very eyes. He had never felt such a heel.

'I'm sorry,' he murmured. 'You see, she was my girlfriend before, but she told me in July that she didn't want to see me again. So when I told you I didn't have a girlfriend, I wasn't lying. But she called me yesterday from Paris and said she had changed her mind.'

'And you invited her to Montvisse?'

'Yes,' he confessed miserably, and lowered his eyes as the horrible burden of shame grew heavier on his shoulders.

For the moment Monique didn't know what to say. It was as though someone had delivered her a physical blow and she was still reeling from the shock. She took a deep breath in an effort to steady herself, but an icy torrent of rage swept through her as once again she saw her happiness slipping away. She wanted to scream; she wanted to fall on her knees and rage against God; she wanted to run, to escape from all the torment welling up inside her. She wanted to thrash out with her hands, kick out with her feet; she wanted to fall to the floor, to clutch at his legs, beg him to love her, make him understand that he couldn't do this to her, he couldn't leave her, not when she had already told Claudine . . .

Suddenly she went very still and her eyes glazed over. Freddy was so horrified that his nerves erupted in a loud guffaw. Then, to his amazement, she took his hand and held it between her own. He looked down, trembling with terror; he felt sure she was going to break every bone in his fingers. Several minutes ticked by and neither of them moved, then, tentatively, he lifted his eyes back to her face. To his overwhelming relief the terrible expression had gone, and in its place was such a heart-rending sadness that it almost moved him to tears.

'It's all right, Freddy,' she said, 'I understand. I am far too old for you really, and I'm sure we would have made one another unhappy in the end. You are wise to take your girlfriend back and I hope she will have a marvellous time here with you. You must take her to the waterfall table, and bring her over to Lorvoire for tea one afternoon; you know how *Maman* loves to have visitors, and I should very much like to meet her myself.' She smiled as she saw the uncertainty in his eyes. 'Don't worry, *chéri*,' she said, 'I won't cause a scene. What we had together was very special, and for me it will always be a wonderful memory, I have no wish to spoil it. You have your whole life ahead of you and I hope that sometimes you will think of me . . .'

'Oh I will!' he cried, hugging her hands to his chest. 'I will!'

She stood up. 'Please don't feel badly over this, Freddy, and please don't think you have hurt me so much that I can't bear it. I am sad, of course, but you must remember that I am used to these things . . .' Her smile almost failed her then, but she swallowed hard, and with a little toss of her head she said, 'She is a very lucky girl, your Teresa.'

'Oh, Monique!' Freddy cried, throwing his arms around her. 'Thank you. Thank you. You are a wonderful woman.'

'Maybe,' she whispered, and gently removing his arms, she turned and started back across the lawn.

Freddy watched her go, dazed by how easy it had been after all, and now not at all sure that he had done the right thing. But it was too late for regrets, Teresa would be arriving in an hour or two and he was rather looking forward to seeing her. He waited for Monique to disappear around the side of the château before wandering off towards the river to pen a verse to his rediscovered love.

Claudine and Armand were standing in the circular cavern at the back of one of the wine caves where potential customers were taken to taste the Lorvoire wine. The only light came from the flickering candles at the centre of a round stone table where glasses and bottles were set out. In the arched recesses around the walls were sample vintages of every year, dating back to the end of the last century.

The air rang with the sound of their laughter as Armand told her stories of the rich and famous who had come pretending to know all there was to know about wine, only to betray themselves with just one inane question, or with obvious ignorance of the way one set about tasting. He was now in the process of showing her how it should be done. Her eyes were shining as she watched him lift the glass to his lips; and when he had finished, he wiped his mouth with the back of his hand and started to refill the glass. 'Your turn,' he said.

'Oh no!' she declared. 'I'll end up as one of your anecdotes.'

Laughing, he handed her the glass, which was almost half-full. 'You will if you don't,' he warned her.

She took the glass and peered into it. 'Why don't you swallow it?' she said, not at all taken with the idea of having to spit it out.

'Because I wouldn't be much use to anyone if I spent the entire day three sheets to the wind.'

'That's an English expression,' she said.

'Stop changing the subject. Now, remember, savour the aroma first.'

She lifted the glass to her nose and inhaled deeply.

He gave an exaggerated sigh. 'You haven't swished it around in the glass,' he said. 'Remember what I told you.'

Pulling a face at him, Claudine sloshed the wine about the glass, and spilt it. 'Before you say anything,' she cried, 'there was too much in there!'

'Well, there isn't now, is there?' he said, handing her a towel. 'Now, swish it gently and release the bouquet.'

This time she was a little more successful.

'Mmm,' she sighed. '*Délicieux.*'

'That's right. Remember, a large proportion of the sense of taste is in the sense of smell. Carry on.'

Looking at him over the rim of the glass, Claudine took a mouthful.

'Roll it around your tongue. That's it. Take in the flavour. Think about it, listen to what your senses are telling you. Now, spit it in there,' he pointed to the bowl on the floor. 'Pathetic!' he cried, as she let the wine go in a dribble. 'What we want is a nice healthy spurt. Now, again.'

She went through the performance again, and this time, at the end, the wine issued from her lips in a veritable fountain.

'Bravo!' he cried, and she looked so thoroughly pleased with herself that he burst out laughing.

'Armand St Jacques, you're trying to make a fool out of me,' she declared.

'Ah, but at least I'm doing it in the privacy of the wine cellar, which is more than I can say for what you have in mind for me. Singing in public! Have you managed to talk François into doing anything for this cabaret of yours?'

'Not yet. But I will.'

'You won't, you know,' he said. 'Because he tells me he's not going to be here. So I'm throwing you a new challenge. If I am to sing with Solange, then you are to invite all the wine-growers in the area and judge their last year's vintage.'

'But I can't do that! I don't know anything about . . .'

'You know what you like the taste of, don't you?'

'Yes, but . . .'

'That's settled, then.'

'All right, I accept the challenge.' Her eyes were dancing with laughter. 'But I'll need some more lessons.'

He nodded. 'Yes, I'll agree to that.'

She watched as he re-corked the bottle, trying to think of

a suitable rejoinder. In the end she gave up and a few minutes later they were strolling in the semi-darkness through pyramids of wine bottles towards the distant sunlight at the mouth of the cave. The constant eleven-degree temperature needed for the wine made Claudine pull her cardigan tightly around her. She glanced absently at the measuring gauges on the huge vats, wondering if she should ask Armand whether François had said where he would be during the harvest.

'I hear you went to see Gertrude Reinberg this morning,' Armand said, interrupting her thoughts.

'News does travel fast.'

'Henri Jallais told me. His wife was watching you from her window.'

He grimaced as he remembered how he had been compelled to reprimand Jallais for repeating what his wife had said about Claudine. It was bad enough that Jallais had repeated it at all, but to do so in front of other estate workers was inexcusable, and made him no better than the acid-tongued harridan he called a wife. Still, being called an interfering, Jew-loving, stuck-up foreigner by Florence Jallais was probably the least of Claudine's problems; he hadn't missed the fleeting look that had crossed her face when he mentioned that François wasn't going to be at the harvest celebration. He wasn't sure whether it had been disappointment or anger, but whatever it was it was only one of several indications that Claudine was having a hard time trying to make sense of her marriage. Well, there was little he could do to help her there – but he would do his utmost to make the harvest celebration a success for her.

Claudine had stopped beside the sixteenth-century wine press. Grinning at him, she started to recite all he had told her earlier about sugar and acidity levels.

'A formidable pupil,' he said when she had finished. 'Now, talk me through the wine year, starting with January.'

She narrowed her eyes in concentration. 'January is the month of pruning and blending. Also there is the sampling of the full-bodied wine, when you invite friends and colleagues to assess the young wines as they develop in the vat. Wines from the previous year are ready for bottling . . .' Her frown deepened as she tried to remember what else he had told her.

He waited, seeing how the beams of sunlight filtering in from the mouth of the cave turned her wild hair to a furnace of blue and gold. He'd thought she looked a little pale earlier, when she drove past him on the way to the village, but now her generous lips were moist and red, and her honey cheeks were flushed with colour. Her eyes were lowered, and he could see the gently curving line of her lashes, thick and glossy and black. She was so beautiful that when he thought of how behind that vibrant, intoxicating energy, she was trying so hard to hide her pain it was only with a tremendous effort that he was able to stop himself from reaching out to comfort her.

' . . . and April,' she was saying, 'is a very tricky time because of lingering frosts as the sap starts to rise in the vine. This is the month when you might sleep out with the vines to keep a check on them.' She turned to look at him, and even before she spoke he was grinning at the mischief in her eyes. 'Do you hug them to keep them warm,' she said, 'or just blow on them?'

Laughing, he moved away from the wine press and started to walk on. 'Remember the smudge pots?' he said. 'At the back of the other cave?'

'The things that look like chestnut braziers?'

He nodded. 'We light them and take them out on frosty nights, to heat up the air around the vines.'

'Amazing. Shall I go on?'

'No, that's enough for today. Some of us have work to do!' They strolled on towards the front of the cave. 'I was talking to Father Pointeau early this morning,' he said, 'and he suggested we hold the celebration on the Sunday following the harvest – after the thanksgiving service.'

'That's a wonderful idea,' Claudine replied. 'Do you know yet which Sunday that will be?'

Armand shrugged. 'François and I took a walk round the vineyards earlier, and we agreed that, providing the weather keeps up, the harvest will take place roughly four weeks from now. So it looks as though we're aiming for the last Sunday in October.'

'Oh, I can hardly wait,' she sighed, hugging herself. 'We're going to have so much fun, I know we are.'

He was about to respond when a sudden, piercing scream resounded through the cave. *'Chienne!'*

Startled, they both looked up to see a silhouetted figure standing at the mouth of the cave.

'Monique,' Claudine breathed.

'I want to talk to you, you bitch!' Monique shrieked, and before either of them could reply she turned on her heel and stormed off towards the house.

Armand saw that the colour had vanished from Claudine's face. 'What on earth was that about?' he said.

'I don't know,' she answered softly, 'but I think I can guess.' And hastily thanking him for his time, she started off after Monique.

'Mademoiselle is upstairs in your apartment, *madame*,' Jean-Paul informed her as she ran through the front door. Claudine took the stairs two at a time, and found Monique pacing the sitting-room, her delicate face ravaged with fury.

'Why?' she screamed as soon as she saw Claudine, 'Just tell me why!'

'You've been to Montvisse?' Claudine said, closing the door behind her and keeping her back against it.

'It was your idea wasn't it?' Monique seethed. 'It was you who put Freddy up to this. But it wasn't enough that he should jilt me, was it? You had to tell him to invite the silly little whore to Montvisse!'

'That's not true. Monique, please listen . . .'

'You're a liar! Everything was perfect between us before you went to see him . . .'

'I was going to try . . .'

'. . . Before you persuaded me to postpone the announcement. I trusted you! I confided in you, and this is the way you repay me. You're a snake, an evil little snake. Just because your own marriage is a farce you can't stand seeing anyone else happy. Well, I'll pay you back for this, Claudine Rafferty, you see if I . . .'

'Her name is Claudine de Lorvoire.'

They both spun round to see François standing in the doorway of his bedroom.

'I don't care what her damned name is,' Monique screamed, 'she's going to pay for what she's done.' She turned back to Claudine, her eyes blazing with hatred. 'You're going to know what it's like to be humiliated, you bitch! You're going to find out just what it is to suffer the way you've made me suffer. I despise you, we all despise you. Even François . . .'

'That's enough!' François' voice cut through the tirade and he turned to Claudine. 'Go downstairs,' he barked.

'But . . .'

'I said, go downstairs. I want to talk to my sister.'

'No!' Monique stalked across the room. When she reached Claudine, she pushed her face towards her and spat, 'Let *her* tell you, François! Let *her* tell you what she's done to me. But I'll tell you this, even if the bitch comes crawling to me on bended knee I'll never forgive her. *Never!'*

She pushed Claudine out of the way, then wrenched open the door and slammed out of the room.

The silence that followed was oppressive. Claudine stared down at her hand, still grasping the edge of the mahogany sideboard, where she had tried to save herself from falling when Monique pushed her. Her mind was in turmoil, and she felt faintly sick. At last she looked up – only to see that François was scowling at her. The day had started out so well, but now a sense of defeat was threatening to overwhelm her.

'Sit down,' François said.

She shook her head.

He took her by the arm, led her to a chair and pushed her into it. Then he turned away towards the window. 'I take it all that was about young Prendergast,' he said, keeping his back turned.

Claudine didn't answer. She felt too miserable even to show any surprise that he knew about Monique and Freddy; she had always abhorred self-pity, but she knew she was coming dangerously close to it at that moment. But Monique's accusations were unjust. She hadn't put Freddy up to inviting Teresa, that had been his own idea. But she could have stopped him, and she would have done if she hadn't been so caught up in her own life.

François turned to look at her. 'Would you like to explain why my sister is so upset?' he said coldly.

'I thought you'd heard all she had to say.'

'I did. Why didn't you defend yourself?'

'I didn't get the chance.'

'I am giving it to you now.'

Claudine looked away.

'Am I to understand from your silence that there is some truth in Monique's accusations?'

She sighed. 'Does it matter? Monique obviously wants to believe I talked Freddy out of marrying her . . .' She shrugged.

'Did you?'

'Why are you asking me these questions?' she suddenly shouted. 'The point is that neither I nor anyone else could have talked him out of it if he'd wanted to marry her, and I resent being treated like an adolescent when none of this is any of your damned business.'

'Claudine,' he said with deliberation, 'if Monique is threatening you, then it is my business.'

'Why? Because, doting husband that you are, you *care*?'

'I told you last night that I want you to be happy here.'

'Then why the hell don't you do something about it!'

'That is precisely what I am trying to do. If there's a rift between you and Monique I want it healed.'

'And what about the rift between you and me? Or doesn't that count? Oh, don't speak to my any more. I've had enough of arguing . . . *I'll* sort things out with Monique and I don't need any help from you.'

'As you wish.'

He started to walk across the room and she expected him to leave, but he stopped at the sofa and sat down. 'How are your plans for the wine feast progressing?' he asked, after a moment or two.

She eyed him suspiciously, wondering if he was now going to tell her that it couldn't happen. 'Satisfactorily,' she said.

He nodded. 'Armand told me about Father Pointeau's suggestion. There'll be a hunt in the Chinon forest before the service of thanksgiving, and I'm sure Georges de Rivet would be willing to donate the catch to the feast if I ask him.'

Barely able to disguise her surprise, Claudine said, 'That's very kind of you.'

'The least I can do, since I won't be here myself.'

'Where will you be?' The question was out before she could stop it.

'Berlin. If you have any letters for your father, than I shall be happy to deliver them.'

'Thank you.' There was a long, uncomfortable pause while she struggled to fight back the loathsome, self-pitying tears that had overcome her at the mention of her father. Then again she had spoken before giving herself time to think: 'Would it be possible for me to come to Berlin with you?'

Sighing, he pulled himself to his feet. 'You have duties here at Lorvoire that preclude that possibility, so I'm afraid the answer is no.' When she continued to stare up at him, he said, 'You can't tell everyone you are going to organize a feast and then disappear on a whim to see your father.'

She knew he was right, but it didn't stop her throwing her resentment at him. 'Of course, it wouldn't have anything to do with you not wanting me in Berlin, would it?' she said nastily.

'As a matter of fact, it would. I don't want you with me. I want you here, where you belong. Now, see that you make amends to Monique before things get out of hand. If I were you, I'd start by getting that young puppy on the next train to England.'

'He's Céline's guest, not mine.'

'Don't be obtuse, Claudine. You have offended my sister deeply; at least have the decency to get young Prendergast as far away from her as you can.'

When the door closed behind him, Claudine sat for some time staring into space and doing her best to stave off the swelling tide of unhappiness. In the end, knowing that she was losing the battle, she jerked herself out of the chair, ran down the stairs and got into the car. She might hate François for the way he had spoken to her, but he was right; having Freddy and his girlfriend at Montvisse would only exacerbate the pain for Monique, and angry as she was with Monique, she had no wish to see her suffer.

11

Claudine's spirits lifted the following afternoon when Lucien arrived home and announced he was staying for at least a week. She and Armand had no trouble in persuading him to help with the preparations for the harvest celebration, and even got him to drive Gertrude Reinberg to Chinon market the morning after his arrival, to purchase fabric remnants for the children's pantomime costumes. As Gertrude loaded him up with crêpes and satins, cottons and lace, Claudine couldn't resist creeping up behind him with a feather headdress from the stall and jamming it on his head. He looked so absurd that everyone started to laugh, and Claudine escaped through the crowd before he could catch her.

Later in the day, Armand began what was to become a daily routine, of driving about the countryside in his Citröen van, persuading the local wine-growers to enter their last year's vintage in the competition Claudine was going to judge. There were snorts and guffaws, loud protests and much waving of hands at the idea of a woman judging their wine – and an English woman at that – but Armand's charm invariably won the day and they grudgingly allowed their names to be put forward.

Meanwhile Claudine was out on a talent hunt – or so Armand thought. In fact she was following after him and informing the wine-growers that whoever donated the largest sum of money for charity would secure first place for his wine. Their donations were to be sealed in an envelope, she told them, so that no one would know what anyone else was giving. This way, she had told herself smugly, she not only got out of judging a contest which would certainly earn her the hostility of half Touraine, she also made money for a good cause. Armand protested strongly when he finally learned what was going on, and to Lucien's great enjoyment told her that she was the most devious and brilliant diplomat he had ever come across.

The Mayor of Chinon agreed to let them use the town hall for auditions and rehearsals, and the hilarity of the days spent there was only surpassed by Armand and Solange's evening sessions at the piano. The first time Armand opened his mouth, he got no further than the opening line of the song they had chosen before Claudine stopped playing and turned to him in horror.

'What's the matter?' he demanded testily.

'You can't sing!'

'I never said I could,' he retorted.

'But your voice is terrible! You sound like a bull elephant with a trumpet in its trunk.'

'Right, that's it!' he said, throwing down his sheet-music. 'I'm not staying here to be insulted. And if you think it's so funny, Lucien de Lorvoire, you get up there and do it!'

In the background Solange started humming tunelessly under her breath, at the same time gliding back and forth across the room with her arms outstretched, her head thrown back and her chiffon dress floating around her.

'What *is* she doing?' Armand said.

Claudine and Lucien glanced at one another – then Lucien leapt from his chair and swept his mother into his arms, while Claudine seized Armand and they all started to dance about the ballroom. Solange was a wily old thing, Claudine thought, who knew as well as anybody how to take the sting out of a situation.

After that the rehearsal went more smoothly, but Armand was always on the watch for Claudine to wince – or worse, laugh – and her struggle to keep a straight face was made only marginally easier by banishing Lucien from the room.

They found him later at the café, drinking *pastis* with half a dozen or so men from the village, who were between them setting the world to rights. They were sitting round a table in front of the roaring fire, and the air was thick with cigarette smoke. Armand and Claudine's arrival brought a cheer of welcome, and chairs were pulled up and fresh glasses called for. Since Claudine didn't much like the aniseed drink Gustave brought her a *pichet* of wine, and she sat between Thomas and Yves Fauberg who started telling her outrageous tales of the things Lucien and Armand got up to as boys.

'And what about François?' she asked, after a time. 'Wasn't he into mischief too?'

'Oh, he was away at the Jesuit school in Paris by that time,' Thomas answered, 'but yes, he always had some scheme going when he was here. I remember the day he took these two for a ride in my tractor – he couldn't have been above ten years old at the time. Caught up with them in the end, halfway to Saumur, after they'd knocked some poor onion seller off his bicycle and squashed his onions.' He gave one of his throatier chuckles. 'The Comte was so angry, we didn't see François again that holiday.'

Everyone laughed; then Claudine, raising her glass, abruptly changed the subject by challenging them all to take part in her cabaret. The response was a unanimous No, but Gustave, refilling their glasses, whispered in her ear that she stood a better chance of talking them into it if they were under the influence, so to speak . . .

'Which means,' Lucien said into her other ear, 'that you are footing the bill.'

An hour later they were all singing, even Armand, but Claudine was no nearer persuading anyone to perform at the harvest celebration. The crafty old rogues told her as she was leaving that if she were to come again the following night, they might reconsider.

'Not one of them is above bribery!' Armand said as

Claudine handed Gustave what money she had and put the rest on account.

Her cheeks were glowing, from the warmth of the fire as much as from the wine, and as she looked up at him she saw the laughter fade from his eyes. Surprised, she paused – but the next thing she knew, Lucien had grabbed her about the waist and was waltzing her towards the door. Once out in the square, she broke free, and then somehow a furious game of chase developed round the well, with Claudine running off at last through the misty night towards the river. Both Armand and Lucien caught up with her at the same time, swept her into the air and threatened to throw her in. Her screams were answered by the lighting up of windows all over the village, and Florence Jallais without knowing whom she was addressing, leaned out and delivered Claudine an extremely savoury piece of her mind.

Still laughing, the three of them finally parted company outside the café, where Lucien and Claudine got into their respective cars and Armand strolled off along the street. Claudine, spinning the car round the well so that she was facing in the right direction for home, called out, 'Don't forget, Armand! We're expecting you at six in the morning.'

'I'll be there,' he shouted back. As she drove out of the village she saw that he was still standing beside the well, watching her go.

Lucien was the first to arrive back at the château, and was waiting for her on the front steps. 'Nightcap?' he said, as she joined him.

'Splendid idea,' she hiccoughed, and laughing they walked into the hall together – where they very nearly collided with François and Captain Paillole who were just emerging from the drawing-room.

It was more than obvious that both she and Lucien had had too much to drink, and Claudine had been quite happy with her condition – until she came face to face with her husband. Now, feeling suddenly hot, she took her arm from Lucien's and tried to concentrate on what he was saying to his brother, but there was a buzzing in her ears and her head started to spin. She took a deep breath, which seemed to steady her for a moment, but still she wasn't listening . . . She was thinking how alike the two brothers were. Both had the distinguished de Lorvoire nose, deep-set eyes and powerful jaw, and both – though François was taller and larger all round than Lucien – had the physique of an athlete: so how could it be that one was so devastatingly handsome and the other so appallingly ugly? And why was it that she felt so drawn to François, when . . .

Quickly she pulled herself together, reminding herself that she hated him. But then he laughed at something Lucien was saying, and she felt horribly light-headed again and started to sway. She blinked, trying to bring his face back into focus, but it only seemed to make her worse. For a moment everything went black, and as if from a great distance she heard François saying, 'It's all right, I'll see to her,' and she was suddenly aware that she was in his arms and he was carrying her towards the stairs.

That night she dreamt that he was holding her and kissing her. That his cruel mouth was soft and warm and moving tenderly over hers. Each time he pulled away, she moaned softly at the way his eyes were looking down at her, suffused with laughter and love, and she pulled him back, wanting to feel his lips on hers again, and the hardness of his body as his passion grew. She shivered as his hands moved to her breasts, stroking and fondling them, then his lips closed around her nipples and she fell back, dazed by the overpowering sensations coursing through her. Then finally he lay over her and pushed himself slowly inside her.

She cried out at the ecstasy of it, lifting her hips to meet his while his tongue probed the depths of her mouth. He moved against her, holding her close, and she clung to him, gripping him with her legs and her arms as he started to push into her with longer, harder strokes. His breath was coming quicker, and the sound of it inflamed her senses and carried her towards a peak of impossible sensation. She arched her back, calling out his name as he took her higher and higher. Then, at the very moment the ecstasy started to explode through her body, he jerked himself away.

She woke with a start and sat bolt upright in bed. All she could see was his hideous face, only inches from hers, looking back at her with contempt. She gasped, blinked hard, and the illusion vanished. Sweat was pouring from her body and her hands, as she lifted them to her face, were trembling uncontrollably. It was some time before she could bring herself to look at the bed beside her, terrified that she would find him watching her, but when she finally reached out to turn on the lamp she saw that the room was empty, and there was no sign that he had been there.

She collapsed against the pillows. So it had been a dream, a terrible nightmare, but her body was still pounding with the sheer power of it.

After that she couldn't sleep, and lay awake embroiled in the chaos of her thoughts. It made her angry and afraid that her body could betray her so cruelly, that even when she was asleep he could torment her. His malice pursued her, forcing her to relive, over and over again, the way he so sadistically denied her the final release of pleasure. Wherever she looked she could see his face, watching her, mocking her, drowning her in the contempt he felt for her.

Just after six the next morning Claudine, Armand and Lucien mounted their horses and rode down over the meadow into the early morning mist of the forest. The air was bracing, and the branches that hung across their path sparkled with dew. They walked the horses to the towpath, then cantered gently along the river bank where the water was still and glassy, with a smoky haze drifting above the surface. Claudine was riding ahead, and surprised the others by turning her horse away from the path, around the edge of the forest to open ground, and urging it gently up the hill. By the time she reached the top, the sun was a glowing ball of orange sitting on the horizon, and as she looked down at the forest behind her she could see the glistening turrets of the château rising proudly through the trees.

Seeing the open countryside had made her horse restless, so glancing challengingly back over her shoulder at Lucien and Armand, Claudine rose in the saddle, dug in her heels and galloped off towards the dawn. As she went, the fresh wind seemed to snatch away the confusion of the night, the thundering hooves seemed to trample her doubts, so that by the time Lucien and Armand caught her, she was laughing loudly at the way she had allowed herself to become so confused when, as Gustave had put it, she was simply 'under the influence'. . . .

It was almost eight o'clock when the three of them, still in their riding clothes, walked into the dining-room, to find Louis humbly sipping his coffee while Solange lectured him about his health. They all enjoyed the look of relief that crossed his face when he saw them come in, and Claudine felt even more cheerful when Monique appeared and told them that François and Captain Paillole had left for Paris half an hour before. For reasons neither of them could have explained, Claudine's and Armand's eyes met; they smiled at each other, shrugged and looked away.

That was the first time Monique had ventured from her room since her terrible row with Claudine, though Claudine knew that François had informed her of Freddy's departure from Montvisse. What else he had said to his sister when they were closeted together in her room, Claudine did not know, but she was relieved to see that Monique was taking an interest in what Armand and Lucien were telling her about the preparations for the wine feast. She tried several times to catch her eye, but without success. Plainly, Monique needed a little more time before she could forgive her.

Over the next two weeks all thoughts of François were banished from Claudine's mind, and the only thing that happened to dampen her spirits was Lucien's departure to rejoin his regiment. Armand missed him too, for the three of them had spent a great deal of time together; though they all had their own business to attend to during the day, they had fallen into the habit of going to the café almost every evening, then riding together the following morning. Sometimes Monique accompanied them, but after Lucien's departure she stopped. However, Armand and Claudine continued with their early morning gallops across the countryside, and their rowdy soirées down at the café, and – to Armand's continuing chagrin – their rehearsals with Solange. During the day, while Armand was working in the vineyards, Claudine busied herself with preparations for the feast, helped by Solange, Louis and Tante Céline.

Monique went to Paris for a few days, and when she returned, to Claudine's relief she started to enter into the spirit of things, and involved herself in the pantomime the children were putting on. Each afternoon she waited at the gates of the château for the school bus to return from Chinon, then escorted the village children to the ballroom where she and Philippe, the footman who had joined the household at the end of September, directed the rehearsals for *Sleeping Beauty*. Philippe had once been a great actor – or so he told the children; and while he took them through their moves and showed them how to deliver their lines – most of which he had written himself – he told them wonderful stories about life in the theatre. He made rehearsals such fun that sometimes only a ride home in

Louis' Bugatti could persuade the children to tear themselves away from him.

Meanwhile Claudine was looking after the adult performers as well as organizing the seating and the staging. Much of her time was spent dealing with the displays of newly acquired artistic temperament; she managed to keep most people happy though, but those who refused to be pacified – mostly men, too chauvinistic to take orders from a woman – she sent over to the vineyards for Armand to cope with.

As the day of the feast drew closer, they all began to pray for fine weather – Father Pointeau had even taken to mentioning it during mass. That the afternoon and evening should remain dry was now of paramount importance, for news of the feast had travelled as far afield as Tours, Châtellerault and Angers, and so many people were expected that it would be quite impossible to hold it inside the château. Tante Céline had invited a party of friends from Paris, and Claudine had written to Dissy and Poppy. Solange, who was continually surprising Claudine with the people she knew, had succeeded in attracting such diverse celebrities as the authoress Simone de Beauvoir, Madame Lebrun, wife of the President of France – an old school friend – and René Clair, the famous film director. Louis' old comrades-in-arms had all accepted their invitations too, which meant that several generals and even two *Maréchaux de France* would be coming, as would Coco Chanel, Edward Molyneux and half a dozen other dress designers invited by Monique and Céline. The châteaux of Montvisse and Lorvoire would be bursting at the seams by the time the harvest was in, and Claudine didn't know whether she was excited, nervous, or just plain crazy.

On the Tuesday before the feast, Armand announced that the grapes were to be harvested – starting the next day. Already people had begun arriving at de Lorvoire and

Montvisse, and to Claudine's amazement and delight, when the sun rose the following morning aristocrats and peasants alike were gathering in the vineyards ready to pick the grapes. It was back-breaking work, but everyone threw themselves into it with astonishing vigour, and the only person to complain was Florence Jallais.

By this time Claudine had had several encounters with Florence Jallais – a little woman with staring eyes and a vicious tongue – and knew that complaining was about all she did. Over the past few weeks Florence had never missed an opportunity of reprimanding her: Claudine was giving people ideas above their station, and it wasn't right. Claudine wasn't French, of course, so she wouldn't understand, but women didn't go drinking in cafés without their husbands unless they were trollops, and they didn't sit down at the table with the men when the meals were being served up, the way Claudine had the other day at Liliane's. Oh yes, she knew all about that, her husband had been there, he had seen it. No, Claudine should have waited for the men to finish before she ate anything herself – that was how decent Frenchwomen behaved. She was setting a bad example all round, and should be ashamed of herself . . .

Halfway through the final afternoon of the harvest, the day before the feast, it started to rain. A groan went up throughout the valley, but no one – with the exception of Florence Jallais – deserted his post. Even Tante Céline and her friends continued picking, scarves tied around their heads and mackintoshes draped over their shoulders. Not one of them had ever done anything like this before, but tremendous fun though it was, they all agreed later as they rubbed expensive creams into their swollen, scratched and in some cases bleeding fingers, that the novelty had now most definitely worn off – as, thankfully, had the rain.

Everyone retired early to bed that night, exhausted from the day's toil, and Claudine drove down to the village to spend the evening with Liliane and Armand, intending to go over the final details of the next day's festivities. But Liliane took herself off to bed within half an hour of Claudine's arrival, and Claudine, rocking back and forth in Liliane's chair in front of the fire, fell into a deep sleep from which Armand had some difficulty in rousing her.

By three o'clock on Sunday afternoon, everything was ready. Dozens of wooden boxes had been set out to make a stage in front of the caves, lights had been rigged in the trees and on the château walls. In the courtyard more than fifty long tables – borrowed from neighbouring town halls, châteaux and churches – had been set up. A path had been cut into the forest so that young Richard, who was playing Prince Charming, could ride out to his Sleeping Beauty – played by little Janette Reinberg. Wild boar, roebuck and hares were roasting on spits, while in the kitchens Arlette, Liliane and an army of helpers were organizing tureens of broth and platters of vegetables and freshly baked bread. Armand and the estate workers were pouring the wine into pitchers while young Luc, the accordionist who usually played under the statue of Rabelais in Chinon, ran speedily through his repertoire before the guests arrived. And in the ballroom the children were being entertained by Philippe, who had been excused from his duties in order to keep them under control until their performance began.

Claudine felt exhausted already. Since mass that morning she had been driving out to Chinon and the surrounding villages, checking that everyone had transport to Lorvoire and making sure that her performers weren't suffering from last-minute nerves. None were, which was more than she could say for herself . . . Returning to the château just before three o'clock, she got up on the stage and in a cracked and harassed voice declared that there was no more she could do, and heaven help them all for the lunatics they were to have got involved in all this in the first place.

Watching her, Armand thought he had never seen her look so pale. He went over to her, turned her round and pointed her in the direction of the château. 'What you need now,' he told her, 'is a long, relaxing bath. After which I expect to see you in nothing less than the most glamorous dress you possess, and all your jewels.'

She smiled up at him. Then, on impulse, she hugged him, wanting him to know that she couldn't have done any of this without him, and that, for once, she was happy to obey his instructions.

When she finally reappeared, she came out of the darkness of the château and stopped at the top of the steps, waiting for him to look up at her. She was aware of people milling about, shouting and laughing and pushing past him as he stood there, simply staring at her. She smiled, a teasing light in her eyes, but Armand's face had paled . . .

Even in the trousers and shirt she had worn earlier, and with dirt on her face, she had managed to look infinitely appealing. But now, standing there with her glorious raven hair piled high on her head, he knew he had never seen her so lovely. Little defiant corkscrews of hair curled round her long, shapely neck, her luscious mouth was rouged and moist, and her full breasts rose with each breath. She was wearing a black crepe evening dress that plunged to her waist at the back and front, barely concealing the fullness of her breasts and hugging the slender length of her figure. Diamonds glittered at her ears, her neck and her wrists – though nothing, Armand thought, could outshine the dazzling beauty of her sapphire-blue eyes. But it was the way she radiated such naked sensuality that dried the words in his throat and sent the sudden surge of desire swelling through his loins.

'Do you like it?' she said, looking down at her dress.

At first he couldn't answer, but in the end he managed a taut smile, and turned to continue organizing the arrivals.

Claudine wondered what had happened to make him angry. Wandering down the steps, she saw Monique, and realized that she had been watching them. Then Solange appeared, sporting a flapper dress from the nineteen twenties, and Claudine ran to take her arm and carry her off to greet their guests.

It turned out to be an evening none of them would ever forget. It began with a brief speech from Louis, welcoming them all, expressing his regret that his sons could not be present, but assuring them that he would do his personal best to make it up to all the pretty girls. Solange shrieked with laughter at that, which was much funnier than Louis' gentle attempt at humour, and conceding that his wife had upstaged him yet again, he laughingly nodded to Joseph Millerand, the village butcher, to start carving the venison, while Arlette, Liliane and the kitchen maids from Lorvoire and Montvisse swarmed out of the kitchens to serve Liliane's famous broth.

Next, the Chinon school choir filed onto the stage and accompanied by a teacher on the piano and their own tambourines, began to sing songs from the Great War. In no time at all the audience was joining in, waving their hands in the air, swaying from side to side and slapping their neighbours on the back as they bellowed the words at the tops of their voices. The party spirit had infected them all and things were off to a magnificent start. However, there was a chorus of disapproval when after fifteen minutes the children made their bows and left – but good humour was rapidly restored when Basile Juette, a juggler from Thierry, somersaulted onto the stage, caught his nine pins from his wife and started tossing them in the air, while Luc played the accordion.

Basile was followed by Fabien Désbourdes and his performing dog, who caused untold hilarity by sitting with its head cocked to one side and looking bemused while

Fabien shouted instructions. No matter what poor Fabien did, the dog seemed perplexed, which turned out to be far better entertainment than if it had performed the tricks expected of it. Later, the barber-shop quartet from Huîmes suffered badly at the hands of the local lads, who insisted on standing on their seats and howling. At first the quartet was distinctly put out, but then they recovered their spirits and sang louder than ever, and the local lads were shamed into silence.

When the light began to fade, the stage was illuminated by lamps in the trees, and soon it was time for *Sleeping Beauty*. It looked like being a triumph – until young Richard, hotly pursued by Philippe, trotted out of the forest on the pony, wailing that he was frightened. Not a very auspicious introduction for Prince Charming, but somehow the day was saved, he planted a kiss on Janette's lips, and every child present whooped and jeered with delight.

Claudine, who had handed over the stage management to professionals from a theatre in Tours for the evening, was able to relax and enjoy herself. She sat at one of the long tables with Solange, Armand, and Dissy and Poppy, who had managed to come over from London. Every time she caught Dissy's eye, they were on the verge of laughing: all around them, dignified and distinguished guests were having as wild and wonderful a time as the people from the villages. Several of them were only too ready to leave their seats and join in the dancing that was taking place in front of the château between acts. Armand was persuaded to his feet by one of Tante Céline's friends, and after that there was no stopping him as he whirled Solange, then Monique, then Dissy, round and round the forecourt to the music of Luc's accordion. In fact it occurred to Claudine that Armand was asking everyone to dance except her . . .

Then there was more entertainment. Two teenagers from Candés St Martin gave a lively performance of a song from an Italian opera, and after them came Raymond Loiseau from Lémeré who fancied himself as a comedian. His act was greeted with great enthusiasm, and it was while everyone was banging the tables and calling for more that Claudine noticed Armand had disappeared.

'What's the matter?' Dissy shouted above the din.

'Have you seen Armand?' Claudine yelled back.

'He's gone to change – for our song,' Solange cried.

'Oh, of course,' Claudine laughed, and was surprised at how relieved she felt that he hadn't left altogether.

She saw him again a few minutes later, while Luc was playing the accordion and General Weygand was leading the dancing with a young girl from Chinon. Armand was standing in the middle of a crowd beside the stage, talking to one of the stage hands and trying – though not very hard, it seemed to Claudine – to disentangle himself from the arms of Mathilde Dubloc, who had had too much to drink. It was the first time Claudine had seen him in anything but his work clothes, and she didn't know whether it was the white tie and tails or Mathilde's amorous attentions that caused the strange sensation she had when she looked at him. She found she couldn't tear her eyes from him.

After a while he turned and started back to the table, and seeing her watching him, his face broke into a grin. Her heart very nearly turned over then, at how handsome he looked. He came up to her and took her hand – but as their eyes met, something seemed to pass between them and their smiles froze. Again Armand was aware of the burning desire he felt for her, but as the blood began to pound through his body he jerked his hand away and turned to speak to someone behind him.

Shocked, Claudine looked down at her hand. She felt suddenly hot, and it was as though the clatter and laughter around her was fading into the distance. She started when his arm pressed against hers as he leaned forward to pass a pitcher of wine to Dissy; it was as if a current of electricity had shot through her body. She turned to look at him, aghast and confused. He was straining to listen to what Dissy was saying, but she knew he was aware of her. A sudden image of François leapt before her eyes – and then she did something so brazen that when she thought of it later, she wanted to die of shame. But then it was as if she had somehow lost control of herself, and she found her hand slipping gently across Armand's thigh.

He turned to look at her, and when she saw the naked desire in his eyes her mouth began to tremble and her fingers increased their pressure. A soft moan escaped him, and he found himself leaning towards her. Then suddenly there was a blare of sound and a stage-hand caught Armand by the shoulder and told him he was on next.

Claudine was so shaken it was some time before she could look at the stage. When she did, it was to see Armand laughing and bowing, the applause growing more and more deafening as he twirled Solange round the piano before they took up their positions to sing.

'Aren't you supposed to be playing for them?'

Monique's sour face was staring across the table at her. Quickly pulling herself together, Claudine walked up the steps onto the stage.

Armand held out a hand to her, and the smile he gave her was so warm and so intimate that for a moment she was seized with panic. But then he turned away, drawing her with him to present her to the audience who, now that they had seen her, were treating her to such a tumultuous welcome that it brought the smile back to her face and returned the strength to her limbs. Letting go of his hand, she curtsied, and went to take her place at the piano.

The duet was a disaster: Armand got no further than the second line of the first verse before a deathly hush fell over the gathering. Solange sang the next few lines tunefully enough, but when Armand started to crow again Claudine could hear sniggers, and to her dismay she felt her own lips beginning to twitch. She glanced up at him, but he seemed oblivious and continued to sing, then gave a charming smile as he turned to Solange for her to take up the next line.

When it came to his turn again, someone at the back let out a howl. It was echoed by a voice a little nearer, then another and another. By this time Claudine was shaking with suppressed laughter, but there was nothing she could do as one by one the audience joined in the cacophony with caterwauls, yelps, barks and groans. She stole another look at Armand, amazed that he could continue under such protest, but as she caught his eye, he winked, then put his heart and soul behind the flattest top note she had ever heard. And Solange, whose head was vibrating with the energy she was pouring into her own performance, was quite clearly in raptures.

The din was terrible. Tears of laughter poured down Claudine's face. They had known this would happen, Armand and Solange, and were now doing everything they could to encourage it.

When the song was finally over they received a standing ovation, but Armand modestly declined to sing again. Regretfully, he said, he must now stand down – to make way for the surprise they had for Claudine. And it was then that Thomas Crouy, Yves Fauberg, Gustave from the café, and four other men from Lorvoire bundled out of the kitchens dressed as can-can girls, lifted their skirts and began to kick their legs in the air in time to Luc's accordion.

Claudine had never seen anything so hilarious in her life as those seven old men in their curly wigs, beauty spots, fishnet stockings and farmyard boots. To think that, while flatly refusing to do anything, they had all the time been planning to steal the show! And steal it they did as they cavorted round the stage wagging their feet, gleefully exposing their lace-clad buttocks and throwing saucy kisses to the young men. They responded handsomely to six encores, but the seventh was too much and Gustave collapsed in a heap, taking Thomas and Yves with him.

The only thing left after *Les Filles du Moulin Macabre*, as they called themselves, was the fireworks. It was a magnificent display, set off by the firemen of Chinon at the bottom of the meadow. Claudine watched Armand fetch his mother from the kitchens to come and watch, and then, resisting the urge to join them, she wandered round to the front steps of the château where Dissy and Poppy were sitting huddled in a blanket.

'Tired, darling?' Dissy asked, as she made room for her.

'Mm, a little.'

Poppy chuckled. 'You've surpassed yourself, Clo, old girl. I can't think of anyone alive who could have mixed the classes as successfully as you have today. You'll be the talk of the countryside for a long time to come – though I gather you're the talk of the countryside already.'

Claudine smiled, and looked up as a rocket screamed loudly overhead, then exploded into a thousand stars. There was a loud chorus of approval, and as she lowered her eyes Claudine saw Armand strolling down over the meadow with his mother and the men from the village.

'It was a shame François couldn't be here,' Dissy said. 'He'd have been proud of the way you brought all this together.'

'Do you think so?' Claudine whispered. And as she rested her head on Dissy's shoulder, there was nothing she could do to stop the tears of all the pain she harboured inside from flowing silently down her cheeks.

12

It was approaching two in the morning as the black Citröen glided smoothly over Chinon bridge, then turned and headed for the forest road leading to Lorvoire. In just over a week it would be Christmas. The rain was coming down in torrents, and the rising mewl of the wind was the only sound that could be heard above the monotonous scraping of the windscreen-wipers. François had left Heidelberg over twenty-four hours before, stopping only for gas and a bite to eat at an inn near Châlons, and now he was tired, unshaven and in a foul temper.

He had known of Hitler's intention to annex Austria for over six months now, but the French government, true to form, were refusing to see what such a move could mean, not only for France but for the rest of Europe. Even the generals were dragging their heels – though that didn't surprise him either, it merely infuriated him. Very few men in positions of power these days would allow themselves actually to believe that there would be another war – which meant that even Louis Rivet and Paul Paillole of the French Secret Service were unable to instill a sense of urgency into the Defence Ministry. Still, that was their problem. What concerned François now was his forthcoming trip to London.

His chance meeting with Lord Halifax, who had been in Berlin recently attempting to persuade Hitler not to help himself to the Sudetenland, had proved rather more profitable than his dealings with the French. Again, that didn't surprise him. The British often were prepared to listen, and Halifax had now, via the British Embassy in Berlin, extended him an invitation to meet that old sparring partner of his father's, Winston Churchill.

It wouldn't be the first time François had met Churchill; they'd come across one another many times over the past five years, and François knew that while the old man grudgingly admired him for the way he acquired information, he was also offended by François' continuing refusal to work solely for the British. The very idea, of course, was laughable – but François was in no mood for humour just at this moment. The British Ambassador in Berlin had superciliously informed him that he would not be welcome in London without documentary evidence to back up his claims – which was why he was returning to Lorvoire in the dead of night, to steal into his own home and take the relevant papers from his father's safe.

Silently cursing, he swung the car into a clearing in the forest, just beyond the gates to the château. He had to have the documents. They included the minutes of a recent secret meeting between the Führer and his staff, which François had obtained in Berlin and sent to Lorvoire by courier; documents his father had obtained, and refused to give him, on the German Enigma coding machine – these would impress the British no end; and a detailed plan of the Maginot Line. This last would impress the Germans when next he returned to Berlin.

The rain was still beating down. Hunched into his voluminous black coat, he made his way stealthily through the forest to the bridge at the back of the château. It was more than two months since he'd last seen his family, he realized, but he'd been away much longer than that in the past – the only difference now was that his father would take a dim view of the way he was neglecting his wife.

The bunch of keys was already in his hand as he walked over the bridge and, selecting the one he wanted, let himself quietly in through the door. He waited a moment for his eyes to adjust to the darkness, then he removed his shoes and started across the landing. The door to Claudine's bedroom was ajar. He hesitated, listened for a moment, then hearing the steady sound of her breathing, he walked on.

For such a big man he moved with surprising agility, stealing through the house as silently and smoothly as the distorted shadow he cast before him. He knew every nook and cranny of the château, every stair that creaked and every door that groaned. In no time at all he was slipping quietly into the drawing-room, closing the door behind him, then crossing to the library.

He approached his father's desk and took the bunch of keys from his pocket, slid the smallest one into the lock and eased open the bottom drawer which housed the document safe. Then he sat down and turned on the desk lamp. The safe combination was easy to remember, it was his and Lucien's dates of birth in reverse order.

In less that five minutes he had everything he had come for. The documents were on the desk, the safe was closed and the drawer locked.

Now, the only thing left to be dealt with was the gun which was pointing straight at his head . . .

He glanced again at the shadow splayed across the wall, then swore under his breath as he sank back in the chair. The man was standing over him. The lamp was between them, so that the man's face was lost in shadow, but François knew who it was, and his mouth curled in a grim smile as he waited to be recognized.

'Monsieur de Lorvoire!' Philippe gasped.

François' eyes narrowed, and he watched with callous amusement as the footman's mouth begin to twitch.

'I – I heard a noise, *monsieur*,' Philippe stammered, feeling himself break into a cold sweat under that terrible gaze. 'I didn't know it was you.'

'You weren't supposed to.' He nodded towards the gun. Philippe started as he realized he was still pointing it, and his boyishly middle-aged face was white and trembling as he placed it on the desk.

François stood up, then sweeping the documents into the deep pocket inside his coat, he turned off the lamp.

Philippe's heart started to pound as his eyes adjusted to the eerie blue darkness. François' face was hidden in shadow, but Philippe could see the whites of his eyes and the vicious silvery gash that tore across his cheek. Ordinarily Philippe was a brave man, but faced with such menace he was terrified, not only for his life, but also, he suddenly realized, for his immortal soul. Involuntarily his hand moved to make the sign of the cross, but before he could even begin François had grabbed it and twisted it behind his back.

'God won't save you!' he hissed. Then he laughed, a low, demonic sound, and Philippe felt the air around him turn chill. 'Pick up the gun, Philippe, and return to your room. Forget you have seen me tonight . . . if you can.' Again François laughed, and Philippe needed no second bidding. He picked up the gun, and fled from the room.

Once he was in the hall he stopped, and took a deep breath in an effort to steady his nerves. His fear had been genuine enough, his heart was still thudding like the drums of hell and that diabolical laugh still rang in his ears, but petrified as he was, he could still rejoice in the immense good fortune he'd had to stumble upon François de Lorvoire in the dead of night, stealing documents from his father's safe. The content of the documents was of no concern to Philippe, nor did it interest him that de Lorvoire obviously didn't want his family to know he was here. All that concerned him was the fact that, just as his employer had suspected, François de Lorvoire was no longer in Germany. Now all Philippe had to do was to get the information through.

Having given Philippe enough time to return to his room,

François let himself out of the library and started back up the stairs. He'd been in half a mind to dispense with the footman there and then, but since he didn't present any immediate danger, either to himself or his family, he'd decided not to bother. However, the very moment Philippe looked like becoming a problem, his stay at the château would be cut dramatically short. François liked that 'dramatically'; given the man's theatrical background, it was peculiarly appropriate. He allowed himself a quiet chuckle as he considered how Philippe's employer might respond to the bogus footman's hasty despatch.

Dismissing the man from his mind, François made his way back to the nursery landing. Once again he hesitated at Claudine's door, and this time, instead of walking on, he pushed the door wider and stepped into the moonlit room.

He walked to the foot of the bed, his hands in his pockets and a heavy frown between his eyes. He looked down at her for some time before allowing himself actually to see her. When he did, the frown deepened as he became aware of his response. Her tousled raven hair tumbled over the pillows, and her sleeping face looked vulnerable in the soft grey light from the window. Her shoulders were bare, and he could see the gentle curve of her breasts beneath the flimsy silk of her nightgown.

There was no denying her sensuality, and his body craved the release, but even as the thought entered his mind, he discarded it. Quite apart from the need to keep this visit secret, any encounter with his wife meant walking into an emotional minefield . . . But his need was pressing, which made him wonder how long it was since he had seen Élise. Six weeks – six long weeks since they had lain in her bed and she had told him how all Paris was talking about the success of the Lorvoire wine feast for which Claudine had been responsible. The memory brought a grim smile to François' face as he recalled how his response had dissolved into a groan when Élise's succulent mouth closed over his genitals.

His eyes were now on Claudine's mouth, and he nearly laughed aloud at the idea of her satisfying him in that way. He wondered then if he had ever kissed her; he couldn't remember. If anything, that pleased him – he had done everything in his power to make her despise him, and hoped that by now he had succeeded. It would make life a great deal easier if he had, but he had never met a woman of such infuriating tenacity. Under different circumstances he might have admired her for it, for no matter what he did to her, it seemed that nothing would break that intransigent spirit of hers. But since he had learned of the Abwehr's intention to recruit him, and knowing only too well the methods German Intelligence employed to achieve what they wanted, the dangers and decisions that faced him during the years ahead were such that he could not allow himself the luxury of the kind of wife she so obviously wanted to be.

What a fool she was, he thought, for not having listened to him at the outset! She could have saved herself so much pain. But he had never done anything to encourage her love, and the responsibility for her suffering must be hers alone. She meant nothing to him, she was there only because his father wanted her to be.

Not wanting to waste any more time, he turned away from the bed and went back to the landing to recover his shoes. He stopped for a moment, sensing suddenly that the night sounds had changed. But it was only that the rain was lighter now, and raking his fingers quickly through his damp hair, he let himself out into the night.

As she heard the door to the bridge swing closed, Claudine opened her eyes. She had known he was there. She had been in the nursery, not in bed, when he came out of the forest; she had seen him crossing the bridge from the window, and had run back to her bedroom so he should not find her awake. She had heard him go downstairs, then come up again. She had felt him standing at the end of her bed, watching her, but she had not stirred. She didn't want him to ask why she had been in the nursery, and she didn't want to know why he had entered his own home like a burglar. Not that he would have told her, of course, but he would have been angry that she had seen him. And something she couldn't face just now was François' anger.

Ever since the night of the wine feast she had felt as though her life was crumbling to pieces. The confusion and pain she had suffered as a result of François' indifference was now exacerbated by her feelings for Armand. During her waking hours she could think only of him, and there was little release to be found in sleep, for the dream she had had the night she returned from the café with Lucien, when François had carried her up the stairs to bed, was waiting to taunt her every time she closed her eyes.

She knew now that the man making love to her in the dream wasn't François at all, it was Armand. François was only there at the end, looking down at her with contempt, as if warning her that no matter who she made love with, no matter how passionately she wanted them, she would never be rid of him.

Perhaps the dream would have been easier to bear if she hadn't spent so many hours asleep. At first when she had taken to her bed, the day after the wine feast, she had thought she was simply tired after all the exertion. But when she was still sluggish and lifeless after two weeks, Solange had wanted to call in the doctor. Claudine had refused, knowing that there was nothing Doctor Lebrun could do to ease the hurt of Armand's silence: he had not sent a message, had not even asked how she was, it seemed. But of course he knew, just as she did, that it was madness to think that there could ever be anything between them. So he was avoiding her, just as she was avoiding him.

For a while it had seemed as if she was avoiding life altogether. She continued to sleep, and was unable to dress herself or even find the energy to speak to her aunt. In the end Solange had called in Doctor Lebrun, and it was then, just over a week ago now, that Claudine had discovered the cause of her lethargy. She was carrying François' child.

That was why she had been in the nursery earlier; she went there often now, to think about the future. And that was why she had pretended to be asleep when François came in. She didn't want to have to tell him, she didn't want it to be happening at all. She had sworn everyone to secrecy, saying that she wanted to tell him herself – and not on the telephone, but when they were together. But she dreaded telling him, almost as much as she dreaded giving birth, because François had left her in no doubt that if the child was a boy, then their marriage would be at an end. But still she would have to live here, pretend that she was happy, pretend she was fulfilled, when all she wanted in the world . . .

She turned her face into the pillow as she thought of Armand, remembered how he had responded to her touch on the night of the wine feast, how she had longed to go to him, to feel his arms around her. But was it really his arms she craved, or did she just want to make François jealous? She laughed bitterly to herself. Nothing she did would ever make François jealous. So why shouldn't she try to find happiness in the arms of another man? After all, hadn't he as good as told her to himself?

It was the second week of the New Year, 1938, and Armand was standing in the chill morning air in front of the wine caves, laughing at something one of his assistants was telling him. Though he hadn't seen him yet, he knew that François had returned to the château the evening before, just as he knew that Claudine was, at that very moment, standing at the window watching him. If he looked up she would wave, and he would wave back. They did this almost every morning, but today he couldn't bring himself to do it; he didn't want to see the heart-rending pretence of happiness in her eyes, and he didn't want her to see the hunger in his own. This morning, knowing that François was back, he could feel the anger and torment surging through his veins, and knew that if he looked at her he would be in danger of losing control, of doing something he might bitterly regret. And so clapping a hand on Michel's shoulder, he turned into the cave where she could no longer see him.

As he disappeared into the darkness, Claudine tore herself from the window, picked up a newspaper and left the room. She abhorred the weakness in her that made her watch him as she did – it was as if she was deliberately intensifying her pain by feasting her eyes on him during the day, so that at night she could lie in her bed and fantasize about him. She didn't know any more what she loved most about him, whether it was his thick blond hair, his laughing, tender blue eyes, his sensitive mouth or the muscular contours of his body. Or maybe it was that crazy woollen hat he pulled tightly over his head to keep out the cold. Or perhaps what she liked best was picturing him in Liliane's wonderful kitchen, with its smells, its warmth and its homeliness that must contrast so painfully with the bleakness of his heart. She thought often of the wife and child he had lost, and wished that in some way she could make it up to him. Perhaps if the child she was carrying were his . . . She tried to imagine what François would say – or do – if she ever told him that, and as the thought intensified her misery her head started to spin.

When François had returned the night before, it was just as they were finishing dinner. He hadn't wanted anything himself, and after handing gifts to her, Solange and Monique he had closeted himself in the library with his father. She knew they had had a terrible row; before they lowered their voices she had heard Louis shout something about papers, and François answer that he had had his reasons for taking them. This morning François had not come down for breakfast, and Louis had seemed distracted.

She had mentioned François' fleeting visit to no one, and she wasn't going to ask him about it. She wanted nothing to do with him now, and wished with all her heart that she didn't have to tell him about the baby. Somehow, when François knew, it would make it all seem real in a way that neither her lethargy nor her expanding waistline had succeeded in doing.

She let herself quietly into their apartment, and found to her relief that his bedroom door was still firmly closed. But when, an hour later, she came out of her own room wearing the sable coat he had given her the night before, she saw to her dismay that he was in the sitting-room reading the newspaper she had brought up with her. She was going to the beauty salon with Tante Céline. She was early, but she had hoped to get away before she was forced to confront him.

She stood in the middle of the room, waiting for him to look up, but when he merely continued to read she turned towards the door.

'Where are you going?'

'To the beauty salon,' she answered, and tucking her purse under her arm, she opened the door.

'When, precisely, Claudine, are you intending to tell me?'

She stopped as the full impact of his question reached her. He couldn't know about the baby, he couldn't possibly, no one would have betrayed her . . . He was still looking down at the paper. After a moment or two, he turned the page, and without looking up said, 'Close the door, Claudine.'

Automatically, she did as he told her.

'I'm still waiting,' he said a few moments later, and when at last he did look up she felt a spasm of fear at the terrible expression in his eyes. 'When are you planning to tell me?' he said again.

'Does it matter, if you already know?' she snapped.

'Perhaps not. But what does matter is that you have known you were pregnant since the beginning of December and haven't yet seen fit to inform me. Why?'

She flinched, but she had no answer to give, and wanting only to get away from those appalling eyes, she started back to the door.

'Is it because you are unsure of the father's identity?' he said.

It was as if he had struck her. She spun round, her face ashen and her eyes flashing with rage. 'How dare you!' she hissed.

His eyes darkened, but his voice remained level as he said, 'I should like an answer. I should also like the truth.' He smiled coldly. 'Do you have the courage for it?'

She was speechless, and could only stare at him. He actually believed he might not be the father.

After a while he said, 'Perhaps it would help you if I were to phrase the question another way. Are you, Claudine, hoping to pass Armand St Jacques' child off as a de Lorvoire?'

His tone was so affable that for a moment she felt she was losing her sanity. She opened her mouth to speak, but still the words wouldn't come. This was a nightmare, it was worse than anything he had put her through before.

'How long have you been lovers?' he demanded.

Her head snapped up and her eyes were blazing with hatred as she screamed, 'We're not lovers! But don't think it's because I don't want him. I want him more than I've ever wanted anyone in my life. And I would have gone to him, I would have left you to rot in your jealousy if this child I'm carrying wasn't yours.'

'Jealousy?' he repeated, clearly both surprised and amused.

'Yes! Jealousy! Why else would you accuse me . . .'

'Claudine,' he interrupted, 'I am guilty of a great many feelings towards you, but . . .'

'*Feelings!* You don't have any feelings!'

'. . . jealousy is not one of them. I'm sorry if that disappoints you, but it is the truth. Now, is the child mine?'

'Of course it's yours, damn you! You're the one who's been raping me these past months. And for your information, I probably fell pregnant the night we got married. How does that make you feel, to know that your child was conceived in such bitterness?'

He rubbed a hand over his jaw as he regarded her with evident amusement. 'If only we'd known at the time,' he drawled, 'you might have been spared my rapacious visits in the weeks that followed. But that wasn't what you wanted, was it?'

In a flash she was across the room and had dealt a stinging blow to his face. 'You're sick! Do you hear me, *sick*!'

'I hear you, Claudine,' he answered mildly. 'But try, for your own sake, never to do that again.'

'Why? Would you hit me back?' she spat, her eyes glittering. 'It's just the kind of thing you would do, isn't it? Strike a pregnant woman.'

'Don't think to hide behind your pregnancy, Claudine. If I wanted to strike you, then neither that nor anything else would stop me.'

'What kind of a man are you?' she cried.

He stood up, towering over her. She took a step back, but he grabbed her by the shoulders and pulled her so close that his mouth was very nearly on hers. 'The kind of man you want so desperately that you can't sleep at night for the sheer hell it puts you through.'

Her eyes blazed into his, and she could feel his fingers

digging into her arms. She lifted her hands to push him away, but he caught them and wrenched them behind her, bringing the full length of her body against his.

'Deny it!' he hissed. 'Let me hear you tell me it's not true.'

She opened her mouth, but her breath locked in her throat as wave after wave of paralysing desire rushed through her.

'Tell me you don't want me!' he raged, and clutching her wrists in one hand, he brought the other to her hair and jerked her head back.

'Let me go!' she cried. 'François, let me . . .' Her words were drowned as he crushed his mouth against hers.

She twisted her hands free and slammed them into his chest, struggling to push him away. But he was holding her against him, pressing his body into hers and probing the depths of her mouth with his tongue. Her hands flew to his face, raked at his skin and tore at his hair, but he wouldn't let her go. Then his hands were beneath her skirt, pulling it to her waist, pushing inside her knickers. He grabbed her buttocks so hard that he lifted her from the floor, and he kissed her as though he would devour her.

She moaned and gasped and fought his tongue with hers, holding his face between her hands, coiling her fingers in his hair and panting for breath. Then she was tearing at his trousers, pulling the buttons apart, and she heard the silk rip as he tore her knickers from her. He lifted her onto the table and pulled her legs wide.

'Do you want me?' he growled.

'Yes,' she gasped. 'Yes, I want you.'

'Where do you want me?' And she cried out as he thrust his fingers inside her. 'Here? Is this where you want me?'

'Yes. Oh my God, yes.' She writhed madly beneath the pressure of his fingers, jerking her hips, pushing herself onto them, feeling them probe even deeper inside her.

He pulled his penis from his trousers, and as she saw him

come towards her she sobbed out his name, opening her legs wider and twisting them about his waist. He withdrew his fingers and caught her by the hips, dragging her towards him, ready to enter her.

Then suddenly their eyes met and he stopped.

For a long moment he looked down at her. She held her breath, unable to read his expression as her blood pounded savagely through her body. Then his face changed, and suddenly she wanted to scream. The bitterness, the loathing, the contempt that glittered in his eyes was unmistakable.

'No!' she cried. 'François, no!' But he had already turned away.

'Cover yourself up,' he growled, rearranging his own clothes.

'François, why are you doing this? *Why*, when . . .'

He turned back, and she flinched at the malicious smile on his lips. 'I did it to show you what a fool you are. To show you . . .'

'No! You did it because you wanted me. François I saw it, I felt it.'

'You saw and felt what you wanted to,' he snarled. 'Now, cover yourself!'

'I won't! I want you and I'm not afraid to say it. You want me too . . .'

'*No!*' he roared. 'I don't want you, Claudine. I've never wanted you. If I did I'd have taken you, just as you wanted me to. But you disgust me, do you hear? You disgust and repel me!'

For one dreadful moment she thought he was going to hit her, but then the anger suddenly died in his eyes, and in its place was a sinister light of pleasure. She stared up at him, too shocked to speak – and then he turned away and started towards his bedroom.

'François,' she said.

He looked back at where she stood beside the table, her coat covering the skirt that was hitched around her waist. Her face was pale, but her voice was perfectly steady as she said, 'I want you to know, François, that I wish with all my heart that the child I am carrying was Armand's. But it's not, it's yours. It can only be yours because until I married you, I was a virgin, and since I married you I have never slept with another man. I don't care if you believe me, I don't care what you think or do any more, but I want to know one thing. I want to know whether, if the baby had been Armand's, you would have let me go.'

The corner of his mouth lifted in a ghastly smile as he took his time contemplating her. In the end she could stand it no more.

'*What would you have done?*' she screamed.

Finally, with a diabolical lowering of his eyebrows, he said, 'Remember Hortense?' And chuckling quietly to himself, he walked into his room.

– 13 –

Claudine was now in her sixth month of pregnancy, and though there were still times when she felt listless and depressed, on the whole she was coping much better than she had in the earlier stages. She never allowed herself to think about François now, and had firmly banished from her mind the memory of that terrible day when she had told him she was pregnant. Instead she concentrated on Armand, doing everything she could to recapture the friendship they had had before the harvest celebration. Of course, things were different now, they both knew that. There were times when her need for his love, his kindness, his comforting arms, reached such a pitch that, but for the fact that they were careful never to be alone together, she would have been unable to stop herself touching him.

As news of her pregnancy spread people had started to come from the nearby châteaux to see her, and some even motored down from Paris. She was happy to see them, but knowing that their presence was a constant reminder to Armand of the great difference between their lives, she was always relieved when they left. And in fact she was never happier than on the quiet days, when she could drop in to see Liliane and relax in the rocking chair beside the fire, while the old lady chattered on and the early spring sunlight shone in through the open window.

Little Janette and Robert Reinberg always kept a look out for her car, and if they saw it outside the St Jacques' house, would come bounding along the street to see her. Madame Reinberg's tailoring business was now beginning to thrive, and Claudine loved the way Armand spent whatever time he could with the two children, trying in his own way to make up to them for the loss of their father. They adored him, and Janette, who had discovered that one coy look from under her outrageously long lashes could persuade him to do anything, used her charms shamelessly.

Whenever Claudine went to the village she invariably arrived at midday, knowing that Armand and several other men from the vineyards would come in soon afterwards for their lunch. Sometimes, as she watched Armand helping himself to food or tossing back his wine, the coarse golden hair on his arms glinting in the sunlight, his handsome face intent on the business at hand, she would imagine what it would be like if it were just the two of them there, safe and secure in their love, with their child growing in her womb. It was a fantasy which she knew would only distress her later, when she was forced to return to the reality of her marriage, but she couldn't deny herself the happiness of those few minutes spent dreaming of how things might be.

Sometimes, rocking in the chair, she fell into a doze; then feeling a hand on her arm, she would look up and see Armand standing over her, his eyes alight with laughter and love as he gently teased her for snoring through her dreams. How she managed to stop herself reaching out for him then, she never knew.

But there were days when Armand was bad-tempered and snapped at everyone. When he was like that, Janette and Robert would take themselves off, the meals would pass in silence and Claudine would watch him with a heavy heart. It was always when François was at home that he was like this. She came less often then, knowing that during those times it hurt him, rather than pleased him, to see her.

The night before her birthday was one of the occasions on which François was at home. He gave her a diamond and ruby necklace in a Mauboussin box – at least, he left it on the table in their sitting-room for her to find. She hadn't realized he even knew it was her birthday, but of course Solange or Louis would have told him. When she opened the box, she gasped. The necklace was the most beautiful and unusual she had ever seen, with three ruby crosses of Lorraine hanging from a three-tiered diamond neckband. It must have cost him a fortune.

She had intended to thank him over dinner, but he was so engrossed in talk with his father – France was being torn apart between the Left and Right, they were saying, and Louis was highly critical of Léon Blum's intention of forming a new Popular Front government – that she decided to leave it until the next morning. But immediately after dinner, François informed them that he must return to Paris that night.

She allowed herself no feelings about the fact that he wasn't intending to stay for her birthday, though somewhere in the deepest recesses of her mind, she thought she was pleased. Perhaps she was at last beginning to overcome her obsession with him. And besides, if he had stayed she would have had to cancel the party she was planning with Solange and Monique, for his presence would have made it impossible.

The morning of her birthday was the morning the Germans finally marched into Austria. But no one at Lorvoire heard the news that day, for it was the day Claudine had her accident.

She was woken early by the baby, who was being even more active than usual, and laughing, she clutched her hands to her belly and started to scold it. Then, thinking of Armand and the day ahead, she felt a sudden rush of happiness. She got out of bed and strolled onto the balcony outside her room, where the branches of the forest were almost close enough to touch and the sun glittered through the leaves.

A little while later she heard the sound of the door opening and then Magaly's gasp of alarm. It wasn't the fact that she was outside that had dismayed Magaly, it was that she was wearing nothing more than a rapturous smile.

'*Madame*!' Magaly cried. 'You will catch a cold! Think of the baby!'

'I am,' Claudine said. 'It's so restless this morning, it's as if it knows it's my birthday.' She ran her hands over her swollen stomach and started to murmur softly to her child. 'I wish I could walk like this through the forest, Magaly,' she said. 'It seems so right to be naked with nature when I am carrying a baby.'

By the time Claudine was ready for breakfast, she was so happy she felt she might burst with it. She could hardly wait for midday, for all the vineyard workers had been invited to take their lunch at the château today, and so too had the children who were too young to be at school, their mothers and grandmothers, Father Pointeau and Doctor Lebrun. Even Florence Jallais was coming, though only because

Armand had agreed to drive her in his van. So, apart from her family, all her guests would be village people, and she was looking forward to it so much that the only thing that had come close to upsetting her was that she couldn't find François' necklace. Never mind, she was too excited to worry about that now. And she began to sail down the stairs in her crimson wool maternity dress, looking, as she had told Magaly, exactly like someone in a bell tent.

It was as she reached the second flight that she heard the noise behind her. Everything happened so quickly then that no one had the chance to shout a warning. Yet when she remembered it later, it was as if it was all happening in slow motion – the clatter of china and silver making her pause, then turn, then she opened her mouth to scream as the footman's body came thundering towards her. As she hit the stairs she felt something sharp dig into her shoulder, then her body seemed to be twisting away from her as the chandelier above started to spin. The last thing she knew was a blinding, star-spangled pain as her head struck the bottom stair.

Hearing the noise, Solange and Louis ran out into the hall, followed by the servants. Monique and Magaly came flying down the stairs, and the instant Magaly saw her mistress's inert body entangled with the footman's, and surrounded by the remains of a breakfast tray, she started to scream.

'Jean-Paul!' Solange barked. 'Find Marcel . . .'

'I'm here, *madame.*'

'Marcel. Go for Doctor Lebrun. Monique! Get away, don't move her. Tilde, Fabienne, fetch some blankets. Louis, take your medication. Now!'

The footman started to groan with pain. 'It's all right, Philippe,' Solange told him, bending down to take his hand. 'Marcel's gone for the doctor. He'll be here soon. Just lie still.'

It seemed an eternity before the doctor arrived, but in that time Solange managed to ascertain that Philippe had probably broken his leg. There was also a deep cut on his jaw, and an angry swelling had started over one eye. He was conscious, though it was clear from the way his head kept rolling from side to side that he was dazed and disoriented.

However, he would live – as would Claudine, Solange told herself vehemently. But her daughter-in-law's lovely face was so pale, and though she had been rubbing her wrists for some time, and wafting smelling-salts under her nose, Claudine showed no signs of coming round.

Monique's hands were resting gently on Claudine's stomach, and when she met her mother's eyes she shook her head. 'It's not moving,' she whispered.

After leaving the château the night before, François had driven straight to the avenue Foch. Almost two months had passed since Élise had told him of Claudine's pregnancy, and her affair with Armand, and he hadn't seen her again in all that time.

Élise had been uneasy at his prolonged absence, particularly since he hadn't even telephoned to say where he was. She knew he was in communication with his courier, Erich von Pappen, but for once von Pappen had refused to divulge François' whereabouts – and her other methods of finding out had, on this occasion, failed her.

By way of comfort, she had reminded herself that a great deal had been happening in Europe over the past couple of months to interest François. Adolf Hitler had pronounced himself Germany's Supreme Military Commander, and Lord Halifax was now the British Foreign Secretary. Most important of all, perhaps – at least, as far as François was concerned – the Nazi plot to annex Austria had been made public. Though the exposé had obviously come far too late, Élise thought, because Erich von Pappen had told her that the Germans were poised to walk into Austria the very next day.

She wondered how many other people knew that – and how much von Schuschnigg, Austria's Chancellor, had paid François for information on the Nazi plot. But that was the kind of detail François never disclosed to anyone, and in truth it didn't really interest Élise. All that mattered to her, as she sat alone in her drawing-room, was that at last he had telephoned to say he was coming.

Beneath her oyster silk peignoir she wore nothing but a pearly-white basque and gartered stockings. Her wonderful golden hair was loose and curling around her shoulders; her pale, luscious skin glowed in the amber half-light, and her ripe lips glimmered a delicate peach-colour. She knew it was the way he would want to find her, she knew too that tonight after such a long absence, he would simply take her, with no thought for her pleasure or care for his own savagery. But the very fact that his body craved such a release was enough to inflame the desire in her own, even if she must wait until the following morning for total satisfaction.

He arrived just after midnight. Hearing his key in the lock, she rose to her feet and, checking herself quickly in the mirror, turned to watch him walk in. The instant she saw his face, her heart contracted so painfully that it was all she could do to stop herself running to him. She had tried so hard to pretend she hadn't missed him; that she wasn't afraid he was angry with her because of what she'd told him about his wife; that she wasn't terrified she might be losing him. But she had been all of those things – and more. It was impossible for her to forget how much she loved him, or how vulnerable that love made her.

But what she did sometimes forget was the way the air, the light, even the temperature, suddenly seemed to change when he walked into a room, and though outwardly she gave no sign of it, inside she was already melting under the burning heat of his eyes. He didn't have to touch her for her to feel him, he didn't have to speak for her to know what he wanted.

Her hand trembled slightly as she poured him a brandy, but her voice was steady as she said, 'It is good to see you.'

He nodded, then reaching inside his coat, he took out a Mauboussin box and put it on the table. She eyed it greedily, knowing that whatever trinket lay inside would be exquisitely expensive.

'The child is mine,' he said.

Startled, she looked up – she hadn't expected him to mention it so soon after arriving. They held one another's eyes, and in the dim golden light she looked more like a mythical goddess than ever, and he more like a demon. Slowly her lips curled into a derisive smile. 'That's what she told you?'

'Yes.'

'And you believe her?'

'Yes.'

She handed him the brandy, then sauntered across to the sofa but didn't sit down. 'François de Lorvoire, the cuckold,' she jeered in her deep, throaty voice. She turned to face him. He was watching her, his eyes as inscrutable as ever and his lips wet from the brandy. 'That is what you are, you know?'

He inclined his head, then put his glass on the mantleshelf beside him.

'You're going to let her get away with it?'

'With having my baby? Of course.'

'If it is your baby. And what about St Jacques?'

'What about him?'

A quick temper flashed in her eyes. 'He is her lover,' she snapped.

'Is he? And just how would you know something like that, Élise?'

He appeared unruffled, but she hadn't missed the dangerous edge in his voice. But it was a question she was prepared for, and was amazed he hadn't asked it before.

'Because it's the talk of the countryside,' she answered disdainfully, 'and fast becoming the talk of Paris. Céline has visitors down there at Montvisse, they're not blind to what goes on under their noses.'

'I should have thought you were above idle gossip, Élise,' he remarked equably. 'However, there is a little truth in the rumours. My wife is in love with St Jacques – or so she tells me.'

'And knowing that, you're prepared to accept that the child isn't his? You're a fool, François.'

All the time they had been speaking, he had been moving towards her. Now he took his hand out of his pocket and pushed her peignoir down over one shoulder. 'Do you think so?' he murmured, feeding his eyes on the ample softness of her skin.

'Do you care what I think?'

'The only thing I care about, Élise, is that the child is mine.' And peeling the peignoir from her other shoulder, he watched it drop to the floor. She looked down at his hand as he trailed it gently over the fine lace of her basque, then watched as he hooked his fingers into a cup of the brassière and eased it down over her plump breast to expose the achingly distended nipple. She took a breath to speak, but his fingers closed over the nipple, and with his other hand he grabbed her hair and tilted her face back to look at him. For a fleeting moment he saw Claudine's lips before him, red and full and trembling, and as his mouth closed angrily over Élise's he released her nipple and started to unbutton his fly.

He took her there on the sofa, so urgently and so swiftly that he didn't even bother to take off his coat. The second time he pushed her over the dining table and took her from behind. Then he led her into the bedroom where he finally removed his clothes and lay down on the bed.

For a while they talked about what he had been doing while he was away, then he flicked back the bedclothes and pulled her on top of him. She rode him with a mounting frenzy while he looked up at her, his hands clasped behind his head, his face expressionless. His climax took longer to achieve that time, but when finally his eyes closed and she saw the muscles in his neck start to tense, she reached behind her and pushed her hand between his legs. His hips suddenly jerked from the bed, and as the semen started to shoot from him, he circled her waist with his hands and slammed into her so hard that she screamed for mercy. When he had finished he let her go, and within minutes he was asleep.

When Élise awoke the following morning she found herself wrapped in his arms, her back pressed against his chest, her bottom resting on his thighs and her head nestling against his shoulder. She lay quietly for some time, listening to his breathing and feeling the warmth of his skin on hers. She knew it was unlikely they would leave the room much before lunch, and for her, lying here like this was the first part of the love-making that would keep them there. This morning he would devote himself to her pleasure, just as last night she had given herself to his.

The fact that he believed Claudine's child was his still rankled with her, but she knew better than to broach the subject again. She would decide later how best to handle Claudine's pregnancy – she had only refrained from interfering until now because she had fully expected François to believe that St Jacques was the father. If he had believed that, she was certain that in one way or another he would have ended his marriage.

For her part, she had no idea whether St Jacques was the father or not. All she knew was that The Bitch was stealing the hearts of everyone she met, and though there were times when Élise doubted if François had a heart to steal, she had only to feel the way he was holding her now to know that, if he chose, he was as capable of love as any man. She also knew that if The Bitch gave birth to an heir, her hopes and dreams of one day becoming the Comtesse de Rassey de Lorvoire, and the mother of the future comte, would be destroyed.

Deciding it was time to wake him she looked at his arm, stretched out across the pillow, and slipping her fingers between his she pushed back against him, gently wriggling her hips. After a moment she did it again, and this time she knew she had woken him.

She turned to face him, and taking his bottom lip between her own, she sucked at it gently. Eventually she pulled away and looked into his eyes. She saw his sardonic smile as she threw off the blankets, then pushed him onto his back so that she could watch him come to full erection. Already his penis was hard, but she waited until it was straining to his navel before lifting her eyes to his. For a while they simply looked at one another, until he lifted a hand and pulled her to him, moulding his lips around hers. It was a long, succulent kiss which seemed to last forever. He drew her body closer so that she could feel the strength of his desire, before, keeping his lips on hers, he rolled her onto her back.

It was as he lowered his mouth to her breasts that the telephone started to ring. Élise groaned and started to sit up, but he pushed her back against the pillows. Smiling salaciously, she relaxed again, and allowed her legs to fall open as his fingers stroked her thighs. Any moment now it would be as if she had left her body, as if there was no room for anything but the overpowering sensation of his touch. But as her eyes fluttered closed, there was a knock at the door. Again she groaned, but this time in anger as her maid called, 'Monsieur de Lorvoire! It is the telephone for you, *monsieur*. Your father wishes to speak to you.'

François had been on the point of telling her to go away, but hearing that it was his father, he pushed himself quickly from the bed and unhooked the robe he kept on the back of the door.

He was back within minutes. Élise was sitting up in bed, the blankets covering her to the waist, her beautiful yellow hair tumbling over her breasts. She smiled as he came in, but as she saw his thunderous expression her face froze.

'What is it?' she breathed.

Ignoring her, he started to pull on his clothes.

'François! What is it? What's happened?'

He didn't answer until he was fully dressed, then he rounded on her with a fierceness that struck terror to her heart. 'My wife has had a fall,' he snarled. 'The footman dropped a breakfast tray, slipped and collided with her on the stairs.'

'What? But . . . Is she all right?'

'I don't know. The doctor's with her now. But you, Élise, had better start praying that she is.'

'François! What do you mean? Where are you going?'

He stopped at the door, then swung round to face her. 'I don't know how much you know about this, Élise, but I'm warning you, have that man out of my home before I arrive there, or so help me, I'll kill you both.'

The door slammed behind him and she was left kneeling on the bed, her exquisite face ashen and her wide green eyes leaden with fear.

There were four of them: General Rudolf von Liebermann, Max Helber, Walter Brüning and Ernst Grundhausen. They were at a secret address in Berlin, in the sleazy, garbage-strewn backstreets of the city's red light district. Apart from the chairs they were sitting on, there was no furniture in the room, and the two sash-windows which overlooked the striptease clubs, the shady bars and the rancid market stalls four floors below, were smeared with the filth and slime of several years.

Von Liebermann, the eldest and heaviest of them, and also the most senior in rank, waited for the others to complete their perusal of the documents he had handed them on their arrival. It was his way to present his *Komitee* with a chronicle of recently acquired intelligence at the start of each meeting, which they were required to read, without comment, from beginning to end. Then, when they had finished, he would address them. On this occasion, however, he had information over and above what was contained in the documents, and as he sat waiting patiently for his men to finish reading there was a hint of a smile on his pale lips. How convenient that a meeting had been arranged for today, – it had saved him the trouble of locating the men in order to pass on the news which had reached him in the early hours of that morning.

At last it was time for him to speak. Lifting a hand to his mouth, he cleared his throat, and with no reference to anything they had read, he said, 'The Wine Supplier's wife has had a fall.'

The three faces staring back at him remained bland, and he experienced a quick thrill of satisfaction that he had chosen his men so well. Then he raised his brows, an indication that they were now permitted to speak.

'Did the child perish?' Grundhausen enquired.

'Possibly,' von Liebermann answered.

'Possibly?' repeated Max Helber, the man sitting to his right.

Looking at Helber's youthful face and thick, full-blooded lips, von Liebermann felt a gentle stirring in his loins. He ignored it, and said, 'For the moment, all I know is that his wife took a fall on the stairs at the Touraine château yesterday morning.'

'Was it an accident?' Helber asked.

'If one were to take into account the fact that Philippe Mauclair has sustained a broken leg and dislocated his shoulder, then yes, one could refer to it as an accident.'

'Clumsy of him,' Helber remarked. 'Where is he now?'

'He has been removed from the château to a nearby hospital.'

Helber started to speak again, but was interrupted by Walter Brüning. 'Was Mauclair acting under the instructions of the Pascale woman?' he wanted to know.

Von Liebermann rubbed his jaw. 'No,' he said, drawing out the word.

Brüning smirked. 'Halunke's?'

Von Liebermann nodded, and shifted his corpulent frame.

'Well,' Brüning said with a sigh, 'whether she ordered Mauclair to do it or not, La Pascale will no doubt be pleased to learn of the accident.'

'No doubt,' General von Liebermann agreed. 'And I am thinking that the time is fast approaching when one of our people should pay her a visit.'

'The Wine Supplier won't like that,' Helber commented.

'He won't know about it. He is extremely valuable to us, but his allegiance is to none but himself. It has long been my intention to change that, to put our friend in a position where he can be persuaded to see the wisdom of placing the Nazi cause a little higher on his list of priorities. We may well be able to achieve that through the Pascale woman. We are fully aware of her ambitions where the Wine Supplier is concerned – we may be in a position to help her, if in return she is prepared to help us.'

'Do we take it that Mauclair is no longer of any use to us?' Grundhausen enquired.

'Not as he is, but when he has recovered I think he could prove extremely useful in representing us to La Pascale. As we know, she believes herself to be his sole employer. It should come as something of a surprise to her to learn that she is not. Incidentally, Halunke informs me that de Lorvoire was at the apartment on the avenue Foch when he learned of his wife's accident. Before he left, he ordered the Pascale woman to remove Mauclair from Lorvoire.'

'De Lorvoire *knew* of Philippe Mauclair's association with his mistress?'

'It would seem so, Max, my friend. Let it be yet another lesson to us never to underestimate this man. However, I think we can remain confident that he knows nothing of *our* association with Mauclair, which is all that concerns me.'

Ernst Grundhausen spoke again. 'In acquiring the services of the Pascale woman we shall presumably become obliged to arrange the death of the Wine Supplier's wife – and child?'

'The child may already have been taken care of,' von Liebermann reminded him. 'However, Halunke gave his instructions without authorization. I shall speak to him about it. It is of little concern to me personally whether the Wine Supplier's wife lives or dies, but as it is of the utmost concern to the Pascale woman, I believe the wife should not be introduced to her Maker just yet. In other words, Élise Pascale will be more inclined to help us while she has something to gain.'

'But if the Wine Supplier believes Pascale to be behind Mauclair's "accident", doesn't that make life rather complicated?' Brüning pointed out. 'After all, the Wine Supplier wants – wanted? – that child.'

Von Liebermann smiled. 'When Élise Pascale pleads her innocence, it is my belief that the Wine Supplier will know she is telling the truth. However, we must hope that the child survives, for he will feel better disposed towards his mistress's pleas if it does.'

Inwardly, Helber shuddered. Since joining the *Komitee*

he had encountered a great many unscrupulous men, but not one of them came even close to disturbing him in the way the French Wine Supplier did. If that child died, he most certainly wouldn't want to be in Élise Pascale's shoes. 'Do we have any immediate plans for Mauclair?' he asked.

'Halunke advises that we leave him to the Pascale woman for the time being, and I am inclined to agree.'

'Do we need to replace him inside the château?'

Von Liebermann shook his head. 'Halunke informs me that the situation there has changed so much over the past few months that we no longer need an agent *in situ*. Of course the situation could change again – but Halunke will keep us posted. In the meantime he has devised a way to observe the Wine Supplier himself, and once we have Élise Pascale working for us, between them they should be able to keep us adequately informed of de Lorvoire's movements.'

'Have you a meeting scheduled with de Lorvoire?'

'I have.'

Helber knew better than to ask when, and Grundhausen returned to the subject of the child.

'In Mauclair's last report he mentioned that there was some doubt as to the father's identity,' he said.

'Halunke is satisfied that it is the Wine Supplier's,' von Liebermann answered with a smirk.

'When do you expect the Pascale woman to be at our disposal?' Brüning asked.

'As soon as Mauclair has recovered and Halunke has had an opportunity to apprise him of our intentions. And now, gentlemen,' von Liebermann said, sliding his own copy of the documents he had presented earlier out of his attaché-case, 'I suggest we return to matters closer to home.'

An hour later, all four members of the Abwehr – the German Intelligence organization whose ruthlessness made the Gestapo's seem like child's play – rose from their chairs and dropped their documents in the fireplace.

Grundhausen struck the match, and they waited until every inch of paper had been devoured before they prepared to leave. Von Liebermann went first, the others followed at intervals of an hour or more – which gave two of them time to avail themselves of the services of the prostitute on the floor below. Helber and von Liebermann would meet later at another secret address.

For more than twenty-four hours Claudine drifted in and out of consciousness, dimly aware of the worried faces looking down at her, and the hushed voices that floated around her but never quite reached her. She knew her baby's life was in jeopardy, but it was as though it was happening to someone else – she was unable to focus her attention for more than a few minutes at a time. Once or twice she thought she heard François speaking to her, thought she could feel him holding her hand, stroking her face and whispering to her that it would be all right. But whenever she managed to force her eyes open, the room was empty.

It was another three days before she was able to sit up without feeling faint, and a further two before Doctor Lebrun dared to admit that it seemed the baby would survive. However, he refused point-blank to allow her out of bed; she must stay there, he told her, for at least another week. By now her strength had returned sufficiently for her to protest loudly at this ruling, but when François appeared at the door and informed the doctor that his wife would of course take his advice, she decided to give in gracefully. Arguing with François when her condition was still so delicate would be foolish in the extreme. She would simply wait for him to leave – as he no doubt would, now that the immediate danger had passed – and then she would vacate her bed as and when she pleased.

However, she soon began to realize that François had no

intention of leaving just yet, and though he hardly ever came into her room, she could feel his presence as oppressively as if he were a gaoler.

'As you are carrying my child,' he said, on one of the rare occasions when he visited her, 'you will do as I say. If you wish to exercise your legs, you can walk about the apartment, and if you want fresh air, the windows will be opened. But until Doctor Lebrun is satisfied that you are strong enough to leave this room, you will stay where you are.'

Afterwards, she heard him outside, telling Magaly that if he found out that his wife had disobeyed him, he would hold her responsible.

Magaly came into the room a few minutes later, having first made certain that François had left the apartment. When she pulled an envelope from her apron pocket, Claudine very nearly snatched it out of her hand.

She didn't even wait for Magaly to leave the room before tearing the letter open, but when she read the few words it contained, she fell back against the pillows, tears welling in her eyes. *I am thinking of you.* She whispered the words aloud. 'Oh, Magaly, this must be so terrible for him.'

Magaly walked back to the bed and took Claudine's hand between her own. They had never discussed Armand before, but Magaly had known Claudine since she was six years old and didn't need to be told what was going on in her mistress's mind.

'Would you like to write to him, *chérie?*' she said. 'I will take the letter for you.'

Claudine opened her eyes, and smiling through her tears, she said. 'Do you think he knows that I love him, Magaly?'

Laughing, Magaly said, 'I am in no doubt of it.'

But then Claudine's face fell again. 'What are we going to do, Magaly?'

Magaly gave her hand a comforting squeeze. 'It is very hard for you now, *ma petite*, but one day you will find a way.'

Again she laughed. 'When have you not?' And taking a handkerchief from her apron pocket, she started to wipe away her mistress's tears.

'Stay and talk to me, Magaly,' Claudine whispered. 'Talk to me about him.'

It was dark outside by the time Magaly left. Claudine was at last sleeping peacefully, Armand's letter tucked beneath her pillow. Magaly would deliver her answer the next morning – she had written the same as him, *Je pense à toi*.

She was still fast asleep when François let himself into the room just after midnight and stood at the foot of her bed, staring down at her with a hard, impenetrable look in his eyes. He had stood there like this every night since her fall, and he would continue to come until the doctor pronounced his child sufficiently out of danger for Claudine to leave her bed.

That happened ten days later, by which time Erich von Pappen had told François that his presence in Berlin was requested urgently. He waited another two days, during which time he provoked everyone's curiosity by spending many hours with Liliane. Then, on the first morning Claudine was allowed downstairs, he prepared to leave.

Solange walked with him to the car, her arm through his. During the crisis she had behaved with perfect sanity, but now that the danger was past she had returned to her old eccentric self. What had happened, she told François as she stood with him by the car, her crazy hair wildly on end, was something they could now all forget about. It was an accident which, thank God, had done nothing more than shake them all up a little.

Her words stayed with him throughout the journey to Paris. She was right, it had shaken them all. But he alone knew how much; he alone knew that the very thing he had been dreading since Claudine first came into his life, had finally started to happen. Which was why he now wanted to

get as far away from her as he could, for as long as he could –
and why he would pray every day to the Holy Mother that he
had done the right thing in talking to Liliane.

Élise hadn't had to arrange for Philippe Mauclair to be
removed from the château, Doctor Lebrun had done that
for her. But, she had organized his transfer to a hospital in
Paris just as soon as he could be moved, and from there to a
clinique privée in the thirteenth arrondissement. It was there
that she visited him, almost two weeks after Claudine's fall.

'Why?' she seethed, the moment the doctor had moved
out of earshot. 'Why did you do it when you had received no
instructions from me?'

Philippe gazed up at her with an expression of intense
irritation on his face. He was still in pain, and could do
without the tantrums of Élise Pascale. 'I am feeling much
better than I was, thank you for asking, Élise,' he remarked
acidly.

'Don't be clever with me!' she snapped.

'I thought you would have been pleased,' he said. 'Didn't
you want . . .'

'Pleased! How can I be pleased when the baby is still alive
and you are lying here strung up like a turkey?'

'Yes, well, that wasn't supposed to happen,' he admitted.

She glared at him. 'How can you call yourself a
stuntman,' she sneered, 'when you can't even fall down the
stairs in one piece? And why the hell did you do it without
talking to me first?'

'I saw the opportunity, I took it.'

'And broke her fall by letting her land on top of you!'

He looked at her with genuine surprise. 'How do you
know that?'

'I'm asking the questions,' she snapped.

He nodded. 'François de Lorvoire. He told you.'

'I haven't spoken to François since the day it happened. I

won't repeat what he said when he left me, just suffice it to say he knows about you.'

'Knows what about me?' Philippe asked cagily.

'That you were sent to Lorvoire by me, you fool.'

'How did he find out?'

'How the hell do I know? It must have been something you did or said.' She waved away his attempts to defend himself. 'I don't care about that. All that matters is that you're of no more use to me. Just thank God that baby didn't die, or I should have lost François for good. And you, Philippe . . .'

'But that was what you sent me there for – to get rid of the child,' he snarled.

'But since you let François know who you were working for,' she snarled back, 'it was just as well you didn't succeed, wasn't it? Now, you can start saying your prayers that when I tell him I knew nothing about the fall, he believes me – because if he doesn't, I swear you'll go out of this clinic in a coffin.'

His top lip curled in an ugly sneer. 'Same old Élise,' he spat. 'But you don't frighten me with your threats . . .'

His scream of agony reverberated through the corridors as she wrenched back the toes of his broken leg. 'You're finished,' she hissed, as an army of nurses came running. 'You'll never work again, Philippe Mauclair, do you hear me? And if François wants to know where to find you, be in no doubt that I shall tell him.'

Still wincing with pain, Philippe watched her stalk out of the ward, and for a fleeting moment remembered the time when that proud, sashaying little rump had been exposed for his pleasure – his recruitment fee. But then her parting words came thundering back to his brain, and the throbbing in his leg became unbearable. He knew that his only protection from François de Lorvoire was Rudolf von Liebermann, and he hoped to God that the man sent someone soon. With equal fervour, he hoped it wouldn't be that bastard Halunke.

When Élise returned to her apartment she found François waiting for her. He was standing at the window, wearing his heavy black coat and Homburg hat. His hands were stuffed into his pockets and his dark, aquiline face bore an expression of murderous, though carefully controlled, rage. He waited until the door had closed behind her, then turning from the window, he said, 'There is a part of me that would like to kill you, Élise, and make no mistake, if my child had died I wouldn't hesitate. I perfectly understand why you wanted to kill it, and I also understand that you hoped to deprive me of my wife at the same time. I will make you no threats – you know me well enough to appreciate the danger you have now put yourself in – but I do strongly advise you not to try again. And I give you my solemn vow, Élise, that no matter what happens to Claudine, you will never be the Comtesse de Lorvoire.' He raised his hand and slapped her hard across the face. '*Never!*' And he walked out of the room.

It took a few moments for her head to stop spinning, but then, with surprising calmness, Élise crossed to the window. By the time François emerged from the building into the street below, a knowing smile had settled on her lips.

He'd be back – if for no other reason than that she knew too much about him for him to have her as an enemy. And as for his vow that she would never become the Comtesse de Lorvoire . . . Here her lips did tremble and a look of pain crossed her face. But once she had devised an efficient way of disposing of The Bitch, she could use her knowledge, to blackmail him into marrying her. François de Lorvoire was a traitor to his country, and she knew it, and would make good use of the power that knowledge gave her.

The following week, at four o'clock in the afternoon, François met Rudolf von Liebermann in the garden of the General's Muncheberg home. Max Helber was there too, and since they had already exchanged perfunctory greetings, François came straight to the point. 'It is my belief,' he said, 'that should the Führer wish to take the Sudetenland he will meet with little resistance from the Allies.'

'Your belief?' Helber repeated, with marked cynicism.

Von Liebermann put a hand on Helber's arm. The Wine Supplier would never reveal his sources, and Helber should know by now that de Lorvoire always prefaced his intelligence reports in that fashion. 'How little is little?' he asked.

'There will be a show of protest, naturally,' François answered, 'but it will be no more than that. Neither country wants a war – particularly France.'

'Yet France has deployed a number of her factories for rearmament,' von Liebermann pointed out.

'She is also about to call up her reservists,' François told him, unperturbed.

Von Liebermann nodded. He already knew that. 'Do you have details of these factories?'

'Yes.'

Von Liebermann glanced at his watch. 'I have an appointment at four thirty. Afterwards I am meeting with the Foreign Minister. You will give the information to Max, who will bring it to me before I see von Ribbentrop.'

François nodded, then wandered on through the garden while von Liebermann took Helber to one side.

'You have the information he requires in return?' von Liebermann asked. 'That is good. We shall see what he can do with it. My belief is, nothing.'

Helber smiled, and von Liebermann patted his arm. Turning to leave, he remembered there was something else he had to say concerning the Wine Supplier. 'I have had a request from Halunke. He wants to make contact with the Pascale woman personally. I see no reason why he shouldn't, do you?'

'Is there any danger that she might recognize him?'

'Halunke assures me not.'

'Then I see no objection.'

'Good. Give him the authorization.'

Helber waited until von Liebermann's chauffeur had closed the car door before turning to follow François to the end of the garden. 'Shall we go inside?' he said affably.

François eyed him with distaste; he would have preferred to remain outdoors but he knew Helber would not allow it, so he nodded curtly and followed him into the dark, oak-panelled library.

Here, Helber handed over the documents he and von Liebermann had prepared as an exchange for the information François was about to supply. Helber's cherubic face was smiling. He was afraid of the Wine Supplier, but would never let it show, and besides, being the kind of man he was, his fear only made what he was about to do all the more pleasurable.

He remained standing at the desk as François settled into a chair and started to read. Helber watched him, his body beginning to tremble with lust. He had never come across a man who exuded such potent sexuality as François de Lorvoire, and he had promised himself that one day, when the time was right, he would have him. But for now he had to content himself with taking his penis from his trousers so that he could fondle himself under the gaze of those darkly hooded eyes.

Knowing precisely what Helber was doing, François continued to read to the end of the documents before looking up and asking Helber to clarify several points.

Helber answered, and they continued to conduct their meeting as though both men were as composed as François.

François knew that he would have to stay until Helber ejaculated, for it was Helber's way to hold back a vital piece of information until he had climaxed. So he waited, watching the man's fumblings with a cold detachment – if he turned away it would only lengthen the process. Sometimes, he thought, as Helber's eyes began to roll back in their sockets and the sweat oozed from his face, the price of obtaining information was almost too high. But when Helber finally handed him the last paper, he was in no doubt that on this occasion it had been worth waiting for.

– 14 –

Nothing in the world could have prepared Claudine for the way she felt when her baby boy was put into her arms. Her skin was still coated with sweat, her hair plastered to her head, but she was conscious only of the beautiful, puckered little face with its mop of inky-black hair and anger-reddened cheeks. Even the indescribable agony of the past twelve hours was forgotten, and laughing at her son's furious objection to being tugged so unceremoniously into the world, she surprised everyone by pushing aside her nightgown and putting his mouth to her nipple. Almost immediately he started to suckle. She stared down at him, mesmerized by the perfection of his tiny limbs. Then her heart stood still as his eyes suddenly opened and he seemed to look straight into her own.

'*Mon Dieu!*' she breathed. Then she looked up at Doctor Lebrun and burst into tears . . .

Later, she slept. When she woke the doctor and midwife had gone, and François was sitting on the edge of the bed. He was holding his son, and was apparently engrossed in the way he was opening and closing his eyes. Claudine lay quietly watching them, captivated by the comparison between François' big hand and the tiny head it cradled. It was the first time she had ever seen her husband not perfectly in control of a situation. Even now he seemed to be coping remarkably well, but the expression on his face suggested that his son's presence in the world was having a profound effect upon him.

After a time she reached out a hand and pulled aside the baby's blanket so that she too could see his face. As she gazed down at him she could feel François' eyes on her, but she wouldn't allow herself to look up in case he said something to spoil the moment. In the end it was the baby who broke the silence, and Claudine couldn't help laughing at the look of horror that came over François' face.

'I think he's hungry,' she told him.

'Of course,' he said, clearly amused by his own stupidity. He placed the baby carefully in her arms. 'Shall I call Magaly?' he offered.

'Why?'

'For his milk.'

'But I have it here,' she said, starting to smile. This was the first time, too, that she had ever seen François embarrassed.

'I'm afraid I have no experience of babies,' he said awkwardly. 'Would you like me to leave the room while you feed him?'

She wasn't sure whether she wanted him to go or not. 'Only if you want to.'

He too seemed undecided, but then Magaly came in and he left.

'Is *monsieur* happy?' Magaly asked, when the door had closed behind him.

Claudine thought for a moment. 'I think so. When did he arrive?'

'About an hour before the baby.'

'Did he come up at all? I mean, while it was happening?'

Magaly shook her head, and Claudine's face hardened for a moment. 'Have you seen Armand?' she asked then.

'I went to Liliane's as soon as the baby arrived, to give her the news. Armand is still in Tours, but she expects him home soon.'

Claudine looked down at the baby and a lump rose in her throat preventing her from saying any more.

Later, François came back. The baby was asleep in his cradle, and after gazing down at him for a time he said, 'Words seem inadequate at a time like this, but I want to thank you. He's a fine son.'

'Isn't he?' she smiled. Then, for no apparent reason, she remembered the necklace he had given her on her birthday. 'There was a time, a few months ago, when *I* wanted to thank *you*.'

'Oh?'

'For the necklace. The one you left on the table for me.'

She watched him as he turned back to the cradle. 'Where is it now?' she ventured, when it was evident he wasn't going to speak.

'I presumed, when you didn't mention it, that you didn't want it,' he answered. 'So I gave it to someone else.'

An icy heat flared in the pit of her stomach, and she turned away before he could see her eyes.

'I take it from your reaction,' he said, 'that I made a mistake.'

'Not at all,' she answered quickly. Then, unable to stop herself, she said, 'Did she like it? The woman you gave it to, did she like the necklace?'

'As a matter of fact, she didn't say, but I imagine she did. Naturally, if there's anything you want by way of replacement you have only to ask.'

'There's nothing, thank you,' she said, and picked up the pile of telegrams she had been reading when he came in.

A few minutes later he said, 'The baby will be baptized Louis François.'

She looked up. 'Is the matter open for discussion?'

'No. You already know that the first-born son of the de Lorvoires is called either Louis or François. Each generation alternates, so our son will be Louis.'

'And if I want to call him after my father?'

'We should be obliged to have another child for that. But as I have every intention of keeping to my promise, that's unlikely. The sexual side of our marriage is now over.'

He looked at her, and when she saw the expression in his eyes her heart suddenly swelled in her chest. She stared back at him, and though neither of them moved she could feel herself going to him as though he were pulling her into his arms, enclosing her in a passionate tenderness he had never shown her before. But as quickly as it had come, the feeling between them vanished and he said, 'You are free to live your life as you please, Claudine. You may even leave the château and live elsewhere if you wish. My son, of course, will stay.'

Her cheeks were suddenly suffused with colour, and fury flashed in her eyes. 'Nothing on God's earth will part me from my son,' she said, 'not even you. And if you're hoping to be rid of me, if you think you can throw me off now that I've served my purpose, then you're seriously mistaken. We will call him Louis, we will have him baptized and brought up the way you want – not because I'm afraid to stand up to you, but because I know that you'll do what is best for him. But you will never again refer to him as *your* son, François, because he is not your son. He is *our* son.'

'Indeed,' he conceded. 'And I'm glad that you have decided to stay at the château. *Our* son will need his mother.'

'I'm staying because I have no choice. I resigned myself to that some time ago.'

'Very wise. Now, if there's nothing I can get you I shall bid you goodnight.'

'Goodnight,' she snapped.

But when he reached the door, he turned back. 'In case you are interested,' he said amiably, 'I thought I should let you know that Armand will not be returning from Tours. He will be taking the train to Burgundy, and when he has finished his business there he will go on to Bordeaux. But before you accuse me of trying to come between you, perhaps you should know that, though it is de Lorvoire business he is engaged on, he is doing it at his own request. It seems that he wanted to be away from Lorvoire for a while.'

Then, treating her to one of his more odious smiles, he closed the door.

As soon as she was able, Claudine went to see Liliane. She had intended to make her enquiries very casual, but she should have known that there was little point in pretending with a woman like Liliane St Jacques.

'He has left a message for you, *chérie*,' Liliane said, the moment she saw Claudine's anguished face. 'Now sit down, and I'll pour you some coffee before I tell you what it is.'

Struggling with her impatience, Claudine pulled out a chair and took off her hat and gloves. Liliane seemd to take an age, and suddenly, unable to bear it a moment longer, Claudine said, 'Can I have the letter now, Liliane? Please!'

Smiling, Liliane put the coffee on the table. 'I didn't say a letter,' she answered, 'I said a message, and it is here.' She tapped the side of her head, then pulling out a chair for herself she sat down next to Claudine. 'He has gone away for a while,' she began, 'because he is afraid. Afraid of his feelings for you, and yours for him.'

'But why should he be afraid? I love him, Liliane. I know it might sound crazy when . . .'

'No, it doesn't sound crazy. I knew, probably before either of you, what was happening between you. I saw it, and knew that you were powerless to stop it. I don't know if there is a solution for you, I cannot even begin to predict a future that would see you together, especially now you've had the baby.' She sighed. 'Of course, it is wrong even to be thinking like this – but we none of us can choose with whom we fall in love.'

She stared distractedly down at her hands. 'He wanted to give you both some time to think,' she went on. 'He wanted you to have the chance to see how it would be if he were no longer here. He has the freedom to leave Lorvoire, and you do not. That's why he is prepared to leave for good if that is what you want.'

'But how could I want that?'

'You don't now, but you might one day. Armand believes that you will always love each other, but that your love might destroy you. You are married to François, Claudine, and François will never let the baby go, and nor will you. That means you will always be married to him. Armand is prepared to live with that, to settle for whatever you can give him, but he is afraid that what he can give in return may not be enough for you. He will return to Lorvoire sometime in August, by which time you may have decided what you want him to do. If you decide he must leave, I shall do nothing to stand in his way . . .' She bowed her head as her eyes filled with tears.

'Please don't be afraid,' Claudine whispered, reaching for her hand. 'I won't ask him to go, I couldn't. Perhaps it's selfish of me, but . . .'

'You may think it is selfish, but it isn't, *chérie*, not really. You deserve to be loved, and so does my son. But my poor Armand has been through so much already . . . I can't help wishing that François had found it in himself to love you, for then, perhaps . . .' She smiled sadly and squeezed

Claudine's hands. 'The ways of fate are strange, Claudine. Who knows, maybe one day you and Armand will find happiness together. One day . . .'

She stopped, and as Claudine met her wise, knowing eyes she suddenly had the feeling that Liliane was holding something back from her.

'What is it, Liliane?' she whispered softly.

Liliane shook her head. 'Nothing,' she answered. 'Nothing more than the silly fears of an old woman.'

'Fears? Oh, Liliane, I will never do anything to hurt him, I swear to you . . .'

'That's not what I'm afraid of. It's . . .'

Again she looked into Claudine's eyes, and instinctively Claudine knew what she had been about to say. 'It's François, isn't it?' she said.

Liliane looked away, but Claudine knew she had been right. She knew because suddenly she could sense François' presence, as though he were sitting there in the room with them.

She didn't press Liliane any further that day, but she was sure now that in some way she didn't yet understand, François was manipulating all their lives.

Élise had never been so relieved to see anyone go. Monique had been in her drawing-room the whole afternoon, harping on about her conscience in a way that made Élise want to slap her.

'I don't have the stomach for this sort of thing, Élise,' she had wailed. 'I can't carry on with it. If you'd seen her body lying there at the foot of the stairs you'd know how I feel. I should never have talked Jean-Paul into employing Philippe, I should never have allowed you to talk me into any of it. I . . .'

'Just a minute!' Élise interrupted. 'As I remember it, *you* came to *me* asking how we might be rid of The Bitch.'

'Yes, but I was angry then, and jealous. I suppose I still am jealous of her, but I didn't want the baby harmed, not really. I know that now; just holding him in my arms, I could die to think of what almost happened to him, and that I was partly responsible. I hope you don't think that Philippe can come back to the château, because . . .'

'He's not coming back!' Élise snapped.

'That's good, because if he did I should feel obliged to tell François who he is.'

'You're too late for that, François already knows.'

Monique's eyes rounded with horror. 'He knows?' she gasped. 'Oh my God, he doesn't know I had anything to do with it, does he? Élise, you didn't tell him?'

'Of course I didn't tell him. And as far as I know, he has no idea of your involvement. Now, if it's all the same to you I'm expecting a visitor.'

Monique stood up and pulled on her gloves. 'Before I leave I should like to have your word that no more harm will come to Claudine,' she said.

Élise didn't even bother to hide her contempt as she swept her eyes over Monique's petite frame. 'You have my word,' she said, 'for what it's worth to you.'

'I confess, not a lot,' Monique retorted stiffly. 'In fact, if anything does happen to my sister-in-law I shall know where to come.'

'Go home, Monique,' Élise sighed. 'Go home and ponder on what François would say if I were to tell him how his precious sister tried to kill his son. And while you're about it, do something about that pathetic jealousy of yours. If you haven't got the guts to use it, Monique, it's not worth having.'

'And you would know, wouldn't you, Élise?'

'That's right.'

'And if I were to tell Claudine about you?'

Élise burst out laughing. 'Is that the best threat you can

come up with? Go home to your precious nephew, and if I were you I would start guarding him with my life.' She smiled at the way the blood drained from Monique's face. 'Now that's what you call a threat!' she sneered.

Of course, Élise thought when she had slammed the door behind Monique, she would have to make it up with her. After all, who knew when she might need her again? But this afternoon she wasn't in the mood to soothe Monique de Lorvoire's peevish conscience.

She had been on edge ever since she had received the mysterious telephone call from a man with a German accent telling her someone would be coming to see her on a matter concerning François de Lorvoire. She wasn't too sure why, but a sixth sense seemed to be warning her that whatever her visitor had to say, she should have nothing to do with it . . . But she had been intrigued, all the same, and had arranged the meeting for this afternoon. Her unknown visitor was due in less than fifteen minutes.

An hour later, Halunke let himself quietly out of Élise's apartment. He noted with distaste the blood on his gloves, and peeled them off, looking cautiously along the grey marble landing as he did so. In an apartment downstairs someone opened and closed a door, and he moved instantly back against the wall. Then, when all was silent again, he stripped off the black woollen mask and tripped lightly down the stairs. As he reached the bottom his stomach growled with hunger, and he chuckled quietly to himself; raping de Lorvoire's mistress had given him quite an appetite.

A fleeting image came to him then, of the way he had left her; sprawled across the floor, her mouth swollen and bloody, her clothes in tatters and her eyes still glazed with terror. He had given her a taste of what would happen if she ever double-crossed the *Komitee*. But she wouldn't do that, not now they had guaranteed the death of de Lorvoire's wife in return for her services.

He grinned. The Pascale woman might have thought herself clever and cunning enough to accomplish that alone – and who could say, perhaps she would have succeeded – but she could be in no doubt now that there was a far, far greater force controlling the fate of de Lorvoire and his family than Élise Pascale. She, like him, was no more than an instrument, a card in the pack, to be played when von Liebermann judged the time right. But he, Halunke, constrained as he was by von Liebermann, would deal the final hand, because for him this vendetta with de Lorvoire was as personal as it was deadly.

He got into his car and started the engine. Checking his mirror to pull away, he was surprised to see de Lorvoire's sister making her way along the street towards the Pascale woman's apartment. He'd seen her leave, just as he arrived, and wondered what had brought her back. But then he dismissed her from his mind. His main concern now was Armand St Jacques, the *vigneron*, who, according to the villagers of Lorvoire, was somewhere in Burgundy. Laughing at that he pulled out into the traffic, and wondered how long it would be, now that the child was born, before St Jacques succeeded in seducing de Lorvoire's wife. Not long, he decided, as de Lorvoire himself had seen to it that she was easy prey. Halunke's laughter died and his hands tightened on the wheel. The situation between the *vigneron* and de Lorvoire's wife suited him perfectly, for now, but what he really wanted to know was how long would de Lorvoire allow it to continue?

15

Armand had been away from Lorvoire for almost three months, but now he was back. He had returned three days ago. Claudine knew because Liliane had told her, but she hadn't seen Armand, nor had she heard from him. She knew he was deliberately avoiding her – and today she had decided to put an end to it. She had left the château half an hour ago and come to stand here, in the shade of the forest, just beyond the waterfall. At the heart of the valley the church clock rang out the midday hour, and a few minutes later, just as Liliane had told her he would, Armand started up through the vineyards.

Claudine watched him as, engrossed in thought, he strolled towards her. He couldn't see her, the sun was behind her; and besides, he was staring down at his feet as the baked earth coated them in dust. Every now and again he waved a hand through a cloud of clinging insects as they swarmed about his face, or stopped to check on the ripening grapes. She could feel the tension mounting in her body, her heart was pounding with apprehension, but as he drew closer she summoned all her courage and disappeared into the shadows.

It wasn't until Armand reached the long grass at the edge of the forest, and felt the welcome coolness of the shade beneath the densely locked branches, that he finally looked up. It took a moment for his eyes to adjust from the blinding glare outside to the silvery sunlight dappling the lake, and he was on the point of stripping off his shirt when he suddenly stopped.

He didn't move. He couldn't. It was as if he was entranced, and could only watch. Claudine was swimming through the lily pads, gliding gently towards the bank.

Slowly she pulled herself up and let the water cascade in tiny beads of silver over her naked body. She stood for a long time, letting him look at her, until finally she started to move towards him. Her breasts were large and firm, and the brown nipples stood out proudly. Her belly was flat, her hips gently rounded, and as her long legs moved smoothly through the water he could see the black, curling thatch of pubic hair. In that moment he knew desire as he had never known it before in his life.

Neither of them spoke as she stepped from the water. It was as if nature itself was holding its breath, as if the air between them had fused with the power of her sensuality.

She stood in front of him, her arms hanging loosely at her sides, her lips slightly parted. He searched her eyes with his, then, starting to unbutton his shirt with one hand, with the other he drew her into the circle of his arm and pressed his lips hard against hers. She moaned softly as his tongue entered her mouth, then put her hands around his face, holding him to her as he shrugged off his shirt and let it fall to the ground. The feel of his hard, bare skin pressing against hers was almost too much for her, but he pushed her away, holding her at arm's length and looking down at her breasts.

They were heavy with milk, and for a moment she felt embarrassed, but as if he had read her mind he lifted them in his hands and gently squeezed. The warm liquid flowed from her nipples, and bending his head he took one in his mouth. Her head fell back, and as she ran her fingers through his hair she felt his hands circle her waist.

When he stood up again his lips were red and moist, and as he sucked her lips between his own he started to unfasten his belt.

She watched until he stood naked in front of her, and moving into his arms, she gasped as his hardness pressed against her belly. She clung to him, never taking her mouth from his as he laid her down on the grass. Again he kissed her breasts and smoothed his hand over the satin smoothness of her thighs. Then her breath caught in her throat as his fingers slipped between her legs and began moving back and forth.

As if they had a will of their own her hips lifted from the ground and his fingers slid gently inside her. 'Oh, Armand,' she murmured, 'Armand.'

His mouth came down on hers, and now his tongue was hard and demanding. He rolled onto her, and as he felt her legs part beneath him he raised his head and looked deep into her eyes.

'*Je t'aime*,' he whispered. Then very slowly, very gently, he eased himself inside her, watching her face as her eyes closed and her breath stopped coming. He waited, and when her eyes finally opened she saw that he was smiling.

'I love you,' she smiled back, then she whimpered and gasped as he pulled back and pushed into her again. Still holding her eyes with his, he pushed in and out of her with long, tender strokes while she ran her fingers over the contours of his face.

'Never stop doing that,' she sighed.

'I think I'm going to have to, quite soon now!' he said.

She laughed with him. 'Oh, I love you,' she said, wrapping her arms around him, and as he started to move more rapidly she felt her hips responding to the rhythm. Gradually the sensation in her loins started to swell through her body: it was as if it was invading her, pushing her away and pulling her back until she no longer knew what was happening to her. She could hear him breathing, feel him beginning to tense, and as he started to murmur her name she lifted his face between her hands. She wanted to see him when he let go, she wanted to be there, with him, she wanted him to look at her. But as the sounds started to come from the back of his throat and he ground into her, his eyes were tightly closed. And she was glad. Because for those few blinding seconds, as ecstasy gripped her so savagely that she cried out with the force of it, it wasn't his face looking down at her, it was François'. The shock ripped through her, and her whole body stiffened as the tidal wave of her climax evaporated. She blinked, and suddenly it was Armand again looking down at her, his eyes suffused with tenderness.

'Oh, Armand,' she cried, pulling him to her and burying her face in his neck. 'Armand, I love you.'

'I love you too, *chérie*,' he whispered.

She knew he thought she had reached her climax, and she would have done if it hadn't been for . . . Again she tensed, and she hated François in that moment as she had never hated him before. It seemed that she could never be rid of him, no matter what she did.

A long time later they were still lying in the grass. Her head was resting on his shoulder and they were staring dreamily up at the sunlit trees. She looked down as he lifted one knee and felt a thrill run through her at the masculine hardness of his thigh. Idly she ran her fingers through the coarse golden hair, and turned her face to look at him.

He gave her a quick hug, then said softly, 'We must talk, *chérie*.'

'I know,' she whispered. 'I know, but don't let's spoil today. Today let's pretend that everything is all right, that I am yours, that nothing can come between us.'

She heard him laugh. 'If that's what you want.'

'It is,' she said, lifting herself up to look at him. 'And I want you.'

'Again?' he teased.

'Yes.'

'Then kiss me.'

She did, and as his arms encircled her she trailed her fingers from his thigh to his penis. He groaned into her open mouth and pulled her closer. And as they started to make love, lazily and languorously, she suddenly knew it would be all right this time.

But it wasn't. François was there again, at the very moment when she was reaching her climax. She wanted to scream as rage tore silently through her body. Why was he doing this to her? Her pleasure had never mattered to him, so why should he be there now, taunting her, denying her what he wouldn't give her himself?

Armand kissed her, and as she felt his love embrace her she told herself that perhaps it needn't matter. Every other moment they spent making love was so wonderful, why should it be so important that she achieve the final release?

'I'm going to take a swim,' he said. 'And then I'm going to leave you.'

'Leave me?'

'I have work to do. For your husband.'

'Don't!' she cried. 'Please don't let's ever mention him.'

'Ssh!' he said, stroking her hair. 'I'm sorry. It was meant as a joke, but it was in very bad taste.' He kissed her on the mouth, then drew back to look into her eyes. 'But we will have to talk about him one day, *chérie*, you know that.'

'Yes,' she said, 'but not now.'

They saw each other every day after that, meeting at the waterfall to talk and laugh and swim; to begin the picnic Liliane had made for them, and then leave it unfinished because their impatience for one another was greater than their hunger . . . For the time being Armand gave up trying to make her talk about the future. The day would come soon enough when they would have to decide what to do. For now, it was enough to be happy.

The harvest came and went. They joined the festival at Chinon this year, as Claudine and Louis had decided to hold the Lorvoire feast on alternate years only. Soon, with the coming of autumn, the weather started to change, and since they could no longer meet at the waterfall Armand began repairs to an old cottage at the far side of the forest. It became their home, and Claudine went shopping like the housewives of Chinon for bread and cheese, lace curtains and rugs. She bought a wireless too, and the first thing they heard on it, sitting together in a deep armchair, was the voice of Edouard Daladier, the French Prime Minister, telling them that an agreement had been reached in Munich, and the threat of war in Europe was over. The following day they heard that, under the terms of the Munich Agreement, the Germans had entered the Sudetenland, but as Armand had bought a new bed they were too preoccupied with trying it out to care what was going on in the rest of the world.

A week later Liliane returned from the market at Saumur in Thomas' lorry, with a peculiar contraption she insisted was a stove. Now at last Claudine could try her skill as a cook. But when the big moment came, her fish stew was a disaster. Armand couldn't bear to see her so disappointed and going to stand behind her at the door where she had wandered in a huff because he'd laughed, he slipped his arms around her waist. She leaned her head back against his shoulder.

'It doesn't matter, really,' he said. 'You'll get it right by the time we're together, you see.'

She smiled, and they stood quietly watching the rain falling over the forest. Night was beginning to draw in and she would have to return to the château soon, but later, after everyone was in bed, Armand was going to meet her at the bridge and bring her back so that, for the first time, they could spend a whole night together. Meanwhile, the smell of wet earth, mingled with her scent, was beginning to arouse him.

She turned her face into his neck, moaning softly as he started to unbutton her blouse, and when he pushed his hands inside he could feel the hardened buds of her nipples.

He knew she enjoyed their love-making just as much as he did, but he also knew she continually failed to reach her climax. He had never questioned her about it, guessing that it had something to do with François. He was afraid that if they spoke of it, the spectre of her husband would destroy everything else they had too.

She unfolded her arms as he eased her blouse over her shoulders, and her breath started to quicken as he unhooked her brassière and let it drop to the floor. Then he pulled her back into his arms and they continued to watch the rain as he gently fondled her breasts.

Suddenly she shivered, and pulling away from him, turned back indoors.

'Cold?' he said, closing the door.

'A little.' She picked up his coat and draped it over her shoulders.

'Shall I light the stove?'

She nodded. 'It'll make it nice and warm for later.'

She stood watching him as he picked up the coal-scuttle and began emptying it into the furnace. 'Do you want to tell me what's on your mind?' he said, after a time. 'It isn't just tonight – you've been edgy for weeks now. What is it?'

She wandered over to the window. 'You're probably going to think I'm crazy, that I'm imagining things,' she said, pulling aside the curtain and peering into the gloom, 'but I keep getting this feeling that someone is watching us.'

'You too?' he said.

'You mean . . . ?'

He nodded. 'Like you, I thought I was imagining things, but at the same time I couldn't seem to be rid of the feeling.'

'When did it start?' she asked him.

He shrugged. 'Several weeks ago, I guess.' Suddenly his eyes shot to hers, and she felt a chill of alarm. 'What is it?' she said, edging away from the window.

'Nothing,' he smiled. 'Sorry, I didn't mean to frighten

you. It was just something that occurred to me, but it doesn't matter.' He'd been about to tell her that he had had the feeling while he was in Burgundy, but then he thought better of it.

'It does matter,' she said. 'Was it to do with François? Do you think it's François who's watching us?'

Armand shook his head thoughtfully. 'I don't know,' he said finally. 'It could be, but we'd know if he was in Lorvoire, wouldn't we?'

'He could be paying someone else to do it.'

'Yes, he could.'

She sat down at the table and pulled Armand's coat tighter around her shoulders. It was a long time since she'd thought about Hortense, but every time the feeling of being watched came over her she instinctively connected it with François, then found herself remembering what he had told her about Hortense.

Armand sat down and reached for her hands. 'What are you thinking?' he said gently.

She took a while to answer, but finally she said, 'I was thinking about a woman called Hortense de Bourchain. Have you ever heard of her?'

'Yes,' he answered, and she thought she sensed him withdraw.

'What do you know about her?' she asked.

'Why do you ask?'

'She's dead, isn't she?'

'Yes.'

Armand saw that this answer had unsettled her even further, but he still wasn't sure what direction her thoughts were taking.

'I didn't believe him,' Claudine said at last. 'When he told me, I thought he was just saying it to try and stop me marrying him. Then after we were married, I thought . . .' She shook her head, as if trying to clear it. 'I keep telling myself that if he had killed her, someone would have . . .'

– 285 –

'Just a minute,' Armand interrupted. 'Are you saying that François *told* you he killed Hortense?'

She nodded. 'But if he had, surely it would have gone to trial? People don't get away with murder, do they?'

Her eyes were beseeching him for the reassurance she craved, but as he continued to say nothing he felt her horror as if it was almost tangible. 'Did he kill her, Armand?' she whispered.

When again he didn't answer she felt a scream of denial curl through her gut. 'He did, didn't he?' she croaked.

'Yes. I saw him do it.'

'You saw him!' she gasped. 'But how? What happened? Oh my God, I can't believe it. I don't want to believe it.'

'Ssh,' he said, trying to calm her.

'But why?' she cried. 'Why did he kill her?'

'All I know is that it had something to do with Lucien. I don't know what exactly, but when I heard them fighting in the wine cave, I heard Lucien's name . . .'

Her mind was racing and her skin was beaded with a cold sweat. She took a deep breath. 'You'd better start at the beginning, Armand.'

He nodded slowly, then letting go of her hands he stood up and started to pace the room. Her eyes never left him, following him back and forth as he told her everything he had seen and heard that night in the wine cave. He even told her of Louis' involvement, and his own reasons for not informing the police.

'Maybe if Jacqueline hadn't been so close to giving birth,' he said, as he reached the end of his story, 'I'd have acted differently, but I'm not sure. The de Lorvoires are a powerful family, to stand against them alone would have been madness. Then when Louis told me Hortense's family did not want to press charges, it showed me more than anything else what pressure the de Lorvoires could bring to bear. But even then I might have done something if I hadn't known that a scandal would break Solange's heart – not to mention what it would do to Lucien's career and Monique's hopes of marriage . . . I've known that family all my life, I just couldn't do it to them.'

She was silent for a long time, trying to take it all in. Finally she said, 'Does François know that you know?'

'I don't think so. If he did . . .' He left the sentence unfinished as he suddenly realized what she was getting at. 'You think that perhaps he does, that that's why he's having us watched? But why should he be afraid of me telling you when he's already told you himself?'

But as she continued to look at him he saw that her mind was travelling much further than that. As reassuringly as he could, he said, 'You aren't in any danger from him, *chérie*. He must be only too aware that if he did anything to you, his father wouldn't stand by him again. Besides, he has no reason to want to harm you.'

'So why is he having us watched?'

'We're only assuming that it's him.'

'But who else could it be?'

He smiled. 'I'm afraid there are people with some rather odd sexual habits. It could be one of them.'

She laughed half-heartedly, and got up to put her arms around him. He held her tightly, stroking her hair as he mulled everything over in his mind. Then, deciding that there was only one way to take her mind off her fears, he took his coat from her shoulders and lowered his mouth to the most beautiful breasts he had ever touched.

16

'Aren't you going to say *anything*?' Élise asked, pulling down the sun-visor and checking her lipstick in the mirror.

François took their passports back from the sentry, and sliding the car into gear, drove across the border into France. 'What about?' he said.

'I don't know. The fact that there isn't going to be a war, I suppose. I take it that's why we were in Munich at the same time as all those leaders – so that you could get your information first-hand?'

'We were there for the opera,' he said, keeping his eyes fixed on the road ahead. 'Did you like it?'

'As a matter of fact, I did.'

'Good.'

Knowing she was unlikely to get any further than that, Élise lapsed into silence, and running a finger under her chin to loosen the ribbon of her hat, she turned to look out at the passing countryside.

She was managing to hide it well, but she was still quite shaken by this trip to Germany, not least because of what she had seen while she was there. Two weeks ago they had driven to Berlin, and after checking them into a hotel near the American Embassy, François had disappeared for two days. Élise had used the opportunity to try and make contact with von Liebermann, as she had been instructed, but it transpired that he was away. So, with nothing else to do she had gone shopping, and it was while she was wandering about on foot that she had come across the bands of young men who called themselves the Hitler Youth.

Their behaviour had astonished her. She had seen them kick down doors, smash windows, throw a woman and and her children into the gutter, and beat one old man half to death in front of her eyes. Someone told her later that the victims were all Jews, and though she had no great love of the Jews herself, she was still sickened by what she had seen. However, when François eventually returned and told her they were to be guests of Hermann Goering at his forest lake home of Karinhall, where the Nazi leader was holding a weekend party to celebrate the birth of his daughter, Edda, she promptly forgot the plight of Berlin's Jews in her eager preparations for the visit.

After Berlin they had headed for Munich, making several stops along the way, the last at a place called Dachau. There they met the dashingly handsome Reinhard Heydrich, a young SS officer who proudly showed them the Death's-head Unit in training. At first Élise was fascinated by the strength and fitness of Heydrich's nubile young men, but when she was confronted with the ruthless discipline inflicted on the prisoners in the camp – most of whom were Jews, Heydrich told her – she was horrified. She stayed no longer than ten minutes before returning to the car and waiting until François had finished whatever business he had come to conduct. So far, neither of them had mentioned what they had seen.

Once in Munich she had settled into their hotel, made love with François in the shower bath, and then, while François was out purchasing their opera tickets, she had received a telephone call from von Liebermann asking her to meet him the following day.

She had behaved with extreme caution on her way to von Liebermann. She had taken a taxi, then a tram, then another taxi; she had entered a hotel, walked through it, and taken a third taxi which finally delivered her to her destination. She was afraid François might be having her followed.

Ever since he had first suggested she accompany him, she had been suspicious. In the past she'd asked on a number of occasions if she could go with him to Germany, but she had always met with a point-blank refusal. So why now? she wondered. And why, after what had happened to his wife and the things he'd said as a result, was he being so exceptionally attentive? Could it be, perhaps, that Monique had told him about the rape? But she had seen Monique before she left, and Monique had assured her she'd said nothing. She had no reason to disbelieve Monique, for they were now friends again, Élise having promised Monique that she meant the child Louis no harm. But even if Monique had relayed to her brother the carefully edited story Élise had given her – how an old flame had broken into her apartment and raped her – Élise couldn't imagine for one moment that sympathy and concern were behind François' motive for taking her with him. There was something else behind it, there must be, and her great fear was that he must know of her intention to meet von Liebermann. But the General had assured her that was impossible, and when she'd returned from her meeting with him there had been nothing in François' manner to suggest the least suspicion.

Later, after he had gone out to have dinner with the French Foreign Minister, she had telephoned Max Helber, and using the code von Liebermann had given her, had told Helber who François was with. She disliked making these calls, chiefly because she didn't know why she was making them. Oh, she knew what they had told her, that in return for information they would help her be rid of The Bitch, and she was more than happy to have them do that for her, but she wanted to know why the Abwehr were so interested in François. They didn't trust him, that much was obvious. But what was it von Liebermann had said? 'We want only to make certain that he does not waver from the path.' The only path von Liebermann could have been referring to was his own, the Nazis', which could only mean that François . . .

'As a matter of fact,' François said, startling her with his abrupt break into her thoughts, 'there will be a war.'

As she turned to look at him, he smiled, and reached out for her hand. 'But Daladier said . . .'

'I know what Daladier said,' he interrupted, 'but I can assure you that our German friends will not be satisfied with the Sudetenland, and Daladier, Chamberlain, and everyone else who was at that conference, knows it. In short, *ma chérie*, to use an American expression, the Allies have just sold Czechoslovakia down the river. The problem is that by doing it they think they have rescued themselves from the brink of war.'

'And they haven't?'

'No. Hitler has no intention of stopping at Czechoslovakia.' He paused, as if uncertain whether to continue, then puzzled her by saying, 'If he doesn't, or even if he does, I'm sure you saw enough in Berlin – and in Dachau – to make you share my sentiments.'

'Which are?'

'God help the Jews.'

Again François smiled, and bringing her hand to his mouth, he kissed it. He enjoyed feeding her titbits of information like that; he was fascinated to see how long it would take her to work out what he was up to. He was also intrigued by her meeting with von Liebermann in Munich. He had no intention of revealing that he knew about it, of course, and he didn't know how their association had come about – though he was fairly sure it had something to do with the rape Monique had told him about. That was what had prompted him to take Élise to Germany with him. Once there, he was convinced she would betray herself somehow, and she had proved him right.

Élise too was thinking of von Liebermann at that moment; she was wondering who her new Paris contact would be. She hadn't actually seen the man Halunke since the day he raped her, but just the sound of his voice on the telephone sent a chill of revulsion slithering down her spine. Von Liebermann had been most sympathetic when she told him what Halunke had done to her, and promised that her contact would be someone quite different. 'I'm afraid Halunke is not always an easy man to control,' he had said. 'In fact there are times when he reminds me a great deal of your lover.'

As she recalled those words now, Élise turned to look at François. With his hawk-like features and long black hair, he was not an attractive man, though how he compared with Halunke she had no idea, for Halunke had worn a mask. But of course von Liebermann had not been referring to physical characteristics. Well, there might be similarities between them, but ruthless as François could be, Élise could never imagine him perpetrating such a vicious act of sodomy as Halunke had visited upon her. Which led her to wonder if François was aware of the designs Max Helber had on him. Of course, Helber was wasting his time, François would kill him before he allowed Helber's fat little hands anywhere near him. But for a moment she almost pitied Helber, for she knew exactly what he was missing.

'François,' she said, slipping her hand out of his and pushing it between his legs.

'Mm?'

'I want you to know that no matter what you do, whoever you decide to follow – the French, the Germans, Italians, even the British – I will support you.'

'Will you, *chérie*?' he smiled. 'I am touched. But what makes you feel you have to say that now?'

She chuckled. 'To be frank, your display of affection these past few months has unnerved me. It makes me feel as though you don't trust me. I doubt if I'll get a straight answer, but *is* there anything behind it?'

He laughed, then cast her a quick look as she started

unbuttoning his fly. 'I told you while we were in Berlin, Élise, I have come very close to falling in love with you. It is true I don't want you as my wife, but I have no intention of losing you as my mistress.'

She was right, she hadn't received a straight answer, but resigning herself to the one she'd got, she lifted his penis from his trousers and said, 'You'll never lose me.'

He picked up his cigarettes from the dashboard and lit one while she moved her hand back and forth.

'What are you doing?' she asked a few minutes later as he pulled over to the side of the road.

'It is not what I am doing, Élise,' he answered, turning off the engine. 'It is what you are going to do.'

'But I've still got my hat on,' she protested, as he put a hand behind her head.

'So you have,' he replied, and pulled her face down to his lap.

Six months later, as François had predicted, German troops marched into Prague. The following day Hitler declared that 'Czechoslovakia has ceased to exist'.

Élise heard the news while entertaining the contact von Liebermann had supplied her with – Philippe Mauclair. Now she was over the shock of discovering that he had been the Abwehr's spy as well as hers, they met on a regular basis, though she had had very little to report since returning from Germany as François had taken himself off to Lorvoire and showed no signs of leaving. However, von Liebermann didn't seem to mind, and sticking to his side of the bargain, he kept Élise abreast of The Bitch's movements via Philippe. It seemed she was still engaged in a torrid affair with the *vigneron*. She saw him almost every day in a house at the edge of the forest, where she cooked for him, swept floors, sewed his shirts and bathed him in an old tin bath in front of the stove.

Playing at peasants was hardly the way for a future comtesse to be conducting herself, Élise thought spitefully, but she could see that the rusticity might have a certain appeal for someone who wasn't born to it. Around two in the afternoon, apparently, The Bitch returned to the château to receive her afternoon callers, and spent two or three hours in the nursery with her precious son before dining with her parents-in-law. Then, at about ten o'clock, she met the *vigneron* at the bridge and went back with him to their house. Until François returned they had often spent the whole night together, with St Jacques taking her back to the château at dawn, but now she stayed no later than midnight. They made love on a bed in the corner of the kitchen, St Jacques always rode her, and she had a mole on the underside of her left breast. In fact Élise knew everything about The Bitch, right down to the fact that she was using a diaphragm. She and the *vigneron* seemed so much in love that there were moments when Élise could almost feel jealous, until she remembered that it was that snake Halunke who was crawling about the forest watching their every move.

Hungry as Élise was for details of Claudine's life, when it came to François she preferred to remain in ignorance. She did not like him spending so long at Lorvoire. If he had still been travelling about the Continent 'selling his wine' she would have been much happier, but since Krystalnacht – the night when the anti-Semitic pogroms had begun in Germany – he had made only two trips to Paris and three to London. She wondered what François felt about what was happening to the Jews, and whether he was making any money out of them. He might be warning them of their fate or, on the other hand, he might be supplying the Nazis with information. Whatever he was doing, there wasn't much chance of finding anything out about it when he was apparently so besotted with his wretched son.

*

François' interest in his son at first confounded Claudine, not least because young Louis, who had not seen his father more than half a dozen times since he was born, responded to him as though he saw him every day. What made the situation feel even stranger was that she had almost forgotten François was her husband – he had been away for so long that the life she had made for herself with Armand now felt more real than the one at the château. Day after day she waited for François to ask her about Armand, but as the weeks passed she realized he wasn't going to. She knew it was irrational, but she was annoyed by his silence. She was burning to ask him if he was responsible for having them watched; though neither she nor Armand had actually caught sight of anyone, the feeling that they were being spied on never left them.

'Do you think François is waiting for something to happen?' she asked Armand one evening as they were settling down to listen to a play on the wireless. 'I mean, why do you think he's here?'

'It is his home,' Armand pointed out. 'And Louis is his son. Maybe he wants to get to know him better.'

'If it was anyone else but François I'd say you were right, but . . .'

'But what?'

She shook her head. 'Nothing.' She didn't want to talk about her fear that François was trying to ease her out of her son's life. In fact she tried not to think about François at all, so she said, 'Do you love me?'

'Yes.'

'Kiss me, then.'

He groaned. 'But you know what'll happen if I kiss you!'

Her eyes were dancing. 'You're like an old married man, Armand St Jacques.'

'And you, Claudine de Lorvoire, are insatiable.'

In fact Claudine had found to her dismay that François' presence at the château made her climax more elusive than ever. She had finally confessed the failure to Armand, suggesting that it might be because they were being watched. He said he understood, admitting that knowing someone was watching sometimes made it more difficult for him too.

'We will overcome it, you know,' he told her later that evening.

She looked down at him, lying on the bed, so handsome and relaxed in his nudity that her heart turned over.

'I know,' she whispered. 'And it's not because I don't love you, you know that, don't you?'

He smiled, then got up and started to pull on his trousers.

It was approaching midnight by the time Claudine crossed the bridge into the château. Armand waited until the door had closed firmly behind her before he turned back into the forest.

Halunke stole quietly through the night. The moon was covered by cloud, but the gurgle and hiss of the waterfall guided him through the trees. As he slithered down the bank into the moonlit glade, the distant sound of thunder rumbled through the heavens. He pulled his collar higher, and hunching his shoulders against the chill night air, moved silently on through the long grass.

He was on the point of making the descent into the vineyards when he suddenly stopped. He waited, then edged towards a tree, sinking into the darkness and pressing his slender body against the rough bark. He listened, his eyes and ears alert to the eerie sounds of shifting night shadows – an animal feeding? His white teeth gleamed in the darkness as his tension suddenly eased – the only person out that night was the *vigneron*, returning home after his rendezvous with de Lorvoire's wife.

He felt a momentary stab of irritation. De Lorvoire had been at the château for months now, and still he had done nothing about his wife's affair. The man's indifference was proving tiresome; if it continued, there would be little satisfaction to be gained from killing her. But then he reminded himself that much could change before he got as far as de Lorvoire's wife.

He moved on, his thoughts turning from de Lorvoire to von Liebermann and he swore viciously under his breath. If it wasn't for the German he'd have struck at de Lorvoire's family long ago, but von Liebermann had threatened to reveal his identity if he acted again without authorization, and Halunke could not risk de Lorvoire finding out who he was. If he did find out, Halunke knew beyond doubt that he would not live long enough to achieve his revenge.

Dimly he wondered why von Liebermann was so interested in de Lorvoire, but he had never asked, and he didn't really care. What mattered was that von Liebermann had discovered his burning hatred for de Lorvoire and was now putting it to his own use. For now, all von Liebermann required was information on the comings and goings at the château. Halunke grimaced. He had no taste for espionage, but he was trapped in the Abwehr net, and his only hope now was that there would be a war between France and Germany. Then, with other things to occupy von Liebermann, he might regain his autonomy. And once he did, how easy it would be to make de Lorvoire suffer!

Again Halunke broke into a smile: François de Lorvoire had made a grave mistake fathering a son on a woman as beautiful and hungry for love as Claudine.

Reaching up and removing the clip from her hair, Claudine shook out her curls and stared dispassionately at her reflection in the dressing-table mirror. She looked older, she thought. Perhaps it was the strain of leading a double-life these past few months. It did not suit her, and what she wanted more than anything else, she realized, confronting her own pale face in the glass, was that François should leave. His presence confused and infuriated her. He could have no doubts about the nature of her relationship with Armand, but he continued to say nothing. Nothing! And she was so consumed with rage at his indifference that she was quite unable to concentrate on what really mattered: how to find a way for her and Armand to be together – always. And when she did manage to focus on the problem, it seemed insuperable. How could she even contemplate leaving François when she knew how hurt Solange and Louis would be. It would break their hearts to lose their grandson . . . But of course, if she took little Louis away François would pursue her to the ends of the earth to get him back.

She sighed wearily. Every time she tried to think any further than that about herself and Armand, it was as though her mind threw up a barrier, blinding her to a solution that she was sure was staring her right in the face . . .

Still looking in the mirror, she put her head on one side and forced a wide smile. Perhaps it was all this talk of war that was making her feel so gloomy this morning – or perhaps it was François' behaviour towards her at dinner the night before.

Ever since his return to the château, each week had seen the arrival of someone new – politicians, generals, diplomats; Poles, Belgians, even one or two Germans. Like Solange, she enjoyed visitors, but François' attitude towards her when he had guests was nothing short of humiliating, and his behaviour last night had been frankly outrageous. When for the second time he casually dismissed a contribution she had made to the general conversation, she had been so incensed that she had waited in their sitting-room until the early hours of the morning for the express purpose of hurling a book at him.

She grinned; it hadn't hurt him a bit, and his response had been maddening. He'd simply picked up the book, replaced it on the shelf and walked into his bedroom. Not even a goodnight.

She put down her hairbrush, and was on the point of opening a drawer when she suddenly sensed that someone was standing at the door. That was one of the things she detested most about François, the way he could make her so acutely aware of his presence without even having to speak.

'Do you want something?' she said coldly, not bothering to turn round.

He smiled at her hostility. 'Yes. I'd like your company for breakfast. I've asked for it to be served here, in the apartment.'

'Why?' she said testily.

'There's something I want to show you.' And before she could protest any further, he walked out.

When she joined him five minutes later, he was already at the table, still wearing his dressing-gown over a pair of black pyjamas. He was reading the newspaper, but he put it down when she came in, and poured them both a coffee.

'I hope this isn't going to take long,' she said, sitting down. 'I've promised to take Gertrude Reinberg to see a doctor in Tours this morning.'

'Gertrude Reinberg?' he said. 'The woman who lives next door to the café? She's Jewish, isn't she?'

Surprised, Claudine said, 'I suppose she is. I hadn't really thought about it. Why?'

'No reason.' He passed her cup, then leaned back in his chair. 'This might take a little longer than you would like, but I'm afraid that can't be helped.'

'I'm listening.' She picked up her coffee and, assuming an air of boredom, stared out of the window at the heavily laden branches swaying across the veranda.

He watched her for a moment, then after taking a

mouthful of coffee he came straight to the point. 'I am aware,' he began, 'that you and Armand suspect me of having you watched.'

Her hand froze in mid-air. She could hardly believe it. All these months of saying nothing, and now . . .

'You are wrong, I'm afraid,' he went on, 'at least in suspecting me. But you're right in thinking that there is someone out there in the forest. Regrettably, he is not in my employ. Life would be so much less complicated if we were dealing with nothing more than a jealous husband.'

Deciding to ignore his loathsome irony, she said, 'Then perhaps you would care to tell me what we *are* dealing with.'

'I'm not sure,' he answered pensively. 'But I do know that his interest in you stems from an interest in me. It will probably come as no suprise to you to learn that I have many enemies. So it is my hope that when I leave Touraine tomorrow, whoever is spying on you will leave too.'

'Well, that's what I call a double relief,' she said acidly – and to her annoyance, he laughed. 'And does this person present any kind of threat to you?' she asked coldly.

He grinned. 'I'm touched by your concern. Yes, ultimately I'm sure he does mean me some harm. But I am less concerned for myself than for my family, which is why I intend taking the precaution of speaking to Armand before I leave, to ask him to make sure you are never in the forest alone.'

His casual allusion to her affair was outrageous, but before she could speak he said, 'I have also employed a nanny for Louis. She is not an ordinary nanny, but only you will know that.'

'What's that supposed to mean?' she cried.

'It means that she will be protecting my – *our* son.'

Immediately the blood drained from her face. 'Are you telling me Louis is in some kind of danger from this man?'

'I doubt it, but . . .'

'But you don't know for sure?'

'No.'

She closed her eyes, feeling for a moment on the brink of hysteria. Then suddenly her fists clenched and she slammed them on the table, shouting, 'He's a baby, François! Just a baby. How could you have put him in this position? I thought you loved him!'

He waited for her to look at him, then held her gaze. She felt his power, then oddly felt her panic start to subside. 'I give you my word, Claudine,' he said, in a deep, sombre voice, 'that nothing will happen to Louis. It is a source of relief to me that you have Armand to protect you, but at the same time you must take some responsibility for yourself.' He hesitated for a moment, then said, 'Maybe now is the time to tell you that it was precisely for this reason that I did not want to marry you.'

'What?'

'I was afraid something like this might happen. As my wife you are an obvious target for my enemies, which is why I have gone out of my way to let it be known that I do not love you. It is also why I have done nothing to interfere in your liaison with Armand. So far it has worked.'

'What do you mean?'

'You are still alive.'

'I can't believe what you're saying!' she cried. 'You mean someone is planning to kill me, to kill Louis, because of you? Who are these people who hate you so much? What have you done to them?'

'At this precise moment in time I am unable to answer either of those questions.'

'Unable or unwilling?'

He looked at her.

'I want to know what's going on, François!'

'I know you do. But as I said, it is my hope that when I leave tomorrow, whoever is watching the château will leave too.'

'And what if he kills you? What will happen . . . ?' She stopped as her words were sucked into the horrible drone of fear rushing through her head.

He chuckled. 'I should have thought nothing would suit you better than my untimely despatch, Claudine, but I'm afraid that if they intended to kill me they'd have done it by now. There are, unfortunately, far more effective ways of making a man pay for what he has done than killing him.'

They sat in silence then, and she watched his hands as he started to break a brioche. They were so large, the dark hair on his arms so sinister . . . She lifted her eyes to his and suddenly she felt as though her heart were being torn from her body. Quickly she looked away, dazed by the strength of him, which made her feel both safe and terrified. 'How long will you be gone?' she asked quietly.

'That depends very much on what I can find out.'

He didn't say any more, and nor did she. She knew that once he had left there would be a thousand questions she wanted to ask him, but for now her mind seemed to have gone numb. In the end she dully reminded him that he had said he had something to show her.

'Ah, yes,' he said, suddenly smiling. He got up and left the apartment, returning a little while later, alone and empty-handed. 'Be patient,' he said, and in a couple of minutes the door opened and Magaly came in, carrying Louis.

'Wait,' François said.

Claudine sat back in her chair and watched as Magaly set Louis on the floor and François leaned forward with his elbows on his knees. 'Now, Louis,' he said, 'show *Maman* what you can do.'

Louis' chubby little face was wreathed in smiles as he bounced around on his unsteady legs, shouting and waving his arms in the air.

'No, no, no,' François said. 'You can do better than that. Now come along, come to Papa.'

Claudine looked at François in amazement, but he was still watching Louis. Then Louis gave an ear-splitting screech, and with an exuberant blowing of bubbles he hurtled the few steps into his father's arms.

'That's my boy,' François laughed, swinging him up onto his lap and planting a kiss on his cheek. 'Now, what does *Maman* think of that?'

For a moment Claudine was too overcome to speak. Then, pulling herself together, she reached out for her son, who was straining to come to her. It wasn't only the fact that Louis had taken his first steps at the age of ten months that had so profoundly affected her. It was the way François had behaved, the way he had looked . . .

She looked across at him, but he only raised his eyebrows at her, then returned to his newspaper as though she had ceased to exist.

– 17 –

Monique shrieked as Claudine whirled her round in her arms, then hugged her tightly. 'Congratulations, *chérie*! I wondered what you had been doing in Paris all this time! But how long have you known him? How did you meet him? Come along, sit down and tell me everything.'

Smiling all over her face, Monique allowed Claudine to lead her to the sofa. 'It's a secret, remember?' she said, still breathless from Claudine's embrace. 'You're not to tell anyone about him until I say.'

'Of course I won't. But aren't you at least going to tell Solange and Louis?'

Monique shook her head. 'No, I don't think it's fair to tell them I'm getting engaged to someone they don't know, so we're going to take it slowly, and arrange for them to meet at least once before we say anything. So promise you won't breathe a word.'

'Cross my heart!' Claudine smiled. Then clasping Monique's hands she cried, 'Oh, but look how your eyes are shining! Any fool could see you're in love! And you haven't even told me his name!'

'Karol Kalinowski,' Monique answered, her face flushing with pleasure as she pronounced the name. 'He's Polish. He's left his country because of what's happening there, and now he's trying to get his family to France too. It isn't proving easy, and he misses them terribly. He's a very special man, Claudine, so sensitive, so full of compassion.'

Her eyes drifted towards the open window, and watching her, Claudine was hard put to it not to hug her again. She was so pleased that at last Monique was happy, so pleased that she had confided in her. 'Well?' she prompted. 'What does he look like? How old is he? Does he come from a good family?'

'He's a count,' Monique laughed. 'He's thirty-three, and he's . . . the most handsome man I've ever met!'

'And when did he ask you to marry him?'

'Er . . . the evening before last.'

But Monique's cheeks had turned pink, and suddenly Claudine knew the truth. 'You were in bed with him at the time!' she cried.

'Ssh!' Monique warned. Then 'Do you think me terrible? Going to bed with a man before we are married?'

'Of course not!' Claudine laughed.

'Then I'll let you into another secret. Karol was not the first.'

'*Oh là là!*' Claudine cried, feigning horror.

'I can't help it,' Monique sighed. 'I just get these feelings when I'm with a man and I . . . Well, you know how it is.'

'I do,' Claudine smiled. 'So, when are you going to announce your engagement?'

'The day after the July ball at the Polish Embassy. We thought that would be a perfect opportunity for Karol to meet my family without too much formality, then he can call on Papa the next day. Oh, you will come to Paris for the ball, won't you, Claudine? You've been invited, we all have.'

'I wouldn't miss it for the world. But aren't we going to meet him before that?'

Monique's smile faded. 'He's gone to Poland and won't be returning until the day before the ball. Three whole weeks, Claudine! How am I going to survive without him for so long?'

'We shall shop, that's how!' Claudine decided. 'It's an age since I was in Paris, and it's high time I livened up my wardrobe. I feel positively dowdy beside you. Just look at that dress!'

'Isn't it wonderful?' Monique stood up and twirled round so that her full skirts billowed around her legs. 'It's what they call a surah dress.'

'It's stunning,' Claudine sighed wistfully, taking the black silk jersey between her fingers. 'And it suits you so well. Has Karol seen it?'

'He chose it. But it's only a day dress, *chérie*. You wait 'til you see what Schiaparelli and Alix have for the evenings. *Oh là là*, you will think you are in heaven.'

Suddenly the door burst open and Solange bounced into the room. 'Can I come shopping too?' she cried. 'I shall have to have something new for the ball, won't I? Especially if I am to meet my future son-in-law! Ah, *chérie*, congratulations. What a happy mother I am.' And she folded Monique into an enveloping embrace.

'*Maman*, you have been listening at the door again!'

'No, no, *chérie*. I was merely passing and heard your voice.'

When they had stopped laughing, Claudine said, 'So it is decided. We shall all go to Paris next week and stay until after the ball. Will Louis come too?'

'Which one?' Monique asked, smiling.

'Why, both will come of course,' Solange declared. 'I cannot go anywhere without my grandson, and *grand* Louis must come to meet your intended, Monique.'

As if on cue, an anxious voice sounded from the stairs. 'Solange! Solange!'

Solange giggled, clapping a hand to her mouth.

'I must hide.' And she dived into François' bedroom.

'I know she's in here,' Louis said, appearing in the doorway. 'Wretched woman! She's put my name down for the young men's boules tournament this afternoon. I had the surprise of my life when Claude Villiers turned up just now, but it was nothing compared to the surprise he got when he saw how old I was. Poor man, he was so flustered I had to invite him in for a brandy.'

'And of course you just had to have one with him!' Monique said, grinning. 'But Papa, everyone in the region knows you. This man Villiers must have known you weren't young.'

'He's a newcomer,' Louis said. 'He's getting to know everyone by organizing these confounded tournaments. Armand, I'm relieved to say, has offered to take my place – but that saucy young Villiers has now put me down for the old men's tournament next week.'

While he spoke, Louis had been quietly edging towards the door of François' bedroom, and now he threw it open.

'Ah! Louis!' Solange shrieked. 'There you are. I was looking for you, *chéri*. The girls and I are going to Paris next week, shopping.'

'Oh no you're not,' Louis answered. 'You, Solange de Lorvoire, are staying here until after the boules tournament. As my wife I order you to share in my humiliation.'

'Oh, *chéri*,' she grumbled, 'do I have to? You play so badly. That was why I put you down for the young men's team. I thought you would be able to use your age as an excuse.'

When the laughter had finally died down, Solange said, 'Do you think we shall see François in Paris? I haven't seen him for so long. I do miss him, *chéri*.'

'I know you do.'

'And Louis misses his father, does he not, Claudine?'

Claudine nodded. No one ever asked her how she felt about François' absence, it was assumed that she preferred it. But the fact was that since he had failed to return for Louis' first birthday, after telephoning the week before to say he would try to come, she had hardly slept for worrying about him. That was over four weeks ago, and as far as she knew he hadn't even contacted his father in that time. 'Do you know where he is, Louis?' she ventured.

'As a matter of fact, I do. He's on his way back from London, where I do believe he spent some time with your father. So we might indeed see him in Paris.' He frowned, and peered at Claudine over the rim of his spectacles. 'You look a little pale, *chérie*, are you feeling unwell?'

'No, I'm feeling fine,' Claudine said. 'Perhaps it's your beautiful daughter outshining me with her . . .' She stopped abruptly as Monique dug an elbow in her ribs, but it was too late, Solange had remembered the engagement, and Monique was obliged to sit her father down and tell him all about Karol Kalinowski.

Later, after Solange and Louis had left the apartment, Claudine said, 'You still haven't told me where you met him.'

Monique seemed hesitant.

'Did your eyes meet across a crowded room?' Claudine said, smiling. 'Was it love at first sight? Come on, I'm dying to know!'

Monique sighed. 'I suppose there's no harm in telling you, I'm sure you know about her anyway. We were introduced by François' mistress.'

It was as if something sharp and burning had been

suddenly plunged into Claudine's chest. Then, strangely, it was as though the muscles of her face were trying to drag the smile from her lips, and her heart started to thud monotonously in her ears. 'François' mistress?' she repeated.

'Oh no!' Monique groaned. She had genuinely believed Claudine must know about Élise by now. 'I am sorry, *chérie*. I thought you knew.'

'But of course I knew,' Claudine heard herself say. 'I was just a little surprised . . . Well, surprised that you know her well enough to . . .'

'I don't really,' Monique answered. 'I've only met her a few times, but of course all Paris knows her.' She winced. That wasn't what she'd meant to say at all.

'And does all Paris know she is François' mistress?' Claudine asked.

Monique lowered her eyes. 'I imagine so. But so many men have mistresses, Claudine. It is normal. And you, you have Armand.'

So far, François had been the only member of the family openly to acknowledge her affair with Armand, and for a moment Claudine wasn't sure what to say. Everything seemed to be happening rather too fast. 'Yes, I have Armand,' she said slowly. And then, 'What's her name, Monique? François' mistress? I've often wondered.'

'Élise,' Monique answered reluctantly. 'Élise Pascale.'

Claudine frowned 'Haven't I heard that name before? Do I know her?'

'No. But you did see her once, I believe. At the opera.' At once Claudine remembered. 'You mean . . . ? You mean the woman who was sitting . . . ? But she's so beautiful!'

Monique's laugh was uneasy. 'Yes,' she said, 'my brother seems to have an uncanny knack of attracting beautiful women, doesn't he?'

After Monique had gone, Claudine sat quite still on the sofa, saying the name to herself over and over again, Élise

Pascale. Élise Pascale. Élise ... Of course, she knew now why the woman had been staring at her during the opera. She remembered too, how she had seen François speaking to her after. She wondered if Élise bore her any resentment for being François' wife. She had no need to, since it seemed François had remained as faithful as he could to Élise despite his marriage. For a moment Claudine felt as though she was drowning, then suddenly she jerked herself to her feet, snatched up her purse and stalked out of the room.

Later that day, as they were sitting together outside the cottage, Claudine told Armand Monique's news. Armand, who had grown up with the de Lorvoire children, was almost as pleased for her as Claudine.

'Perhaps this time the relationship will be a success,' he said, stretching out on his back and holding up an arm to shield his eyes from the sun. 'She deserves some happiness after being let down so many times in the past.'

Claudine hugged her knees, and stared thoughtfully into the forest. 'I've never been able to understand that,' she said. 'I mean, she's so beautiful. And she's such a good catch.'

'I think it could have something to do with the fact that she appears so desperate – it really puts men off. For some reason, you know, she's always been like that. There was a time when François and Lucien were afraid to invite anyone home, not only for the embarrassment it caused them later, but because she was so hurt when she was let down.'

'Well, let's hope she's found true happiness at last.' Claudine was silent for a moment. 'I'm envious, you know,' she said.

'Envious?'

She nodded. 'Because she can announce her love to the world and we can't. She told me this morning that François has a mistress, someone the whole world knows about. It just doesn't seem fair, does it? I know it sounds childish, but it makes me hate him even more.' She leaned forward to pick up her wine, her eyes suddenly stinging with tears.

'I wonder how I'm going to survive without you while you're in Paris? Armand sighed. 'It'll be the first time we've been separated and I can't say I'm much looking forward to it. When did you say you were leaving?'

When she didn't answer, he reached out for her hand. To his amazement she snatched it away. 'Don't!' she snapped.

He sat up. 'What is it? What on earth's the matter?' But already she was on her feet and walking back to the house. He went after her. 'Have I done something to upset you?' he asked catching her up and taking her by the shoulder.

'No, no. It's not you, it's . . .' She turned away, looking back at the trees.

'I see,' he said, suddenly understanding. 'You think someone's there?'

'I don't know,' she sighed. 'Maybe it's just that I've become paranoid since François told me. But . . .' She looked up at him. 'Do you feel it too? Do you think someone is still there?'

Slowly he shook his head. 'Not really, no. Or perhaps I've just become used to it.' He pulled her to him and rested her head on his shoulder. 'Didn't you say that you might see François in Paris? You must tell him about this, Claudine. Tell him you think there's still someone here. Then . . .' He stopped, and to her surprise Claudine saw that he was smiling. She turned to follow his eyes and saw walking through the trees towards them Corinne and little Louis.

Corinne's toothy smile was dazzling. If it hadn't been for that, and the yellow softness of her plaited hair, Claudine often thought she might have found her intimidating, for she was bigger and brawnier even than Armand, who, since François had told him of her formidable skills in unarmed

combat, was forever challenging her to a fight. Her name –
Corinne Pichard – was French, and she spoke the language
like a native, but with her green loden suits, feathered
trilbies and bib-front dresses she looked positively
Tyrolean. Claudine had no idea where François had found
her, but she was glad he had, for the nursery had become an
even jollier place since her arrival.

'He was crying for his mother,' Corinne said, 'so I
thought I would bring him to you, *madame*. Mam'selle
Monique told me where to find you. I hope you do not
mind?'

'Of course not, Corinne,' Claudine smiled. She held out
her arms to Louis. 'Hello, my darling,' she said and for the
moment her painful preoccupation with Élise Pascale, and
dangerous strangers in the forest, was forgotten.

Rudolf von Liebermann heaved his bulk from the chair and
moved across the barren room to the window. Through the
grime he could see the blur of red lights and winking signs in
the street below. The depressing sound of a languid female
voice chanting 'Lili Marlene' drifted through the night. He
rubbed a circle in the grime, and followed the progress of a
huddled figure shuffling through the rain until it disappeared around the corner. 'When did he leave England?'
he said eventually, without turning round. Behind him,
Brüning and Grundhausen sat stiffly in their chairs. Max
Helber was in Paris.

'He left four days ago,' Walter Brüning answered.

'And no one knows where he is now?'

Silence.

'You mean to tell me he has disappeared from the face of
the earth?'

Again silence.

Wiping his finger with a handkerchief, von Liebermann
turned back into the room. 'Where is Halunke?' he snapped.

'At Lorvoire.'

'And he doesn't know the whereabouts of the Wine Supplier either?'

'No,' Brüning confirmed. 'But as we know, it is the Wine Supplier's family he is after, not the Wine Supplier himself.'

'Then he must be stopped!' von Liebermann roared.

Nobody spoke. After a while, von Liebermann said more calmly, 'This is a crucial time for the Fatherland. We need de Lorvoire, and if Halunke harms his family we shall lose him. Have we discovered anything further about this nanny?'

Brüning and Grundhausen appeared uncomfortable. As Brüning loosed his collar, von Liebermann's piercing eyes fell upon him. 'Well have we?'

'Not yet, *Herr General*. Max has spoken with both Halunke and the Pascale woman, but neither has been able to throw any light on the nanny's true identity.'

There was a long silence. Brüning and Grundhausen glanced at each other several times, then Grundhausen said, 'The Pascale woman is threatening to stop supplying information if we don't do something about the Wine Supplier's wife. She says we made a bargain, that she is keeping to her side but we are failing . . . '

'Instruct Halunke to pay her a visit,' von Liebermann snapped. Then his gruesome, wart-infested face broke into a smile. 'That is a good idea,' he chuckled. 'It will keep them both quiet for a while – Halunke will enjoy raping de Lorvoire's mistress a second time. But my concern now is the whereabouts of de Lorvoire himself. How long ago did he warn the French High Command of our prospective operations against Belgium and Holland?'

'In January of this year,' Grundhausen answered.

'And the French still disbelieve him? That is good. But what I want to know is, do the British disbelieve him too? Have we any reason to think that he might have gained the information we asked of him from the British?'

'The information regarding the Royal Air Force?' Brüning asked.

'Of course regarding the Royal Air Force! Hermann Goering needs to know its strength before we make an attack on Poland.'

'Then you think the Allies will stand by their promise to defend Poland?' Grundhausen asked – and immediately wished he hadn't.

'You stupid dog!' von Liebermann snarled. 'They are on the brink of signing a formal alliance with Poland. If they do that, they won't back down.' He wiped the saliva from his lips with the back of his hand. 'Find the Wine Supplier! If we need to bargain with him again, give him details of the euthanasia plan for the gipsies and the insane. No one will come to their rescue, any more than they have with the Jews. And remind Halunke that if he wishes his identity to remain secure, he will do nothing to harm the de Lorvoire family until I have the information I require. Then, he may do as he pleases. Unless, of course,' and here his thin mouth broke into a smile, 'de Lorvoire succeeds in proving his fealty to The Reich.'

He paused for a moment, then looked at Grundhausen. 'Tell Halunke not to hold back with the mistress, and this time to leave his calling card. It will do de Lorvoire no harm to understand what lengths we are prepared to go to to get him.'

– 18 –

Paris hadn't been so hot for years. The grey stone buildings shimmered in the heat like desert mirages, insects swarmed over the declining waters of the Seine, and pavement cafés had never seen so much trade or so many lovers. With all the talk of war, love, like everything else, became more urgent; there was a feeling of excitement in the city as children donned their gas masks to frighten their friends, newspaper vendors barked , *'Le Matin! Le Matin! Le Boche arrive!'* and shops on the rue de Rivoli did a roaring trade in china dogs lifting a leg on a copy of *Mein Kampf.* There was a sense of unreality, too, as if all this might be the product of a fever which would soon subside.

The day before the July ball, excited and nervous, Monique took Claudine to meet Karol Kalinowski at his apartment on the avenue Marceau. Claudine liked him on sight. His face was severe and his manner a trifle abrupt, she thought, but the twinkle in his green eyes was constant and there was no mistaking his devotion to Monique. They spent a cheerful two hours together, listening as Karol told stories of his homeland and plied them with refreshments almost as lavish as his compliments. Claudine was enjoying herself so much that she almost forgot Karol and Monique had not seen each other for three weeks, and that it might be tactful to leave them alone together.

She rode back to the Bois de Boulogne in a taxi, feeling very happy – almost as if she must try to keep her spirits from soaring too high. She was missing Armand dreadfully, of course, but it was so wonderful to be in Paris, away from the prying eyes that followed her about Lorvoire. And she could hardly wait to get home to see if her ball gown had been delivered yet . . . Again she sighed as she pictured the yards and yards of black rayon satin, the strapless cross-over bodice and daringly low back. Monique and Solange had shrieked with laughter during her final fitting, for when she stooped to pick up the hem, her breasts had broken free of the bodice.

'It is no matter,' Coco had assured her, 'we shall merely stiffen the whalebone and tighten the cross-over.'

'But will I be able to breathe?'

'I doubt it, but which do you wish to secure, your modesty or your life?'

'My life, I think. Even if I remain covered, this gown leaves very little to the imagination!'

'Then we shall do our best,' Coco laughed. 'And perhaps, before you return to Lorvoire, you will do me the honour of being photographed in the dress. I am very proud of this creation.'

When she arrived home Claudine ran straight up the stairs to the nursery, but only to find that Louis was asleep. She stood over him for several minutes, looking at his adorable little face, the tousled mop of black hair, the long dark lashes curled over the silky smoothness of his cheeks. She loved him so much she ached with it.

'He has worn himself out playing with all the new toys Madame la Comtesse has purchased,' Corinne said, coming into the room and standing beside her at the cot.

'She spoils him,' Claudine said softly. 'We all do.' She turned back to the nanny. 'Corinne, if anything were to happen to him . . .'

'There now, *madame*,' Corinne soothed. 'Nothing is going to happen to him. Has your husband not given you his word?'

It was clear from Claudine's expression that she needed more reassurance than that. Corinne pressed her hand. 'Why don't you go down to the sitting-room? The Comtesse is about to take tea with her visitors and I believe your aunt is amongst them.'

Immediately Claudine's face brightened. 'Tante Céline!' she cried. 'I had no idea she was in Paris.' And after casting another lingering look at her son, she ran off down the stairs.

The following morning she was standing at the mirror in the hall, arranging her hat before joining Corinne and Louis for their walk, when she was drawn to the sound of voices coming from the study.

'. . . so I am afraid, *Monsieur le Comte*, that I am unable to tell you any more than that.'

She frowned. It was a voice she recognized, but for the moment she couldn't place it.

'Have you sent anyone to Brest?' Louis enquired.

'Of course, *monsieur*. But it is over fourteen days now since the Royal Navy landed him, he is unlikely still to be there.'

'But someone there must have seen him?'

'There is a garage mechanic who was holding François' car. François collected it, as arranged, and the mechanic has every reason to believe he then drove out of Brest.'

Claudine edged closer to the door.

'You're taking the word of a garage mechanic?'

'We have no choice, *monsieur*. No one else has seen him, no one has heard from him.'

'Have you tried Élise Pascale?'

'Naturally. She is as baffled as we are.'

'This isn't good enough, Paillole,' Louis said. 'I don't need to remind you what a dangerous game my son is playing and it is one of which I strongly disapprove. I want him found, and I want him found alive '

'Of course, *monsieur*. We all want that. But the reason I have come here today is to prepare you for the worst.'

Claudine's heart stood still.

'So you think he is already dead?' Louis snapped

'No. That is not what we think at all. What we think is what we have always feared.'

There was a long silence, then Louis spoke again. 'Are you saying what I think you're saying, Captain Paillole?'

'We have no confirmation, *monsieur*, but I'm afraid, yes, that is what we suspect.'

'Get out of here!' Louis roared. 'Get out and don't come into my house again!'

Claudine fled across the hall to the sitting-room.

Thankfully no one was inside. She heard the front door slam, then Captain Paillole's footsteps in the drive. She crossed quickly to the window and watched as he drove out of the gates.

She could make nothing of what she had heard, nothing except that François had vanished – and somewhere inside her a knot of fear started to tighten. If she asked Louis to explain, it would mean admitting to eavesdropping. But did that matter? It was her husband they had been discussing – she had a right to know what Captain Paillole suspected him of.

Louis was still in his study when she knocked, but as she pushed the door open Monique came flying down the stairs crying, 'Papa! Papa! Is he there, Claudine? Oh Papa! You are the most generous man in the world,' she gushed, sailing into the room. 'Did you see what he has given me, Claudine? Look here,' and she passed Claudine a small leather case. Inside was an emerald necklace, earrings and bracelet. 'Won't they match my dress perfectly this evening? Oh Papa, you are so clever.'

To Claudine's amazement there was nothing in Louis' manner to suggest that only a few moments ago he had lost his temper; as he accepted his daughter's gratitude his face was a picture of pleasure.

'It's stunning, Louis,' Claudine said. 'Absolutely . . .'

'Just a minute,' he interrupted. 'Have you not found your own? I instructed Magaly to leave it on your dressing table.'

Claudine shook her head, bewildered.

'Then I suggest you return to your room and inspect my choice. If it is not suitable we shall need to change it before tonight. And you, Monique, why don't you go with her while I make a telephone call?'

The rest of the day was so taken up with last-minute house guests arriving and then their own preparations for the ball, that it wasn't until late afternoon that Claudine had an opportunity to speak to Louis again. However, when she knocked on the study door there was no reply, and when she turned the handle she found that it was locked. Puzzled, she went back upstairs, and had got as far as the first landing when she heard the study door open, and saw Louis cross to the front door and open it. He spoke briefly to a man she couldn't see, closed the door again and returned to the study.

There was obviously something strange going on, and as the evening went on Claudine found herself increasingly unnerved by it. Uppermost in her mind was the fact that François had disappeared. What he had done, or what Captain Paillole suspected him of, had for the moment ceased to matter: she just wanted to know where he was. Then it occurred to her that Corinne might know.

'Yes, as a matter of fact I do know where he is,' Corinne said. 'But I'm afraid he has instructed me to tell no one. The only reason I know is so that I can reach him if I feel Louis is in any danger.'

'But what about François? Is he in any danger?'

Corinne smiled. 'Not now, *madame.*'

'Meaning he was?'

'I think a little, yes.'

Claudine's eyes narrowed. 'Corinne! I want to know where he is!'

'*Madame, monsieur* gives his orders for his own safety as well as yours, and I should be in breach of my duty to you both if I went against his wishes.'

'I want to know, Corinne!'

But just then, to Corinne's evident relief, the door opened and Solange came in with Louis.

Claudine had no choice but to accept her defeat and several minutes later took Louis off to her own room so he could join her in the bath. And after all, she thought as she lay back in the scented water while Magaly handed her a glass of champagne and Louis sailed his toy boats around her, if Corinne believed François to be safe then he probably was. And she had no intention of spoiling this evening by worrying about a husband she detested.

The ball was in full swing by the time the Polish Ambassador led his staff, bare-footed, in a polonaise across the Embassy lawn. The watching crowd gasped in admiration as the macabre glow of red Bengal lights illuminated the dancers, bejewelled women glittered in the darkness and coloured smoke entwined itself around them. It was as though they were dancing on fire.

Guy de Maulevrier, a family friend who was Claudine's escort for the evening, ushered her to the front of the audience, and seeing her, Monsieur Lukasiewicz, the Polish Ambassador, took her by the hand and drew her into the dance. Others were joining in too, and as the music swelled to a deafening pitch and the rhythm quickened to a polka, beautiful women frolicked about the gardens in the arms of their dashing young courtiers – while inside the statesmen talked soberly of war.

At the end of the dance, breathless and laughing, Claudine fell back into the arms of Guy de Maulevrier, who whisked a glass of champagne from a passing tray for her, then stooped to kiss her shoulders. She was enjoying herself, surrounded by friends. There was singing; only the Poles knew the words, but everyone joined in, making as much noise as they could so that the surrounding streets rang with their merriment. Guy's hands were again on Claudine's shoulders, making her feel reckless and carefree and happy. Then suddenly there was someone tugging at her wrist, and looking round she saw Tante Céline.

'It's Monique,' Céline shouted above the din. 'You'd better come.'

She hurried through the embassy after her aunt until they

reached the Ambassador's outer office, where Monique was sitting alone. She looked up when they walked in, and as her black bobbed hair fell back from her face, Claudine almost gasped aloud.

'What is it?' she cried. 'What's happened?'

'It's Karol,' Céline answered. 'He hasn't arrived. I sent my chauffeur round to his apartment, and he's just returned. There's no sign of Karol, and it's past midnight.'

Claudine sat down beside Monique and took her hand. 'There will be an explanation, *chérie*.'

'That's what Céline keeps saying,' Monique wailed, 'but what explanation can there be? He knew how important tonight was to me. He was to meet *Maman* and Papa. Oh, Claudine, you don't think he's changed his mind about me, do you?'

'No, of course I don't,' Claudine assured her. 'He's in love with you. He . . .'

'But I've thought men were in love with me before,' Monique cried, wrenching her hands away and burying her face in them. 'Oh God, I can't believe this is happening to me again. Why does it have to be like this for me? I can't have him, he can never be mine, that's why I try so hard to fall in love with other men. And I thought Karol was the man, I thought that this time . . .'

'Monique, what are you saying?' Claudine interrupted. 'Who can never be yours?'

Quickly Monique shook her head. 'No one, nothing. I didn't mean anything. Oh, Claudine, what have I done to deserve this?'

Claudine looked at her aunt for help, but Céline only shrugged. 'All right,' Claudine said decisively. 'Tell me who Karol's friends are, Monique, and I'll go and ask them if they know where he is.'

'Here,' Céline said, taking a pad and pen from the desk behind her, 'write them down, Claudine.'

Monique knew only three of Karol's friends, and they had a good deal of trouble over the spellings, but Claudine took the list back to the party and began to ask about Karol. No one knew where he was. She stopped for a word with Monsieur Reynaud, the French Finance Minister, and was just turning away from him when she became uncomfortably aware that someone was watching her. Fear shot through her: the man in the Lorvoire forest had followed her here to Paris . . . And then, as her body began to tingle in that horribly disturbing way it often did when under his scrutiny she turned round, and found herself staring straight into François' eyes.

Until that moment she had not understood just how afraid she had been for his safety, or how badly she had missed him. Now seeing him, all she wanted was to run to him, hear him tell her that he was all right. But she remained where she was, strangely unable to move.

He made his way through the crowd towards her, and as though she was drifting somewhere apart from herself, she watched him come, feeling his black eyes sink deep into hers and hearing her breath whisper from her lips.

'What a fortunate man I am to have such a beautiful wife,' he murmured as he reached her, bringing her hand to his lips. 'These are the diamonds my father gave you today?' He fingered the bracelet on her wrist. 'He always has had a remarkable eye for quality.'

There was an ambiguity to his remark that Claudine thought she understood, but she said, 'When did you arrive in Paris?'

'Earlier today. I'm afraid I had business to attend to before . . .'

'What business?'

'Business.'

'Don't treat me like a fool, François!' she snapped, suddenly angry. 'I want to know what's going on. I have a

right to know. If you have put my son in any more danger.'
She broke off as he tilted her face up to his.

'*Our* son,' he reminded her.

For a moment her eyes were locked on his, and she felt
her lips parting as though waiting for his kiss; but then,
slapping his hand away, she said, 'If you've put him in any
more danger François . . .'

'He is in no more danger than he was before.'

'Then where have you been? Everyone has been looking
for you . . .'

'Ah, so you did overhear the conversation in my father's
study today. He thought you did.'

'Then would you mind explaining . . . ?'

'I'm not explaining anything in the middle of a crowd
like this. Now, I rather feel the desire to dance with my
wife.' And taking her by the elbow, he led her into the
garden.

She could hardly believe what was happening to her.
With one hand he held the small of her back, and with the
other he twined his fingers through hers. Her body's
response to him was so strong that she could barely move.

'You don't appear to dance as well with me as you do with
others,' he remarked. 'But that is hardly surprising.'

She looked up into his face, but as he started to smile at
her she turned quickly away.

'How is the situation at Lorvoire?' he asked, after a
minute or two.

'To be truthful, I'm not sure,' she said, mentally shaking
herself out of her trance. 'I still have the feeling of being
watched – but Armand doesn't seem to feel it at all. He
thinks whoever it is has gone away. Has he?' she asked,
when François didn't answer.

'I'm afraid I don't know, *chérie.*'

She faltered at the endearment, and anything she might
have been about to say was snatched from her mind.

'Have you come across any strangers at Lorvoire?' he asked.

'No,' she answered. But then, thinking about it, 'Actually, there is someone. His name is Claude Villiers. He's been organizing boules tournaments.'

François nodded thoughtfully, then returning his attention to her, he pulled her closer and said, 'I shall have him checked out. I can't have anything happen to my beautiful wife, now can I?' His white teeth flashed a smile. 'Armand is taking good care of you?'

'Yes,' she breathed, feeling hopelessly dizzy at the way his body was pressing against hers. She blinked, trying to bring herself back to reality. This couldn't be desire she was feeling, not now, after all this time, when she had fought so hard to conquer it and when Armand had shown her what it was to be truly loved. Yet the feel of his legs moving against hers was quickening her heartbeat and locking the breath in her lungs. She looked up at him, and her heart turned over at the harsh, disfigured face that tonight seemed so strangely alluring.

He was looking down the length of his nose at her, his thick black brows ironically raised. 'If you continue to look at me that way, *ma chére*, I shall feel obliged to do something about it.'

It was as if all the blood in her body had suddenly rushed to her loins, and she found herself clinging to him as though trying to stay on her feet.

'In fact,' he went on, 'since our home is filled with guests I shall indeed have to come to your bed tonight. However, I'm not sure I feel inclined to make love to a woman who whores like a peasant with my own *vigneron*.'

He grabbed her as she made to break away. 'Does Armand know that you lust after your husband?' he said, laughing.

'You're insane if you think that!' she spat. 'I loathe and detest you, and I don't care who knows it!'

'Evidently,' he remarked, looking around to see who had heard, but as she made to wrench herself away again, he pulled her back. 'I haven't finished.'

'Let go of me!' she seethed. 'Let go or I'll scream!'

'Scream by all means, if you want everyone present to witness your face being slapped.'

She was silent, staring stonily past him as she waited for him to continue.

'Where is Monique?' he said, after a while.

'Inside.'

'Then I want you to go to her and tell her that Kalinowski will not be coming tonight.'

Claudine's eyes shot to his. 'How do you know? Where is he?'

'There will be no engagement,' he continued, as if she hadn't spoken. 'Kalinowski has returned to Poland and I have no reason to believe that he will set foot in France again.'

'*What*? Why?'

'Because I have seen to it that he will not,' he answered. 'Break the news gently to my sister. I believe she thought herself in love with him.'

'What have you done?' she hissed. 'Why have you interfered when he's asked her to marry him?'

'He was in no position to ask her. He already has a wife.'

'Oh no!' Claudine groaned. 'But if he already has a wife, why did he ask Monique to marry him?'

'Did he?'

'Well, of course he . . .' The words dried on her lips as she remembered Freddy.

'Precisely,' François said. 'I'm afraid Monique has a way of reading things into a situation that simply aren't there. But that's no excuse for the way he allowed her to believe he was a free man. He is notorious for his conquests, and my sister, I'm sorry to say, is easy prey.'

The dance ended then, and François led her to a shadowy corner of the garden. As they passed through the crowd Claudine couldn't help noticing the way heads turned – it was rare to see François and Claudine de Lorvoire together in public. Strangely, even after the way he had behaved, she felt a thrill at the interest they provoked, but then she snatched her hand from his as her body threatened once again to betray her.

'This won't be easy for you, Claudine,' he said, when they were away from the crowd. 'I know Monique will take it hard, but I think your approach will be far gentler than mine, which is why I've asked you to break it to her.'

'Your consideration for your sister does you credit,' she said tartly. 'Will you show your mistress the same consideration when you ask her why she introduced Monique to Kalinowski in the first place?'

'My mistress is not as guilty as you might think,' he answered, quite unperturbed. 'Monique happened to be at Élise's apartment when Kalinowski arrived. She made all the running, I gather, and sadly Élise could do little to stop her.'

François knew that his discussing – and defending – his mistress in such a matter-of-fact way was incensing Claudine beyond words. Looking down at her, he saw the way her breasts were heaving with indignation, the way her eyes were flashing in the darkness, saw the moistness of her soft, sensuous mouth. He put a hand on her shoulder and started to caress her.

She shrugged him off. 'Are you touching me while your mind is on *Élise*, François?' she sneered.

He laughed. '*Touché*. But I was thinking that maybe I will come to your bed tonight after all, if only to remind you how repulsive you find me.'

'I don't need reminding!' she spat, and turning on her heel she stalked imperiously back into the crowd.

The following night François' impassive black eyes were watching Élise as she entertained Max Helber. As always when she entertained his guests, nothing was too much trouble, and he was amused to see German dishes being served one after the other. She was, he thought, putting up a remarkably good performance of feigning a first encounter with Helber.

He glanced at his watch, then set his glass back on the table and rose to his feet. It was time now for Élise to disappear, as he had confidential matters to discuss with the German. Knowing how she would enjoy being seen with the man whose current success with the economy was likely to make him the next Prime Minister of France, he had arranged for her to join Paul Reynaud's opera party. Reynaud's mistress would be there too, and knowing how much Élise disliked Madame des Portes, François was almost sorry he wouldn't be there to see the fireworks.

Élise was still listening raptly to Helber's flowery opinions on French literature as François walked over to the fireplace and rang for the maid. 'Fetch *madame*'s cloak,' he said, when she came in.

Immediately Élise looked up, and he could see her irritation at being dismissed so unceremoniously. Ignoring it, he poured a cognac for Helber and himself.

'François, may I have a word?' Élise purred through her teeth.

'Certainly, *ma chére*, if it won't take long.'

'It won't,' she snapped, and he followed her through into the bedroom.

'Well?' he enquired, closing the door behind him.

'I wish to know if you will be here when I return?' she said testily.

'No.'

'Why?'

– 326 –

'I don't propose to give you a reason.'

The pain she felt at his words showed in her eyes, but her tone was brittle rather than peevish as she said, 'You haven't made love to me since you returned from Lorvoire, François – over three months ago. What's happened? Have I done something . . . ?'

'Élise,' he interrupted smoothly, 'surely you don't need reminding that you tried to kill my son.'

'But I thought we had put that behind us! When we were in Germany . . .'

'Are you really so stupid as to think I could forget something like that?'

'No, of course not. But . . .'

'But what, Élise?'

She had known his coldness so often in the past, but lately it had begun to frighten her. 'I would never do anything to hurt him now!' she cried 'I swear to you, François. Upon my mother's grave I swear it!'

He seemed amused by that. 'Wouldn't you, Élise?' he said. 'Then tell me, who is having him – and my wife – watched?'

'You've asked me that before, and the answer is still the same. I don't know, François. Truthfully, I don't know.'

'Is it the man who raped you?'

She gasped at the deliberate brutality. Then suddenly he grabbed her by the hair and pulled her face very close to his. 'Don't bother to lie, Élise,' he said. 'Just tell me who he's working for.'

'I don't know! I don't know who he is, he just came here and . . .'

He smiled grimly at her hesitation. 'Does he have any connection with von Liebermann?' he asked.

He knew about her contact with von Liebermann! Again she shrank from him, and he tightened his grip on her hair as he saw she was about to deny the association. 'I am fully aware of your links with the Abwehr, Élise, so just answer my question.'

'Yes!' she cried. 'Yes, he has!'

He let her go. 'Thank you. That was all I wanted to know. However, you have succeeded in confirming something else I have long suspected.'

'What?' she asked, dreading the answer.

'That you are unable to keep your mouth shut when subjected to what our friend Liebermann calls coercion.'

She turned away, too confused for the moment to see where all this might lead. She expected him to leave the room, but then he came behind her, and holding her by the shoulders he pulled her back against him. 'So you see, *ma chérie*, why I have told you nothing these past months. What you do not know you cannot tell.' She drew in her breath sharply as his hand slipped inside her dress. 'Now all you have to do, Élise, is decide whether your allegiance is to me, or to the Nazis.'

'It is to you, François! It has always been to you.'

'But when I join with them, your conscience will not be troubled? You will come with me?'

'Yes! I've told you before . . .' She gasped as his fingers closed over her nipple, and she wanted him so desperately that she could think of nothing else.

'Do you want to make love, Élise?' he murmured in her ear.

'Yes, oh yes,' she moaned, turning in his arms.

He looked down at her, and when he saw the lust in her eyes an ugly sneer curled across his lips. 'Then as a professional whore you should have no trouble in finding someone to satisfy you,' he said, and letting her go, he turned and walked out of the room.

'I have all the information you require,' François told Max Helber moments after Élise had left them.

Helber's wide eyes gleamed, then looking about the room, he said, 'We are alone?'

'The maid has left too,' François confirmed.

'Then begin.'

François sipped his cognac, relaxing back into his chair. He eyed the German for some time, inuring himself to the revulsion he felt for that smooth, fleshy face with its half-timid, half-greedy smile. He had never understood how one man could be attracted to another, and that he should find himself the object of such perverse fantasy disgusted him like nothing else. But these were Helber's terms for tendering his invaluable morsels of intelligence, and François had no choice but to accept them.

When finally he spoke, his voice had a rich, mellifluous tone guaranteed to make Helber squirm in his chair. 'I have in my possession,' he began, 'a series of maps indicating all factories in Great Britain involved in the manufacture of munitions.'

'And France?' Helber said, uncrossing his legs.

'Not yet.'

'But you will be able to supply them?'

'I believe so.'

'Good.' Helber considered for a moment. 'And now perhaps you would like to tell me where you have been these past weeks?'

'Certainly. But before I do I want some information from you.'

A lascivious light leapt into Helber's eyes as it always did when his turn came to impart intelligence. 'So soon?' he said, running the tip of his pink tongue over his lips. 'Then of course I shall oblige. What would you like to know?'

François watched as the loathsome man set down his glass and started to unbutton his fly. 'I want to know who von Liebermann has employed to watch my family.'

Helber showed no surprise. His plump lips parted in a

smile and his girlish fingers pulled his penis from his trousers. 'Does it matter who it is?' he said, resting his hands on the arms of the chair.

'Yes.'

'But why? You must surely be aware that it is in all of our interests to know where you are at all times. Your safety is of the utmost concern to the General.'

François let that pass. 'I want to know the name of the man snooping about Lorvoire,' he said.

'I fail to see why his name should be important. He is there merely to ensure that you do not act in the interests of anyone but The Reich.'

'Have you any reason to believe I have ever done otherwise?'

'Plenty, my friend,' Helber laughed, only just managing to resist the urge to start stroking himself. 'You act in your own interests, we know that, we accept it. But there is a war approaching, a time when each and every man must declare his fealty to one side or the other.'

François' jaw tightened and his eyes narrowed. 'This man, he has a personal vendetta against me, does he not?'

This time Helber allowed his surprise to show. 'What makes you ask such a question?'

'Because it is your style to ferret out these people. They are easier to control when their motives are personal.'

Hearing the turbulent note in the Wine Supplier's voice, Helber could restrain himself no longer, and almost groaned aloud as his fingers circled his penis. 'How is that so?'

'You simply offer to assist them in their revenge in exchange for a little something you need to know. Then, once you have the man – or woman – working for you, you threaten to inform their victim of their identity if they don't continue to do so. It's an old trick, Helber, but a good one. So, who is he?'

'I cannot tell you that, my friend.'

François lowered his gaze to Helber's hands and held it there for some time before looking back to the fleshy, womanish face. 'Then tell me if he means any harm to my family,' he said.

Helber was beginning to pant. 'I believe he does, yes,' he answered.

Now he was getting somewhere. Dropping his eyes again to Helber's erection, François said, 'Why don't you join me on the sofa, Max?'

For one dreadful moment he thought Helber was going to ejaculate on the spot, but he managed to contain himself and settled beside François on the sofa. François said, 'You understand what I am offering for this information, Max?'

Helber nodded, but for the moment, with François' powerful body so temptingly close, he was unable to speak.

'Tell me what I want to know, Max,' François coaxed.

Still Helber was unable to speak as François' hand waited to take his penis. 'Is he German?' François said.

Helber shook his head.

'French?'

Helber nodded.

'His name, Max,' François said, fighting the nausea as he took the man's penis in his hand.

Helber's breath wheezed from his lungs and he started to grunt.

'His name,' François encouraged, starting to move his hand.

Helber's lips were trembling, and a high-pitched sound was coming from the back of his throat. François lowered his hand to the man's testicles and Helber started to splutter.

'His name!' François roared, and he clenched his fist so viciously that Helber screamed, and François leapt to his feet as the semen spurted over his hand and onto his shoulder. Snatching a handkerchief from his pocket, he wiped his fingers, and saw Helber's eyes roll back in their sockets in the dying throes of his ecstasy. Christ, he should have known that wouldn't work with a creep like Helber. The man was a Goddamned masochist.

He went to the bathroom and scrubbed his hands under scalding water. By the time he returned, Helber had regained his composure and was sipping another cognac. François never failed to be surprised by Helber's lack of shame for his disgraceful behaviour; somehow it made the man more intolerable than ever.

'So,' Helber said cheerfully, 'you were going to tell me where you have been these past weeks.'

François' hard eyes contemplated him for several minutes before he walked across the room and settled against the edge of the table. He was weighing up in his mind the little information Helber had ceded. He knew only that the man watching him and his family was French, and that his motives for doing so were personal. It didn't narrow the field greatly, but he would get Erich von Pappen onto it and see what he came up with. He could start with Villiers, the man Claudine had mentioned. In the meantime, he knew exactly what it was going to take to persuade von Liebermann to keep the man at bay.

'I have been in Moscow,' he answered.

Helber was immediately interested, but tried not to show it. 'Tell me more,' he said casually.

'As you are aware, Britain and France have opened negotiations with the Kremlin in order to strengthen their guarantee to Poland. Marshal Voroshilov, the principal Soviet negotiator, informed them that his government has a complete plan, with figures, for co-operation.'

'The details?'

'They have, ready to put into the field, one hundred and twenty infantry divisions and sixteen cavalry divisions; five thousand heavy and medium cannon, and approximately ten thousand armoured vehicles.'

Helber nodded. 'Impressive. How did the Poles react?'

François raised his eyebrows. Helber might be a disgusting man but he wasn't a stupid one. 'Colonel Beck's government has refused to allow the Red Army into Poland under any circumstances. To quote Marshal Smigly-Rydz, "With the Germans we risk losing our liberty, but with the Russians we would lose our souls." '

'A shrewd man, Marshal Smigly-Rydz,' Helber commented. 'And what chance, in your opinion, do the Allies stand of changing the minds of the Polish government?'

'In my opinion, little or none. However, talks are still taking place.'

Helber got up and helped himself to yet another cognac. 'I take it you have a full report on what you discovered, both in England and Russia? And you can give me the charts you mentioned earlier?'

François nodded. 'They will be handed to you when you cross the border back into Germany. Someone will telephone you tomorrow, to tell you which station they have been left at.'

'Good. Good.' Helber appeared extremely happy. 'General von Liebermann will be most grateful to you, my friend. Now, is there any further information you require from me? Free of charge,' he added, catching François' eye.

'You won't have come empty-handed,' François answered, 'so I'll take what you've got – for what it's worth.'

Helber opened his case and pulled out the documents Brüning and Grundhausen had sent by courier the week before. 'I think you will find them interesting,' he said.

François took the papers and put them on the table. 'One thing before you go, Helber,' he said. 'Having now committed myself to the Nazi cause, I expect von Liebermann to keep control of this Frenchman.'

'Oh, he will, my friend, have no fear of that. As long as you continue to prove your loyalty to the Fatherland, your family will be safe. Incidentally, I am intrigued to know: how does it feel to be a traitor to your own country?'

'I imagine as good as it felt when I squeezed your balls.'

Helber left soon after, not entirely sure he understood François' answer. But the dull ache between his legs not only reminded him that the Wine Supplier's fingers had, for the first time, been there, it also increased his determination to see the man's total surrender one of these days. And the way things were developing, he might not have long to wait.

Twenty minutes later, as François followed Helber out into the street, Halunke slithered down behind the steering wheel of his car and watched the dark figure of his nemesis get into his Citröen and drive off into the night. As he disappeared from view, Halunke's fingers tightened on the *rossignol* he would use later to pick the locks of La Pascale's apartment. She was small compensation for his patience when the great prize of de Lorvoire's wife still remained so elusive; but for now she was as far as von Liebermann would allow him to go, and tonight she would bear the full brunt of his frustration.

– 19 –

They had been back at Lorvoire for over a week now – and it was as if the excitement of early July had never been. Already, on the journey from Paris back to Touraine, they had felt the change: war, for so long a remote possibilty, had become a real and imminent threat, and the countryside had an eerie, almost end-of-the-world feel about it. As the hot summer days passed, a hush seemed to settle all over France, a terrible, portentous gloom. On the surface people went about their normal business, but there was an undercurrent of horror and disbelief. Few dared to voice it, but everyone knew that France had neither the spirit nor the strength to defend herself – even Lucien, who had arrived unexpectedly in Paris for three days, had been unable to kindle a spark of hope.

Within an hour of arriving at the château Claudine had sent Magaly to find Armand, telling him to meet her at the farmhouse. Their reunion was as passionate as their parting had been, but Claudine sensed almost immediately that something in him had changed.

'The young men have gone,' he said sadly, when she questioned him. 'They have been leaving every day for the past week. I'd have gone myself, but I'm too old. Too old at thirty-two, I ask you.'

Knowing now was not the moment to express her relief, Claudine tried to tease him out of his dejection, but even she was finding it difficult to remain unaffected by the pervading air of pessimism. 'Shall we sit outside, under the trees?' she said, and they took a rug and sat in the shade, her head resting on his shoulder while she told him about Monique and Karol Kalinowski.

'Poor Monique!' he said. 'Where is she now?'

'At the château. She clings to Solange like a frightened child, and Solange talks to her and listens in a way that tears at your heart. She's the most wonderful mother, you know. Crazy and capricious as she is, she loves her family to distraction, and in their times of crisis her strength is amazing.' She sighed. 'You know, François has seen to it that Kalinowski is never allowed back into France. But I can't help thinking about his wife and children – it could be that their only means of escaping the Germans is to seek asylum in France. He should have told Monique from the start that he was married.'

Armand nodded soberly. Then he chuckled. 'I shouldn't

have liked to be in Kalinowski's shoes when he came face to face with François!'

They sat quietly then, and as Claudine trailed her fingers lazily over his bare arm, inhaling the acrid smell of sun-dried grass and listening to the buzz and rustle of the forest, she felt herself beginning to relax at last. Bringing his hand to her mouth, she kissed it, almost in gratitude – she had been half-afraid that nothing, not even Armand's love, would be able to exorcize the restlessness and doubt that had plagued her since the night of the July ball.

At first she had told herself that she had drunk too much champagne, that it was because she was missing Armand that she had felt that dreadful, demeaning desire for François again. But in her heart she knew that didn't explain it. It didn't explain why she had lain awake night after night, waiting to hear his footsteps on the stairs, dreading, and hoping that he would come to her bed. He had not come, and on the few occasions when their paths crossed she had had to turn away, terrified he might detect the anarchic lust she experienced whenever he looked at her. But it was a feeling that was mercifully starting to fade as she sat with Armand's arms tight around her and the breath of his kiss on her cheek.

'Did you talk to François about the other matter?' he asked.

She nodded. 'He wanted to know if there had been any strangers in the area, but there's only Claude Villiers. He said he would have him checked out. What do you think? D'you think there's still someone here?'

'While you were away I did get the impression I was being watched once or twice, but it's difficult to know whether one is imagining it or not. Is François intending to return to Lorvoire?'

'He didn't say. But I don't think so.'

'Mm. A pity. I wanted to talk to him.'

'What about?'

It was some time before he answered, and in the silence a strange foreboding stole over her. She felt his mood beginning to change, she felt him withdrawing from her into the sadness she had detected in him when she arrived. She waited, hardly daring to breathe lest it should inject further life into her dread.

'Well,' he said finally, 'if they do raise the age for recruitment, I want to go, Claudine. I shall have to discuss it with François first, because it'll mean there's no one here to run the vineyards, but I don't imagine he will raise any objections – except that neither of us will feel happy about leaving you here unprotected. Which reminds me, you shouldn't have come through the forest alone, however eager you were to see me. Don't do it again.'

'No sir!' she said, saluting. But there was more to come, she knew it.

'Why didn't you write while you were away?' he said suddenly.

She was stunned. Not only because of the reproach in his voice, but because it hadn't even occurred to her to write.

'I take it you did miss me?'

She sat up and turned to look at him. 'Of course I did,' she answered, her voice imbued with feeling. 'I'm surprised you even need to ask.'

He smiled. 'That's all right then, isn't it?'

But it wasn't. There was something in his voice . . . 'What is it?' she said. 'What are you thinking?'

He lifted a gentle hand to her cheek. 'Of how much I love you.'

'No. There's more, Armand. Tell me, what is it?'

He laughed, and turned his eyes into the forest. 'The truth,' he said. 'I've been so terrified of losing you these past weeks that somehow, in my mind, I've managed to convince myself that it has already happened, but I'm refusing to see it.'

'But Armand, I love you!' she cried. 'You know I do. Nothing has changed, except perhaps that having been away from you, I love you more than ever.'

'Even though I can never give you the life you have now? Balls at the Polish Embassy, soirées at the Bois de Boulogne, visits to the opera, a household of staff? They will all be things of the past if you come to live with me.'

'But they don't mean anything! All the time I was in Paris I wanted to be here, with you, the way we are now. I love you, Armand. You're all that matters to me.'

He shook his head. 'No, Claudine. I know you'd like that to be true, but it isn't. I've been thinking about it while you were away, and I know, as you do too in your heart, that there's no future for us, and if we go on like this I'll only make you unhappy. That's why I want to talk to François. I want him to pull strings for me to join the army, because that way it will be easier for us to say goodbye.'

Her face was ashen. A terrible panic was beginning to stir inside her. 'No!' she cried. 'No, you don't mean that!'

He held her away as she made to throw herself against him. 'I do mean it, Claudine. This time apart has shown me how futile our love is. You don't belong to my world, any more than I do to yours. I want you to think about that, and I want you to be honest with yourself. You can't leave your family, and you know it.'

'But we'll think of a way, Armand! We've always said that, that one day we'll find the answer. I couldn't bear to lose you. If you want to go and fight for France, I'll even talk to François myself for you, but if you're going just to be away from me, then I beg you not to do it.'

He looked away, but she saw the tears in his eyes and threw her arms around him. 'I beg you, *chéri!*' she cried. 'I beg you. Don't do this.'

He buried his face in her shoulder, and suddenly he started to sob. 'Dear God, if only I had the guts!' he said savagely. 'If only I had the courage to walk away from you now. I want to fight for my country, but I'm afraid to leave you. Afraid you won't be here when I get back. I love you so much I can hardly think straight. I wanted you to beg me to stay. I needed to know that you love me that much. I'm so afraid of losing you, of having you tell me that it's over. I thought about nothing else while you were away. I waited for your letters, and when they didn't come I thought you'd stopped caring, that maybe you'd found someone else. Someone who is worthy of you, who can give you the life and happiness you deserve. Claudine, hold me, please, hold me. Tell me you love me. I've got to hear it. I know I'm a coward, that I don't deserve your love, but without it I'm nothing.'

'Oh, *mon chéri*,' she cried, lifting his face and holding it between her hands. 'Of course I love you. And you're not a coward. You're wonderful and kind and the biggest idiot I've ever met in my life. How could you have put yourself through such torment? But I'll never go away again, and nor will you. We'll find an answer. *I* will find the answer. Trust me.'

His eyes were still clouded with uncertainty as he looked at her, and she smiled at the way his tears had left furrows in the dust on his cheeks. 'Will you spend the night with me tonight?' he asked.

'Yes,' she whispered.

By the time he left her at the bridge he was more his old self, and was even laughing about his 'pathetic display of tears'. Whereas, in the past, she had always been the one who was reluctant to let go, this time it was Armand who found it hard to part. Claudine wondered if he had noticed the change. But inside the château, on the nursery landing, Magaly was waiting with news which pushed all thoughts of Armand from her mind. She flew down the stairs to the family sitting-room, where she found Louis and Solange talking quietly.

'Magaly told me,' Claudine said. 'But what does it mean?'

Louis took off his spectacles, and her heart almost ground to a halt as she saw the terrible anguish in his eyes. 'It means that in a matter of days France will be at war,' he answered soberly.

'But Communist Russia and Nazi Germany!' she cried. 'It doesn't make sense. How could this have happened?'

'Nobody knows,' Louis said in a voice that cracked with fatigue. 'Maybe the details will come out later, but it will be too late to change anything. A non-aggression pact between Russia and Germany means that Poland and all her people are already lost.' He turned to Solange and gripped her hands between his own. 'I'd like to lie down for a while, *chérie*,' he said. 'I'd like you to come with me.'

'Is Monique in her room?' Claudine asked. 'I'd better go and tell her the news.'

As Claudine walked up the stairs in front of Solange and Louis, she was thinking again of Armand. She had never seen him like that before, so uncertain of himself, nor had she ever seen Louis anything but strong – and the bewildering change in two men she had come to depend upon so much was in its way as horrifying as the imminence of war. But it wasn't until later that night that she began to feel the full impact of the day's news; to face up to the chilling reality of war with Germany, and even the possibility of defeat.

The nation's mood over the next eleven days vacillated between dread and hysteria as Britain and France signed a formal alliance with Poland, then tried to persuade her to negotiate with Germany. Poland refused, and in the early hours of Friday morning, September 1st 1939, German troops crossed the frontier into Poland.

François telephoned at eleven thirty on the morning of September 3rd and asked to speak to his father. Claudine took the call, since Louis was in the chapel with Solange. 'Where are you?' she asked him.

'In Paris.'

'Are you coming home?'

'No. I can't. But I'm glad to talk to you, Claudine, because I want you to start packing, now. I want you and Louis to come to Paris, and from here I'll see you on a flight to the United States. I don't want you to argue, I just want you to get out of France while you still can.'

'No!' she cried. Tears were stinging the backs of her eyes and the ghastly panic she had been trying to stave off over the past eleven days suddenly threatened to overwhelm her.

'Claudine, listen to me,' he said. 'Neville Chamberlain is going to broadcast to the British nation at twelve fifteen on the BBC. It will be a declaration of war on Germany. France will follow within hours. So please, start packing.'

There was a pause as she took in the full impact of his words. Then, as she slowly started to come back to life, her shoulders straightened, her head lifted, and in a voice of inflexible resolve she said, 'No, François.'

'Claudine . . .'

'No, François! I won't discuss it any further. I'm not coming to Paris. I'm staying here where I belong.' There was a fierce determination in her voice that she had never used with him before, and she thought he was smiling as he said, 'All right, I won't force you, though I ought to. But if it is your wish to remain in France, you'll have to understand what it will mean. This is a war we cannot possibly win, Claudine. Now the Russians have signed their pact with Germany, our case is hopeless – unless the United States decides to back us. So far they have not committed themselves, and I don't believe they will until forced. By then France will probably be a defeated nation.'

She could hear him breathing at the end of the line, and

for a moment, more than anything else in the world, she wanted him to come home.

'I will, as soon as I can,' he answered her. 'But I don't want you looking to me for your strength. You have your own strength, Claudine, and if you stay at the château you're going to need it. Our son is safe as long as Corinne is there, but you are a different matter. I'll come home as often as I can, but I have no idea yet what will be required of me in the months ahead. If Armand stays he will give you the support you need, for as long as he is able.'

There was a choking dryness in her throat as she said, 'What do you mean, as long as he is able?'

'I'm saying that I am doing all I can to see he stays at Lorvoire, at least for the time being. But the day is not far off when France will need all her men – no matter what their age – to defend herself. Armand will have to go, he'll want to go. It may seem petty, just at this moment, to remind you of the man who is watching you, watching all of us, but when I tell you that he's working for the Abwehr – German Intelligence – you will understand why you're in danger if you stay in France. Will you reconsider your decision now?'

'The Abwehr?' she breathed. 'He's working for the Abwehr? My God, François, what have you been doing? Why have you put us in this danger?'

'Will you reconsider your decision?' he repeated firmly.

'No! No, damn it, I won't! And I want you to come home. I want you to explain this to me, and make me understand. Do you hear me?'

'I hear you,' he said, 'but I won't be coming. You have to stand on your own feet and take responsibility for your decision. I've tried to help you, and believe me, if I was there I'd force you to leave. Listen to your Prime Minister at twelve fifteen, maybe he will change your mind.'

'François! Don't go!'

'I'm still here,' he answered.

- 342 -

She didn't know what she wanted to say, but just knowing he was at the end of the telephone gave her sense of security that would start to crumble the moment he rang off. She needed to hear his voice again. 'Where can I contact you?' she said.

'You can't. I shall contact you.'

'Why?' she shouted. 'All I need is a telephone number!'

'Listen to Chamberlain,' he said, and the line went dead.

She turned as the door opened and Louis and Solange came into the library. 'What is it, *chérie?*' Louis asked, alarmed by her stricken face. 'Who was that on the telephone?'

'François,' she answered.

Louis and Solange exchanged glances. 'Did he say where he was?' he asked.

'In Paris,' Claudine said – and Louis seemed almost to crumple with relief.

'Louis,' Claudine said, putting a hand to her head as if trying to hold in her sanity. 'Can you tell me what's going on? What is François doing? Who is he with?'

'*Chérie*, please don't ask questions you would rather not know the answers to,' Louis said.

'Don't patronize me! I have a right to know. He's my husband, for God's sake!'

'In name only, Claudine.'

She looked from Louis to Solange, then back to Louis. For a moment it was as if they were strangers instead of the people she had come to love as her own parents. She took a step back, as if to run away, then checking herself, she raised her chin and said, 'I didn't deserve that, Louis. Your son has never shown me a moment's affection in the entire two years we have been married. I tried to love him at the beginning, I tried, but he pushed me away, he didn't want me. He still doesn't want me. So if there are accusations to be made, they should be made at him. And if I'm facing danger because of something he has done, and you know what it is, then I think you owe it to me to tell me.'

Louis looked at her for a long moment. 'I think we could all use a little brandy, *chérie*,' he said to Solange, and while Solange went to fetch the cognac, he beckoned Claudine to the chair beside him. 'Sit here,' he said. Then he turned to face her and removed his glasses.

'If I knew what François had done, Claudine,' he said earnestly, 'I would tell you. You have my word on that. But as it is, I would only be guessing. And I beg your forgiveness for what I said earlier. You are right, you didn't deserve that. There are difficult times ahead, and François will be involved in a way I neither understand nor approve of . . .' He paused, and turned his pale grey eyes to the hearth.

'Louis,' Claudine ventured, 'François mentioned something about the Abwehr. Is that . . . ? Does that mean . . . ?'

Louis shook his head. 'If you're going to ask me if he is working for them, then the answer is that I don't know, Claudine. I hope to God he isn't. He's my son, and I love him, but if I ever learned that he'd become a traitor to his country . . .'

Claudine looked at him, aghast. She hadn't been going to ask that at all, it had never even crossed her mind that François might be *working* for the Abwehr. 'Did you know we're being watched?' she said. 'All of us.'

Louis nodded.

'François says the man is affiliated to the Abwehr. So surely that must mean he is as much their enemy as we are?'

'If only it were as simple as that, *chérie*,' Louis sighed. 'There was a time when François always took me into his confidence. Now he tells me only what he wants me to know, which over these past few months has become less and less.'

'Why were you so relieved just now, when I told you he was in Paris?' she asked, after a pause.

'Because I was afraid he had gone to Berlin.'

Solange came back into the room then, with a decanter of brandy and four glasses. 'Monique is about to join us,' she told them.

'Good.' Then turning back to Claudine, Louis said, 'There's always the hope that he's keeping us in the dark for our own protection. That there's a method in the madness of what he's doing which one day we will understand.' He looked away, and the tired lines around his eyes visibly deepened. 'But you have my solemn promise, Claudine, that as soon as I find out exactly what he's doing, and for whom he's working, I will tell you. As you said before, you have a right to know.'

Solange handed them both a brandy, then sweeping the morning's papers from the sofa, she sat down herself. Claudine watched as with a trembling hand she lifted her glass to her lips. Of all of them it was Solange who had taken the greatest strain these past few weeks. Monique's broken heart was as big a sorrow to her mother as it was to Monique, and with her constant, almost irrational, terror for Lucien, her fears for François and her anxiety over Louis' obviously diminishing health, Claudine wondered how much longer her mother-in-law would be able to hold on. She knew then, as she looked into that beloved, startlingly jovial face, that no matter what Neville Chamberlain had to say, and whether François' morbid predictions came true or not, she had been right to tell him she wouldn't leave Lorvoire – and she would stay as long as Solange needed her.

She went to sit beside her on the sofa. 'François says that Britain is about to declare war,' she said in a trembling voice to no one in particular. 'Apparently Mr Chamberlain is making a broadcast at twelve fifteen.'

Louis nodded. 'And France?'

'Later today, François says. He didn't say what time.'

Solange looked at her watch. 'It's almost one fifteen,'

she said. 'I wonder if François gave you British or French time?'

'Well, there's only one way to find out,' Louis said, pulling himself from his chair and walking across to the wireless. As they listened to the crackling and whining of his search for the BBC's World Service, Monique came in and took the remaining glass of brandy from the tray.

They had no more than two minutes to wait before Neville Chamberlain's sombre voice came over the crackling air-waves. 'I am speaking to you from the Cabinet Room at Ten Downing Street,' he began. 'This morning the British Ambassador in Berlin handed the German Government a final note, stating that, unless the British Government heard from them by eleven o'clock that they were prepared at once to withdraw their troops from Poland, a state of war would exist between us. I have to tell you now that no such undertaking has been received, and that consequently this country is at war with Germany . . .'

There was more, but none of them heard it. Louis looked at Solange, and with tears running down his face, said, 'In nineteen eighteen I looked around for the men I'd known, but they were all gone. The battlefields were strewn with their brave young bodies. One and half *million* of them gave their lives in that war, Solange. Their hearts numbed by the cold, their skin crawling with filth, their nostrils filled with the stench of blood and decaying flesh. I never thought we would come to this again, Solange, I never thought . . .'

Solange wiped the tears from his eyes, and as the British National Anthem started to play on the wireless, Claudine let herself quietly out of the room and went upstairs to the nursery. Louis was playing with his toy car, but when he saw her come into the room he ran into her arms.

'Corinne,' Claudine said, settling Louis on her hip.

'*Madame?*'

'I want you to teach me the skill of unarmed combat.'

François' black eyes moved meditatively about the room. The creamy-white walls were unadorned, apart from a crucifix between the windows, and the bare tiled floor was scrupulously clean. The smell of disinfectant lingered in the air churning his empty stomach, making him feel bilious. Next to the brown leather armchair in which he sat was a small iron-framed bed, and through the windowed walls facing him he could see white-overalled doctors and nurses in stiff uniforms going about their business.

Earlier, the air-raid sirens had sounded, and he had heard the commotion in the street outside as Parisians rushed panic-stricken to the shelters. When it was over several women had been brought to the hospital, stifled and half-fainting in their gas-masks. It had been another false alarm.

He closed his eyes as the Herculean burden of his tiredness weighted his limbs. But still sleep eluded him, as it had done for days. He was now a machine, operating ceaselessly, monotonously, without feeling . . . All the same, he grinned when he recalled his conversation with Claudine that morning. Her passionate refusal to leave France had not surprised him, but he would telephone again later for her final decision. If she was determined to stay he wouldn't argue, he had no time for it now . . . Just as he had no time for the self-recrimination that was razoring his mind of sleep. It was too late now to regret the path he had chosen, to regret his marriage, to regret, most bitterly of all, what had happened to Élise.

He turned to look at her, but she was still sleeping, and resting his head against the winged back of the chair, he stared sightlessly up at a corner of the room. A few days ago the doctor had told him that she was at last out of danger, but the road to recovery was going to be a long one, he had warned, and she might never reach the end of it. Her breasts and her buttocks would always bear the scars of the knife, but that was nothing to the way her insides had been ripped. It was doubtful if she would ever be able to make love again, and the memory of the last words he, François, had spoken to her on the night they entertained Helber would remain forever branded on his mind.

'Do you want to make love, Élise?' he had asked her.

'Yes, oh yes,' she had moaned, turning in his arms.

'Then as a professional whore you should have no trouble in finding someone to satisfy you,' he had said, and letting her go, he had turned and walked out of the room.

He would never have said that if he had not known Helber was listening at the door, and now that he knew the extent of Élise's injuries he had vowed that one day he would sever the man's genitals from his body, so that he too should be denied the pleasures of love.

But that would never give Élise back what she had lost. He sighed, and again closed his eyes as the choking monster of guilt heaved in his chest. He had tried everything he could to stop her falling in love with him; at times he had disgusted even himself with his brutality. But despite all his efforts he had failed. To her he had been the ultimate challenge, and she had believed herself strong enough, clever enough, brave enough to take him on, together with the world of intrigue in which he moved. She had never stood a chance. Her sophistication lay in her body, not in her mind; in her beauty and her matchless bedroom skills. Yet for a while she had held her own, had surprised even him with her determination and her ruthlessness.

But he should have known that something like this would happen in the end – that von Liebermann would find her Achilles heel. She had wanted to become the Comtesse de Rassey de Lorvoire, and no doubt that was what von Liebermann had promised her. If only she had listened to him, believed him, when he told her he would never marry her! But the blame was his, he should have acted the moment he realized von Liebermann had got to her. Instead he had merely kept her ignorant of what he was doing, thereby letting the Abwehr know that he no longer trusted her.

And it was that, as much as anything else, that had sealed her fate. Knowing that Élise was no longer in his confidence, could supply no more useful information on him, von Liebermann had unleashed on her the man Helber had told him about, as a warning of what would happen to those he loved if he failed to co-operate . . .

Now, hearing Élise stir, he braced himself for the thin, frail sound of her voice. Every time he heard it, it was as though he was reliving the violent, vindictive slashing of the knife that had ruined her body.

'François, are you there?'

'Yes, I'm here,' he answered, sitting forward and taking her hand. It was limp and cold, and his heart contracted as he looked down at her terrible caved-in cheek. 'How are you feeling?' he asked softly.

'Quite good.' She tried to smile, and the gruesome twist of her face made him wince. It was only in the last two days that she had started to speak coherently, and though he longed to ask her about her attacker, he couldn't bring himself to make her relive even a moment of what had happened. Of course he knew who had done it, but he needed the man's name.

He looked at her, but as she gazed up at him from the valley of swellings around her eyes, he said simply, 'Would you like me to read to you?'

'Can it be Perrault?'

He smiled. It had been Erich von Pappen's idea that he should read her fairy tales, and now she wanted nothing else. He kissed her hand and then picked up the book, but as he opened it at the first page she said, 'You'll have to go away soon, won't you?'

'For a while,' he answered.

'Will you come back?'

'Yes.'

She lowered her eyes as a tear rolled over her bruises and fell onto the pillow. 'I know you have to go, but I don't want you to. I'm afraid without you.'

'Erich will be here, *chérie*,' he said, putting down the book and taking her hands again. 'Nothing will happen to you. And when you're well enough to leave, I've arranged for someone to watch over you.'

Again she smiled, and he lifted his hand to stroke the hair from her face. Then suddenly her eyes were wide and terrified; her lips parted and she started to mumble.

It was often like that, and the doctor had warned him that it might never change. The trauma she had suffered had tragically affected her brain as badly as her body.

He waited, unable to understand her ramblings but knowing that in a few minutes she would be with him again. Yet when her eyes focussed at last, they were still glazed with terror.

'Halunke?' she gasped. 'Are you Halunke?' And then she screamed.

The piercing cry whipped round the room, and he grabbed her as she tried to sit up. 'Élise!' he cried. 'Élise! Stop!'

The door flew open and a doctor ran in, followed by three nurses. They held her to the bed while a needle was pushed into her arm, and within seconds she was sinking into oblivion. The doctor turned to François, an accusatory frown on his face, but he said nothing and left the room.

François stood to one side as the nurses checked Élise's wounds to see that none of them had opened. That strange word Élise had uttered ... *Halunke*. It was the German word for rat, yet she had used it as a name. 'Are you Halunke?' she had said.

He glanced at his watch, and as he did so Erich von Pappen walked into the room, five minutes later than expected. François motioned for the nurses to leave, then turned to his courier.

Von Pappen was an odd-looking man, whose eyes and mouth formed three circles above and below a thin, upturned nose. He had no hair, no earlobes and no neck, and his short, scrawny body was racked with alarming frequency by a nervous twitch.

'Well?' François said.

'The same,' von Pappen answered. 'Liebermann wants you in Berlin.'

François nodded, and rubbed his fingers over the black shadow on his chin.

'I don't think you can ignore this summons any longer,' von Pappen told him. 'He wanted you there three weeks ago, his patience is wearing thin.'

'Have you contacted Captain Paillole?'

'Yes. He'll see you at nine o'clock tonight at the avenue de Tourville.'

François' eyes were hard. '*Les Services de Renseignements*' headquarters? That must mean he intends to tape the meeting.' He gave a mirthless laugh. 'So he no longer trusts me! Very wise of him.' Then, looking up, 'Contact von Liebermann as soon as you can after midnight. Tell him I'm on my way.'

'It may take you some time to get there,' von Pappen warned. 'The roads out of Paris are blocked for miles. Everyone's fleeing the city, there's pandemonium out there.'

Dismissing this with a wave of his hand, François said, 'Have you visited the Jews?'

'All except two, and I'm told they're in the United States. I doubt if they'll come back.'

'I see. And the others?'

'I have their valuables already. They'll be transported to Lorvoire sometime over the next few weeks.'

François smiled. 'And the Jews themselves?'

'Everything is as you instructed.'

François turned back to Élise. As von Pappen walked round to the other side of the bed and gazed down at her too, he said, 'Claude Villiers?'

'I'm afraid not,' von Pappen answered.

Though he hadn't expected to find his nemesis so easily, François' spirits sank. They were still no closer to discovering the man's identity. 'Halunke,' he said. 'Does that mean anything to you?'

Von Pappen shrugged. 'It means rat.'

'His code name,' François said, digging a hand into his pocket and pulling out the note he had received the morning after Élise's mutilation. It contained only one word – ÉLISE. 'I think he meant to kill her,' he said.

'Maybe it would have been better if he had,' von Pappen answered solemnly.

François scowled at the little man, then pushed the note back into his pocket. 'Have we any idea where he is now?'

'None.'

François looked back once more at Élise, then turned abruptly away. 'Stay with her, Erich. When she comes round, read to her from Perrault, and if she asks for me, tell her I'll be back as soon as I can. If need be, swear on your mother's grave that I have not abandoned her.'

Von Pappen's bony limbs twitched in answer.

François drove to the house in the Bois de Boulogne, where he took a long bath, shaved, changed, and ordered an early dinner. In the study he placed a person-to-person call to Lorvoire. Knowing it would take some time to come through, he decided that the long-overdue explanation to his father must be dealt with now. As it turned out, it covered only one page, but more than an hour passed before he was ready to sign his name to the most soul-destroying letter he would ever write. At that very instant, the telephone rang.

When he heard Claudine at the other end, he felt the weariness pull at his bones – God, how he longed to hold her! But the sudden and unwelcome weakness angered him, and his voice was like steel as he said, 'Have you changed your mind?'

'No,' she answered stiffly, 'I'm staying at Lorvoire.'

'Then you're a fool.'

There was a pause before she said, 'A fool maybe, but better that than a traitor.'

His eyes narrowed as her accusation bit into him. He would have liked to ask her how she had found out, but as it made little difference, he simply replaced the receiver.

As he walked from the room, his face turned even uglier as he watched a valet deposit his bags at the foot of the stairs, ready for his departure. With the advent of war, the tightrope he walked had been drawn impossibly tight, and already the fraying strands were beginning to snap. And he was in no doubt that the safety net which had always been there to catch him would, that very night, be removed by Captain Paul Paillole.

He toyed then with the idea of putting a call through to London. But on a night like this the connection would take hours, if he got one at all. And even if he did, the chances of finding Beavis at home were so slim as to be virtually non-existent.

– 20 –

The morning sun was bright, the air pungent with the smell of autumn. On the hillsides the Lorvoire vines were weighted with clusters of luscious purple grapes, now almost ready for harvest, and the trees were tinged with gold as they prepared for their seasonal change.

Claudine, Solange and Liliane were walking down over the bank outside Liliane's house to the cobbled street. Claudine, leading her horse, was thankful for the small veil on her riding hat, which partially concealed the mirth she could not suppress. Solange had come to the village in her nurse's uniform, which she had been wearing for the past three weeks, ever since war had been declared. Her tufts of grey hair sprouted from under her cap and her busy fingers were constantly lifting the watch pinned to her apron, but the chief source of Claudine's mirth was the stethoscope draped importantly around Solange's neck. It was the first time Claudine had seen it, and she had no idea where Solange had got it, but it wouldn't suprise her in the least to discover that Doctor Lebrun had inexplicably lost one . . . Heaven help them all, she thought, if Solange managed to get her hands on a syringe!

'It's a pity I'm too old to go off to the front,' Solange was saying. 'I did in the last war, you know. So did you, Liliane. Don't tell me you'd forgotten!'

Liliane had confessed to no such thing. Her watery eyes met Claudine's as she said, without a trace of irony, 'It must be my age, Solange. I'm forgetting everything these days.'

'Poor Liliane,' Solange soothed – and Liliane's eyes widened in horror as Solange started fingering her stethoscope with obvious intent.

Fortunately, Liliane was saved from an impromptu

medical examination by a sudden stampede of small feet. The village children had spotted Claudine and her horse, and come running over to beg a ride.

'Splendid idea!' Solange cried, instantly forgetting Liliane, and ignoring Marcel who was standing to attention at the open door of the Bentley. 'I'll take them. Sit them on, Claudine. Two at a time, and I'll lead them round the square.'

With a grin, Claudine watched Liliane hurry back up the bank to the safety of her kitchen, then turned to lift Thomas Crouy's grandchildren into the saddle. As Solange took the reins and led the horse steadily into the square, Claudine wandered over to the well to wait with the other children, enjoying their chatter as they told her how their older brothers and fathers had gone off to fight the Germans, and asked if Captain Lucien was going to be a hero.

'I hope so,' she told them, glad that Solange was out of earshot. No one had mentioned Lucien since the outbreak of war, but they all knew he was the reason why Solange was slipping from the rails again. He was stationed at Metz with Colonel de Gaulle's tank brigade, and Metz was far too close to Germany for Solange's peace of mind.

As Claudine sat perched on the edge of the wall, the children started to play at soldiers, running around the well, shouting and screaming as they fired imaginary guns, then pretended to fall down dead. Robert Reinberg looked on blankly, every now and again pointing his fingers like a gun and waiting for someone to react. The other children ignored him, and Claudine's heart went out to him as he threw himself awkwardly to the ground beside his sister, who put a protective arm round him to shield him from the enemy.

'Are you going to be a hero too?' she said, lifting him onto her lap and ruffling his wispy fair hair.

'He can't be a hero!' one of the other boys shouted. 'He's too stupid.'

Claudine's face tightened, but before she could speak Janette Reinberg had thrown herself at the boy, beating him with her fists. 'He's not stupid!' she cried. 'He's not! He's not!'

'He is! Everyone knows he is! Even the grown-ups say so.'

Claudine reached out for the boy and pulled him in front of her. 'Which grown-ups?' she demanded.

The little boy's face turned crimson and he hung his head.

'Which grown-ups?' Claudine repeated with delibera-tion.

'Madame Jallais,' another boy answered. 'She said that Robert was silly in the head. She said it was because Robert was a Jew. She said that Jesus was getting his own back.'

'Did she indeed,' Claudine said, through gritted teeth. She looked across at the Jallais cottage. The shutters were closed – she had passed Florence earlier, on her way to Chinon with her husband. It was high time, she decided, that that bitter, twisted old harridan was taken to task. She would return to the village immediately after lunch and deal with her then. She would even, if it proved necessary, ask Armand to dismiss Monsieur Jallais from the vineyards.

Gustave appeared, strolling over from the café. 'And how are you, Gustave?' she said, smiling up at his jolly round face.

'Getting poorer by the minute, *madame*,' he complained. 'All the men have gone except us old ones. There's no one to buy my drinks.'

Taking the hint, Claudine sent the children off to get some lemonade and followed Gustave to a table outside the café. Across the square she could see Solange talking animatedly over her shoulder to the children on the horse.

'Queer kind of war, this, don't you think, *madame*?' Gustave said, putting a large glass of wine in front of her. 'Three weeks and almost nothing has happened.'

Claudine gave him a droll look as she picked up the unordered wine and took a sip. 'I had a letter from my aunt this morning,' she told him. 'She's still in Paris. She says all the cinemas and theatres have reopened, that people are even walking about the streets without gas-masks.'

'Mmm,' Gustave grunted. 'Maybe Hitler has lost his nerve. What does the Comte think?'

'I'm not sure what he thinks,' Claudine answered. 'He hasn't been well these past few weeks.'

'So I hear,' Gustave said mournfully. 'How is he now?'

'A little better, I'm glad to say.' Then in a whisper she added, 'Well enough to ask for cigars.'

Gustave's face brightened at the prospect of making a sale, and as Solange approached with the horse and its two mounts, he cried, 'A glass of wine for you, *Madame la Comtesse?*'

'Certainly not, Gustave!' she cried. 'I'm on duty.'

'*Madame la Comtesse* is going to play war,' Thomas' grandson informed everyone as Claudine lifted him down from the horse. 'She said that her car is the ambulance and the café is our hospital.'

'There you are, Gustave,' Claudine said, 'you have plenty of customers now. So,' she turned back to Solange and the children, 'do I take it you've finished with my horse? I'd better be getting home to see my own little boy, then, or he'll think I've forgotten him.'

No one waved as she trotted off down the street, they were all too busy fighting for a place in the ambulance. She could hardly wait to tell Louis what his wife was up to; already she could hear him chuckling as she described how Solange was lining up the injured and bullying them with her stethoscope . . . Louis would be as glad of the diversion as she was. If only for a little while, it would keep Solange from thinking about François.

Since he had telephoned her that night, when she had all

but accused him of being a traitor, Claudine had heard nothing from him. Nor had Louis, though he had somehow managed to discover that François was no longer in Paris and suspected he was somewhere in Germany.

That her husband was a traitor was something Claudine could not allow herself to think about – it dragged emotions from too deep within her. Armand was certain it wasn't true, that somewhere there was an innocent explanation for François' behaviour. But he hadn't even bothered to refute her accusation. He hadn't cared enough even to let his father know where he was or what he was doing. She knew it was breaking Louis' heart. And, if Louis really did disown his eldest son, as he had threatened to do if François' treachery was proved, Solange's heart would be broken too.

Trying to dismiss her misgivings Claudine rode round the corner to the gates of the château. Suddenly her horse reared as it came face to face with a lorry. She managed to keep her seat, and leaned forward, soothing her mount, while the lorry, the first of a convoy of four, turned into the drive.

Claudine followed them up to the château, and once she had dismounted at the stables, walked back to the front of the house just as Louis was coming down the steps.

'What on earth are all those lorries doing here?' she asked.

Taking her by the elbow Louis led her round to the small courtyard in front of the wine caves where the lorries were now parked. 'I received a message from François' courier, Erich von Pappen, this morning,' he told her. 'François wants the contents of these lorries stored.'

'But what's in them?'

'I don't know.'

One of the drivers approached and asked for the Comte de Lorvoire. 'That's me,' Louis informed him. Then turning to Jean-Paul, who had followed at a distance, he said, 'Show the men where to take the . . . ?' But the driver simply started unloading. Jean-Paul unlocked the arched door at the side of the château which led down to the cellars, and Louis and Claudine stood at the top of the steps hoping to have their curiosity satisfied. But all that came out of the lorries were wooden crates, dozens of them, tall and flat, small and square, crate after crate.

'Can't you ask what's in them?' Claudine whispered, as they stepped back to let one of them pass.

Louis shrugged, but when two men struggled by with the next one, he did.

'*Je ne sais pas, monsieur,*' the man answered, giving Louis an incredulous look as if to say, 'They're yours, aren't they?' Louis shrugged again, then beckoning Claudine after him, he started down the steps into the wine cellar.

The endless racks were illuminated by bare bulbs, thick with dust, hanging from the ceiling. Through the gloom Claudine saw Jean-Paul and one of the lorry drivers gingerly shifting a rack from the back wall.

'The inner cellar is behind,' Louis explained. 'It's where François wanted the – er, boxes, to be stored.'

They remained in the cellar until the last crate had been carried through, their breath forming clouds in the chill air. 'Thank you, Jean-Paul,' Louis said, as the butler edged the wine-rack back into place. 'Perhaps you would like to offer the men some refreshment?'

The drivers' grimy faces visibly brightened, and brushing the cobwebs from their clothes, they followed Jean-Paul back up the stairs.

'What are we going to do now?' Claudine asked as the door closed behind them.

'We're going in there to find out what's in those boxes, of course.'

The musty smell of the inner cellar was stifling, and the wall lamp cast a weak, dull light over the imbroglio of wooden crates. Louis handed Claudine a handkerchief to cover her mouth with, and pointed to the box nearest them. 'Did you see this, written on the side? There are letters like this on every one.'

'Yes, I noticed,' came her muffled voice. 'I wonder what it means?'

'No idea. Probably some kind of code. We don't stand much chance of deciphering it, though, so we'll just have to break the boxes open.'

'But how?' Claudine asked, tilting one of the smaller boxes. 'They're sealed very securely.'

For a moment Louis seemed defeated, then peering at her through the darkness he said, 'Run upstairs to the caves and see if Armand is there. If he is, get him to bring some tools down here and he can give us a hand.'

Claudine was back within five minutes, carrying Armand's tool bag. 'Armand has gone into Chinon,' she told Louis. 'I found this under the workbench.'

'Try this one here,' Louis said, tipping up one of the boxes. 'One of the nails isn't quite in, it should be easy to pull.'

It turned out to be more difficult than they expected, but eventually they managed to prise the lid off, and reaching into the box Louis pulled out a large cloth bag.

'*Mon Dieu!*' he spluttered as he peered inside.

'What is it?' Claudine whispered. Despite the dim light she could see that his face had turned quite pale. 'Here.' He passed the bag over. 'Take a look.'

Claudine could hardly believe her eyes. She pulled out glittering diamond tiaras, ruby necklaces, sapphire rings, emerald brooches and gold earrings. She looked at Louis. 'Where can he have got them?' she whispered.

Louis shook his head.

'But not all these boxes can be filled with jewellery,' she said, looking at the bigger ones. 'What do you suppose is in them?'

'There's only one way to find out.'

It was the middle of the afternoon by the time they slid the wine-rack back into place and went upstairs.

'What are we going to do?' Claudine asked, as Louis closed the drawing-room door behind them and went to pour himself a brandy.

'What can we do? Those paintings are even more valuable than the jewellery, you know.'

'But where have they all come from?'

'I don't know. I don't even know if they're his. We'll just have to wait until he comes to Lorvoire and ask him to explain.'

'Did this von Pappen man say where he is now?'

'No. But he'll know. Erich von Pappen always knows where François is.'

'Can't we get on to him again?'

'Easier said than done, *chérie*.'

There was a queasy feeling in the pit of her stomach, and as Louis took a sip of his brandy Claudine went to pour one for herself. 'Are you going to tell anyone about this?' she said.

'No. And nor should you. I can't for the life of me think what it might be, but there could be a perfectly reasonable explanation.'

His voice held no conviction, and knowing what he was thinking, Claudine felt herself overtaken by an engulfing dread. What else was there to think, after all? Rumours of Nazi looting had long been rife in the salons of Paris.

Not for the first time, Claudine felt the incongruity of standing at the dilapidated stove of a rundown farmhouse, heating a midday meal for a man who was not her husband. It wasn't simply that the novelty had worn off – it was that the impropriety of it had recently started to bother her. Why that should be, she didn't know. She preferred not to ask herself the question, because she had an uncanny feeling she wouldn't like the answer. So, attempting to put her unease aside, she continued to stir the cassoulet as Armand strolled listlessly across the room and went to sit at the foot of the broken staircase.

'I can't fire Henri Jallais, Claudine,' he said, wiping crumbs from his mouth with the back of his hand. 'I've lost half the workers as it is. Besides, he wasn't the one who said it, it was his wife. And you've certainly made yourself an enemy there. What exactly did you say to the woman?'

'It hardly matters what *I* said,' she retorted. 'It's what Florence Jallais said that matters.'

'But no one takes any notice of her.'

'They do!' she flared. 'The children are repeating it, and Gertrude Reinberg has enough to contend with without Florence Jallais' spiteful little mind making things worse.'

'But there was no reason for you to get involved,' he said wearily.

'There was every reason!' she shouted. 'I happen to care about that little boy. I thought you did too.'

He sighed. 'All right. All right. I'll speak to the man if that's what you want.'

Swallowing hard on her anger, Claudine turned back to the stove. She knew that if Armand didn't do something soon to pull himself out of his apathy, she would end up saying something they would both regret. His depression since the declaration of war was getting on her nerves. Every time she saw him it was as though another layer of his self-esteem had been peeled away – and she wasn't sure that she particularly liked the man being revealed underneath. It was so at odds with the man she had known before, the man she loved; she simply didn't know how to react to him any more.

She carried a bowl of cassoulet over to the table, and seeing his bowed head her impatience flared again; but as he looked up at her, his bronzed face creased with hopelessness, her irritation gave way to pity. She knew he was suffering badly – but if only he would tell her why! She was certain there was more to his despondency than the fact that he was unable to fight, but how could she help him when he refused to talk about it?

'You haven't told me why you didn't come yesterday,' he said, as he pulled out a chair and sat down at the table.

'As a matter of fact, I did,' she answered, 'but you obviously weren't listening. I was helping Louis with some things and time just ran away with us.'

'What things?'

'We were putting some boxes into store for François.' She didn't know what she was going to say if he asked what was in the boxes, but he seemed to lose interest then, and picked up his spoon to begin eating.

'Did you make this?' he said, after the first mouthful.

'No. Your mother did.'

'I thought so,' he said, and put down his spoon.

'What's the matter with it? Why aren't you eating?'

'Have you given up cooking for me yourself?'

'No, but there isn't always time.'

'Yet you can make time to help Louis or interfere in the affairs of the village.'

'Don't be childish, Armand!' she snapped, and turned back to the stove to ladle herself a helping of stew.

'Is there any more news regarding François' whereabouts?' he asked as she sat down.

'No.'

'I was wondering,' he said, 'if he might do us the favour of getting himself killed in this war.'

Her spoon clanged against the dish as she slammed it on the table. 'I've had about all I can take of this!' she cried.

'Well, that's the answer for us, isn't it?' he said. 'That François should die?'

'Stop it!' she shouted. 'Just stop this now or I'm leaving.'

He was silent then, and as he poured himself some wine she picked up her bowl and carried it to the stove.

'What are you doing?'

'I've lost my appetite,' she answered, pouring the cassoulet back into the pot.

'I'm sorry.'

She turned to face him, ready to forgive – but had to grit her teeth as she saw his head was again buried in his hands.

'I'm sorry,' he said again. 'I didn't mean it. I shouldn't have said it. God knows, this business is difficult enough for you without me making it worse.' He looked up, and his handsome face was drawn with guilt. 'You care about what happens to him, though, don't you?'

She was suddenly gripped by an overpowering need to escape. But it wasn't Armand she wanted to run from, she realized, it was herself.

'So do I,' Armand sighed, as if she had spoken. 'There have been times when I've come very close to hating him – for what he did to Hortense, for what he's done and is still doing to you – but I can't forget the man he used to be, the way he was before.'

A bell of recognition clanged in her head, and she remembered that Lucien had once said something very similar about François. 'Before what?' she prompted, going to sit back at the table.

He shook his head. 'I don't know. All I know is that something happened to change him. About five years ago. But I suppose there was always something different about him, even before that, something that seemed to set him apart from everyone else. People were frightened of him even then. Except Lucien, of course. And me. They used to say he was the devil.' He laughed, without humour.

'We certainly made some capital out of that,' he went on. 'We were very close, the three of us then. There was nothing we didn't know about each other; even when Lucien joined the army and I married Jacqueline, the bond between us remained. Then, as I say, about five years ago François suddenly changed. He stopped confiding in us, he became secretive, withdrawn even, and that mean look of his became a permanent expression. He started to spend more and more time in Paris; he didn't even come to Lorvoire when Lucien was at home, which I know hurt Lucien a great deal. At first we thought it was his mistress keeping him away, but there was never a woman born who could make François do something he didn't want . . .'

Armand looked at her, then looked away again. 'We've drifted a long way apart, the three of us, but there's nothing we wouldn't do for each other, even now. At least, that's the way I feel, and I'm sure Lucien does too. That seems an odd thing to say, doesn't it, when I'm committing adultery with François' wife, but I mean it. And besides, there's been precious little of that of late, hasn't there?'

She looked back at him, her lovely blue eyes hard and uncompromising. She wasn't going to take the blame for that. He was the one who had lost his appetite for love-making, and even now, irritated with him as she was, if he were to take her in his arms with something of his old charm, she knew she would respond.

'Warsaw has surrendered,' he sighed. 'The Soviets and the Germans are carving the country up between them. It's only a matter of time now before they turn to the West. And what am I doing to stop them?' His face was suddenly contorted with self-disgust. 'Of the three of us, Lucien is the only one who'll be able to hold his head up when this war is over.'

'I thought you didn't believe François was a traitor,' she said.

'I didn't. But Louis told me what was in those boxes.' There was no recrimination in his voice, but it was there in his eyes when he looked at her.

'Louis swore me to secrecy,' she said.

'And that's the reason you didn't tell me?'

'Of course. Why else would I hide it from you?'

'Think about it, Claudine, and I'm sure you'll come up with the answer.'

She shook her head. 'I don't know what you're talking about, Armand, but I'm glad Louis told you. I don't want there to be any secrets between us.'

'Then be honest with me now, Claudine.'

She frowned. 'I am being honest with you,' she declared, but she was baffled by the way she was suddenly unable to meet his eyes.

'Louis knows, Claudine. I know, and I wouldn't be surprised if François knows too.'

'Knows what? What do you know? What are you talking about, Armand?'

He smiled, but there was a sadness in him that unnerved her. 'Armand, you're talking in riddles,' she snapped. 'What are you trying to tell me?'

'It's not for me to tell you, Claudine. It's for you to tell me.'

Suddenly she didn't want this conversation to go any further, and snatching his bowl from the table, she said, 'I haven't the first idea what you're talking about, and I don't think you have either.'

'All right!' he roared, and she jumped as he slammed his fist on the table. 'We'll change the subject. We'll run away from the truth. We'll pretend none of this is happening. If that's what you want, then that's what we'll do.'

There was the sound of someone clearing his throat. Claudine spun round, and to her amazement saw Louis standing at the door.

'I'm sorry if I'm interrupting,' he said. 'I knew I'd find you both here at this time, and as I didn't want anyone to overhear our conversation . . .' He looked from Claudine to Armand and back again. 'May I come in?'

'Of course.' Claudine cast a quick glance at Armand. 'Nothing's happened, has it?' she said, a slight catch in her voice. 'Everything . . . ? Everyone . . . ?'

Louis held up his hand. 'Everyone is fine,' he said.

Armand offered Louis his chair and passed him a glass of wine. 'I think I have some of Gustave's cigars somewhere.'

'No, thank you,' Louis said, cupping a hand round his glass but making no attempt to drink.

For a few moments no one said anything. Then Louis said to Claudine, 'I think you'd better sit down too, *chérie*.'

Claudine felt a jolt of alarm, but she said nothing and pulled up a chair.

'I made you a promise,' Louis began, gazing solemnly down at his wine, 'that as soon as I learned anything concerning François, I would tell you. I have just this morning received a letter from him.'

Armand started to rise. 'Perhaps it would be better if I left,' he said.

'No,' Louis answered. 'François mentions you in the letter, so I think you should read it too.' He reached into the pocket of his jacket, pulled out a folded envelope and passed it to Claudine.

Her hands were unsteady as she opened it, and fear was turning her blood to ice. She cast another look at Louis, then started to read,

Mon cher Papa,

I can offer no apology for what I am about to do, for I believe it to be right. The only regret I have is for the pain I know it will cause you. I am leaving France tonight, and have no idea if, or when, I shall return. I imagine it will come as no surprise to you to learn that I have allied myself to the Nazi cause. As you know, I have on many occasions attempted to persuade key figures in the French High

Command to adopt Hitler's policies, since I believe them to be the only way forward for our country. That I have not been successful in this is a source of deep regret to me, and will continue to be until France falls to the Germans, as she eventually must.

You will, I am sure, take the action you must now feel to be appropriate. I ask only that in disinheriting me you arrange for Claudine to obtain her freedom. Together we have given you an heir; she has done what was required of her and should now be free to go to the man she loves. Armand, I know, loves her and Louis, and will undoubtedly prove a better husband and father than I could ever be.

It grieves me that I am not the son you wanted, Papa, but I must be true to myself. François.

As the letter fell from her fingers, Claudine turned to look at Louis, and saw her own horror and despair mirrored in his eyes. They had had their suspicions, both of them, but she realized now that neither of them had allowed themselves to believe they might really be true. And if they had been able to they would have carried on like that, nurturing the doubt like a withering flower. But now they had read the confession in François' own hand and were forced to face the facts. And François himself had told them what they must do. His father was to disown him, and she was to gain her freedom. While he, her husband, the father of her son, the man . . .

As she leapt up from her chair Louis caught her, hugged her to him, and whispered to her to remain calm. But the panic in her would not be stilled. This couldn't be happening! It couldn't be true! François' name screamed across the front of her mind: he was gone, he had left them, he was never coming back! His ideals and beliefs meant more to him than his own son . . .

But that wasn't true. She didn't believe it. François loved his son, she knew he did. And then she felt a sudden intensifying of her pain as she wondered if he had taken his mistress with him. That beautiful, golden woman she had seen at the opera. The woman he loved. The woman for whom he was forsaking his family . . .

She closed her eyes, trying to get a grip on herself. He had made no mention of Élise so she must stop torturing herself this way. She must remember that he was giving her her freedom. He was telling her to go to Armand, to allow Armand to take his place. It was what she had always wanted . . .

But it wasn't what she wanted!

She looked at Louis again, and seeing the terrible grief in her eyes he buried her face in his shoulder.

'Why did he do it, Louis?' she breathed. 'Why?'

'He gave us his reasons, *chérie*.'

'But I don't believe them. I *won't* believe them!'

She felt Armand's arms going round her, taking her from Louis. 'It's all right, Claudine,' he whispered. 'You don't have to hide it any longer.'

'Hide what?' she cried.

'Ssh!' he soothed, stroking her face. But as he looked down at her, his eyes speaking the words more clearly than his voice, she started to shrink away. 'No!' she cried. 'It's not true! It's not! Do you hear me?' But her heart told her that it was.

'You've always loved him,' Armand whispered, 'and now is the time for you to face the truth. I know it'll be hard, but I'll be here for you. So will Louis, so will Solange. We all know, Claudine, we've always known. And in your heart, so have you.'

'No, Armand, no. I love you.'

He shook his head. 'I've tried to make you love me, Claudine, and for a while I think that maybe you did, but I knew when you returned from Paris that it was only a matter of time . . .'

He looked away, and Claudine felt the first stirring of an unbearable pity. Now she knew the reason for his apathy and despair. And now, with the shadow of dread removed and his worst fears realized, at last he had regained his strength. All he needed now was to hear her admit it – that she loved François.

But she couldn't, she wouldn't. If she did she would fall apart.

Taking a deep breath, she said, 'You're wrong, both of you. He's a traitor. He's a murderer. And as far as I'm concerned, he's dead.'

Armand's eyes met Louis', but before either of them could speak she pulled back a chair and sat down. 'We have now to decide what we are going to do about this,' she said firmly. 'Please sit down.'

When they were seated, she continued. 'We must decide what we're going to tell Solange. And Monique. And Lucien.' She saw Louis flinch as she mentioned Lucien, and suddenly realized what all this might do to his career. 'We can't afford to wait,' she went on. 'Louis, I think you should leave for Paris in the morning. François' contacts in the Government must be told at once, in case he tries to return to France. And if we don't pass this information on, it makes us traitors ourselves.'

She knew her words must be like acid on Louis' wounds, but she was carried along on the tide of her resolve, determined to make them all face up to the horror of it. 'I imagine,' she continued, 'that whoever has been watching us will be removed by the Abwehr, now that François' loyalty to them is no longer in question.'

To her surprise, her speech was greeted with silence. Then Louis said slowly, 'What you're saying makes sense, Claudine, but I wonder if perhaps we're not being a little too hasty. You see, I don't want to raise false hopes, but . . .'

Claudine stiffened, and Armand put a hand over hers as if to steady her. Her powers of resilience were remarkable, he knew, but he also knew that she couldn't take much more. 'I think we should know everything,' he said.

Louis looked down at the letter lying on the table in front of them. 'It may be nothing,' he said, 'it may be only the hope of a desperate father. But I think there's another message in that letter besides the obvious one. Look at the date. You see, François wrote this letter almost four weeks ago.'

'I don't understand,' Armand said.

'It doesn't take four weeks for a letter to arrive from Paris, not even in these times. Claudine received one from Céline only yesterday that Céline had written five days before. It's my guess that François expected someone to read this letter before me. That he was telling someone else, not me, that he has defected to the German side. It would explain the delay. And never in his life has François written to me using the address *Mon cher Papa*.'

'No!' Claudine shouted, slamming her hands on the table. 'He can't do this to us! He can't! He's confessed his treachery and we must act upon it.'

'Claudine,' Armand said softly, 'I think Louis might have a point. And we owe it to François to see . . .'

'We owe him nothing!' she cried. 'He has deserted us! He has deserted his country and I won't help him!'

'You must, *chérie*,' Armand replied. 'We all must. He could be in a great deal of danger . . .' He stopped as the blood drained from her face, but forced himself to go on. 'I know that the torture of not knowing is going to worsen the pain for you, but if we have any doubt at all about this letter, I don't think we should do as François asks.'

'I agree with Armand,' Louis said.

Claudine's beautiful face was ravaged with grief and as she turned her eyes to Louis a silent scream erupted from the core of her despair.

Later that night Claudine sat on the edge of François' bed, hugging a pillow and gazing sightlessly down at the floor. 'I hate you,' she said into the darkness. 'I hate you for what you're doing to me. I don't know who I am any more, I don't know what I want. But I don't love you, François. Do you hear me? They're wrong! I don't care what happens to you! I don't want you to come back. I never want to see you again . . .

'Oh, François, I can't love you, it hurts too much . . . I can't hope that you'll come back, because if you don't . . . Oh, my love, where are you? Where are you?' She pressed her face into the pillow as the tears started to stream down her cheeks.

'If you didn't want me,' she sobbed, 'why didn't you let me go at the beginning? Why did you have to do it like this? But if you can't love me, then please find it in your heart to love Louis. Come back for him, François, he needs you. I'm crying now, François, but I won't cry again. After tonight there will be no more tears, there will be no more love. There will be nothing, after tonight.'

– 21 –

After scanning the bookshelves for some time, François pulled out a volume of Goethe's poetry. He yawned. His hair needed cutting, he thought, catching a glimpse of his reflection in the brass lamp-stand beside him, and perhaps he should go upstairs and change out of the grey wool sweater and brown corduroy trousers before dinner. But it didn't really matter whether he did nor not, and he strolled listlessly back to the fireplace and sat down heavily in the chair where he had spent the best part of the afternoon.

He had been here, at von Liebermann's country residence, since France declared war on Germany – just under four months ago now. During this time his anger over what had happened to Élise had given way first to frustration at his enforced inactivity, then to utter boredom. He couldn't deny that von Liebermann was the most generous of hosts; intellectual soirées were arranged for him, there were visits to the theatre and the opera, and any number of women were brought in for his entertainment; every French and British newspaper was delivered on a regular basis as well as the German ones, and he had free access to the wireless, and even a chauffeur at his disposal twenty-four hours a day. But despite all that, there was no getting away from the fact that he was a prisoner.

After Poland's defeat he had been taken to Warsaw, where he had seen for himself the effectiveness of the Blitzkrieg. The city was in ruins, and God only knew how many had died. But they were the lucky ones; over a million men, women and children had been captured and taken to prisoner-of-war camps in Eastern Europe. François had assumed that after this von Liebermann would send him to France so that he could report on what he had seen and try once again to persuade the French to capitulate. But he was still, as the Christmas festivities approached, imprisoned in this cell of luxury – knowing as well as von Liebermann that to escape would be the easiest thing in the world, but that he wouldn't even attempt it while the Abwehr controlled Halunke.

He rested his feet on the fender in front of the log fire and pondered the situation. Even now, von Lieberman still did not trust him. Of course, the Abwehr would have intercepted his letter to Louis; so far so good, they must be thinking, but why has the Comte de Lorvoire not now disinherited his elder son? Which was exactly what he himself was thinking: why in God's name had Louis not gone ahead and disowned him, as instructed? The disinheritance was crucial, as the French Secret Service, under whose auspices he had been toiling for the last five years, had agreed. It would finally convince the Abwehr that he was to be trusted, but at the same time it would negate his usefulness to them as a spy by letting the French and British know he was considered a traitor. It was a complex and dangerous game they were playing, and one in which he might well lose his life.

He stirred irritably in his chair. Why was his father taking so long? Unless the Germans were convinced they could trust him, what happened to Élise could happen to Claudine. Halunke might well have intended to kill Élise, but undoubtedly von Liebermann was much gratified that he hadn't, for she was now a living reminder of the threat his family was under if he didn't co-operate. And the hell of it was, Captain Paillole and his agents couldn't go anywhere near Lorvoire now, either to protect the family or see what was delaying Louis, because their presence would immediately alert German suspicions.

François sighed quietly to himself, then looked up as the door opened and von Liebermann walked in.

'Ah, there you are, my friend,' said the German, his narrow eyes shining with pleasure. His corpulent frame moved to the row of decanters on the heavy mahogany table. 'Would you care for a drink before dinner?'

François declined with a shake of the head. 'And what are you reading there?' von Liebermann asked, glancing back over his shoulder.

François grimaced as he realized the significance of the title he had chosen, which would not be lost on the General. '*Roman Elegies*,' he answered, putting the book to one side.

Von Liebermann's fat shoulders shook as he turned back and saluted François with his glass. 'Poems written for a mistress who eventually became a wife,' he chuckled. 'How very fitting.'

François didn't comment. When he first arrived he had made his feelings about what had happened to Élise quite clear. As a result he had seen nothing of Helber since, for he had told von Liebermann precisely what he intended to do to the manhood of his toady.

Von Liebermann had merely smiled. 'All I can say is, do not pursue your revenge too soon, my friend, or it will be the worse for others.'

'I take it you are threatening me with Halunke?' It was a stab in the dark, but von Liebermann's thin eyebrows had lifted.

'So you have discovered his code name,' he had said. 'Most diligent of you.'

François had let the matter drop then, and neither man had mentioned either Halunke or Élise again, until now.

'I must say, it surprises me that you have expressed no interest in the welfare of Mademoiselle Pascale since arriving,' von Liebermann said, easing his bulk into the chair opposite François'.

'As she is of no further use to you, I imagine she is quite safe,' François answered.

Von Liebermann nodded. 'You are correct in your assumption. So why are you bothering to have her watched?'

'For her own peace of mind.'

'Very commendable. Particularly since her injuries mean that she is of no further use to you either.'

François' jaw tightened, but he bit hard on his anger, knowing there was little point in giving vent to it now.

'But the affair was over anyway, was it not?' von Liebermann smiled. 'So all we have to do now is discover which fortunate lady has succeeded to your affections?'

'You can try, but as there is no such lady you'll be wasting your time.'

Von Liebermann laughed. 'Very wise, my friend. A man in your position cannot afford the luxury of love, as you have discovered. Now, I have some good news for you. You are to return to France in the New Year. Or rather, in the spring. You have not been kept in the dark on the matter of *Weser* – the plans for the Norwegian operation – though I imagine you would appreciate more details. Alas, I cannot furnish them, though with a mind as brilliant as yours you will have already taken into account the fact that Swedish supplies of iron-ore travel to Germany through Norway. Therefore, it is necessary for us to turn our attention to Norway before executing *Fall Gelb*.'

François knew that *Fall Gelb* – Plan Yellow – was the invasion of the Low Countries. As far as he knew, this had been planned for January, but if the Norwegian operation had to come first it would obviously be postponed. However, this information would be useless by the time he got to France; unless the Nazis were stupid, *Weser* would already be well under way.

'I'm afraid your bargaining power in France will be limited,' von Liebermann continued. 'However, it is not Herr Himmler's wish that you obtain intelligence from the French, he merely requires that you use your remarkable talent for persuasion to convince them that they cannot possibly win this war.'

'It will not have escaped your notice that I have failed to achieve this in the past. What makes you think I can do so now?'

'In the past there was no war between Germany and France. You have seen what happened in Poland, a most lamentable defeat for that nation. But if the Poles had not fought the inevitable, they would not now be in the situation they are in. I'm sure that Monsieur Daladier and Monsieur Lebrun have no desire to see their country suffer such a fate. Have you asked yourself why France and Britain, having declared war on the Fatherland, did not attack from the west at a time when it would have been most prudent to do so?'

François had, many times, but he said nothing.

'The only conclusion we can draw from this near-passive observation of Poland's fate,' von Liebermann went on, 'is that France – and maybe Britain – do not, despite their declarations of war, want to fight.'

'You are less certain about Britain?'

'A cunning nation. They have their Expeditionary Force in what they feel to be strategic position in northern France. We shall see whether they will fight. Naturally, we shall try to persuade them not to, we have no desire for further bloodshed. But you know the British as well as I; not nearly as pragmatic as the French. So perhaps your first job as an officer of the Abwehr will not be such a difficult one.'

'An officer?' François repeated.

'That is the other good news I have for you. Herr Himmler has seen fit to bestow the rank of major upon you.'

'I am honoured,' François murmured. 'Please thank Herr Himmler on my behalf when next you see him.'

'You can thank him yourself,' von Liebermann grinned. 'We are to spend the Christmas period at Karinhall as the guests of Herr Goering and his estimable lady wife. Herr Himmler is also invited. As is the Führer.'

'It will be an honour indeed to spend time in such distinguished company,' François remarked, getting to his feet.

Von Liebermann's beady eyes watched him as he walked across the room and helped himself to a cognac. Like Helber, he was not unaffected by de Lorvoire's potent sexuality, there were times when he had only to raise an eyebrow for von Liebermann to experience a stirring in his groin. But unlike Helber, he had his carnal desires well under control – as de Lorvoire quite simply terrified him.

'I presume,' François said, turning round and perching on the edge of the table, 'that any preference I might have for where I spend the festive season is unlikely to be considered?'

'Aaah,' von Liebermann sighed mournfully. 'You would like to be with your family? I understand only too well, my friend. However, I am afraid that is not possible. Herr Himmler feels it would be unwise for you to return to France before the spring.' He paused. 'By which time it is our hope that the question of your fealty to the Reich will have been finally settled.'

François thought about this. 'Do I understand,' he said carefully, 'that there is something you wish me to do between now and the spring to prove, yet again, where my loyalties lie?'

Von Liebermann tutted and sighed. 'You have such an astute brain, my friend. It pleases me so much not to have to spell things out. Incidentally, before we move any further from the subject of your family, I am able to give you news of them if you wish.'

François' hand hesitated as he lifted the cognac to his lips.

'No,' von Liebermann laughed, reading his mind, 'we have not obtained this information from Halunke, my friend. But it may interest you to know that your wife has taken the news of your defection rather well. She is even now making preparations for her marriage to the *vigneron* . . . I'm afraid his name escapes me.'

'St Jacques,' François supplied. His eyes narrowed. So the Abwehr had read his letter, and they had also passed it on to his father – there were times when he'd wondered whether Louis had ever received it. But if he had received it, why hadn't he disinherited him?

'Yes, St Jacques,' von Liebermann nodded. His eyes shot to François', then with a smirk he said, 'A rather odd choice of lover for a woman in your wife's position, wouldn't you say?'

François was not deceived. This was von Liebermann's way of trying to find out whether he harboured any secret feelings for his wife. 'Had you met St Jacques,' he said, smiling straight into von Liebermann's eyes, 'you might not think so. He has a certain appeal for the ladies. And who knows, perhaps my wife will find in her second marriage the happiness she failed to find in her first.'

'But not the status.'

François smiled. 'If there's one thing my wife cannot be accused of, it is snobbery.'

Von Liebermann sighed. 'It is a sorrowful thing when our wives do not live up to our expectations, is it not?' he said.

'But mine did,' François answered. 'She has delivered an heir, which was all that was required of her.'

'Quite so. And now, like the rest of her sex, she is not only dispensable but replaceable.'

'As I said earlier, there is no one else,' François said. 'So shall we get on with the task you have in mind for the proof of my fealty?'

'Of course,' von Liebermann smiled. 'Come, sit down again, and I shall tell you what it is. I think, considering your reputation for ruthlessness, that it is a task you are going to enjoy.'

Holding the pistol with both hands, Claudine raised it, lowered it very slowly and took aim. All around her there was an unnatural silence, as if nature itself was holding its breath. She squeezed hard on the trigger. The explosion reverberated round the valley as though echoing through the very bowels of hell.

'Bravo!' Lucien cried, as one of the wine bottles balanced on a ledge between the two caves smashed to a thousand pieces. 'You're a natural, *ma chérie*.'

Claudine's face was aglow with pride, until she saw how Armand was laughing at her. 'Your turn,' she said, handing him the pistol.

'But I'm such a miserable shot,' Armand protested.

She gave him a sceptical look, and obediently Armand raised the gun the way Lucien had shown them, lowered it, took aim, and missed.

'Such humiliation!' he groaned. But Claudine had seen the way his eyes met Lucien's, and before Armand could do as much as turn to her for sympathy, she had grabbed his arm, twisted it behind his back, kicked his legs from under him and toppled him to the ground.

'Bravo!' Lucien exclaimed. 'I didn't know you were that good at self-defence, Claudine.'

She stood over her victim with her hands on her hips. 'Don't think you can fool me, Armand St Jacques. I've seen you both practising out here so I know what a good shot you are. And I'm ready to take on anyone,' she said, grinning meaningfully at Lucien.

Despite the biting March wind, the three of them had spent a happy and sometimes hilarious morning at shooting practice in the courtyard. A few yards away, wearing a multitude of coloured scarves, a woollen hat tugged down to her eyebrows and thick leather gloves which certainly belonged to Louis, Solange sat reading a book that had been sent to her by her friend Simone de Beauvoir. It was not one of Simone's own books, but the Marquis de Sade's *One Hundred and Twenty Days of Sodom* to which Simone had written an introduction. As she slowly turned the pages, Solange's normally mobile face was frozen in an expression of total incredulity.

'Good book, Solange?' Claudine called.

Startled, Solange peered out from under her hat as though she had forgotten where she was. 'Astonishing, *chérie*,' she said. 'Altogether astonishing.'

'What's it about?' Armand said. All three of them knew perfectly well what it was about.

'Oh, I couldn't say,' Solange answered, quite flustered. 'I mean, I'm not really sure . . .'

'Does Papa know you're reading that, *Maman*?' Lucien called.

Solange glanced anxiously over her shoulder. 'I don't think so.'

'No, I don't think so either,' Lucien grinned. 'So don't, whatever you do, ask him to explain it.'

Suddenly young Louis appeared round the corner of the château. '*Grand-mère! Grand-mère!*' he cried, and hurled himself into Solange's lap.

'*Chéri!*' she shrieked, giving him a big wet kiss on the cheek.

'Wait for this, he's sure to ask her to read to him when he sees the book,' Claudine whispered. And when this was exactly what happened, and Solange turned puce with discomfort, the three of them roared with laughter.

'Come along, young man,' Lucien said, swinging his nephew up onto his shoulders. 'I have a book for you that comes all the way from Denmark. And if we ask *Grand-père* nicely, perhaps he'll let us look for Denmark on his globe so you can see how far away it is.'

Claudine watched as Lucien and Louis disappeared through the kitchen door. Any minute now Solange would get up and follow them inside, so that she could continue to keep Lucien under her maternal eye. Instead of irritating Lucien, his mother's protectiveness seemed to amuse him; he'd turned it into a game of hide-and-seek which Solange, with her usual sense of fun, had entered into gladly. Of them all, it was his father who had been most surprised to see Lucien when he arrived three days ago – but things were so quiet at the front, Lucien explained, that there were now serious doubts as to whether there really would be a war after all. And over the past forty-eight hours many of the young men from Lorvoire and the surrounding villages had started to reappear too. The generals, deciding that there was little point in them kicking their heels at the lines, had sent them home on leave.

Lucien's first dinner at home had been a sober affair, for he had spent the afternoon in the library with his father, being told about François. Lucien's handsome face had been pale and drawn when the two of them finally emerged, but it soon became clear that his concern was not for his own career, but solely and wholeheartedly for his brother. A concern he was simply not worthy of, Claudine had told him when he joined her later in her sitting-room for a nightcap.

'But how can you say that?' Lucien had protested. 'You haven't heard from him for almost seven months. God only knows what might have happened to him in that time.'

'Does it matter?' she had retorted. 'He made his choice, he knew what he was letting himself in for.'

'You don't mean that. And besides, you don't know if it was his choice,' Lucien pointed out. 'I know your marriage hasn't been all you might have hoped for, but . . .'

'There are no buts, Lucien. He's done nothing to make me care for him and everything to make me hate him. And if I ever see him again I shall take great pleasure in telling him how well he's succeeded. I loathe and detest him to the very depths of my soul. The only decency in him was his love for his son, but now even that's gone.'

'I don't believe that, and neither do you.'

'How can I not believe it!' she had cried. 'Your father showed you the letter, you read what he said. How can any man of principle and integrity consider handing his own son to another man?'

'And his wife?' Lucien said gently.

'Yes! And me!' she had yelled. 'But don't think I care about that! I've never in my life wanted to be free of him more than I do now. He's a traitor! A murderer! A sadist! He's vile and evil, and I don't know how you can defend him when we both know that he has very probably ruined your career.'

'Oh, I'll survive,' Lucien had said. 'But will you,

Claudine? With so much bitterness wrapped up inside you . . .'

It had been a painful conversation, and now, as Solange rose to her feet and went into the château – still clutching her book to her chest – Claudine resolved to put all uncomfortable thoughts out of her mind. She turned to Armand.

'Come to the cottage,' she whispered, 'and let me make you some lunch.'

By the time they had finished eating the sky outside was so black and thunderous that Claudine had to light the oil lamps. The rain was beating rhythmically against the windows and the wind shrilled through the cottage's battered roof, almost drowning the sleepy sound of an American band playing on the wireless. They sat side by side at the old table, sipping their coffee.

'Kiss me,' Claudine said.

Armand knew it was an invitation to more than a kiss. They often made love in the afternoons, slowly savouring one another's bodies in the long, languorous hours between lunch and Claudine's return to the château. But now he only brushed his lips lightly across hers, then turned to take another sip of coffee.

'Is something the matter?' she said. And then, feeling her heart start to pound, 'Don't you want to make love?'

'It's not that I don't want to,' he said. 'It's just that we have to talk, Claudine. We have to talk about us.'

This, he had decided, was the time to have it out with her. Today, this afternoon, he was going to force her to face the truth. Since the day Louis had come to the cottage with François' letter, François' name had not been mentioned between them, and they had gone on with their pretence of love as if nothing had happened. But they were living a lie, and now he was going to put an end to it.

When he looked up, Claudine was staring at him with an almost petulant expression on her face. 'Are you trying to tell me you don't want to marry me? Is that what this is all about?'

He sighed. 'It's not a case of whether I want to marry you, Claudine,' he said. 'You know I do. But you have to face the fact that that will never happen so long as François . . .'

'I don't want to talk about François!'

He pulled his chair closer to the table. 'That's not going to be easy when we both know that he's the reason for things being the way they are between us.'

'What do you mean, "the way they are"?' she said in a tight voice.

'You know what I mean, but if you'd prefer me to spell it out . . .'

'Perhaps you'd better.'

'Well, to begin with, this pretence is tearing us both apart. I love you, Claudine, you know that, but if you care anything at all for me you'll understand that the time has come – no, is long overdue – for you to let me go.'

'No!' she cried. 'No, I can't.'

'Then ask yourself why you can't. And please don't say it's because you love me.'

'But it is.'

'No, Claudine! You've never loved me, at least not in the way you love . . .' He held up his hand as she started to protest. 'All this time, what we've had here in this cottage, it's all been a game. It's a game that has meant a great deal to you, I know, but it's a game you would never have played if you hadn't been lonely, if François hadn't turned his back on you the way he did.' He sighed, and looked away from the pain in her eyes. 'I'm going to end our affair,' he said, quietly but firmly. 'It's the only way I can see of saving my own sanity. You have to let me go, Claudine. You have to.'

'No, Armand! Stop saying these things.'

'Claudine, please think about what this is doing to me. I can't go on making love to you knowing that all the time you're thinking of him. You must try to accept that it's because you love and want him so desperately that you can't dispel him from your mind even when . . .'

'That's not true,' she said fiercely. 'I've told you how things were between us. He didn't bother to hide his distaste even at having to touch me.'

'But was it so distasteful for you?'

She drew breath to speak, then lowered her eyes to her hands. 'Yes,' she murmured. 'Yes, it was.'

'Look me in the eye and tell me that. Tell me that it was you who brought that side of your marriage to an end.'

'Does it matter which of us brought it to an end?' she cried. 'The fact is, François loves someone else. He's been sleeping with Élise Pascale since before we were married! He loves her so much that now he's abandoned his own son and gone away to Germany with her! How can you believe I could either want or love a man who has treated me like that?'

Armand smiled. 'Very easily,' he said. 'And perhaps now is the time to tell you that he didn't take Élise Pascale to Germany with him as you suspect. In fact, his affair with her is over.'

His words seemed to hit her a stultifying blow. Suddenly, she felt as though every ounce of energy she possessed was being wrung from her limbs. 'How do you know that?' she breathed.

'Louis told me, just after he received the letter from François.'

'Why didn't he tell me?'

'Because with François being in Germany, with the future so uncertain, he though it would only make things worse for you.'

They were strange, the feelings that were running amok

through her body. She felt dizzy, disoriented. Outwardly she was calm, but inside the feelings were beating at her heart, drumming at her mind. She must try to understand what they were telling her.

He hadn't taken her. He hadn't taken Élise Pascale to Germany, he had gone alone. But didn't that only make it worse? Because though he had given up his mistress, he had still tried to give her, his wife, to another man. So ending his liaison with Élise had made no difference at all. Still he didn't want her. And she would rather die than admit she wanted him, even though every fibre of her body was crying out for him.

Hardly knowing what she was doing, she got up from the table and put a shaking hand on Armand's shoulder.

'I'm sorry,' she whispered. 'I'm truly sorry – for everything.'

'There's no need to be,' he said, rising too and taking her in his arms. 'I'm just glad I was there for a while to ease your loneliness.'

'And I yours?' she said.

'Oh yes. You certainly did that. But now I feel more lonely when I'm with you than I do when we're apart.' He pulled her head from his shoulder and looked into her eyes. 'Are you ready to admit now that you love him?'

'No,' she said, shaking her head.

'Why?'

'Because I can't. Because I can hardly think of him without wanting to scream, or cry, or . . . I don't know. I don't understand the way I feel. We've never shared even a moment of affection, yet . . .' She looked away. 'I can't, Armand. It's as if there's something deep inside me, so deep and so powerful that . . . I don't know . . . All I know is that it frightens me and that I've got to keep it buried.'

She moved away and went to stand at the window. 'I knew the day I married him the way I felt about him, but then I thought, after the way he made love to me that night . . . He was so cruel, so unfeeling, and yet, you're right, the desire didn't go away. It's never gone away. But I've tried to bury it, along with the pain. It was the only way I knew how to survive my marriage. He never wanted a wife, he made that plain from the start, and he wanted me to despise him as he despises me – so I did. Then, when I met you, and you were so kind, so gentle and caring . . . I truly believed that it was you I wanted, you I loved. But I suppose now, looking back, that all I wanted, even then, was that François . . . That seeing me with another man, he would . . .'

She shrugged, but there were tears on her cheeks. 'He didn't care, though. His only concern was that the child I was carrying was his. And after Louis was born, when I saw the tenderness in his eyes every time he looked at him . . . Oh, Armand you don't know how I've longed for him to look at me like that. I'm guilty of being jealous of my own son because his father loves him, can you imagine? But I still hate him, Armand. And it's that hatred that will keep me together, that will stop me from throwing myself at him and begging him to love me. Because that's what I want to do. I've failed in every other way, and now I want to beg him . . . But I'll never do it, because if I did I'd end up despising myself as much as he does.'

She sat down then, and buried her face in her hands. 'He's a traitor, and a murderer, I know that, so why can't I make myself believe it? Why can't I just accept the fact that he doesn't love me, and get on with my life? It's as though he has some kind of hold over me, as though he won't let go of me. But that's not true! I'm the one who won't let go – and I *must*! Yet even as I say all these things, I still don't know what to do. It's as if I'm drowning. As if someone has pushed me from dry land and now I'm being submerged by waves I can do nothing to control. But I will control them, Armand. I will! And the only way I can do that is to deny, to ignore, everything that's happening inside me. So please, Armand, don't force me into saying something I just can't allow myself to feel.'

When she had finished there was a long, long silence. The rain had stopped, and the only sounds were of water running from the guttering into the barrels beneath, and the fire crackling in the hearth. She had said a great deal, much more than she had intended, but she could not allow herself to go any further. So many times in the past she had opened herself to receive his love – the day she married him, the day Louis was born, the night of the July ball – and on each of those – and on others too painful to recall – he had pushed her away. She couldn't let that happen again.

Armand's voice seemed to come from a great distance as he spoke into the darkness. 'You're only making it worse by hiding from it.'

'Maybe you're right,' she sighed. 'But I don't know any other way. How can I even begin to understand my feelings when they just don't make sense? But I suppose that trying to tie love to logic is like trying to pin the sun to the moon. Once in a while they will meet, but even then one will always eclipse the other.'

'You shouldn't try to make sense of the way you are feeling,' he said. 'You should simply accept it. Maybe then you can decide what to do.'

'Hasn't he made that decision for me?'

'Only if you let him.'

She turned in her chair to face him, and her heart contracted as she saw the tears on his cheeks.

'No, don't look at me, Claudine,' he said, hiding his face. 'I don't want you to see me like this.'

She started to get up, but he held out his arm to keep her away. 'Don't touch me,' he sobbed. 'Please, just leave me alone now.'

'But Armand . . .'

'I've tried to be strong for you,' he wept, 'but I can't take any more. I can't listen to any more.'

'I'm sorry!' she said. 'Oh my God, I didn't think. I . . .'

'No, you didn't, did you?' he said. 'Because all you've ever thought about is him. Well, I can't live in his shadow any longer. Find him, wherever he is, and go to him. I don't want you near me. I can't stand you looking at me with those accusing eyes, hating me because I'm not him.'

'I've never done that!' she cried.

'Oh, but you have. And me, pathetic, used little man that I am . . .'

'I've never used you!'

'For Christ's sake! What do you think you've been doing here today? You've used me from the start. You admitted as much yourself: you wanted to make him jealous. But it didn't work, did it? But even then you couldn't bear to be alone, so you kept coming. But what would have happened if he'd lifted just one finger to call you back to him? You'd have gone! You'd have left me as cruelly as he left you. You're two of a kind, you and François, Claudine. You deserve one another. But don't ever forget what happened to Hortense. She paid the price of loving him, and she paid it with her life. Now get your coat, because I'm taking you back to the château for the last time.'

She was dumbfounded, and could only stare at him. At last she got up from the chair and lifted her coat from the bed. 'Armand,' she said, as they started out into the forest. 'Armand, you're wrong, you know. I did love you. Perhaps not in the way you wanted me to, but I'd never have left you the way you say I would. Armand, I couldn't bear it if we parted like this.'

'Oh, you'll learn to live with it,' he said bitterly. 'Just as you've learned to live with François' rejection. You'll bury it all, as though none of it has happened. And if anyone reminds you of it a few years from now, you'll shudder with revulsion at the idea that you allowed your husband's *vigneron* even to come near you. And where will I be? I'll be there, tending the vines, looking after your estate and you won't even be able to bring yourself to speak to me.'

'That's not true!' she cried. 'I don't know why you're saying all these things.'

He drew breath to speak, but she put her hand over his mouth. 'No, stop! Please, stop it now, before we both say things we'll only regret later.'

He shoved her hand away. 'Are you giving me orders, *madame*?' he sneered.

'Armand! What's got into you? Just now you were so . . .' She shook her head. 'I understand that you're hurting, that it's all my fault, but I had no idea you were capable of such bitterness.'

He closed his eyes. 'I'm not,' he growled, his voice thick with self-disgust. 'I'm not even capable of that. But I'm trying to give myself something to hold onto.' Suddenly he clutched her to him and buried his face in her hair. 'Don't desert me, Claudine!' he sobbed. 'Don't leave me altogether, because I don't think I could bear it.'

– 22 –

François hadn't really expected Paris to look any different from the last time he'd seen it, but seven months is a long time, and he was relieved, and in some way comforted, to find that the city hadn't changed. Perhaps there were many more bicycles than he remembered, a result of the petrol rationing no doubt, but otherwise the tree-lined avenues, the pavement cafés, the grey still waters of the Seine, the hurrying people –unmistakably Parisians – were the same.

Inwardly he shuddered as he remembered Warsaw: the smoking ruins, the terrified faces, the jack-booted German soldiers as they looted the debris and beat innocent people half to death. It all came so vividly to his mind that for a moment it was as though it were happening right in front of him. That Paris should suffer in that way was unthinkable. He hoped to God that if it ever came to it, someone would have the foresight to declare her an open city before the Germans razed her glory to ashes.

As he drove past the Tuileries Gardens, heading towards the Champs Elysées, he stole a quick glance at Erich von Pappen who was sitting beside him, his peculiar face turned towards the window. Von Pappen had been at the border to meet him when he drove through at five o'clock that morning in his own black Citröen, which von Liebermann had returned the day before. Thank God von Pappen had brought him a change of clothes, or he might still be wearing the commandant's uniform the Abwehr had supplied him with before he left. Von Liebermann had insisted he wear it, no doubt to titillate his own perverted sense of humour, as very few members of the Abwehr wore uniform.

Once von Pappen had filled him in on what had been happening while he was away, they had spent most of the journey in silence. As yet neither had mentioned Élise, or François' family. Now as François swerved to avoid a cyclist on the Place de la Concorde, von Pappen was the first to break the silence.

'Do you think you've gained their trust yet?'

'Only they know the answer to that, *mon ami*,' François replied.

'Max Helber tells me that they set you a test before you left.'

'Mmm.' François' hooded eyes narrowed, and von Pappen felt rather than saw their virulence.

'Did you pass?'

'If you can call torturing two Frenchmen to the brink of death passing, then the answer is yes.'

Von Pappen twitched. 'Did you know either of them?' he asked, after a pause.

'Yes.' Then abruptly changing the subject, François said, 'What have you discovered about Halunke?'

'Not very much, I'm afraid,' von Pappen confessed. 'I've been through the list you gave me, I've even come up with some suggestions of my own as to who might have a grudge against you, but as yet I have nothing conclusive.'

'Did you check on Hortense de Bourchain's family?'

'Yes. They're all still in Tahiti, with the exception of her brother, Michel. He's serving with the Seventh Army under General Giraud, and hasn't taken leave since arriving in France.'

'When did he arrive?'

'Early in October. Two months after the attack on Élise.'

'You're certain of that?'

'Absolutely.'

François didn't bother to ask how von Pappen had got his information; he trusted him implicitly, and had never yet had reason to doubt him. 'Is Élise up to giving a dinner party?' he asked.

'I think so. I think she'll be glad of something to do. She rarely goes out these days.'

François' mouth was set in a grim line. 'How does she look?' he asked.

'Better than you might think. Naturally, I haven't seen her body, though I imagine the scars are as yet barely healed. But her face is good. Her left eye is partially closed, but you have to look closely to notice. She walks with a slight limp.'

'And her mind?'

'She still has occasional lapses of memory, forgets what she's saying or who she's talking to. The nightmares, as you might expect, are still giving her trouble.'

François nodded. 'Have you told her I'm coming?'

'No.'

'Then I'll drop you at the avenue Foch now, and you can tell her.' He leaned across von Pappen and, opening the glove compartment, pulled out a handwritten list of names. 'I'd like you to arrange for as many as possible of the people on this list to come to dinner tonight.'

'Your brief?' von Pappen enquired, his face twitching as he looked down the list.

'To persuade France not to go to war,' François answered prosaically. Then drawing up the corner of his mouth in a smile, he glanced at von Pappen and said, 'An easy enough task, wouldn't you say, Erich?'

Von Pappen chuckled. He knew precisely what François meant. He would talk about capitulation tonight, of course, but neither he nor the Germans expected him to succeed in this mission – it was widely known in political circles that France and Britain were on the verge of agreeing that neither country should conclude peace separately. And if Winston Churchill had anything to do with it, the British would fight to the bitter end. No, the real reason why von Liebermann had sent François to France now was to discover how many of the country's politicians and generals were still prepared to listen to a man who – according to rumour, at least – was a traitor.

'There's one other thing I'd like you to do, Erich,' François said as they drove round the Arc de Triomphe and filtered off into the avenue Foch. 'I'd like you to travel to Lorvoire tomorrow morning and speak to my father. Try not to be seen, the château will be under heavy surveillance now that I'm back in the country, which is why I can't go myself. Use the bridge at the back and speak first to Corinne. She'll arrange for my father to see you.'

'You have a particular message for the Comte?'

'I just want him to do as I instructed in my letter and

disinherit me. It's the only way I know of preventing the Germans from sending me back into France again. If I've been denounced, publicly, as a traitor, then I'll be worthless as a spy against my own countrymen. It will cause my father a great deal of pain to do this, so you must make certain he knows all the facts. I want you to do this in person, so I can be sure it's handled properly.'

'Understood.'

'And before you go, Erich,' François said, pulling in to the side of the road outside Élise's apartment. 'D'you know if anything's been done about my other instruction in the letter?'

Von Pappen pursed his lips. 'You mean, concerning your wife? I've heard nothing.' Then, when it was clear François was going to say no more, 'You're going to the Bois de Boulogne now?'

'Yes.'

'The staff are expecting you. I shall telephone you there later.' And slamming the car door, he walked off across the pavement, his hairless head exposed unflinchingly to the wind.

When François arrived at the Lorvoire house in the Bois de Boulogne he found that fires had been lit in the drawing-room and study, and when he went upstairs to his bedroom, there was Gilbert, his valet, pumping the bellows at the hearth. François almost laughed then, as he thought how old Gilbert might have reacted if he had walked into the house wearing his German staff-officer's uniform. He greeted him fondly, for he had known the old man since he was a child; then he went back downstairs to the study, where he ate the late lunch which had been prepared for him, and looked at the morning's newspapers.

Afterwards, he went to sit in a chair beside the fire, intending to consider how best to approach the task in hand for the evening. But instead, he found that his tired mind was continuously and disturbingly arrested by a sense of impending doom that had been with him from the moment he set foot back in France. The mind very often played tricks when starved of sleep, he knew that, but the sense of foreboding was so strong that he found himself sitting forward in the chair and holding his head in his hands. He wished to God now that he'd killed those two Frenchmen before he left Germany. Never leave your man alive to tell tales, one of the first rules of the game. But von Liebermann had particularly required that they be left alive – and by now would almost certainly have tortured them himself and discovered exactly who they were. And once he knew that, he would understand why François had had no compunction about dealing with his fellow-countrymen in the brutal, merciless manner he had. In other words, torturing two French agents whom he knew for a fact to be working for the Soviets, was going to do nothing to prove his fealty to the Third Reich.

So now the question was, what would von Liebermann do to make his displeasure known? To teach him what a madman he was even to consider deceiving the Abwehr . . . Which led François to the most pressing question of all: where, and who the hell, was Halunke?

'I don't like it, Lucien,' Claudine sighed. 'Armand said he thought he saw someone this morning. I know it could have been anyone, but who in their right mind is going to go into the forest with this fog still hanging around? And what does this man want? What is he doing here when he must know that François is in Germany?'

'Assuming you're right, and there *is* someone out there,' Lucien answered, lighting two cigarettes and handing one to her, 'then I guess François is the only one who can answer those questions.'

Claudine turned to scan his handsome face. 'What's he

done, Lucien?' she said. 'Do you know? He told me he thought this man had some kind of grudge against him . . .'

Lucien shook his head. 'There's a whole side to my brother that's as much of a mystery to me as it is to you, Claudine,' he said. 'I imagine there are any number of people who think they have cause to hate him.'

'But so deeply that they must terrorize his family like this?' She shivered. 'Do you really think this man intends to harm us?'

Lucien smiled, and getting up from the sofa, strolled across to the fire. 'Who can tell what's going on in his mind?' he said. He turned back to look at her and took another draw on his cigarette. 'Perhaps you should go away for a few days, *chérie*. You haven't seemed at all yourself lately. Why not go up to Paris? A change of scene might do you good. Take Monique with you.'

'I couldn't leave Louis. Not when that . . . that man is outside.'

'Then take Louis too. Though he's quite well taken care of here, you know. François has seen to that, remember?'

She nodded. 'Yes, Yes, he has, hasn't he?' She looked down at her cigarette as she flicked the ash into an ashtray beside her. Lucien's suggestion was tempting, though perhaps not for the reasons he thought. Oh, she would certainly like to escape from the loathsome prying eyes that she felt were following her everywhere – but what she really wanted was to get away from Armand for a while. For his sake more than her own. Since they had broken off their affair, he had withdrawn so deeply into himself that any attempt she made to be friendly was met with just a stony glare. And if he did reply, it was in a voice so thick with pain or sarcasm that she could hardly bear it. And as well as Armand, there was François; her fears for his safety, her anger at what he had done, her feelings for him – so many thoughts whirling frenziedly around in her mind that the

– 396 –

prospect of getting away from the château, of being somewhere else for a few days, was extremely inviting.

'Monique is going to Paris anyway,' Lucien said. 'And I do believe she has arranged to meet your aunt to go and rattle tins at the Ritz with her, for refugee relief and soldiers' canteens.'

That settled it. Why on earth it hadn't occurred to her before to go and talk things over with Tante Céline, she couldn't imagine.

'Then yes. Yes, I'll go too,' she said decisively, getting up to ring the bell for Magaly. 'Why don't you come too?' she said.

'I can't. My leave is over at the end of the week, and I don't think *Maman* would appreciate it if I spent my last few days anywhere but with her. Anyway, *ma chère*, what you need is time for yourself – so go to it! And by the way, the uniform for tin-rattling is a simple black dress, or so they tell me.'

'I'll tell Magaly,' she laughed.

He walked across the room, but at the door he turned back. 'Claudine,' he said, a serious note to his voice that belied the twinkle in his eyes, 'you'll work it out in the end, you know.'

She lowered her eyes, not wanting him to see the sudden and terrible desperation that had rushed from nowhere to swamp her. 'But it's not that easy, is it?' she whispered, 'when I don't even know if I'll ever see him again?'

'Oh, you will. And if I know my brother, much sooner than you think.' He grinned. 'And don't be too surprised, either, if one of these days you discover that he loves you every bit as much as you do him.'

Her hand reached out to grab the back of a chair. 'No!' she cried. 'No, Lucien don't say that! Please!' But it was already too late. That tiny, withering seed of hope that she had tried, since the day she married him, to destroy, had absorbed the words so greedily that it was already starting to thrive again.

It was just past five thirty in the evening when the telephone rang. François, heaving himself from the chair where he had fallen into an uneasy slumber, got up to answer it himself.

'Good news,' von Pappen's voice came down the line. 'There will be eight guests for dinner this evening, including Paul Reynaud, Captain Paillole and William Bullitt, the American Ambassador. Every one of them has cancelled other engagements; they're obviously keen to hear what you have to say.'

François wasn't sure how he felt about that, and made no comment.

'I have also taken the liberty of inviting someone not on your list,' von Pappen continued. 'I'm sure you would have invited him if you'd known he was going to be in Paris.' He paused. 'It's Colonel de Gaulle.'

François' eyebrows flickered. 'What is he doing in Paris?'

'He's here only for the day. There was talk that he was to be made Under-Secretary for Defence, but Prime Minister Daladier has vetoed it. As you can imagine, Monsieur de Gaulle is not in the best of humours.'

François grinned, already looking forward to seeing his old friend. 'How is Élise?' he asked, his smile fading.

Von Pappen lowered his voice, and faintly François could hear the sound of Élise singing in the bathroom. 'Excited,' Erich answered. 'And nervous.'

'You're sure she's up to this?'

'Positive. She's looking better than I've seen her for a long time. Would you like to have a word?'

'No. But tell her I'm looking forward to seeing her.'

Throughout the evening, François could feel Élise's eyes on him down the polished length of the dining table. Once in a while he smiled at her, but as yet they had done no more than exchange a formal greeting when he arrived. Through the din of deep male voices and the clatter of cutlery he could hear her frantic laughter, and he saw the way her fingers trembled when she lifted her glass to her lips. He wondered why Erich hadn't told him how her eyes had lost their lustrous sparkle, her hair its soft, golden sheen, and how she winced with pain every time she made a sudden movement.

The evening passed much as he had expected. There was a great deal of talk, but nothing much was actually said, and he gleaned little information that he didn't already know. He exchanged a word or two with de Gaulle about Lucien, who, the Colonel informed him, was currently at Lorvoire on leave. François felt a pang of regret; he would very much have liked to see his brother.

'I'm glad to say that it's official leave this time,' de Gaulle remarked.

'This time?' François said curiously.

'I had to reprimand him some time ago,' de Gaulle explained, 'for taking off without permission. I left it at that, for he's not one to desert his post in a time of crisis, which is when it counts. But it wasn't the first time he'd disappeared for a few days; his pursuit of the ladies is going to land him in deep trouble if he doesn't watch out.'

A little while later François heard Paul Paillole asking Élise if she was all right, and as he looked up she caught his eye, and he felt the full force of her adoration. How it tugged at his heart! Yet the affection he felt for her now was almost paternal, the painful love of a father for a damaged child. As the evening wore on, none of the guests had failed to notice her periodic moments of confusion. Her green eyes would glaze over, and the smile on her lips would start to quiver as she was sucked into the grip of some terrifying vision. It lasted only a matter of seconds, but afterwards she would be disoriented, off-balance. What was to become of her? François wondered despairingly. Not that he had any intention of deserting her, but how was she going to fill the rest of such a blighted life?

At ten o'clock Charles de Gaulle got up to leave. He wanted to be back with his regiment before morning, he told François, 'And as for thinking you're going to persuade the French army to lay down their arms,' he growled, 'I can tell you that I for one have no intention whatever of handing my country to the *Boche*.'

'Hear, hear,' Paul Reynaud said, helping himself from the cigar box.

'And that possibility would not even have arisen,' de Gaulle went on passionately, 'if France had prepared herself for this war – which men like you and me, François, were predicting as long ago as thirty-three. It is a tragedy that our country should be blighted with generals who have blinkered themselves to events in Germany for so long. They cannot even begin to imagine what this war will be like, their methods are outdated, their strategy is prehistoric. And even now, is anything being done to expand our Air Force? I tell you, my friend, I shudder for the fate of this nation. And much as I detest the British, at least they will fight, and fight to the bitter end.'

It was another two hours before the others could be prised from their brandy and cigars and the comfort of Élise's sitting-room, but eventually they departed – encouraged on their way by François, who could see that Élise was beginning to tire. He talked to Erich at the door for a few moments, then turned back into the apartment.

Élise was pouring him another drink. He took it from her, put it on the table beside him and pulled her into his arms. 'How are you, *chérie*?' he murmured.

'Better now you're here,' she answered.

He noticed how careful she was not to press her body

against his. 'I've missed you,' he said. 'Have you been well looked after in my absence?'

She lifted her face to look at him, and there was something of the old light in her eyes as she said, 'If you mean, how am I getting along without sex, then the answer is that it's not as difficult as you might think.'

He chuckled. 'That's not what I meant at all,' he said. But how much he admired her courage in coming straight to the point of a subject that would have proved extremely difficult for him to broach.

'That is,' she said, 'it hasn't been difficult until now, because you haven't been here to tempt me.'

He looked at her warily, not knowing quite how he should respond. Then, to his surprise, she drew his mouth down to hers and kissed him tenderly on the lips.

'What you meant,' she said, letting him go and handing him back his brandy, 'was, how am I getting along with my nursemaid? And the answer is, she has proved an extremely diverting companion. Where did you find her?'

'I didn't,' he confessed. 'Erich did.'

'Oh. My other nursemaid.' She grinned up at him. 'Little Erich clucks around me like a mother hen,' she explained. 'I think in some bizarre way he feels responsible for what's happened – there are even times when I find myself comforting him, and telling him everything will be all right! Isn't that funny? But I wouldn't be without him for the world.'

François grimaced. 'If anyone is responsible,' he said darkly, 'I am.'

She patted her hair, and stole a quick, nervous glance at herself in the mirror over the hearth. 'No, *chéri*, you mustn't blame yourself,' she said. 'It's done now, and no amount of self-recrimination from you is going to change it. I'm just glad that you're here. I was afraid I might never see you again.' Her lip trembled. 'You did want to see me again, didn't you?' she said, her eyes widening like a child's.

'Of course.'

'Only I got the impression, before . . . before you went away, that perhaps things had changed between us. That you were going to tell me it was over for us.'

Pulling her back into his arms so that she could no longer see his eyes, he said, 'No, I wasn't going to do that.'

'I'm so relieved.' She laughed uneasily. 'I don't think I'd want to carry on if that were true. And thank you for holding the dinner here tonight. It meant a lot to me to know that I was still of some use to you. You made me feel needed again. It's important to feel needed, don't you agree?'

'Yes,' he whispered. 'Yes, it's important.'

'But you don't like discussing feelings, do you?' she said, breaking away from him. 'So shall we change the subject?'

'Aren't you tired?' he asked, watching her as she went to sit down.

'Not really.' Then her face suddenly changed, and she peered up at him from under her lashes and started to giggle. 'Oh, I see,' she said. 'You want to go to bed. Why didn't you say? Oh, François! You haven't forgotten the other things I can do for you, have you? Shall we go into the bedroom, or would you prefer it here?' And getting up from the sofa, she started towards him.

'Élise,' he said, closing his hands over hers as she started to unbutton his fly.

'Yes, *chéri*?' she murmured, putting her head back and gazing up into his eyes.

Dear God, how was he going to tell her? How could he explain that he simply couldn't let her do this?

To his eternal relief the door opened at that moment, and a plain, large-faced woman he had never seen before came into the room.

'*Bonsoir, monsieur*,' she said. 'I am Béatrice.' And from the barely perceptible lift of her eyebrows he realized that she was Élise's 'nursemaid'.

'Béatrice!' Élise cried, turning round. 'What are you doing here?'

'I've come to put you to bed, Élise,' Béatrice answered. 'It is past midnight.'

'But François is here,' Élise said truculently.

'And he will still be here in the morning,' Béatrice declared, looking meaningfully at François. 'So come along now, no arguing.'

Élise shrugged, and giving François a sheepish, naughty look, she obediently walked off to the bedroom.

'I'll be with you in a minute,' Béatrice called after her. Then turning back to François, she said, 'I hope you didn't mind me interrupting, *monsieur*. I'm afraid she is like that with most men who call. She needs to know that they – you – still find her attractive. I say you, because she calls them all François when she is trying to seduce them.'

'Oh, God!' François groaned. 'I had no idea.'

'No. Well, how could you? I hope you don't mind staying the night. The maid has prepared the spare room for you. It's only that if Élise wakes in the early hours and remembers that you were here, then discovers you have left, I'm afraid she won't take it too well. Frankly, I'm surprised I managed to get her off to bed so easily now. She got herself quite worked up earlier when she knew she was going to see you.'

Béatrice hesitated a moment, then said, 'I'm afraid there's no easy way of telling you this, *monsieur*, but I think you should know that she has convinced herself you are going to marry her. She tells me at least a dozen times a day how much she loves you, how much you love her, and that you will find the man who attacked her and kill him. Erich reassures her on this point, since it is something she needs to hear, but as far as you marrying her is concerned, she refuses to understand that it is not possible. She says you don't love your wife, and she has all but begged Erich to arrange for someone to "remove" her, as she puts it. She even goes so far as to insist that he will be doing you a favour if he does so. Of course,' she went on, when she saw how strained François' face had become, 'she only says these things when her mind is obscured from reason, but nevertheless I thought I should warn you.'

'Warn is a strong word to use, Béatrice,' he said.

'She can be very determined, *monsieur*, as I'm sure you know. And with the contacts she has, she doesn't necessarily need Erich to carry out her wishes.'

He closed his eyes as the memory of the movie stuntman, Philippe Mauclair, swelled to the front of his mind. 'No, she doesn't,' he said. 'And I thank you for telling me this. I shall rely on you to inform either Erich or me if you feel there is any danger of her pursuing this plan.'

'Of course,' she said. Then, after a pause, 'Maybe now is not the time, *monsieur*, but perhaps we should at some point discuss the possibility of having her institutionalized.'

'No!' he said sharply. 'No. If she had no clarity of mind at all, I might agree – but she has already suffered so much because of me . . . I will not even consider the idea. Now, I think I'll take myself off to bed.'

'*Monsieur*,' Béatrice said, as he reached the door. 'There is one other thing, I'm afraid. It is concerning Halunke.'

François turned back. 'Yes?' he said in a tight voice.

'Corinne, your son's nanny, managed to get a message to me which I received earlier this evening. It would appear that your wife thinks Halunke might be back at Lorvoire.'

François closed his eyes. 'Might?' he said.

'No one has actually seen him.'

'No one has ever seen him, apart from Élise.'

'And then he was wearing a mask.'

'Yes,' he said. 'Have you told Erich?'

'I caught him as he was going down the stairs. He told me to tell you he has already set out for Lorvoire.'

- 404 -

François knew he must not over-react, but knowing how he had deceived von Liebermann, his instinct was to follow von Pappen to Lorvoire immediately.

As if reading his thoughts, Béatrice said, 'Erich also told me to advise you not to go to Lorvoire. At least, not until you hear from him. Your presence there would negate the purpose of his visit.'

François seemed thoughtful, almost as if he hadn't heard what she'd said. 'I'll give Erich until tomorrow evening to contact me,' he said. 'If I haven't heard from him by then, I shall go to Lorvoire myself.'

It was a decision he would regret for the rest of his life.

Claudine burst out of her bedroom onto the landing of their Paris home, fastening her watch around the wrist of her black glove and struggling to keep purse and hat under her arm. She and Monique had taken the early train from Chinon, and had arrived at the Bois de Boulogne around eleven o'clock. Now it was fast approaching one, Monique had already gone out to meet an old school friend at the Ritz, and if she, Claudine, didn't hurry she was going to be late for her lunch with Tante Céline.

Finally snapping the watch into place, she started down the stairs just as Magaly called out after her.

'Yes, I have it!' she cried in answer. 'I should be back around four, but if Solange telephones tell her she can reach me at Tante . . .' She stopped dead. Standing at the front door, looking up at her with his piercing black eyes, was François.

Her first instinct was to turn and run back up the stairs. She couldn't face him now, not when she was so unprepared. But his eyes held her, and she felt the blood running hotly in her veins. Longing filled her, so powerful that she had to grip the bannister to stop herself falling.

'What are you doing here?' she said, her voice barely above a whisper.

Her question seemed to amuse him. 'I live here, remember?'

She was in such turmoil that she hardly knew what she was saying, 'But . . . the letter. In the letter you said . . .'

'You thought I was never coming back?' he said. 'So did I. At least, I hoped I wasn't.'

His words viciously stripped away her panic, leaving her with a raw, aching emptiness. 'Are you all right?' she heard herself ask.

'As you can see,' he answered. 'And you? How are you?'

'I'm well. Louis misses you,' she added, after a pause.

He looked away, but not before she had seen the quick pain in his eyes.

He knew he should walk into the study now, get away from her before . . .

'François . . .'

He looked up, but the hunted, almost desperate look retreated from her eyes and she only smiled and shrugged awkwardly.

'You look lovely,' he remarked, noting that she was wearing the short sable coat he had bought her. 'But then you always do.'

She watched him take off his hat and put it on the table beside the front door. Then he looked at her again, measuring her with an arrogant smile.

'If you have an engagement, don't let me keep you,' he said abruptly. Then he turned and walked into the study.

How could seven months away from her have done this to him, he wondered angrily. How could that look in her eyes, the one he had seen so many times before, have suddenly now the power to crack the barrier he had always held between them? What was happening to him that he should want so desperately to take her in his arms, when before he had always managed to resist her?

He tensed as the door opened, and felt the anger spring to

his lips as he turned to look at her. But when he saw the temper flash in her eyes, his own evaporated, and he relaxed, smiling, against the edge of the desk. This was the Claudine he knew, the Claudine he could handle.

'Whatever engagement I have can wait,' she snapped. 'You owe me an explanation, François, and I want to hear it now.'

He nodded. 'I take it you are referring to the contents of the letter I sent my father?'

'Naturally.'

'Then I think you can be in no doubt . . .'

'But how dare you!' she seethed, slamming the door behind her. 'How dare you think you could dismiss me like a servant? I am your wife! Louis is your son! Have you no conscience, François?'

'You need to ask?' he remarked dryly. 'And what is all this anger anyway? I thought I'd given you what you wanted. The freedom to marry Armand.'

'The Catholic church does not permit divorce,' she cried.

'But it does permit annulment,' he said, not without irony.

'It's too late for that! We have a son, remember!'

'Non-consummation is not the only grounds for annulment,' he answered. 'And if my father disinherits me, which I have good reason to believe he will in the next few days, I think you will find the Bishop of Touraine sympathetic to your cause.'

She stared at him in horror. He meant it. He did want to be rid of her. Her feelings were in turmoil. She wanted him. God, she wanted him so much . . . But she wouldn't think about that now. 'So you are a traitor?' she breathed.

'I'm working with the Germans, yes,' he said, folding his arms. 'In fact they have promoted me to the rank of commandant.'

'No!' she cried, clasping her hands to her head. 'No. You

can't! You're French, your family are French! Haven't you considered what this will do to them?'

'I have considered,' he said, taking a cigarette from the box on the desk and lighting it. 'But we're getting away from the point. Which is, that you now have grounds for your annulment, and this time I will do nothing to stand in your way.'

'I don't want an annulment!'

She cried out as he suddenly gripped her arm and dragged her towards him. 'You do!' he said viciously. 'Do you hear me? You do!'

She looked up at him, frightened and bewildered. There were tears in her eyes, and as her lips started to tremble he suddenly pushed her away. 'Go, Claudine,' he growled. 'Go back to Armand. I don't want you. I never have.'

She stood staring at the window, tears rolling down her cheeks. 'But I want you,' she said quietly, unable to stop herself.

'*No!*' he roared.

There was a long, long silence. The clock over the mantle ticked away the minutes, and François ground out his cigarette. It was tearing him apart to hurt her like this. But why was this happening now? Why was he allowing her to break down his defences at a time when it was more important than ever that they remain invincible? And why, now, was he so longing to tell her how much he wanted her too? How much he loved her. The words were there in his throat, clamouring to be spoken, but he wouldn't, he couldn't, utter them. As von Liebermann himself had pointed out, he was a man who could not allow himself the luxury of love . . .

And yet, how could he carry on like this? Looking at her now, he saw how straight she held herself, how she averted her head so he could not see her pain, and her courage and dignity wrenched at his heart. He had always known how much she loved him. He had known it, probably, before she knew it herself. But he had hardened his heart, pushed her away – though there were times, so many times, when it had half-killed him to do it. It had never been easy, even at the start, before he loved her, but most difficult of all had been the times when he made love to her, when her exquisite body moved beneath his with such hunger that it was enough to seduce his very soul. But still he had held back, even though her every move, every breath, every murmur, was a source of unbearable torture for him. She was his wife, and he longed for her with an ache that knew no threshold of pain.

And as that ache once again surged through his loins, he closed his eyes and willed her to leave. But still she didn't move. He wondered how much longer he could hold on. The desire to touch her, to feel her mouth beneath his, was becoming so intense that it was almost beyond his control. Then suddenly his feelings threatened to overpower him. He knew if she didn't leave now, that very instant, there would be nothing he could do to stop himself pulling her into his arms and crushing her with the full force of his love.

She told herself that soon, any minute now, she would be able to walk away. She must go, and she must not turn back, because if she did she knew she would tell him. She knew that she would be unable to stop herself falling to the floor in front of him and confessing how deeply she loved him. How the need to feel his arms around her was tormenting her beyond endurance. But she would rather die than let him see her like that. And rather die than see the contempt in his eyes as she begged him.

She started to move, and for one terrifying moment felt that she couldn't. It was as though the tension between them was holding her back, pulling her to him; but taking a breath, she willed herself to try again. She heard him move, and as she felt his hand on her shoulder the breath locked in her throat. His fingers brushed against her neck, and as her head fell back she gave a tortured, choking sob.

He grabbed her into his arms, holding her against him, pressing her face to his neck and breathing the scent of her hair. He could feel her trembling, just as he could feel his own need tearing through him. He lifted her face, and as desire engulfed them he covered her mouth with his.

She clung to him, pushing hard against him, wanting to lose herself in him so that he would never let her go again. Her body shook. She could feel his hands in her hair, his mouth covering her face with kisses, and all she could hear was the agony in his voice as he repeated over and over again, 'Oh my God, my God, Claudine. I love you. I love you.' Then his mouth was on hers again, sucking her lips between his own, thrusting his tongue into her mouth.

The telephone behind them started to ring, and there was nothing in the world that could have torn him away from her then – except his fear of Halunke. But as he started to pull away she clung to him, begging him with her eyes to stay with her. He kissed her again, more urgently and more passionately than before, then he gently removed her arms from his neck and turned back to the desk.

He picked up the receiver, his eyes on Claudine as she walked to the window. Instead of von Pappen's voice, as he had expected, he heard Lucien's. 'Yes,' he said gruffly. 'Claudine is here.'

She looked up, and the way he was looking at her sent a shock of such commanding hunger through her body that she felt herself start to sway.

'Yes, Lucien, it is François,' he said. Then after a pause, 'I arrived yesterday.'

He said no more after that, listening to his brother, and Claudine watched him, unable to tear her eyes away. Then she saw the blood drain from his face, his knuckles whiten with the tension of his grip, and in his eyes, as he looked back at her, a sudden appalling rage. Her heart leapt into her throat and she started towards him.

'We'll be there as soon as we can,' François said finally, and replaced the receiver.

Already her eyes were wide with terror as she whispered, 'It's Louis, isn't it? I know it. François, what's happened to him?'

'Sssh,' he said sharply. 'Calm yourself. Louis is all right.'

'Then what is it? What's happened? Why are you looking like that?'

'It's Papa,' he answered, dashing a hand savagely through his hair.

'What about him?' she cried.

He raised his eyes to hers, and his haunted, murderous face sent a jolt of pure terror searing through her veins. 'What about him?' she cried again – then she screamed as he swung round and smashed his fist into the mirror behind him.

'He's dead!' he roared. 'My father is dead!'

– 23 –

By the time they arrived at Lorvoire it had been dark for some hours. From where she was sitting in the back of the Citröen, Claudine had watched François throughout the journey, every now and again catching a glimpse of his thunderous face in the mirror as he drove furiously through the night. Before they left she had telephoned Tante Céline to ask her to go to the Ritz for Monique. She would have gone herself, except that she didn't want to leave François. But as she'd bandaged his hand and they'd waited for Monique, she had watched him withdraw so deeply into himself until he had appeared almost oblivious to her presence.

Absently, she stroked Monique's hand where it was resting in her lap. She knew from the steady sound of her breathing that she had finally fallen into a doze. She had taken the news badly; as they set out she had become almost hysterical, recalling the last time they had all been in Paris, when her father had stood at the drawing-room window with an arm round Solange, waving her off . . . To where? She couldn't remember. All she remembered was that he had been standing there, his kind, smiling face reflecting all the love he felt for his daughter . . . At that point she had collapsed into Claudine's arms, and Claudine had stopped trying to persuade François to let her drive.

Now, as he steered the car into the drive of the château, he said in a voice made hoarse by too many cigarettes, 'I'm sorry. I know how much you loved him. You must be hurting too.'

She was, but that didn't matter when she could see how brutally he was fighting his own pain. For now she had to be strong, and keep herself together for him, and for . . . She closed her eyes as she wondered how Solange had taken the news, and she knew that was uppermost in François' mind too as he pulled the car to a halt outside the front door.

As they got out, Lucien came down the steps to greet them. He took Monique in his arms, then turned to François.

'How is *Maman*?' François asked.

'She hasn't cried yet,' Lucien answered. Then with a sigh he added, 'I wish she didn't worry about me so, it's only that that has stopped her. She feels she has to be strong for me.'

François nodded, then turning to Claudine he took her by the elbow and ushered her into the château.

They found Solange in the semi-darkness of the family room, sitting beside the fire in the deep, worn armchair Louis had always used. Her eyes were wide and staring, and Claudine's heart turned over as she saw how harshly she was wringing her hands. As they walked in, Doctor Lebrun and Father Pointeau got to their feet, but François ignored them as his mother's tormented eyes met his. They all heard her choke, then turned away as a heart-rending cry broke from her lips and she stumbled into her son's arms.

Solange's body was racked by sobs as François led her from the room, and as the door closed behind them Monique turned to Claudine, burying her face in her hands.

'Poor *Maman*!' she cried. 'Oh, poor, poor *Maman*! What is she going to do without him, Claudine? He was her whole life.'

'Ssh,' Claudine whispered, putting her arms around her. 'François will take care of her. So will we.' She took the glass of brandy Lucien held out, and put it to Monique's lips. 'What was it?' she said quietly, looking at Doctor Lebrun. 'How did he die?'

'He had a heart-attack,' the doctor answered, shaking his head sorrowfully.

'It could have happened at any time,' Lucien added. 'We all knew that. But it still comes as a shock.'

They all looked up as the door opened and Jean-Paul, the butler, came in. '*Monsieur* asks if you will wait to speak to him,' he said to Doctor Lebrun.

Doctor Lebrun nodded, and Jean-Paul went quietly from the room. Many of the staff had left now, either to join the army or to go to work in the factories, but there was still Arlette, the cook, and the ladies' maids who would need his comfort that night.

'I want to go to *Maman*,' Monique said, but as she started towards the door Father Pointeau put a hand on her shoulder.

'Leave her for now,' he said. 'She needs to cry, and François is the only one she feels she doesn't have to be strong for. She'll sleep soon anyway, the doctor has given her some pills.'

Monique allowed Claudine to lead her to the sofa. Lucien came to sit the other side of her and Claudine held them both as they wept and talked of their memories, laughed, and wept again.

It was long past midnight by the time Claudine and Lucien took Monique up to bed. Then, hugging each other, they parted outside her door and Claudine went up to her apartment.

Despite her tiredness and the dull, distant ache around her heart, she could feel the gnawing pangs of hunger. It was hours since she had had a meal, but she knew that if she tried to eat she would be unable to. François was with Doctor Lebrun now, they had been together for some time but it wasn't only that which told her there was something odd about Louis' death, it was the way François himself had reacted to the news.

More than an hour passed before she heard his footsteps on the stairs, and as the door to the sitting-room opened she turned away from the fire to look at him. His anger seemed to have abated, but his pale, scarred face was ravaged with exhaustion.

'You should have gone to bed,' he said.

'I wanted to wait.'

His eyes were blank as they looked into hers, but when she took a step towards him he turned away. 'Go to bed,' he said.

'François,' she pleaded.

'No!' he cried angrily. 'Just go to bed.'

But she put her arms around him anyway, and to her relief he pulled her against him and buried his face in her neck.

They stood like that for a long time, neither of them speaking or moving. The only sound was the wind outside and the gentle tick of the clock.

'Come along,' she said finally. 'Come to bed.'

As he raised his head she looked up into his face and saw that his eyes were dry and empty.

'I can't,' he said gruffly.

'But you must, you're exhausted.'

He shook his head. 'I mean, I can't come with you.' And before she could protest, he pulled away from her, saying, 'Go to your room. Go now, before . . .'

'But François . . .'

'No, Claudine! I know what you're going to say, but you must forget what happened between us today. You must put it from your mind, pretend it . . . Get your annulment, marry Armand. Then get as far away from me as you can, do you hear me? As far away as you can.'

'No!' she cried. 'I can't pretend that I don't feel the way I do, and neither can you. We've got to stop this, François! You love me, I know you do . . .'

He put his fingers over her lips. 'Don't say any more. Just do as I tell you, Claudine. Please!' And before she could protest any further, he walked into his room and locked the door behind him.

He knew that it was going to take a great deal more than a mere door to shut her out now, and as he stood in the middle of his darkened room, staring sightlessly down at the bed, he could still feel the softness of her body against his and the raging need to hold her again. But the death of his father had been a cruel and senseless reminder of why he could not give in to the demands of his heart. He still had no way of knowing if Halunke had been responsible, but the timing was too much of a coincidence for him to ignore, despite what Doctor Lebrun had told him. It seemed Louis had been down at the chapel, praying, when his heart went into arrest. There had been no one around to help him, but he had managed to drag himself to the door, where Armand had found him. By then he was already dead.

His one hope now was that Erich had managed to get to

him before he died – he simply could not bear the thought of Louis going to his grave in the belief that his eldest son was a traitor. But whether Erich had reached him or not, there was no possibility now of being disinherited. He was already the Comte de Rassey de Lorvoire, and nothing he or anyone else could do would change that.

And that was why, in his heart, he knew that there was more to his father's death than Doctor Lebrun realized. Halunke was here, he could feel it in his bones. Von Liebermann had sent him as retribution and reminder.

Squeezing his eyes tightly closed, he let his head fall forward. Dear God in heaven, how was a man to choose between his family and his country? He would never dare to risk deceiving the Germans again, not after this. And yet . . . perhaps he was wrong. Perhaps the death had been as Doctor Lebrun said. As long as there was doubt, there might still be a way . . .

He was woken early the following morning by a knock on his door, and as Jean-Paul came in with the letter on a silver salver, he knew even before he opened it that the shred of hope he had clung to was already gone. Inside the envelope was a single sheet of paper, and on it was written just one word – LOUIS.

Over the next few days, as first Tante Céline arrived and then her father, Claudine watched François build a barrier around himself so invincible that she feared she might never get through to him. He went out of his way to avoid her, and though it hurt her deeply to do it, she decided to keep her distance too, knowing that her presence only brought him pain. But she always knew where he was, and if he wasn't with Solange or in the nursery with Louis and Corinne, he was out riding in the forest. When he returned, soaked by the rain or frozen by the wind, she could see he was still no closer to sorting out the confusion in his mind than when he had set out. Occasionally she would find him watching her, maybe at the breakfast table, or as she walked up the stairs to their apartment – but the instant she met his eyes he turned away. They had barely spoken since the night of Louis' death, yet somehow she knew that she was almost constantly on his mind, and instinct told her that he was trying to reach a decision concerning their marriage.

Then one morning she saw him talking to Armand outside the wine caves. She watched from an upstairs window, dreading to think what he might be saying. But no matter what, and even if he told her there could never be anything between them, she had made up her mind that she would remain his wife until the day she died. He couldn't stop her loving him – but how much easier it would be for them if he could find it in himself to trust her! To tell her what was going on ... When he left, as she was sure he would sooner or later, and Lucien rejoined his regiment, she would be responsible for Solange and Monique. And if they faced a threat as dangerous as she now suspected, then the only way she could see of combating it was to know precisely what it was.

It was in the early hours of the morning following the day of the funeral that Erich von Pappen finally came to the château. François let him in through the nursery landing and led him past Claudine's bedroom to the sitting-room.

'How is Élise?' he said, knowing that von Pappen had been with her for the past five days.

'Better now,' von Pappen answered, taking the cognac François held out. He went to sit on the chair beside the fire. 'It was the worst I've seen her,' he said with a sigh, 'or I would have come sooner.'

'She was bad the night I was there,' François said, lighting a cigarette. 'She woke up screaming, but when I went into the room she wouldn't let me near her. She thought I was Halunke.' He drew on his cigarette and inhaled deeply. 'It was terrible, I've never seen anything like it. It was as though she was possessed by some kind of demon. I guess she is, if fear is a demon.' He paused for a while as he remembered that night, and how she had gnashed her teeth, torn her hair and thrown herself savagely against the wall. But once she recognized him she had allowed him to carry her back to bed, where he had lain with her, holding her in his arms until she had finally fallen asleep again.

From the corner of his eye von Pappen watched François curiously. He had been in François' employ for five years now and probably knew him better than any man, which was why he was so quick to detect the change in him. He wasn't sure yet what it was, except that the customary harshness was absent from his eyes. Perhaps the death of his father had in some way softened him – which, von Pappen decided, was no bad thing, providing it didn't in any way affect his judgement.

'I just wish to God she knew who he was,' François sighed. 'What about you, have you come up with anything yet?'

Von Pappen twitched as he too lit a cigarette. 'No. But I think I'm a little closer now than I was before.'

'Oh?'

'I still have no idea who he is, but I think his revenge could have something to do with Hortense de Bourchain after all.'

François showed no sign of surprise. 'What makes you say that?' he asked, going to sit on the sofa.

'I don't know. It's just a hunch, but it's one I'm going to pursue a little further.'

François said no more on the matter. This was von Pappen's way; and as soon as he had anything worth reporting, he would do so. 'Did you see my father before he died?' he asked, feeling himself tense in dread of the answer.

– 418 –

'Yes.'

'You told him everything?'

'Yes.'

François' relief was evident. Grinding out his cigarette and lighting another, he said, 'So what happened that morning?'

Von Pappen twisted in his chair so that he could see François better. 'I did as you said, and made contact with Corinne,' he told him. 'She arranged for me to meet the Comte down at the *mairie* first thing in the morning. The Mayor of Chinon was due to arrive at eleven, with a delegation of officials from Tours, to discuss the distribution of rations. I was to go in as an early arrival from the delegation – in disguise, of course – which I did. By the time the delegation arrived I had managed to persuade your father to disown you, and though he was unhappy about it, he was finally persuaded that it was the only way. I stayed for the meeting, and as we left the Comte whispered to me that he was going over to the chapel to pray for you, and that I was to tell you that he loved you deeply. That was the last time I saw him. I knew nothing of his death until Béatrice told me when I arrived back in Paris.'

François' face was strained. He took a deep breath and let his head fall back against the sofa.

Von Pappen waited quietly, puffing on his cigarette and staring down at the flickering flames in the hearth. 'I am truly sorry, François,' he murmured finally. 'I know how much he meant to you.'

They both looked up as the door opened and Claudine, pulling a blue satin negligé around her, came into the room.

Von Pappen immediately got to his feet, and as François looked at her, her beautiful face flushed from sleep and her raven hair tousled around her shoulders, he felt the pain of his love shoot straight through his heart.

'I heard voices,' she said, looking at him.

He smiled, and keeping his eyes on hers, said, 'Erich, I don't believe you have ever met my wife. *Chérie*, may I introduce you to Erich von Pappen.'

'*Madame la Comtesse*,' von Pappen said, walking over to her and taking her hand.

François smiled again as he saw her confusion. This was probably the first time anyone had referred to her by her title, and it was also the first time since the day his father died that he had shown her any affection. But he had done a lot of thinking over the past few days, and had now reached a decision. He hoped to God it was the right one, for it entailed telling her everything. It would be a tremendous burden for her, he knew that, but of all the qualities she possessed, the two he admired perhaps the most were her resilence and her determination. Later, no doubt, von Pappen would accuse him of insanity for listening to his heart rather than his head, but that would only come once Erich was over the shock of seeing him do something he had never done before – which was to trust a woman, and more particularly, a woman he loved.

'Come and sit down,' he said, surprising both Claudine and Erich. And as she walked uncertainly towards him, he patted the cushion beside him and pulled her into the circle of his arm. 'I'm sorry if we woke you,' he murmured, kissing the top of her head as she rested it on his shoulder – and he almost laughed to see the astonishment on von Pappen's face.

He knew that for a while Claudine would be too dazed to take in much of what they were saying, but he would go over it again in detail when Erich had left. For now, he could feel the barrier he had built around himself over the past few days begin to re-erect itself – this time to include Claudine. And he was amazed and gratified by how right it felt.

'Have you any messages for me?' he said to von Pappen, who had returned to his chair.

'You mean from. . . ?' Von Pappen's eyes moved incredulously to Claudine.

'Yes, I mean from von Liebermann,' François said, keeping his eyes on von Pappen and at the same time running his fingers lazily through Claudine's hair. 'Erich,' he added, looking down at her, 'is my courier.'

She nodded, remembering now where she had heard the name before. Louis had mentioned it the day the lorries full of boxes arrived.

'Go ahead, Erich,' François encouraged.

'Er well, yes,' von Pappen stammered. 'Er, he sympathizes over the loss of your father, but would like you to return to Berlin within the next week.'

Claudine stiffened, and François hugged her. 'His condolences are somewhat out of place, Erich,' he said. And suddenly he wished Claudine wasn't there to hear this; he would have liked to break it to her more gently. 'The General, by way of Halunke, is responsible for my father's death.'

Claudine gasped, and von Pappen's queer face froze.

'But it was a heart-attack,' von Pappen finally uttered. 'Béatrice said that he had a heart-attack in the chapel.'

'He did,' François confirmed. Then reaching out for the envelope on the table, he handed it to von Pappen. And when von Pappen saw what it contained, he was clearly too stunned even to twitch.

He looked at François, and when François nodded, passed the note to Claudine.

'I will explain it later, *chérie*,' François told her. 'I don't know how Halunke managed to bring on the heart-attack, but that's clearly what he did,' he went on. 'And just as clearly, he wanted me to know it.'

Von Pappen sucked in his round lips and bowed his head thoughtfully. He didn't like what he was hearing. Things were starting to add up in a way he didn't like at all. But for now he would say nothing. Although François was suffering from the temporary insanity of trusting his wife, he was willing to stake every franc of the considerable salary François paid him that she knew nothing about Hortense de Bourchain – and he was most definitely not going to be the one to tell her.

When he lifted his head again he saw that François was whispering to her, their faces so close that for a moment he thought they were kissing. Then, as François' hand took hers and their fingers entwined, von Pappen could feel the magnetism between them as though it were alive in the air. Quickly he averted his eyes, wishing he could remove his entire self with such speed and silence. Of course he had always known that François loved his wife, he could even pinpoint the day François had realized it himself. But he had never dreamt that François would let it get the better of him like this.

Hearing François give a low, intimate laugh, he fumbled in his pocket for another cigarette. It was only as he lit it and stole another quick look at them that he realized François was laughing at him. And when he saw the way Claudine's magnificent blue eyes were glittering, how her full lips, so red and enticing, were parted in a smile, he found himself wondering how François had managed to resist her for so long.

'Are you going back to Paris tonight?' François asked him. 'Or would you like to stay here?'

'I think I'd like to get back, thank you,' von Pappen answered. 'If I leave now I should be there by dawn.'

'As you please,' François said, getting to his feet. 'I'll see you out.'

'Are you sure this is wise?' von Pappen hissed, as François walked him round to the nursery landing.

'I take it you're referring to my wife?' François answered with a smile. 'Well, the answer is, I don't know Erich – but

I'm going to tell her anyway. She has a right to know. Meanwhile, tell Élise I shall be in Paris sometime in the next few days, but at the same time prepare her for my hasty departure. And Erich,' he said, as he pulled the door open, 'thank you for looking after her.'

Von Pappen blinked, then turned to cross the bridge into the forest. Not only was François de Lorvoire's wife one of the most beautiful creatures he had ever seen, he thought, but she must also be a remarkable woman. In the space of a few short days she had changed her husband beyond recognition. Never, in all the time he had known him, had he seen François display anything approaching the kind of tenderness he had shown that night.

François was still grinning to himself as he walked back into the sitting-room. 'Well,' he said, 'I imagine I've got a lot of explaining to do now.' He turned to look at Claudine, and the smile fell from his lips.

She was standing before the dying embers of the fire, lit only by the amber glow of a lamp behind her, so that her hair, cascading over the blue satin on her shoulders, was like the blaze of a setting sun. She was so beautiful that all he could do was look at her. She turned to face him, almost in a dream. She could hardly dare to believe the depth of the love she sensed in him now. She had waited so long, had wanted him so much, and now he wanted her too.

Suddenly an overpowering surge of longing swept through her body, and as if he felt it he moved swiftly towards her, lifting his arms to take her. As their lips met, he eased her head onto his shoulder, pulling her body round so that he could untie the ribbon at her throat. She moaned softly as he drew the robe from her shoulders, then gasped as his hand lifted her breasts free of her nightdress. She looked down at what he was doing, but he took her chin and lifted her mouth back to his. Then, as he pushed his tongue between her lips and sought her nipples with his fingers, a sudden blaze of passion soared through her and she fell against him, sobbing. He pushed her nightgown to the floor, running his hands over the satin smoothness of her thighs.

'Oh François!' she choked as he drew her to him. 'François. Please! Take me here. I want you now. Oh my God!' she cried, as his fingers found the opening between her legs.

'Be patient, my darling,' he whispered, and lifting her up in his arms, he carried her into the bedroom.

'I want to see you,' she murmured, as he laid her down on the bed, and she reached out to turn on the lamp.

She watched him strip away his clothes, feasting her eyes on the powerful muscles of his arms, his shoulders, his abdomen. And when he removed his trousers a cry escaped from her lips as she saw the sheer magnitude of his erection.

'François,' she sobbed, as he lay on the bed beside her and she turned to push herself against him. 'Please! Don't make me wait any more. I want you now.'

The turbulence in her voice so inflamed him that he knew he could not hold back any longer, and quickly he rolled her onto her back, pushed his legs between hers and positioned himself over her. Then, sliding a hand under her hips, he lifted her to meet him, all the time looking down into her face. He eased himself slowly, slowly into her, watching her eyes widen and her head press back into the pillow as he filled her. But before he reached the full depth of penetration, he pulled back and started to push again.

'Yes, oh, yes,' she moaned, arching her back to take more of him, but again he pulled away. Then he thrust himself so violently into her that she screamed. He pulled back, and thrust again, and again and again until the storm of their passion broke, engulfing them in a love and desire so all-consuming that it was though they had become one. Her nails dug into his back, her legs encircled his waist, and her breasts bounced over her ribs as he slammed into her harder and harder. He held himself up on his arms and they watched him pump in and out of her, so savagely, so hungrily that her breath stopped and her limbs started to lose power.

He was shooting sensations through her that shattered and exploded and soared into every corner of her body. She was on fire, she could neither see nor speak, all she knew was the unbearable, exquisite sensation that burned around the pulsating stem of his penis. She tried to hold onto him, tried to utter his name, but her breath wouldn't come and her arms fell away as the blinding rapture of what he was doing shuddered through her in great spasms of ecstasy.

Then she heard herself sobbing, knew that her head was twisting from side to side. Then his mouth was crushing hers, his hands were pushing her legs wider, and as he began to thrust into the core of her orgasm it burst against him, gripping him, pulling him, commanding the seed from his body.

'Claudine,' he groaned. 'Oh my God! Claudine. God help me!' And with an agonized cry he ground into her with such fury, knowing such ecstasy, that the seed spurted from him. His heart was thumping, his skin glistening with perspiration, and still his seed came. He pulled back, pushed into her again, waiting for the blinding climax to leave him.

When finally it did he lay over her for a long time, struggling to regain his breath and feeling her heart pound against his. He held her tightly in his arms until the strength started to return to his limbs, but when he tried to pull away she clung to him, holding him with her legs. 'No,' she murmured, 'don't leave me. Don't go.' And as her fingers slipped down over his buttocks and pushed between his legs, he knew that he was going to take her again.

Quickly he turned her over, raised her buttocks and buried himself to the full length of his penis. Again she cried out, screaming through clenched teeth, and he took her heavy breasts in his hands, tugged hard at her nipples, squeezing them between his fingers, then pulled her face round to his and sucked greedily at her lips. Then, as he started to circle her clitoris with his finger, she pushed her face into the pillow and sobbed.

A long time later she lay sprawled across him, her arms and legs entwined in his and every pore of her body still tingling with fulfilment. He watched her try to lift her head, but she was still too weak and he chuckled as she gave up. She sank her teeth gently into his arm and idly he traced his finger through the crease between her buttocks. The bed was in turmoil, but he managed to wrench a sheet from the chaos to cover them. Then finally she managed to pull herself up, and looked down at him with eyes that were still dazed.

'I don't know what to say,' she whispered. 'I never knew it could be like that. I never knew . . . Oh, François . . .'

He put a finger over her lips, and lifting his head from the pillow, took first one nipple, then the other gently into his mouth. Then, pulling her down beside him and turning her so that he could see her face, he said, 'There's something I've forgotten to do.'

'There can't be anything else,' she murmured.

'Oh there is, believe me,' he laughed. 'But I wasn't thinking of that.'

'Then what were you thinking of?' she smiled sleepily.

'I was thinking of telling you I love you.'

Her eyes opened, and as she gazed back at him she felt a choking knot of emotion swell in her throat.

'And that I'm sorry for all I've put you through.'

'It doesn't matter,' she whispered. 'Nothing matters except that you love me.' She snuggled back into his arms, thrilling at the feel of his hard body next to hers, the way its strength and power made hers seem so soft and vulnerable.

She was, at long last, where she had always belonged, in his arms and in his heart, and it was as though she had finally found a part of herself that had always been missing. She felt complete.

After a while she looked at him again. His eyes were closed, and her heart tightened with love as she took in every inch of his face: the thick, heavy brows, the hooked nose, the thin lips, powerful jaw, and the unsightly scar. Then, as he opened one eye and smiled, her heart turned over.

She moved onto him, and he put his hands behind his head, looking up at her and watching her face as she sat astride his legs. She ran her hands over his chest, then lowered her eyes to his penis, and as it started to grow she glanced up at him. His eyebrows flickered, and she could see that he was amused by her fascination. Then, taking him in both hands, she caressed him to full erection.

When Claudine woke in the morning the room was flooded with sunlight, and it was several seconds before she realized why her body was aching so. With a smile she turned over – and then her heart contracted with love. For there were her husband and her son together, little Louis' sleeping face resting on his father's shoulder. Her eyes filled with tears. Louis came in to her most every morning, but that morning, having found François there, he had obviously climbed into the other side of the bed. He was curled into the crook of François' arm, his tiny fist bunched under his cheek and his raven black curls tumbling over his forehead. He looked so small beside his father . . . she could hardly believe this was happening, had never dared to believe she could be so happy.

She looked down at the black mass of hair on François' chest and tried to resist the urge to touch him. But when she remembered the things he had done to her the night before, desire surged so fiercely through her loins that her hand reached out for him. And when her eyes moved back to his face she found he was watching her.

She followed his hand as she lifted it to cup her breast, and watched the way he rubbed his thumb over her achingly hard nipple. Her eyes closed and her head fell back, but she knew she must try to control herself while Louis was still there. Then she started to laugh as she heard his melodious little voice ask François what he was doing to *Maman*.

'She's a little sore there and I'm making her feel better,' François laughed, swinging him up in the air and shaking him. 'And now, young man, it's time you went back to your own room to get dressed.'

'But I don't want to,' Louis protested, as François deposited him on the floor. 'I want to stay here with you.'

'Go and dress!' François said sternly.

'But Papa . . .'

'Louis!'

Louis hung his head dolefully then promptly sat himself down on the floor.

Claudine saw François' lips twitch, and had to turn away to hide her own smile.

'Well, there's nothing else for it,' François said, flinging back the sheets and getting out of bed. 'I'll just have to throw you out.'

'But why can't I stay?' Louis groaned, still hanging his head.

'Because *Maman* and I have something we need to do. Now stop arguing.' And taking him by the arm, François pulled him to his feet. He realized immediately that it would have been better to pick him up, but it was too late now, and Louis' black eyes, on a level with his thigh, were round with wonder. François stole a quick look at Claudine and saw that she was convulsed with laughter.

'I'm glad you found that so amusing,' François said, when he had closed and locked the door behind his son. And glowering at her darkly, he added, 'Now I'd better deal with you.'

'Or I with you,' she said, still laughing. He came to stand beside the bed and she sat up and put her arms around his waist. 'I love you,' she smiled, looking up at him. His hands moved into her hair and she heard his breath quicken as she ran her tongue the full length of his penis.

'You don't need to do that, *chérie*,' he murmured, pulling her head back.

'But I want to,' she answered, and lowering her mouth to his testicles, she took them between her lips and started to suck gently. She had never done anything like this before, it had never even occurred to her, but now it seemed the most natural thing in the world, and when she finally looked up at François' face she could see what an effect it was having on him . . . But he had a similar surprise in store for her, and it was almost midday by the time they finally left the bed.

When she joined him an hour later in the sitting-room, he was sitting at the table reading that morning's newspaper. She sensed immediately that his mood had changed, and when he looked up she saw the deep frown between his eyes. She made to kiss him, but he turned his head so that her lips connected with his cheek. Panic flashed through her; she was afraid that even now, after all that had happened between them, he was going to push her away again. But he saw her fear, and pulling her onto his lap, kissed her full on the mouth.

'I don't know what everyone's going to think,' he said, when at last he let her go. 'We've been here all morning . . .'

'Does it matter what everyone thinks? After all, we are married.'

'Yes, it does matter,' he answered. 'That's why we have to talk. That's why we – *I* – was insane to run the risk of staying in bed with you last night. I should have returned to my own room.'

'I should have taken a very dim view of that,' she said, going to sit at the other side of the table.

'I daresay you would.' And to her delight, he laughed. He laughed so rarely, but when he did his whole face was transformed.

'Are you hungry?' he asked.

'Ravenous.'

'Good. Arlette is preparing something for us now. I've asked for it to be served here. I've also asked Corinne to keep Louis occupied. Your father is taking the others to Montsoreau for the day; I don't want us disturbed while we talk. Perhaps by the time I've finished you'll understand why our marriage has been the way it has. Why it was necessary for me to hide my feelings, not only from you but from the rest of the world. It is still necessary, I'm afraid. I don't have to hide them from you any more, but I do from everyone else. And you must do the same.'

She had already decided that she must be pragmatic, that she must respond calmly and reasonably to whatever he was going to tell her, and she started now. 'I'll do whatever you say. But can I ask why you've decided to confide in me? And I'm not searching for compliments, only answers.'

He smiled. 'I took the decision because now that Halunke – that's the code name for the man who's been watching you and Armand – now that he's struck at my family you need to know what danger you face if you stay here.'

'If?'

'We'll come to that later. For now I think it's better if I start at the beginning, which means going back five years to the time when your father introduced me to espionage.'

'My father?' she echoed.

He nodded. 'He's not the diplomat you think him, I'm afraid. He too works in Intelligence. In his case, British Intelligence, naturally. In mine, French.'

'Papa is a *spy*?' she said, hardly able to believe it.

– 430 –

'For want of a better word, yes.'

'Did *Maman* know?'

'No. She died with a great many things unexplained, and that's something he has never been able to forgive himself for. Which is why I've decided that mustn't happen to us. Not,' he added quickly, 'that you are going to die; at least not this week.'

'I hope that was a joke!'

He laughed, but then his face became serious again. 'You're facing a very real danger, Claudine. The man the Germans have employed to ensure my commitment to them is also waging a personal vendetta against me. Who he is, and what is at the root of his vendetta, I haven't yet been able to discover. But I will, I promise you. It's too late for this now, but I wish to God you had listened to me before we were married and had gone back to England as I advised. Of course you didn't then face the danger you do now, at least I wasn't aware that you did, but I still didn't want you in my life. I was committed to my work and wanted nothing to disrupt it. However, your father, and my own, were determined we should marry, as you know, even though your father knew the risks as well as I. And I had made a promise to my father which I couldn't go back on. Nevertheless, I tried everything I could to dissuade you from marrying me – but your determination was even greater than theirs!' He threw her a look to which she responded in kind. 'So, once we were married,' he went on 'the only way I could see of avoiding explanations for my absences was to keep you at a distance. Of course, I didn't love you then, so hurting you was much easier than it has been since.'

'Since when? When did you start loving me, François? I'd like to know.'

'It was the day you almost miscarried with Louis. In fact it must have been before then, but that was when I thought, irrationally, that you were going to die, and then I realized how much you meant to me.'

He stopped as the door opened and Arlette brought in their meal. François continued to talk as they ate, going steadily over the past five years, what he had done, the people he had become involved with.

It was past five o'clock and already growing dark by the time he said, 'So, as Erich told us last night, I have to be back in Berlin by the end of the week. You understand now why I have to go, and you also understand why our feelings for each other must remain a secret from everyone. And I mean everyone. If you ever feel the desire to confide in someone, don't. Not even your aunt. It is the only way I can see of keeping you alive. If Halunke found out that I love you, he wouldn't hesitate to kill you. I'm very much afraid he'll try anyway, sooner or later – he can't be so stupid as to think you don't matter to me at all.'

'I'm afraid,' she began, clearing her throat, 'that Lucien and Armand both know I'm in love with you. Come to that, Erich knows that you're in love with me.'

'That doesn't matter. Erich can be trusted. They all can, but I still don't want Lucien or Armand to know how I feel. It's simply safer that way. Lucien will be rejoining his regiment tomorrow anyway, but Armand is still very upset about the break-up of your affair. If he knew how I feel about you, he might tell his mother, who might tell someone else. And so it goes on. It's better not to put the burden on anyone – because that, *chérie*, is what it is. A burden. However, I want to ease it for you as much as I can, which is why I've spoken to Armand. I've asked him to take you and Louis to America, and he has agreed. I'd like you to go, Claudine.'

'No.' She shook her head firmly. 'I don't want to, and even if I did, I couldn't.'

'Why?'

'You know why, François. I can't leave your mother and Monique, not now Louis is . . .' She paused and turned her head away for a moment. 'So I shall stay,' she said. 'Please, don't let's argue about it.'

He had known that that would be her answer, so he didn't waste time arguing. 'Both Armand and I guessed what you would say,' he said, 'so Armand has agreed that he won't attempt to join the army again, but will remain here to protect you as best he can. I'd never have asked him if there had been anyone else, but there's no one. And of course he has a very real affection for *Maman* and Monique. And I presume I can trust you to remain faithful to me from now on?' he added, with an ironic lift of his eyebrows.

The look she gave him in response was so blatantly seductive that he stood up, walked round the table and gave her a lingering kiss on the mouth.

'Let's go back to the Germans,' she said shakily, as he strolled over to the fireplace and took his cigarettes from the mantleshelf. 'You say they control Halunke, but I don't understand how.'

'It's very easy. The hold they have over him is simply that if he doesn't do as they say, they will reveal his identity to me. And he will know only too well that once I know who he is, his days are numbered and he'll never accomplish his revenge.'

'But why do the Germans want you so badly? Surely they have their own agents?'

'Naturally they do. But the contacts I have here in France, in Britain, Italy, North Africa, make me an extremely valuable commodity to them. And having this kind of hold over me – someone endangering my family the way Halunke is – suits them perfectly.'

'And they gave him permission to kill your father because you deceived them over these Frenchmen? I can hardly believe it. It seems . . . Well, it seems so extreme.'

'Their methods are extreme, *chérie*. Which is why I can't run the risk of deceiving them again.'

'So what are you going to do?'

'God only knows,' he sighed. 'All the information I have given them to date has come from the French Government itself. Or in some cases, the British. But since the Allies have discovered that someone has a personal vendetta against me, they've closed ranks – wisely, I must admit – which means they are no longer prepared to give me information to feed to the Germans. And if the Germans don't get what they want, they'll tell Halunke he's free to do as he pleases. Of course, this game we've played – the SR, the *Services de Renseignements* and I – with the Germans was bound to come to an end sooner or later, and it's my guess the Germans have known for some time they were being duped, not only by me but by three or four other French agents as well. Until now it has suited the Germans to play the game too, but things are changing fast and already the French Secret Service have pulled my colleagues out of Germany. They, of course, don't face the threat of Halunke. For me, there's nothing the French can do. They can't even run the risk of trusting me any longer. And nor should you.'

'But surely you're not saying that you're going to become a traitor?'

'Who knows? In a month, a year from now they may force me to make a choice between my family and my country. And when it comes to the crunch – which it will do, if we don't discover Halunke's identity – there's no knowing which I shall choose.'

She took a moment to digest this, then looking at him again, she said, 'Do you have *any* idea who Halunke might be?'

He shook his head. 'No. Erich has a hunch, though I think he's heading down the wrong path.'

'Have you told him that?'

'No, because there have been times in the past when I have been wrong and Erich right. That's why I trust him so implicitly. However, there is someone else, besides von Liebermann, who knows who Halunke is.'

'Well?' she said, when he stopped.

'His name is Max Helber – also a member of the Abwehr.'

'Will he tell you?'

'Perhaps. In return for certain . . . shall we say, favours?'

'What kind of favours?'

'The kind of favours I would rather not discuss.'

She looked puzzled for a moment, then her eyes dilated. 'Do you mean . . .? Is he . . .?'

He nodded slowly. 'Yes, my darling, he is a homosexual.'

'But you can't do it!'

'I may have to if Erich doesn't come up with an answer soon.'

They were both subdued when they went to join the family for dinner, and later, as she lay in his arms, she wanted to weep for the choices that lay before him. She knew from the way he made love to her, without the urgency of the night before, but with a tenderness and feeling that filled her heart with love, that he was thinking the same. If only there was something she could do! But she had no means of providing him with the information the Germans required, nor was she equipped to satisfy the desires of Max Helber.

She lay awake for a long time, listening to the steady rhythm of his breathing and thinking back over the three years she had known him. It was a terrible pass they had come to now, but nothing, nothing in the world, would ever make her regret marrying him.

Halunke's breath thickened the fog around his face as he pressed through the forest, his feet slithering in the slimy undergrowth. Once or twice he chuckled aloud to himself, elated by his discovery. So, de Lorvoire did love his wife after all! Even so, there was no reason to make a move on her just yet. It would be much more intriguing to see how far down the road of traitordom he could push de Lorvoire before letting him know that it had all been for nothing ... And in the meantime, should von Liebermann for any reason require that de Lorvoire be taught another lesson, why not remove his beloved brother? Or better still, his wife's protector the *vigneron*? The perversity of this idea appealed to him strongly, and he laughed even louder.

Pity, he thought, as he got into his car, that the old man had died of his own volition – well, almost. For it was the revelation of his, Halunke's, identity that had jolted the old Comte's heart into arrest.

– 24 –

In the weeks that followed François' departure from Lorvoire, Claudine experienced such paradoxes of emotion that she often found herself laughing and crying at the same time. Things had moved so quickly between them in such a short time that she couldn't get used to the idea that he loved her, and there were times when she was half-afraid it had all happened in a dream. But then she had only to picture his face in her mind's eye – to see the tenderness of his smile as he gazed into her eyes, to feel the power of his touch as he caressed her, to hear the humorous lilt in his voice when he told her he loved her – for her heart to fill with love and certainty. That he trusted her, that he had chosen to draw her so securely into his life, made her almost dizzy with joy and relief.

But euphoric as she was, she never allowed herself to lose

sight of the danger they faced. In a way she felt almost grateful for the danger, for that was what had finally brought them together; but she was never so blinkered by love that she forgot the terrible dilemma it had forced upon François.

As time passed she became increasingly frustrated by all the things she had forgotten to ask him. The boxes in the cellar still remained a mystery, and she would like to have known what lay behind his break-up with Élise. But what she now longed most desperately to know was why he had killed Hortense de Bourchain. She couldn't explain it, but she had an uncanny feeling that what had happened then might somehow lie at the root of what was happening now. She was even tempted to ask Armand to tell her again what he had seen, but somehow that seemed disloyal to François. She would ask him herself, the very next time she saw him – she was in no doubt that he would come back, simply because she refused to consider the possibility that he might not. That he had gone to Berlin was all she knew; she could not contact him, and he had made it plain that, except in case of dire emergency, he would not contact her.

She had no idea if Halunke was still in Lorvoire. Lately, she had not seemed to sense his presence. And events in the world outside were taking such a horrifying turn that even the threat Halunke presented seemed mild by comparison.

The *Boches* were coming. Everyone in France knew it, and the nation was edging towards the brink of panic. Claudine felt it in the air every time she went out, and inside the château the talk was of little else. It was as though they were all bracing themselves for the day when their lives would be trampled by the advancing German army. Again, people were fleeing Paris, and refugees from the north streamed through Touraine, leaving a trail of terror in their wake.

Solange, still heartbroken over the death of Louis, waited every day for news of Lucien. Claudine did her best to comfort her, and telephoned their contacts in Paris, but without Louis to pull strings for them there seemed no hope of getting any information. All she could gather was that the Government was in chaos, and though she did her best to hide it, that alarmed her even more than the whooping cry of air-raid sirens and the eerie silence that followed. The fear was becoming oppressive, it seemed to be closing in from all sides – the Germans, Halunke, and the constant dread of what might be happening to François.

Then one day while she, Solange and little Louis were helping the one gardener left at Lorvoire to dredge the pond at the edge of the forest, Magaly called her inside and handed her a letter.

'A peculiar little man, with the most dreadful nervous affliction, just knocked on the bridge door and gave this to Corinne,' she said.

Claudine knew at once who it was from. Thrusting her gardening gloves into Magaly's hands, she dashed up the stairs to the privacy of her bedroom, where she tore the letter open and with her heart in her mouth feasted her eyes on the words François had written.

Chérie, I know I said I would contact you only in an
emergency, but I feel I must tell you this, if only to
reassure you. General von Liebermann has sworn
that for as long as I remain with the Abwehr,
Halunke will cease to be a threat. Naturally I have
reaffirmed my allegiance, though I still have no idea
what will be expected of me. My only hope is that
when I finally come out of this I will be worthy of
your love. I think of you night and day, my love. If I
had known what a difference you would make to my
life, I would never have embarked upon my present
road. But it is too late now for regrets, we must
think only of the future.

You will know by now that Belgium has surrendered and that the Germans are already on French soil. I hear talk every day, here, how soon France will be conquered and how poor the morale of our troops is. Try to prepare yourself, and those around you, my love, for the fall of our nation, as it is almost sure to come.

And yet, in spite of this, you must keep heart, my darling, and please take care of yourself and of our son. You mean more to me than I can even begin to express. I wish I could have held you in my arms to tell you this, but try to imagine I am there, and be in no doubt of how much I love you. *Ton mari*, François.

She swallowed hard on her tears, and walking over to the bed, lifted the pillow where his head had lain and hugged it to her. This moment of weakness would pass, she knew, but dear God, she missed him! Maybe if they had had more time together, had shared their feelings sooner . . . She felt so cheated, so unfulfilled . . . She pulled a face, as if mocking her self-pity, and looked down at the letter. She longed to keep it, to hold it to her heart and read it over and over again, but he had told her before he left that she must destroy any written communication as soon as she had read it. As she put a match to it, watching it curl and twist in the flames, she wished her dread were as easy to destroy.

That afternoon she, Monique and Solange went to the little cinema in Chinon to watch the newsreels. They went almost every day now, standing in the aisles when there were no seats to be had, cheering and booing with the others who had come from miles around to watch the progress of the war. Sometimes Claudine discussed the war with Armand, but she always came away angry at his lassitude. He had changed so much since they had parted: he was a bitter, rejected man and did little to disguise it. His sarcastic remarks about François sickened her, but she said nothing, torn by guilt at the way she had so selfishly used him.

Then, at the beginning of June, even Armand was forced to look beyond himself. The Germans bombed Paris. Of the two hundred and fifty-four people killed, almost two hundred were civilians and a great many of them were children. National outrage was swiftly followed by panic. Ten million people in the north abandoned their homes, left production lines unmanned, crops untended, houses deserted in a bid to escape the enemy. Meanwhile the Germans were claiming one victory after another, and the Allies, so rumour had it, were engaged in the most humiliating retreat. Solange was prostrate with fear as news of French casualties started to reach them.

'These are the ones the Government is admitting to!' she wailed. 'How many men are really dead or wounded? Or captured!' she screamed, burying her face in her hands.

'I'm sure Lucien and François are safe,' Claudine said gently, with a confidence she was far from feeling. 'We'd have heard by now if anything had happened to Lucien, and François will get word to us somehow, I promise you.'

'I wouldn't be too sure of that,' Tante Céline, who had stayed on at the château after Louis' death said later, when Claudine related this conversation to her. 'François has never shown any such consideration for anyone in the past, so I fail to see why he should do so now.'

The hell of being unable to defend him was terrible, but somehow Claudine managed to bite back an angry retort. Then the door flew open and Monique came running in. 'Quick, turn to the BBC!' she cried. 'Something incredible has happened! I was just listening in my room and came to find you. No, no, it's too late now, the broadcast is over.' She was so agitated that Claudine poured her a cognac and made her sit down.

'Well, what is it? What did you hear?' Céline asked, waiting only as long as it took for Monique to take a first sip.

'It's terrible!' she answered. 'Or is it? I don't know! The British have taken over a quarter of a million troops out of France.'

'What!' Celine and Claudine gasped in unison.

'No! No, it's not like that,' Monique said hurriedly. 'They've saved them. That's what they said, they've saved them. They sent the Royal Navy and, oh everyone, all their small boats, hundreds and hundreds of them . . .' Tears started to stream down her face. 'They didn't only rescue their own men, they took ours too. They've been saving our men, Claudine. For the past ten days they've been sailing to Dunkirk and rescuing them.'

'So who is to defend us now?' Céline asked indignantly. 'We're just sitting here like hens in a coop, and the damned British have opened the door to the fox.'

'Be quiet!' Claudine interrupted firmly. 'If the British really have got so many men out, at least they're alive to fight another day. Remember that!'

'Yes, but what about us? The women and children left here in France?' Céline argued.

'Our army won't abandon us,' Claudine answered. 'Nor will the British.'

'For heaven's sake, child, be realistic! They aren't in France any longer, so how can you say they haven't abandoned us?'

'Look, I'm not going to argue about it,' Claudine declared fiercely. 'I'm going down to the café to see Gustave. Are you coming, Monique?'

'No, I'll go and break the news to *Maman*. I don't know how she'll take it, but she must be told.'

The café was crammed with the old men of Lorvoire and the surrounding villages, and the talk was solely of the evacuation of troops from Dunkirk. Opinion was as divided as it had been at the château, some felt deserted, other were hopeful. Armand was one of the hopeful ones, and to

Claudine's relief she saw that something of his old spirit had returned. Nevertheless, she was wary; his mood could change at a moment's notice.

'You hold me responsible for your not being able to fight, don't you?' she said, when later he walked her back through the dusk to her car. 'I don't blame you. After all, it is my fault really. If it weren't for Halunke . . .'

'It's too late for recriminations now,' he interrupted. Then he laughed softly. 'No longer your lover, but still your protector. Ironic, isn't it?'

Despite the warm night, she shivered. It wasn't the first time he'd said that, and there was an undercurrent to it that left her with a distinct feeling of unease.

'There's something I want to tell you,' he said as they stood beside the Lagonda. 'I've been meaning to tell you for some time . . .' He paused. 'I've met someone else. Actually, I've known her for some time. Her name is Estelle. You know her too, she works at the beauty parlour in Chinon.'

'Yes, yes, I know her,' Claudine said, unable to hide her surprise.

'It might seem a bit sudden to you,' he went on, 'but the truth is, I was seeing her before you came to Lorvoire. In fact, I never really stopped seeing her, even when we were together.'

Claudine couldn't have been more shocked. 'I see,' she said, wondering if what she was feeling was jealousy. 'Well, under the circumstances I suppose I have no right to be angry.'

'No, you haven't,' he said. 'But I wouldn't blame you if you were. After all, there were times when I was making love to her within hours of making love to you.'

His bluntness took her breath away. 'Why are you telling me this?' she asked, after a pause.

'For two reasons. The first is because I don't want you to think that, if François doesn't return, you and I can ever go back to the way we were. Once everything is sorted out, the war and Halunke, I'm going to ask Estelle to marry me, so that will be an end to it. *La belle dame du château* can find herself another lover. In the meantime I'll carry out François' dirty work for him for as long as it takes, but after that I want no more to do with you – either of you. And the second reason is because Estelle and I would like to use the old cottage. It's on your land, so I need your permission.'

Inwardly she was appalled, but her voice was perfectly steady as she said, 'If Estelle doesn't mind that you once shared the cottage with me, then please feel free to use it.'

He nodded, and their eyes met. There were several moments of silent antagonism between them, then Claudine saw the hostility retreat from his eyes. 'I'm sorry,' he sighed. 'I shouldn't have told you like that. But we should be honest with each other, and . . .'

'Armand,' she interrupted, 'if you feel so badly about carrying out François' wishes, perhaps we should try to come to some other arrangement.'

He shook his head. 'I gave him my word, and despite what I said just now, I'd never forgive myself if anything happened to you.'

Smiling, she put a hand on his arm. 'I'm glad about Estelle,' she said – and immediately could have kicked herself. That wasn't what he wanted to hear, he wanted her to be jealous. And she was jealous, a little. For much as she loved François she could not deny that for a while she had loved Armand too, and the days and nights they had spent together in that cottage would always be a very special memory for her.

'Have you had any news of François or Lucien?' he asked, opening the car door for her.

She shook her head. 'Nothing.'

'I'm sure there will be some soon,' he said comfortingly. 'Meanwhile, what are you doing driving about in this vehicle when no one else can get petrol for love or money?'

'We found some that Louis had stored in the stables,' she answered. 'But you're right, I should only be using it for emergencies.'

'I'll tell you what, we'll get you a bicycle. And one for Solange too. I rather think she'll enjoy being a cyclist. Why don't we go into Chinon tomorrow, the three of us, and see if we can fix you up?'

'It's a date,' Claudine smiled. 'And I think we should put it to Tante Céline as well. I can just picture her cycling down the hill into Lorvoire, can't you?'

'No, but I'd like to!' And he waved her off into the night, then turned to walk back across the square towards home.

He knew it was pointless trying to hurt her as he had with talk of Estelle. It was only driving them further apart, which wasn't what he wanted at all. Not that he'd been altogether lying about Estelle; he had been seeing her before Claudine came to Lorvoire, and he was seeing her again now, but he had always been faithful to Claudine during the time they were together.

And he would continue to be faithful to her, if only as a friend. He would control this loathsome bitterness – he would stick to the promise he had made François, and do all he could to protect Claudine from Halunke. And there was always the timid, submissive little Estelle to provide a frequent and welcome escape from his pain.

'You must be out of your mind if you think I'm getting onto that contraption,' Céline declared the following day, as they stood in the middle of the bicycle shop in Chinon.

'It's either that or roller-skates,' Claudine informed her.

'Roller-skates!' Solange cried. 'Now why didn't I think of that?'

'No, *Maman*, I strictly forbid you even to entertain the idea,' Monique said firmly. 'Now, is that the bicycle you like best?' She nodded towards the gleaming red machine poised between Solange's legs.

'I think so. But I shall have to buy some trousers. No, I shan't, I shall wear Louis'. Come along, Céline, lift up that dress and get onto the saddle. Oh, don't mind old Claude there, he's seen plenty of pretty legs in his time, haven't you, Claude?'

'*Si, si, madame,*' Claude chuckled, quite overcome by the fact that for the first time in months someone had come into his shop with real money to spend. He held the bicycle steady, and Armand offered Céline his hand. Both men caught a glimpse of her suspenders, but only Armand and Claudine realized that this was what Céline intended; she was extremely proud of her legs.

Their bicycles were delivered the following day, and by the time they had finished practising – in the ballroom, because the gravel outside was too difficult for beginners – Céline was as dedicated a cyclist as any of them. Liliane, who watched from the piano stool, bemoaned the fact that she was too fat to ride one herself, and Solange instantly told Armand that he was to build a box to put on the side of hers, so that she could cycle her friend about the countryside.

Claudine caught Armand's eye, and he winked. 'Thank you,' she said, walking her bicycle across the room to join him. 'It was your idea, and Solange likes nothing more than a new challenge.'

'She does look better, doesn't she?' he said. 'And do you know, I think I will build the box. Even if she can't manage it with my mother inside, it'll always come in useful for carrying things.' He glanced at his watch, and seeing the time Claudine clapped her hands and cried, 'The news! Everyone into the sitting-room to listen to the news!'

The headline that day was that Monsieur Paul Reynaud, who had succeeded Edouard Daladier as Prime Minister two months before, had appointed General Charles de Gaulle as Under-Secretary for Defence. Then Solange's hand found its way into Claudine's as it was reported that, despite the unprecedented success of the Dunkirk evacuation, forty thousand prisoners had been taken. It wasn't yet known how many of them were French.

The last part of the bulletin was given over to a speech made the day before in the British House of Commons by Prime Minister Churchill. His strange, hypnotic voice came over the airwaves in tones of such passionate patriotism that it seemed to hang in the air like the thin, curling tendrils of cigarette smoke, and not one of them remained unmoved.

> 'We shall not flag or fail. We shall go on to the end.
> We shall fight in France, we shall fight on the seas
> and oceans, we shall fight with growing confidence
> and growing strength in the air. We shall defend our
> island, whatever the cost may be. We shall fight on
> the beaches, we shall fight on the landing grounds,
> we shall fight in the fields and in the streets, we
> shall fight in the hills. We shall never surrender!
> And even if, which I do not for a moment believe,
> this island or a large part of it, were subjugated and
> starving, then our empire beyond the seas, armed
> and guarded by the British fleet, would carry on the
> struggle until in God's good time the New World,
> with all its power and might, steps forth to the
> rescue of the old.'

For the listeners who did not understand English the speech was delivered again in French, spoken by an actor.

Claudine got up and turned off the wireless.

'He speaks as though France were already lost,' Liliane said, speaking the thought uppermost in everyone's mind.

Claudine looked at her aunt, and Céline looked away. 'The speech was made for the benefit of the British,' Claudine declared. 'And let's not forget that their Government has a pact with France that neither country will agree to peace without the other.'

'But even so, he talked only of "this island",' Armand reminded her. 'I think *Maman* is right, he already believes France to have fallen.'

'We don't know that for sure,' Claudine retorted. 'And now that General de Gaulle is Under-Secretary perhaps we shall see some changes.'

'If it's not already too late,' he said sourly. And as if to add menace to his pessimism, the distant wail of an air-raid siren started its eerie crescendo across the countryside. They quickly made their way down to the cellar, but Claudine handed Louis to Monique and waited at the top of the steps with Armand, where they watched the enemy aircraft soar overhead and a few minutes later heard the dull boom of exploding bombs reverberate through the hills. The munitions factory on the road to Tours was undamaged, they discovered later, but a busful of workers arriving for their evening shift had perished.

In the end, the boys at the Army Cadet School, not ten kilometers away in Saumur, were among the last to make a stand against the great might of the German army. They fought on, despite the fact that the Government had fled first to Briare, then to Tours, then to Bordeaux and that rumours of an armistice were growing stronger by the minute. At the château, with the battle raging almost on their doorstep, Claudine and the rest of the family went on with life as best they could. Every day now was filled with the doom-laden roar of Allied and enemy aircraft flying overhead, gunfire echoing through the countryside, and the acrid stench of explosives lingered in the still, hot air of summer.

On 18th June, General Charles de Gaulle made a broadcast from London calling upon all Frenchmen to remember that '. . . whatever happens, the flame of French resistance must not and shall not die!' But apathy and a sense of defeat were spreading now like a disease, and four days after de Gaulle's speech, Marshal Henri Philippe Pétain – the proud, erect man with pale blue eyes whom Claudine had met once in Paris, and who had taken over the Government after Paul Reynaud's resignation six days before – signed the armistice that betrayed Great Britain and brought peace to France. But not even the indignity of seeing its national representatives forced to return to the railway carriage in the Forest of Compiègne where France's Marshal Foch had dictated terms to a defeated Germany in 1918, seemed to bother the French. There was a new sound ringing through the countryside now – the sound of rejoicing. The war, for France at least, was at an end.

Claudine was stupefied. That the French should welcome surrender was horrifying enough, but when that surrender called for three-fifths of France, including Touraine to be occupied and governed by the German army; when it called for four hundred million francs to be paid every day to the Reich, and for over a million and a half Frenchmen to be deported to prisoner-of-war camps – the sheer atrocity of it was inexpressible.

The first Germans arrived in Chinon at four in the morning on August 5th. There were no more than five of them and they came on bicycles – so Monsieur Bonet, the melon farmer informed Claudine.

'They reached the statue of Jeanne d'Arc, fired guns into the window of the laundry, then went away again,' he said, scratching his head in bewilderment.

He cycled off then, but returned at six that evening to tell her that the *Boches* were back, this time with the rest of their company. They had taken over the Hôtel de France on the square, the Hôtel Boule d'Or on the quay, and many of the desirable residences on the rue Voltaire.

The following day Claudine and Monique cycled into Chinon, neither of them knowing quite what to expect, but unable to contain their curiosity. Nothing could have prepared them for the shock of finding scores of young men in dull grey uniforms swarming all over the town, wearing rifles slung over their shoulders and thick leather belts full of ammunition. The infamous jackboots were much in evidence, as were Nazi flags, draped from the windows of requisitioned buildings or fluttering triumphantly from flag poles which only a week ago had flown the *tricolore*. But more than all these things, what really shocked them was that every soldier they came across was brandishing a camera or licking an ice-cream, or shielding his eyes from the sun as he admired the castle ruins on the hill.

'Anyone would think they were on holiday,' Claudine said, and her look of incredulity turned to a scowl as she read a notice in the florist's window: *Ici on parle allemand*.

They turned their bicycles at the statue of Jeanne d'Arc and pedalled into the square. Three young German soldiers saluted them cheerfully from the side of the street, and several more who were sitting outside Madame Desbourdes' café laughed and joked with the locals as though they were prodigal sons returned. None of them could be in any doubt that they were welcome, or why: they had money to spend, and the French, as ever, were only too willing to take it.

'They're so good-looking,' Monique murmured, as one of them caught her eye and smiled broadly. 'And so young.'

'And so damned arrogant,' Claudine seethed, turning her back as another invited them to sit down. 'Look, what's that, over there on the wall?'

They wheeled their bicycles over to the Town Hall to get a closer look at the posters. They showed a German soldier holding two children in his arms, with the slogan, 'Abandoned population, put your trust in a German soldier.'

'That's sick!' Claudine spat, strongly tempted to tear

them down. 'How dare they exploit children like that! And how dare they call us an abandoned population.'

'But that's what we are,' Monique said softly. 'We have no army now.'

Claudine's eyes were blazing with indignation. 'Come along,' she snapped, 'let's go home. I feel unclean just being on the same street with them.'

But it was plain that no one else in the area shared Claudine's scruples, and when eventually the defeated army started to drift back from the front, returning to their work in the factories and on the land, the occupying forces behaved with such extravagant civility that after a while even Claudine found it difficult to dislike them. How could you hate General Kahl, their commanding officer, for example, who roamed the cobbled streets of Chinon each morning with his pet poodle on a lead?

Then, to her amazement, she found herself inviting one or two of the lower-ranking officers to drive out to Lorvoire and join her and Armand at Gustave's café. Armand, who had teased her relentlessly about her sense of outrage at the German presence, immediately accused her of fraternizing, but when it came to it the afternoon passed perhaps more pleasantly for him than for anyone else. In the end Gustave, aided by one of the German youths, had to carry him home. Claudine followed, and couldn't help laughing at the look on Liliane's face when she saw her son draped over the shoulder of a German officer. But to her surprise Liliane invited him in, and in less than ten minutes had learned that Einrich was nineteen years old, came from Hamburg, and had four brothers, two of whom had been killed in the fighting near Amiens. Also that his mother had suffered a heart-attack when she heard of her second son's death.

'General Kahl for me to go home is to arrange,' he told them in his awkward French. 'For few days only, but my mother . . .' He broke off, his eyes filled with tears, and

Claudine guessed that the lump in Liliane's throat was as large as the one in her own. They were men like any others, she grudgingly admitted – in fact boys, most of them, a long way from their families and only too grateful for any little kindness shown them. All the same her feelings towards the Germans *en masse* had not changed. They had no right to be in France, and if their families back in Germany were suffering they had no one but themselves to blame; they were the ones who had brought Hitler to power.

Then, to her surprise, graffiti declaring allegiance to General de Gaulle started to appear, with the cross of Lorraine scratched underneath. They were scrawled on posters, on walls, even on the backs of German cars and the façade of the Hôtel de France, where most of the senior-ranking officers were billeted. Claudine wanted very much to know who was doing it.

'I've absolutely no idea' Céline sighed when she asked her. 'Why on earth d'you want to know?'

Claudine paused in her weekly chore of polishing the silver. 'Perhaps because it tells me that there are some people in France with a degree of integrity left.'

'Meaning? No, no, I know what you mean. But this is the way life is now, Claudine, you have to accept it like everyone else.'

'I have accepted it, as far as I can, but they're still the enemy, Tante Céline. And you've heard General de Gaulle on the wireless these past weeks, he's calling for all Frenchmen everywhere to resist. And someone's listening to him, the graffiti proves it. I just want to know how to make contact with them.' She was silent for a moment. 'Maybe I could help them,' she said.

Céline crushed out her red-tipped de Rezske cigarette, put down her magazine and turned to face her niece. 'Claudine,' she began, 'the war is over. The Germans are here, and they are making life as pleasant as they can for us under the circumstances. If you do anything to disrupt that you won't be doing anyone any favours, least of all yourself. Now, take my advice and let it be.'

'If Louis was here, d'you think he'd let it be? No, of course he wouldn't, it would make a mockery of all the lives given in the last war, and this one too. François and Lucien would feel the same.'

'*Oh là là!*' Céline laughed scornfully. 'As far as we know, Claudine, your husband is a traitor . . .'

'And I'm beginning to feel like one too, socializing with the Germans the way I do.'

'Keep it that way! Make friends, not enemies, it will be wiser in the long run.'

Claudine sucked in her cheeks thoughtfully as her aunt confirmed the feeling she had had herself. 'You're right,' she said in the end, 'but our lives aren't our own any more. We have to have so many passes and identity cards in order to be able do anything or go anywhere. We have to queue for our food – waiting for the Germans to take their pick of everything first, of course. We have to be indoors by ten every night . . . Oh, I don't know, the list is endless, and it makes me furious . . .'

'All right,' said Céline, 'so life is difficult. But no one is going to thank you for making things even harder, are they? Which you will do if you antagonize the Germans.'

'Hear! Hear!' Monique said, walking into the drawing-room just then. 'Speaking personally, I'm rather glad they're here, they've certainly livened things up a little.' She held out a card to Claudine. 'It's an invitation to a dance at the Hôtel Boule d'Or tomorrow evening. Shall we go?'

'No,' Claudine answered with finality. Then, seeing the plea in Monique's eyes, 'You haven't got an escort, so how can you go?'

'Armand says he'll arrange one for me.'

Claudine threw up her hands. 'Go then! There's nothing I can do to stop you, but I won't be there.'

Just then they heard several vehicles coming up the drive. It was such a rare sound these days that both Claudine and Monique went to the window to look. A black Mercedes and four outriders emerged from under the trees and swept grandly across the top of the meadow.

'What do you think they want?' Monique asked, her eyes searching the faces beneath the round tin helmets of the German motor-cyclists.

'There's only one way to find out,' Claudine answered tightly. 'You two stay here.'

As the car came to a halt outside the front door, she walked down the steps. 'Can I help you?' she said, shielding her eyes against the dazzling sun as a uniformed figure sporting an extravagant array of medals alighted from the rear of the car.

The man nodded to one of his subordinates, who quickly stepped forward. 'Colonel Blomberg wishes to speask with the Comtesse de Lorvoire,' he barked.

'I am she,' Claudine said frostily, aware that her casual attire and the duster she still held in her hand had fooled them into thinking her a servant.

The Colonel removed his cap, revealing a balding head, thick grey eyebrows and piercing yellow eyes. His bottom lip protruded, and whiskers sprouted from the nostrils of his bulbous nose. '*Madame*,' he said, having to tilt his head to look up into her face, 'it is a pleasure to make your acquaintance.'

Claudine took the hand he offered and was immediately revolted by its limp and sweaty grasp. 'What can I do for you, Colonel?' she said, forcing a smile.

The Colonel turned again to the sergeant beside him, spoke rapidly in German, then waited while the officer explained the purpose of their visit.

As she listened, Claudine's heart sank. Friends of theirs in other parts of northern France had been forced to evacuate their homes to make room for German officers, and she knew there was no appeal.

'May I ask why you have chosen to come to Lorvoire?' she said. 'There are many other châteaux in the region, some of them unoccupied.'

'I think,' the Colonel answered, sweeping an arm towards the imposing façade, 'that must speak for itself. However, as your menfolk are not at present in residence, we shall not require you to move out. There will be room for us all.' His smile sent a shiver down Claudine's spine. 'I have been assured of the most excellent hospitality here,' he continued, walking past her and up the steps into the château. 'I am told there is an apartment on the second floor that will suit my needs admirably.'

For a moment, as the Colonel gazed at the paintings in the hall, then ran his finger over the highly polished sideboard, Claudine could only look on. Then, with an effort, she pulled herself together. 'I think you will find our circular guest room much more to your liking,' she said equably. 'I will ask the butler to show you the way.'

'There is no need, *madame*, you can show me to the *apartment* yourself.'

'I have no intention of doing any such thing,' she retorted grandly. 'As a guest in my home you will reside in a *guest* room.'

'I think you misunderstand, *madame*. I am not a guest in your home, it is you who are the guest, and as such . . .'

He broke off as Solange, an apron over her dress and a scarf wound like a turban round her head, came out of the dining-room, waving her hands in the air and gabbling under her breath. She stopped suddenly when she saw the German, then with her eyes nearly popping from her head she barked , 'Who are you?'

'This is Colonel Blomberg, Solange,' Claudine answered for him. 'He is going to be staying with us for a while, in the circular guest room.'

'Enough of this!' Blomberg bellowed, marching past them and starting up the stairs. 'Bring in my baggage,' he called to the officer who was standing to attention at the top of the steps.

Claudine and Solange glanced at one another, then Claudine went swiftly up the stairs after the Colonel.

'Your room is this way,' she snapped as they reached the first landing, but ignoring her the Colonel walked the few steps to the second flight of stairs and continued up.

Gritting her teeth, Claudine watched him, his long black boots creaking as he moved, and tried to decide what the hell she should do. But come what may, she wasn't going to give up her rooms for anyone, least of all a despicable little toad like Blomberg.

'This is your bed-chamber, I take it?' he said, as she came into the sitting-room of the apartment and found him on the threshold of her room. 'So over there must be your husband's,' he went on, not waiting for her to answer.

How on earth did he know so much, she wondered as he walked across to François' room, threw open the door and looked in. 'Mm, this should suit me well,' he grunted. 'In fact, it is all I shall need, so I see no reason for you to leave your room.' He turned to look at her, and she felt herself shrink from the gleam in his eye. 'We could become very good friends, I think. As a matter of fact, your husband assures me we shall. A most obliging man, your husband. Not only does he offer me his home, but he has offered me his wife too. Most generous, don't you agree? I had thought to refuse the offer, but now I have met you, *madame* . . .' He ran his tongue over his lips and lowered his hungry eyes to her breasts.

Claudine's head was spinning. This disgusting little man knew François! Claimed that François had . . . She took a breath to try and steady herself. François would never, never have made such an offer. Unless . . .

Oh, dear God, the very thought that he had undergone any degree of torture made her feel faint. Her eyes moved back to Blomberg. He was so unlike the other Germans she had met, but she had heard plenty of rumours of how they were behaving in other places. It was incredible, he hadn't been in her home five minutes, and already . . .

Mentally, she shook herself; she must think, and think fast. If she was right, and François had been forced into making the offer, what might happen to him if she refused? On the other hand, Blomberg could be lying . . . There was nothing for it, she had to try to bluff it out.

She turned away and walked imperiously towards the door. Then, with her head held so high that she had to look at Blomberg down the length of her nose, she said in a dangerously low voice, 'May I remind you, *monsieur*, that you are not in a bordello, but in the ancestral home of the Comtes de Rassey de Lorvoire. If you are intending to stay, therefore, I suggest you learn some manners. Now, remove yourself from this room before I am forced to send someone to Chinon to report your outrageous behaviour to General Kahl.'

Blomberg's repulsive face contorted in a snarl as he started towards her. Somehow she stood her ground. When he reached her he lifted a hand to strike, but when she didn't even so much as flinch he turned away, snorting with digust, and stumped out of the room.

Shaking with relief, Claudine leaned back against the wall. Her bluff had worked – so far – and silently she thanked God for General Kahl, for it was undoubtedly his name that had saved the day. But François, where was he, and what in God's name was happening to him?

She found Blomberg in the circular room, where Solange was bustling around him, patting his arm, pulling back the covers from the bed and calling him *Monsieur Allemand*. Claudine couldn't resist a smile. Solange was playing her part well, and the Colonel was clearly irritated beyond words.

'Get this confounded woman out of here!' he roared, when he saw Claudine at the door. 'And tell your cook I'd like dinner served at seven o'clock sharp.'

'Of course, *Herr Colonel*,' Claudine said smoothly. She had scored her victory for that day and wasn't inclined to fight again – or not just yet. However, there was one point she couldn't resist scoring. Taking Solange by the hand, she arched her brows, and again making him aware of his lack of height, said, 'Monsieur, I'm sure you won't mind my pointing out that it would be more suitable to address my mother-in-law as *Madame la Comtesse*.'

As she closed the door, she clapped a hand over Solange's mouth so the Colonel wouldn't hear her shriek of laughter. 'Dignity, *Maman*,' she hissed. 'We're going to make that appalling man shrivel in the face of it.'

Knowing that for all sorts of reasons it would be unwise for her to enquire about François herself, Claudine left it to Solange, who brought the subject up over dinner that very night.

'My daughter-in-law informs me that you are an acquaintance of my son's,' she began, peering with keen interest at the fork the Colonel was holding.

Reddening, Blomberg looked at it too, and Claudine turned away before he could see her smiling. Solange was purposely unnerving him, making him question his table manners, though in fact had been using the correct implements throughout the meal.

'May I ask when you last saw him?' Solange continued.

'At the end of June,' Blomberg replied, dabbing the corner of his rubbery mouth with a napkin.

'And where was that?' Solange said pleasantly.

'In Germany, of course.'

'Where in Germany?' Monique enquired.

Blomberg gave a haughty smile. 'I am not at liberty to say,' he answered, nodding to Magaly who was standing at his elbow with the coffee pot.

Solange yawned. 'In my experience,' she said, 'when someone gives that answer it is because they don't know.'

Watching her over the rim of his cup, the Colonel took a sip of coffee, then set it back in the saucer. 'As a matter of fact,' he said 'I spent rather a pleasant evening in *Monsieur le Comte*'s company – at the home of my brother-in-law.'

'Are we acquainted with your brother-in-law?' Solange asked grandly.

'I should think it unlikely. His name is Max Helber.'

Somehow Claudine managed to keep an expressionless face, as she made a series of quick deductions. If anything had passed between Helber and François, François had clearly not managed to obtain Halunke's identity or he would have sent word by now. It was appalling to think that François might have submitted himself to Helber to no purpose . . . She would not even consider that possibility, she must put it out of her mind.

'No, we don't know him,' Solange sighed. She inhaled the delicious smell of freshly mown grass wafting in through the open window. 'I take it my son was in good health when you saw him, *Colonel*?'

'He was – then,' Blomberg answered.

Not one of them missed the emphasis.

'What do you mean, *then*?' Solange barked.

'*Maman*, I think the Colonel is playing games with us,' Claudine interrupted. 'As he said, he hasn't seen François since June and it is now the beginning of September. It is my belief that he doesn't have the first idea where François is now, so shall we save our breath for a stroll in the water-garden?'

The four of them walked out into the cool evening air,

and Tante Céline shook her head warningly at Claudine. 'He is not a man to cross, *chérie*,' she warned. 'He may be a German, but he is also a colonel. As such, he is used to respect.'

'Respect is something you earn, Tante Céline,' Claudine answered crisply, 'not something you demand.'

She hadn't told any of them what had passed between her and Blomberg in her apartment that afternoon. Nor would she – because if it ever came to the point where François' life depended on it, she would be forced to succumb to his loathsome blackmail, and she would rather die than have anyone in the world know about it. And now that he had mentioned Max Helber's name, she could no longer be under any illusion that his presence at the château was a mere coincidence. But what he hoped to do or discover here was something she could only guess at . . .

The evening had turned chilly. Claudine, looking up at the peachy-yellow sky, suddenly felt her skin start to prickle. She spun round, half expecting to find someone behind her, but there was no one. Even so, she was certain that someone was following her progress through the garden, if only with his eyes, and if it hadn't been so close to curfew she would have sent someone to the village for Armand.

– 25 –

It was a morning in mid-November. Claudine and Monique were in the village, watching with much amusement as Solange pedalled unsteadily round the square, with Liliane's bemused face poking up over the rim of the box Armand had attached to the bicycle.

'It's a triumph!' Claudine declared, delighted to see Solange back in spirits again. She had cried herself to sleep in Claudine's arms the night before, not only because she missed Louis so terribly, but because not one of the young village men who had returned from the front in the past weeks had been able to give her news of Lucien.

'Isn't it?' Solange called back. 'We can even go into Chinon together,' she told Liliane. 'Of course, we shall have to walk up the hill, but going down the other side will be no problem.'

'It might be wise to get Armand to adjust the brakes,' Gustave muttered. 'That hill is quite steep, you know.'

'Good idea,' Claudine laughed. 'I'll talk to him.'

Her relationship with Armand was easier now. He hadn't mentioned Estelle since the night he first talked of her, but he definitely seemed calmer, more his old self. It was over two months since she had had that feeling that Halunke was back, watching her, but both she and Armand were still on edge. At least Armand told her he was, but she'd got the impression lately that Armand's concern was merely a pretence. But then, how could she expect him to care so much any more.

'How is your colonel settling in at the château?' Gustave asked as they strolled over to the café.

'I think he's comfortable,' Claudine answered demurely.

Monique gave a shout of laughter. 'Don't you listen to a word of it, Gustave! One glance from *Madame la Comtesse* here, and our Colonel simply withers.'

'Monique's exaggerating,' Claudine grinned. 'We've hardly seen him since the day he arrived.'

'He's avoiding you, that's why!' Monique said. 'He really is the most repellent man to look at, though, so perhaps it's just as well. Have you noticed the way he breaks into a sweat when he's angry? And he's always angry with you, Claudine. Incidentally, Hans, his chauffeur, told me he still suspects that you're responsible for the acts of sabotage on his car.'

'I'd hardly call three flat tyres and a leaking petrol tank sabotage,' Claudine protested. 'Unfortunate, perhaps . . .'

'Have you managed to discover who really is doing it yet?'

Claudine shook her head. 'I thought it might have been Armand, but . . .'

She turned, hearing someone call her name, and saw Janette and Robert Reinberg running across the square from the river bank, followed by their mother. 'Ah, seeing Gertrude reminds me,' she said. 'I need some new trousers. What about you, Monique? Didn't you say wanted some too?'

'I'll say. The last pair Gertrude made were marvellous. So comfortable. Does she have any fabric, though?'

'Let's ask her.'

But as they walked over to talk to her, they were astonished to see Florence Jallais come out of her front door and spit on the cobbles right in front of her.

Both Claudine and Monique were outraged, and seeing Claudine storm across the square towards her, Florence Jallais scuttled back into her house and slammed the door. 'Open this door now!' Claudine shouted, banging it with her fist.

'No, leave it,' Gertrude said softly. 'Please, *madame*.'

'But she can't do that to you!'

'I'm afraid she can.'

'What's going on?' Solange cried, bringing her bicycle to a halt beside them.

Claudine swung round 'Florence Jallais just *spat* at Gertrude.'

'*Oh là là!*' Liliane said, opening the little door in her box and climbing out. 'I spoke to her the last time.'

'You mean she's done it before?'

'What's that you're wearing?' Solange asked suddenly, seeing the yellow badge on Gertrude's cardigan.

They all looked at it. There was one word on the badge: *Juive*. Jewess.

'We all have to wear them now, *madame*,' Gertrude said, averting her eyes to hide her misery.

'By whose orders?' Claudine wanted to know.

'I believe, by Hitler's own.'

Claudine's nostrils flared. 'Monique! Solange! Come along, we're going to Gertrude's,' she ordered.

'Please, *madame*,' Gertrude begged. 'We don't want any more trouble. The children are suffering enough as it is.'

'I'm not going to make trouble, Gertrude,' Claudine assured her. 'At least, not for you.'

That evening, when Colonel Blomberg returned to the château for dinner, he found the four women already halfway through their meal. His protruding bottom lip quivered with fury, but he took his seat silently at the head of the table.

It was as the watery vegetable soup was being ladled into his bowl that he noticed the badge Solange was wearing. His eyes narrowed as he looked at each of the other women in turn. They were all sporting the same badge of bright yellow card with the word *Catholique* emblazoned across it.

The meal continued in silence until the women finished and stood up to leave the room.

'*Madame*,' Blomberg said then, looking at Claudine. 'I should be obliged if you could spare me a few moments in my room later. I will send for you when I am ready.'

Claudine nodded curtly and followed the others out into the hall.

'It's sure to be about our badges,' Céline whispered, pushing open the door to the sitting-room.

'Well, I for one am not taking mine off until Gertrude Reinberg is allowed to take hers off,' Solange stated.

'Me neither,' Monique said, looking back over her shoulder at the German soldier stationed outside the dining-room. It was Hans, the one who generally acted as Blomberg's chauffeur.

Claudine didn't miss the smile that passed between them, and was glad to think that Monique had won his friendship.

They needed all the allies they could get when Blomberg resented them so bitterly. Then she shuddered. Having the Germans in their own home like this, invading their privacy, contaminating their daily lives, was intolerable.

There was no wireless to listen to now; wirelesses had been confiscated soon after the occupation began. Monique, however, had managed to secrete one in her room, but they listened to it only rarely: the penalty for keeping a wireless was twenty-one days' imprisonment.

'What do you think Blomberg does all day?' Céline wondered as she selected a record to play on the gramophone.

'He goes to the Château d'Artigny,' Claudine answered. 'It's been taken over by the Germans since Admiral Darlan left, it's their regional headquarters.'

'Oh? How do you know that?' Monique enquired.

'Armand followed him,' Claudine answered simply.

'But why?'

'Because I asked him to.'

There was a tap on the door, and Hans, the handsome young German officer came in. 'The Colonel wishes to see you now, *madame.*'

'Tell the Colonel I will be with him shortly,' Claudine answered.

'But . . .'

'I'm going to say goodnight to my son. I will be with the Colonel shortly,' she said with deliberation, and sailing past him, she went upstairs to the nursery.

'So, you think yourself clever for keeping me waiting?' Blomberg said when he opened his door to her ten minutes later.

'Colonel,' she replied in a bored voice, 'running this château keeps me extremely busy and you simply have to wait your turn. Now, what is it you would like to discuss with me?'

Scarcely managing to contain his anger, Blomberg said, 'The badge, *madame*. Take it off!'

'There is no law prohibiting the wearing of badges,' Claudine said coolly.

'It is a deliberate insult to the Reich.'

'That I am a Catholic?' she said incredulously. 'How can that be?'

'I am not arguing with you on this matter! Take it off, or I shall take it off for you.'

Claudine looked at him with evident amusement, then calmly folding her arms, she turned to look out of the window.

He caught her a blow to side of her head that made stars dance before her eyes, but she gritted her teeth and turned to look him straight in the eye. 'Only a coward strikes women,' she began – then gasped as he took hold of the badge and tore it from her blouse. The fabric ripped, exposing the silk of her camisole underneath.

'I hope that makes you feel better,' she said. 'Now, if you have quite finished I should like to return to my family.'

'Don't you mean your *husband's* family?' he said, as she reached the door.

His emphasis on 'husband' made her turn back. There was a new glint in his eyes, and she suddenly realized they were only now coming to the point of why he had asked her here. 'I have news of your husband,' he said, strolling across the room and settling himself on the sofa beneath the window. Behind him the sun was setting in a blaze of orange, and she could no longer see his face. 'How long has it been since you saw him now?' he said. 'Six months? Seven?'

'I have no idea,' she replied. 'I don't keep count.'

Blomberg chuckled. 'I was told there was no love lost between you. So I take it you are not in the least interested in knowing what he is doing – or where he is?'

'Not in the least,' she confirmed.

'Then I shall inform my brother-in-law that the efforts he has made to keep you abreast of your husband's career are wasted.'

'Yes, you tell him that,' she smiled, and opened the door to leave.

'Oh, no, no, no,' Blomberg's voice said behind her, and immediately the German officer Hans stepped into her path, indicating that she should return to the room.

Claudine sighed with exasperation as the door closed behind her. 'All right,' she said, folding her arms. 'You clearly want to tell me something regarding my husband, so get on with it.'

'I must inform you, *madame*, that this is the last time I shall overlook your insolence. If you speak to me in that tone again, it is not you who will suffer but your husband.'

Claudine closed her eyes. 'As I have no regard for my husband, or his welfare,' she said through gritted teeth, 'you are wasting your time . . .'

'I doubt if your mother-in-law would take that attitude,' Blomberg interrupted. 'I heard just the other day that the fingers of *Monsieur le Comte*'s left hand have been broken, and I could not help wondering how his mother would react to a graphic description of his – what shall we call them? – injuries, and how they were obtained. There are other injuries too, of course, but I shall save the details for *la Comtesse*. Unless you would prefer I didn't tell her at all. The choice is yours, *madame*.'

Claudine's face had paled. 'You're lying!' she hissed.

'Am I?'

'I know why you are doing this,' she seethed, 'but unlike you, Colonel, I don't make threats. I make promises, and here's one for you. If you lay so much as a finger on me, I give you my word I'll kill you.'

Blomberg laughed. 'I think not.'

'Then you're a fool.'

'Even if you were able to carry out your *promise* – which I doubt – think what repercussions such an act would have on your family, Claudine.' He saw how her nostrils flared at his use of her Christian name, and could not suppress a smile. 'Oh,' he went on, 'and before you threaten me again with the intervention of General Kahl, I should inform you that I have now been given sole – and unequivocal – authority to deal with this family as I see fit. I have no intention of, as you put it, laying a finger on you; I want only to see you humiliated, in the way you have tried to humiliate me. You may start by removing your clothes.'

'You must be out of your mind!' she sneered.

'*Madame la Comtesse*, your mother-in-law,' he said, getting to his feet, 'is not of stable mind, is she? It would be a shame, would it not, to unhinge her further for the sake of your dignity? After all, that is all I require from you, *madame*. Not such a great price, when one weighs it against the one *la Comtesse* would have to pay if you refuse me.'

'You are a disgusting little man!' Claudine spat.

'You make things worse for yourself by addressing me in that fashion,' he replied smoothly, and with a quick flick of his wrist he slapped his gloves across her face.

Claudine saw red. Before she could stop herself, she had twisted his arm so brutally behind his back that she heard the bones crack.

'Hans! Hans!' he squealed, and the door flew open to admit the young soldier. A gun was pressed between Claudine's shoulder-blades, and knowing she could do nothing else, she let the Colonel go.

'All right, Hans,' Blomberg said, purple in the face and puffing as he massaged his shoulder. A thin film of sweat had broken out on his skin, and his grotesque bottom lip was coated in saliva.

Hans went away again, and Claudine knew she had made

a grave error. That Blomberg had had to call for a junior officer because he had been attacked by a woman would make him the laughing-stock of the Château d'Artigny. But she refused to flinch as he approached, and when he grasped the rip in her blouse and tore it right down the front, she only looked back at him with contempt.

'Undress yourself, whore!' he snarled. 'Do it now, or I shall instruct my colleagues in Germany to step up the torture of your husband. And then I shall tell your mother- in-law why I have been obliged to take that step. I'm sure you can imagine how she will feel to know that you might have saved him.'

Staring into his eyes with unmitigated loathing, Claudine peeled away the shreds of her blouse, then unfastened her skirt, telling herself all the time that her body was merely a product of nature, that it meant nothing to reveal it. But if he made one move to touch her, she would break his neck . . .

'All right,' he rasped, when she stood naked in front of him. He loosened his collar and tried to speak again. 'Walk over to the window.'

She sauntered to the window, turned, and walked back again. Then, remembering that his intention was to humiliate her, she decided to let him believe he had succeeded. That way, it might be over sooner.

'Can I put my clothes back on now?' she said meekly, covering her breasts with her hands and crossing her legs.

'No!' she answered. 'Go and stand by the mirror.'

She did as he instructed, forcing tears into her eyes to add to her masquerade of disgrace.

'That's it,' he said, 'turn so I can see you from behind as well as in front. Good. *Hans!*'

Again the door opened, and when Hans came in and saw the lady of the house standing naked in front of the mirror, he quickly averted his eyes.

'Look at her!' Blomberg growled. 'That's what she's there for.'

Hans's young face was beet red as he obeyed the order and allowed his pale blue eyes to travel the length of Claudine's exquisite body. Claudine hung her head in mock shame. She wondered if Hans was clever enough to realize that this was something he *was* expected to tell his fellow officers about.

'You may go closer, Hans,' Blomberg panted.

Claudine froze. Blomberg was keeping his promise not to lay a finger on her all right, but the promise had not extended to the junior officer.

'She's a fine specimen, don't you agree, Hans?' Blomberg asked him.

'Yes, sir,' he replied in a strangled voice.

'All right, you may go now.' Claudine almost fell to her knees with relief. 'And you,' Blomberg said to her, 'where is your pride now?'

Claudine kept her eyes lowered and Blomberg laughed.

'I shall see to it that your husband is told how obliging his wife has been. I daresay he will enjoy the joke. Now, put your clothes on and get out.'

When Claudine left, she went straight to her room and doused her face in cold water, hoping it might calm her anger. After all, she told herself, if that was all she had to suffer to prevent any more harm coming to François, she would gladly do it again.

She looked at herself in the mirror, and suddenly his name erupted from the depths of her buried fear. *François!* she cried silently. *Oh, François!* She sank onto the edge of the bath and bowed her head over the washbasin. It was as though some barricade she had erected against pain was suddenly being cleaved from around her heart and in one almighty surge the terror of what might be happening to him rushed to every corner of her body. It was seven months since she had seen him, over five since he had written. Where was he now? What were they doing to him? Oh dear

God, please let Blomberg have been lying. Please, please, God, let him be safe.

The following night Claudine was in the drawing-room, helping Jean-Paul to black-out the windows, when Corinne came down from the nursery to find her.

'Erich von Pappen is here, *madame*,' she whispered.

Claudine's heart leapt into her throat, but her face remained calm. In the hall she smiled politely at Hans, who was standing to attention outside the dining-room, and wished him goodnight. Then she followed Corinne at a leisurely pace up to her apartment.

'I cannot stay above a few minutes, *madame*,' Erich said, as she burst into her bedroom.

'François!' she cried in a heavy whisper. 'Is he all right? What. . . ?'

Von Pappen shook his head. 'I have not come for that reason,' he said. 'I need to know if you have heard from Lucien?'

'No,' Claudine answered. 'No, nothing. Why?'

Again von Pappen shook his head. 'He has been missing for some time and we – I – am concerned.'

She didn't miss the way he had changed the 'we' to 'I' and her heart started to pound. 'Where is François, Erich?' she said.

He looked away, but she caught him by the shoulders and turned him back to face her. 'Where is he? *Tell me!*'

He stared dumbly into her eyes and she felt suddenly dizzy with fear. 'Erich,' she said steadily, 'I think, I'm not sure, but I think Halunke is back. So tell me, what has happened?'

She heard him groan under his breath, then he snatched himself away from her and started to beat his hands against his head.

'Erich!' It came out almost as a scream. 'Where is he, Erich? You've got to tell me.'

'I can't,' he whispered. '*Madame*, I can't.'

'Is he with Max Helber?'

Von Pappen seemed surprised, and quickly she told him about Blomberg and what he had said to them.

'No,' von Pappen said when she had finished, 'François left Helber some time ago. But you're right, Blomberg is here for a reason. I don't know what it is, but if you're thinking that he is Halunke, you are wrong.'

'Then who is Halunke? Do you know? In his letter François said . . .' She swung round as the door opened and Corinne came in.

'I am sorry, *madame*,' she said, 'but Colonel Blomberg wishes to speak with you, immediately.'

'Tell him to go to hell!' Claudine spat, and turned back to von Pappen.

'*Madame* I am sorry,' he said, backing away, 'I should not have come.'

'No!' she cried. 'You can't go now!'

'I must. I shall return when I have some news. In the meantime, please stay out of the forest and keep all the doors and windows locked.'

'Just tell me if he's all right, Erich?' Claudine pleaded. 'Please, I beg you . . .' But as she started after him, Corinne caught her by the arm and pulled her back.

'He does not know where your husband is, *madame*,' Corinne said softly. 'He has not known for over three months.'

– 26 –

Sweat was pouring down his face, and the blinding pain racked every nerve in his body. After a while a shadow started to creep over his brain, but as he was sucked into the blessed release of oblivion a wall of icy water hit his face. He was too exhausted even to lift his head. A few minutes later he heard a door open and close, muted voices, then footsteps receding into the distance.

His left arm hung lifelessly at his side, the broken bones of his fingers jutting out at right angles where they had been snapped back. His right hand was resting on the table, but as far as he could tell the bones remained intact. His arms, like his back and legs, were covered with burns, but the true extent of his injuries, internal and external, was unclear to him; he was long past the point of being able to distinguish one part of his body from another.

He had no idea where he was, or how long he had been there. All he knew was that he had been in this dazzling pool of light at the centre of this windowless room for so long now, inhaling the stench of his own burning flesh, his own blood, that it could only be a matter of time before he lost all sense of reason, if not his life.

He had believed himself to be alone, but suddenly someone coughed. François carefully raised his eyes until he saw the feet of his companion. He willed himself to try again, and got as far as the man's waist before his head fell back onto his chest. He had not slept for days. It felt like months.

The door opened again, and as if they were approaching down a long, dark corridor of confused consciousness, the sound of footsteps he both recognized and dreaded came to him. For a moment the tiled floor started to swim, the blood on it – his blood – was rising like waves. He blinked hard, and it was steady again.

Walter Brüning, a member of General von Liebermann's élite *Komitee*, glanced at the officer partially hidden in the shadows. Then he pulled a chair up to the table so that he was facing François, and said, 'So, at last you have admitted to working for the *Services de Renseignements*.'

'Yes,' François answered, with difficulty. 'But I have sworn allegiance to the Reich. I no longer work for France.'

Brüning rested his arms on the table and eyed the ropes binding François to his chair. They were so tight that the man could barely breathe. 'I am glad to hear this,' he said. 'But if it is true, why will you not tell us from whom you obtained the information you so misguidedly passed to the Führer?'

'I gave him no information,' François answered in muted tones. 'I had none to give.'

Brüning nodded to the man beside him. The man lifted a wafer-thin knife from the table and went to stand beside François.

'Again, *monsieur*,' Brüning said. 'From whom did you acquire the information?'

François didn't answer. They had been through this a thousand times, and would probably go through it another thousand before they were done with him, but his answer would remain the same. He had given no information, he had had no information to give.

A gasp burst from his lips as the knife slid smoothly under his thumbnail. His head flew back and his teeth bared in agony. Again Brüning nodded, and the man slowly peeled the nail from the skin. A white-hot blaze of pain shot through François' arm, and blood started to stream from the wound. He braced himself, waiting for his index finger to suffer the same fate, but nothing happened.

Finally, as the searing pain dulled to an excruciating throb, he lowered his head to look at them.

'Are you prepared to talk now?' Brüning enquired.

'For God's sake,' François muttered, 'I've got nothing to say.'

A peculiar smile twisted Brüning's mouth. 'All right, we shall return later, *monsieur*,' he said.

When they had gone, François let his head fall back to his chest and tried to wrench his mind away from the pain, but it was a long time before he was capable of coherent thought.

It was pointless, he knew it and they knew it. He was here because someone had to be blamed for Hitler's astonishing error back in May, when he had halted his army for those three vital days – days in which the British had managed to mount one of the most extraordinary rescue operations the world had ever seen. As soon as Hitler realized what was happening he had given the order to mobilize again, but by then it was too late. The British were snatching their troops from under the Germans' noses, and despite the fierce battle that raged in the sky, on the sea and on land, they had managed to rescue over three hundred thousand men, who now lived to fight another day. The Germans' three-day halt was likely to prove one of the greatest strategic errors in history, and Hitler had been persuaded to attribute it to false information supplied by the Abwehr. And he, François, was the Abwehr's chosen scapegoat. Not only because his loyalty was still in question, but because while he was on a visit to the Franco-Belgian border in May, von Liebermann had introduced him to the Führer. Now the Abwehr were claiming that he had somehow succeeded in passing information to their leader in a three-minute encounter during which any number of generals could have heard his every word.

It was fatuous – and yet, despite everything, it still gave François a certain satisfaction to know that Hitler's bull-headed refusal to mobilize sooner had had such dire consequences. He knew that France had fallen, but he also knew that Operation Sealion – the plan to invade Britain – had been postponed. That was undoubtedly one consequence of that extraordinary three-day halt – and there were sure to be others.

His mind blurred for a few minutes, then his eyes opened again and he tried to ease himself to a more comfortable position. But his broken ribs and the vice-like ropes intensified the pain as soon as he moved. The scar on his face was once again a fresh, open wound, and blood trickled down his cheek. He wondered dimly if they were going to keep him here until he finally expired from the injuries they were inflicting. He would be of little use to them then – but better that than become a traitor.

His mind, as it always did when he was left alone for any length of time, turned to Claudine. How he wished he had allowed himself the luxury of her love sooner! Perhaps then the thought of dying would be easier to bear. As it was, he wanted more than anything to live, to turn those ten days they had known into a lifetime. He closed his eyes and swallowed hard on the choking emotion. Lack of sleep and food had weakened him, and the desire to see her again, to hold her in his arms and breathe the fragrance of her hair as he told her over and over how much he loved her, was as vivid and unrelenting as the pain.

He had no idea what was happening in France, what she was having to face under the occupation, but he knew that she would find the courage for whatever ordeals she had to meet. The thought reassured him a little, even though he knew how headstrong and impulsive she could be. He just hoped to God Helber's brother-in-law, Fritz Blomberg, wasn't carrying out the threats he had made before departing for Lorvoire. Though she would put up a fight, he knew that if she thought his life depended on it she would do whatever Blomberg asked of her, and he had no way of telling her that he would rather die than have her submit to him. As it was, he had contemplated suicide as a means of rescuing her from the threat of Halunke – but he did not have the means for suicide here. And he had no idea where Halunke was, or whom he was planning to strike at next.

François groaned as his frustration fired the physical pain through his body. He had brought her to this, to a point where she was trapped, hemmed in by Blomberg's lechery and Halunke's revenge. If anything happened to her . . .

The worst of it was, if he hadn't been so insanely foolish as to let von Liebermann know how he felt about Max Helber, he might by now have discovered Halunke's identity. As it was, during the three days he had spent at Helber's Berlin apartment, Helber had seen to it that they were never alone together; and though he had managed to push a note under Helber's door telling him that he was now prepared to do whatever Helber wanted in return for the information he required, Helber hadn't trusted him. And Helber's instincts were right, because the day would come when he *would* carry out the threat he had made. Even now, even in here, the thought of Élise's injuries incensed him beyond words.

Outside in the corridor, at a distance from the room where François was being held, von Liebermann was talking quietly with Brüning.

'It is hardly surprising that he continues to deny it,' he wheezed, still breathless from his climb up the stairs. 'No one in the world knows why the Führer took that decision, least of all de Lorvoire. But we have to make a show. How is he bearing up?'

'Any other man would be close to death by now,' Brüning answered. 'The only thing de Lorvoire has come close to is unconsciousness.'

Von Liebermann scratched the warts on his chin. 'I did not go to all this effort so that he could be used as a scapegoat for . . .' He stopped before the treasonous words were spoken. 'Everyone knows there can be no confession, and I have plans for de Lorvoire that require his health. So, I am ordering you to leave him be for a while. I will speak with Herr Himmler and see what can be done. How long, in your estimation, will it take for his wounds to heal?'

'If it was any other man,' Brüning said with a smirk, 'I should say six months, possibly more. As it is de Lorvoire, three months.'

Von Liebermann nodded thoughtfully. 'That will take us

into the New Year.' Annoyance flashed in his eyes. 'We might have had him sooner if the Luftwaffe's defeat in the sky battle hadn't been presented as a direct result of halting our troops for those damned three days. Why, oh why, did I introduce him to the Führer? If I hadn't, someone else's neck would be on the block and we wouldn't be here now, wasting our time. And if you repeat one word of that, Brüning, I'll have your tongue cut out.'

Brüning saluted. 'Yes, sir.'

Von Liebermann chuckled. His *Komitee* were loyal, but it amused him to make that kind of threat. 'Get a doctor to de Lorvoire,' he said, starting back towards the stairs and gesturing to Brüning to follow, 'and keep me abreast of his progress. In the meantime, I have something of a more personal nature to discuss with you concerning de Lorvoire. I have heard from Fritz Blomberg. He has, as we instructed, made contact with Halunke.'

'Ah! And how is our friend Halunke?'

'Worried. He believes that de Lorvoire's courier is getting a little too close for comfort. It would appear von Pappen has been asking questions of the right people, and is presumably coming up with the right answers. Naturally, I share Halunke's concern. It would be most inconvenient if his identity were to be discovered now. Fortunately he is not planning a *Blitzkrieg* on de Lorvoire's family because de Lorvoire is not there to witness it – which, as we know, is something our friend Halunke prefers. Even so, his next subject, I believe, will be the *vigneron*.'

Both men laughed. 'It will shake de Lorvoire considerably when his wife's protector is slaughtered,' von Liebermann continued. 'He will really feel the net beginning to close then, and that will give us even greater leverage on him.' Again he laughed, and clapped Brüning on the shoulder as they reached the bottom of the staircase. 'I do hope I can obtain de Lorvoire's release soon; I'm looking forward to the time when those two men are forced to pit their skills against one another. It will be a most interesting spectacle, don't you agree?'

'You are intending to send de Lorvoire back to France?' Brüning said, surprised.

'Most certainly.'

'But how will that serve us?'

'All in good time, Walter. All in good time.'

'And the courier? Are we going to do something about him?'

'I'm giving the matter some thought,' von Liebermann answered.

Two junior officers helped them into their coats, then they went out into the biting wind that swept through the bleak grounds of Belsen concentration camp.

'Incidentally,' Brüning said, as they approached von Liebermann's Mercedes, 'has de Lorvoire's wife succumbed to Blomberg yet?'

'I have no idea, Walter. Blomberg's designs on the Comtesse's honour are of no interest to me. However, he did have a rather interesting encounter with Élise Pascale when passing through Paris a while ago.'

'Oh?'

'I will let Max tell you. He's waiting in the car. It is most amusing, my friend. Most amusing.'

Béatrice Baptiste, Élise's 'nursemaid', knew only too well what was going on in the sitting-room now that the voices had stopped. Nevertheless she stole a quick look round the door to reassure herself that no harm had come to her charge. Everything was as she had expected. The two Abwehr officers whose chauffeur had driven them over from their headquarters on the avenue de l'Opéra for the third time that week, were seated side by side on the sofa, and Élise, *comme d'habitude*, was on her knees in front of them, providing them with oral stimulation.

Béatrice closed the door quietly, and sat down on a chair to wait. Today Élise was playing the part of Agnès Sorel, the mistress of King Charles VII. The last time she had been Diane de Poitiers, mistress of King Henry II, and the time before that she had been the most famous of all French mistresses, Jeanne, Marquise de Pompadour. She had had clothes made up to suit each part, which was how Béatrice could tell that she was Agnès Sorel today: the only portrait they had been able to find of Agnès was one in which her bodice was unlaced and her left breast revealed. Élise had been delighted when she saw it was the left breast, for she would never have been able to show her right one; the nipple had been severed by Halunke's knife.

Béatrice and Erich had decided some time ago that they should allow Élise to do as she pleased with her German visitors. Erich had been against it at first, not only because of what François might say, but because he couldn't begin to understand why Élise should want to do it. But Béatrice had understood. Élise needed to know that she still had the power not only to arouse a man, but to satisfy him too. If she couldn't do that, she had wept when explaining it to Béatrice, then she might as well be dead. She had gone on to tell Béatrice how, even as a child, she had idolized the powerful courtesans of the French court. She had modelled herself on them for so long, Béatrice realized, that now, in the troubled recesses of her poor, deranged mind, she had become them – all of them. Naturally, François was the monarch at whose throne she knelt, and like the concubines of old she continued her scheming and conniving to gain what she wanted. Which was, of course, to become his queen.

Madame la Comtesse had little to fear from her, though, for Béatrice never let Élise out of her sight. And as for the German officers Élise was rewarding for their part in her conspiracy to kill Claudine, it was evident that they didn't know what she was talking about, and didn't care either. But Élise, poor, tortured, lonely Élise, knew such a sense of purpose to her life again now that, just as Béatrice had hoped, the nightmares and visions had begun to subside.

'It's tomorrow!' Élise hissed, half an hour later as Béatrice closed the door behind the Germans. 'We're going to kill her tomorrow!'

Béatrice smiled. She had heard it a hundred times before. Tucking Élise's breast back into the bodice of her dress, she led her into the sitting-room.

For several minutes she listened as Élise told her, in frenzied detail, what she had discussed with the Germans. It was obvious that she had forgotten precisely what she was talking about. Then at last the glassy look came into her eyes, signalling an imminent return to sanity.

'I know they're laughing at me, Béatrice,' she said, her long skirts sweeping across the floor as she limped to the window. 'But I have to do it. You understand that, don't you?'

'Yes, I understand, *chérie.*'

'But will François?' She turned to look at Béatrice, and Béatrice's heart turned over at the haunted, childlike look in her eyes. 'Has there been any word from him?'

Béatrice shook her head.

After a while Élise smiled and said, 'There will be, soon.' Then her face darkened. 'Has Erich found out who Halunke is yet?' And fully expecting Béatrice to say no, she turned to gaze out of the window. But when Béatrice's soft voice answered in the affirmative, Élise's eyes dilated and she turned back again.

'What!' she gasped. 'Why didn't you tell me before? Who? Who is it?'

'He won't tell me,' Béatrice said apologetically. 'He says that . . .'

'No, I don't believe you,' Élise said, shaking her head

rapidly from side to side. 'If he knew he would have told you, I know he would, and I have a right to know, Béatrice.'

'I won't deny that, Élise, but I swear it's the truth. I don't know who Halunke is.' She sighed. 'I've already gone too far in telling you this much. It was only that I wanted you to know that he'll be caught soon. But until Erich has actual proof, and until he talks to François, he's refusing even to tell me.'

Erich von Pappen was sitting in his shabby studio room in the Residence Domance on the Left Bank, staring down at the papers in front of him. His eyes were sore from lack of sleep and his fingers stained with nicotine. He had been over it time and time again, sifting through lists of names and dates until his head ached and his vision blurred, but always the result was the same. And he knew he now had finally to admit that he was never going to come up with the answer.

He gazed despondently down at the single sheet of paper he had placed on top of the pile. There was no longer any doubt that Halunke's true identity belonged to one of the two men whose names were written on it. He gained no satisfaction from knowing that he had been right to think Hortense de Bourchain's murder was at the root of it, but if he lived to reach a hundred he would never understand why either man should feel the need to seek such bitter revenge. François would not understand it either; von Pappen knew that he had never for a moment considered that Halunke was a man as close to him as this.

He stood up, walked over to the bed and sat down with his head in his hands. He knew now that François was being held in Belsen. He also knew that he would be returning to France within a month – his source inside the Abwehr had given him the information a week ago. The question was, how the hell was he going to tell François about Halunke?

And what the hell was François going to do when he found out that the man who had butchered Élise, who had killed his father, who had driven him into the hands of the Abwehr, and who could even now be threatening the lives of his wife and son, was either his brother, Lucien de Lorvoire, or his *vigneron*, Armand St Jacques?

Everything fitted for both men, the dates, the times, the places. The only thing he could not get straight was motive. Lucien had been Hortense de Bourchain's lover, and Armand had witnessed François killing her. But why in God's name would Lucien kill his own father? And why should Hortense's death matter to Armand? But there could no longer be any doubt. At the time Élise was attacked, Lucien was in Paris and Armand, von Pappen had since discovered, was absent from Lorvoire. At the time Louis died, both men were at Lorvoire. And every time Claudine had experienced that extraordinary sense of being spied on, Lucien had been absent from his regiment and Armand had been there in the forest with her.

Von Pappen glanced at the window and saw that it was beginning to get dark. He heard the dull clatter of wooden shoes on the cobbles as the people of Montparnasse hurried to get home before curfew. Knowing that very soon now the *concièrge* would go outside to check that there was no light escaping from the Residence windows, he got up to close the shutters and pull the heavy black drapes. The power had been off all day; he struck a match and lit both a candle and a cigarette.

He didn't hear the footsteps on the stairs, or the bare boards creaking on the landing outside. Even if he had, he would have presumed they belonged to one of his neighbours. He drew deeply on his cigarette and asked himself for the thousandth time where Lucien de Lorvoire was now.

The door handle behind him started to turn. Unaware of it, his mind moved to Armand St Jacques, the man François had allowed to have an affair with his wife in order that he should protect her. Which of these two hated François so much that they could do this to him? Which one of them was Halunke?

Von Pappen felt a cold draught blow into the room. It unsettled the curtains and made him shiver. Then he realized that he was no longer alone. He turned round. A sad, crooked smile came to his face. So now he knew who Halunke was, and his last thought before the bullet tore through his brain was one of desperate sorrow that he would never be able to tell François.

– 27 –

Claudine was in the kitchen with Arlette, grinding acorns to make coffee and discussing that week's menus, when the door opened and Louis toddled in, followed by Corinne.

'*Maman*, we have a surprise for you,' he said.

'You do?' she smiled, sweeping him up in her arms. He was so like his father now that her heart turned over every time she saw him. She hadn't heard from François in almost a year. There had been no news either from Erich von Pappen, though she couldn't make up her mind whether that was good or bad.

For weeks, following his last visit, she had tried to obtain an *Ausweis* in order to travel to Paris, but her application was constantly refused. What she hoped to achieve once she was there, she wasn't sure, for she had no idea where Erich lived; what she did know was that sitting around at Lorvoire tearing herself to pieces with worry was serving no purpose at all. However, in the end she had no choice, because as Armand pointed out, if she defied the Germans there was no telling what reprisals would be visited on the family.

With Armand, it was a different matter. Since he had taken over the selling of the wine he found it much easier to obtain travel documents, so, only the week before, he had gone to Paris himself. He was there for five days, by which time the date on his permit had expired and he was forced to return to Lorvoire. He hadn't managed to find Erich von Pappen.

'And what is the surprise, *chéri*?' Claudine said, swallowing the lump in her throat and kissing Louis' cheek.

'You have to come upstairs,' he said, frowning and rubbing his fist over the wet patch her kiss had left.

'Right now?'

He turned to look at Corinne and she nodded. 'Yes, now,' he confirmed. He wriggled to be put down, then held out his hand to lead her from the kitchen. Claudine gave Arlette a mystified shrug and told her she would be back.

'I've painted a picture for you,' Louis told her as they started up the stairs, 'but you're not to keep kissing me for it.'

'I wouldn't dream of it,' Claudine answered, grinning as she caught Corinne's eye.

'But that isn't the surprise,' Louis added.

Claudine wondered why he didn't seem very excited: giving her a surprise was usually a source of tremendous glee. This time he seemed, if anything, rather bemused, and she was more than a little intrigued to find out what was waiting for her in the nursery.

As they crossed the landing to take the stairs to the second floor, they passed the door to Blomberg's room. Claudine felt a sudden blaze of hatred. Only the night before he had made her kneel in front of him to polish his boots, then he had called in Hans and made her clean his too. But that was nothing to what he had forced her to do the week before. He had returned from the Château d'Artigny very nearly drooling at the mouth because he had only that day discovered she was half-English. In graphic detail he told her then what was happening to other dual-nationals – and their children – in the rest of occupied France. Of course, he said, it was his duty to pass this information to the Gestapo, but as they had become such good friends he was willing to overlook his duty in this instance, providing . . .

He had laughed so hard then that he had started to choke, so it was some minutes before he was able to tell her the price of his silence. An hour later she was in the drawing-room, the door was locked, and she was performing for three German officers, whom Blomberg had invited to watch the Comtesse de Lorvoire crawl about on all fours, naked.

She was now deeply suspicious of how much Blomberg actually knew about François and what he was doing, but she dared not run the risk of defying him until she had definite proof he was lying, but even then there was now this added complication of her being half-English. So for the time being at least she had no choice but to do as he said, but one day he would pay. He would pay with his life and she personally was going to take it.

'There's no need to look so gloomy,' Corinne whispered in her ear, 'it's really quite a nice surprise.'

Claudine forced a smile, but she doubted whether anything short of François' return would cheer her up today. But she was wrong.

When they reached the nursery playroom, Louis positioned her in the middle of the floor and Corinne closed the door. Then someone came up behind her, and put a hand over her eyes and said, 'Guess who?'

She spun round, her eyes wide and her heart racing. 'Lucien!' she cried, and flung her arms around him. 'Oh Lucien, we thought you were dead! We thought, oh, I don't know, we thought so many things . . . Let me look at you! Oh, you don't know how good it is to see you! Solange will

be ecstatic. We'll have to break it to her gently, but even then
. . .' Suddenly the smile fell from her face and she looked
from his empty sleeve back to his laughing eyes. 'Lucien!
What happened to your arm?'

'Careless of me, I know,' he answered, 'but I lost the
darned thing and couldn't find it anywhere.'

'But how?'

'It's a long story. I'm just glad it was my left arm and not
the right, or I'd be really stymied. Anyway, I'm getting used
to it now, I hardly notice it's missing.'

'Are you Papa?' Louis asked, gazing up at him curiously.

Grinning, Lucien lowered himself to Louis' height and
said, 'No. I'm your Uncle Lucien. Don't you remember
me?'

Louis pulled a face, then looked at Claudine. 'I think so,'
he said. Then turning back to Lucien, 'Do you know where
Papa is?'

It was Lucien's turn to look at Claudine. 'No,' he
answered.

'We haven't heard from him in almost a year,' Claudine
said. 'I'll tell you about it later. First, I'd better go and break
the news to Solange.'

'No,' Lucien said, standing up and lifting Louis with him.
'We're not going to tell *Grand-mère* I'm here, are we,
Louis?'

Louis' face took on a conspiratorial look and he solemnly
shook his head. Then Corinne took him into her own arms
and reminded him that they had the chickens to feed.

'We only have two horses now,' Louis told Lucien, 'the
Germans took the others. So we keep chickens in the stables
instead.'

'I see,' Lucien nodded, 'that seems to make sense.'

Louis drew back as Claudine went to kiss him goodbye,
but then, relenting, he offered her his cheek on the
understanding that she didn't make it wet.

'He's grown so much,' Lucien chuckled as the door closed behind Louis and Corinne, 'I can hardly believe it. I'm sorry he saw me, by the way, but he happened to walk out of the nursery just as I let myself in from the bridge. Gave him the fright of his life, I think. Thank God Corinne was behind him or he might have screamed. You have Germans living here, I'm told?'

'Just the one. And his chauffeur. They're out all day.'

'What's he like?'

'Don't ask,' Claudine said. She sat down on the sofa, and Lucien joined her. 'Now what's all this business about not telling Solange?'

He glanced at his watch. 'You won't be missed?' he said.

'No.' Arlette would carry on without her.

'All right. I'd better start at the beginning.'

'Start with the arm.'

He nodded. Then, as if rattling off a shopping list, he said, 'I was engaged in the fighting at Abbeville with the Fourth Armoured Division under de Gaulle. Then the Germans pushed through, cutting us off from the main British Expeditionary Force, and I was injured – not seriously, but enough to put me out for several days. The next thing I knew I was at Dunkirk, being piled into a stinking fishing boat along with dozens of others. As we started into the Channel our boat collided with another, and my arm, which was hanging over the side at the time . . .' He made a slicing motion with his hand and grinned as Claudine winced.

'Anyway,' he went on, 'we got to England and I was carted off to hospital, which was where one of de Gaulle's men found me. He took me off to London as soon as I'd recovered, and that's where I was until January. In January I sailed back to France with a couple of others, again in a stinking fishing boat. We made our way to Paris, holed up there for a while, and now I'm here.'

'Why do I get the impression you've missed out the most important bit?'

Lucien grinned. 'Because I have. And because I have to know that I can trust you before I tell you anything else.'

'And what am I supposed to do to convince you of that?'

'I guess nothing, because I'm going to trust you anyway. I have to. The reason I'm here in France is to help organize an escape route for the British pilots who are shot down or forced to bail out of their aircraft. It's imperative that we get them back to England as quickly as possible so that they can continue the fight.'

'And where do I come in?'

'We need safe-houses for the pilots right the way through the country down into Spain. We also need couriers to let the safe-houses know when to expect the pilots. But that's only the beginning. We need clothes, documents, guides, doctors, medication and as much information about the movement of German troops as we can get. You have contacts in this area, so does Armand. Where is he, by the way? Perhaps we should call him in?'

Claudine shook her head. 'He went to Blois yesterday and won't be back until Friday.'

'I thought he was supposed to be protecting you from François' nemesis?'

'Life has to go on, Lucien.'

He nodded. 'Has anyone discovered who Halunke is yet?'

'I don't think so. But as I said, we haven't heard from François for almost a year.'

'What about von Pappen?'

'He came here a few months ago. Looking for you, as a matter of fact.'

'Did he?' Lucien said thoughtfully. 'Did he say *why* he was looking for me?'

'No. He just said he was concerned.'

Lucien laughed. 'Probably thought I'd got myself killed.

Well, we can put his mind at rest now. So what's all this about Armand going to Blois?'

'He travels quite a lot to sell the wine.' She shrugged. 'Someone has to, now François isn't here to do it.'

His eyes narrowed as he looked at her, and he wondered if he should tell her that he knew how in love she and his brother were, so there was no need to hide it from him. But he decided not to. She was handling it in her own way, and now wasn't the time to be having that kind of conversation. 'So who's running the vineyards?' he asked.

'Armand. Solange, Monique and I help as much as we can. But that's not important. What is important is that Armand finds it much easier than most to obtain a *laissez-passer*, or an *Ausweis* – the documents we need to travel about the country. So he could be invaluable as a courier.'

'He most certainly could,' Lucien agreed. 'Pity he's not here now. I have three airmen at a safe house in La Flèche, and I need to get word to their next safe-house which is just outside Loudun. I can't go myself because I have to return to La Flèche before curfew to get them.'

'I'll go,' Claudine said, without even thinking about it.

'You would?' Lucien exclaimed. 'That's just what I was hoping you'd say.' And putting his arm round her, he gave her a smacking kiss on the forehead. 'You're a remarkable woman, Claudine!'

She pulled a face, and extricating herself from his embrace, said, 'So, what do I do, and who should I speak to?'

'First things first,' he chuckled. 'You have to think of a cover-story for why you're going to Lémeré.'

'Lémeré? But I thought you said Loudun?'

'I did. But we're introducing a system of cut-outs, which means you never actually meet the person you're trying to contact. That way, if the Gestapo get hold of you you won't be able to betray anyone. So, you are to go to the post office in Lémeré and ask to send a long cable including the words

"Grandfather is sick", then make a fuss about the charge. That way the postmaster will pay extra attention to your cable, and when he sees the code he'll know he has to pass the message on to the next cut-out point.'

'But that way I know who my contact is. And he'll know me.'

'As I know you, etc. It's not a perfect system, but we're working on it. However, if the Germans rumble you and torture you, which they will if they catch you, you will be able to tell them only of the post office in Lémeré. And if you disappear, I will know, so I can warn the postmaster.'

'And if I tell them about you?'

'What can you tell them? You have no idea where I'm going from here.'

'La Flèche.'

'That's what I've told you.'

She grinned. 'I'm with you.'

'Good. So all you need now is a cover-story, and a cable.'

'The cable is easy enough. I'll simply address it to some friends in the south and tell them how sorry I am to learn their grandfather is sick.'

'And sign it with a fictitious name. The last thing the postmaster will want to know is who you really are.'

She nodded. 'And the reason I'm going to Lémeré, if I'm stopped along the way? I know, Liliane has a friend in Lémeré, I'll say I'm taking her some eggs because Liliane can't ride a bicycle.'

'Pretty thin,' Lucien said.

'You know, we spend half our time pedalling round the countryside delivering farm produce to old folk.'

'All right. But keep to the back roads, and if there's a German anywhere near the post office, don't go in. Just deliver the eggs and come home. If you succeed in passing the message, then black-out your bedroom window at curfew as normal, but leave the shutters open. If you fail, close the shutters. That way, I'll know.'

'So you're going to be passing through the forest. Should you really be telling me that?'

Lucien laughed and got up. 'I can see you're going to make an excellent agent! But even agents have to tell one another something. Now, I'm going to make my way back to La Flèche,' he gave her a comical look, 'and you should go to see Liliane and tell her you're taking eggs to her friend. And you'll have to do it, too.'

Claudine walked with him to the bridge door.

'One other thing before I go,' he said, pulling the door closed behind them. 'I don't know when I'll be able to get here again, but if I need you to relay another message, Jacques will come. It's not his real name, of course, and you should think of a pseudonym too, by the way. Do it now.'

'Antoinette,' she said, immediately giving her mother's name.

'Good. I'll tell him to give an owl hoot from the forest if he needs to contact you. When you hear it, go to the edge of the bridge and wait. When he's sure you haven't been followed and aren't being watched, he'll come out of hiding. Then he'll give you a password. *It is snowing in Paris*. You answer with, *It often does in spring*. If you hear anything but that, scream! Make it look as though you were waiting for a lover or something – but if you have to, kill him. Do you have a gun?'

Claudine shook her head.

'I'll get one to you.' He grinned. 'Do you think you're up to it?'

'Killing?'

He nodded.

'Yes,' she answered without hesitation, thinking of Blomberg.

Laughing, he dropped a kiss on the tip of her nose and loped off into the forest. She waited until he had disappeared, then turned back inside. Just as she was closing the door she saw him come back through the trees. She waved, and he blew her kiss, mouthing the words, '*Bonne chance!*'

Several days later, Claudine was in the library reading the newspaper Gustave had slipped her that morning. It was by now three months old, the date at the top of the page was December 1940; but the clandestine newspapers often were well out of date by the time they received them. Circulating newspapers like *Résistance* – the one she was reading now – was an extremely risky business, and if the publishers, or indeed the readers, were caught, they would almost certainly be delivered into the hands of the Gestapo. Particularly if the paper carried a message on its front page like this one: 'Resist! This is the cry that comes from the hearts of all of you who suffer from our country's disaster. This is the wish of all of you who want to do your duty.'

A few minutes later Claudine pushed the newspaper back into the drawer of Louis' desk and locked it. Then, resting her chin on her hands, she started to think. Her little venture for Lucien the other day, which had passed without incident, had sharpened her appetite for action. She hadn't heard from him since, so she had no idea if he had managed to get the pilots to their next safe-house or not. But either way, she knew she couldn't just sit around waiting for him to make contact. The time had come for a more organized resistance, and instead of talking about it she must actually *do* something about it.

The problems were manifold, that much was clear. To begin with, though there were obviously plenty of people who would be willing to help, there were many more who wouldn't, and who would even betray those who did. Nevertheless, she made a mental list of those she felt sure she could rely on. Armand, naturally. Then there was his mother, who could possibly be persuaded into making her home a safe-house. And of course the cottage in the forest could be used too. There was also Gertrude Reinberg, who would undoubtedly be willing to make clothes for the pilots. And Doctor Lebrun, who had already volunteered the information that the telephone operator in Chinon was listening into German telephone calls, and said how frustrated he felt at having no one to pass the intelligence on to. So what they needed was to co-ordinate and extend this little network in such a way that it would not only help Lucien and the pilots, but would to some degree harass and thwart the Germans.

She must begin with a recruitment programme. Potential resisters should be given a rigorous interview and various tests of loyalty, and must be initially recommended by someone already known to be trustworthy. What then? Defacing German posters, cutting telephone lines, re-hoisting French flags and slashing tyres was hardly going to send the Germans scuttling back to the Fatherland. Annoyance wasn't enough; they must be inconvenienced. But how? They, the resisters, had no weapons, no training, no underground experience . . .

Claudine's eye suddenly widened, and she couldn't imagine why the idea hadn't occurred to her before. Corinne. She would know exactly how to go about this, she could even help train the recruits in unarmed combat.

Excitedly, Claudine got up from her chair and began to pace the room. She must think this through a little more, because Corinne's job was to protect Louis, and that must come first. But Corinne could act as an adviser; the training she, Claudine, would carry out herself. She would need someone to head their little group, too, once it was under way. Most of their members would probably be men, and knowing the French as she did, it would be fatuous of her to expect them to take orders from a woman. Lucien's visits were going to be erratic, but Armand was both liked and respected and, as she had pointed out to Lucien, he had the perfect excuse for travelling about the countryside, and *bona fide* documents that would even take him over the demarcation line and into Vichy France if necessary.

Yes, it was all beginning to shape up nicely. There was no point in thinking about the danger, if she did that she would become one of the *Attentistes* she accused Tante Céline of being. Sitting around waiting to see what would happen wasn't good enough. They had to *make* things happen, and the sooner they started the better. Armand was due back later that day, so she would cycle into the village, return the newspaper to Gustave ... Gustave! There was another recruit. A café was the perfect place to pass on information.

'Ah! I was just coming to see you,' Armand said as she walked out of the café an hour later.

'And I you,' Claudine said. 'How was Blois?'

'Successful.'

'Good. Did Estelle enjoy her trip?'

'I think so.'

His face had turned slightly pink at the mention of Estelle, but if he hadn't told her himself that he was taking Estelle to Blois she would never have mentioned it. 'And what were you coming to see me about?' she asked, as they turned to walk across the square.

'Two things. First, I wanted to know that you were all right.' He grinned. 'That the big bad wolf hadn't come out of the forest to get you.'

They often joked about Halunke now, it was probably one of the best ways of dealing with it, she'd decided. 'As a matter of fact,' she said, smiling, 'someone did come out of the forest.'

Immediately he was angry. 'I've told you time and time again that I shouldn't be leaving you to go and sell wine. We should employ someone else to do it ...'

'Oh, do be quiet, Armand, and stop fussing,' she laughed. 'Now, don't you want to know who it was?'

'Well?' he said.

She put her head to one side, caught her scarf as it took off in the wind, and said, 'Lucien.'

'What!'

'Yes, our very own Lucien. Alive and kicking and in need of our help. Which is why I was coming to see you.'

'Help? What kind of help?'

Claudine glanced about her, and seeing that there was no one in sight decided that here was as good a place as any. She perched herself on the edge of the well, and began.

'. . . So what d'you think?' she said, when she had finished. 'It'll be risky, I know, but . . .'

'Risky! It'll be downright dangerous,' he cried. 'We might just as well go and put ourselves in front of a firing squad now.'

'Oh, Armand,' she groaned. 'Please don't . . .'

'Count me in,' he laughed. 'When are you seeing Lucien again?'

Resisting the urge to hug him, she said, 'I don't know. He didn't say. But that's no reason for us to wait. We can have everything organized by the time he returns.'

'All right. I'll make a start by going to ask my mother about this safe-house business, and you can talk to Gustave. Then I want you to meet me on the bridge at eleven thirty tomorrow morning.'

'Oh?' she said curiously.

'It's the second reason I was coming to see you this afternoon. But it can wait until then.'

Claudine shivered and pulled her waterproof hat tighter onto her head. It was a horrible, dreary day, the sky was leaden grey and the wind bitingly cold. Armand was leading the way through the forest, and though she was trying to concentrate on what he was saying, the fact that they were clearly heading towards the old cottage was unsettling her.

He had so far refused to tell her why they were going there, except to say that he had something to show her.

They reached a dip in the path and she slipped in the slimy undergrowth, her scarf getting hooked on the spiky branches of a low-hanging tree.

'Armand, I do wish you would tell me what's going on,' she said, exasperated.

'You'll see soon enough,' he answered, helping her to untangle her scarf, then winding it about her neck. 'Now come along, we're almost there.'

A few minutes later they approached the clearing in front of the cottage, and Claudine saw straightaway that there was smoke coming from the chimney. Her heart sank. It was days like this that she and Armand had found so romantic, making love in front of the fire and huddling into the coarse blankets they took from the bed . . .

'Wait!' Armand put out a hand to stop her going any further. 'Wait here,' he whispered, and hunching his shoulders against the rain, he crept quietly across the clearing.

She watched, not a little irritated, as he pressed himself against the wall of the cottage and edged towards the window. He peered inside, then looked back to where she was standing and signalled her to join him.

'What is it?' she whispered as she walked into the circle of his arm. But he only put a finger over his lips then pushed her towards the window.

At first she couldn't see anything through the steam on the glass, but Armand pointed to a clear patch near the bottom and she stooped to look through.

Her eyes scanned the room. It hadn't changed a bit since she was last there; even her amateurish portrait of Armand still hung over the fireplace. The table was laid for lunch, with pieces of broken bread, a half-empty bottle of wine and – considering the ration per person per day was a quarter of an ounce – a surprisingly generous wedge of cheese. She could hear voices, but she couldn't actually see anyone until she re-positioned herself and looked over into the far corner where the old bed was pushed up against the wall. On it were two naked figures in the final throes of making love. Immediately Claudine drew back and turned an angry face to Armand.

He shook his head. 'Look closer,' he hissed.

Her face was taut with disapproval, but she dragged her eyes back to the window, and as she looked in again the man rolled over onto his back. Claudine's stomach gave a sickening lurch. It was Hans, Blomberg's chauffeur, and the woman he had been making love to was Monique.

It was almost four o'clock by the time Monique let herself in through the bridge door. Claudine was waiting for her. Without uttering a word, she grabbed Monique by the arm and hauled her into her bedroom.

'What the hell's going on?' Monique cried, snatching her arm away and glaring at Claudine defiantly.

Claudine slammed the door. 'I'd like *you* to tell *me* that!' she said, trying to keep her voice down. 'I saw you, Monique. I saw you with my own eyes, so don't bother to deny it. Now what the hell do you think you're doing fornicating with Germans? You know what could happen . . .'

'How *dare* you speak to me like that!'

'I dare. And if need be I'll keep you locked in your room to stop you seeing him again.'

For a moment Monique was speechless with rage. 'Just who do you think you are!' she shouted. 'I'm not a child . . .'

'No! You're a damned fool. You know as well as I do what the penalty is for sleeping with a German. They call it "polluting the master race", Monique, and for that you can be shot.'

– 496 –

'But we're in love!' Monique cried, tears starting to pour from her eyes. 'You know what it's like to be in love, so how can you . . .'

'Stop it! Stop it now!' Claudine shouted. 'If he's in love with you, why is he putting you in this danger?' An image of François flashed into her mind and for once she was relieved that no one knew how they felt about each other. 'If I can find out so easily what's going on,' she continued, 'then so can others. The worst that can happen to Hans is that he'll be transferred elsewhere. But *you*, you could find yourself facing a firing squad and there won't be a damned thing he can do to help you.'

Burying her face in her hands, Monique started to run from the room, but Claudine caught her and pulled her back. 'No!' she said firmly. 'You are not going to run away. You're going to sit here and talk to me, and I'm not letting you leave until I have your word that you won't see him again.'

'You can't stop me!' Monique sobbed.

'I can stop you, and I will. I care a great deal about you, Monique, so do the rest of your family, and think what it would do to your mother if she were to find out.' Then, realizing that she was being perhaps a little too harsh, she softened her voice and said, 'Come and sit down, Monique. Sit down and listen to what I have to say.'

Once they were sitting side by side on the bed, she took a handkerchief from her pocket and wiped the tears from Monique's cheeks. 'I'm sorry I flew off the handle,' she said gently, 'but I was afraid for you. I still am.'

Monique's wide, amber eyes looked at her, searching her face as if she might find the answers to the misery of her life. 'Oh, Claudine,' she said, her voice catching in her throat. 'Claudine, I don't know what to do any more. I'm so lonely. I can't find anyone to love me, to care about me. What's wrong with me? Please tell me. Why is this happening?'

'I don't know, *chérie*,' Claudine answered, hugging her. 'I wish I did. But you can't go on seeing Hans, you know that, don't you?'

'But what if he's the right one for me? What if we're meant to be together?'

Claudine shook her head. 'He's not, Monique. This may hurt you, but I have to make you understand that he is simply using you. Armand tells me that Hans has quite a reputation in Chinon, that he sleeps with a lot of the girls.'

'That's not true!' Monique wailed. 'How would Armand know, anyway?'

'Estelle told him. She was the one who first saw you at the cottage with Hans. Now listen, I'm going to let you into a secret. It won't exactly make up for anything, but I think it'll make you a little happier than you are now. But you have to swear to me first that you won't tell Solange.'

'I swear,' Monique said.

Claudine took a deep breath, sent up a silent prayer that she was doing the right thing, then put her hands on Monique's shoulders and said, 'I've seen Lucien. He's been here . . .' But she got no further, for Monique let out a howl and fell sobbing into her arms.

'Lucien!' she cried. 'Lucien! Where is he now? Oh, Claudine, why didn't he see me too? But I know why. Oh, Claudine, I can't bear it. I love him so much. And François. They love me, they're the only men who love me. I want them back here, Claudine. I want François. François makes everything all right. He understands. He knows about Lucien and he understands the way I feel. But I can't feel it, Claudine. I mustn't. It's wrong, but I can't help it. I love him so much . . .'

A cold dread was starting to run through Claudine's veins, and pulling Monique away from her shoulder she looked into her eyes. 'What are you saying, Monique?' she whispered. 'What do you mean, it's wrong?'

Monique started to shake her head, and tearing herself away, she pushed her face into the pillow. 'Nothing!' she cried. 'I don't mean anything. I can't tell you. I can't tell anyone. Only François knows.'

'Knows what, *chérie?*'

'Nothing! I shouldn't have said . . .' Her body was convulsed with sobs and Claudine could only stare at her in horror.

'Monique, are you in love with Lucien?' she said finally, staggered that she should even be thinking such a thing.

The silence that followed was confirmation enough, and for the moment Claudine felt too shocked to move. She looked at Monique. She was so still that for a moment Claudine thought she might have fainted. 'Does Lucien know?' Her voice was like an echo inside her head.

After what felt like an unbearably long time, Monique pulled herself up and looked into Claudine's eyes. But she couldn't hold the gaze and lowered her head. 'No one knows,' she said huskily. 'Except François.'

'How does he know?' Claudine whispered.

Monique blew her nose noisily. 'I told him. When I was fifteen. He found me crying one day and made me tell him why. I'd just come from Lucien's room where I'd caught him making love to the maid. They didn't see me, but I stood there for a long time watching them, and I was so jealous that I just wanted to kill her. François said it was natural for me to be jealous. He said that it had come as a shock to me to realize that Lucien could love another girl. He said that when I was older and had a relationship of my own, I'd understand how it was possible to love in two different ways. But I knew the way I was feeling wasn't normal. Lucien's my brother, my own flesh and blood, and I wanted him to hold me the way he . . .

'Oh Claudine, I tried so hard to believe what François had told me, but I knew I couldn't wait until I was older, I had to find out then. So I got one of the men from the vineyards to make love to me, but it was no good, I couldn't get Lucien and the maid out of my mind. I kept imagining that Christophe, the man from the vineyards, was Lucien . . . I told François, but he only said that it was because I didn't really love Christophe. He dismissed Christophe then, I know he did, though he told me that Christophe had left of his own accord . . .'

She looked up and Claudine's heart turned over at the anguish in her eyes. 'The worst thing,' she went on, 'is that François said the memory would fade – but it hasn't. Every time I make love with someone I see them together, her legs wrapped around Lucien's waist, Lucien's back, his shoulders, the sweat glistening on his skin . . . and I start to imagine that I'm the maid and the man I'm with is Lucien. I've tried so hard not to, I keep trying, but it's all I can think of. I so desperately want to fall in love with someone else, to prove to myself that I'm normal, but . . .' She looked off into the distance and swallowed hard on her tears. i don't know what to do, Claudine. I just don't know what to do.'

Claudine felt a gurgle of laughter in her throat as relief overcame her. 'Oh Monique!' she said, taking her hands, 'Monique. It's not what . . .'

'Don't! Don't say anything. I should never have told you, but I . . . It's so horrible and it's never going to change. I know you despise me now, I don't blame you! I despise myself. I want to die, so many times I've just wanted to . . .'

'Ssh!' Claudine soothed. 'Just tell me, when did you last talk to François about this?'

Monique shrugged. 'I don't know. A long time ago. When I was twenty, I think.'

'Then you're a silly goose. You should have talked to him again.'

'Why? It's his brother I'm talking about as well as mine. And he knows I still feel the way I do, but he's as disgusted by it as you are. But he understood, at first . . . Oh Claudine, so many awful things have happened because of it. François . . . François killed someone because of it.'

Claudine's face turned white. 'What do you mean? What are you saying, Monique?'

'François killed a woman because she loved Lucien. He knew I was jealous, so he killed her. I didn't want him to do it, but it was . . . No, I can't think of it. It was all so terrible. It was all my fault . . .'

'Monique, calm down,' Claudine said firmly. 'Now tell me, who was the woman?'

'Her name was Hortense. Hortense de Bourchain.'

It was the name Claudine had expected to hear, yet still she was stunned. 'No, Monique,' she said slowly. 'You're wrong. I don't know why François killed her, but he wouldn't have done it for the reasons you think.'

'How do you know? You weren't here. He's never told you . . .'

'He told me he killed her, but I know he wouldn't have done it because of the way you feel – you think you feel – about Lucien. Monique, you've got to listen to me, and you must try to understand what I'm saying. François was right when he told you you were shocked by finding Lucien in bed with the maid, and the way you responded was quite natural, given your age and how close you are to Lucien. But somehow you've managed to build it out of all proportion; you're so obsessed by the image of Lucien making love that you can't see beyond it. But you aren't going to exorcise the image by sleeping with every man you meet. Either your desperation will frighten them – as it did with Freddy – or your vulnerability will lead them to use you – as happened with Karol and with Hans.'

'You're not listening to me,' Monique cried. 'I think of Lucien when I'm making love with them, that's why things go wrong. Oh, they don't know it, I can hide it, but it's true, and somehow they must sense it.'

'No! All they sense is that they've got hold of a woman they can turn into a slave. The answer doesn't lie with these men, it lies with you. You have to face the truth – which is much, much easier than the terrible misconception you've been living with. Oh, if only you'd talked to François again. He would have helped you, things might never have gone this far . . . He probably thinks you're over it.'

'Well, I'm *not* over it.' Monique stood up abruptly. 'I don't want to discuss it any more. Please, I beg you, don't ever refer to it again. I'll stop seeing Hans, I'll do anything you ask of me, but please . . .' She broke down again, and before Claudine could stop her she had run out of the room.

If she hadn't at that moment heard the haunting owl hoot that was her signal to receive a message from Lucien, Claudine would have gone after her. She had no intention of letting the matter rest there. Monique was not in love with Lucien, but it was going to take a great deal of time, patience and understanding to help her put that adolescent trauma into perspective. However, for the moment the call from the forest was more pressing, and putting her coat round her shoulders, she let herself out into the icy rain and ran to the far edge of the bridge.

She waited, and after a few minutes a dark figure loomed out of the shadows. Her heart lurched into her throat. He was wearing heavy boots, a belted fur jerkin, and a voluminous black cap was pulled down over his eyes. She dreaded to think what Armand, or more particularly François, would say if they knew what she was doing now, but she pushed the thought to one side and watched the man approach.

'It's snowing in Paris,' he told her, his voice barely reaching her through the howl of the wind.

'It often does in spring,' she answered, her heart thudding wildly.

The stranger smiled briefly, then said, 'Two coming

through tomorrow night. Go to the *tabac* in Monts. Hand over these ration tickets,' he passed them to her, 'and ask for *five packets of Gauloises*. The answer you receive should be *I have only three*. Ask to smoke one there – since women aren't permitted to smoke in public it won't be such an unusual request – and he will take you through to the back of the shop. Smoke your cigarette, tell him two are coming through, then when he gives you the three packets, leave. If he has a message to relay to us it will be in the cigarettes. Don't open them, bring them here.' He took her by the arm and pulled her into the shadows. 'Put them there,' he said, pointing to a hollow in the bole of a tree, 'and I will collect them tomorrow night.' He bent down and reached inside the hole. Then standing up again, he pressed something into her hand. It was a gun.

'*Bonne chance!*' he said. Then he pulled his collar up round his face and sprinted off into the forest.

Claudine returned immediately to her room, secreted the gun beneath her pillow and went off to find Monique. But when she tried the door of Monique's room it was locked, and nothing Claudine said would persuade her to open it.

The following morning, while Claudine was in her sitting-room trying to concoct a reason for going to Monts, Solange came in and told her Monique had gone to stay with some friends at L'Île Bouchard.

'For how long?' Claudine asked, trying to swallow her frustration.

'Two weeks. Now, where is that grandson of mine? I expected to find him here.'

'He's in François' bathroom,' Claudine told her, 'having a shave.'

'What?' Solange shrilled.

'It's all right, there aren't any blades,' Claudine laughed, as Solange hurtled off in the direction of François' room, 'he's just pretending.'

Damn it, Claudine thought, what was she going to do about Monique? It was maddening to think that she was putting herself through such unnecessary misery. But there was nothing she could do about it for the moment, Claudine thought. She would just have to wait for her return.

As it turned out, it was almost five weeks before Monique came back. And the night before she returned, something happened to put Monique's problem, and everything else, right out of Claudine's mind.

– 28 –

Exhausted, and never having been quite so eager to climb into bed, Claudine dragged back the covers. She checked the time on her watch, snapped off the lamp and snuggled down into the crisp linen sheets Magaly had only moments before stroked with the warming pan.

It was approaching one in the morning, and three times during her cycle ride back from Montsoreau she had been forced to throw herself into a hedge to escape a German patrol. She had been terrified, not only of the Germans, but because it was the first time she had been out after curfew without Armand, and the driving rain, coupled with the almost solid blackness of the moonless night, had thrown up all manner of imaginary evils. But Lucien himself had come to the château the night before, to ask her and Armand to attend a meeting of the local resistance group at an old barn on the road between Montsoreau and Saumur. Armand had left for Le Mans that morning and wouldn't be back until the following day, so Claudine had gone alone, her gun tucked safely beneath the blanket in the handlebar basket.

When she arrived at the barn, following the directions Lucien had made her memorize, she had been amazed to count as many as twenty-five faces, although apart from Lucien and the man Jacques – who had come to the bridge several times now – they were all strangers to her. She was introduced as Antoinette, and guessed that all the names she was given in return were also false. The meeting was to tell them of their successes and failures so far, and to see if anyone had any suggestions about how they might improve and expand their network. It seemed that to date they had seen no fewer than twenty-three airmen through their escape-line, and suffered only four arrests – one *Résistant* and three pilots. Lucien had also managed to locate someone with a radio in Saumur, and had made contact with General de Gaulle's London headquarters three times in the past two weeks. He was now looking for a new hide-out for the radio operator, as the detector vans had picked up their last transmission. Claudine had immediately offered the cottage, as it was not only secluded but on high ground, which was vital. So the man would be arriving in the next few days, and would stay for about a week before he moved elsewhere.

'Though we are primarily working for de Gaulle's intelligence service,' Lucien said, 'I have been informed that the British have already started parachuting their own agents into France. I want everyone to dispense with any prejudice they might have towards the British,' he added hastily as several of the men made noises of protest, 'because it's essential we work together. They're bringing arms with them, small guns, hand grenades and the like, radio transmitters, canned food and even bicycles, all of which we need. These agents are going to need safe-houses, though most of them are fixed up before they leave England. But we must put ourselves at their disposal and help them in every way we can. They, like us, are working towards the liberation of France.'

Lucien cleared his throat. 'For now we need to store the

arms and ammunition, and get as much information as we can back to Britain on troop movements here.' He turned to Claudine. 'I want you and the rest of your family to cut all the labels from your French clothes and give them to me. I'm returning to Britain in a few days, so I can take them with me. Also, being half-English, Antoinette, you will know the kind of things British people do that might give them away as not being French. Write them down and let me have that too. They're setting up training centres around the British Isles to educate their agents in, amongst other things, the habits of the French.'

'What, you mean like. . . ?'

'. . . pissing on the side of the road,' Lucien finished for her, and they all laughed. 'Precisely,' he said.

They went on then to discuss the *réseaux* – which was what the resistance groups were collectively known as – in other parts of northern France, and how the British were planning to send in their own agents to head them. There were more grunts of disapproval at that, but Lucien let it go; the agents themselves would have to deal with the discontent when they arrived. It was a pity, he thought, that the British had been compelled to blow up the French fleet at Mers-el-Kabir; it would be a long time before the French forgave them for that. But the British had had no choice, the ships would otherwise have fallen into German hands – and besides, the animosity between the two nations went a lot further back than July of 1940.

'When I return from England,' Lucien went on, 'I fully expect to be asking you to form reception committees. That means that you'll be lighting up fields at night so that the pilots can see where to drop their supplies – and indeed agents. I don't have to tell you how risky that will be, but none of us is in this for the good of his health. In the meantime, Jacques here is arranging for us to join up with the Jupiter *réseau*, and Henri over there has found a printer willing to help us. We need a new forger, because Madame Germond has been arrested. As far as we know she's told the Gestapo nothing yet, but the three men who were in contact with her are now in hiding.'

The meeting broke up soon after that, and Claudine was one of the first to leave. 'I'm glad to have this chance to talk to you,' she said, as Lucien walked outside with her. 'I've told Monique that I've seen you. She's away at the moment, but when she comes back I want to get her involved as a courier. What do you think?'

'I don't know. Armand told me about the business with the German.'

'That's over,' Claudine said. 'It was a touch of summer madness.'

'In the middle of a wintry spring. Well, you're the best judge, you see more of her than the rest of us. But remember, it's not only her life you'll be putting at risk.'

'I'll remember. The other thing is, I think Solange should join us too. She has the perfect cover for going about the countryside, she's always visiting someone or other. And these days she takes Liliane with her in a box Armand attached to her bicycle. Of course, it takes them hours to get anywhere, but the Germans are so used to seeing them, they've become a sort of local attraction. And they look so funny that no one would suspect them of anything but eccentricity!'

Lucien was grinning widely as he pictured the spectacle.

'And,' Claudine went on, 'I hate keeping this from her. She's so worried about you, and I think she should know that at least one of her sons is alive.'

'All right,' he said, relenting. 'But don't tell her until I'm back from England. Then I'll work out a way to see her myself. I take it there's still no news from François?'

Claudine shook her head, and feeling a sudden and unexpected rush of tears she had turned quickly to her bicycle and started to pedal away . . .

Now, as she lay in the comfort and safety of her bed, the dreaded tears started to roll down her cheeks. But again she pushed François from her mind, making a mental note to go and see Gertrude Reinberg in the morning, to find out how she was getting on with the overalls and berets which were the uniform of French farm labourers, but were being made for escaping prisoners and pilots . . .

She had no idea what time it was when the noise woke her but she knew it couldn't yet be dawn because the room was still in darkness. She was lying on her side, and though her first instinct was to reach out for the light, she stopped herself and listened, praying that it had been nothing more than the wind outside. But there was a cold air in the room as though someone had left the door open, then she heard the curtains rustle in the breeze, and the door clicked quietly closed.

Blind terror galloped through her brain. Her hand moved silently to her pillow, and as her fingers searched for the gun she heard the intruder take a breath. He moved about for some time; then, she suddenly realized, he was standing right beside the bed. The gun! she panicked. Where was the gun? Then she remembered she had turned over, it would be behind her head. Oh, dear God, help me, she prayed. Then, bracing herself, she jerked herself up in the bed, jabbed her hand under the pillow and opened her mouth to scream. But before the breath could leave her body, a hand closed over her mouth and she was being pushed back against the pillows. She tried to wrench her hand free because she now had the gun, but his body was pressing down on her and she couldn't move. He gave a low chuckle, then his hand moved from her mouth and his lips were there.

'François!' she whispered.

'*Oui, chérie. C'est moi.*'

'Oh François,' she gasped, and throwing her arms around

him she kissed him savagely. But then she was angry, and pushing him away, she said, 'You frightened me half to death! I could have killed you! What are you doing here? Where have you been? Oh, my darling, hold me.'

Laughing softly, he took her back into his arms and pulled her against him. His lips were almost touching hers as he said, 'How are you, *chérie?* Have you missed me?'

She couldn't speak as the fear and the longing she had bottled up for so long were suddenly unleashed in huge, racking sobs. 'Oh, François,' she choked. 'Tell me you're all right. Tell me everything is all right now. I was so afraid for you. I didn't know where you were. No one knew. Let me turn on the light. Let me look at you.' But as she made to reach across him, he pulled her back.

'Not yet,' he whispered. 'I just want to lie here in the dark and hold you, touch you, breathe you, the way I've wanted to for over a year. Take off your nightdress, let me feel you next to me.'

It was only then that she realized he was completely naked, and sitting up, she pulled her nightdress over her head so she would be too. She was still a little dazed, and part of her was wondering if this was only a dream, but as his hands closed over her breasts she no longer cared whether it was or not.

She had never known herself capable of such passion as she showed then, but just like her fear, her desire had been bottled up too, and as it took hold of her she pressed his hands against her breasts, searched for his lips and buried her tongue deep inside his mouth. Then she was pulling him on top of her, her hands on his buttocks, on his thighs, pushing between his legs and taking him in a firm, demanding grip. A groan escaped her as she felt the size of him, and she writhed madly beneath him. As he pushed his fingers hard into her, she tore his hair, bit his face and begged him to take her now.

'I can feel you,' she moaned. 'I can feel you filling me and filling me and oh . . . *Oh!*' Her scream was drowned by his kiss, and as her legs gripped his waist he pushed his hands beneath her and lifted her to meet his thrusts. And then he was so deep inside her that waves of ecstasy broke through her body and she began to sob and whimper and cry into his open mouth.

'Hold back,' he groaned. 'Hold back . . .'

'I can't. Oh, François!'

'Tell me you love me,' he panted, throwing his full weight behind the pounding of his hips.

'*Je t'aime!*' she cried. But the words were strangled in her throat as she started to shudder and convulse. He pushed her legs up to his shoulders and drove even deeper inside her, and then he was there with her, releasing his seed into the demanding pressure of her climax.

He fell over her, letting her legs go and feeling them slide down his back and over his thighs. Her arms lay limply across the sheets and her heart thudded loudly against his.

'I love you, Claudine,' he murmured, a long time later. 'I love you, but if you make me do that again tonight . . .'

She giggled, and turned her face to kiss him.

Gently he eased himself out of her and rolled onto his back, lifting his arm for her to rest on his shoulder. 'I had envisaged a more tender reunion,' he whispered. 'I knew it would be madness to think we might talk before we made love, but . . . Jesus Christ, Claudine what got into you?'

'I was afraid,' she laughed. 'Afraid that you were only a dream and I had to have you then before you disappeared. You're not going to, are you?'

Putting his fingers under her chin, he lifted her mouth and kissed her. 'No,' he said, 'I'm here to stay. At least, for a while. But I won't make my return for a few days yet.'

'What do you mean?'

'I mean that the need to see you was so great that I

managed to shake off the man who was following me when we reached the outskirts of Paris, and then I drove straight here. I'm not scheduled to arrive until the weekend. The Abwehr are expecting me to report to their headquarters in Paris first thing tomorrow.'

'Are you going to?'

'No. I'm staying here to have a brief honeymoon with my wife.'

'Is that wise?' she said, pushing her body closer to his.

'Probably not. But I'll think up some reason for my mysterious three-day absence, and in the meantime I can make love to you and you can tell me everything that's been happening while I've been away. Incidentally, have you seen Erich?'

'Not for months. When he came he said he didn't know where you were . . .'

'That's strange,' François interrupted. 'I was expecting him to meet me at the border, but he wasn't there. Does Corinne know where he is?'

'I don't think so.'

'I'll talk to her in the morning. Now, how are we going to find a way to be together for three days without raising anyone's suspicions?'

'You can stay right here,' Claudine answered. 'The only person who goes into your room is me, to clean it, and Louis for a shave . . .'

'A what!'

'I'll explain later. But you can stay in the warmth and comfort of your own room, and I shall feed you your meals and we can talk and . . . François, what's this on your arm?' She moved her fingers. 'And here, and here.'

'That's something *I'll* explain later,' he said, wrapping her in his arms and yawning.

'No! What is it?' she said, sitting up and reaching out for the lamp.

'Please, *chérie*,' he said, trying to pull her back. 'Not now.' She already had her finger on the switch, but as she pressed it, to his eternal relief, it was only to find that the power was off.

There was a long silence, then quietly she said, 'They tortured you, didn't they?'

He put his hands into the darkness to find her, but as he tried to pull her back into his arms, she resisted. 'What did they do to you?' she said.

He sat up too, and this time as he pulled her head onto his shoulder, she let him.

'It doesn't matter now,' he whispered. 'The wounds are healing.'

'Do you know why they were torturing you?' she asked, dreading that Blomberg had betrayed her, so that all she had submitted herself to was for nothing.

'Yes.' And in his deep, beloved voice he told her.

She couldn't feel relieved. The thought that he had undergone such pain was terrible.

'You're still weak,' she said. 'I can tell.'

'Yes, a little.'

'Then let me hold you while you sleep.'

They lay down again, and it wasn't long before she heard the steady rhythm of his breathing.

'Are you asleep?' she whispered, and when there was no answer she pressed herself closer against him and kissed his cheek. 'I love you, my darling,' she murmured, and closed her eyes.

'I love you too,' he said.

The next morning started with a heated argument. One look at François' scars was enough to convince Claudine that he must see a doctor, but he was adamant that he wouldn't. He had spent the last three months with doctors, he said, and that was quite enough; and though she shouted, wheedled, cried and even slapped him, he still wouldn't give in. In the end she told him she hoped he was suffering as he deserved to after all he had put her through. He roared with laughter at that, and it was just as well they were in the shower at the time or Magaly, who was just letting herself into the sitting-room, might have heard.

Half an hour later, François was in his own room talking to Corinne while Claudine went down to prepare their breakfast. Fortunately Arlette was too busy to notice how much bread she was taking, but later poor Jean-Paul was accused of stealing other people's rations.

'I was wondering,' Claudine said, as she fed François with her fingers, then kissed him before he had a chance to swallow, 'how you managed to drive through the night without being stopped.'

'I was stopped,' he told her, grimacing as she slid her hand inside his dressing-gown and started to caress his thighs. 'Several times, in fact. But as you haven't yet seen the clothes I arrived in . . . If you keep that up, woman, you'll end up flat on your back.'

'What were you wearing?' she said, grinning.

'A uniform. A German uniform. I am, remember, an officer of the Abwehr.'

She pulled a face, then laughed as he turned in his chair, picked her up and sat her astride him. He ran his hands under her skirt and up over her thighs, then raised his brows as he discovered she wasn't wearing any underwear.

'Was Corinne able to tell you anything about Erich?' she said, taking his penis and beginning to stroke herself with it.

'No,' he answered, picking up his coffee and taking a sip. 'I'm afraid we won't be able to have that honeymoon after all. I shall have to go to Paris and find out where he is.'

'When?'

'Today,' he said, smiling as her breathing started to quicken.

'But not yet.'

'Not quite yet,' he answered, lifting her skirt to watch what she was doing. But as she wriggled forward to take him into her, he pushed her back, lifted her from his lap and walked to the door.

'François!' she declared, then relaxed as she saw him lock it.

'Do you realize,' he said, taking off his dressing-gown, 'that I am a forty-year-old man?'

'What's that got to do with anything?'

'Only that I'm wondering if I have the stamina to satisfy an insatiable wife.'

'Then why don't you lie down and let your insatiable wife satisfy you?'

As it turned out he stayed all day, and Claudine, pleading a headache, pulled the curtains and locked all the doors. She bathed and kissed the angry scars on his body, and told him all she had been doing while he was away, right up to the meeting she had had with Lucien and the other *Résistants* the night before. His relief at hearing that Lucien was still alive was evident, but when she offered to try and get word to him to tell him to come to the château, François said no.

'I'll be back on Saturday,' he said, 'and as far as I know I shall be staying for some time. I'll see him then. Has there been any sign of Halunke?'

'Not since Erich was last here.' She turned to look at him, suddenly alarmed. It had never occurred to her until that moment that Erich's absence might have something to do with Halunke. It was clear from the look on François' face that the same thought was going through his mind.

'Do you think Erich has found him?' she said, getting up from the bed.

François got up too, and she saw the harsh look that had come into his eyes. 'I'm going to get dressed,' he said, starting towards her bedroom. 'If I leave now I should be in

Paris before midnight. In the meantime, you can stop this going out alone after curfew.'

'But . . .'

'I said it must stop!' he barked.

'I've got a gun,' she reminded him, walking into her room after him.

'I don't care.' He pulled open the door to her dressing-room and took down his uniform. 'I know how headstrong, determined and downright stubborn you can be, but in this instance, Claudine, you will do as I say. It may well have seemed that Halunke had disappeared while I was away, but I'm back now, and you can be damned sure he is too. Or soon will be.' Then he saw the look on her face, and laughed. 'Don't you like my uniform?'

'It's horrifying,' she answered, going to put her arms around him. 'But I am not one of your junior officers, so stop ordering me about. When will you be back?'

'On Saturday. And you'd better prepare yourself, because I shall drive up to the front of the house in the jeep the Abwehr have so obligingly given me, and I shall be wearing this uniform. You will of course be horrified and digusted.' He unwound her arms and stooped to pull his boots from under the bed. 'Incidentally,' he said, 'do you have a Colonel Blomberg staying here?'

'Yes.' Claudine shivered, but as she started to turn away he pulled her back.

His black eyes were gleaming horribly as he stared down into hers. 'He made certain threats before he left Germany,' he said carefully, 'I trust he hasn't carried them out.'

'What threats?' Claudine asked innocently.

'Concerning you.'

She shrugged. 'Well, as you can see I'm all in one piece.'

'I can see that very clearly,' he remarked, not without irony as he ran his eyes over her nudity. 'But if he approaches you, if he as much as . . .'

'François, why don't you let me help you on with your boots?' she said, and pushing him onto the bed she knelt at his feet in much the same way as she had knelt at Blomberg's. It had a different feeling altogether when it was her husband watching her, and as she looked up at his sinister face she ran her hands over his legs. The corner of his mouth dropped as his eyes narrowed – but then she remembered that it was already dark outside, he had a long drive ahead of him, and he still wasn't fully recovered from the injuries inflicted by the Abwehr. So letting him go, she stood up, gave him a lingering kiss on the mouth and walked with him to the door.

'*Bonne chance*,' she said, as he let himself out onto the bridge. Then she heard Corinne coming up the stairs with Louis, and ran back into her room to weep with joy – and frustration that he had gone again so soon.

As he had promised, François was back again by the weekend. He came to the front of the château in a jeep plastered with swastikas and wearing his commandant's uniform. It was the middle of the afternoon and Claudine was dusting the books in the library with Magaly. Hearing the commotion in the hall, they both went to see what was happening, and found Solange so beside herself with joy that she had rubbed black lead polish all over her face and hair. Monique was racing down the stairs, and as Claudine watched François embrace her she made a mental note to tell him about the business with Lucien. Tante Céline came out of the kitchens then, her hands covered in flour, and Claudine had to turn away when she saw the look of horror on her face as she took in François' uniform. But she greeted him politely enough, and Claudine was perfectly composed by the time he turned to her. At least, she thought she was, but he looked so fierce, so horribly sinister yet somehow so devastatingly attractive in his uniform, that she found her knees were trembling.

He saw her reaction, and a flash of humour sparked in his eyes. Then suddenly she was so close to laughing herself that they had to turn abruptly away from one another. François started speaking to Blomberg, who had come in with him. 'It is obvious that my wife is less than overwhelmed by my return,' he said, in a voice heavy with sarcasm. 'Never mind. If you'll excuse me, Fritz, I'll go and see my son.' And putting an arm round each of their shoulders, he drew his mother and his sister up the stairs with him to the nursery.

Blomberg, Claudine noticed, seemed nervous, and could not meet her eyes. Had she known it, he was remembering the words of one of his fellow-officers. 'I wouldn't like to be in your shoes, Fritz, if de Lorvoire ever found out how you've been humiliating his wife.' The problem was, knowing that the fun would have to stop now made Blomberg want it all the more. He watched Claudine walk away, tossing her head at him as she went, and swore to himself that he would have the bitch yet.

An hour later, François came down from the nursery alone and went outside. Soon afterwards Corinne and Louis came into the library, and Corinne whispered to Claudine that François wanted to see her in half an hour.

'He said, take one of the horses, as if you were going for a normal afternoon ride, and he'll meet you by the old fishermen's huts on the river bank.'

Claudine kissed Louis, much to his disgust, and went upstairs to change. Within fifteen minutes she was galloping down over the meadow towards the lower part of the forest, then ploughing through the trees on her way to the river.

François was already there by the time she arrived. He held out his arms to catch her as she cantered up to him, and she all but threw herself into them.

'Why are we meeting here?' she asked, when he had kissed her. 'Why not in our rooms?'

'Because they might be bugged and we have to talk.' He glanced at his watch. 'A quarter to five,' he said, 'that gives us a few hours before curfew.'

'Do you think they were bugged the other night?' she said, aghast.

'I've no idea, but I doubt it. They weren't expecting me back until now. God, you're beautiful,' he murmured, running a hand over her hair. 'Come along, we'll go into old Thomas' hut.'

He led her to one of the huts, set back in the trees. Inside, as well as the tangle of fishing rods, nets and baskets, there were two dilapidated armchairs and a damp mattress rolled up in one corner.

'No prizes for guessing where Thomas comes for a bit of peace and quiet,' François grinned, unrolling the mattress and laying his coat over it.

'Well?' Claudine said, sitting cross-legged in front of him. 'Did you find Erich?'

He sat down too, and rested his elbows on his knees. 'Erich is dead,' he said flatly. Then he reached into his pocket and handed her a letter. 'This was waiting for me at the Bois de Boulogne.'

She opened it, read the one word ERICH, and felt a cold finger of dread start to run down her spine. 'Oh God, François,' she whispered. 'I'm so sorry. He was such a good friend to you. Do you know when it happened?'

'The *concierge* at his apartment couldn't remember the date,' he said bitterly. 'All she could remember was that it was before Christmas. She doesn't even know where he was buried.'

Claudine sighed, and taking his hand she gave it a comforting squeeze. 'You know what it means, don't you?' he growled.

She nodded. 'That he had found out who Halunke was.'

'Yes. But he didn't tell anyone, so we're still none the wiser. Now listen, has Lucien returned to England yet?'

'I think so.'

'Damn!'

'Why?'

'When he comes back, I want to see him. I want him to arrange for you to . . .'

'No! I know what you're going to say, but I'm not going, François. We're in this together now, and I'm not leaving you. We'll find out who Halunke is, and we'll find out together. That's my final word on it.'

'Well, it's not mine. You'll do as I say, damn you, and get the hell out of here. I don't want you messing around with this. Two people have already died . . .'

'Ssh!' she said, cutting him off. Making as little noise as possible, she got up and went to peer out of the broken window.

'What is it?'

'Nothing. It must have been the horse.' She sat down again. 'Now, you listen to me. I'm co-ordinating a network of *Résistants* here in this area. They, and Lucien, are depending on me, and I'm not going to let them down. Also, I've been cheated of too much of my married life already by this vendetta, and I won't put up with losing any more. I love you, François, I want to be with you, and I'm going to be. You needed Erich before, which goes to show you couldn't manage on your own. Well, now you've got me. We have to work this thing out together. We'd better begin with what you know, what Erich last told you and . . .'

'Claudine, shut up and for God's sake kiss me.'

'Why?'

'Because I'd like to know that you'll do a least one thing I tell you to.'

'I'll kiss you later,' she said.

He gave a shout of laughter, and just for a moment she was almost light-headed with joy. But as quickly as it had come, the moment passed, and suddenly they were both quiet again, staring down at the letter with Erich's name on it, which was still lying between them.

'We'd better begin with why I'm here,' François said. 'Why the Abwehr have sent me back to Lorvoire. You have to know because it's going to affect you in a way you're not going to like very much. They know there's a Resistance group in the area with the code name Jupiter. No, don't say anything until I've finished. They also know that there are several local escape-lines taking British pilots to safety, and that one of them runs through Touraine. The Abwehr want me not only to destroy the Touraine escape route but to arrest as many as I can of those involved. The same goes for the Jupiter *réseau*.'

'Oh God,' she murmured. 'You do know what you're saying, don't you?'

'I'm afraid I do. But I don't want you to tell me anything. I don't want to know who's involved. You're to tell me nothing, do you understand? And I can't promise that I'll give you information, either.'

'But you have to!' she protested.

'No! If you act on information I give you, the Abwehr will know instantly where it has come from. That doesn't only put me in danger, it puts Halunke back in action. You won't have forgotten what they're doing to keep me loyal. If I make one slip, then God knows what will happen to you.'

He turned away as an image of Élise came to his mind. He had called on her while he was in Paris, and she had been so pathetically grateful to see him that he had ended up staying the night. Béatrice had told him what was happening with the Abwehr officers, and he had known such a murderous rage that it was some time before he had himself back under control. He had decided then that he didn't want her in Paris any longer, where they could abuse her like that, so he had made arrangements to move her out some time in the next few weeks.

'So remember,' he said to Claudine, 'and keep this in your mind the whole time: I am not only a collaborator, I am the very worst kind of collaborator. I shall be wearing a German uniform, and I shall be turning my own country-men over to the Gestapo.'

Her face was ashen. 'You won't!' she breathed. 'You can't do it! François . . .'

'Of course I won't be doing it!' he cried. 'But you have to believe that I am. Everyone must believe it, even the Abwehr. Though God alone knows how I'm going to convince them.'

'What about Lucien?' she said. 'Don't you think we should take him into our confidence? In fact,' she added, 'I think we have to. Maybe I shouldn't be telling you this, but the Resistance already has weapons. Not many, but there could come a time when they start using them . . .'

'The FTP are already using weapons,' François butted in.

'The Communist *Résistants?* There you are, then. And you'll be one of the first targets for the Resistance in this area. We – they – hate collaborators almost more than Nazis. Lucien might be able to tip you off if someone is planning to kill you.'

'I'll think about it,' he said. 'In the meantime, there's Halunke.'

'The last time we spoke about this,' she said, 'you thought Erich was drawing the wrong conclusions. But now he's been killed . . . Well, perhaps he was on the right track.'

François gazed into her vibrant blue eyes, then looked down at the torn and faded patterns of the mattress.

'François,' Claudine said quietly, 'is Halunke's identity tied up with what happened to Hortense de Bourchain?'

His head came up, and she could see that he was both annoyed and surprised. 'What makes you say that?' he asked.

'I don't know. It was just a feeling I had. Has it got something to do with her? *Is* that the line Erich was pursuing?'

François nodded. 'Yes. Yes, it was.'

'Then don't you think it's time, *chéri*, to tell me what happened?'

He stood up and walked over to the door. For a moment she thought he was going outside, but then he turned back to look at her. 'I'll tell you,' he said, 'but I still don't think that's where the answer lies. I hadn't seen Erich for some time before he died, he might have discovered something else, nothing to do with Hortense at all.'

'But we don't know that. All we have to go on is what he said to you when he came to the château. And we have to start somewhere, so it had better be there.'

'All right,' he sighed. He went to sit in one of the chairs. Running a hand over his jaw and fixing his eyes on the fishing paraphernalia at his feet, he began. 'Hortense was in love with me,' he said. 'She wanted me to marry her, she even went as far as getting her father to speak to mine. My father was in favour of the match; it was eminently suitable, and as you know, he wanted grandchildren. I was fond of Hortense, I suppose I did love her in a way. But it was all happening at the time your father was introducing me to the Secret Service. I told her to wait, that maybe in a year or two I would be ready to marry her.'

He sighed. 'Hortense flew into a royal rage at that and told me I was a philanderer. She said we were practically engaged already, and I couldn't treat her like that. Nevertheless, I didn't see her for three or four weeks. Then she came to the house in Paris one night when she knew I'd be there alone and . . . She was a very attractive woman, she wanted me to make love to her, so I did. She said I had to marry her then, that I was honour-bound to do so. It was my turn to fly into a temper and I ordered her out of the house.

She came back the following day, begging forgiveness and promising she would wait for as long as I wanted, provided I did marry her in the end. We continued to see one another, though we didn't make love again. It wasn't that I didn't want to, it was just that I knew she was hoping to become pregnant so that then I'd be forced to marry her. I didn't want to be trapped like that. The truth was, though I did love her in a way, I didn't want to be married at all.

'Over the next year or so, things went from bad to worse. I tried to stop seeing her, but wherever I went she was there. Then one night, when we were all staying at Lorvoire, she asked me to go outside with her, into one of the caves. She told me then that she'd been sleeping with Lucien and that Lucien was in love with her. I made the great mistake of laughing. It wasn't that I didn't believe her, it was simply that her motives were so transparent. And sure enough, she told me that she would continue sleeping with Lucien if I didn't promise to marry her within the month. I told her she could sleep with Lucien as often as she liked, that as far as I was concerned she could sleep with any number of men, and I wished her well.'

François paused, and shifted uncomfortably in the chair. 'It was then that she pulled out a knife. A dagger. God only knows where she got it, but she had it. She said that if I didn't promise, she would kill herself. I tried to get the knife from her, but she just went crazy. In the struggle she managed to slash my face, and it was then, in the moment that I let go of her, that she lifted the knife to plunge it into her chest. Again I managed to get hold of it, but as I wrenched it away from her my hand jerked downwards, she pushed herself against me, and the next thing I knew I had stabbed her. I didn't even give myself a moment for disbelief, I simply picked her up and ran with her to the car. All I could think of was getting her to a doctor. As I drove off I looked in the mirror and saw my father talking to Armand.

I had no idea how much either of them had seen, but it hardly mattered at the time. I had to get Hortense to a doctor.

'It was her parents who wanted the whole matter hushed up. They knew what had been going on, and when my father told them exactly what had happened in the wine cave, well I think they wanted the whole episode to receive as little attention as possible. Armand never mentioned it, though my father told me he had spoken to him, and he had promised to keep everything to himself. Lucien never mentioned it either. Whether he and Hortense had been sleeping together I don't know, it never seemed appropriate to ask. But I think they had.

'So there you have it, the murder of Hortense de Bourchain. Why Erich thought it had some vital connection with Halunke I simply don't know. He checked on Hortense's family and none of them were in France at the times that mattered. The only other people who know what happened are Doctor Lebrun, my father, Lucien and Armand, and as none of them could conceivably be Halunke . . .'

Looking up, François saw in the fading light that Claudine's eyes were shining with tears. 'Why are you crying?' he asked softly.

'I'm not. Not exactly. I just feel so sad. But you're right, none of them could be Halunke. The only one who has anything approaching a motive is Lucien – if he loved Hortense. And Lucien wouldn't have killed his own father.'

'So, we're right back at the beginning. Erich must have discovered something else, and we – I – have to find out what that was.'

'We,' she corrected. 'Will you come here, please? I want to give you that kiss now.'

As he knelt in front of her, she put her arms round his neck and said, 'How does a man with such an ugly face and such a chequered past manage to fill my heart with so much love?'

'I don't know, but I'm glad I do,' he smiled, lowering his mouth to hers.

Five minutes later he was handing her up onto her horse.

'That wasn't enough,' she said, looking down at him sulkily.

'I didn't think it would be,' he answered with a wry smile. 'Can we make love tonight?'

'If you can make it sound like rape.' He thought about that, then his eyes met hers and they laughed.

'How are you getting back?' she asked, turning her horse.

'There's a tunnel. It leads from the river bank over there, into the middle cellar.'

'The middle cellar!' she gasped. 'The boxes!'

'Don't tell me,' he groaned. 'You've opened them.'

'It was your father's idea,' she said sheepishly. 'But where did all those valuables come from?'

'Jews,' he answered. 'They belong to wealthy Parisian Jews. I'm keeping them until they, or their descendants, can come to collect them.'

Claudine smiled widely as tilting her head quizzically to one side, she said, 'Is that a halo I can see shining over your devilish face?'

'Get out of here,' he laughed, and giving the horse a slap, he sent her galloping off into the forest.

– 29 –

During the months that followed François' return to the château it was easy to forget that there was a war taking place beyond the borders of Lorvoire – that was, if you ignored the drone of aircraft passing overhead, the daily wireless broadcasts and the presence of the Germans stationed in

Chinon. Even Claudine's Resistance group went to ground for a time, once she had warned the Jupiter *réseau* that the Germans knew about them. But as soon as Lucien returned from England with news that the RAF were to begin a series of fighter sweeps over northern France, the escape-line went back into operation and the search for safe-houses and couriers began again. At first, though, the number of Allied pilots needing to be escorted through France to Spain was small, and Claudine was more than happy to concentrate on other things.

As those balmy summer days passed, she could feel herself inexorably changing. She was light-headed with love, with a sense of fulfilment, a feeling of well-being. She walked taller than ever, her glorious hair bouncing on her shoulders, and was so unmistakably radiant that François was forced to see that continuing to try and delude the family they were not in love was a waste of effort. But the truth must go no further than that, he warned her. Apart from anything else, her fellow *Résistants* would take a dim view of her attachment to a collaborator.

He told her little about the days he spent at the Château d'Artigny, though she knew that as yet he had been required to do very little. Following the breakdown of the Russo-German non-aggression pact, Hitler had turned his army east, and von Liebermann and his *Komitee* were heavily involved in intelligence-gathering for the planned invasion of Russia. Without von Liebermann's specific instructions it appeared that François' commanding officers in Touraine were at a loss to know what they should do with him. This suited François perfectly, of course – though he was curious to know why von Liebermann – or more accurately, Himmler – had not yet ordered his execution. He had as yet done nothing further to prove his fealty to the Reich, and if he wasn't to be actively engaged on the Abwehr's behalf he couldn't see what purpose his staying alive served. Still, the

German plan for his fate would no doubt be made clear soon enough, and meanwhile he and Claudine determined to make the most of the reprieve.

It wasn't long before Blomberg, whose discomfort since François' return had been painfully obvious, started to spend more and more nights away from the château. This delighted Solange, because it meant that the family – including Lucien – could spend the long, hot summer evenings together, singing and dancing in the ballroom, or simply listening to Edith Piaf's lazy, seductive voice on the gramophone. Lucien couldn't come often, but when he did François allowed Louis to stay up late as a special treat. Solange, whose hair was back on end as though the crazy ideas in her head were pushing up through her skull, played loudly on the piano while Louis sang with Monique and Claudine. And when Louis became tired and snuggled sleepily into his father's lap, the cries for Lucien to sing next were almost as loud as the protests that were made when Armand joined in. Liliane was often there too, and neighbours from nearby châteaux took to bringing their rations to Arlette so that they too could join the de Lorvoire soirées. No one objected to François' apparent allegiance to the German cause since most of them, like Tante Céline, were *Attentistes* – waiting to see which way the war went before deciding which side to take. Besides, most of them played host during the day to hunting and shooting parties in the Chinon Forest which François and many other German officers attended.

During those wonderfully light-hearted evenings Claudine often found herself watching Armand as he laughed and joked with Solange and Monique, twirled them about the room or tossed them into Lucien's arms. He was at last his old self again, and she could see once more why she had found it so easy to love him. She was glad that he now seemed so relaxed – and it was obvious, too, that the worry she had had that he and François would never recapture their former friendship was unfounded. The two of them were as easy in each other's company as they were in Lucien's. There were times, though – particularly when she danced with Armand, when she would catch François staring at them, a black frown between his eyes and his mouth a thin, tight line of concentration. Could her invincible husband actually have fallen prey to jealousy?

'What, when I know how utterly devoted you are to me?' he would say when she challenged him. And then he would pull her onto his lap and kiss her so soundly – in front of the entire family – that she would almost blush.

'*Oh là là*,' Tante Céline would cry at these public displays of affection. She still wasn't quite over the shock of discovering that François de Lorvoire had a heart, or that her niece had, by some miracle, managed to capture it, though like everyone else she was delighted for them, and simply longed to tell Beavis – wherever he might be.

It was only on family evenings, when they had no guests, that Claudine and François felt able to behave so freely with each other, and only on those evenings would they dance together, usually to an over-played, scratched record of Al Bowlly singing 'The Very Thought of You' – the song everyone remembered them dancing to at their wedding. Later, if it was a night when Lucien was there and Louis had stayed up, François would carry his sleeping son to the nursery, then join Claudine in her room where they would spend hour upon hour making lazy, luxurious, and increasingly erotic love. Her room, like his, was bugged, but now that Blomberg knew they were in love there was little point in hiding it from the Germans, and if they had anything of importance to say to one another they would either walk in the forest or meet at Thomas' fishing hut. In truth, their recklessness caused François a great deal of concern, but he said nothing; Claudine was so happy, and he couldn't bring himself to do anything to spoil it.

Summer turned to autumn, and as the German army tightened its stranglehold on Russia, and the British suffered incalculable losses in North Africa, in Lorvoire it was time to harvest the grapes. As they did every year, the locals came to help, and so did the German soldiers who still visited Gustave's café each Friday to drink an endless supply of black-market spirits with Armand. As Claudine had predicted at the outset of the occupation, befriending these officers had proved extremely useful. Surprisingly often they would let little nuggets of information slip to Armand – troop movements, the location of road-blocks, areas of concentration for radio detector vans. These details were enormously useful to the group in their task of escorting pilots through the escape-line, or when they were trying to send messages to London.

On the night of the harvest there was a party. It was nothing like the one in thirty-seven – but it amused Claudine no end to be dancing with German officers when no more than half a mile away, two British pilots and one Canadian were spending the night at the forest cottage. The following morning they were given black felt berets and blue serge overalls tailored by Gertrude Reinberg, and a collection of identity cards forged overnight by Théobald the signwriter. Then, while their uniforms burned in the grate, they ate a heartier breakfast than most of the locals had seen since the outbreak of war, before being transported in broad daylight to the demarcation line by old Thomas in his horse and cart. The escape-line was now running so smoothly that Claudine often had to remind the others – Solange and Liliane in particular, who had appointed themselves her chief couriers – of the danger they all faced if they were caught.

It wasn't until the following week that they heard that while they had been celebrating the harvest, fifty Frenchmen had been shot as a reprisal for the assassination of a

German officer in Nantes. Two days later, fifty more were shot in Bordeaux where another German officer had lost his life at the hands of the Resistance.

From that day on, all fraternizing with the Germans came to an abrupt end. Even the *Attentistes* ceased their hospitality. Resistance groups who had gone to ground over the summer months began to re-form, and techniques of sabotage and assault favoured by the Communists started to catch on. It was a difficult time for François. He became a major target for local hostility, and more than once he arrived home with the windshield of his jeep smashed and his face and hands covered in cuts. Claudine became increasingly afraid for his life, but nothing she said would persuade him to go into hiding with Lucien. There had been no sign of Halunke for almost a year, but until he was caught François was not prepared to do anything to antagonize von Liebermann. And von Liebermann, he told Claudine, was due any time now to arrive at the Abwehr headquarters in Paris.

As it turned out, von Liebermann didn't arrive until early in the New Year, by which time Hitler's invasion of Russia was suffering severe setbacks, and the Japanese had bombed Pearl Harbour, bringing America into the war. This change of fortune for the Allies prompted many *Attentistes* finally to declare their allegiance, and the numbers of men – and women – who went into hiding in the forest after successful sabotage attacks on German bases started steadily to increase. *Léopard*, which was Lucien's code name as well as the name of their escape-line, now prepared to transport American as well as British and Canadian pilots out of the country and back to the war; and though it was a bitterly cold winter, with heavy frosts, snow and gales, neither Claudine nor any of her fellow *Résistants* were deterred.

Keeping busy all day also prevented Claudine from

worrying about François, which was why he made no objection to her becoming one of the vital links between the *Maquis* – the men in hiding – and the 'sleeping' Resistance – those in the towns and villages. However, when it came to going out after curfew he put his foot down. She protested strongly, even going so far as to hit him – which was nothing unusual, for they frequently fought as passionately as they made love – but he would not be moved. So she had to content herself with the daytime activities of ferrying food, drink and the vineyard's smudge-pots to the Forest of Scevolles, where Lucien's *Maquis* group were all but freezing to death beneath tents made from parachutes and old blankets. And when she and Monique weren't running messages, devising passwords and signals, or closeted in the larder making invisible ink with powdered aspirin and lemon juice, they were working on methods of transporting clothing, radio crystals and an ever-decreasing supply of arms from one hide-out to another. All manner of means were invented, from scooping out the centre of Monsieur Bonet's melons to carry radio transmitters and hand-guns, to having fillings removed in order to secrete microfilm in teeth. And now that agents and much-needed supplies were at last being parachuted into France, there were reception committees to be formed and landing grounds to be prepared.

Claudine longed to join the reception committees herself, to watch the parachutes float down from the moonlit sky, to gather them up and bury them, to store the arms and supplies in the *gazogènes* – vans that ran at twenty kilometres an hour on charcoal – and hear them trundle off into the night. She longed to meet the agents and escort them to their safe-houses – she felt she was missing out on the real adventure. But François slept in her bed every night, and there was no way in which she could evade him.

It was one night towards the end of February that François gave Claudine the news she had been dreading. Earlier that day they had had a fierce row because he had found out about her diplomatic mission to the Gestapo headquarters at the Hôtel Boule d'Or, to plead mercy for the seven Chinonais who had been arrested the day before. He still seemed preoccupied at dinner, but it was only when he actually snapped at Monique that Claudine began to realize there was something much more serious than her indiscretion playing on his mind. She knew better than to question him, he would tell her when he was ready. To her relief it turned out to be sooner rather than later: after checking that everyone else was in bed, he came into her room and told her to get her coat.

Claudine hurried into her dressing-room, took off her nightdress and pulled on her fur coat and hat, woollen stockings and old fleece-lined boots, and went to join him at the bridge door. It was a bitterly cold night, but the raging winds of the past few weeks had at last died down, and every now again the moon pushed through the clouds, shedding enough light for them to see where they were going.

They had walked some distance in total silence before François finally said, 'I've received word from von Liebermann.'

Instantly Claudine felt a cold, pinching fear. It was the communication they had prayed would never come.

'What does he want?' she asked, leaning closer as he slipped his hand between her fur collar and hat, and gently massaged the back of her neck.

'He wants me to meet him in Vichy some time in March. He'll let me know when.'

'Did he say why?'

'No.'

Taking a breath, Claudine turned to face him, but before she could speak he put his fingers over her lips. 'I know what

– 532 –

you're going to say, *chérie*,' he said, 'but the answer is no. I won't join Lucien.'

She looked up at him with her wide blue eyes and, smiling, he stooped to kiss her. 'But if von Liebermann asks you to do something dreadful. . . ? she said.

'Let me worry about that.' And pulling her head onto his shoulder, he wrapped her comfortingly in his arms.

She lay against him and he gazed absently out into the shifting tree-shadows behind her. His summons to Vichy had inevitably brought with it the preying spectre of Halunke's revenge. He felt his mind assailed yet again by anguish, fury and incomprehension. What in God's name could he have done to have incurred such a terrible hatred?

'What are you thinking about?' Claudine said.

He let his breath go. 'Von Liebermann,' he lied, still looking past her into the forest.

'Not Halunke?'

He gave a queer sort of half-smile, then lifting her face in his hands, he looked into her eyes and whispered, 'I love you.'

'I love you too,' she murmured, starting to unbutton her coat so that he could slide his hands inside.

'Claudine!' he groaned, as he felt the goosey flesh of her naked body. 'Why have you come out like this? You'll catch pneumonia.'

'Not if you hold me very close,' she purred.

Running his hands down over her thighs, he felt the tops of her woollen stockings. Then, laughing softly, he cupped her buttocks in his hands, pulled her hard against him and pushed his tongue deep inside her mouth.

'Oh, François,' she moaned, snaking her fingers through his hair and rubbing herself against his growing erection. 'I want you, *chéri*, I want you now.'

Sucking her lips and twisting her so that he could push a hand between their bodies, he inserted a finger into the dark thatch between her legs and started to caress the moist skin beneath. 'Is this where you want me?' he said huskily. 'Just here?'

'Mmmmmm.' She lifted her leg, circling it about his waist. 'Oh yes!' she cried, as he found her opening and pushed his finger deep inside.

She moved a hand to his fly and started to unbutton it. Her eyes were fixed hungrily on his mouth while her own lips parted, her nipples puckered with the cold and her chest began to heave. Their breath mingled in clouds about their faces, and her eyelids fluttered closed as he started to move his hand back and forth. Then suddenly she was flying backwards, through the air as if fired from a catapult. Her head struck a tree, and she fell awkwardly into the undergrowth. Through the stars exploding in her eyes, she watched as François heaved something over his shoulder and threw it heavily to the ground. The polished barrel of a gun glinted in the moonlight, and she heard the trigger click as François prepared to fire.

It had all happened in a matter of seconds. If Lucien had not that instant cried out, François would have shot him.

'For heaven's sake!' François snapped, as he took his brother's arm and hauled him to his feet. 'What the hell are you doing creeping about the forest like that? I might have killed you.'

Lucien's white teeth gleamed in the darkness as he watched his brother stoop over Claudine to check that she was all right. 'I was testing you,' he said jauntily. 'The reflexes are still good, *mon frère*.'

'Obviously better than yours,' François remarked dryly, as he covered Claudine's nudity and helped her to her feet. 'Now, perhaps you'd like to tell me what you're doing here?'

'As a matter of fact, I'm here to see Claudine.' There was enough moonlight for François to see the very appreciative way Lucien was looking at her, and when he heard his brother mutter something that sounded like *charmante* under his breath, and Claudine stifled a laugh, he pulled her into the circle of his arm and clamped the front of her coat together with his fist.

Collecting himself, Lucien said, 'I have a message for Claudine. Can I give it to her?'

'If you must. But if it involves her going out after curfew you can save your breath.'

'I know, I know,' Lucien said. Then with a grin he added, 'Sorry if I interrupted. But if you don't mind my saying so, it's a bit chilly to be doing it *al fresco*, isn't it?'

'Mind your own business,' François retorted. 'And don't keep her long. I'll wait at the bridge.'

When he was safely out of earshot, Lucien took Claudine's arm and they started to follow him slowly. 'Jacques is in Paris,' he said quietly, 'and I have to leave tonight, to join him there for a few days. But a message came through earlier from the British, asking for our help. They want to parachute in two agents and a supply of arms at the next full moon, but it seems three of their own people in the district have been arrested, and the others have gone to ground. I've said we'll do it, but as I'm not going to be around for a while I want you to start organizing the reception committee alone. Do you think you can do it?'

Without hesitation Claudine said, 'When's the next full moon?'

'Three weeks tomorrow. Jacques and I will be back by then, so count us in.'

'How many more do we need?'

'Ten. Twelve if possible.'

'Mm,' she pondered. 'Old Thomas and Yves Fauberg have volunteered to help in any way they can. Gustave, obviously. Monique and me. You and . . .'

'Didn't you hear what François said?' he interrupted.

'Armand,' she continued, as if he hadn't spoken. She

turned to face him. 'Leave it with me. I'll come up with five more, don't worry.'

'Not yourself, though.'

'Lucien! If I . . .'

'No! You might be prepared to face François' wrath, but I'm not.'

They had reached the edge of the forest by now, and could see François leaning against the bridge smoking a cigarette. 'Two more things,' Claudine said, tearing her eyes away from the awesome aquiline profile she loved so much and neatly changing the subject. 'First, do you have the map co-ordinates?'

'You'll find them in the usual bible down at the church on Friday morning,' Lucien answered.

'Second, did you get my message about the guns?'

'Yes. I've just put them in the cottage. Who wants them?'

'Someone in Langeais. I'll get Solange and Liliane to take them over tomorrow on their bicycle. Will we have any left after that?'

'No. But we'll syphon some off from the British when they arrive. *If* they bring any.'

'Let me know when you're back from Paris,' she said, and giving him a brief peck on the cheek, she ran off to join François.

Lucien stepped back into the shadows to watch as François threw away his cigarette and folded her into his arms. After a long and unmistakably intimate kiss, François parted the front of her coat to slip his hands inside – but Claudine shrieked and jumped away from him, complaining that he was cold. Lucien continued to watch as François put a hand on the back of her neck and propelled her into the château. Before closing the door he turned, and for a long moment looked straight into Lucien's eyes. Then, as the door closed, Lucien started back into the forest.

The following afternoon, as Claudine was preparing to go down to the café, Magaly came into her room and told her that François wanted to see her immediately.

'He says you'll know where, *madame*,' she added. 'He was in a terrible temper . . .' Her eyes were round and her lips trembling with fear for her mistress.

Claudine gave her a quick hug, told her it would be all right and ran off to the stables.

When she galloped up to Thomas' hut, François was waiting. He all but dragged her from the saddle and spun her round to face him.

'Whose idea was it to use my mother as a courier?' he raged.

'What!' she gasped, wincing as his fingers dug into her arm. She wasn't unduly alarmed, for Solange and Liliane had returned quite safely from Langeais half an hour before. 'But I thought you knew!'

'Of course I didn't damned well know. What the hell has got into you, Claudine? She's an old lady. So is Liliane.'

'We all have to play our part,' she argued. 'And if they're willing, I don't see any reason why Solange and Liliane shouldn't too. Anyway, how did you find out?'

'Never mind that. Does Lucien know they're involved?'

'Of course he does.'

François' face turned to thunder. 'Tell him I want to see him. Tell him to get himself to the château within the week.'

'I'll do no such thing.'

'Claudine!' he said dangerously.

'You don't frighten me with that tone,' she said loftily, all the while thanking God that he didn't appear to know what Solange and Liliane had been carrying when they'd cycled over to Langeais. If he'd known there were guns in the false bottom Armand had made for the passenger-box, she dreaded to think what he might do. And the way Liliane had cheekily informed a German officer at a road-block that she was sitting on a bomb was unlikely to seem as funny to him as it had to her and Monique. 'You're being over-protective, François,' she grumbled.

'Someone has to be; it seems the whole damned lot of you have lost your senses. Do you know how many *Résistants* have been arrested in Touraine during the past four weeks? No, I didn't think you did. Over twenty. And while we're here I'd better tell you that you have a traitor in your midst. The escape-line has to close down, Claudine, before you're all arrested. Has anyone told you that you haven't got one pilot, one agent or one escaped prisoner through in the past three weeks?'

'What!'

'The Gestapo have got them all. They're picking them up at Poitiers.'

'But why didn't you tell me sooner?'

'I've only just found out. There's a weak link in your chain.'

'Do you know where?'

'No, but I don't think it's here, it seems to be further down the line. Nevertheless, if they've got one link in the chain they can trace the whole thing. So I'm telling you, my mother is to stop carrying messages and so is Liliane. *Don't argue!*' he roared as she started to protest. 'Shut down that escape-line and tell Lucien I want to see him.'

He stalked off then, and she knew better than to go after him when he was in that mood.

When Lucien returned from Paris a week later, and she finally got the two of them together, there was another bitter row. In the end Lucien capitulated and told Solange that she wouldn't be able to run any more errands. Solange meekly agreed, then informed Claudine that she was at her disposal as usual.

'François is right about the escape-line,' Lucien said to Claudine later that night, as they stood together just inside the forest at the back of the château. 'If the Germans have managed to infiltrate it, we have to close it down. The problem is, we have a pilot in Neuville who needs to be moved. He can't go on, because we think our "weak link" is just beyond Neuville. I suggest we bring him back here for a while. Can we put him in the cottage?'

'I don't see why not. For how long?'

'A few days, no more.'

But it turned out to be a lot longer than that. While the pilot and his guide were on their way back to Lorvoire they ran into a German patrol and were challenged. The guide panicked and pulled out a gun. The pilot followed suit, shot one of the German officers, and in the mêlée that followed the guide was killed. The pilot, by some miracle, managed to escape and make his way into the forest of Fontevraud, where he was picked up by other fugitives who managed to get word to Lucien. What Lucien didn't discover until he arrived at Fontevraud was that the pilot had been shot in the leg and shoulder. By the time he got him to Lorvoire, the man had lost so much blood that Doctor Lebrun seriously doubted his chances of survival.

The shooting of the German officer had immediate repercussions. Posters were pasted on every wall and lamp-post informing those responsible that if they didn't come forward, twenty of the prisoners held in the cellars of the Hôtel Boule d'Or would be shot. No one doubted that the threat was real; no one had forgotten what had happened at Nantes and Bordeaux.

Those early days of March were the darkest any of them had known, for many people in Chinon and the surrounding villages had loved-ones in the German cells. Most were there for crimes as petty as breaking curfew or failing to salute a German officer, but the Germans had not yet named those who were to be shot. Neighbour suspected neighbour; fights broke out on the street as prisoners' relatives accused lifelong friends of harbouring the culprit.

For Claudine and Lucien the dilemma was terrible. The pilot, Squadron Leader Jack Bingham, remained unconscious, and the idea of handing him over to the Gestapo was utterly abhorrent. But so too was the prospect of seeing innocent men go to their deaths.

In the end Claudine turned to François for help. As she expected, he was furious even to be told that she had the pilot in their cottage, and that Monique and Estelle were nursing him round the clock didn't please him either. Nevertheless, two days after she told him, the threatening notices started to come down. How he managed to achieve this François refused to tell her; he wasn't proud of the fact that he had turned the Germans' attention to a group of Communist *Résistants* he knew to be planning the sabotage of a train out of Tours sometime during the next week. The man they were looking for, he told his colleagues, was with them.

The FTP did sabotage the train, and managed to secure themselves hundreds of gallons of diesel fuel bound for Germany. Their success was due to the fact that they struck a day before the Germans expected them to, and further back on the line, near Chemille.

François hadn't tipped them off; he was fairly certain the informer was a cleaning woman at the Château d'Artigny, who had been sweeping outside his office when he told his fellow-officers of the FTP plan. He was grateful to her for doing it – but the FTP coup also filled him with a gnawing dread. He would have a lot of questions to answer when he met von Liebermann in Vichy. This was just the sort of incident that would prompt the General to start moving the pieces again in his iniquitous game of human chess.

The very next day François was ordered to present himself at the Hôtel Louis XV in Vichy the following Wednesday, at fifteen hundred hours precisely.

Halunke watched from the grime-covered windows of the fishing hut. At the moment there was nothing to see, but he knew that de Lorvoire and his wife were on the point of leaving old Thomas' hut. It was Tuesday morning, the day before François was due to go to Vichy, and though Halunke had managed to overhear very little of their conversation, he knew that de Lorvoire had told his wife a lie. He had told her that he was meeting von Liebermann at nine o'clock in the morning. There was probably a good reason for the lie, and Halunke was fairly certain he knew what it was, but it didn't concern him. All that concerned him was that von Liebermann had given his authorization for another strike while de Lorvoire was away – and de Lorvoire was leaving at noon.

Halunke jerked his head back from the window as the door to the next hut opened and de Lorvoire came out. A few minutes later Claudine followed, by which time de Lorvoire had already disappeared into the tunnel leading back to the château's inner cellar. Careless of him to have left her alone like that, Halunke mused, but of course she always carried a gun, and she certainly knew how to use it. She hadn't brought her horse today, which meant that as she started back through the forest, Halunke was able to follow. He kept at a safe distance all the way, and not once did she turn round – which surprised him, given that curious sixth sense of hers. When she reached the meadow in front of the château, Halunke stayed in the forest, circled the meadow under cover of the trees, made the steep climb to the back of the château and waited.

Half an hour later he heard de Lorvoire drive off, and not long after that Claudine came out onto the bridge, looked around, then started the trek to the cottage. Again Halunke followed.

'Are you sure you don't mind staying on?' Claudine said,

wiping down the table in the kitchen and glancing over her shoulder at Monique.

'No, of course I don't,' Monique answered, sitting back in the chair she had pulled up to Jack Bingham's bedside. 'I like sitting here with him. It's restful.'

'I imagine it is,' Claudine said, with some irony. 'He's still unconscious.'

'But improving,' Monique reminded her.

Claudine started drying the few dishes she and Monique had used for their lunch. 'Are you warm enough?' she said, shivering suddenly. 'There's not much wood on the fire. Shall I put some more on for you?'

'Yes, please.' Monique leaned over the pilot and tucked the blankets closer round his face. 'He's American, you know,' she said.

'American?' Claudine turned round in surprise. 'But he's an RAF pilot.'

'That doesn't preclude him from being an American, does it?' Monique smiled. 'I found a letter from his mother in his wallet, she lives in a place called Missouri. And look, he's got a photograph of his wife and three children too.'

Claudine took the small, disintegrating snapshot and stared at the laughing faces of Bingham's family. Then suddenly she shivered again. This time she cast a nervous glance towards the window, but there was nothing to see.

Monique was looking at the pilot again, and Claudine watched as she stroked a wisp of fair hair from his forehead. It was odd, Claudine thought, how she hadn't noticed his looks before, perhaps because he had been so deathly pale when he arrived. But now that a little colour had returned to his cheeks she could see that he was really quite handsome in, come to think of it, an extremely American way. Her eyes moved to Monique's face, and immediately her heart sank.

François had talked to Monique, some time ago now, about her feelings for Lucien. Exactly what he had said

Claudine wasn't sure, but he had seemed satisfied with the way the conversation had gone. Now however, seeing Monique gaze so adoringly at Jack, Claudine was very much afraid that François had not managed to get through to her at all.

'Monique,' she said softly.

Monique looked up, and her wide amber eyes seemed so innocent in her fragile white face that it was all Claudine could do to make herself go on. 'Monique,' she said again, perching on the edge of the bed and taking her hand. 'He's married, *chérie*.'

'I know,' Monique answered, smiling.

'When he's well he will have to return to his family, or to the war.'

'Yes, I know that too.' Then squeezing Claudine's hands, she said, 'Don't worry. It's only concern I feel.' She turned to look at him. 'And perhaps gratitude.'

'Gratitude?'

Monique nodded. 'He was there to listen and not judge when I needed to talk.' She laughed quietly. 'I've told him about Lucien, and about all the men I've . . . Well, it doesn't matter now, it's in the past. But François made me see how misguided I had been, how there had been no need to search so desperately for love just to convince myself I didn't want Lucien in the way I thought I did. Of course, Jack couldn't hear what I was saying, but it helps sometimes to speak things aloud, don't you think?'

Claudine smiled, then leaned forward to kiss Monique's forehead. 'Estelle should be here soon,' she said, picking up her coat and checking her pocket for the gun. 'Doctor Lebrun said he would stop by later, too. Invite him to join us for dinner this evening, will you?'

'Will anyone else be there?'

'Besides us, only Blomberg.'

Monique grinned. 'What a pity François won't be there. I

so enjoy the way Blomberg squirms every time he brings up the subject of German culture. I'm sure François does it on purpose.'

'Well, the Colonel can rest easy tonight,' Claudine said, laughing.

'If you can call putting up with you, resting easy,' Monique remarked. 'You're as bad as François. And the way you look at him sometimes, Claudine, is enough to make anyone think you'd just scraped him off the bottom of your shoe.'

Again Claudine laughed, and Monique watched her as she buttoned her coat and pulled her fur hat down over her ears. 'Did something happen between you and Blomberg, Claudine,' she said carefully. 'Something you haven't told me about?'

'The short answer is yes,' Claudine answered. 'Please don't ask for the long one, and don't mention it to François either.'

'I won't if you don't want me to, but François asked me that very question himself just after he came back from Germany. I couldn't help wondering at the time why he didn't ask you.'

'He did, but I didn't give him a straight answer.'

'Why?'

'Because he would have taken matters into his own hands – and I'm determined to deal with Blomberg myself, the very minute the opportunity presents itself.'

'You're a mean woman, Claudine,' Monique grinned.

Claudine pointed her fingers at Monique like a gun and made a firing noise. Then, smiling, she let herself out into the forest.

In the little clearing outside the cottage, the sun was bright, making her eyes water. She took a deep breath of the crisp autumn air, slid her hand into her pocket to take firm hold of the gun, and set off into the trees.

She had gone only a few steps when she heard something behind her. In one movement she whipped out the gun and spun round, her nerves like needles and her heart in her throat. Then she saw that it was Lucien, standing at the other side of the clearing. She was about to shout at him for making her jump when Estelle walked out from behind him.

Imagine, Claudine thought as she turned back into the forest, shy little Estelle flirting with Lucien! But then she no longer found it quite so amusing. Armand had had a lot of bad luck where women were concerned, and Lucien had plenty of women fawning after him without having to add Estelle to their number.

She tried to concentrate on this as she walked on through the trees; anything to keep her mind away from the terrible misgivings she had about François' visit to Vichy, and to dispel the sense of unease that had started just after she left Thomas' hut that morning. But her hand on the gun was as tight as the tension in her head. He was back, she knew it. She could feel his eyes on her as surely as she could hear her own voice humming its tuneless melody.

She took the gun out of her pocket and quickened her pace. She should go back, ask Lucien to walk her to the château, but her feet kept moving her deeper into the forest. Everything was so still, not even a breeze moved the branches above her.

Suddenly she slipped in the mud, and as she righted herself a bird fluttered from a branch. She jerked the gun upwards and fired. Then, hearing footsteps behind her, she swung round, both hands on the gun. Again she squeezed the trigger, but there was nothing there. Something slithered in the undergrowth, only feet away. She jerked the gun towards it, slipped and fell. Another bird flew screeching from a tree, and she fired, the din of it drowning the beating drum in her head. Terrified, she pulled herself to her feet, her eyes hunting the shadows. Then suddenly she knew that someone was there, standing behind her. She turned. She tried to fire, but her hands were shaking. She looked up into his face and then her legs buckled under her. 'Armand,' she choked. 'Oh, Armand!'

'Were you expecting someone else?' he said, putting a hand under her arm to help her up and apparently quite unruffled by the fact that she had almost shot him.

'He's back!' she sobbed. 'Armand, he's here. I know it. I can feel it.' She looked up into his face, and suddenly her eyes dilated. 'Armand, why are you looking at me like that?' she cried.

'Ssh!' he hissed.

Then she heard it too. Someone running. They spun round as Lucien came racing through the trees.

'What is it?' he cried. 'What's happening? I heard a shot ...' He looked at Claudine's white face, then at the gun hanging limply in her hand.

'It's all right,' Armand told him. 'No one's been hurt.'

'But what happened, for God's sake!'

'It's Halunke,' Claudine interrupted. 'He's back.'

Lucien's eyes shot to Armand, and Claudine turned to look at him too. Then she moved her gaze to Lucien, and in that instant, as she stared up at their strikingly handsome faces, the world around them started to spin. The gun slipped from her fingers and there was a terrible cacophony in her ears. She covered them with her hands, shaking her head as the two faces seemed to whirl about her, faster and faster, ballooning and shrivelling, writhing and twisting. And through it all the long-forgotten words of the old fairground gypsy returned to her.

She started to back away. She stumbled, picked herself up, then turned and ran. She could hear them coming after her, shouting her name, their voices drowning the terrible words in her head. '. . . He will be like a brother,' the old woman had said. 'Or perhaps it will be his brother.'

The reason François had lied to Claudine about the time he was expected at Vichy was because he had promised to spend the night with Élise. She was now living in the upper two storeys of a town house in Montbazon, overlooking the river Indre, which he had taken for her and Béatrice soon after returning to Lorvoire. The house was forty kilometres from Lorvoire, but little more than a stone's throw from the Château d'Artigny.

When he arrived in the middle of the afternoon, letting himself in with his own key, it was to find Béatrice sitting alone knitting and looking every bit the middle-aged woman she was. How deceptive appearances could be, he thought wryly. Béatrice was as dangerous as her Secret Service name suggested: the Alligator, they had called her.

'It's good to see you, *monsieur*.' She smiled warmly, setting aside her needles. 'We weren't expecting you until a little later. Élise is taking a nap. I'll fetch some coffee.'

'How is she?' François asked when she returned a few minutes later. He took a sip of coffee, and could not hide his distaste. 'Acorns?' he said.

'All there is, I'm afraid,' Béatrice laughed. 'Revolting, isn't it?' She took up her knitting again. 'Élise is much the same. There has been no real change.'

'Has anyone called recently?'

'I'm afraid so,' Béatrice sighed.

François' face darkened. He jerked himself to his feet and walked to the window.

They had been in Montbazon only three weeks when Béatrice first told him that Abwehr officers were paying calls again on a regular basis. François had been livid, but Béatrice had begged for tolerance. Debasing as it was, she told him, Élise needed to do it. It was all part of the fantasy that gave her a reason for living: the services she performed for the Germans were to persuade them to enter into a plot to kill Claudine. If it wasn't so pathetic, François thought bitterly, gazing down at the people milling about on the bridge below, it would be laughable.

He had always known that Élise loved him, but now her love placed on him an almost insupportable burden of guilt. How deeply now he regretted the way he had treated her in the past, how he had used her to the point of abusing her. Almost since he had first known her, he had been aware that behind the sophistication she held like a barrier between herself and the world, there was a child crying out to be loved; but he had refused to acknowledge it. And now it was too late. Nothing he did would ever make up for what she had lost because of him. All he could do was reassure her that he would never desert her – which he wouldn't, anymore than he would allow himself to give way completely to his guilt. It was what Halunke wanted, that he should destroy his own life with self-condemnation and blame for the deaths and mutilations of those he loved.

He looked up as the door opened and Élise walked in. The instant she saw him, her face lit up, and she hurtled across the room into his arms. 'Kiss me, *chéri*,' she said, tilting her face back to look at him. 'Kiss me and tell me how you've missed me.'

He kissed her gently, then took her hands from around his neck and held them between his own. Every time he saw her, he felt the tragedy of what had happened to her more deeply than ever. The doctors had told him that she might never improve, but they had not prepared him for the fact that she might get worse. Her once beautiful green eyes now held the depraved look of a madwoman, and the effort it cost her to control her poor, tormented mind showed in the deep ridges forming round her mouth. Her hair, as ever, was immaculately dressed, but the golden sheen had vanished and the grey strands were thickening. From her dress he could see that today she was the Marquise de Pompadour, though she must have removed the wig before she lay down to sleep.

'How are you, *chérie?*' he asked.

'Troubled,' she said, frowning.

'Why is that?'

'Because you have not been to see me for so long. But I tell myself that it is because you are looking for that man Halunke. Have you found him?'

François' eyes darted to Béatrice, but she too looked surprised. It was the first time for months that Élise had mentioned her attacker.

'No, *chérie*, I haven't,' he said gently.

'It is of no matter,' she trilled. She picked up her skirts and tried to glide across the room in a way her limp would not quite permit. 'You will sleep with me tonight?' she said, suddenly turning round.

Again François looked at Béatrice. 'You know François is staying, Élise,' Béatrice said. 'I have prepared the room next to yours.'

Élise's eyes flashed. 'No! He is to sleep with me!' she declared. 'You want to sleep with me, don't you, François?' But before he could answer, she said, 'Béatrice, fetch *monsieur* some wine.'

Obediently Béatrice got up and left the room. 'Take no notice of her,' Élise said, not even waiting for the door to close. 'She is a prude. But I have laid out my prettiest silk nightgown and perfumed the sheets. You see, I knew you would come. You said you would, and you never let me down, do you François? You never lie to me. Not like the others.' She was moving towards him again, and his heart sank as he saw the smile twitching the corners of her mouth. Any moment now, regardless of Béatrice's imminent return, she would drop to her knees and beg him to let her satisfy him. He often wondered which was worse, that or the hideous embarrassment he felt when she behaved as though he were a king.

But to his surprise and relief she stopped before she reached him, and assuming a coquettish stance, her head lowered so that she was looking at him from beneath her lashes, her hands trailing along the back of the sofa, she said sweetly, 'When did you last make love to a woman, François?'

The question threw him. She had never asked him that before, even though he had never permitted her to 'satisfy' him, as she put it, and he was at a loss to know how he should answer.

'When?' she prompted.

'Does it matter?'

She nodded.

'Why?' He was watching her closely, beginning to suspect that there was more to this than he had realized.

'Because I want to know.'

They eyed one another for a long moment until, to his profound relief, she seemed to lose interest and turned away. But then she looked at him again, and he realized that it wasn't over yet. Her eyes were narrowed, her lips drawn in a tight, bitter smile. Like a striking snake, she rasped, 'You've been making love to *her*, haven't you?'

François was dumbfounded. There weren't many situations he couldn't handle, but this was beyond him.

'You've been making love to her, haven't you!' she screamed, advancing towards him. 'Admit it! You've taken her to your bed. You've given her everything that belongs to me!'

She stopped an arm's length away from him, and her eyes blazed into his. 'Say something!' she yelled, and suddenly she sprang at him, her nails brandished like the claws of a wild-cat, and her teeth bared. 'Answer me!' she screeched. 'Answer me, you bastard!'

He caught her hands, but only after she had scratched his face. 'Élise, calm down!' he barked, trying to take her by the shoulders. But with tremendous strength she threw herself at him again, hitting, kicking, scratching and biting. 'I'm going to kill her!' she spat. 'I'll get her out of your life. She can't have you! You're mine! It's me you love, not her. You despise her!'

He grabbed her arms and twisted them behind her back. The door opened and Béatrice came running in.

'They're going to kill her for me!' Élise screamed. 'Tell him, Béatrice! Tell him they're going to annihilate The Bitch!'

Béatrice rushed across the room as Élise sank to the floor. François let her go, but as she rolled over she struck out with her feet, kicking Béatrice hard in the stomach. Winded, Béatrice fell back, and Élise screeched with demonic laughter. 'They'll get her, François!' she cried. 'They've promised me. They're going to arrest her, and torture her, and then they're going to kill her. They're going to do it tomorrow, François.'

Suddenly her eyes rolled back in their sockets, her back arched and her whole body started to convulse. Immediately François dropped to his knees, taking her in his arms, but Béatrice pushed him away.

'Leave her to me,' she said. But even as she spoke Élise's body went limp as unconsciousness overtook her.

It had happened in a matter of minutes, but it was more than half an hour before Béatrice came back into the room. François was standing in front of the mantlepiece, staring down at the dying fire.

'That's the first fit she's had,' Béatrice said pouring them both a thimbleful of precious cognac. 'But the doctor warned me it might happen if she ever became seriously overwrought.' She passed him a glass and went to sit in the window-seat. She could see how shaken he still was. 'I'm sorry,' she said, after a moment or two, 'it must have been very distressing for you.'

François only sighed. 'How does she know about Claudine and me?' he said.

'Blomberg,' Béatrice answered. 'He was here again yesterday. He must have told her.'

François' face showed nothing of the anger he felt at her reply. He could hardly believe he had been so stupid as not to have realized Blomberg would tell Élise. '*Must have* told her?' he said shortly. 'Weren't you listening?'

Béatrice coloured slightly. 'I was listening,' she said, 'but there does tend to be rather a lot of whispering, and perhaps,' she looked away, 'my hearing is not quite as good as it was.'

François let it go at that, and soon afterwards took himself off to a hotel for the night. His continued presence at the house would only cause Élise more distress, and he couldn't go home because he had lied to Claudine about the time he was expected in Vichy. In fact he did try telephoning her, but the lines were down.

He spent a sleepless night at the hotel, turning over in his mind the painful events of the afternoon. One thing that did not occur to him, or to Béatrice, was that Élise's claims about what was going to happen to Claudine next day should be taken seriously. They had heard it all too many times before to pay any attention to it.

Halunke was counting on the telephone lines between Chinon and Lorvoire not being repaired before tonight. He'd sabotaged them himself, so that Lorvoire and his wife couldn't make contact. If he'd given himself away in the forest yesterday – if Claudine's running away like that meant she knew who he was – it was vital that she didn't pass the information on. But it could be that he was imagining things, that she didn't suspect him at all. At their meeting in old Thomas' barn last night, to finalize preparations for tonight's parachute drop, she had seemed perfectly in control of herself again, and made only a passing reference to the incident by saying that her nerves had got the better of her.

He had been expecting her to say that she no longer intended coming with them tonight – but she was as determined as ever to be there, which was good. In fact, it was vital. The Germans knew about the drop, they were even now making room in the cells for their new prisoners. Later, one of the prisoners would be shot, someone whose death would hurt de Lorvoire more than any other so far.

Halunke grinned, and swung himself up over the fence into the forest. Everything was falling neatly into place. There was just one further task he needed to perform before tonight, then he could focus his mind on the real prize: François de Lorvoire's son and heir.

Claudine hadn't seen anyone for hours. A little while ago, driving the vineyard *gazogène*, she had crossed the Thouet river for the second time that day, heading west along the narrow, winding country roads towards Cholet. There were still another twenty kilometres to cover before she reached the field, just beyond the village of Brossay, where they were going to light the bonfires for the British parachute drop that night. Already logs, dried bracken, cans of paraffin and bicycles were hidden in a nearby barn, and now she was going over the route again to make certain of finding her way in the dark. Not that she would be alone, but old Thomas, Yves Fauberg and Armand were counting on her to know the way. Lucien would lead three others over the route he had chosen, and Jacques would bring the remainder of the party in a small truck he had 'borrowed' from a bakery in

Richelieu, complete with a tank of precious gasoline. The truck would be used later to ferry the parachuted supplies to a hiding-place known only to Lucien and Jacques. Safe-houses were already arranged for the agents, Armand would escort one of them to La Roche-Clermault and she would take the other to St Pierre-à-Champ. Everyone else would take different roads home.

She looked around her at the sprawling, wide open plains, and her stomach gave a lurch when she thought how vulnerable they would be in such unsheltered territory. Illuminated by the glare of a full moon, too – providing the weather held out.

Half an hour later, having driven through the village of Brossay, she passed a disused factory, then started to look out for the crucifix that marked the turning into a cart-track which led to the barn, a nearby copse – and the landing ground. Having satisfied herself that she now knew the way, she drove straight past the crucifix, crossed herself, made a silent prayer that all would go well for them that night, and then set off for home by a direct route.

The roads were almost empty, but a few cyclists saluted her, laughing at the huge balloon of charcoal gas bobbing about on the roof of her Renault van. Her progress was so slow that a couple of them pedalled along beside her to pass the time of day. She was glad of their company, for it stopped her, briefly, from thinking about what had happened in the forest the day before.

She had lain awake all night, thinking about it. The terrible discovery had taken over her mind, forcing her to examine and re-examine every coincidence, every strange glance and every unanswered question. In the end she had felt as though her head would explode with it. She was desperate to speak to François. He would tell her if she was simply making a fool of herself over the incoherent ramblings of an old gypsy, or whether he too could see that the appalling truth might have been staring them in the face all the time.

If the gypsy was right, then there was little doubt in her mind which one of them was Halunke – Lucien would never have killed his own father. But she didn't seem able to think beyond that, for the very idea that Armand, who loved François as a brother, who had been her lover . . . And yet better Armand than Lucien, perhaps. What would it do to François if he learned that his own brother . . . No! None of it bore thinking about, and she would not think about it any more until François returned.

At last she turned the *gazogène* off the forest road and into the drive leading up to the west wing of the château. It looked as if there was something up ahead. She peered through the trees, trying to force the van to go faster, and when she came to the end of the drive and saw what it was, her face drained of colour. Parked right across the front of the château were five police cars.

She leapt out of the car and raced up the steps. As she burst in through the door she ran straight into Solange.

'Oh, Claudine! At last ! Where. . . ?'

'What is it?' Claudine cried, hearing the shrillness in her voice. 'What's happened? What are the *gendarmes* doing here?'

'Oh Claudine,' Solange wailed, 'something terrible has happened! I can't . . .'

'Louis!' Claudine screamed, and pushing Solange out of the way, she dashed towards the stairs.

'No! Stop!' Solange shouted. 'It isn't Louis, Claudine. It's Estelle.'

Claudine's relief gave way almost immediately to fear. She saw again in her mind's eye Lucien and Estelle standing together in the clearing outside the cottage. Maybe Armand had seen them too. 'What's happened to her?' she breathed.

'She's been murdered,' Solange said, crossing herself. 'Come outside, *chérie* and I'll tell you.'

As they descended the steps, Solange said 'The *gendarmes* are at the cottage. It's where she was murdered, outside in the clearing. Monique found her.'

'Where's Monique now?'

'In her room. Céline is taking care of her.'

'And Jack Bingham?'

'We've moved him to Thomas' barn for the time being. Incidently, he regained consciousness this morning.'

While they talked they had made their way between the haphazardly parked cars and now came to a halt at the top of the meadow.

'Tell me what happened,' Claudine said. 'From the beginning.'

Solange turned her face away for a moment, and Claudine suddenly reached for her hand. 'I'm sorry,' she whispered. 'It must have been a terrible shock for you, *Maman*. You don't have to tell me now . . .'

'I do,' Solange said. 'It will help me to get things straight in my own mind. I'll start with when Monique found the body, is that all right?' She took a deep breath, then blinked, and began.

'Well, as soon as Monique found the body she ran back here to raise the alarm. Armand was in the wine caves, so I went straight out to tell him. For a moment I thought he was going to faint, but then Céline came out with some brandy, and once he had himself back under control he sent me for Doctor Lebrun, and Céline to the village to tell Gustave to get a message to Lucien. The wretched telephone still isn't working, you see, and we had to get the American out of the cottage before the police arrived, and Armand thought Lucien should take care of that. When I got back here with the doctor, Armand had disappeared, but we found him at the cottage. He was in such a dreadful state, Claudine, it was terrible to see. He was crying like a baby, holding her body in his arms and . . . He was calling her Jacqueline. It was as though he was reliving the death of his poor wife.' Using her fingers, Solange wiped a tear from under her eye.

'How did Estelle die?' Claudine asked, her voice muted by pity.

'It was unpleasant,' Solange said haltingly. 'It was a knife . . .' And then, to Claudine's horror, she said, 'The *gendarmes* want to question Monique, Claudine. They think . . They are saying . . . One of them is outside her door now. Oh, how can they think she would have done such a thing?'

Claudine put her arms about Solange and said, 'The only reason they want to talk to Monique is because she found the body, *Maman*. Not because they think she did it. You mustn't distress yourself like this.'

Nevertheless, when the *gendarmes* finally left they took Monique with them – for further questioning, they said – and Solange went too, unable to let her daughter face the ordeal alone. Claudine sat with Tante Céline, listening to the wireless in Monique's room and waiting for the *message personnel* on the BBC that would be their final confirmation that tonight's airdrop was going ahead. Just before nightfall, Armand joined them.

It was strange, Claudine thought, that she felt no fear of Armand. And yet a voice, somewhere deep down inside, was telling her urgently that she should withdraw from tonight's reception committee and let them go ahead without her . . . She felt dazed, incapable of decision, as if she was being swept along in a dream. Oh, why did the telephone lines have to be down now? She so desperately needed to speak to François. But she would speak to Lucien instead. Somehow she would find a moment, while they were waiting for the plane to arrive, to tell him that she now knew who Halunke was.

The message they were waiting for, 'Felicity's grand-mother enjoyed Brighton', came over the airwaves just after nine fifteen. Immediately Armand got to his feet. Claudine, still sitting on Monique's bed with Tante Céline, looked up at him for the first time since he had come into the room.

He smiled uncertainly. 'I'll go and see if Thomas and Yves have arrived,' he said quietly.

'Armand.'

He turned.

'I'm sorry about Estelle,' she said.

He bowed his head and left the room.

The journey along the same roads Claudine had travelled that afternoon was untroubled. Thomas and Yves had no difficulty in keeping up on their bicycles, and the two-hour ride passed quickly and in silence. The moonlight seemed dazzling, though the strange shadows of trees and bushes that loomed across the road reminded Claudine of the dark thoughts sheltering in her mind. The wind moaned across the maize fields like an eerie extension of her fear, and it was only now that she was approaching the landing ground – a long way from Lorvoire, too far to turn back – that she began fully to realize what danger she was in. What danger they were all in. If François ever found out that she had disobeyed him . . .

She turned her bicycle onto the cart track, keeping to the ridges made by a tractor. The others followed, and in single file they pedalled between the bushes until Claudine spotted the final landmark on the brow of the hill. She jumped off her bicycle and wheeled it over the grass, making the ascent to the barn with ease.

When they were all inside she said, 'We'll start taking the logs and bracken into the middle of the field. Armand, can you go and see if there's any sign of the others? I presume they'll be coming from the road over there, just beyond the copse.'

It wasn't the first time Armand had been part of a

reception committee, but he didn't mind taking orders from Claudine. 'Is it all right if I smoke a cigarette?' he said.

'Do you normally?'

'Yes.'

'Then carry on.'

Yves and Thomas were already filling their arms with firewood, and Claudine took off her bicycle basket and began to stuff it full of leaves. François' thick leather gloves were hampering her, so despite the bitter cold she tugged them off and pushed them into the pocket of her black sheepskin jacket. She was wearing two pairs of knitted stockings beneath her jodphurs and fleece-lined boots, and the black woollen hat Armand had given her was pulled snugly down over her ears, covering her hair.

Just as they were leaving the barn to make their first trip across the field, Armand came back. 'The others are arriving,' he said quietly. 'Lucien's with them.'

And at that moment Lucien appeared from under the trees. He ran quickly towards them with three others in his wake; he greeted Claudine with a kiss, then they set about helping to build the bonfires.

By the time they heard the distant rumble of a truck, all the hard work had been accomplished and Claudine's hands and face were tingling with the cold. 'At last,' Lucien muttered. 'What kept him?'

'But we don't know if it is Jacques,' Armand warned, and at once they all took cover, behind the bonfires or in the long grass at the edge of the copse.

It seemed an eternity before, with a crashing of gears, the truck finally came round the bend, and Claudine could feel the damp seeping through her clothes. 'It's him,' Lucien said, as soon as it came into view, 'tell him to leave it there in the lay-by.' And not bothering to wait, he ran back to the bonfires.

As the truck came to a halt Claudine dashed over to it,

told Jacques where to park, then took him and the four other men to the barn, where the bicycles they would need later were waiting. She recognized them all, but knew only their codes names.

'Antoinette,' one of them whispered, 'this bicycle has a puncture.'

'Oh no!' Claudine groaned. 'What are we going to do? Well, never mind, one of you will have to go back in the truck with Lucien and Jacques.'

Outside, the wind was picking up, clouds had scudded across the moon. Claudine was freezing, but there was so much adrenalin pumping through her veins that she hardly noticed.

It was just as they finished dousing the bonfires with fuel that Armand heard the drone of an aircraft. Everyone stopped to listen. At first Claudine heard nothing, then after a while she too heard the distant hum.

'Quick!' Lucien said, pulling matches from his pocket. 'Get them alight!'

Within minutes the bonfires were ablaze, roaring like thunder and shooting sparks far into the sky. The whole party withdrew to the shelter of the trees to watch. Surely no one could fail to see the bonfires, Claudine thought fearfully; not the pilot, and not the Germans either.

'Don't worry,' Lucien whispered, seeing her taut face in the firelight. 'It's always like this.'

At that moment Yves, unable to contain his excitement, yelled, 'Look! There it is! The plane!'

And as they all turned their faces to the sky, the nose, then the wings, then the tail of a Whitley bomber emerged from a cloud to glide magnificently across the face of the moon. Claudine's heart flooded with emotion. To think that something like this could happen as a result of a peculiar system of dots and dashes and cryptic wireless messages was so amazing as to be miraculous.

'Here they come,' Armand murmered – and tiny, barely distinguishable black shapes began to fall into the sky. A few minutes later the first parachute ballooned, then another and another.

'*C'est magnifique!*' Thomas exclaimed.

'Shut up!' Lucien hissed suddenly. 'Listen!' Then they all heard it, Jacques' voice screaming, '*Les Boches*! *Les Boches*!'

'Quick!' Lucien yelled. 'Run! Everyone run!'

He dashed towards the truck, but as Claudine made to follow, Armand caught her. 'This way!' he shouted. 'Keep away from the road!'

Black figures were darting in every direction as the *Résistants* tried to escape. Before Claudine had time to argue, Armand was dragging her across the field, past the bonfires towards the open countryside. They were running into the wind and the ground was full of pot-holes, but every time she stumbled Armand pulled her up and forced her on. The cold night air burned in her lungs, and she thought of the agents, even now parachuting down from the sky, helpless and abandoned.

Suddenly it was as though the whole world had been lit up. Armand hesitated and both threw a quick glance over their shoulders, only to be dazzled by the headlights pursuing them.

'*Merde!*' Armand growled. Then, spotting a clump of bushes a few feet away, he pushed Claudine towards them.

She dived in, tearing her hands and face on the brambles. Armand gave her another quick shove, and she was through. He followed, hauled her to the ground and half-covered her with his body. They were in a ditch, thick with mud and rainwater. Claudine's hat had vanished and her hair was trapped beneath Armand's arm. The pain of it was excruciating, but she didn't dare make a sound. The left side of her face was submerged in the icy water, all she could do was twist her neck just enough to be able to breathe, and hold herself there. She could feel Armand's heart pounding against her shoulder, and tried to concentrate on counting the beats, but the pain was agonizing. Through the bushes she could see the bobbing headlights of the German jeep coming towards them. The roar of the engine grew to a peak and she could hear someone shouting above the din, telling them to come out.

'Don't move,' Armand muttered.

With her eyes almost bursting from her head, Claudine watched the lights come straight at the bushes. This was it, they'd been caught, and God only knew what lay in store now . . .

'I don't believe it,' she heard Armand gasp. 'They've gone right past us.'

She lifted her head, and at last Armand shifted his weight onto his other arm, freeing her hair.

'Look, they're going . . . They think we've gone into the village,' he said.

But the words were hardly out of his mouth before they saw that the jeep was turning round. It was heading back towards them.

'Got your gun?' Armand said, grabbing his own from his jacket. 'Then use it!'

But before she could even get her hand to her pocket, the jeep suddenly sped towards them, veered off at the last minute and came to a halt. Then the world was plunged into darkness as the headlights were turned off. There was a deathly silence. Then, as Armand cocked the trigger of his gun, there was a deafening explosion that seemed to echo on for ever.

It was several seconds before either of them pulled their faces out of the water, then Claudine tried to get up.

'What are you doing, for God's sake?' Armand hissed, snatching her back.

'Armand, we don't stand a chance. That was a machine-gun.'

'We are waiting!' a voice sang into the night.

'We can't give ourselves up, Claudine,' Armand moaned, and she suddenly realized that he was shaking all over. But before she could speak there was another volley of machine-gun fire. The bullets splattered into the swamp behind them.

'If we don't go now, they'll kill us with that thing,' Claudine hissed.

'I'd rather that than be tortured,' Armand responded, his voice twisted with fear.

'Pull yourself together!' she spat. 'You shouldn't . . . Oh my God!'

Armand followed the direction of her gaze. Poised on the edge of the ditch, no more that three feet away, was a pair of gleaming black jack-boots.

Claudine started to look up, but before she had raised her head more than an inch Armand was dragged from on top of her. She started to roll over, going instinctively for the gun, but someone caught her by the hair and heaved her to her feet. She was on the point of slamming her foot into his shins when she became aware of the gun digging into her back.

'Let go of my hair!' she hissed.

The grip tightened for an instant, then the German threw her forward onto her knees. She turned to look at him, but he pressed the gun hard against her temple. There was a dull thud, and turning back she saw Armand stagger forward, groaning in agony. His assailant stood over him, the butt of his rifle still brandished. His uniform and status Claudine recognized only too well, it was the same as François', but his face was unknown to her.

'On your feet!' he barked at Armand. Then nodding to the officer standing behind Claudine, he said, 'Check her for weapons, then bring her to the car.'

It was only then, as she glanced about her, that Claudine realized they were completely surrounded. Where so many Germans had come from she couldn't imagine, but as they were jostled about in the jeep on their way back to the road, she could be in no doubt that the whole time they had been building the bonfires and waiting for the aircraft, they had been watched. And once the parachutes had started to come down, when it was too late to stop them, the Germans had struck. And the size and accuracy of their operation could only mean that someone had told them about the drop long before tonight.

They were driven to a lorry which was waiting out on the road beside the crucifix. Shivering and soaked to the skin, Claudine was shoved inside. She fell against the step as she got in, and a hand reached out of the darkness to help her. When she looked up, she saw to her dismay, that it belonged to Thomas.

'Is Armand with you?' he whispered.

'Yes.'

'Then no one's got away.'

'Not even Lucien?'

Thomas shook his head. 'He's here. He's unconscious.' And looking down beside Thomas, Claudine could just make out Lucien, lying pale and still on the floor.

A few minutes later the rear flap of the lorry was snapped into place, and they started to roll down the hill.

It was then that Claudine experienced the first stabbings of real terror. Immediately she thought of François. Which was she more afraid of, she wondered: what François would do to her when he found out, or what the Gestapo would do when they questioned her? A silly grin spread across her face. It was such a preposterous thought that it made her giggle, and the German officer sitting beside her threw her a nasty look. She tried to stifle it, but without success, and this time the officer told her to shut up. But by now the entire lorry was filled with the sound of her screaming, brittle laughter, and it was evident to everyone on board that she was on the edge of hysteria.

A sharp crack on her skull brought her reeling back to reality. As the blood trickled down her face she suddenly remembered what torture had done to François' body, and dimly she wondered if she would be able to tolerate the pain that lay in store for her.

– 31 –

By the time dawn broke Céline had to admit to herself at last that something had gone terribly wrong. She had waited throughout the night for Claudine to return, but in vain, and when she cycled down to Liliane's cottage an hour after daybreak, her worst fears were confirmed. Gustave was there, trying to comfort the old lady. He was able to tell Céline everything.

And now Céline had not only to break the news of Claudine's and Lucien's arrest to Solange, she had to get word somehow to François. But she didn't know where he was staying, all she knew was that he was somewhere in Vichy. And even if she did manage to find him, what could he actually do? Claudine, Lucien, Armand – they had all been caught redhanded.

It was not until she was cycling back up the drive to the château that she suddenly thought of Beavis. Her heart gave a leap, and immediately she turned her bicycle round and started back to the village. Gustave would know how to get a message to London, and if she could somehow make contact with Beavis, then maybe – just maybe – he could find a way of getting to Lorvoire. Céline didn't stop to think of the difficulties involved, nor of how Beavis would be putting his own life at risk if he did come; all she knew was that in order to rescue Claudine and the others François was going to need all the help he could get.

'Ah, Max, there you are,' von Liebermann said, as Helber walked into the General's room at the Hôtel Louis XV in Vichy. 'Did you make contact with Blomberg?'

'Yes, General. My brother-in-law informs me that everything went according to plan. De Lorvoire's wife and her Resistance group are all in custody.'

'Good,' von Liebermann said, eyeing his reflection critically in the mirror. Satisfied, he removed his cap, smoothed down his hair and turned back to his desk. 'Did you manage to discover who was behind the killing in the forest?'

'It was Halunke, as we suspected.'

'Do we need to concern ourselves with it?'

'I think not.'

Von Liebermann nodded, then looked down at the document lying on his desk. It was an order he had received from Herr Himmler, dated 9th April 1941. The instruction was brief and to the point: François de Lorvoire was to be shot.

It was now March 23rd 1942, almost a year later, and still von Liebermann had not carried out the order. Of course, Herr Himmler knew he hadn't; when von Liebermann pleaded for execution to be delayed, Himmler had been pleased to indulge the General in his whim. Von Liebermann badly wanted to see the game with Halunke played out to the end. It amused him. It intrigued him. It also gave him a feeling of inordinate power to be in control of two men whose intellect, cunning and physical strength were superior even to his own.

However, things had not gone well for von Liebermann in Russia, and now Himmler had seen fit to withdraw his indulgence and had reinstigated the order of execution on de Lorvoire. It was to be carried out in any way von Liebermann desired – but it was to be carried out.

'So,' he sighed, turning his pale eyes back to Helber who had quietly taken a seat in front of his desk, 'things have gone well for Halunke these past few days. He deserves it. Thanks to him, our colleagues in Touraine have not only closed down an escape-line but have made over forty arrests. And now they have made twelve more, including de Lorvoire's *vigneron*, de Lorvoire's brother and de Lorvoire's wife.' He chuckled. 'Quite a coup. When will the shooting take place?'

'Within the week.'

Von Liebermann grunted. Then shifting his bulk a little more comfortably in the chair, he said, 'I am of the opinion that things are a little unevenly balanced. I think it is time we gave de Lorvoire his share of our help. We know, from the treasures stored beneath his château, that the orders we have given him during this visit to Vichy will be utterly abhorrent to him, but he has agreed to carry them out. I wonder if he will. I also wonder if he will find a way round them. He has a brilliant mind, most enviable, but most dangerous. But I would never have put him down for a Jew-lover. You must warn your brother-in-law to keep a very close eye on him. As Monsieur Laval said at our meeting yesterday, it is high time this nation was cleansed of the Jews, and we don't want any of them escaping, do we?

'Now, back to Halunke. You may inform him that he now has a free hand to do as he wishes. But at the same time I am going to give you, Max, the pleasure of revealing his identity to de Lorvoire. You may do it in any way you wish,' he continued as Helber's cheeks turned pink with pleasure, 'but be on your guard at all times. I'm sure you won't have forgotten what de Lorvoire has threatened to do to you . . . But you must tell him soon. He leaves for Lorvoire in three days, tell him before he goes. Then take yourself off to the Hôtel Boule d'Or in Chinon. I will join you there as soon as I am able. I have no intention of missing the final confrontation.'

The throbbing in Claudine's head had not let up since she'd arrived. Added to it now was the appalling ache in her limbs brought on by the fact that she still wore the same clothes she had been captured in. She was filthier than a street urchin. Her hair was caked with mud, her face and hands smeared with blood from the wound on her temple, and her left eye was badly bruised and swollen.

She had been incarcerated in this cell for two days now – though with its rough stone walls and stench of decay it was more like a dungeon. Through its single barred window, so high that she couldn't reach it even by standing on the bed, she occasionally heard the sound of marching jack-boots.

She had spent most of the time lying on the iron bed, her arms clasped about her body in an effort to keep warm, trying to summon all her resources for the interrogation to come. During the night, howls of agony had reverberated through the cells. When she realized that they were Lucien's, her terror, and her blinding hatred of Armand, had made her vomit again and again until there was nothing left in her body.

What an actor he was, she thought now. He had even gone as far as faking cowardice the night they were arrested, when he had orchestrated the arrest himself! He had revealed his true self only once, with that look of raw hatred, of pure savagery, that had come over his face that day in the forest. Then, she had known beyond doubt that he was Halunke; her hackles had risen like a cat's in the presence of evil. But great actor that he was, he had never given himself away until that day. And perhaps his best performance of all had been at dawn this morning, when he cried out as if under an extremity of torture. Even so, his cries had not had the same chillingly authentic ring as Lucien's. Lucien's screams could even now, hours after they had ceased, send a shiver of terror down her spine.

After that, it had been quiet. Then, an hour or more ago, there had been some kind of commotion at the other end of the passage – footsteps up and down the stone steps, heavy whispers and the clanging of doors. She wondered where Yves and Thomas were being held, and her heart filled with pity for the two old men who had been drawn into this horrifying web of revenge.

She still had no idea what motivated Armand. Certainly he hated her for the way he felt she had treated him, but there was something else, something darker and deeper. She had been nothing more than an instrument of his revenge – but how he must have enjoyed it that François de Lorvoire's wife had given herself to him so willingly! And her usefulness as a means of inflicting pain on François was certainly not exhausted yet. She would be tortured, and François, when he heard of it, would find that even more insupportable than his own sufferings at the hands of the Abwehr.

She tensed suddenly. In the distance she heard a door open and close, a heavy, echoing tread in the stone passage outside. She knew, even before the bolts were scraped back on her door, that they were coming for her.

The door creaked open, and only then did she hear the other, lighter footsteps. The uniformed guard snapped at her to get up, and obediently she forced her aching legs to move. She could smell the foul odour of her clothes as she unwound her arms and dragged her head from the pillow, and once again her stomach was gripped with nausea.

'You may remain seated,' a voice barked as she started to pull herself to her feet, and looking up, she saw her interrogators standing at the door. There was no mistaking the Gestapo, she thought grimly, in their black Homburg hats and leather overcoats.

Now that fear was starting to pump adrenalin through her body, she was feeling stronger. She watched as the man who had spoken to her clicked his fingers at his companion, and pointed to a spot beside the bed. Immediately a chair was produced, and the guard bolted the door.

Claudine studied the face of the man who sat down beside her. His skin was pale and slightly pockmarked, his eyes a translucent blue and his mouth a narrow band of concentration. There was no hint of the brutishness she had expected to see, but there was no trace of compassion either.

He smiled, revealing an ugly gap in his front teeth. 'So,' he said, 'you are the Comtesse de Lorvoire. I have heard a great deal about you, *madame*.'

She said nothing, and he smiled again. Then they both turned as the grid in the door scraped open and the guard's face appeared.

'Everything is ready, Herr Schmidt.'

The grid remained open and Schmidt's companion went to stand beside it. Schmidt folded his arms, crossed one leg casually over the other and said, '*Léopard*.'

Claudine stared at him.

'All you have to tell us, *madame*, is *Léopard*'s identity and the location of his camp. Then you may go home.'

Claudine was astonished. Surely Armand had already told them all about Lucien? And as for going home, the circumstances of her arrest proved she was a *Résistante*, and *Résistants* were never released – unless of course they turned collaborator.

'I should tell you, *madame*,' Schmidt continued, 'that you will make it much easier on your *vigneron* if you co-operate.'

Her eyes narrowed for an instant, then she smiled. They were simply trying to throw her off the scent. Well, let them go ahead with their macabre pantomime. Unless she saw Armand suffer with her own eyes, she wasn't buying it.

'I repeat, *madame*,' Schmidt said affably, '*Léopard*'s identity and the location of his camp, if you please.'

Claudine's face was expressionless as she gazed back at him.

Schmidt cast a look at his accomplice, who nodded to the guard. A few moments later she heard Armand scream.

She flinched, and waited for the echo to die away before turning back to Schmidt. She was on the point of telling him that she was not convinced, when she stopped. If she let them know that she knew who Armand really was, they would undoubtedly abandon this farce and subject her to a much more personal method of torture.

'We know, *madame*,' Schmidt said, 'that you are in regular contact with *Léopard*. So please, think of your *vigneron* and tell us where we can find him.'

Her silence brought another scream of pain from the adjacent cell. Schmidt looked at her expectantly, but when she still remained silent he scratched his nose and said, 'Perhaps I should tell you exactly what my colleagues are doing to your *vigneron*.' He raised his eyebrows questioningly, and she did the same. 'They are removing his teeth,' he said bluntly.

Claudine suppressed a shudder and reminded herself that this was all a sham.

'All right,' Schmidt sighed, uncrossing his legs. 'Let's talk about the destination of the British agents who landed outside Brossay the other night. Where were you intending to take them?'

'Home,' Claudine answered.

'Ah, a joke. Very amusing. Shall we see if your *vigneron*, your ex-lover, is entertained by your misguided sense of humour?'

Armand's cry howled through the cells. Claudine visibly

blanched as she heard him cough and splutter, as though choking on his own blood.

'Where were you taking them!' Schmidt barked.

'Nowhere!' she shouted back.

'Where were you taking them?'

'Nowhere!'

Armand screamed again.

'Where?'

'I don't know!'

'Where?'

'I don't know!'

Armand's agony bounced from the walls. The noise was unbearable, Claudine covered her ears.

'Names and addresses!'

'I don't know!'

It went on like that, a steady crescendo of interrogation, denial, agony. The screams became inhuman. Scream after scream after scream, a never-ending explosion of noise.

At last Schmidt stood up. 'You have until five o'clock this afternoon to tell us what we want to know,' he said, looking down at Claudine's bowed head. 'If you do not tell us, the *vigneron* will be shot.'

The door swung open and he left. The other man stayed, no doubt to await her confession. But shaken as she was, her resolve was as firm now as it had been when they began. She hadn't been taken in, not even for a moment. It was all a farce! Why else were they torturing him in another cell? And nothing short of seeing Armand drop before the firing squad would convince her now that he wasn't Halunke.

Helber was standing just inside the door of François' hotel room. François himself was seated in a winged armchair near the window, his head almost imperceptibly bowed. Helber was watching de Lorvoire's face very closely. It gave nothing away, but Helber knew he was on extremely dangerous ground now, for he had just informed de Lorvoire of his wife's arrest.

If he had been able to look inside François' mind he would have seen the final pieces of an almost complete jigsaw being fitted into the unholy pattern that made up Halunke's revenge – until the only piece missing was the one that gave Halunke his motive. Only that piece would tell François for certain whether his suspicion was correct. It was a suspicion that had taken root in his mind some time ago now; a suspicion so abhorrent, so devastating, that he had refused to give it the nourishment of thought.

At last he turned to look up at Helber, almost paralysing him with his terrible eyes. Helber could feel the hatred as though it were twisting round his neck. After a while François spoke. 'You say my brother was arrested too?'

'And your *vigneron*.'

François turned to stare sightlessly at the bed where his luggage was piled ready for his departure. Then, in his deep steady voice he said, 'It's one of them isn't it?'

Helber nodded.

There was a long, asphyxiating silence. 'How do I know I can trust you?' François said.

'You have no choice,' Helber answered. 'But I give you my word I will tell you.'

François threw him a look of such violent loathing that Helber's pulsating erection momentarily lost its urgency. 'And if I tell you that I am not prepared to do what you want, you will remind me that you are holding my wife?'

Helber only looked at him.

François stood up, towering monstrously over Helber's plump little body. 'Then we'd best get on with it,' he said, and turned to pull the curtains, shutting the daylight from the room.

Twenty minutes later François emerged, fully clothed, from the bathroom. His face was strained, his mouth compressed with loathing. Helber was sitting on the edge of the tousled bed, still naked, and to François' unutterable disgust the man's flabby penis started to respond to his presence. His eyes bored into Helber's, and Helber knew that if de Lorvoire's wife had not been in captivity, his genitals would have undergone a very different experience from the one they just had. As it was the ravishment of François de Lorvoire's body, inanimate as it had remained throughout, had surpassed all expectation. Helber's only regret was that it would never happen again.

François picked up his luggage and moved it to the door. He wasn't sure why von Liebermann, using Helber as his messenger, had decided to tell him now who Halunke was, but he could guess. He had long outlived his usefulness to the Abwehr, so the execution order he had been expecting must have arrived. Which could only mean that von Liebermann wanted to bring Halunke's revenge to its climax.

He turned to face Helber. Helber looked up at him, and every cell in François' body suddenly recoiled from hearing the word Helber was about to speak. It was unthinkable that Halunke should be either of them, but worst of all was that it should be Lucien. Why should he, why should either of them, feel the need to exact such a terrible revenge? What in God's name had he done?

Then, from the darkest corner of his mind, a terrible flame of suspicion suddenly roared like the inferno of hell. It was as though Erich von Pappen were standing there in the room with him, telling him that it was all because of Hortense de Bourchain's death. And if that was true . . . But it couldn't be! Lucien could not possibly have inflicted the kind of mutilation Élise had suffered; he could never have gunned von Pappen down in cold blood, terrorized his own family – killed his own father.

But he had, Helber had just confirmed it.

Blomberg was contemplating a map of Touraine, propped on an easel in front of him, when Hans knocked on his office door. Scowling, Blomberg barked admittance, but when he saw who was standing on the threshold his face visibly brightened. 'Ah, *Madame la Comtesse*,' he said, 'come in. Thank you, Hans, you may go.'

Claudine took a few paces into the room and stopped. The only colour in her face, apart from the caked blood and dirt along her hairline, was the blueish-black of the swelling over her left eye, where the German soldier had hit her with the butt of his rifle the night she was captured. Her jacket had been taken away from her before she entered the room, and now she wore only her jodhpurs, boots and a thick sweater. She smelt dirty and stale, and her hair fell in matted strands about her shoulders.

Blomberg walked to his desk and sat down, not taking his eyes off her for a moment. Beneath her feet, sunlight dappled the thick blue carpet, and particles of dust floated in the rays that streamed across her body. The room was long and airy, and the tall windows behind her looked out onto gardens which sloped in tiers down to the River Indre.

Claudine knew where she was; they had driven through the outskirts of Montbazon to get here. Of course she might have guessed, when they'd come to get her from her cell an hour ago, that they were bringing her here – to the Château d'Artigny, to Blomberg – but weary and worn down as she was, she hadn't really cared where they were taking her.

She had lain awake all the previous night, too numb to think beyond the gnawing pangs of her hunger. Just before five in the afternoon they had come to take Armand from his cell. Schmidt had been with her then, giving her the chance, right up to the last, to change her mind and talk. But she had remained silent, still not for one minute believing that any of it was real.

The firing squad had assembled in the yard above her cell, so she had heard every command, every footstep – and every shot. She was too tired even to be amused by the lengths they were going to to convince her that Armand was paying the price of her silence. Though the gunfire, when it came, had shaken her. But not enough to shatter her resolve, and when Schmidt finally left her he had told her not to make the mistake of believing her ordeal was over.

In the hours that followed she had tried to close her ears to the sickening sounds of torture going on in cells around her. She knew she must try to sleep because she would need all the strength she could muster to face her own when it came. But every time she closed her eyes, the sounds of gunfire seemed to echo mercilessly through her brain. It wasn't that she believed they had shot Armand; on the contrary, to her the sound meant that he had been released – and now there was nothing and no one to stop him, because no one, apart from her, knew who he was. She had wept for a while, feeling like a child and longing for the comfort and safety of François' arms. But she wasn't going to give the Germans the satisfaction of seeing her weakness, so she had let the tears dry on her cheeks and lain quietly on the bed, praying that François would come . . .

Blomberg's scrutiny continued. His desk was at the other end of the room, beneath a massive portrait of the Führer, and despite the ache in her neck she held her head high as she regarded him, not bothering to hide her repugnance.

'Come forward,' he said eventually.

Keeping her eyes defiantly on his, she walked towards the desk.

'Good,' he said, his protuberant bottom lip trembling as he smiled. He dropped the pen he was holding and sat back in his chair. Then, taking a sheet of paper from the drawer in front of him, he put it on the desk and said, 'Herr Schmidt informs me that you do not believe we have shot the *vigneron.*'

Claudine's nostrils flared over an insolent smile.

'Perhaps you will tell me why you refuse to believe this?' he said, folding his hands over his belly.

'I'm not a fool.' she said, biting out the words.

'Perhaps not. But I must inform you that you are gravely mistaken in your refusal to believe he was shot.'

'I'll believe it when you show me the body.'

Blomberg sucked his bottom lip thoughtfully. 'Would I be correct in thinking that you suspect him to be the man who is avenging himself on your husband?'

Now how would they know that, she thought, unless Armand had told them? 'No,' she said, 'I don't suspect it. I know it.'

Blomberg's body rocked back and forth as he nodded. 'You seem very certain, *madame.* Are you equally certain of your husband's fidelity? That *Monsieur le Comte* puts your safety above all else? That he loves you, *madame?*'

Her eyes darted to his. 'Yes,' she said carefully, wondering what this could possibly have to do with anything.

'I see.' He looked down at his hands. 'And if I were to tell you,' he continued, raising his head until his malicious eyes connected with hers, 'that for the past ten months your husband has been regularly visiting his mistress, Élise Pascale, who now resides in a house he has leased for her in Montbazon, what would you say then?'

'I would say you were lying,' Claudine snapped.

'But I am not lying,' Blomberg smiled pleasantly. 'And I shall prove it.'

She stared at him. Weak with hunger as she was, her legs began to tremble with the effort of holding her steady.

'Your husband told you, did he not,' Blomberg

continued, 'that his rendezvous in Vichy was at nine o'clock in the morning. It was a lie, I'm afraid.' He leaned forward and pushed the sheet of paper across the desk. 'There is the memorandum instructing him to present himself at three in the afternoon, six hours later than he told you. He lied so that he could spend an uninterrupted night with his mistress. Oh dear, you look a little shaken. Would you like to sit down, *madame*?'

Claudine glared at him, inwardly struggling to fight back the panic – and persuade herself that it was only tiredness that was making her react like this.

'Suit yourself,' Blomberg shrugged. 'But maybe you will change your mind when I tell you that not long after your husband arrived at Élise Pascale's house, on the afternoon when you supposed him to be travelling to Vichy, Élise Pascale informed him of our intention to arrest you. She knew, because I had told her myself. Your husband had ample opportunity then to return home and try to prevent it happening, but as you know, *madame*, he continued on to Vichy. Now, are you still as firm in your belief that your husband loves you?'

She wished her head would stop spinning, then she would be able to think. As it was, tears were welling in her eyes, bitter, desperate tears. But she wouldn't listen to him. He was lying. François would never . . .

'No, of course you aren't,' Blomberg answered for her. 'So now I return to the matter of Armand St Jacques, though I am sure it must have already occurred to you, *madame*, that you may have made a terrible mistake there too.'

Everything inside her suddenly froze. Her lips were parted to scream the denial, but nothing came out. She mustn't listen to him. She must trust her instincts, and every instinct in her body screamed that he was lying. Why, then, was she suddenly so afraid?

Blomberg got up from his chair and walked round his desk. 'I see you are not quite so sure of yourself now, *madame*,' he said, his little round eyes gleaming with pleasure. 'What is more, you appear to have mislaid that arrogance I find so offensive. And what has happened, I wonder, to that acerbic tongue? The one you used with such contempt when addressing *me*, an officer of the Reich. Perhaps you do not feel so superior now. Perhaps you are beginning to understand what it means to ridicule a German officer. You surely didn't think you were going to get away with it, did you?'

He lashed out with his fist, so fast that Claudine didn't even see it coming. She staggered across the room, fell against a cabinet and struck her head on the corner.

'How does it feel, *madame*,' he said, advancing towards her, eyes glittering and lip trembling, 'to know that your husband has betrayed you?' He caught her by the collar and rammed her head against the cabinet again. 'Does it feel as good as knowing that you have sent an innocent man to his death?'

Tears of pain were streaming through the grime on her cheeks, but she didn't make a sound as he hit her again, so hard that stars exploded before her eyes.

'No, you're not so proud now, are you?' he jeered, letting her go and slapping her to the floor. His boot smashed into her thigh, then he grabbed her hair and jerked her to her knees.

'You know what you're going to do now, don't you?' he growled, and slammed his fist into her face.

Blood spurted from her nose and mouth, but as she made to cover them he caught her hair again and yanked back her head.

Oh God, let me die, let me die now, she prayed, squeezing her eyes shut against the searing pain. He slapped her again and again, harder and harder, until she started to gag on her own blood.

At last he let her go. She fell back to the floor, blood and saliva trickling from her mouth, her head rolling from side to side as she moaned softly at the terrible pain in her head. It was nothing compared to the pain and confusion in her heart, but still she wouldn't let go, still she wouldn't allow herself to believe that François had betrayed her, or that she had sent Armand to his death. 'Lying,' she mumbled through her swollen lips. 'You're lying.'

Blomberg seemed not to hear as he loomed over her, unbuckling his belt. 'Take off your trousers,' he snarled. 'Take them off!' And when she made no move and her eyes stayed closed, he whipped his belt from its loops and smashed his foot into her again.

She dragged her eyelids apart and watched as his hand reached inside his trousers. As he pulled out his penis her mouth flooded with bile.

'Do as I say!' he roared, and the belt slashed across her thighs.

Her fingers moved to her waist, but before she could get the first button undone the buckle smashed into her hands.

She screamed, which only seemed to excite him more. 'Get on with it!' he panted, and lifted his hand to strike again.

She cowered away, curling herself into a ball, and as his hand came down again and again, flogging her mercilessly with the belt, she willed herself to pass out. But she remained conscious, choking as she felt his hands fumbling with her trousers and breathed the nauseating stench of his sweat. She heard the fabric rip as he lost patience and tore her trousers open. Using his foot, he pushed her over and dragged them to her knees. The belt whistled through the air as he brought the buckle down on her naked buttocks.

He raised his arm again and again, so aroused now that he was on the point of ejaculating. He circled his penis with his other hand and frenziedly jerked it back and forth. Her white flesh quivered beneath the strap, and huge red weals striped her buttocks and thighs. Feeling the semen start to leap from his body, he triumphantly raised his arm again. He heard a noise behind him, but he was too far gone now to care. He jerked the belt for one last savage assault, saliva dribbling from his mouth. Then an unholy scream erupted from his lips as his arm was wrenched over his shoulder, and with a sickening crunch the bone was snapped clean from the joint. Then a fist smashed into his face. He flew across the room and sprawled in a heap on the floor.

For a moment François stared down at him. Then, slapping down on the floor beside him the order von Liebermann had issued for Claudine's release, he turned to his wife.

With the utmost gentleness he covered her nudity. Then he lifted her carefully into his arms, and without uttering a word to any of the officers who had followed him, carried her from the château. He put her into the jeep, smoothed the blood-sodden hair from her face and closed the door. Then getting in beside her, he started the engine and drove away.

Claudine was barely conscious. She felt as if she was inside a dream. Sometimes she could not seem to understand what was happening. They passed a river, the evening sunlight dancing on the water, and French people and German soldiers walking together along the embankment. Surely that was the bridge at Chinon? What was happening to her? But behind the confusion, and the terrible pain of her bruised and bleeding body, there was a sense that she was safe. And though she could barely manage to turn her battered head to look at him, she knew he was there beside her. François.

Only one thing she said before they reached the château. 'Have I been released?' she croaked. 'Are we going home?'

'Yes,' François said. 'Yes. We're going home.'

He carried her from the jeep and up the steps. She was dimly aware of people in the hall – Solange, Tante Céline, Jean-Paul – of shocked faces, cries of alarm. And then of everyone receding, and François carrying her up the stairs to their apartment.

She shut her eyes then, and tears of exhaustion started to seep from under her lids. She felt him lay her down on the sofa, and heard him close the door behind them. Then she opened her eyes. He was standing beside her, looking down at her.

She heard herself say, her voice so constricted with misery that the words were barely audible, 'Did you spend the night with Élise before you went to Vichy?'

He only looked at her, but there was such love and passion in his eyes that she could not bear it. 'Oh, François!' she choked. 'François. François.' And suddenly he was on his knees beside her, and she was in his arms, and he was saying. 'It's all right now, my darling. It's all right now.'

'I thought you loved me,' she said, her face buried in his neck. 'I thought it was over, you and Élise . . . Tell me it's not true . . . Tell me you don't love her . . .'

'Sssh,' he said gently, sliding his hand under her hair and stroking her neck. 'Sssh. I love *you*, Claudine. I love you with all my heart.'

She clung to him then, and cried as he had never known her cry before. He held her tight, feeling the tortured sobs shudder through her body and into his. And Claudine felt the warmth and strength of his body draw out her fear, as if he was telling her to let it go, to let him take it, and just to let him love her.

But she couldn't. Armand. Armand. Armand. His name echoed round her head as if it was blasting from the guns that had shot him. But it couldn't be true, what Blomberg had said. *It couldn't.* She concentrated on François, pressing herself to him, pushing her face into his neck and choking his name.

At last she grew a little calmer, and taking her ravaged face between his hands, François said, 'We have to talk, *chérie*. I have a great deal to tell you. But I don't think you are up to it now. Let me . . .'

She was shaking her head. 'No, François. I don't want to wait. I have to know . . . about you and Élise, I have to know now.'

He looked hard into her grimy, battered face. 'All right,' he said at last, and sitting beside her on the sofa he told her about Halunke's attack on Élise, how damaged Élise's mind had become as a result, and the terrible burden of responsibility it had laid upon him. All the more terrible now, because he knew that it had been carried out by his own brother – but he wasn't going to tell Claudine that part of it yet.

'So that's why I lied to you about the time I was expected in Vichy,' he said. 'She needs me to spend time with her whenever I can, and I simply can't refuse it, not after all she's suffered. And because of the way she so often claims that she's arranged to have you killed, neither Béatrice nor I took any notice of her warning.'

He was holding her hand, and watching her. When finally she looked up at him, her eyes were swimming with tears, tears that he knew were for Élise. 'Why didn't you tell me all this before?' she said huskily.

He sighed deeply. 'I don't know. I suppose I was afraid you would want to see her, that you'd want to try and help her in some way, and I had to keep you away from her.'

Claudine smiled briefly. 'You're right,' she said, 'I would have wanted to help her. I still do. But if you forbid it I won't argue. I won't ever disobey you again.'

François couldn't help smiling at that. 'I know you don't believe me,' she said solemnly, 'but if I'd done as you told me before, if I hadn't gone out after curfew, none of this would have happened.'

'It would,' he said. 'Maybe not in quite the same way, but it would have happened. It was all arranged by Halunke.'

Claudine's heart lurched. 'François, there's something I have to tell you – about Halunke,' she said. She could feel the hammer of dread start up in her head again, but she pressed on, telling him everything, from the day she had first suspected Armand, to Estelle's murder, right through to the moment the guns had fired outside her cell. Yet all the time she was speaking, she could hear Blomberg's voice. 'I am sure it must have already occurred to you, *madame*, that you may have made a terrible mistake there too.'

'But I didn't *see* a thing,' she finished. 'And I think, no I know, that it was all a sham right from the minute they started torturing him. It was, I know it was,' she cried, her voice beginning to shrill as François' expressionless eyes stared into hers. 'Why else wouldn't they let me see him? Why else wouldn't they let me see the body? It was a trick, François, don't you see? They wanted me to think . . . François! Why are you looking at me like that?'

'I'm sorry, *chérie*,' he said sadly.

Panic threatened to engulf her. 'He's dead, isn't he?' she breathed. 'Armand is dead.'

Slowly, François nodded.

'Oh my God!' she spluttered. 'No! François, you're wrong! Don't you see, everything I told you, everything . . .'

'*Chérie*, Lucien escaped from the Château St Hilaire where they were holding you. He escaped the morning after you were all arrested. In other words, they let him go.'

'No!' She buried her face in her hands, wishing this nightmare would end.

François rose, and pulled her gently to her feet so that she stood facing him. 'You must be strong, *chérie*' he said, taking her hands in his. 'You must listen to what I tell you now, and you must be strong.'

Her tormented eyes gazed up into his as, sparing her the details of his degradation, he told her everything Max Helber had told him the previous day. 'And when I returned to the château last night,' he finished, digging his hand into his inside pocket, 'this was waiting for me.'

He passed her the note, and her fingers started to shake uncontrollably as she unfolded it. She looked down, and as Armand's name danced before her eyes it was as though the hands of death had closed around her heart. 'No,' she whispered brokenly. 'François . . . Oh my God, what have I done?'

She slumped forward against him, and for a moment he thought she had fainted, but then she straightened herself and looked at him. And it was only then, when she saw the anguish and bewilderment in his eyes, that she realized what all this meant to him. She was stunned by her selfishness. She had thought no further than her own guilt and grief, but what must he be feeling, knowing that his own brother. . . ?

'Did Helber tell you why?' she said.

'Apparently Lucien himself will tell me, when he is ready.'

A silence fell between them, and Claudine shivered. 'Does that mean. . . ?'

'Oh yes,' said François. He looked away, and for a moment he could not speak. 'Oh yes, I'm afraid Halunke is still intent on his revenge, my darling.' He looked back at her, and in the fading light she could see how he was suffering. 'I want to kiss you,' he said, forcing himself to smile, 'but your mouth looks too painful.'

She touched her fingers to her swollen lips, then pressed them to his. But it wasn't enough, so she took him in her arms and kissed him.

When finally she let him go, the cuts on her mouth had

reopened and he dabbed at them gently, saying, 'For the first time in my life, Claudine, I know what it is to need someone. And I need you, my darling. I need and love you so much that if anything were to happen to you I know I couldn't go on living.'

'Nothing's going to happen to me, François,' she whispered. 'Not now.'

He gave her a bath then, dispensing with Magaly's services and undressing her himself. Now that she was in the sanctuary of her own home, her exhaustion had finally caught up with her, her head lolled against his shoulder and her arm hung limply in the air as he carried her into the bathroom. But she was still fighting it, he could see her eyelids fluttering as she struggled to keep them apart. What strength and resilience she had. Her head was painfully cut and bruised, and there were terrible weals on her buttocks and her hands where Blomberg's belt had caught her – but she had not once complained. He must get Lebrun to her in the morning . . .

He wondered about the internal wounds. It would be a long, long time before she came to terms with Armand's death – sometimes, scars like those never healed. He'd already decided that it would be better if she never told Liliane what she had believed, just as he would never tell his mother about Lucien. Of course Solange already knew that Lucien was being hunted for Estelle's murder, but she was convinced the *gendarmes* had made a mistake. However, if Lucien were caught . . . Well, that was a bridge they would have to cross when they came to it.

'I got Magaly to put some salt in it,' he said, lowering her gently into the bath. 'It'll help those wounds to heal.'

Claudine looked up at him. She felt her heart might almost dissolve with love, just as her body felt as if it was dissolving in the healing warmth of the water. 'Have I ever told you,' she said, 'how much I love you?'

François smiled. 'Several times,' he said. 'But I don't mind hearing it again.'

Claudine didn't wake the next morning until nearly eleven, and she made sure that the very first thing that happened – even before Magaly brought in her breakfast – was a visit from Louis.

It almost broke her heart to see how solemn-faced he was when he came in to her. He was used to a Papa who came and went, but not a *Maman* – and *Maman* had been gone for almost a week, and he had felt how frightened everyone in the house was; and he had been frightened too, but had known he must not show it because he was a big boy now, and a de Lorvoire. All this Claudine read in his face, and as she lifted him onto the bed and held his small body close to hers, it was all she could do not to cry.

'I don't like it when you go away, *Maman*,' he said, looking her straight in the eye, 'so please don't do it any more.'

'Oh no, I won't, my darling, I promise you I won't,' she said, kissing him.

He looked at her consideringly. 'You're allowed to make my face wet this time,' he said, 'because you've got a bad bruise and I expect it hurts. But you're not to do it again.'

When Louis had gone, François came in with her breakfast tray and sat with her while she ate. When she had finished she leaned back against the pillows and sighed.

'Feeling better?' François asked, one eyebrow raised.

'Mm,' she answered. 'Real coffee. I'd almost forgotten what it tasted like. Where on earth did it come from?'

'It's some Solange has been saving for a rainy day.' He smiled. 'She's longing to see you, of course, and so is Céline. Do you feel strong enough?'

'Almost!' she said. 'And I want to see Monique, too. Is she here?'

'Ah, Monique!' François said with a smile. 'Yes, she's been released, and now she's at Rivau.'

'Rivau?' Claudine was mystified. 'Why Rivau?'

'Because Rivau,' François said, 'is where Jack Bingham is. He's been moved to safety to an old tower there and Monique's keeping house for him.'

'But . . .'

'And before you say any more, it appears that Jack Bingham's wife died three years ago, and Bingham himself is improving every day, and Monique is very happy.'

Claudine was stunned. 'I feel as if I've been away a year, not a week!' She thought about it for a moment, then her smile faded, and her eyes met François'. 'You haven't told me anything about yourself yet, *chéri*,' she said. 'What happened in Vichy? Why did von Liebermann want to see you?'

François' face was suddenly expressionless. 'I and four others,' he told her, 'one of whom is Blomberg, are to oversee the rounding up of Jews from this area for transportation to an internment camp at Beaune-la-Rolande.'

She groaned inwardly. How much more could he take? 'But do you have to do it, François?' she said, 'now that you know who Halunke is?'

'If I don't, von Liebermann will ally himself with Lucien again.' He paused, then said quietly, 'But there may be a way round it.'

She waited.

'You remember Bertrand Raffault, at the Manoir de Pontoise? Where we spent the first night of our honeymoon?'

'I remember,' she said dryly.

'I found out some time ago that he spends half his time working with the Resistance in Paris, and the other half in Poitiers smuggling pilots and agents through to the Free

Zone. The trains carrying the Jews from Touraine will have to pass near Paris on their way to the internment camp, and if I can get a message through to Bertrand, he and his group may be able to ambush them.'

Claudine thought of the Jews she knew, of Gertrude Reinberg, little Janette and Robert. 'Isn't there anything else we can do to help them?' she said. 'Can't we get a message through to the British?'

'They already know. Jews are Jews, Claudine, and the British, French, Americans, Russians, all of them will save their own skins before they do anything to help the Jews. And even then . . .'

He left the sentence unfinished, and they sat for a long time, thinking their own thoughts. Then François reached over and took her hand. 'I have a surprise for you,' he said quietly. 'Would you like to see it?'

'A surprise?' Claudine said, intrigued. 'Yes, of course I'd love to see it!'

'I think it's downstairs. I'll just go and get it for you.'

A few moments later, she heard footsteps crossing the sitting-room to her bedroom door. Then the door opened.

'*Papa!*' she cried 'Papa! What are you doing here? Oh Papa, if only you knew how pleased I am to see you!'

'Not half as pleased as I am to see you,' he answered, holding her tight. He looked searchingly into her face. 'Was it very bad *chérie*?'

The surprise and joy of seeing him had unsettled her, so that for a moment she was on the verge of tears. 'Terrible!' she said, with a lop-sided grin. Then she kissed him again, to hide her distress, and said, 'But you, Papa, how did you get here?'

'Céline got me here,' he said, grinning.

'Tante Céline?'

'She managed to get a message to me in London. Used one of your Resistance operators to do it. It took me a couple of days to organize things, but I parachuted in the night before last. *Et voilà*, here I am!' He saw no point in bothering her with details of the difficulties he had had to overcome, and the loud disapproval of his colleagues in Whitehall. 'So what's been happening here?'

'Oh Papa,' Claudine sighed, 'I hardly know where to begin. But this afternoon, after I've seen Solange and Tante Céline, and we're all a bit calmer, François wants me to sit down with him and see if we can work out what's the best thing for us to do. I'm sure he will want you there too, and then we can tell you everything, and perhaps you can help. You are here to help, Papa, aren't you?' she said, giving him another hug. 'That's why Tante Céline sent for you, isn't it? Or no,' she looked at him with a sudden glint of mischief in her eyes, 'perhaps it was just that she couldn't stand being without you any longer!'

She watched delightedly as her father's normally calm and dignified face came as near as it could to looking embarrassed. He cleared his throat loudly, but when she caught his eye she saw that he was smiling.

'Oh Papa,' she said, 'I'm so glad you're here!'

'There's something I want to ask you,' he said suddenly. 'Something personal. May I?'

She nodded. 'Yes, of course.'

'Are you ... you and François, are you happy?'

Despite the bruises on her face the smile she gave him was so radiant that he could almost feel the warmth of it – and felt the secret knot of doubt that had tormented him since the day he first brought his daughter to Lorvoire, begin to unravel. It was clear, from what conversation he had had with his son-in-law over the last twenty-four hours, that François loved Claudine with extraordinary depth and intensity, but Beavis had wanted to make sure for himself that his daughter returned that love. Now, there could be no doubt of it, and though he was not a religious man he found

himself sending up a silent prayer of thanks to God that he
had done the right thing in bringing them together.

Later that afternoon, Claudine, François and Beavis sat
down in the library.

Of course, Beavis knew through his Intelligence contacts
a great deal of what was happening now in France, but he
did not know precisely how François stood with von
Liebermann and the Abwehr, and the Halunke situation
was entirely new to him. He sat and listened while François
filled him in, his face growing steadily more grave.

'So that's how things are at the moment,' François
finished. 'I'm no more use to the Abwehr as a spy, and von
Liebermann knows it. In fact, I suspect he's got an
execution order on me from Himmler in his pocket now.
But he wants us alive, and available for Halunke. That's why
he ordered Claudine's release, and that's why he's making
me useful round here, with the Jews. What he really wants is
to see his iniquitous little game with Halunke played out to
the end. He wants to be in at the kill.'

There was a heavy silence in the room. 'And Halunke
himself?' Beavis said, not using Lucien's name in order to
spare François' feelings. 'Is there any news of him?'

François shook his head. 'He's out there somewhere,
watching and waiting. Biding his time.' He turned to
Claudine. 'I hope you meant it when you said you don't
intend to disobey me again, chérie, because I want you never
to leave the château alone, and preferably not without me. Is
that understood?'

'Understood,' she said, giving him a mock salute. But her
face was serious.

'So the question is,' Beavis said, 'what do we do now?'

There was another long silence. Then François said,
'There is one step I've taken already. I've asked Bertrand
Raffault to see if he can arrange to get Claudine and Louis,

and possibly Solange and Céline too, across to England – perhaps in a boat out of Nantes.' He looked at Claudine waiting for her response. She returned the look steadily, then to his relief, she got up from her chair and planted a kiss on his forehead. 'It's all right, François,' she said. 'I'm not going to argue. Only . . .' she looked at him '. . . will you be coming too?'

François put his hand over hers. 'We'll talk about that later, *chérie*,' he said, looking back at her.

'But in the meantime, what else can we do to protect you?' Beavis said.

After a long moment, François shook his head. 'I think we can only go on as we are. Lie low, not attract attention, not run unnecessary risks – no more Resistance activity, Claudine, not of any kind.'

'How soon will it be before Bertrand contacts you?' Beavis asked.

'I don't know,' François answered, 'but I hope to God it's not long.'

Somehow the days of waiting passed. At the château, the family went about their daily tasks mostly in silence, none of them wanting to burden the others with their inner fears and anxieties. During the day François was at the Château d'Artigny, or at Camp Ruchard where the Jews were held before being transported to Beaune-la-Rolande. He came home in the evening depressed beyond words by the gruesome tasks he was required to perform, but his day didn't end there, and though Claudine begged and pleaded with him not to, he went out into the forest in the hope of finding Lucien. But there was not a sign of him, and the *gendarmes*, who were hunting him for Estelle's murder, had drawn a blank too.

Claudine herself spent much of the time trying to fight the debilitating depression that came over her every time she thought of Armand. She did everything she could to fill her days, keeping herself so busy that there wasn't time to think, for the guilt was always there, ready to pounce every time she stopped. She had let him die, a man whose only crime was to love and protect her. Despite François' assurances she knew she would never forgive herself, *never*! It didn't matter that she had been a weapon in Halunke's – Lucien's – grotesque bid for revenge. There was no excuse, no forgiveness. Armand was dead. Sometimes she woke in the night, sweat pouring from her skin and the deathly echo of gunfire still sounding in her mind. François was always there to hold her until she slept again, but she hated inflicting her suffering on him when his own was beyond anything she could begin to imagine.

But worse, perhaps, even than this, was the fear they both shared: that Lucien would strike again before she, and the rest of the family, could be got from the country.

One evening, François and Claudine were sitting reading in the family room. It was still early, but Solange and Céline, and even Beavis, had gone to bed soon after dinner; hard as they all tried, an evening's light-hearted conversation was beyond them. Claudine was idly turning over the pages of a magazine – a fashion magazine from the old days, before the war – how strange and silly it seemed now! – when she thought she heard a knock on the door.

'Did you hear anything, François?' she said, half-rising from her chair. 'I thought . . .'

Immediately, he was up and out of his chair and striding across the room. These days, any strange noise, any unexpected happening was cause for instant alarm, and sensing the fear in his reaction, she rose too.

François flung open the door, and a woman almost fell into the room – a middle-aged woman, her grey hair in disorder and her face drawn with anxiety. 'Oh, *monsieur*!'

she said, 'I am so glad I have found you. I have travelled across country from Montbazon, it has not been easy, and then I could not get into the château. Your servants are all gone, no doubt, because of the war, and your doors are very well secured – but the Alligator is not so easily defeated, and at last I found a window that would let me in . . .' She smiled, but it was a weak, half-hearted smile, and when the woman looked up at François, Claudine could see that her eyes were full of grief and pain. 'I could not telephone, you see, *monsieur*,' the woman went on. 'Such news has to be given in person.'

'Who is this?' Claudine said quietly to François. She saw that his face was dark with anxiety.

'This is Madame Béatrice Baptiste,' François said. 'Élise's "nursemaid", formerly known to the Secret Service as the Alligator. Béatrice, this is my wife, Claudine.'

Claudine took Béatrice's hand and led her over to the sofa. 'Haven't we any brandy left, François?' she said. 'Madame Baptiste has come a long way, and . . .'

'Oh, *monsieur, madame*,' said Béatrice, looking from one to the other and unable to contain her distress any longer. 'I am so sorry. I am so sorry to be the bearer of such tidings, but I have to tell you. Élise is dead, *monsieur*! Élise Pascale is dead.'

There was a long and terrible silence, until at last François said heavily, 'Tell us how it happened.'

Gathering herself together, Béatrice began to tell them. Watching her, Claudine could see how deeply Élise's death had affected her; there was no doubt that Béatrice had loved and cared for her, and as she listened to the tragic story Claudine's heart was full of pity for them both.

'It was at a café in Montbazon, Monsieur,' Béatrice said, addressing herself chiefly to François. 'A café that the Germans frequented – that Blomberg, and others. I did not like to take her there, *monsieur*, but the soldiers had not come to the house since she got worse, and she missed them so much. So I took her to the café . . .'

'She had got worse?' François said sharply.

'Yes, *monsieur*, there had been more convulsions, and the soldiers witnessed one of them. She was definitely deteriorating. I sometimes wondered, you know, if she was deliberately withdrawing into a shell of madness, unable to face her life the way it was, her inadequacies, her disfigured body – her insatiable hunger for you, *monsieur*. Perhaps it was the only way she could mask the horror of all she had lost. There were still moments of lucidity, you know, when she would speak rationally and her eyes would reflect all the pain she felt inside, but they were becoming fewer and fewer.'

Béatrice paused. 'You know what she said to me only the night before, *monsieur*? She said, "I want to die, Béatrice. Please let me die. Let me go to a place where I can be rid of this torment. There's nothing anyone can do to help me now, not even François. I know he tries, but it hurts him to see me, as much as it hurts me." It was truly pitiful, *monsieur*. "Only God has the answer for me now," she said. "Let me go to Him. Please Béatrice, help me to go to him." '

She stopped to wipe away her tears, and they were all quiet then, feeling Élise's tragedy strike at their hearts – the tragedy of her life, and of her death.

At last Béatrice continued. 'Blomberg was there at the café and two of his officers. They were not really interested in Élise, *monsieur*. She batted her eyelids at them, tried to whisper in their ears, but they shoved her away so that she almost fell from her chair. She just laughed, you know, as if it was some kind of joke. She seemed so lost sometimes, *monsieur*, so uncertain, so lonely . . .'

Again, Béatrice was overcome, and Claudine's heart swelled with pity for her.

'Then,' Béatrice said, 'Blomberg started talking about

you, *madame*.' She looked at Claudine. 'Forgive me, *madame*, but he said such dreadful things. About how he had whipped you, and . . .' she looked at François unsure whether to continue.

'It's all right,' Claudine said quietly. 'Go on.'

'Élise loved what Blomberg was saying. She bounced in her chair, and applauded and wanted to hear more, and of course the Germans roared with laughter at that, and Élise laughed too.

'Anyway,' Béatrice went on, 'after about an hour, I went to the lavatory, and when I came out, Jean, the proprietor, was waiting for me in the corridor. I had noticed at the beginning that he didn't give us our usual welcome, *monsieur*. He is a man of few words, and slow-witted, but usually he was eager to serve us and cold with the Germans, and today it was the other way round. And when I came out of the lavatory he was there in the corridor, and he said, "You must get Élise out of here now!" "Why, what is it, Jean?" I asked. He was ashen-faced and trembling. "*Madame*," he said, "it is the Resistance. They are coming here! You must get Élise away, immediately, but you must not alert the *Boches* . . ."

'Well, *monsieur*, as you can imagine I started back to our table at once. But even before I could reach it, the firing had started, *monsieur*. Even before I could reach it . . .'

Claudine and François waited, imagining only too easily the horrific scene inside the café, the deafening noise as machine-gun bullets drove into walls and tables, the screams, the blood, the splintered glass . . .

Béatrice's mouth was trembling, so that she could hardly get the words out. 'When it was over,' she said carefully, 'I got up off the floor and looked for Élise. She was not hard to find, *monsieur*. She was lying on the floor, beside Blomberg's table. She was covered in blood, there was no doubt that she was dead. And the bodies of Blomberg and his friends were sagging over her in their chairs, *monsieur*, like ... like ...' She shivered, 'Like puppets. Grisly, abandoned puppets.'

She looked up at them, and now the tears were coursing shamelessly down her cheeks. 'It was terrible. I made the sign of the cross over her, *monsieur*. And you know, I cannot help thinking that maybe it is better this way. Maybe now God will take away the pain and the torment and give her peace. And I shall pray every day,' she said, in a voice so quiet now that it was almost inaudible, 'that He loves her enough to forgive her. Do you think he will, monsieur? Do you think he will?'

François did his best to comfort her and much later that night, after they had made up a bed for Béatrice in the west wing, he and Claudine sat together on the sofa in their sitting-room.

'I was thinking,' Claudine said, as François stroked her hair. 'I know that in your own way you cared a great deal for Élise, so perhaps she should be buried at Lorvoire, in a family plot. I think she would have liked that.'

'Claudine,' he said gruffly, 'I love you so much that I ...' But his voice was too full of emotion to continue.

The next day, a message came through from Bertrand. He could arrange passage to England, from Nantes, for three. Within the next couple of days they were to expect a messenger who would tell them where to rendezvous for the trip across country.

They decided that the passengers would be Claudine, Louis and Solange. Céline was under no threat from the Germans, and Beavis said that, of all of them, he was the one best equipped with the knowledge and experience to enable him to get out of France on his own. François would not go; Claudine had known that from the beginning. But he had promised her that he would go into hiding as soon as she left, and she had to be content with that.

They had another piece of news that day, too. Though François had not seen them at Camp Ruchard, they heard that Gertrude Reinberg and her two children had been arrested. They had been hiding out in the deserted château of Montvisse, and Florence Jallais had betrayed them to the Gestapo.

That night, knowing that it might be their last night together, Claudine's heart felt close to breaking, and when François made love to her there was a tenderness and passion in it that they had never known before. Afterwards, they lay silently together, holding one another close; there were no words to say what they felt – their bodies had spoken for them.

Just before noon three days later without knocking, Corinne burst into Claudine's sitting-room. '*Madame*, the messenger has come!'

'The messenger? From Bertrand? Where is he?'

'He could not stay, *madame*. He came over the bridge, and he has already gone back again into the forest. But he says the rendezvous with Bertrand's guide is in the big barn opposite the château of Rigny-Ussé. The barn is deserted now, and you and Louis are to go there as soon as you can. Madame Solange is to follow before nightfall – you are to go separately, you understand, so that you do not arouse suspicion.'

Claudine nodded, her thoughts in a whirl. She would go on Solange's bike, that would be the easiest thing, with Louis in the passenger-box.

'Corinne,' she said, 'do you think Solange can ride my bicycle?'

'What? Oh yes,' Corinne said, rapidly realizing how her mind was working. 'Yes, I'm sure she can.'

'Good. Then we must hurry. There's no time to lose.'

Half an hour later, having said an emotional farewell to

Tante Céline, Beavis and Corinne, Claudine helped a delighted Louis into the passenger-box of Solange's bicycle, and began to pedal off down the drive. All she could think of was when, dear God, when, would she see François again?

She was already out of sight by the time Lucien let himself into the château.

– 33 –

Claudine was looking at her son. His child's body was dwarfed by the powerful arm holding him from shoulder to groin, and his face was frighteningly pale, making his eyes seem wider and blacker than ever. The long lashes were beaded with tears and his chin wobbled with the effort of holding them back. His hair needed cutting, she thought, noticing the way his curls fell haphazardly over his forehead, and really she should wipe his nose. Then a fat tear dropped onto his cheek, and it was as though a terrible fist of fear had smashed through the irrelevance of her thoughts, forcing her once again to confront the horrifying reality of what was happening to them. She closed her eyes, unable to bear the gun pointing at his delicate little face a moment longer.

She was sitting on a cold, dusty floor, propped against two bales of hay, her face dazzled by the brilliant streams of sunlight coming through the arch at the front of the barn. She was within reaching distance of Louis, but she dared not hold her arms out to him again. The last time she'd done it he had been hit across the face.

Panic swelled, then subsided, then swelled again in her chest. She shifted her feet in the scattered strands of hay, and tightened the clench of her hands, willing herself to keep calm. She could feel Armand watching her, but she couldn't bring herself to look back. The lying, the deceit, the treachery, the murders, the mutilations were all there, like phantoms dancing a macabre, malefic dance in the space between them. She could still hardly believe it. When she had first come into the barn with Louis and seen him, it was a moment of such incredulous horror that she almost fainted. The Germans had deceived them, and her instincts had been right all the time. It was Armand. Halunke was Armand.

Finally she forced her eyes to meet his. He was crammed up against a corner of the barn, facing the arch. His face was unshaven, his eyes bloodshot and ringed with shadow. He stared back, and after a while a curl of malicious amusement started to hover about his lips. Her skin prickled. It was a stranger looking out of a familiar face.

'Why?' she breathed at last. 'Just tell me why?'

He laughed, an arid, mirthless sound, and his eyes glittered as he swept them over her body, then back to her face. 'You think it's because of you, don't you?' he sneered. 'You think it's because I still want you.'

'No. No, I don't, but . . .'

'The arrogance!' he spat, covering her words with his own. 'The conceit! You thought you could use me, didn't you, thought you could satiate the lust for your pig of a husband on me – the poor, peasant *vigneron*. The man who had lost his wife and son, who needed someone to love, someone to heal his wounds – I was easy prey for a woman like you, that's what you thought, didn't you? He didn't love you, and you thought to make him jealous by turning to me. But it didn't work, did it? He didn't care, and you, you could never get him out of your mind.'

He laughed, nastily. 'But it's not you, Claudine, you aren't the reason I'm making him suffer. You and your son here are merely the instruments with which I can inflict the greatest torture of all. What a pity for your sake that he fell in love with you in the end, but what a Godsend for me! He tried not to, though, didn't he? He tried everything in his power not to succumb, but finally even he couldn't resist you. Who would have thought it? That François the Invincible could actually fall prey to his own heart. But then, how could any of us resist you – those tempting eyes, that succulent mouth, and that exquisitely hungry body? Hah! what a prize that was, knowing that I, Halunke, the man François feared above all others, was all the time copulating with his wife – and with his permission! He even asked me to protect you, how I laughed at that. He never suspected me once. But you did, didn't you? In the end. You worked it out. But François, he believed Helber when Helber told him that Lucien was Halunke. Did he ever tell you the price he paid for that information?'

Again, Armand snorted with laughter. 'Such a pity that after you two are dead I am forced to kill François too. I wanted him to see his brother hang for a murder he didn't commit. A murder I set him up for. But an even greater pity is that he won't know what it is to live without you, to know what it is to suffer the way he's made me suffer. That he won't . . .'

Suddenly, Armand's eyes shot to the arch. It was only the breeze rustling a piece of litter across the wasteland outside, but it had broken his concentration, and Claudine seized her chance to speak, to bring him back to the present.

'Armand, please,' she begged. 'Louis – he's just a child. Please let him go.'

'Papa,' Louis sobbed. 'I want my Papa.'

Claudine gasped as Armand slapped him across the face – but as she sprang towards them Armand jammed the gun into Louis' neck.

'All the unarmed combat in the world won't save you now,' he snarled, kicking her back against the bales, 'so don't even try it.'

Claudine looked helplessly at her son as tears rolled down his cheeks and little sobs choked from his throat. She had never in all her life felt so desperate or so impotent. 'Papa will come, *chéri*,' she said, trying to force some comfort through the anguish in her voice. 'He will be here soon.'

'Yes, he will be here,' Armand jeered. 'Von Liebermann will send him. This is a set-up, *Madame la Comtesse* – or didn't you realize that?'

'Armand, tell me what he's done,' Claudine pleaded. 'Tell me, and perhaps we can ...' She stopped as his stranger's eyes shot back to hers.

'Nothing,' he snarled. 'He's done nothing. It's what *I've* done because of him.' The light suddenly dimmed in his eyes and he looked down at Louis, fixing on the point where the gun met his jaw.

Claudine watched him, seeing his concentration slip again as he became engulfed in his thoughts. She started to edge towards him, sliding her feet under her, trying to position herself to dive straight for the gun. But then he turned back, and though his eyes were unfocused she didn't dare to make another move. 'What did you do?' she asked, sinking hopelessly back against the hay.

When at last he spoke, his voice trembled. It was as though each word he uttered came from the core of a wound so deep, a pain so profound, that she couldn't begin to comprehend it. 'I killed my son,' he said. 'I murdered my own son.'

For a long time she simply looked at him, and he stared back, watching the shock register on her face, until finally his own stiffened with contempt. She whispered, 'But I thought ...'

'I know what you thought,' he snapped. 'It was what everyone thought. He was a weak child, his health gave out, *that's* what everyone thought. But he died because I put a pillow over his face and smothered him.'

Claudine squeezed her eyes tight shut. 'Why?' she gasped, forcing herself to think rationally. 'You must have had a reason.'

'Oh yes, I had a reason. I did it because he wasn't my son at all. He was your husband's son. The son of François de Lorvoire.'

Outside, birds were chattering in the trees, the river bubbled and gushed, and in the distance, the town hall clock was chiming the midday hour. Claudine's head had started to throb. She looked around for something to hold onto, but the dizziness was coming over her in such paralysing waves that she was afraid to move.

Seeing her reaction, Armand gave a dry, caustic laugh. 'That's what I thought,' he sneered, 'because that's what she told me. But he wasn't. He was *my* son. *I* was his father, but I only found that out when it was too late.'

'I don't understand,' she cried. 'What are you talking about?' Oh, François! If only he would come and deliver her from this nightmare! Then Armand started to speak again, and she bit her lips to stop herself screaming as his voice washed over her in gentle, familiar waves. It was a voice as sweet as honey, a voice she knew and had once loved.

'I'll go back to the day it all really began,' he said, 'to the day Hortense de Bourchain died.'

Claudine lifted her head and looked into his face. He was gazing absently at the floor, a strange smile on his lips and a frown creasing his forehead. 'Hortense?' she breathed, now more confused than ever.

He went on as if she hadn't spoken. 'He killed her because she loved him, but you know that, don't you? You know how she wanted to die rather than live without him – so he put her out of her misery.' Suddenly his head snapped up and the savagery had returned to his eyes. 'Tell me, Claudine, what is it about him? What is it that makes women half-demented with love for him? I want to know why you've loved him ever since you came to Lorvoire. We both know how he treated you, the contempt, the abuse you suffered in those early days. Yet you loved him. Oh, you tried not to, you even managed to convince yourself you detested him, but I knew. I always knew. Even when we were making love, I knew you were thinking of him, wishing I was him. So tell me, Claudine, how is it that François de Lorvoire can command love as though he were God Almighty Himself?'

'He can't,' Claudine answered, echoing his anger.

'He can create love, he can manipulate it and destroy it. I know, because I've seen him do it. He destroyed my wife's love for me and made her love him. He possessed her. Like a demon, he consumed her from within and turned her into a monster. Until she met him she was content, fulfilled, happy. She loved life, she loved me. Then she met him, and everything changed. She started to despise me because I wasn't strong like him, I wasn't brilliant like him, not an aristocrat like him. She ridiculed me because I cared about her and loved her when all she wanted was him. She adored him, there was nothing she wouldn't do for him. Can you explain that to me, Claudine? Can you explain how a woman can turn her life inside out, yearning for a man who hardly knows she exists?'

Claudine looked down at Louis' pale, frightened face. 'I didn't know Jacqueline,' she answered. 'So no, I can't explain it.'

'She said I was jealous of him,' Armand went on. 'She taunted me day and night with it, comparing me with him. She drove me half out of my mind. But I loved her, I couldn't stop loving her. And I began to hate him. I hated him more and more, until I wanted to kill him. Then she became pregnant and I thought then that maybe things would change, that at last she would stop torturing herself with wanting him. But if anything it became worse. She was obsessed with him. On any pretext she would go to the château, just to look at him. Then she would come back and tell me how she had felt when she'd seen him, what she had wanted to do to him. She fantasized about him all the time.

'Then Hortense started to come to Lorvoire. At first Jacqueline was beside herself with jealousy. It was all I could do to restrain her from going to the château and causing a scene. Then she locked herself in the bedroom and refused to come out. She stayed there for almost a week, until one morning she came downstairs, put her arms round me and cried as though her heart would break. She begged me to forgive her and swore she would never try to see François again. Of course I forgave her, and I thanked God that she was at last back to her normal self. She was calmer, easier to live with, and she never went to the château at all.

'It was some time before I realized she had stopped eating. I thought, in my ignorance, that the pregnancy was making her weak. In the end she became so ill that I was afraid she would die, or lose the baby, or . . . I don't know what I thought. I never knew in those days. All I knew was that my life had become a nightmare, and that François de Lorvoire was the cause.

'Then one night Jacqueline and I had a terrible fight. It was about François, of course, though it was the first time his name had been mentioned for weeks. I could see she was no closer to getting over him than she'd ever been. We both said some terrible things that night, things I shall never forget. Finally she worked me up to such a pitch that I had to leave the house. I went to the wine caves to escape. That was how I came to see what happened between François and Hortense. Another woman driven half out of her mind for wanting François de Lorvoire. What is it about him?' he groaned. 'Why do you all love him so much?'

'Did François ever know how Jacqueline felt about him?' Claudine asked gently.

'Even if he did, what would he have cared for a woman like her? What does he care for anyone?'

'Go on,' she said. 'What happened after you saw Hortense and François?'

He bowed his head for a moment. Then taking a breath, he looked at her again. 'When Louis finally let me go, having sworn me to secrecy about what had happened, I went home and told Jacqueline everything I had seen. I knew François hadn't killed Hortense intentionally, but I told Jacqueline he had. I asked her how it felt to be in love with a murderer. I asked her if she felt the same way now, knowing that he could kill a woman just for wanting him? And do you know what she said?'

Claudine was very still, her face drawn with pity.

'She said, how could she stop loving him when he was the father of her baby? And how did I feel now, to know that every day I looked upon my child I would know it wasn't really mine? That I was so inadequate that . . .' He broke off, pushing his fingers hard into the sockets of his eyes. 'She even described the way he made love to her, the way he made her feel, she went on and on and on until I finally lost control and hit her. She laughed. So I hit her again. She fell down the stairs, and when I got to her she was still laughing. She was hysterical – and delirious with joy, because Hortense de Bourchain was out of his life.

'She gave birth two weeks later, and with every contraction, every push and every breath she called his name. She screamed at the top of her voice that she was giving birth to his child – that I should never forget that it was *his* child.

'When the baby was born, after Doctor Lebrun had severed the cord, she told me she wanted to call the baby after his father. I didn't argue, I couldn't. There was no fight left in me. My mother sent me out. I walked around for hours, trying to tell myself she had been lying, that the child was mine, but I couldn't make myself believe it. I knew, because I'd always known, what power François had over women. He had no morals, no scruples, he wouldn't have thought twice about fornicating with my wife.'

Again Armand rubbed a hand over his eyes, and for a moment Claudine thought he was crying. But then Louis, seeing his chance, tried to break free – and when Armand grabbed him back she saw that his eyes were as dry as the dust at his feet.

'When I got back to the house, Father Pointeau was there,' he went on, 'Jacqueline was already dead. She had haemorrhaged just after I'd left. The last words she said to me were, "I want to call *his* son François."

'I lived with it for a year, but as the child's features began to form, all I could see was François. I know now that it was Jacqueline he resembled, his dark complexion, his black hair, his deep brown eyes, they were all hers, but at the time all I could see was François. What was more, François visited us a lot that year and the child took to him – more than he did to me. I would watch François swinging him up on his shoulders, and the child would laugh in a way he never laughed for me.

'Then one day, as I was returning from the vineyards, I saw François carry him from the house and put him on a pony. He couldn't walk, he wasn't strong enough, he'd been sickly since birth, but François thought he could learn to ride. The child was more excited than I'd ever seen him. He cried when François left, and he wouldn't stop crying. I put him to bed and sat with him until finally he fell asleep, then I took the pillow, covered his face and held it there until I knew he was dead.'

His last word fell into silence. His hands were shaking and now there were tears on his cheeks. He was trapped, Claudine knew, in the nightmare of the past, unable to bring himself back to the present, unable to escape the stalking shadow of guilt. In the end, her voice so thick with emotion she could barely speak, she said his name.

He looked up in surprise, almost as if he had forgotten she was there. Then his face contorted. 'A sorry tale, isn't it?' he said scathingly. 'One that I thought was going to end there, because I thought I was finally rid of him, that he couldn't torment me any more. That living each day in the knowledge that the person I loved most in the world loved François de Lorvoire – that nightmare was over. You see, I couldn't take that any more. I'd lived with it for two years. Two years of unadulterated hell, when first my wife, then my son ...' He started to sob, and Claudine moved to comfort him. But he pushed her away, wiping the back of his hand over his eyes.

'But he was your son?' she prompted gently.

'Oh yes, he was my son all right. Father Pointeau told me. But it was too late by then. I'd already killed him.'

'But how did Father Pointeau know?'

'She'd confessed. Before she died, Jacqueline had confessed her sins and told him how she'd lied to me. She also told him never to tell me – never to let me be certain that I was the father of my own son. How she must have hated me to do that to me! Father Pointeau, of course, tried to reason with her, tried to make her understand that she must make peace with the world before going to meet her Maker. But she refused. So, obeying the laws of confession, Father Pointeau kept her secret – until the morning after I had killed my son. He told me then, he said, because for a whole year he had witnessed my misery and he couldn't bear to see me suffering any longer. The Good Lord would not want him to keep such a secret, he said, so he told me.

'Of course he didn't know then that the child was dead, I hadn't told him. Can you imagine how I felt then, Claudine? Can you even begin to understand? It was too late, the child, my son, was already dead. My son who loved François, whose mother loved François. And I, who had once loved him too, swore that day that he would pay for what he had done to my family. I sat there, in the confessional, and told Father Pointeau everything. Then I told him what I intended to do. How I would make François de Lorvoire suffer as I was suffering, how I would kill those he loved until he, like me, had no one. But more than that, I vowed that if he ever had a son I would make him kill that son, as he had made me kill mine.'

Claudine looked at Louis. 'I am so sorry, Armand,' she whispered. Words seemed so inadequate. 'I didn't know. Neither of us did. If we had . . .'

'If you had, then what? There was nothing you could do, it was already too late. The damage was done, my wife and son were dead, and François de Lorvoire was going to pay. Nothing, *no one* would have changed my mind. Don't you think Father Pointeau tried? I let him think he'd succeeded, of course. I was a fool ever to have told him. And I was to find out just how big a fool within a matter of days. Von Liebermann had one of his snoops listening in to the confessions. He'd had someone there for a long time, it was just one of his many methods of getting information about François. Of course, von Liebermann didn't know then that François was working for the Secret Service, but he suspected it. So I, just like François, became a pawn in von Liebermann's game. And whenever François didn't play to his rules, that was when I got my chance. But even so, von Liebermann never did manage to turn François, make him the double agent he wanted him to be. Because François is meaner, uglier and cleverer than any man alive.'

Armand's voice was thick with scorn, his mouth twisted with venom. 'The man isn't human, he's a devil, *the* devil. His only weakness is that he loves, and that is why I've used it as my weapon against him.'

'But so many people, Armand! Not only those François loved, but Yves and Thomas, the pilots and agents who were captured in the escape-line, Estelle ... Why did you kill Estelle?'

'You saw her that day in the forest, cavorting with his brother. Another de Lorvoire. I'd lost my wife to one, I'd lost my son because of one – I wasn't going to lose her to one as well. She paid, you'll all pay, but this will be the bitterest price. As for the others ... Regrettable, but there was nothing I could do. I was a tool of the Abwehr. They made me do it. Stinking, filthy Germans, I despise them. They've manipulated me all the way. But not any more. They won't be able to control my life ever again, because after today they'll have nothing on me. Because François will be dead. It will all be over, and at last I shall be free.'

'No, Armand, you won't be free. No matter what you do to François you'll never be free, because nothing you do is going to bring your son back.'

He stared at her, blinking as though she had delivered him a brutal blow.

'She's right, Armand.'

A shadow fell across the barn, and they both spun round to see François standing at the centre of the arch.

'Papa!' Louis shrieked. And oblivious to the gun pressed against his head, he started to struggle over Armand's leg to get to François. Then, to Claudine's amazement, Armand lowered his leg and let Louis go.

She watched as he flew across the barn into his father's arms. François scooped him up and Louis clung to him, sobs shuddering from his little body as he buried his face in François' shoulder. But François wasn't looking at Louis, his eyes were fixed on Armand.

Claudine turned back, then started as she saw Armand's gun only inches from her face. 'So,' Armand hissed, looking at her but speaking to François, 'you've come at last.'

François didn't answer.

Armand shifted so that his back was against the wall

beside Claudine. Then gesturing towards the floor in front of him, he made her lie down.

'On your front!' he growled. 'Put your hands under your body and turn your face to me.'

She did as he told her, and then, keeping the gun out of her reach but still aimed at her head, Armand lifted his eyes to François. 'I take it you've been there for some time,' he sneered.

'Long enough,' François replied.

'So tell me. How does it feel to know that Halunke, the only man you've ever feared, was all the time fucking your wife? Does it feel good, François? Or do you want to kill me for it? I even drank your son's milk from her breasts. I suckled her, François. How does that make you feel? Does it get to you, right deep down inside?' He twisted a hand into his gut. 'Because that's where it got me, François. It got me, and ate me like a cancer. But we're equal now, aren't we? You made my wife love you, and I made yours love me. But it doesn't end there, does it? *It doesn't end there François, because you made me kill my son!*' Armand stopped and wiped the saliva from his lips with the back of his hand. 'So you know what you have to do. You've ruined my life, de Lorvoire, and now I'm going to ruin yours. So kill him, kill him now, or I'll kill her.'

For a long moment François merely stared at him. Then, without uttering a word, he put Louis on the ground, took him by the hand and walked away.

Claudine knew they had gone, she could hear their footsteps crunching on the gravel. Her heart started to pound in her chest. He had gone; he hadn't spoken a word, he had just walked away.

Armand swore violently under his breath, and her eyes dilated as his hand tightened on the gun.

Then he started to laugh, a low rumbling sound that seemed to creep into every shadowy corner of the barn. 'So he's fooled us both! He's fooled you, and me, he's fooled us all. François de Lorvoire has won again! Yes, he even managed to convince me that he loved you. But he doesn't love you, does he, Claudine? Because he's left you here to die. He's walking away. He's made his choice, and he's left you. But as far as he was concerned there never was a choice, because all that matters to him is his son. You don't matter at all, you never did. So how does it feel, Claudine, to know that he's tricked you as foully and as ingeniously as he's tricked everyone else? How does it feel to be one of his victims? Hurts doesn't it? It hurts *here*.' He thumped his fist into his heart. 'So why don't I put you out of your misery?'

He hooked his thumb over the cock and drew it back. Claudine closed her eyes, and through the horror of what was happening to her she started to pray.

The shot blasted into the silence, ricocheting from the walls, vibrating from the beams and echoing out into the field where it finally faded into the chill, empty air.

Still holding Louis' hand François kept on walking, not betraying, even by the twitch of a muscle, that he had heard the shot.

Minute after minute ticked by. The wind rustled the trees behind the barn, and the magnificent château of Rigny-Ussé slumbered peacefully on the opposite bank of the Indre. Besides François and Louis, the only other sign of life was inside the Mercedes, parked on the cart track halfway between the field gate and the barn. From behind the open window in the rear seat von Liebermann and Max Helber watched as de Lorvoire finally stopped at his jeep, stooped to speak to his son, then handed him up to his sister. Then she drove away.

Another ten minutes slipped by. Clouds massed angrily overhead; the rain didn't come, but the sky darkened about the sun covering its face with black, bulbous warts of cloud.

Inside the barn, Armand stood up. A sheen of sweat

glimmered on his face, but his senses were brittly alert. He stepped over Claudine and stole quietly across the barn to the arch. As he peered outside, he prepared the gun to fire again. Then his eyes narrowed dangerously as he saw someone sitting on the bank of the river with a fishing rod.

'Get over here,' he hissed to Claudine.

Too terrorized to do anything other than obey, Claudine got up and went to stand beside him.

'Who's that?' he growled.

Claudine turned to look where he was pointing and as she recognized the man sitting nonchalantly on the riverbank, a sob gurgled in her throat. She had no idea how he had got here, but it was her father, and she was so swamped by relief that it was all she could do to stop herself collapsing. She knew she should never have doubted François, but when she had heard his footsteps retreat, when he had gone with no arguments, no protests, no attempt even to reason with Armand, she had believed ... But now she knew that somehow he was in charge of the situation. Somehow he had found out about the torturous climax Armand and von Liebermann had plotted between them, and had laid his own plans. And if Beavis was here, perhaps there were others.

'Who is it?' Armand seethed.

'It's my father,' she answered, knowing that he would recognize him sooner or later.

Armand uttered a stream of obscenities, then pushing her in front of him and jamming the gun into her neck, he edged a short way out of the barn. Seeing von Liebermann's car, he waited for a sign to tell him what was happening, but the General's face was lost in shadow.

Then suddenly both Armand and Claudine spun round as they heard a footstep behind them. It was Lucien, standing at the corner of the barn.

'At last,' Lucien said, starting towards them. 'We were

beginning to think you would never come out. Now put the gun down, Armand, and let's talk.'

Before Armand could answer, someone else was striding up behind him, and he twisted round again to see a masked figure coming from the other side of the barn. 'Hand it over, there's a good chap.' The American accent was strong – Claudine suddenly realized that this must be Jack Bingham.

Armand took a step back, pulling Claudine with him, his eyes darting between Lucien and Bingham. Then he noticed that Beavis had gone. 'Get away from me!' he growled. 'Get away or I'll kill her.'

'And what then?' Lucien said mildly.

Armand stared at him.

'And what then, Armand?' he repeated. 'Tell me, *Armand!*'

Armand flinched as Lucien boomed out his name, then he staggered as the cry started to echo through the valley like the deathly chant of ravens. Voices, hundreds of voices, resounding from the trees, from the barn, from the river, from the château. They were coming from everywhere. Below him, above him, in front of him, behind him, from every side. Shouting his name: *'Armand! Armand! Armand!'*

At the side of the barn François was climbing swiftly and quietly from the ladder into the hay loft.

'It won't work, de Lorvoire!' he heard Armand scream into the cacophony.

'Armand!'

'Armand!'

'Armand!'

The noise rose to a deafening crescendo. François stole through the hay, then lowered himself into the barn. He could see them now, grouped in a pool of sunlight on the waste ground.

'Kill him, de Lorvoire!' Armand roared to the sky. 'Kill your son or I'll kill her.'

– 614 –

'Armand!'
'Armand!'
'Armand!'
'Shut up!' he bellowed. 'Shut up or I'll fire.'

More voices, flat, monotonous, menacing voices. No faces, only Lucien and Bingham and . . . Armand stepped back, looking for Claudine. Then he saw her. She was on the floor, covering her head with her arms. He raised the gun, aimed it straight at her, then screamed as a foot crashed into his wrist. Then he became aware of the pressure on his spine, and he clenched his teeth as the agony tore through his limbs. But he still had the gun, and he fired it, again and again . . .

He couldn't move his arm; the bullets were blasting randomly into the air. Armand jerked his body forward – then screamed as François' hands tightened their grip. But now the gun was pointing right at her . . . A splintering pain seared through his skull. His knees were sagging, but he tightened his finger on the trigger. He tried to throw the weight from his back. It shifted and he staggered, then the gun was on her again. He fired – and in that same instant François broke his neck.

Claudine stared at the bullet, buried in the ground only an inch from her face. She couldn't move, her whole body was frozen in terror. She knew François was there, she could feel him holding her, lifting her, but she couldn't tear her eyes from the bullet.

'It's all right,' he soothed. 'It's all right, *chérie*, it's over.'
'Louis,' she mumbled. 'Where's Louis?'
'With Monique. He's safe.'
'Oh François!' she gasped, then fell sobbing into his arms.

Then she opened her eyes and stared down at Armand's limp, broken body lying at her feet. His eyes were still open, staring back at her. She shuddered, and François stooped to close them.

'Did you know?' she said. 'About Jacqueline?'

'No.'

He looked at her, and her heart twisted as she saw the torment in his eyes. She could read his thoughts, almost as if he were speaking them aloud. Hortense, Jacqueline and Élise. Three women whose lives had been ruined because of him, because he had been unable to love them. He would never forgive himself, yet there was nothing he could have done to prevent it. Claudine choked back her tears, and pulled him tightly into her arms. He pushed his face into her hair and clung to her the way Louis had clung to him.

Finally he pulled away and gazed searchingly into her eyes. 'Are you all right?' he whispered.

She nodded.

He brushed her cheek with the backs of his fingers, then turned to Armand's body.

'What are we going to tell Liliane?' she asked.

'Nothing, if we can avoid it. It's better that she thinks he died by the firing squad.'

'Do you think she knows? About all this.'

He shook his head. 'I doubt it. Except about Jacqueline, she must have known about that. But she would never have imagined him capable of doing all he's done. What mother would?'

'A mother who persuaded me to have an affair with her son?'

François lifted his head. 'I asked her to.'

Claudine shook her head in dismay, then, as she started shakily to pull herself to her feet a voice boomed into the stillness.

'*François!*'

Both she and François swung round. Then François flew back as a stultifying blow crashed into his chest. Claudine

– 616 –

started for the barn as first one shot, then another and another blasted through the air. Then suddenly she staggered to the ground beside François as both *Résistants* and Germans emerged from the woods, from the barn, from the river bank and from the road, until the whole world was alive with the sound of machine-guns, pistols, rifles, even grenades.

Bullets tore through the air above their bodies, plunging into the earth all around them. Black smoke curled round the barn as canisters were thrown from the woods to disguise the emergence of the *Résistants*. The air rang with shouts, barked orders and the sound of running feet. Men in berets and masks swooped into the field, while the German soldiers in their tin helmets and uniforms flattened themselves to the grass and blasted bullets into the mêlée.

Lucien and Beavis, crouching low with guns slung over their shoulders, waded through the river to the bridge. Jack Bingham, Pierre Bonet the melon farmer, and three others, crawled through the next field's vines towards the road. Still more withdrew into the woods, firing and shouting and holding cover for those gone to circle the Germans.

François turned his head to look at Claudine, half expecting her to have crawled into the barn. But she was still there, lying only an arm's length away. He twisted himself a little further so he could see her face. Her arms were spread out, her hair was tangled around her mouth and her eyes were wide, staring straight into his. His lungs turned to pockets of ice as the whole world tilted on its axis. Then she blinked, and he breathed again.

Almost from the moment he'd fallen, he had realized that the hammer-blow to his chest had come from Claudine as she'd knocked him to the ground, but he continued to lie where he was, unmoving. Von Liebermann and Helber must think he was dead.

'Are you all right?' he hissed.

'I think so.'

'Stay right where you are. For God's sake let them think you're dead.'

She blinked again, not daring to move another muscle, as the battle raged on around them. Then she watched, as François slid his hand carefully beneath him and pulled out his gun.

He waited until there was a drift in the smoke, then aimed directly at the Mercedes. Again he waited, until von Liebermann's eyes finally came to rest on his, but before von Liebermann had a chance even to register surprise, the bullet ripped through his face.

And there was still one more score to settle. From the rear door on the other side of the car, Max Helber emerged, his face splattered with von Liebermann's blood. As he staggered round the car, dazed and disoriented, into full view, François took aim again, pointing the gun this time between Helber's legs.

As Helber screamed, chaos broke loose. The Mercedes roared off, and what seemed like an entire battalion of Germans closed in around the woods. No one thought to look in the direction of the barn, no one knew that the bullets which had killed the General and his henchman had come from François de Lorvoire.

Still neither he nor Claudine moved, but lay there feigning death until finally the battle was drawn into the depths of the wood and the gunfire started to recede into the distance.

After a while they heard footsteps running towards them.

'François!' Lucien called in a heavy whisper.

'It's all right, I'm alive,' François answered, recognizing his brother's voice.

'I thought you must be. I saw what Claudine did. Are you all right?' he added turning to her. 'Come on, let's get you both out of here.'

François was already on his feet. The smoke had all but disappeared by now, and for the moment there was no sign of the *Boches*.

'It's all right, *chérie*, you can get up now,' he said, starting to help Lucien drag Armand's body into the barn.

When she didn't move, he looked up. 'Claudine, you can get up,' he said, a hammer of alarm suddenly starting to thud in his chest.

'I can't,' she answered.

Dropping Armand, he threw himself down on his knees beside her. 'What is it?' he said.

'Oh François, I'm sorry,' she gasped. 'I'm so sorry.'

And then he saw the pool of blood, spreading thickly across the ground beneath her.

– 34 –

It was the first real day of summer, warm and tranquil. François was standing on the hillside, gazing out at the valley of Lorvoire. It was a very different view now from the one he had looked out on a week ago when the fire had heaved its massive chest and roared through the vineyards, curling great tongues of flame round every root and leaf of the vines. The village was unharmed, so too was the château, but the sloping banks of the valley were now a blackened mass of destruction. He could still smell it, the pungent aroma of fuel that the Germans had thrown on the vines before setting them alight, and the acrid stench of the ash that drifted lazily on the breeze. He raised his eyes to the trees at the top of the hill opposite, where he could see the coned turrets of the château shimmering like silver in the sunlight. No one was inside now, it had been closed and boarded-up just over a month ago. Jean-Paul had seen to it, but there had been nothing Jean-Paul could do to stop the Germans raiding it first. They had even helped themselves to the Jews' property stored in the cellar. Since then the servants had dispersed, and the family, all of them, had been living in the chapter-house at the Royal Abbey of Fontevraud –the abbey where he and Claudine had married.

Now the family had gone too. The night before, Beavis had taken Solange, Céline and Louis to England in a Lysander, which had landed in a field near Angers, bringing in two more British agents. And Lucien had taken Jack Bingham and Monique to Poitiers, where Bertrand Raffault was to arrange their safe passage through France and into Spain. Lucien himself would return in a few days, but he wouldn't stay long, Lorvoire was too dangerous a place for any of them to stay now. Reprisals for the battle which had raged on the field at Rigny-Ussé – a battle which had claimed the lives of five German soldiers – had been severe. Twenty of the twenty-five *Résistants* captured had been shot, and God only knew what hell the remaining five were now having to endure. Lucien and Gustave had put it about that he, François, was dead, but it was clear that the Germans didn't believe it. Why else had they razed the vineyards? Why else had they pasted up reward posters all over the district? If he had believed that the *Résistants'* lives would be spared in exchange for his surrender, he would have given himself up long ago, but he knew the Germans only too well – no one was going to be released from the bowels of the Hôtel Boule d'Or, and his family needed him, not only now but in the future, when this bloody war finally came to an end.

He sighed – and then the ghost of a smile crossed his face. It was on this very spot that he had found Claudine, the morning after they were married. He remembered how young she had seemed then, how angry, hurt and confused.

Then the harshness returned to his face as he thought of all she had suffered since. All she had suffered because of him.

Until he fell in love with her he had always held himself aloof from the world, believing himself immune to the vagaries of love. Nothing could touch him, he was an island remote in an ocean of humanity, and just like waves lapped at a shore so emotion never stole beyond the surface of his heart. But Claudine had changed all that. She had reached into his heart, shown him that love, the kind of love he had for her, was not a weakness at all, but a strength. She had tamed him, mellowed him, warmed the fires of his soul. She had ignited his passion with love, tempered his fury with laughter. It was as though she had brought summer to a winter-torn land, rain to a desert. He loved her so much. She was the reason he laughed, the reason he raged. He lived for her. And it was the knowledge of how much she loved him in return that would give him the strength to carry on. To accept all that had happened and one day put it behind him.

He closed his eyes and let the faces of his past crowd in. There were so many, but some of them would haunt him maybe until the end of his days. Hortense. Élise. Jacqueline. Jacqueline who, in wanting him, had driven her husband to madness. And that was the greatest mystery of his life. Why had Jacqueline loved him like that? Why had Hortense? Élise? Why, even, had Claudine?

He knew he would never understand it. He had never shown any of them affection, encouragement or concern, yet they had all loved him. Claudine was different, of course, because he had fallen in love with her. But at the beginning, when she had first come to Lorvoire, he had failed to drive her away even though he had treated her to all the vileness he was capable of.

Was it true that no woman could resist a challenge? That not loving them was the surest way to win them? It would seem so. But that did not really explain what had happened to Jacqueline, Hortense and Élise. Why was it that they had all but lost their minds for wanting him?

There were no answers, there was only punishment. The punishment of guilt, confusion and . . . He threw back his head and gazed up at the sky. He had known during all those weeks when Claudine fought for her life that he would lose her in the end. That God would take her to punish him for what he had done to the others. No one had given up hope, not his mother, not Lucien, not even the doctor – but he, he had known she would go. As he'd held her in his arms and told her over and over how much he loved her, he'd known that in the end she would leave him. But he had never told her that; instead he had made her smile with the awkwardness of his words, and had brought colour to her cheeks when speaking of their love. And he had made her cry because he cried, and now he wondered if he was going to cry forever.

'I love you, François.'

He heard her voice, and the grief locked in his throat, choking him. 'I love you too, Claudine,' he whispered. And closing his eyes, he turned his face to heaven and started to pray. Thank you, he said, over and over. Thank you, Mary Mother of Christ, for the love. Thank you for her beauty, for her strength, her will and determination. Thank you for letting her be mine, for the love in my own heart. . . He looked down at where she was sitting on the grass at his feet, and as his eyes blurred he added, but thank you most of all for sparing her.

Her pale, tired face was gazing up at him, and he smiled. 'What are you thinking?' she said softly.

'I'm thinking of how merciful God is,' he answered, reaching out for her hands and pulling her to her feet.

'For letting me live?'

He nodded.

She looked lovingly into his eyes, then pulled his mouth to hers. 'You were crying,' she said.

'Yes.' And his mouth tilted in an ironic smile.

She watched him, knowing that it had taken great strength for him to give in to his tears. This wasn't the first time he had wept, nor would it be the last. What had happened to him, to those he loved, would have broken any other man, and if she had died maybe it would have been the end for him. When she was so ill she had seen the spirit fading in him, dulling his eyes and extinguishing the light in his soul – and it was that that had given her the will to wrest herself from the hands of death. And now she would be there for him always, to soothe his wounds, those terrible internal wounds that were going to take many years to heal. Outwardly there would be no sign of them, and there would be times when he would try to hide them even from her. But she knew him too well – and she knew too that the way to treat him was not only with sympathy and understanding, but with defiance. Which was why now, as he told her that he was sending her to England, she protested.

'No buts, Claudine,' he said, smoothing the hair from her face. 'This war is far from over, and you have stayed too long already. I should have been firm at the outset – I shall not make that mistake again.'

'I won't go,' she said. 'If you stay to fight on with Lucien, then so do I.'

'Claudine,' he said, trying to inject a little menace into his voice.

'No, I told you before, you don't frighten me with that tone. Besides, bombs are falling all over England. It's safer here.'

'With every German from here to Paris and beyond looking for you?'

'And for you. So, if you stay, I stay with you.'

'Don't think I'm afraid to argue just because you're not

– 623 –

fully recovered,' he warned. 'You'll do as I tell you and that's final.'

'No. My mind is made up, I'm not being parted from you.'

His eyes rolled in exasperation. 'I reminded you once before, on this very hillside, that you promised before God to love, honour and *obey* me. The first you do admirably, but your efforts on the second and third counts are deplorable. You are going to England.'

'But my instincts are telling me . . .'

'Oh, no, no, no, no!' he laughed. 'You'll be telling me next that the gypsy foresaw this hillside scenario and strongly advised you not to give in.'

'She did.'

He shook his head. 'No. I don't believe it. And even if I did, I wouldn't listen. You are going to England.'

'Then so are you.'

'That's right.'

'I won't argue any more if . . . What did you say?'

'I said, that's right.'

'Meaning?'

'That I'm going to England too.'

Her face started to beam. 'François!' she cried, throwing her arms around him. 'So you won't let us be parted after all?'

'Of course not.'

'Then why didn't you say so?'

'Because I love the way your eyes flash when you're defying me,' he grinned.

'Oh, kiss me, François,' she cried. 'Kiss me before I hit you.' It was a long and tender embrace that filled both their hearts with such love that neither wanted to stop. So it was a long time later when she turned in his arms to look down at the valley. He pulled her back to lean against him, resting his chin on her head.

'We'll go soon,' he said. 'Maybe in a week. Do you think you'll be up to the journey?'

'I think so. Will we be following the same route as Jack and Monique?'

'Yes.'

She pondered quietly for a moment, then said, 'Do you think anything will come of their relationship?'

'Yes.'

She tilted her head back to look at him. 'You seem very certain.'

'I am. Jack talked to me before they left. The only thing they have to decide is whether they live in France or America.'

'But Monique is so French, I can't see her living anywhere else.'

'She's in love, Claudine. She'll live where Jack wants her to live. You see, some wives do obey their husbands.'

'But most wives don't have such a tyrant as I have.'

She laughed as he dug her in the ribs, then purred softly as he pulled back her hair to kiss her neck.

'Will you join de Gaulle when you get to England?' she asked.

'Yes. I have a great deal of information that will be extremely valuable to the Allies.'

'But after the war, when it's all over, will you stop then?'

'Do you want me to?'

'I don't want you to be in any more danger.'

'Then I shall stop.'

'Just like that?' she said, amazed.

'Just like that,' he confirmed.

'Which means you had already decided to anyway. We'll come back here though, won't we? To Lorvoire?'

'Of course. If we're all still alive.'

'Don't be so gloomy. Do you think you'll be able to stand doing nothing?'

'I think so. What about you?'

'I think so.'

He chuckled. 'You couldn't do nothing if your life depended on it. Which is why I have decided that you will run the vineyards.'

'Me?' she gasped.

'Yes, you. You know a great deal already, and while they're being re-planted we'll send you to the agricultural college to find out the rest.'

'And what will you be doing?'

'Me? I shall be selling the wine, of course. And when I'm not doing that, I shall be sitting in the bosom of my family trying to cope with an overworked wife and over-active children.'

She smiled at the improbable picture he painted, and relaxed against him. 'I'm glad you're coming to England,' she said a few minutes later. 'It's easier that way. You see, I really wouldn't have been parted from you, no matter what you said, but I do think it's better that I don't give birth to this baby in a barn.'

His hands, which had been idly stroking her arms, suddenly stopped. Then taking her by the shoulders, he turned her to face him. 'You mean. . . ? Are you telling me. . . ?'

She nodded.

'Oh, Claudine,' he breathed, clasping her in his arms. 'Claudine, *chérie*. Why didn't you tell me before?'

'Because I only found out a few weeks ago. Doctor Lebrun told me, on one of his visits.'

'Doctor Lebrun knew? But why didn't he tell me? All the time he's been coming to the Abbey to see you . . .'

'Because I asked him not to. I was afraid that if I died, you'd see it as a Divine punishment for what had happened to Armand. He had lost his wife and child, you'd have lost yours too. I didn't want you thinking that way. I didn't want you to go on blaming yourself for something you could have done nothing to prevent. Jacqueline is dead now, so too is

Armand, and we must bury the past with them. *You* must bury the past. You must let it go, my darling, and stop torturing yourself with all the questions that keep spinning around in your head.

'I know what you ask yourself, you want to know why those women loved you so much. Well, all I can tell you is that you are different. That there is something in you that sets you apart from other men. I don't know why that should be, but you must just accept it. God made you the way you are. He gave you the heart of a lion, the mind of Machiavelli, and the face of a devil. But he gave you something else too. He gave you a presence and a power. But it is a power, a presence, a mind and a heart that I love more than any other in the world. And I didn't want you to suffer any more if I died. I couldn't bear to think of you tearing yourself apart with guilt. And that's what you would have done if you'd known that our child had died too.'

'Oh, Claudine,' he breathed, taking her face between his hands.

For the moment he couldn't speak, his heart was too full, but at last he said, 'Some people believe that love, real love, is experienced by very few, and that to attain that love you must know pain and suffering and heartache. If they are right, if the depth of love is measured by the depth of suffering, you can be in no doubt that what I have for you is a very great love indeed.'

'No, I am in no doubt,' Claudine said. 'No doubt at all. We have suffered, we have loved, we have been happy and we have been sad. And all those things are waiting for us in the future too. I know, when you thought I would die, that you wanted to die too. It was then that I decided I must live. I wanted to live for you, for our children and for all that the future will bring. And I wanted to live so that you could never be in any doubt that what *I* have for *you* is a very great love indeed.'

A French Affair

Susan Lewis

When Natalie Moore is killed in a freak accident in France her mother – the very poised and elegant Jessica – knows instinctively there is more to it. However, Natalie's father – the glamorous, high-flying Charlie – is so paralysed by the horror of losing his daughter, that he refuses even to discuss his wife's suspicions.

In the end, when their marriage is rocked by yet another terrible shock, Jessica decides to go back to France alone in search of some answers. When she gets to the idyllic vineyard in the heart of Burgundy she soon finds a great deal more than she was expecting in a love that is totally forbidden and a truth that will almost certainly devastate her life . . .

'One of the best around' *Independent on Sunday*

'Spellbinding! . . . you just keep turning the pages, with the atmosphere growing more and more intense as the story leads to its dramatic climax' *Daily Mail*

arrow books

The Mill House

Susan Lewis

Julia Thayne is a valued and loving wife, a successful mother and a beautiful woman. She is everything most other women strive to be. But beneath the surface is a terrible secret that threatens to tear her perfect world apart.

Joshua is Julia's husband – a dynamic, devastatingly handsome man with great style, charisma and humour. He is utterly devoted to his wife and children, but as the ghosts of Julia's past begin to move into their marriage, he finds himself losing the struggle to keep them together. Then two telephone calls change everything.

Julia moves from London to a remote mill house in Cornwall, determined to break free from the past and save her fractured relationship with Josh. But it is here that she makes her own fatal mistake, and once more her marriage is rocked to its very foundation . . .

'Mystery and romance *par excellence*' Sun

'Erotic and exciting' *Sunday Times*

arrow books

Intimate Strangers

Susan Lewis

Investigative journalist, Laurie Forbes, is planning her wedding to Elliot Russell, when she receives a tip-off that a group of illegally smuggled women is being held somewhere in the East End of London. During her search unexpected and devastating events begin throwing her own life into chaos, so fellow journalist, Sherry MacElvoy steps in to help. Taking on undercover roles to get to the heart of the ruthless gang of human-traffickers, neither reporter can ever begin to imagine what dangers they are about to face.

Neela is one of the helpless Indian girls being held in captivity. Her fear is not only for herself, but her six-year-old niece, Shaila. A disfiguring birthmark has so far saved Neela from abuse, but she knows it is only a matter of time before she is sent for – and worse, before Shaila is taken. Her desperate bids to seek outside help are constantly thwarted, until finally she, and the women with her, agree there is only one way out . . .

'Spellbinding – you just keep turning the pages, with the atmosphere growing more and more intense as the story leads to its dramatic climax' *Daily Mail*

'Mystery and romance *par excellence*' *Sun*

arrow books

The Hornbeam Tree

Susan Lewis

Just as celebrated columnist Katie Kiernan thinks life is over, it suddenly arrives on her doorstep in the shape of her sister Michelle, and all the intrigue she brings with her. Friction, resentment and old jealousies make life in their house doubly challenging, as Katie struggles to cope with a rebellious teenager and Michelle longs for the man she left behind.

After a devastating betrayal Laurie Forbes is trying to rebuild her relationship with Elliot Russell, when she is plunged into a whirlwind of passion that threatens to tear them apart completely.

Top journalist, Tom Chambers, the man Michelle left behind, faces the greatest challenge of his career when highly classified documents fall into his hands. Realizing how explosive the material is, Tom calls upon Elliot Russell to help with the investigation, and very quickly they are caught up in the deadly efforts to stop them going to print . . .

'A multi-faceted tear jerker'
heat

arrow books

Just One More Day: A Memoir

Susan Lewis

In 1960s Bristol a family is overshadowed by tragedy . . .

While Susan, a feisty seven-year-old, is busy being brave, her mother, Eddress, is struggling for courage. Though bound by an indestructible love, their journey through a world that is darkening with tragedy is fraught with misunderstandings.

As a mother's greatest fear becomes reality, Eddress tries to deny the truth. And, faced with a wall of adult secrets, Susan creates a world that will never allow her mother to leave.

Set in a world where a fridge is a luxury, cars have starting handles, and where bingo and coupons bring in the little extras, *Just One More Day* is a deeply moving true-life account of how the spectre of death moved into Susan's family, and how hard they all tried to pretend it wasn't there.

'Susan Lewis fans know she can write compelling fiction, but not, until now, that she can write even more engrossing fact. We use the phrase honest truth too lightly: it should be reserved for books – deeply moving books – like this' Alan Coren

arrow books

ALSO AVAILABLE IN ARROW

Obsession

Susan Lewis

Corrie Browne is an ordinary girl with extraordinary ambitions. Determined to find the father she has never known, her search takes her from the quiet Suffolk village where she lives, to a new life in London, a fastpace television career – and to three people who come to dominate her life.

Luke, charismatic, blond and charming, is the only one to make Corrie feel welcome at TW TV and the only one to recognise her talent. Cristoff, an internationally famous film director, is the man who teaches her everything he knows about sex and passion. And Annelise is her boss and friend – a woman about whom Corrie knows a secret that must never be revealed. Three colleagues – all of whom are to play an important role in Corrie's search for love and success. One of whom intends Corrie's ultimate destruction.

arrow books

Strange Allure

Susan Lewis

Carla Craig is passionately in love with Richard Mere, in an affair that is like no other. Richard has a hold over her, both physical and intellectual, which she can't resist. Then her world is blown apart, her career crushed. Carla finds herself alone and devastated. Her oldest friend Avril sweeps back into her life like a storm of fresh air. Flamboyant and sensual, she is intrigued by the mysterious connection between Carla and Richard – a connection that won't go away.

As Carla starts to rebuild her life and her company, she tries to put her affair with Richard behind her. But she can't resist the mind-games he plays, the connection she feels with him. Then certain things stop adding up. The teasing games become too bizarre, and vital questions remain disturbingly unanswered. And as hidden truths are finally revealed, intrigue turns quickly to fear, and risk to terrible danger . . .

arrow books